broadview editions

D1427494

000070

Black-and-white crayon drawing executed when Ouida was 39.

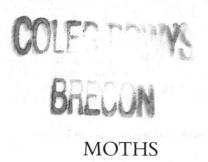

MOTHS

Ouida

edited by Natalie Schroeder

broadview editions

Library and Archives Canada Cataloguing in Publication

Ouida
    Moths / Ouida ; edited by Natalie Schroeder.

(Broadview editions)
Includes bibliographical references.
ISBN 1-55111-520-4

    I. Schroeder, Natalie, 1941-   II. Title.   III. Series.

PR4527.M68 2005   823'.8   C2004-905691-3

Broadview Editions

The Broadview Editions series represents the ever-changing canon of literature by bringing together texts long regarded as classics with valuable lesser-known works.

Advisory editor for this volume: Michel Pharand

Broadview Press Ltd. is an independent, international publishing house, incorporated in 1985. Broadview believes in shared ownership, both with its employees and with the general public; since the year 2000 Broadview shares have traded publicly on the Toronto Venture Exchange under the symbol BDP.

We welcome comments and suggestions regarding any aspect of our publications—please feel free to contact us at the addresses below or at broadview@broadviewpress.com.

North America
Post Office Box 1243, Peterborough, Ontario, Canada K9J 7H5
3576 California Road, Post Office Box 1015, Orchard Park, NY, USA 14127
Tel: (705) 743-8990   Fax: (705) 743-8353
e-mail: customerservice@broadviewpress.com

UK, Ireland, and continental Europe
NBN Plymbridge, Estover Road, Plymouth PL6 7PY UK
Tel: 44 (0) 1752 202301   Fax: 44 (0) 1752 202331
Fax Order Line: 44 (0) 1752 202333
Customer Service: cservs@nbnplymbridge.com Orders: orders@nbnplymbridge.com

Australia and New Zealand
UNIREPS, University of New South Wales
Sydney, NSW, 2052
Australia
Tel: 61 2 9664 0999   Fax: 61 2 9664 5420
email: info.press@unsw.edu.au

www.broadviewpress.com

Typesetting and assembly: True to Type Inc., Mississauga, Canada.

PRINTED IN CANADA

Contents

Acknowledgements • 7
Introduction • 9
Ouida: A Brief Chronology • 37
A Note on the Text • 41

Moths • 43

Appendix A: Contemporary Reviews of *Moths*
1. *The Athenæum* 7 (February 1880) • 545
2. *The Saturday Review* 49 (28 February 1880) • 546
3. *The Westminster Review* 113 (April 1880) • 550
4. *The North American Review* 285 (July 1880) • 550

Appendix B: The Novels of Society
1. From Vincent E.H. Murray, "Ouida's Novels," *The Contemporary Review* 22 (1878) • 555
2. From "Contemporary Literature," *Blackwood's Edinburgh Magazine* 125 (March 1879) • 556
3. From Harriet Waters Preston, "Ouida," *The Atlantic Monthly* 58 (1886) • 558
4. From [Oscar Wilde], "Ouida's New Novel," *Pall Mall Gazette* (May 1889) • 561
5. From Ouida, "The Sins of Society," *Views and Opinions* (1895) • 561

Appendix C: Contemporary Responses to Ouida
1. From Ella, "Ouida," *The Victoria Magazine* 28 (March 1877) • 565
2. From "The 'Whitehall' Portraits. XCVIII.—Ouida," *The Whitehall Review* (5 October 1878) • 566
3. From Marie Corelli, "A Word about 'Ouida,'" *Belgravia* 71 (March 1890) • 567
4. From G.S. Street, "An Appreciation of Ouida," *The Yellow Book* 6 (July 1895) • 570
5. From Willa Cather, "The Passing Show," *The Courier* (23 November 1895) • 573
6. From Max Beerbohm, "Ouida," *More* (1899) • 575
7. Obituary, *The Times* (27 January 1908) • 577

Appendix D: Marriage and Divorce in the Nineteenth Century
1. Ouida on The Marriage Market and her "Philosophy of Marriage"
   a. From *Granville de Vigne* (1863) • 583

    b. From *Princess Napraxine* (1884) • 584

    c. From *Guilderoy* (1889) • 585

  2. From George H. Lewis, "Marriage and Divorce," *The Fortnightly Review* 37 (1885) • 585

  3. From Charles Dickens, *Hard Times* (1854) • 589

  4. Reports of Divorce Cases, 1884

    a. Cranfield v. Cranfield, *The Times*, 4 April 1884 • 590

    b. Wilson v. Wilson, Grille, and Morley, *The Times*, 10 May 1884 • 591

    c. Stent v. Stent and Low, *The Times*, 19 June 1884 • 593

  5. From Mona Caird, "Marriage," *The Westminster Review* (August 1888) • 594

  6. From Marie Corelli, "The Modern Marriage Market," *The Lady's Realm* (April 1897) • 597

Appendix E: Ouida and the New Woman Debate

  1. From Eliza Lynn Lynton, "The Shrieking Sisterhood," *The Saturday Review* (12 March 1870) • 599

  2. From Sarah Grand, "The New Aspect of the Woman Question," *The North American Review* 158 (March 1894) • 601

  3. From Ouida, "The New Woman," *The North American Review* 158 (May 1894) • 605

  4. From Mrs. M. Eastwood, "The New Woman in Fiction and in Fact," *The Humanitarian* 5 (1894) • 612

  5. From Ouida, "Female Suffrage," *Views and Opinions* (1895) • 615

  6. From Mrs. Morgan-Dockrell, "Is the New Woman a Myth?" *The Humanitarian* 8 (1896) • 619

Select Bibliography • 625

Acknowledgements

I would like to thank the following people for their help and support. My husband Ronald A. Schroeder for all around assistance—answering questions, making suggestions, and checking translations. My mother Mollie Antler for proofreading. My research assistants Lorraine Dubuisson and Corrie Cattlett for typing and final manuscript preparation. J.R. Hall, Michael Danahy, Gregory Heyworth, and Karen Raber for help with translations and answering annotation queries. Jane Jordan for supplying information on the publishing history of *Moths*. Cheryl Coleman, Benjamin Franklin Fisher IV, and Shari Hodges Holt for help editing my introduction. Joe Urgo, for his encouragement. The staff of the University of Mississippi Department of Interlibrary Loan for their efficiency and promptness. The Department of English at the University of Mississippi.

Introduction

Ouida's Life

Ouida was born 1 January 1839, in Bury St. Edmunds, Suffolk. Her mother Susan Sutton was the daughter of a wine merchant. Her elusive father Louis Ramé may or may not have been the son of a tailor and a secret agent for the then exiled Louis Napoleon. While he never totally abandoned his wife and child until his final disappearance in 1871, Ramé did not often live with them.[1]

The name "Ouida" derived from an infant attempt to pronounce Louisa. Her generally happy childhood was marred only by her father's frequent mysterious absences. When he was present in the Ramé household, he taught French to Ouida and other young ladies in Bury St. Edmunds. He also instructed Ouida in literature, history, math, and politics. From him she developed her love for reading.

At age eleven, Ouida began acting out stories with painted cardboard figures as characters. Her vibrant imagination led her to live in a narcissistic fantasy world, a world she occupied for the rest of her life. She believed, for example, that every man she met was in love with her. In 1857, when Ouida was 18, she moved to London with her mother, her 85-year-old maternal grandmother, and her dog Beausire. Their new conventional neighbors in Hammersmith gossiped about the three women who lived alone without a man in the house. To make matters worse, Ouida's long walks with only her dog as a companion raised Victorian eyebrows.

Inspired by her new surroundings, Ouida determined to support her mother and grandmother by writing short stories. Their family doctor and neighbor, Francis Ainsworth, introduced Ouida to his cousin, William Harrison Ainsworth, the editor of *Bentley's Miscellany*. When Ouida sent him her stories, Ainsworth promptly published *Dashwood Drag; or the Derby and what came of it* in the April and May 1859 issues of the *Miscellany*. For the next few years he continued to publish her "society stories," peopled with rich aristocrats and set in foreign places like Bohemia, Vienna, Germany, and France.

---

1 The material in this section derives from Ouida's two most recent biographies: Monica Stirling's *The Fine and the Wicked* and Eileen Bigland's *Ouida: The Passionate Victorian*.

When Ouida was twenty-two, Ainsworth serialized her first full-length novel, *Granville de Vigne; a Tale of the Day*, along with Ellen Wood's *East Lynne* in *The New Monthly Magazine*. When her novel was published in three volumes in 1863, she changed the title to *Held in Bondage*. At first reviewers classified Ouida as a sensation novelist like Wood and Mary Elizabeth Braddon. Most of Ouida's novels, however, focus mainly on romance and on foibles of fashionable society rather than mystery and intrigue. Readers devoured her stories, an escape from stuffy middle class morality. Her first novel was immediately followed by *Strathmore* in 1865 and *Chandos* in 1866. Fueled by Ouida's unorthodox behavior, rumors spread about the "mysterious" new best-selling author.

Ouida's love and pampering of animals—especially dogs—was excessive throughout her life. When Beausire died in 1866, both Ouida and her mother grieved as much as they did at the death of Mrs. Sutton later that year. After her period of mourning, the young author moved to the luxurious Langham Hotel where she spent money recklessly, behaved outrageously, and hosted elaborate dinner parties and evening receptions, often smoking cigars with the men. With the exception of her mother and Lady Burton (wife of the explorer and writer, Sir Richard Burton), all her guests were male. What's more, Ouida was often coarse and rude. Her voice was unpleasantly rasping and her appearance eccentric. She demanded to be addressed as Madame de la Ramée or Madame Ouida. Although Ouida was nearly thirty years old, Bigland states that she "persisted in wearing her hair down her back, and whether it was the mode or not M. Worth had to design her gowns with shortish sleeves so that she might show off her tiny wrists and hands, and with shortish skirts so that she might display her incredibly small feet which were always shod in satin slippers" (53).

Under Two Flags (1867), featuring the unconventional heroine Cigarette, mascot of the French Foreign Legion, became Ouida's greatest success to date. That same year, Mario, a sixty-one year-old tenor, came to London. He was the first of the three passionate infatuations of Ouida's life. This first one, however, was with a man whom she never even met. In an essay written later in her life, "O Beati Insipientes!," Ouida describes Mario as "a man of genius in every way, apart from the art in which he was unsurpassed ... yet, he was a singularly handsome man, and possessed of magical seduction for women" (*Views and Opinions* 74). At Mario's farewell performance at Covent Garden, Ouida threw a bouquet of flowers onto the stage containing an ivory cigar-case with her card and a note in it. When

Mario left London soon after, never acknowledging her gift, Ouida "invented another and greater fiction to account for his silent departure." He became her fantasy-lover (Bigland 73). Later Ouida modeled Corrèze, the hero of *Moths*, after him.

Following Mario's departure, Ouida and her mother traveled to the Continent, and Italy became her home for the next twenty-three years. She leased the Villa Farinola in Florence and surrounded herself with ostentatious luxuries. Ouida was rich, earning five thousand pounds a year, but she spent the money from her book royalties faster than she wrote the novels. In England, Ouida had shunned the companionship of women, but in Florence she befriended several female acquaintances. Her most intimate friends were Emilie de Tchiatcheff, Lady Orford, and Lady Paget, the latter of whose "circumstances, looks, and character were remarkably like those of what came to be considered a typical Ouida heroine" (Stirling 102).

Within a few months she met the Marchese Lotteria Lotharingo della Stufa, a gentleman in waiting to the King of Italy, who "aroused in Ouida the greatest passion of her life" (Stirling 89). Unlike Mario, who never acknowledged Ouida's existence, Stufa apparently was fond of her. They shared a love for animals, politics, and nature, and for several years he showered her with attention. Ouida was unaware, however, of Stufa's long term love affair with Mrs. Janet Ross, and her friends did not want to disturb her happiness by enlightening her. During those "blissful" years, Ouida continued to pen novels, and she modeled the heroes on Stufa: *Idalia* (1867), *Tricotrin* (1869), *Puck* (1870), and *Folle-Farine* (1871). Her popular children's tale, *A Dog of Flanders*, was published in 1872, followed by *Pascarel* (1873), *Two Little Wooden Shoes* (1874), *Signa* (1875), *In A Winter City* (1876), and *Ariadne* (1877).

Ouida had become famous and wealthy, but she continued to live far beyond her means and spent money recklessly. Fancying herself a romance heroine, she dressed accordingly, often in expensive, flowing white dresses. Ouida treated her gaggle of dogs like royalty, serving them boiled liver and bread in the morning, beef and rice in the evening, and any extras they wanted from her dinner table. She insisted that her guests and servants conform to her dog-worship:

> [The dogs] occupied the best chairs, they lay on the beds, they chewed the carpets, they lapped cream out of the priceless Capo di Monti tea-cups. One servant groomed them daily under Mme Ramé's vigilant eye, another spent his entire time exercising them. Ouida refused to have any of them house-trained because she

thought it cruel and any servant caught "ill-treating" a dog—even if, as often happened, the animal had bitten him—was instantly dismissed. (Bigland 102)

After a ten year relationship with Stufa, Ouida learned about his ongoing affair with Mrs. Ross. Stufa's lover immediately became the model for Ouida's fictional adulteress Lady Joan, while Ouida cast Stufa as Prince Ioris, and herself as Étoile in her scandalous *roman à clef, Friendship* (1878). The main characters were compromisingly recognizable. Furthermore, Ouida declared that except for setting the novel in Rome rather than Florence, everything in the novel was true.

Ouida only escaped her severe depression, caused by the discovery of Stufa's affair, when she was writing *Moths*, which financially and artistically became her greatest success. The novel was in such demand that libraries could not get enough copies of it. However, after Mudie[1] threatened to remove *Moths* from their stock (presumably as a result of the reviewers' objections to Ouida's offences against propriety—See Appendix A), her publisher ordered the type to be broken up, and a cheap edition was published four months later. As a result, copies of the original edition cost three guineas. Ouida was concerned that bringing out a cheap edition of *Moths* only four months after the first issue "makes the novel look like an old one" and it would suggest that interest in the novel had declined. Ouida wrote to her publisher Chatto: "I wish you had said something in the advertisements to the effect that the 3 vol form being all sold off, to supply the demand the new edition etc., etc.," and concluded, "I saw a letter the other day from Mudie regretting he had not enough Moths to supply the incessant demand for it."[2] Despite these reservations, Ouida received enthusiastic fan mail, and according to Stirling, "the book's influence can be discerned in Bernard Shaw's early novels and Oscar Wilde's society comedies" (137). Moths was adapt-

---

1 Charles Edward Mudie (1818-90), was the owner of the famous "Select Circulating Library" to which thousands of families in England subscribed. He had strict Evangelical convictions, and he could make or break an author's book by accepting or rejecting it. According to Altick, "His favor could mean the sale of several hundred copies ... added to this would be a boost in retail sales if the size of Mudie's purchase were well publicized" (196).
2 New York Public Library, Berg Collection, Ouida to Chatto and Windus, 7 June 1880; qtd. in Jordan, "The Writings of 'Ouida.'"

ed as a play and successfully produced at the Globe Theatre in London in 1883.

Despite the sensation she aroused by exposing Stufa's affair in print, Ouida still aggressively pursued him, following him twice to Rome until he finally "looked straight through her when she addressed him, and walked on" (Bigland 143). But she continued penning stories.

A Village Commune (1881) and *In Maremma* (1882) (Italian peasant novels), followed *Moths,* and then *Wanda* (1883) and *Princess Naprax-ine* (1884). Despite her productivity and success, Ouida still found herself in difficult financial straits. For years she had been spending money extravagantly, dodging creditors, and borrowing heavily. According to Bigland,

> When Ouida received a cheque she simply had to spend it at once, usually on some costly bit of bric-à-brac which had caught her fancy. At a moment when creditors were hammering at the back door she would dash out of the front one and buy great arm-fuls of hot-house flowers. If a peremptory note from the landlord warned her that the rent was overdue she felt compelled to spend what she owed him on anything from a piano to a pedigree dog. (200)

In 1881, the Marchese Farinola, the owner of her rented villa, sent a group of peasants and village police to evict Ouida forcibly. Her creditors seized most of her possessions, and Ouida and her mother were forced to move from one residence to the next. She relied on loans from friends, but still refused to practice prudence or frugality.

In 1884, Ouida fell in love again, this time with Robert Lord Lytton, the son of the novelist Bulwer-Lytton. Despite the fact that Lytton was married, Ouida created a fantasy relationship with him. When she spent a weekend as a guest in his home in Knebworth she was temporarily disillusioned. To avoid a private interview with the overbearing writer, Lytton locked himself in his room, pointedly signaling that he did not want her love. But Ouida quickly rallied and resumed her imaginary love affair. In those years she published: *Othmar* (1885), *Guilderoy* (1889), *Syrlin* (1890), and assorted short fiction. In 1891, she was stunned to learn that Lytton, her imaginary lover, had died of a heart attack.

Ouida's financial straits reached a crisis in 1893. Her friend Lady Paget described visiting Ouida, who was then living in the dilapidated Villa della Corona:

Her only furniture seemed to be a plaster cast of Gay's bust, for which she asked me years ago. There were only two or three chairs in the many rooms I traversed, a pink-and gold paper hung in rags from the wall, there were no fires, no carpets. A troupe of fluffy and rather dirty white dogs barked at me and then rolled themselves under Ouida's feet, amongst the folds of a draggled black-lace skirt. She wore a mantelet of some once bright but now faded colour, out of which her arms and tiny but ugly hands protruded. Her legs were encased in very bright blue stockings, and her feet in very thin white slippers. She insisted on walking through the lanes with me in this costume, with a whitey-browney hat with many feathers superadded, and a spotty veil. (qtd. in Stirling 181)

When her mother died later that year, Ouida kept the body in the villa for ten days because she was ashamed to have her buried in a pauper's grave.

Penniless, alone, and "weary of everything" but her dogs, Ouida was evicted again (Bigland 211). She moved to Lucca in 1894, where she rented the Villa Massoni. She forced herself to continue writing, but with less success. In the last decade of her life, Ouida focused more on essay and letter writing than on fiction. She wrote a series of short articles for *The Fortnightly Review*, several of which expressed her strong anti-vivisection, anti-feminist, and political beliefs. A collection of her essays, published as *Views and Opinions* (1895), contains her indictment of fashionable society and her attack on the New Woman. *The Massarines* (1897), her first novel in several years, is another scathing attack on "smart society." It inspired Sir Max Beerbohm's[1] laudatory essay, "Ouida," published in his collection of essays, *More* (1899) and dedicated to her:

<blockquote>
to
Mlle de la Ramée
With the author's compliments
and to
Ouida
With his love (See Appendix C.4)
</blockquote>

---

1 Max Beerbohm (1876-1956) was a renowned drama critic, caricaturist, playwright, and wit.

Nevertheless, Ouida's circumstances continued to be desperate. Mme Grosfils, the owner of the Villa Massoni, evicted Ouida and sent her sons to take possession of the villa by force. They kicked her dogs and ransacked the rooms, confiscating her paintings, books, unpublished manuscripts, and letters. Ouida won a lawsuit against the Grosfils family, but they never paid her the damages. She spent her final years impoverished, living alone with her dogs and her faithful peasant maid. To feed the dogs, she practically starved herself. Her eyesight was failing, she had chronic bronchitis, and her debtors clamored to be paid. When a muzzle law was passed and Ouida refused to muzzle her dogs, she was again evicted. She spent a cold night in a cab, alone with her dogs. When her maid found her the next morning, Ouida's right eye was inflamed, and she was deaf. Her eye grew worse, and eventually she lost sight in it completely.

In her last years Ouida's health continued to decline. In 1907, she became infuriated by a letter Marie Corelli wrote to *The Daily Mail*, sympathizing with Ouida for her poverty and asking for charity for her. Vernon Lee's subsequent article in *The Westminster Gazette* also insulted the aged writer. Her final humiliation was the publication of a picture of a peasant woman in *The Daily Mail*, said to be Ouida.

Ouida died of pneumonia in 1908, at the age of sixty-nine "in a house crowded out with dogs—not the prize breeds of her heyday, but 'stray curs taken out of the streets to rescue from vivisection ... in a room bare of furniture—with hardly a vestige of clothes, and inadequate bed-covers, and only with the assistance of a rough Italian peasant-woman, whose ideas of cleanliness and order left the place in a condition difficult to describe but easily imagined'" (qtd. in Elwin 310).

Ouida was a phenomenon. During a career spanning almost forty years, her novels were read by all social classes: males and females, youths and adults, working girls and elevator boys, canonical novelists and European statesmen. She was legendary for her audacity, eccentricity, and extravagance. Despite her financial difficulties, especially in her later years, Ouida supported herself and her mother for over thirty years.

Historical and Cultural Contexts

Russia

From the time of Peter the Great (1689-1725), the Russian nobility became increasingly Westernized, modeling themselves on wealthy

Europeans. The nobles spoke French, danced, and fenced. They were familiar with the latest trends in art, music, and culture. They lived in vast landed estates, with formal gardens and opulent furnishings, where they hosted elaborate house parties. Hunting was the primary pastime for men during the daytime, and at night visitors were privy to regal entertainments by musicians, actors, and dancers. The nobility regularly traveled on the Continent, and many of them had homes in Paris, Normandy, and the Riviera.[1]

With the defeat of Napoleon in 1812, Russia emerged as the dominant country in Europe. When Nicholas I became Czar in 1812, he claimed that his authority was derived from God. He established a chancery to run the Imperial household and set up "sections" to deal with laws and internal security. This led to what we would call now a police state. The Third Department (or Third Section—as it is referred to in *Moths*) was a political police organization that uncovered plots against the czar and conspiracies against the government. It also enforced strict censorship laws. Although Nicholas was fluent in English, German, and French, he was decidedly anti-Western. His secret police arrested hundreds of students and professors who fostered Western ideals.

Russia had earlier gained control of Poland after three partitions (the division of Poland to various countries), and Nicholas was determined to Russify it. After he had himself crowned king of Poland in 1830, the resentful Poles tried to rebel. The Russians recaptured Warsaw, however, and Russian generals were rewarded with the estates of Polish nobles who had supported the rebellion. (At one point in *Moths* the heroine is banished to a Polish estate.)

At the death of Nicholas in 1855, his son Alexander II took the throne. He fostered Russia's interaction with the European community, lifted the restrictions on foreign travel, and removed the police spies from the universities. He also relaxed the censorship laws. His decision to emancipate the serfs in 1861 significantly changed Russia. The serfs looked on their freedom, however, as another form of bondage. Expecting to get free land, they instead foresaw themselves in debt for years in order to purchase land. In addition, revolutionaries were opposed to the autocratic political and social system. In 1873 and 1874, thousands of young people preached revolution to the peasants, but that effort failed when the peasants remained passive.

---

1   The information in this section derives from Roosevelt, Heyman, Duffy, and Seton-Watson.

After a revolutionary shift to terrorism in the 1870s, the government adopted repressive measures. Many youths and members of smaller underground organizations were condemned to hard labor in Siberia; others became Administrative Exiles. They were sent to remote spots where, homeless, many of them starved.

At first Poland regained some of its autonomy under the rule of Alexander II. But discontent with Russian rule led to another Polish Rebellion in 1863, which was suppressed the following year. Freed serfs were given generous land allotments that penalized Polish landowners. Britain and France were, however, openly sympathetic to the Poles.

France[1]

The Revolution and the First Empire (1789-1848)

The storming of the Bastille on July 14, 1789, began the French Revolution (1789-1804). The First Republic of France was established, but early Republican ideals led to the Reign of Terror. There were widespread political executions (Louis XVI and Marie Antoinette were guillotined in 1793) followed by executions of the leaders of the Terror (1794).

Napoleon Bonaparte seized control (1794-1804), and ruled over a short-lived empire during the Napoleonic wars (1804-14). He remained powerful until his disastrous invasion of Russia in 1812. The allied coalition defeated him in 1814, and he was exiled to Elba.

Following Napoleon's defeat, Louis XVIII (brother of Louis XVI and of the Bourbon family) took the throne. During "the Hundred Days," Napoleon came out of exile and regained power for a brief time, but he was finally defeated at Waterloo. Upon the death of Louis XVIII, his younger brother Charles X reigned as the last Bourbon king of France. From 1828 to 1842, political and urban discontent led to riots and uprisings in the streets. Bonapartist insurgents finally replaced Charles X with Napoleon II in 1830. After several unsuccessful coups, Louis Napoleon seized control from his cousin and was elected president of France in 1848.

---

1   The material in this section derives from Burchell and Guedalla.

The Second Empire (1848-70)[1]

The era of Napoleon III was a time of flamboyance and extravagance. According to S.C. Burchell, "The imperial court created by Louis Napoleon ... soon emerged as the most splendid in Europe, if not the most splendid in French history" (58). A mania for amusement characterized the whole period and lasted through the Third Republic. Clothes and make-up became unduly important: "Women were first of all objects of decoration and then objects of pleasure" (62). Immorality was the climate of the age. The theatre, where viewers were exposed to one salacious musical comedy after another, was very popular. The king, who was notorious for his sexual excesses, had several permanent mistresses.

During the modernization of Paris, which Louis ordered, work began on a new opera house. The "vulgar and materialistic" Théâtre de l'Opéra.... [was] a gay and careless mixture of periods in which form has nothing whatever to do with function. Elaboration grew from elaboration and ... [t]he resulting mélange is an expression of Second Empire materialism in its purest form" (Burchell 95). The Opéra Garnier finally opened to public acclaim in 1875, and it became the focus of upper class society.

Like the Russian nobility, the French regularly traveled on the continent. They discovered Deauville and Trouville, seaside resorts in Normandy where *Moths* opens. By the end of the Second Empire, Deauville was *the* beach of the upper classes.

All this appalling excess and luxury existed side by side with poverty. The living conditions of the lower classes became more and more desperate, which led to an atmosphere of rebellion. Following several attempts on his life, Louis Napoleon established a secret police and censored the press. But unlike in Russia, only the most outspoken critics were forced into exile or imprisoned (Burchell 146-47).

Believing that he was commander of the finest army in Europe, Napoleon III became active in foreign affairs. Burchell calls the atmosphere of the Second Empire's military establishment "flamboyant and unreal." In fact he says that it was similar to the atmosphere of the military in Ouida's *Under Two Flags*. He quotes from a battle scene in her novel and states: "Over-romantic and bathetic and pre-

---

1   *Moths* is set during the Third Republic, but the lifestyles of the members of the fashionable society who people the novel are characteristic of the Second Empire.

posterous—all this is true enough. However, in a curious way Ouida was almost a realist, and there is more than an element of truth in her description of an era when bravura was a military virtue. It was not all fiction: Others had cried '*Vive la France*' and fallen...." (303-04).

Authors like Victor Hugo and painters like Honoré Daumier created a new school of realism, which focused on poverty and the more sordid aspects of life. The government attacked these artists because their works revealed the truth behind the flamboyant facade of opulence. In 1857, Charles Baudelaire (*Les Fleurs du Mal*) and Gustave Flaubert (*Madame Bovary*) were prosecuted for public immorality (quite ironic considering the decadence of the king and his nobility). After the publication of *Les Misérables* in 1862, Napoleon III ordered Victor Hugo exiled.

By 1870, the king's popularity began to decline, and failures in foreign affairs led to more anti-imperial opposition. After he was defeated in the Franco-Prussian War, Louis Napoleon was deposed and the Third Republic declared.

The Third Republic

The Paris Commune of 1871, a citizens' attempt to take power, resulted in the destruction of the Tuileries Palace. In a bloody battle, about 10,000 people were killed and 40,000 arrested. The government became split between the "Legitimists," those who wanted an absolutist Catholic monarchy and who viewed the representatives of the house of Bourbon as the rightful rulers of France, and the "Orléanists," those who wanted a British-style parliamentary monarchy and a descendent of the house of Orléans to assume the throne. With the capitulation of the Emperor and the army, however, the Republic was claimed without further violence. Adolphe Thiers served as President from 1871-73, succeeded by Marshall MacMahon from 1873-79.

Ouida and the Novel of Society

Although critics at first branded Ouida a sensation novelist, her works are actually romantic novels of fashionable society or "the high life," which derive from the "silver-fork" novels of the 1820s and 1830s. Novelists such as Bulwer-Lytton and George Lawrence, two regular guests at Ouida's London dinner parties, were among the earliest writers of this sub-genre. Their works are snobbishly preoccupied with aristocratic opulence and the development of the foppish young hero. The silver-fork novel stemmed from the middle-class fascination with the Regency period and "with the quintessential Regency figure, the dandy: the cool, crisply dressed, affectedly unaffected man-about-town" (Gilmour 16).

Although the guardsmen-heroes of Ouida's early fiction have characteristics of the silver-fork dandy, her works focus more on fantasy, romance, and passion from a female, rather than male point of view. A reviewer for *Blackwood's Edinburgh Magazine* attributed Ouida's popularity with the reading public to her pictures of high society: "There is nothing the middle and the lower classes care for more than to be introduced to these unfamiliar splendours which Providence has placed beyond their reach, and, necessarily, they can never be very critical as to the beings who people these dazzling realms of mystery" (Appendix B.2).

Editor Anthony Powell included *Moths*, along with Disraeli's *Henrietta Temple* and Lawrence's *Guy Livingstone*, in *Novels of High Society in the Victorian Age*, an edition of three nineteenth-century novels which he published in 1947. In his "Introduction," Powell states:

> Since all but purely snobbish considerations were rejected by Ouida in her approach to society, she naturally depicts a somewhat unpleasing world, the disagreeable features of which are in no way ameliorated by the fact that they are drawn largely from her imagination. Her position as a well-known novelist allowed her opportunities of meeting and mixing with many of the people whom it was her ambition to know.... [F]or Ouida, society was the firmament of the charity-bazaar, the gossip column, and the illustrated papers, the promised land of those who could dream only of its splendours. (xii)

Ouida is not always snobbish, however, nor are her depictions of the high life always unpleasant. She has a somewhat ambivalent attitude to society in her fiction. At times she seems the romantic dreamer who, like her readers, longs for "splendours," a princess waiting for "a fairy prince who would live with her for ever and a day on the peak of some rosy and ethereal mountain" (Bigland 126). At other times, her satiric treatment of society is as witty and caustic as Thackeray's in *Vanity Fair* and Dickens's in *Little Dorrit*. Ouida's *Puck*, for example, published in 1870, is a scathing attack on an age where a vain, cruel peasant girl can rise to become a Marchioness, where pure innocence and honor is easily destroyed. It is a "society that is artificial, passionless, and insincere" (352-53).

Similarly, in *Moths* Ouida exposes society for its artificiality, hypocrisy, cruelty, and immorality. Early in the novel, Corrèze the hero warns the heroine to keep herself "unspotted from the world." He goes on to use moths as metaphors for society and women:

> [This world] is a world of moths. Half the moths are burning themselves in feverish frailty, the other half are corroding and consuming all that they touch.... The women of your time are not, perhaps, the worst the world has seen, but they are certainly the most contemptible. They have dethroned grace; they have driven out honour; they have succeeded in making men ashamed of the sex of their mothers; and they have set up nothing in the stead of all they have destroyed except a feverish frenzy for amusement and an idiotic imitation of vice. (97-98)

The heroine's mother Lady Dolly is case in point. She has at least two lovers during the course of the novel and has had many former liaisons. She remains "respectable" because she is married and because both her husband and society close their eyes to these affairs: "Everyone knew [Lady Dolly] was a naughty little woman, but she had never been ... coldly looked on by anybody" (236). Because she has her charities and occasionally feigns religious reverence (she wears a large silver cross and hangs a silver-bound prayer book on her belt), she protects her "reputation." Society forgives her indiscretions because it promotes artifice:

> In her frothy world there is no such thing as wickedness, there is only exposure; and the dread of it, which passes for virtue.
> She lived, like all women of her stamp and her epoch in an atmosphere of sugared sophisms; she never reflected, she never admitted, that she did wrong; in her world nothing mattered much unless, indeed, it were found out, and got into the public mouth.
> Shifting as the sands, shallow as the rain-pools, drifting in all danger to a lie, incapable of loyalty, insatiably curious, still as a friend and ill as a foe ... the woman of modern society is too often at once the feeblest and the foulest outcome of a false civilisation. (431-32)

The character of Lady Dolly is, however, dramatically unlike Ouida's earlier villainous adventuresses—stock figures drawn from melodrama. She is much more realistic. Deceitful, vain, selfish Lady Dolly is also one of Ouida's comic masterpieces. The novel opens with Lady Dolly on a beach in Trouville, fretting about the impending arrival of her sixteen-year old daughter, who had been raised by her grandmother:

> It ruined her morning. It clouded the sunshine. It spoiled her cigarette. It made the waltzes sound like dirges. It made her chief rival look almost good-looking to her.... It was so sudden, so appalling, so bewildering, so endless a question; and Lady Dolly only asked questions, she never answered them or waited for their answers.
>
> After all, what could she do with her? She, a pretty woman and a wonderful flirt, who liked to dance to the very end of the cotillon, and had as many lovers as she had pairs of shoes. What could she do with a daughter just sixteen years old?
>
> "It makes one look so old!" (48)

Although the narrator says that Dolly is a conscienceless product of society, occasional glimpses of the inner Lady Dolly suggest that she does have one. After she manipulates Vere to accept Zouroff's proposal, Dolly's conscience is very much present: "It was dawn when [she] crept away from her daughter's chamber; shivering, ashamed, contrite, in so far as humiliation and regret make up contrition; hiding her blanched face with the hood of her wrapper as though the faint, white rays of daybreak were spectators and witnesses against her" (173). But she is quick to rationalize away the guilt. After she drowns her conscience in ether, for example, she reminds herself that society dictates that it is a mother's duty to find a good match for her daughter: "She had betrothed her daughter to one of the richest and best-born men in all Europe. Was it not the crown of maternity, as maternity is understood in society?" And like Thackeray's Becky Sharp, she concludes that had *she* married a very rich man: "how easy it would have been to have become a good woman!"[1] (175). Although she is perpetually haunted by a vague sense of guilt for forcing Vere to marry Prince Zouroff, she repeatedly reassures

---

1 In *Vanity Fair* (1847-48), Thackeray's roguish character Becky (Sharp) and her husband Rawdon Crawley have been living in London on nothing a year. They are invited to the family estate, Queen's Crawley, where Becky rationalizes: "I think I could be a good woman if I had five thousand a year" (495).

herself that she did the right thing and continues on with her shallow life of gambling, flirting, and self-indulgence.

Ouida also ends *Moths* with her comic villainess. "Poor Dolly" juxtaposes the rules of society that will not allow her to associate with her divorced and remarried daughter, her disappointment in the latest hair fashions, and the news of her former lover's suicide:

> "Everything is so dreadful," she says with a little sob and shiver. "Only to think that I cannot know my own daughter! And then to have to wear one's hair flat, and the bonnets are not becoming, say what they like, and the season is so stupid; and now poor dear Jack has killed himself, really killed himself, because nobody believes about that rifle being an accident, he has been so morose and so strange for years, and his mother comes and reproaches *me* when it is all centuries ago, centuries! and I am sure I never did him anything but good!" (543)

And the great ladies of society sympathize with the "dear little woman," who "is so kind, so sweet" and who "has so much to bear"... "So the moths eat the ermine; and the world kisses the leper on both cheeks" (543).

Finally, in Ouida's lengthy 1895 essay "The Sins of Society," she again indicts society. She uses butterflies and locusts (rather than moths) as metaphors. "The butterfly," she says, "is a creature of the most perfect taste, arrayed in the most harmonious colours," which "is always graceful, leisurely, and aerial," no longer exists. Instead, society has become like locusts—"jammed together in a serried host," tearing "forward without knowing in the least why or where he goes, except that he must move on and must devour." She points to the practices of European society that she finds particularly vulgar: overeating and smoking, gathering in crowds, drinking and gambling, living beyond one's means, holding vulgar weddings and funerals, and dressing in ugly clothes (i.e., women wearing dresses and bonnets decorated with dead birds). Smart people, she says, are not necessarily elegant people and many "leaders of the smart set are wholly unrefined in taste, loud in manner, and followed merely because they please certain personages, spend or seem to spend profusely, and are seen at all the conspicuous gatherings of the season in London and wherever else society congregates. This is why the smart sets have so little refining influence on society." She concludes that society could save itself "if it became something which money cannot purchase, and envy ... cannot deride" (Appendix B.5).

Ouida and "The New Woman"

In response to an article by Sara Grand, Ouida coined the term "New Woman" in an essay published in May 1894 (see Appendix E.2 and 3). Although Ouida is credited for naming the New Woman, the term actually appeared first in *The Westminster Review* in 1865, in an article objecting to sensation fiction: "The New Woman, as we read of her in recent novels, possesses not only the velvet, but the claws of the tiger. She is no longer the Angel, but the Devil in the House" (qtd. in Helsinger, Sheets, and Veeder 125). Between the 1860s and the 1890s, however, most of the articles about the woman question and women who wanted more autonomy referred to real women, rather than to fictional characters. According to Ann Ardis aggressive women's "violations of the social code were viewed as a serious threat to bourgeois culture's hegemony." She goes on to point out that after Ouida named the New Woman, "the New Woman novel, not real New Women, became the center of controversy" (12; see also Cunningham, Heilmann, E. Jordan, and Schaffer, "Nothing but Foolscap and Ink"). Lyn Pykett points out that the New Woman novels, like the sensation novels of the 1860s, focused "on the constraining and claustrophobic nature of the domestic space" (146).

Although Ouida ridiculed the New Woman as "an unmitigated bore" who "violated in her own person every law alike of common sense and of artistic fitness," she contradicts these sentiments in her fiction. Pamela K. Gilbert says that "many of Ouida's characters anticipate the New Woman ... [H]er portrayal of women often licenses extramarital sexuality as an expression of a higher ethical standard in a world wherein marriage is corrupted by the profit motive. Further, many of her women reject traditional gender roles, being active, heroic, able to fight men and win" ("Ouida and the Other New Woman" 170). Carol Poster also points to three of Ouida's heroines who "appropriate all the characteristics of the male hero, including physical courage, strength, and intelligence" (300).

In *Moths* Ouida depicts a number of strong women: Lady Dolly, Nadine Nelaguine, Jeanne de Sonnaz, and Fuschia Leach (the American). They are "sexually active, strong female characters who do not die decorously after a period of hideous suffering repudiating the errors of their ways" ("Ouida and the Other New Woman" 173). And the passive, often Griselda-like heroine Vere, is far from being "ice cream in substance," as Stirling suggests (134). Vere submits to her husband's tyrannies because she has been raised to believe that a wife's sacred duty is to obey her husband. But she stands up to him on numerous occasions. Vere adamantly refuses to have a booth at a charity bazaar when she learns that Croisette, one of Zouroff's mistresses, will be there; and she refuses to ride with her husband on the Promenade des Anglais after she meets him riding there with his other mistress, Casse-une-Croûte. Later, after Zouroff smashes Vere's medallion of the moth and the star, he sees a "new power in her glance" a "new meaning in her voice" (454). Vere's real strength surfaces when she learns that Jeanne de Sonnaz is also Zouroff's mistress and that they have been sleeping together in her home. She threatens to leave her husband, steadfastly refuses to receive his lover again, and accepts banishment to one of his Polish estates. Zouroff, however, is unable to break her will, and when she learns that her husband shot her lover Corrèze, she courageously travels alone by sledge and then by train from Poland to Paris to be with him. She is subsequently divorced and remarried—a key issue in the battle for female autonomy. Sally Mitchell points out that "Vere breaks free of her marriage because—however tormented and provoked she has been, and though Correze [sic] has constantly been presented as Saint Raphael while the Prince is unmistakably the prince of darkness—she loves another man. And with him, in the seclusion of an Alpine valley, she prospers" (141-42).[1]

As mentioned earlier, Ouida herself was a strong, aggressive, unconventional woman. Schaffer agrees that Ouida's "own life follows a New Woman pattern; as an unmarried woman who supported herself through writing, who initiated relationships with men outside of marriage, and who stubbornly followed her own rules for fashion and etiquette in spite of social norms, she might even have been a role model" ("Nothing but Foolscap and Ink" 47).

Ouida's naming of the New Woman sparked an important controversy. In "the process of rejecting, affirming, decrying, or defining the 'New Woman,' writers were able to enunciate where they stood on various issues.... The 'New Woman' furore may have helped the multitudinous groupings of the *fin de siècle*[2] settle down into the dominant 'feminist' and 'anti-feminist' camps which would dominate the twentieth century" (Schaffer, "Nothing but Foolscap and Ink" 49). The debate significantly influenced the public attitude to

---

1 For a different reading of Vere as heroine, see Schaffer. She states that "Vere is an eminently passive heroine" and that "her only tool against the threatening world is her feminine passivity, and she utilizes it until she becomes virtually autistic" (*The Forgotten Female Aesthetes* 128-29).
2 End of the century.

women's roles in society and ultimately resulted in sexual and social changes for women such as divorce law reform, the right to vote, career choices, the double standard in sexual relations, and the dress code.

Marriage and Divorce in Nineteenth-Century England

Few lifestyle options were open to women in the Victorian Age. The only "respectable" alternatives for an unmarried woman were to marry, to remain a spinster, or to become a governess, schoolmistress, or companion.[1] When a young woman was considered of marriageable age, usually at seventeen or eighteen, she was "presented" (formally introduced into society at a ball) and placed on the "marriage market." It was considered good fortune if a young woman could find an eligible husband in one fashionable "Season" in London or on the continent. But generally these matches were loveless ones, in which young adolescents were married off to older men.

Wives were both economically and legally dependent on their husbands. The legal doctrine of *coverture* stated that the husband and wife were one, but that *one* was the husband. The prime duty of the nineteenth-century wife was to provide her husband with "the pleasure of her society.... These obligations were legally designated the husband's right to his wife's *consortium* and meant in effect that the wife was physically tied to the home and that her energy and time were at her husband's disposal" (Lewis 120; see also Shanley 8-9).

Before 1857, there were two types of divorce in England: judicial separation (divorce *a mensa et thoro*)[2] and divorce (divorce *a vinculo matrimonii*).[3] Only an ecclesiastical court could grant a separation. Divorce required suits in both ecclesiastical and common law courts and an act of Parliament. Because court costs were prohibitive, only the very rich could obtain divorces. After the Matrimonial Causes Act was passed in 1857, judicial separation could be obtained by the husband or the wife for adultery, desertion for over two years, or physical cruelty. To obtain a divorce, the husband could sue simply on grounds of his wife's adultery. He could also sue his wife's lover, and if he was convincing, he could get the jury to award him "damages"

---

1 Writers, like Ouida, the Brontës, George Eliot, Mary Elizabeth Braddon, Ellen Wood, and Margaret Oliphant, were exceptions, and there were strong prejudices against women writers.
2 Separation from bed and board. These couples could not remarry.
3 Divorce from the bond of matrimony.

(see Appendix D.2 and 4). The wife, on the other hand, had to have grounds of adultery and an additional offense: physical cruelty, incest, rape, or desertion. The divorce procedure was still expensive, and "as late as the nineties less than six hundred divorce cases went through the courts in a year" (Altick 58).

Moths

In *Moths* as in her other fiction, Ouida presents marriage as a badly tarnished ideal. She develops what she refers to in her fiction as a "philosophy of marriage": First of all, marriage laws were originally created simply for the sake of passing on property to successive generations—not for the union of two people in love. Second, familiarity produces boredom and infidelity, and marriage laws are unnatural because they bind two people together for life (see Appendix D.1). Thus marriage vows contain within them the seeds of their own destruction, and even some marriages based on love are bound to fail. For the most part either one party or the other will soon be disappointed with a union which he/she had expected "to be a primrose path, whilst it is only a common highway" (*Princess Napraxine* 732).

Because marriages are often arranged for mercenary reasons, they typically exclude affection and fulfilling intimacies. Both husbands and wives almost casually deceive their spouses with lovers and mistresses. Sexual norms are strained, corrupted, and distorted. In marriage, Ouida says, "The dangerous romance [adultery] begins afterwards, in life as in novels" (*Princess Napraxine* 567).

Moths is a romantic love story, but it is also one of Ouida's most vehement condemnations of marriage as a social evil. She attacks the marriage market, the institution of marriage, and socially accepted adultery. The novel is riddled with actual and metaphorical references to prostitution and bondage—to the buying and selling of adolescent women. The only married women in the novel who have total autonomy are the American heiress Fuschia Leach (free by nature of being American) and the adulteresses.

Lady Dolly is the first of several "Femme Galantes" in the novel, a female type Ouida introduced in *In a Winter City* (1876):

[She is a woman who] neither forfeits her place nor leaves her lord; who has studied adultery as one of the fine arts and made it one of the domestic virtues; who takes her lover to her friends' houses as she takes her muff or her dog ... who challenges the world to find a flaw in her, and who smiles serene at her husband's table on a society she is careful to conciliate ... who uses the sanctity of her maternity to cover the lawlessness of her license; and who, incapable alike of the self-abandonment of love or of the self-sacrifice of duty, has not even such poor, cheap honor as in the creatures of the streets....

This is the Femme Galante of the passing century, who, with her hand on her husband's arm, babbles of her virtue in complacent boast, smiles in her lover's eyes, and, ignoring such a vulgar word as Sin, talks with a smile of Friendship. (540)

The femme galante character evolves from the unmarried adventuresses of Ouida's earlier fiction and from Stufa's lover Mrs. Ross. Ouida learned about the love affair in 1876, and she became so obsessed with hatred for her rival that she repeatedly attacked her in her fiction.

When Vere comes to France to live with her mother, Lady Dolly consults her friend, Lady Stoat of Stitchley, the voice of society. Lady Stoat pontificates on marriage as the first duty of a woman and teaches girls to accept that "as the gospel of their generation" that "love and honour were silly things, and all that really mattered was to have rank and to be rich, and to be envied by others" (111, 110). In other words, to uphold society, adolescent females must be sacrificed on the marriage market. From the beginning Vere resists the two women's machinations to marry her off. She equates an arranged marriage to being sold. In Lady Dolly's defense, she is a product of society, and she does not fully understand her daughter's objections. She equates money with freedom and power and considers love and marriage two different things that kill each other.

To Prince Zouroff, marriage is purely an economic transaction. He knows that Vere loathes him, which increases his desire to buy and commodify her—to have total ownership until he tires of her. He is ready to "pay a high price for innocence, because it was a new toy that pleased him. But he never thought that it would last, any more than the bloom lasts on the peach" (176). He reduces Vere to an object—an "it" rather than a her: "Since it would be agreeable to brush *it* off himself, he was ready to purchase *it*" (176). The institution of marriage in his eyes is a socially approved means of acquiring a sexual slave:

Only a generation or two back his forefathers had bought beautiful Persian women by heaping up the scales of barter with strings of pearls and sequins, and had borne off Circassian slaves in forays with simple payment of a lance left in the lifeless breasts of the men who had owned them: his wooing was of the same rude sort. Only being a man of the world, and his ravishing being legalised by society, he went to the great shops of Paris for his gems, and employed great notaries to write down the terms of barter.

[Vere's] shrinking coldness, the undisguised aversion of his bethrothed only whetted his passion to quicker ardour, as the shrieks of the Circassian captives, or the quivering limbs of the Persian slaves, had done that of his forefathers in Ukraine. (195)[1]

It is no wonder that when Vere receives Zouroff's gift of pearls, they seem to her to be the same as "the chains locked on slave-girls bought for the harem" (180).

The narrator ironically notes that by forcing Vere to marry Zouroff, Dolly is actually consigning her daughter to a life of prostitution: "The streets absorb the girls of the poor; society absorbs the daughters of the rich; and not seldom one form of prostitution, like the other, keep its captives 'bound in the dungeon of their own corruption'"[2] (187). The institution of marriage then is no longer a sacrament, but legalized bondage and prostitution.

Vere's grandmother "reared her in old-world ideas of duty" (230); thus she submits to her husband's carnal demands. Afterwards she feels that she has been sentenced to a lifetime of perpetual degradation. She walks "with a step that was slow and weary, and yet very restless, the step of a thing that is chained" (197). She considers herself so vile and degraded "that the basest of creatures would have full right to strike her cheek, and spit in her face, and call her sister" (198). Yet Vere has only followed what society decrees the proper duty of women—to marry and obey her husband:

Society had set its seal of approval upon this union, and upon all such unions, and so deemed them sanctified. Year after year, one

---

1 See also Jane Jordan's ("Ouida: the Enigma of a Literary Identity" 96-97) and Talia Schaffer's (*The Forgotten Female Aesthetes* 128-29) discussions of Vere's oppressive marriage.

2 From John Ruskin's *The Two Paths*, Lecture 1, January 1858. He was referring to the art of India, which "never represents a natural fact" because the artists are "cut off from all possible sources of healthy knowledge or natural delight."

on another, the pretty, rosy, golden-curled daughters of fair mothers were carefully tended and cultured and reared up to grace the proud races from which they sprang, and were brought out into the great world in their first bloom like half-opened roses, with no other end or aim set before them as the one ambition of their lives than to make such a marriage as this....

Pollution? Prostitution? Society would have closed its ears to such words, knowing nothing of such things, not choosing to know anything.

Shame? What shame could there be when he was her husband? Strange fanciful exaggeration!—society would have stared and smiled....

To marry well; that was the first duty of a woman. (199)

To make matters worse, Zouroff sexually, mentally, and physically abuses Vere: "Sometimes he liked to hurt her in any way he could" (206). Unaware that Lady Dolly forced her daughter to accept his proposal Zouroff believes that Vere has sold herself like all other women he knows—that she married him for his money and social position. Therefore, he treats her accordingly: like a whore. He sadistically forces her to abase herself and obey his obscene demands, and he triumphs in exposing her to bawdy drama and erotic fiction: "It amused him to lower her, morally and physically, and he cast all the naked truths of human vices before her shrinking mind, as he made her body tremble at his touch" (225). Vere was not tempted by a serpent, nor has she eaten a forbidden fruit, but the marriage strips away her innocence: "She had drunk of the cup of knowledge of good and evil, and, though she had drunk with sinless lips, she could not entirely escape the poison the cup held" (263). She learns just how corrupt the society that sanctioned her marriage is: "Sin she heard of for the first time, and it was smiled at; vice became bare to her, but no one shunned it; the rapacity of an ignoble passion let loose and called 'marriage' tore down all her childish ignorance and threw it to the winds, destroyed her self-respect, and laughed at her, trampled on all her modest shame, and ridiculed her innocence" (205).

Zouroff, however, soon wearies of his cold, beautiful young wife—his new toy. Because it is not in Vere's nature to behave like his wanton mistresses, he turns more frequently and flagrantly to them. But he never lets Vere forget that he is her master, and he takes sadistic delight in forcing her to submit sexually—to raping her.

Humiliated by her husband's debauchery and the "emptiness and nothingness" in her oppressive life, Vere gradually rebels. The institution of marriage ironically both imprisons and, to a certain extent, empowers her. First she asks for a partial separation—to live one half a year alone on one of his estates. This only causes her husband to remind her forcefully that he owns her soul and body:

> He took the loose gold of her hair in his hands with a sudden caress and drew her into his arms....
> "A very calm proposition for a separation! That is what you drive at, no doubt; a separation in which you should have all the honours as Princess Zouroff still! No, my lovely Vera, I am not disposed to gratify you,—so. You belong to me, and you must continue to belong to me, nilly-willy. You are too handsome to lose.... Pshaw! how you shudder! You forget you must pay now and then for your diamonds."
> There are many martyrdoms as there are many prostitutions that law legalises and the churches approve. (390)

Jane Jordan points out how sensational Ouida's portrayal of Zouroff's sexual abuse was in 1880: "There is excessive rhetoric of brutality, of bestiality, and of unspecified male vices, which suggest indeed vices which could not be uttered ... perhaps including vices such as marital rape, denied a name under British law" ("Ouida: the Enigma of a Literary Identity" 96).

Although Vere is strong-willed and rebellious, when faced with having to acknowledge publicly her husband's three mistresses (even to the point of threatening to leave him), she refuses to consider divorce as an option. She remains firm even when Zouroff gives her grounds and taunts her to divorce him. She cringes from the publicity of the Divorce Court, which "literally rewrote sexuality in the English public sphere" (Leckie 109). To sue for a divorce, Vere would have to expose her private life to the public. She would have to charge her husband with adultery and physical cruelty, and the lurid details of the marriage would be published in the daily newspapers. Even though she has been defiled by the marriage, Vere believes that "The woman who can wish for a divorce and drag her wrongs into public—such wrongs!—is already a wanton herself.... A woman who divorces her husband is a prostitute legalized by a form, that is all" (422-23).

Eventually Zouroff has their marriage annulled, and Vere is rewarded with a happy marriage—the first time in the English novel that "a divorced woman [is] utterly happy" (Mitchell 140). Nevertheless, she still remains permanently scarred from the first marriage: "for no fault of her own, the weight of a guilt not her own lies heavily, and the ineffaceable past is like a ghost that tracks her steps; from her memory the pollution of her marriage never can pass away, and to her purity her life seems forever defiled by those dead years, which are like mill-stones hung about her neck" (541).

Ouida ultimately remains ambiguous about marriage and divorce. Like marriage, divorce is "no primrose path." Suffering or committing adultery are the only two options in *Moths* for a woman trapped in a marriage like Vere's. With the exception of rich American women like her cousin's wife, in the society of Ouida's fiction only Femme Galantes have freedom and power; ironically, they are rewarded, not punished. Both Nadine Nelaguine and Lady Dolly remain content with their husbands and lovers. Jeanne de Sonnaz, newly widowed, vengefully entraps her lover Zouroff into marrying her and plans to make him dance for her like a bear on a rope. Vere remains innocent, but "when the moths have gnawed the ermine, no power in heaven or earth can make it ever again altogether what once it was" (541).

Critical Responses to Ouida's Work

Contemporary Responses

Nineteenth-century critics generally either praised Ouida for her brilliant poetic use of language and her romantic, escapist plots, or mocked her absurd caricatures, her repetition and poor style, her mawkish sentimentality, and her prurient exposures of society. Reviewers were often patronizing and contemptuous (see Appendix A.2). Her novels were called vulgar, nasty, and immoral. A.K. Fiske, for example, berates *Moths*, along with Zola's *Nana*,[1] as offenses against propriety that promote gross sensuality. He insinuates that because of Ouida's "foreign" upbringing, she had no knowledge of domesticity, which produces "the graces of character." He adds that Ouida attacks society because it "is not openly tolerant of a disregard of the canons of morality" and concludes that she "turns the gutters into our wholesome gardens and casts the uncleanliness of the divorce court among our hearthstones" (Appendix A.4). In another review Willa Cather also calls Ouida's novels sinful, not for her

---

1 Émile Zola's *Nana* (1880) is the story of a prostitute in Paris. The novel was shocking in its day because of its strong emphasis on the sordid side of life.

sensuality, though, but because the novelist didn't use her "great talent." Her novels, Cather states, "are the work of a brilliant mind that never matured" (Appendix C.5).

Another major objection was the effect Ouida's novels supposedly had on the lower and middle classes: "Foolish lads and girls fancy they have a reflection of society in the most ludicrously distorted pictures and caricatures" (Appendix B.2). Fiske faults the reading public who, "[t]ormented with prurient longings," encourage the publication of novels like Ouida's.

On the other hand, Ouida had her supporters who argued that her "great talent" compensated for weaknesses, such as repetition and florid language. Marie Corelli, for example, says that without the exaggerated characters, sensuous suggestions, and the recklessness of writing, she would rank Ouida's fiction "in the highest rank of modern literature" (Appendix C.3). "Ella" praises Ouida for her vigorous vivacious language and the richness of her imagination, and *The Whitehall Review* compares Ouida with the composer, Frédéric Chopin. The reviewer says that Ouida is original and superb: "a constellation of surpassing brilliance, an author whose light will never be put out" (Appendix C.2). G.S. Street objects to the "contemptuous patronage" of reviewers: "I enjoyed them [her novels] as a boy, and I enjoy them now; I place them far above books whose praise is in all critics' mouths" (Appendix C.4). Finally, Max Beerbohm's tribute to Ouida is perhaps the most complimentary. He calls her "one of the miracles of modern literature" and states that Ouida towers "Head and shoulders over all the other women (and all but one of two of the men) who are writing English novels." He says that her sustained vitality is the strongest aspect of her work. He also praises her for her wit, poetry, philosophy, psychological analysis, and her "diatribes against society for its vulgar use of luxury" (Appendix C.6).

Twentieth-Century Responses

Malcolm Elwin in his *Victorian Wallflowers* (1930) repeats many of the objections to Ouida's fiction that her contemporary reviewers voiced, but he does praise the merits of her critical essays, concluding: "Her worthlessness and artificiality are qualifications [for her to appear in his book], for they typify the taste and mentality of the new reading public, created by the industrial development and cheap education" (311). In 1970, on the other hand, Bonamy Dobrée echoes Beerbohm's earlier praise. He speculates why a writer as popular as Ouida was in her day is neglected in the twentieth century and concludes that readers today are not in tune with her "lavishness," her "immense torrent of words." He concedes that Ouida has flaws, but says that her dazzling fantasy world is a "delicious escape" (194) and concludes by saying, "Her work will not stand the test of actuality, but it will stand that of an undisciplined imaginative truth" (198).

In *Women and Fiction* (1979) Patricia Stubbs faults Ouida because her heroines do not challenge "patriarchal stereotypes of feminine character or behavior" (39). Although Stubbs admits that Ouida did deal with some important feminist issues, such as the marriage market, the legal position of women in marriage, and the double standard, she claims that *Moths* is "timid in its treatment of women and sexuality" (48). Sally Mitchell (1982), on the other hand, says that Ouida is a transitional novelist because of her unconventional treatment of love and sex and calls *Moths* a "shocking book.... [A] novel with a purpose, and the first in England to show a divorced woman utterly happy" and remarried (140).

In a 1988 article, I argue that both Ouida and Mary Elizabeth Braddon challenged the conventional feminine ideal, voicing fantasies of their reading public. By being self-assertive and using their sexuality, their fictional characters gain power and a "taste of independence" (90). Pamela K. Gilbert concurs, stating that although Ouida is decidedly anti-feminist and denigrating to women in her fiction, "she grants these women a remarkable power and energy in manipulating and controlling their environment, and a capacity for doing damage that may have been a potent attractant for female readers who felt that their own control of their lives was at best tenuous" (*Disease, Desire, and the Body* 144). In an important 1995 essay on Ouida, Jane Jordan specifically praises *Moths* for its reflection of "the contemporary debate about the status of women in marriage.... [I]t created a critical furor because of the openness with which it treated of women's sufferings at the hands of unscrupulous husbands" (97). Finally, in *The Forgotten Female Aesthetes* (2000), Talia Schaffer notes that: "Ouida's position as a best-selling writer who cared about art uniquely positioned her in both circulating-library and high-culture camps, which gives her a vital role in literary history" (123). She classifies *Moths* as "a classically Ouidean Gothic tale," in which her heroine is forced "into a state of pathological perpetual childishness" (131-32).

Works Cited

Altick, Richard D. *Victorian People and Ideas.* New York: W.W. Norton, 1973.

Ardis, Ann L. *New Women, New Novels: Feminism and Early Modernism.* New Brunswick: Rutgers UP, 1990.

Bigland, Eileen. *Ouida, The Passionate Victorian.* New York: Duell, Sloan and Pearce, 1951.

Burchell, S.C. *Imperial Masquerade: The Paris of Napoleon III.* New York: Atheneum, 1971.

Cunningham, Gail. *The New Woman and the Victorian Novel.* London and Basingstoke: Macmillan, 1978.

Dobrée, Bonamy. "Ouida." *Milton to Ouida: A Collection of Essays.* London: Frank Cass, 1970.

Duffy, James P. and Vincent L. Ricci. *Czars: Russia's Rulers for More Than One Thousand Years.* New York: Facts On File, 1995.

Elwin, Malcolm. *Victorian Wallflowers.* London: Jonathan Cape, 1934.

Gilbert, Pamela K. *Disease, Desire, and the Body in Victorian Women's Popular Novels.* Cambridge: Cambridge UP, 1997.

—. "Ouida and the Other New Woman," *Victorian Women Writers and the Woman Question.* Ed. Nicola Diane Thompson. Cambridge: Cambridge UP, 1999.

Gilmour, Robin. *The Novel in the Victorian Age: A Modern Introduction.* London: Edward Arnold, 1986.

Guedalla, Philip. *The Second Empire: Bonapartism, the Prince, the President, the Emperor.* New York: G.P. Putnam's Sons, 1922.

Heilmann, Ann. *New Women Writing: First-Wave Feminism.* New York: St. Martin's P, 2000.

Helsinger, Elizabeth K., Robin Lauterbach Sheets, William Veeder. *The Woman Question: Society and Literature in Britain and America 1837-1883.* Vol. 3. Chicago: U of Chicago P, 1989.

Heyman, Neil M. *Russian History.* New York: McGraw-Hill, 1993.

Jordan, Ellen. "The Christening of the New Woman: May 1894." *Victorian Newsletter* 63 (Spring 1983): 19-21.

Jordan, Jane. "Ouida: the Enigma of a Literary Identity." *Princeton University Library Chronicle* 57 (Autumn 1995): 75-105.

—. "The Writings of 'Ouida' (Marie Louise de la Ramée, 1839-1908)." PhD Thesis, Birkbeck College, University of London, 1995.

Leckie, Barbara. *Culture and Adultery: The Novel, the Newspaper, and the Law, 1857-1914.* Philadelphia: U of Pennsylvania P, 1999.

Lewis, Jane. *Women in England 1870-1950: Sexual Divisions and Social Change.* Bloomington: Indiana UP, 1984.

Mitchell, Sally. *The Fallen Angel: Chastity, Class and Women's Reading 1835-1880.* Bowling Green, OH: Bowling Green University Popular P, 1982.

Ouida. "Female Suffrage." *Views and Opinions.* London: Methuen, 1896.

—. *Guilderoy.* Ouida Illustrated. Vol. 12. New York: P.F. Collier, 1893.

—. *In a Winter City*. Ouida Illustrated. Vol. 6. New York: P.F. Collier, 1890.

—. *Moths*. Copyright Edition. 3 vols. Leipzig: Bernard Tauchnitz, 1880.

—. *Moths*. Ouida Illustrated. Vol. 12. New York: P.F. Collier, 1893.

—. "O Beati Insipientes!" *Views and Opinions*. London: Methuen, 1896.

—. *Princess Napraxine*. Ouida Illustrated. Vol. 10. New York: P.F. Collier, 1889.

—. *Puck*. Ouida Illustrated. Vol. 9. New York: P.F. Collier, 1892.

Poster, Carol. "Oxidation is a Feminist Issue: Acidity, Canonicity, and Popular Victorian Female Authors." *College English* 58.3 (March 1996): 287–306.

Powell, Anthony. "Introduction." *Novels of High Society in the Victorian Age*. London: Pilot P, 1947.

Pykett, Lyn. *The 'Improper' Feminine: The Women's Sensation Novel and the New Woman Writing*. London: Routledge, 1992.

Roosevelt, Priscilla. *Life on the Russian Country Estate: A Social and Cultural History*. New Haven and London: Yale UP, 1995.

Schaffer, Talia. "'Nothing But Foolscap and Ink': Inventing the New Woman." *The New Woman in Fiction and in Fact: Fin-de-Siècle Feminisms*. Eds. Angelique Richardson and Chris Willis. New York: Palgrave, 2001.

—. *The Forgotten Female Aesthetes: Literary Culture in Late Victorian England*. Charlottesville: UP of Virginia, 2000.

Schroeder, Natalie. "Feminine Sensationalism, Eroticism, and Self Assertion: M.E. Braddon and Ouida." *Tulsa Studies in Women's Literature* 7 (1988): 87–105.

Seton-Watson, Hugh. *The Russian Empire 1801-1917*. Oxford: Oxford UP, 1976.

Shanley, Mary Lyndon. *Feminism, Marriage, and the Law in Victorian England*. New Jersey: Princeton UP, 1989.

Stirling, Monica. *The Fine and the Wicked: The Life and Times of Ouida*. New York: Coward-McCann, 1958.

Stubbs, Patricia. *Women and Fiction: Feminism and the Novel 1880-1920*. New York: Harper and Row, 1979.

Thackeray, William. *Vanity Fair*. Harmondsworth: Penguin, 1983.

Thompson, Nicola Diane. "Responding to the Women Questions: Rereading Noncanonical Victorian Women Novelists." *Victorian Women Writers and the Woman Question*. Ed. Nicola Diane Thompson. Cambridge: Cambridge UP, 1999.

Ouida: A Brief Chronology

1839   Born New Years day in Bury St. Edmunds, Suffolk, Ouida is christened Maria Louisa Ramé.

1850   Her father takes Ouida and her mother to Bologne for a summer holiday.

1851   The family visits the Great Exhibition in London.

1854   The Crimean War sparks Ouida's interest in foreign affairs and the military.

1857   Ouida, her mother, maternal grandmother, and Beausire (the dog) move to London. Ouida meets William Harrison Ainsworth.

1859   *Dashwood Drag; or the Derby and What Came of It* serialized in the April and May numbers of *Bentley's Miscellany*.

1861   *Granville de Vigne; A Tale of the Day* [later named *Held in Bondage*], Ouida's first full-length novel, serialized in *The New Monthly Magazine*, January 1861-June 1863.

1863   *Held in Bondage* published in three volumes. *Strathmore* serialized in *The New Monthly Magazine* until 1865.

1865   *Strathmore* published in three volumes. Mme. Ramé is convinced Louis Ramé will never return. *Idalia* is serialized in *The New Monthly Magazine* until 1867.

1866   Grandmother and Beausire die; *Chandos* published.

1867   *Under Two Flags*, Ouida's fourth novel, published and becomes her greatest success to date. Ouida moves to the Langham Hotel and establishes herself as a hostess. *Idalia* and *Cecil Castlemaine's Gage and Other Novelettes* published.

1869   *Tricotrin* published.

1870   *Puck* published.

1871   Ouida falls in love with sixty-one year old Italian tenor Mario. *Folle-Farine* published; Ouida and her mother travel to Brussels, Germany, and arrive in Florence. She is so charmed with the city that they rent an apartment. Ouida meets Marchese Lotteria Lotharingo della Stufa and falls in love.

1872   Ouida makes female friendships. *A Dog of Flanders* published.

1873   Ouida and her mother visit Rome. Bulwer-Lytton and Napoleon III die. Ouida meets Lady Paget. *Pascarel* published.

1874   Ouida rents the Villa Farinola and holds Monday receptions. *Two Little Wooden Shoes* published.

1875   Ouida gets diphtheria. *Signa* published.

1876   Ouida learns Mrs. Ross is della Stufa's mistress. *In A Winter City* published.

1877   Ouida follows della Stufa to Rome and they resume their friendship. *Ariadne* published.

1878   *Friendship* published. Ouida's *roman à clef* causes a scandal by exposing della Stufa's and Mrs. Ross's affair.

1879   Ouida turns 40 and begins *Moths*.

1880   *Moths*, Ouida's fifteenth novel published. *Pipistrello and Other Stories* published.

1881   Della Stufa "cuts" Ouida in Rome, and she suffers a mental and physical breakdown. *A Village Commune* published. Italy joins Austria and Germany in the Triple Alliance.

1882   *In Maremma* published.

1883   *Wanda* and *Frescoes* published.

1884   Ouida meets and falls in love with Robert, Lord Lytton. *Princess Napraxine* published.

1885   *Othmar* and *A Rainy June* published.

1886   Ouida spends part of the summer in Hamburg. An invitation from Lord Lytton prompts her to visit London. At his home in Knebworth, Lytton locks himself in his room to avoid a private interview with Ouida. *Don Guesaldo* published.

1887   *A House Party* published.

1888   A group of peasants and carabinari, sent by the Marchese Farinola, force their way into the Villa Farinola and evict Ouida and her mother. They lease Palazzo Ferroni.

1889   *Guilderoy* published.

1890   Ouida and mother forced to leave the Palazzo. Their furniture is seized and manuscripts are auctioned. They move from hotel to hotel—from villa to villa. *Ruffino and other Stories* and *Syrlin* published.

1891   Learning of Lord Lytton's death, Ouida grieves. *Santa Barbara and Other Tales* published.

1892   Ouida rents the Villa della Corona, Bellosguardo. *The Tower of Taddeo* published.

1893   Madame Ramé dies. Destitute, Ouida at first refuses to part with the body to avoid its inevitable burial in a pauper's grave. *The New Priesthood: A Protest Against Vivisection* (pamphlet) published.

1894 After being evicted again, she moves to Lucca. *Two Offenders and Other Tales* and *The Silver Christ and a Lemon Tree* published.

1895 Ouida rents the Villa Massoni at Sant' Alessio. *Views and Opinions* and *Toxin* published.

1896 *Le Selve and Other Tales* published.

1897 *The Massarenes, Dogs*, and *An Altruist* published.

1899 Max Beerbohm dedicates *More* to Ouida. *La Strega and Other Stories* published.

1900 *The Waters of Edera* and *Critical Studies* published.

1901 *Street Dust and Other Stories* published.

1903 Madame Grosfils, the owner of the Villa Massoni, pressures Ouida to leave her residence of eight years. The sons take possession of the villa and steal Ouida's paintings, china, books, and manuscripts. She lives in distress at the Hotel de Russie at Viareggio for seven months.

1904 Ouida sues the Grosfils family. She takes a small villa at Camaiore, but when the leash laws are enforced, she moves back to Viareggio. She spends the night in a cab and loses sight in one eye and hearing in one ear. She makes her final move to Mazzarosa.

1907 Ouida becomes infuriated by Marie Corelli's letter to *The Daily Mail* about Ouida's poverty.

1908 Ouida dies of the effects of pneumonia. Her body is taken to the Protestant Cemetery at Bagni di Lucca. An anonymous admirer has a marble tomb erected showing Ouida in effigy lying with a little dog at her feet. The inscription reads "IN MEMORY OF LOUISE DE LA RAMÉE/ OUIDA/WRITER OF INCOMPARABLE NOVELS." *Helianthus* published posthumously and unfinished.

1909 Memorial drinking fountain for horses and dogs unveiled in Bury St. Edmunds. The inscription reads "Born at Bury St. Edmunds, January 1st 1839. Died in Viareggio, Italy, January 25th, 1908. Her friends have erected this fountain in the place of her birth. Here may God's creatures whom she loved assuage her tender soul as they drink."

A Note on the Text

The text of *Moths* used in this edition is based on the Copyright Edition, the 1880 Tauchnitz Collection of British Authors Edition, vols. 1878, 1897, and 1880. In 1841, Freiherr von Tauchnitz started the collection with Bulwer-Lytton's *Pelham*. He paid the authors for an exclusive right to publish their works on the continent. He had been the European publisher for Disraeli, Tennyson, Dickens, and George Eliot before he discovered Ouida. He approached her in 1865 and offered to publish her works in his collection. They remained friends and contemporaries until his death in 1895.

I chose this edition because it was the earliest one I could locate and it was in the original three-volume format. I also consulted the 1893 Peter Fenelon Collier Edition (New York) when I found errors in Tauchnitz that might have been due to type-setting. As many of Ouida's contemporary reviewers noted, her novels were filled with grammatical errors in English, French, and Italian. I have not attempted to correct grammatical errors, but I have silently corrected punctuation, spelling, and misplaced or missing accent marks.

Ouida was also criticized for padding her novels with obscure allusions. I have made every effort to identify the allusions with the help of colleagues, friends, and members of the Victoria listserv. Unfortunately, some of them proved to be so obscure (as in the case of Chaucer's heroine "with strait glaive and simple shield") that they remain a mystery.

MOTHS

A NOVEL

BY

OUIDA

"Like moths fretting a garment." (PSALM)

COPYRIGHT EDITION.

IN THREE VOLUMES

Le monde aime le vice et hait l'amour; le vice est un bon enfant, un viveur, un drôle, un gourmet; il tient bonne table, et vous invite souvent; l'amour, au contraire, est un pédant, un solitaire, un misanthrope, un va-nu-pieds; il ne vous amuse pas; vous criez vite, "à la lanterne!"—RIVAREZ.[1]

---

1 The world loves vice and hates love; vice is a good child, a pleasure seeker, a rascal, a glutton; he keeps a good table and invites you often; love, on the contrary, is a pedant, a hermit, a misanthrope, a beggar; he doesn't amuse you; you shout quick, "hang her!"

Inscribed

To

MY OLD FRIEND

ALGERNON BORTHWICK[1]

IN MEMORY OF THE DAYS OF

"PUCK"

AND AS A SLIGHT TOKEN OF AN

UNCHANGED REGARD

AND ESTEEM

---

1 Sir Algernon Borthwick, Lord Glenesk (1830-1908) was the proprietor/ editor of *The Morning Post*. The newspaper maintained a reputation for covering society events and as an advocate of a forward foreign policy. Borthwick attended many of the dinner parties Ouida hosted at the Langham Hotel in London.

VOLUME 1

CHAPTER I.

Lady Dolly ought to have been perfectly happy. She had everything that can constitute the joys of a woman of her epoch.

She was at Trouville.[1] She had won heaps of money at play. She had made a correct book on the races. She had seen her chief rival looking bilious in an unbecoming gown. She had had a letter from her husband to say he was going away to Java or Jupiter or somewhere indefinitely. She wore a costume which had cost a great tailor twenty hours of anxious and continuous reflection. Nothing but *baptiste* indeed! but *baptiste* sublimised and apotheosised by niello buttons, old lace, and genius. She had her adorers and slaves grouped about her. She had found her dearest friend out in cheating at cards. She had dined the night before at the Maison Persanne and would dine this night at the Maison Normande. She had been told a state secret by a minister which she knew it was shameful of him to have been coaxed and chaffed into revealing. She had had a new comedy read to her in man-uscript-form three months before it would be given in Paris, and had screamed at all its indecencies in the choice company of a Serene Princess and two ambassadresses as they all took their chocolate in their dressing-gowns. Above all, she was at Trouville, having left half a million of debts behind her strewn about in all directions, and stand-ing free as air in gossamer garments on the planks in the summer sun-shine. There was a charming blue sea beside her; a balmy fluttering breeze around her, a crowd of the most fashionable sunshades of Europe before her, like a bed of full-blown anemones. She had float-ed and bobbed and swum and splashed semi-nude, with all the other mermaids à *la mode*,[2] and had shown that she must still be a pretty woman, pretty even in daylight, or the men would not have looked at her so: and yet with all this she was not enjoying herself.

It was very hard.

The yachts came and went, the sands glittered, the music sound-ed, men and women in bright-coloured stripes took headers into the tide or pulled themselves about in little canoes; the snowy canvas of the tent shone like a huge white mushroom, and the faces of all the houses were lively with green shutters and awnings brightly striped

---

1 A fashionable seaside resort in northwest France (Normandy).
2 As is the fashion.

like the bathers; people, the gayest and best-born people in Europe, laughed and chattered, and made love, and Lady Dolly with them, pacing the deal planks with her pretty high-heeled shoes; but for all that she was wretched.

She was thinking to herself, *"What on earth shall I do with her?"*

It ruined her morning. It clouded the sunshine. It spoiled her cigarette. It made the waltzes sound like dirges. It made her chief rival look almost good-looking to her. It made a gown combined of parrots' breasts and passion-flowers that she was going to wear in the afternoon feel green, and yellow, and bilious in her anticipation of it, though it was quite new and a wonder. It made her remember her debts. It made her feel that she had not digested those *écrevissses*[1] at supper. It made her fancy that her husband might not really go to Java or Jupiter. It was so sudden, so appalling, so bewildering, so endless a question; and Lady Dolly only asked questions, she never answered them or waited for their answers.

After all, what could she do with her? She, a pretty woman and a wonderful flirt, who liked to dance to the very end of the cotillon,[2] and had as many lovers as she had pairs of shoes. What could she do with a daughter just sixteen years old?

"It makes one look so old!" she had said to herself wretchedly, as she had bobbed and danced in the waves. Lady Dolly was not old; she was not quite thirty-four, and she was as pretty as if she were seventeen, perhaps prettier; even when she was not "done up," and she did not need to do herself up very much just yet, really not much, considering,—well, considering so many things, that she never went to bed till daylight, that she never ate anything digestible, and never drank anything wholesome, that she made her waist fifteen inches round, and destroyed her nerves with gambling, chloral, and many other things; considering these, and so many other reasons, besides the one supreme reason that everybody does it, and that you always look a fright if you don't do it.

The thought of her daughter's impending arrival made Lady Dolly miserable. Telegrams were such horrible things. Before she had had time to realise the force of the impending catastrophe the electric wires had brought her tidings that the girl was actually on her way across the sea, not to be stayed by any kind of means, and would be there by nightfall. Nightfall at Trouville! When Lady Dolly in the deftest of summer-evening toilettes would be just opening her pret-

---

1   Crawfish.
2   Formal balls, especially ones where young girls are presented to society.

ty mouth for her first morsel of salmon and drop of Chablis, with the windows open and the moon rising on the sea, and the card-tables ready set, and the band playing within earshot, and the courtiers all around and at her orders, whether she liked to go out and dance, or stay at home for poker or *chemin de fer*.[1]

"What in the world shall I do with her, Jack?" she sighed to her chief counsellor.

The chief counsellor opened his lips, answered "Marry her!" then closed them on a big cigar.

"Of course! One always marries girls; how stupid you are," said Lady Dolly peevishly.

The counsellor smiled grimly, "And then you will be a grand-mother," he said with a cruel relish: he had just paid a bill at a *bric-à-brac* shop for her and it had left him unamiable.

"I suppose you think that witty," said Lady Dolly with delicate contempt. "Well, Hélène there is a great-grandmother, and look at her!"

Hélène was a Prussian princess, married to a Russian minister: she was arrayed in white with a tender blending about it of all the blues in creation, from that of a summer sky to that of a *lapis lazuli* ring; she had a quantity of fair curls, a broad hat wreathed with white lilac and con-volvulus, a complexion of cream, teeth of pearl, a luminous and inno-cent smile; she was talking at the top of her voice and munching chocolate; she had a circle of young men round her; she looked, per-haps, if you wished to be ill-natured, eight-and-twenty. Yet a great-grandmother she was, and the "Almanach de Gotha,"[2] said so, and alas! said her age.

"You won't wear so well as Hélène. You don't take care of your-self," the counsellor retorted, with a puff of smoke between each sentence.

"WHAT!" screamed Lady Dolly, so that her voice rose above the din of all the other voices,—the sound of the waves, the click-clack of the high heels, and the noise of the band. Not take care of her-self!—she! who had every fashionable medicine that came out, and, except at Trouville, never would be awakened for any earthly thing till one o'clock in the day.

"You don't take care of yourself," said the counsellor. "No; you eat heaps of sweetmeats. You take too much tea, too much ice, too much soup, too much wine; too much everything. You—"

---

1 A version of baccarat.
2 Publication giving statistical information on European royalty.

"Oh! if you mean to insult me and call me a drunkard—!" said Lady Dolly, very hotly flushing up a little.

"You smoke quite awfully too much," pursued her companion immovably. "It hurts us, and can't be good for you. Indeed, all you women would be dead if you smoked right; you don't smoke right; you send all your smoke out, chattering; it never gets into your mouth even, and so that saves you all; if you drew it in, as we do, you would be dead, all of you. Who was the first woman that smoked I often wonder?"

"The idea of my not wearing as well as Hélène," pursued Lady Dolly, unable to forget the insult. "Well, there are five-and-twenty years between us, thank goodness, and more!"

"I say you won't," said the counsellor, "not if you go on as you do, screaming all night over those cards and taking quarts of chloral because you can't sleep? Why can't you sleep? I can."

"All the lower animals sleep like tops," said Lady Dolly. "You seem to have been reading medical treatises, and they haven't agreed with you. Go and buy me a 'Petit Journal.'"

The counsellor went grumbling and obedient—a tall, good-looking, well-built, and very fair Englishman, who had shot everything that was shootable all over the known world. Lady Dolly smiled serenely on the person who glided to her elbow, and took the vacant place; a slender, pale, and graceful Frenchman, the Duc de Dinant of the *vieille souche*.[1]

"Dear old Jack gets rather a proser," she thought, and she began to plan a fishing picnic with her little Duke; a picnic at which everybody was to go barefooted, and dress like peasants—real common peasants, you know, of course,—and dredge, didn't they call it, and poke about, and hunt for oysters. Lady Dolly had lovely feet, and could afford to uncover them; very few of her rivals could do so, a fact of which she took cruel advantage, and from which she derived exquisite satisfaction in clear shallows and rock pools. "The donkeys! they've cramped themselves in tight boots!" she said to herself, with the scorn of a superior mind. She always gave her miniature feet and arched insteps their natural play, and therein displayed a wisdom of which it must be honestly confessed, the rest of her career gave no glimpse.

The counsellor bought the "Petit Journal" and a "Figaro"[2] for himself, and came back; but she did not notice him at all. A few years

---

1 Old family.
2 French newspapers.

before the neglect would have made him miserable; now it made him comfortable—such is the ingratitude of man. He sat down and read the "Figaro" with complacency, while she, under her sunshade beamed on Gaston de Dinant, and on four or five others of his kind; youngsters without youth, but, as a compensation for the loss, with a perfect knowledge of Judic's last song, and Dumas' last piece[1] of the last new card-room scandal, and the last drawing-room adultery; of everything that was coming out at the theatres, and of all that was of promise in the stables. They were not in the least amusing in themselves, but the chatter of the world has almost always an element of the amusing in it, because it ruins so many characters, and gossips and chuckles so merrily and so lightly over infamy, incest, or anything else that it thinks only fun, and deals with such impudent personalities. At any rate they amused Lady Dolly, and her Duc de Dinant did more; they arranged the picnic,—without shoes, that was indispensable, without shoes, and in real peasant's things, else there would be no joke—they settled their picnic, divorced half-a-dozen of their friends, conjectured about another half-dozen all those enormities which modern society would blush at in the Bible but, out of it, whispers and chuckles over very happily; speculated about the few unhappy unknowns who had dared to enter the magic precincts of these very dusty sands; wondered with whom the Prince of Wales would dine that night, and whose that new yawl was, that had been standing off since morning flying the R.Y.S. flag;[2] and generally diverted one another so well, that beyond an occasional passing spasm of remembrance, Lady Dolly had forgotten her impending trial.

"I think I will go in to breakfast," she said at last, and got up. It was one o'clock, and the sun was getting hot; the anemone-bed began to heave and be dispersed; up and down the planks the throng was thick still, the last bathers, peignoir-enwrapped, were sauntering from the edge of the sea. The counsellor folded his "Figaro," and shut up his cigar-case; his was the useful but humble task to go home before her and see that the Moselle was iced, the prawns just netted, the strawberries just culled, and the cutlets duly frothing in their silver dish. The Duc de Dinant sauntered by her with no weightier duty than to gaze gently down into her eyes, and buy a stephanotis or a knot of roses for her bosom when they passed the flower-baskets.

---

1 Anna Judic (1849-1911) was a French singer and song writer; Alexandre Dumas *fils* (1824-95) was a French playwright who was obsessed with the theme of illicit love.
2 The Royal Yacht Squadron was a club that sponsored races.

"What are they all looking at?" said Lady Dolly to her escort sud-denly. Bodies of the picturesque parti-coloured crowd were all streaming the same way, inland towards the sunny white houses, whose closed green shutters were all so attractively suggestive of the shade and rest to be found within. But the heads of the crowd were turning back seaward, and their eyes and eye-glasses all gazed in the same direction.

Was it at the Prince? Was it at the President? Was it the Channel fleet had hove in sight? or some swimmer drowning, or some por-poises, or what? No, it was a new arrival. A new arrival was no excite-ment at Trouville if it were somebody that everybody knew. Emper-ors were common-place; ministers were nonentities; marshals were monotonous; princes were more numerous than the porpoises; and great dramatists, great singers, great actors, great orators, were all there as the very sands of the sea. But an arrival of somebody that nobody knew had a certain interest, if only as food for laughter. It seemed so queer that there should be such people, or that existing, they should venture there.

"Who is it?" said Trouville, in one breath, and the women laughed, and the men stared, and both sexes turned round by common con-sent. Something lovelier than anything there was coming through them as a sunbeam comes through dust. Yet it wore nothing but brown holland![1] Brown holland at Trouville may be worn indeed, but it is brown holland transfigured, sublimated, canonised, borne, like Lady Dolly's *baptiste*, into an apotheosis of écru[2] lace and floss silk embroideries, and old point cravats, and buttons of repousse work, or ancient smalto;[3] brown holland raised to the empyrean, and no more discoverable to the ordinary naked eye than the original flesh, fish, or fowl lying at the root of a good cook's *mayonnaise* is discernible to the uneducated palate.

But this was brown holland naked and not ashamed, unadorned and barbaric, without any attempt at disguise of itself, and looking wet and wrinkled from seawater, and very brown indeed beside the fresh and ethereal costumes of the ladies gathered there, that looked like bubbles just blown in a thousand hues to float upon the breeze.

"Brown holland! good gracious!" said Lady Dolly, putting up her eyeglass. She could not very well see the wearer of it; there were so

---

1 A cotton cloth treated to produce an opaque finish.
2 Raw, unbleached.
3 Colored glass used in mosaics.

many men between them; but she could see the wet, clinging, tumbled skirt which came in amongst the wonderful garments of the sacred place, and to make this worse there was an old Scotch plaid above the skirt, not worn, thrown on anyhow, as she said pathetically, long afterwards.

"What a guy!"[1] said Lady Dolly.

"What a face!" said the courtiers; but they said it under their breath, being wise in their generation, and praising no woman before another.

But the brown holland came towards her, catching in the wind, and showing feet as perfect as her own. The brown holland stretched two hands out to her, and a voice cried aloud,

"Mother! don't you know me, mother?"

Lady Dolly gave a sharp little scream, then stood still. Her pretty face was very blank, her rosy small mouth was parted in amaze and disgust.

"IN THAT DRESS!" she gasped, when the position became clear to her and her senses returned.

But the brown holland was clinging in a wild and joyous kind of horrible, barbarous way all about her, as it seemed, and the old Scotch plaid was pressing itself against her *baptiste* skirts.

"Oh, mother! how lovely you are! Not changed in the very least! Don't you know me. Oh dear! don't you know me? I am Vere."

Lady Dolly was a sweet-tempered woman by nature, and only made fretful occasionally by maids' contretemps, debts, husbands, and other disagreeable accompaniments of life. But, at this moment, she had no other sense than that of rage. She could have struck her sunshade furiously at all creation; she could have fainted, only the situation would have been rendered more ridiculous still if she had, and that consciousness sustained her; the sands, and the planks, and the sea, and the sun, all went round her in a whirl of wrath. She could hear all her lovers, and friends, and rivals, and enemies tittering; and Princess Hélène Olgarouski, who was at her shoulder, said in the pleasantest way—

"Is that your little daughter, dear? Why she is quite a woman! A new beauty for Monseigneur."

Lady Dolly could have slain her hundreds in that moment, had her sunshade but been of steel. To be made ridiculous! There is no more disastrous destiny under the sun.

---

1 British: a person of odd or grotesque appearance or dress.

The brown holland had ceased to cling about her, finding itself repulsed; the Scotch plaid had fallen down on the plank; there were two brilliant and wistful eyes regarding her from above, and one hand still stretched out shyly.

"I amVere!" said a voice in which tears trembled and held a struggle with pride.

"I see you are!" said Lady Dolly with asperity. "What on earth made you come in this—this—indecent way for—without even dressing! I expected you at night. Is that Fräulein Schroder? She should be ashamed of herself."

"I see no shame, Miladi," retorted in guttural tones an injured German, "in that a long-absent and much-loving daughter should be breathless to flee to embrace the one to whom she owes her being—"

"Hold your tongue!" said Lady Dolly angrily. Fräulein Schroder wore a green veil and blue spectacles, and was not beautiful to the eye, and was grizzle-headed; and the friends and lovers, and courtiers, and enemies, were laughing uncontrollably.

"What an angel of loveliness! But a woman; quite a woman. She must be twenty at least, my dear?" said Princess Hélène, who always said the pleasantest thing she could think of at any time.

"Vere is sixteen," said Lady Dolly sharply, much ruffled, seeing angrily that the girl's head in its sun-burnt sailor's hat, bound with a black ribbon, was nearly a foot higher than her own, hung down, though it now was, like a rose in the rain.

There was a person coming up from his mile swim in the sea, with the burnous-like folds cast about him more gracefully than other men were able ever to cast theirs.

"How do you manage to get so much grace out of a dozen yards of bath towelling, Corrèze?" asked an Englishman who was with him.

"*C'est mon métier à moi d'être poseur,*"[1] said the other, paraphrasing the famous saying of Joseph the Second.[2]

"Ah, no," said the Englishman, "you never do *poser*; that is the secret of the charm of the thing. I feel like a fool in these *spadilles* and swathings;[3] but you—you look as if you had just come up from

---

1 "It is my calling to be a poser"; to affect an attitude or manner to impress others.
2 Joseph II (1741-90) was the Holy Roman emperor and king of Bohemia and Hungary who tried unsuccessfully to reform and unify the Austrian Hapsburg domains.
3 Beach shoes and (towel) wrappings.

a sacred river of the East, and are worthy to sing strophes to a Nourmahal."[1]

"*Encore une fois—mon métier*,"[2] said the other, casting some of the linen folds over his head, which was exceedingly handsome, and almost line for line like the young Sebastian of Del Sarto.[3] At that moment he saw the little scene going on between Lady Dolly and her daughter, and watched it from a distance with much amusement.

"What an exquisite face that child has,—that lovely tint like the wild white rose, there is nothing like it. It makes all the women with colour look vulgar," he said, after a prolonged gaze through a friend's field-glass. "Who is she do you say? Miladi Dolly's daughter? Is it possible? I thought Miladi was made herself yesterday in Giroux's shop, and was kept in a wadded box when her mechanism was not wound up. Surely, it is impossible Dolly can ever have stooped to such a homely unartificial thing as maternity. You must be mistaken."

"No. In remote ages she married a cousin. The white wild rose is the result."

"A charming result. A child only, but an exquisite child. It is a pity we are in this costume, or we would go and be presented; though Miladi would not be grateful, to judge by her face now. Poor little Dolly! It is hard to have a daughter—and a daughter that comes to Trouville in August."

Then he who was a figure of grace even in white towelling, and had a face like Saint Sebastian, handed the field-glass back to his friend, and went to his hotel to dress.

Meanwhile Lady Dolly was saying irritably: "Go home to my house, Vere,—the Châlet Ludoff. Of course you ought to have gone there first; why didn't you go there first and *dress*? None but an idiot would ever have allowed you to do it. The idea! Walk on, pray—and as quickly as you can."

"We went to the house, but they said you were on the beach, and so, mother—"

"Pray don't call me mother in that way. It makes one feel like What's-her-name in the 'Trovatore,'"[4] said Lady Dolly, with a little laugh, that was very fretful. "And be kind enough not to stand here and stare; everybody is listening."

---

1 Sultana; light of the harem.
2 "One more time—my calling."
3 A Roman martyr who was a favorite subject of Renaissance painters.
4 An opera by Guiseppe Verdi (1813-1901), an Italian composer. *Il Trovatore* premièred in 1853.

"What for should they not listen?" said Fräulein Schroder stoutly. "Can there be in nature a sweeter, more soul-inspiring, and of-heaven-always-blessed-emotion than the out-coming of filial love and the spontaneous flow of—"

"Rubbish!" said Lady Dolly. "Vere, oblige me by walking in; I shall be with you in a moment at the house. You'll find Jack there. You remember Jack?"

"What an angel! anyone would give her twenty years at least," said Princess Hélène again. "But your German, in her blue glasses, she is a *drôlesse*—"[1]

"A very clever woman; dreadfully blue and conscientious, and all that is intolerable; the old duchess found her for me," replied Lady Dolly, still half willing to faint, and half inclined to cry, and wholly in that state of irritation which Fuseli[2] was wont to say made swearing delicious.

"I always fancied—so stupid of me!—that your Vere was quite a little child, always at the Sacré Coeur,"[3] continued the Princess musingly, with her sweetest smile.

"I wish to heaven we had a Sacré Coeur," said Lady Dolly devoutly. "We wretched English people have nothing half so sensible; you know that, Hélène, as well as I do. Vere is tall and very like her poor father and the old Duke."

"But Vere—surely that is not the name of a girl?"

"It was her father's. *That* was the old Duchess's doing too. Of course one will call her Vera. Well, *au revoir ma très chère, à ce soir*."[4]

"With nods and becks and wreathed smiles," and many good-days and pretty words, poor Lady Dolly got away from her friends and acquaintances, and had the common luxury of hearing them all begin laughing again as soon as they imagined she had got out of earshot. Her young courtiers accompanied her, of course, but she dismissed them on the doorstep.

"I can't think of anything but my child to-day!" she said very charmingly. "So glad you think her nice-looking. When she is *dressed*, you know—" and she disappeared into her own house with the phrase unfinished, leaving all it suggested to her hearers.

"Where's Vere?" she said sharply to her counsellor, entering the breakfast-room, before the empty stove of which, from the

---

1 Hussy.
2 John Henry Fuseli (1741–1825) was a British Romantic painter.
3 Sacred Heart, a church in Paris.
4 "Goodby, my dearest. Until this evening."

sheer fire-place club-room habit of his race, that person stood smoking.

"Gone to her room," he answered. "You've made her cry. You were nasty, weren't you?"

"I was furious! Who wouldn't have been? That vile dress! That abominable old woman! And kissing me too—me—on the beach!"

Her companion smiled grimly.

"She couldn't tell that one mustn't touch you when you're 'done up.' You didn't do up so much three years ago. She'll soon learn, never fear."

"You grow quite horribly rude, Jack."

He smoked serenely.

"And quite too odiously coarse."

He continued to smoke.

She often abused him, but she never could do without him; and he was aware of that.

"And what a height she is! and what her gowns will cost! and she must come out soon—and that horrid Hélène!" sobbed Lady Dolly, fairly bursting into tears. She had been so gay and comfortable at Trouville, and now it was all over. What comfort could there be with a girl nearly six feet high, that looked twenty years old when she was sixteen, and who called her "Mother!"

"Don't make a fuss," said the counsellor from the stove. "She's very handsome, awfully pretty, you'll marry her in no time, and be just as larky as you were before. Don't cry, there's a dear little soul. Look here, the cutlets are getting cold, and there's all these mullets steaming away for nothing. Come and eat, and the thing won't seem so terrible."

Being versed in the ways of consolations, he opened a bottle of Moselle with an inviting rush of sound, and let the golden stream foam itself softly over a lump of ice in a glass. Lady Dolly looked up, dried her eyes, and sat down at the table.

"Vere must be hungry, surely," she said, with a sudden remembrance, twenty minutes later, eating her last morsel of a truffled *timbâle*.[1] Come and eat, and the thing won't seem so terrible."

The counsellor smiled grimly.

"It's rather late to think about that; I sent her her breakfast before you came in."

"Dear me! how very fatherly of you!"

The counsellor laughed. "I feel like her father, I assure you."

---

1 A custard-like dish baked in a pastry mold.

Lady Dolly coloured, and lit a cigarette. She felt that she would not digest her breakfast. Henceforth there would be two bills to pay—the interest of them at any rate—at all the great tailors' and milliners' houses in Paris and London; she had an uneasy sense that to whirl in and out the mazes of the cotillons, or smoke your cigarette on the smooth lawns of shooting-clubs, vis-à-vis with your own daughter, was a position, in the main, rather ridiculous; and she had still an uneasier conviction that the girl in the brown holland would not be taught in a moment to comprehend the necessity for the existence of Jack—and the rest.

"That horrid old duchess!" she murmured, sinking to sleep with the last atom of her cigarette crumbling itself away on the open page of a French novel. For it was the duchess who had sent her Vere.

CHAPTER II.

Lady Dorothy Vanderdecken, who was Lady Dolly to everybody, down to the very boys that ran after her carriage in the streets, was the seventh daughter of a very poor peer, the Earl of Caterham, who was a clever politician, but always in a chronic state of financial embarrassment. Lady Dolly had made a very silly love-match with her own cousin, Vere Herbert, a younger son of her uncle the Duke of Mull and Cantire, when she was only seventeen, and he had just left Oxford and entered the Church. But Vere Herbert had only lived long enough for her to begin to get very tired of his country parsonage in the wilds of the Devonshire moors, and to be left before she was twenty with a miserable pittance for her portion, and a little daughter twelve months old to plague her farther. Lady Dolly cried terribly for a fortnight, and thought she cried for love, when she only cried for worry. In another fortnight or so she had ceased to cry, had found out that crape brightened her pretty tea-rose skin, had discarded her baby to the care of her aunt and mother-in-law, the old and austere Duchess of Mull, and had gone for her health with her own gay little mother, the Countess of Caterham, to the south of France.

In the south of France Lady Dolly forgot that she had ever cried at all; and in a year's time from the loss of Vere Herbert had married herself again to a Mr. Vanderdecken, an Englishman of Dutch extraction, a rich man, of no remarkable lineage, a financier, a contractor, a politician, a very restless creature, always rushing about alone, and never asking any questions—which suited her. On the other hand it suited him to ally himself with a score of great families, and obtain a lovely and high-born wife; it was one of those marriages which everybody calls so sensible, so suitable, so very *nice!* Quite unlike the marriage with poor Vere Herbert, which everybody had screamed at, as they had not made up five hundred a year in income, or forty-five years in age, between them.

Lady Dolly and Mr. Vanderdecken did not perhaps find it so perfectly well assorted when they had had a little of it; she thought him stingy, he thought her frivolous, but they did not tell anybody else so, and so everybody always said that the marriage was very nice. They were always seen in the Bois and the Park[1] together, and always kept house together three months every spring in London; they went to country houses together, and certainly dined out together at least a dozen times every season: nothing could be nicer, Lady Dolly took care of that.

She thought him a great bore, a great screw;[2] she never had enough money by half, and he was sometimes very nasty about cheques. But he was not troublesome about anything else, and was generally head over ears in some wonderful loan, or contract, or subsidy, which entailed distant journeys, and absorbed him entirely; so that, on the whole, she was content and enjoyed herself.

This morning, however, she had gone down to the shore not indeed fully anticipating such a blow as had fallen upon her, but ruffled, disgusted, and nervous, conscious that her daughter was travelling towards her, and furious with the person she termed a "horrid old cat."

The old cat was the now dowager Duchess of Mull, who for fifteen years had kept safe in Northumbria the daughter of poor Vere, and now had hurled her like a cannon-ball at Lady Dolly's head in this hideous, abominable, unforeseen manner, straight on the sands of Trouville, in sight of that snake in angel's guise, the Princesse Hélène Olgarouski!

Lady Dolly, who never would allow that she gave up her maternal rights, though she would never be bored with maternal responsibilities, had quarrelled for the nine-hundredth time (by post) with the Duchess of Mull; quarrelled desperately, impudently, irrevocably, quarrelled once too often; and the result of the quarrel had been the instant despatch of her daughter to Trouville, with the duchess's declaration

---

1 The Bois de Boulogne was a splendid park built during the Second Empire. An afternoon ride on the Bois was one of the great spectacles in Paris.

2 A stingy bargainer.

that she could struggle for the soul of her poor son's child no longer, and that come what would, she consigned Vere to her mother then and for ever more.

"The horrid woman will be howling for the child again in a week's time," thought Lady Dolly, "but she has done it to spite me, and I'll keep the child to spite her. That's only fair."

The duchess had taken her at her word, that was all; but then, indeed, there are few things more spiteful that one can do to anybody than to take them at their word. Lady Dolly had been perplexed, irritated, and very angry with herself for having written all that rubbish about suffering from the unnatural deprivation of her only child's society; rubbish which had brought this stroke of retribution on her head.

She had pulled her blonde *perruque*[1] all awry in her vexation; she did not want that *perruque* at all, for her own hair was thick and pretty, but she covered it up and wore the *perruque* because it was the fashion to do so.

Lady Dolly had always been, and was very pretty: she had lovely large eyes, and the tiniest mouth, and a complexion which did not want all the pains she bestowed on it; when she had not the *perruque* on, she had dark silky hair all tumbled about over her eyebrows in a disarray that cost her maid two hours to compose; and her eyebrows themselves were drawn beautifully in two fine, dark, slender lines by a pencil that supplied the one defect of Nature. When she was seventeen, at the rectory, amongst the rosebuds on the lawn, she had been a rosebud herself; now she was a Dresden statuette; the statuette was the more finished and brilliant beauty of the two, and never seemed the worse for wear. This is the advantage of artificial over natural loveliness; the latter will alter with health or feeling, the former never; it is always the same, unless you come in on it at its toilette, or see it when it is very ill.

Lady Dolly this morning woke up prematurely from her sleep and fancied she was in the old parsonage gardens on the lawn, amongst the roses in Devonshire, with poor Vere's pale handsome face looking down so tenderly on hers. She felt a mist before her eyes, a tightness at her throat; a vague and worried pain all over her. "It is the prawns!" she said to herself, "I will never smoke after prawns again."

She was all alone; the counsellor had gone to his schooner, other counsellors were at their hotels, it was an hour when everything

---

1 Wig.

except Englishmen and dogs were indoors.[1] She rose, shook her muslin breakfast-wrapper about her impatiently, and went to see her daughter.

"He used to be so fond of me, poor fellow!" she thought. Such a pure fond passion then amongst the roses by the sea. It had all been very silly, and he used to bore her dreadfully with Keble, and his namesake, George of holy memory, and that old proser Thomas à Kempis;[2] but still it had been a different thing to all these other loves. He lay in his grave there by the Atlantic amongst the Devon roses, and she had had no memory of him for many a year, and when he had been alive, she had thought the church and the old women, and the saints, and the flannel, and the choral services, and the matins—and vesper—nonsense, all so tiresome; but still he had loved her. Of course they all adored her now, heaps of them—but his love had been a different thing to theirs. And somehow Lady Dolly felt a tinge and twinge of shame.

"Poor Vere," she murmured to herself tenderly; and so went to see his daughter, who had been called after him by that absurd old woman, the Duchess of Mull, with whom Lady Dolly in her dual relation of niece and daughter-in-law had always waged a fierce undying war: a war in which she had now got the worst of it.

"May I come in, dear?" she said at the bed-chamber door. She felt almost nervous. It was very absurd, but why would the girl have her dead father's eyes?

The girl opened the door and stood silent.

"A beautiful creature. They are quite right," thought Lady Dolly, now that her brain was no longer filled with the dreadful rumpled brown holland, and the smiling face of Princess Hélène. The girl was in a white wrapper like her own, only without any lace, and any of the ribbons that adorned Lady Dolly at all points, as tassels a Roman horse at Carnival. Lady Dolly was too lovely herself, and also far too contented with herself to feel any jealousy; but she looked at her daughter critically, as she would have looked at a young untried actress on the boards of the Odéon.[3] "Quite another style to me, that

---

1   This may refer to a proverbial Italian expression: "Only Englishmen and dogs walk in the sun" or to the Indian proverb: "Only mad dogs and Englishmen go out in the noon-day sun."

2   John Keble (1792-1866) was a British clergyman and poet; George Herbert (1593-1633) was a British metaphysical poet; Thomas à Kempis (1379-1471) was a German priest, monk, and writer. He was the author of a manual of spiritual advice, *The Imitation of Christ* (c. 1427).

3   The Odéon Théâtre de l'Europe was a theater in Paris.

is fortunate," she thought as she looked. "Like Vere—very—quite extraordinarily like Vere—only handsomer still."

Then she kissed her daughter very prettily on both cheeks, and with effusion embraced her, much as she embraced Princess Hélène or anybody else that she hated.

"You took me by surprise to-day, love," she said with a little accent of apology, "and you know I do so detest scenes. Pray try and remember that."

"Scenes?" said Vere. "Please what are they?"

"Scenes?" said Lady Dolly, kissing her once more, and a little puzzled as everybody is, who is suddenly asked to define a familiar word. "Scenes? Well, dear me, scenes are—scenes. Anything, you know, that makes a fuss, that looks silly, that sets people laughing; don't you understand? Anything done before people, you know: it is vulgar."

"I think I understand," said Vere Herbert. She was a very lovely girl, and despite her height still looked a child. Her small head was perfectly poised on a slender neck, and her face, quite colourless, with a complexion like the leaf of a white rose, had perfect features, straight, delicate, and noble; her fair hair was cut square over her brows, and loosely knotted behind; she had a beautiful serious mouth, not so small as her mother's, and serene eyes, grey as night, contemplative, yet wistful.

She was calm and still. She had cried as if her heart would break, but she would have died rather than let her mother guess it. She had been what the French call *refoulée sur elle-même;*[1] and the process is chilling.

"Have you all you want?" said Lady Dolly, casting a hasty glance round the room. "You know I didn't expect you, dear; not in the least."

"Surely my grandmother wrote?"

"Your grandmother telegraphed that you had started; just like her! Of course I wished to have you here, and meant to do so, but not all in a moment."

"The horrid old woman will be howling for the child back again in three weeks' time," thought Lady Dolly once more. "But she has done it to spite me: the old cat!"

"Are you sorry to come to me, love?" she said sweetly meanwhile, drawing Vere down beside her on a couch.

---

1 Closed in on herself; she had held her feelings inside, a state which could go on for days.

"I *was* very glad," answered Vere.

Lady Dolly discreetly omitted to notice the past tense. "Ah, no doubt, very dear of you! It is three years since I saw you; for those few days at Bulmer hardly count. Bulmer is terribly dull, isn't it?"

"I suppose it is dull; I was not so. If grandmamma had not been so often—"

"Cross as two sticks, you mean," laughed Lady Dolly. "Oh, I know her, my dear: the *most* disagreeable person that *ever* lived. The dear old duke was so nice and so handsome; but you hardly remember him, of course. Your grandmamma is a cat, dear—a cat, positively a cat! We will not talk about her. And how she has dressed you! It is quite wicked to dress a girl like that, it does her taste so much harm. You are very handsome, Vere."

"Yes? I am like my father they say."

"Very."

Lady Dolly felt the mist over her eyes again, and this time knew it was not the prawns. She saw the sunny lawn in Devon, and the roses, and the little large-eyed child at her breast. Heavens! what a long way away all that time seemed.

She gazed intently at Vere with a musing pathetic tenderness that moved the girl, and made her tremble and glow, because at last this lovely mother of hers seemed to feel. Lady Dolly's gaze grew graver, more and more introspective.

"She is thinking of the past and of my father," thought the girl tenderly, and her young heart swelled with reverent sympathy. She did not dare to break her mother's silence.

"Vere!" said Lady Dolly dreamily, at length, "I am trying to think what one can do to get you decent clothes. My maid must run up something for you to wear by to-morrow. It is a pity to keep you shut up all this beautiful weather, and a little life will do you good after that prison at Bulmer. I am sure those three days I was last there I thought I should have yawned till I broke my neck, I did indeed, dear. She would hardly let me have breakfast in my own room, and she *would* dine at six!—six! But she was never like anybody else; when even the duke was alive she was the most obstinate, humdrum, nasty old scratch-cat in the county. Such ideas too! She was a sort of Wesley[1] in petticoats, and, by the way, her gowns were never long enough for her. But I was saying, dear, I will have Adrienne run up something

---

1   John Wesley (1703-91) was a British theologian, evangelist, and founder of the Methodist Church

for you directly. She is clever. I never let a maid *make* a dress. It is absurd. You might as well want Rubinstein[1] to make the violin he plays on. If she is inferior, she will make you look dowdy. If she is a really good maid she will not make, she will arrange, what your tailor has made, and perfect it—nothing more. But still, for you, Adrienne will go out of her way for once. She shall combine a few little things, and she can get a girl to sew them for her. Something to go out in they really must manage for to-morrow. You shall have brown holland if you are so fond of it, dear, but you shall see what brown holland can look like with Adrienne."

Vere sat silent.

"By the bye," said her mother vivaciously, "didn't you bring a maid? Positively, not a maid?"

"Grandmamma sent Keziah: she has always done very well for me."

"Keziah!" echoed Lady Dolly with a shudder. "How exactly it is like your grandmother to give you a woman called Keziah! That horrible Fräulein one might dismiss too, don't you think? You are old enough to do without her, and you shall have a nice French maid; Adrienne will soon find one."

The girl's eyes dilated with fear.

"Oh! pray do not send away the Fräulein! We are now in the conic sections."[2]

"The what?" said Lady Dolly.

"I mean I could not go on in science or mathematics without her, and besides, she is so good."

"Mathematics! science! why, what can you want to make yourself hateful for, like a Girton College guy?"[3]

"I want to know things; pray do not send away the Fräulein."

Lady Dolly, who was at heart very good-natured when her own comfort was not too much interfered with, patted her cheek and laughed.

"What should you want to know?—know how to dress, how to curtsey, how to look your best; that is all you want to know. Believe me, men will ask nothing more of you. As for your hideous Schroder, I think her the most odious person in existence, except your grand-

---

1 Anton Rubinstein (1829-94) was a Russian pianist, composer, and educator. Though he was mainly known as a virtuoso of the piano, he wrote three violin sonatas.
2 She is referring to geometry.
3 A women's college established in Cambridge in 1869.

mother. But if her blue spectacles comfort you, keep her at present. Of course you will want somebody to be with you a good deal: I can't be; and I suppose you'll have to stay with me now. You may be seen here a little, and wherever I go in autumn; then you can come out in Paris in the winter, and be presented next spring. I shall do it to spite your grandmother, who has behaved disgracefully to me— disgracefully. I believe she'd be capable of coming up to London to present you herself, though she's never set foot there for fifteen years!"

Vere was silent.

"What do you like best?" said her mother suddenly. Something in the girl worried her: she could not have said what it was.

Vere lifted her great eyes dreamily.

"Greek," she answered.

"*Greek!* a horse? a pony? a dog?"

"A language," said Vere.

"Of course Greek is a language; I know that," said her mother irritably. "But of course I thought you meant something natural, sensible; some pet of some kind. And what do you like best after that, pray?"

"Music—Greek is like music."

"Oh dear me!" sighed Lady Dolly.

"I can ride; I am fond of riding," added Vere; "and I can shoot, and row, and sail, and steer a boat. The keepers taught me."

"Well, that sort of thing goes down rather, now that they walk with the guns, though I'm quite sure men wish them anywhere all the while," said Lady Dolly, somewhat vaguely. "Only you must be masculine with it, and slangy, and you don't seem to me to be that in the least. Do you know, Vere—it is a horrible thing to say—but I am dreadfully afraid you will be just the old-fashioned, prudish, open-air, touch-me-not Englishwoman! I am indeed. Now you know that won't answer anywhere, nowadays."

"Answer—what?"

"Don't take my words up like that, it is rude. I mean, you know, that kind of style is gone out altogether, pleases nobody; men hate it. The only women that please nowadays are Russians and Americans. Why? Because in their totally different ways they neither of them care one fig what they do if only it please them to do it. They are all *chic*[1] you know. Now you haven't a bit of *chic*; you look like a

---

1 Stylish.

creature out of Burne-Jones's[1] things, don't you know, only more—more—religious-looking. You really look as if you were studying your Bible every minute; it is most extraordinary!"

"Her father *would* read me Keble and Kempis before she was born," thought Lady Dolly angrily, her wrath rising against the dead man for the psychological inconsistencies in her daughter; a daughter she would have been a million times better without at any time.

"Well, then, my love," she said suddenly; "you shall ride and you shall swim; that will certainly help you better than your Greek and your conic sessions, whatever they may be, they sound like something about magistrates, perhaps they have taught you law as well?"

"May I swim here?" asked Vere.

"Of course; it's the thing to do. Can you dive?"

"Oh yes! I am used to the water."

"Very well, then. But wait; you can't have any bathing-dress?"

"Yes. I brought it. Would you wish to see it? Keziah—"

Keziah was bidden to seek for and bring out the bathing-dress, and after a little delay did so.

Lady Dolly looked. Gradually an expression of horror, such as is depicted on the faces of those who are supposed to see ghosts, spread itself over her countenance and seemed to change it to stone.

"That thing!" she gasped.

What she saw was the long indigo-coloured linen gown—high to the throat and down to the feet—of the uneducated British bather, whose mind has not been opened by the sweetness and light of continental shores.

"That thing!" gasped Lady Dolly.

"What is the matter with it?" said Vere, timidly and perplexed.

"Matter? It is indecent!"

"Indecent?" Vere coloured all over the white rose-leaf beauty of her face.

"Indecent," reiterated Lady Dolly. "If it isn't worse! Good gracious! It must have been worn at the deluge. The very children would stone you! Of course I knew you couldn't have any decent dress. You shall have one like mine made to-morrow, and then you can kick about as you like. Blue and white or blue and pink. You shall see mine."

She rang, and sent one of her maids for one of her bathing costumes, which were many and of all hues.

---

1 Sir Edward Burne-Jones (1833-98) was a British Pre-Raphaelite painter, illustrator, and designer.

Vere looked at the brilliant object when it arrived, puzzled and troubled by it. She could not understand it. It appeared to be cut off at the shoulders and the knees.

"It is like what the circus-riders wear," she said, with a deep breath.

"Well, it is, now you name it," said Lady Dolly amused. "You shall have one to-morrow."

Vere's face crimsoned.

"But what covers one's legs and arms?"

"Nothing! what a little silly you are. I suppose you have nothing the matter with them, have you? no mark, or twist, or anything? I don't remember any when you were little. You were thought an extraordinarily well-made baby."

Might one then go naked provided only one had no mark or twist? Vere wondered, and wondered at the world into which she had strayed.

"I would never wear a costume like that," she said quietly after a little pause.

"You will wear what I tell you," said her sweet little mother sharply; "and for goodness' sake, child, don't be a prude whatever you are. Prudes belong to Noah's Ark, like your bathing-gown."

Vere was silent.

"Is Mr. Vanderdecken here?" she asked at length, to change the theme, and, finding her mother did not speak again, who, indeed, was busy, thinking what her clothes were likely to cost, and also whether she would arrange a marriage for her with the young Duc de Tambour, son of the Prince de Chambrée. The best alliance she could thing of at the minute—but then the poor child had no *dot*.[1]

"Mr. Vanderdecken?" said Lady Dolly waking to fact. "Oh, he is on the sea going somewhere. He is always going somewhere; it is Java or Japan, or Jupiter; something with a J. He makes his money in that sort of way, you know. I never understand it myself. Whenever people want money he goes, and he makes it because the people he goes to haven't got any; isn't it queer? Come here. Do you know, Vere, you are very pretty? You will be very handsome. Kiss me again, dear."

Vere did so, learning, by a kind of intuition, that she must touch her mother without injuring the artistic work of the maids and the "little secrets." Then she stood silent and passive.

"She is an uncomfortable girl," thought Lady Dolly once more.

---

1 Dowry.

"And dear me, so like poor Vere! What a tall creature you are getting," she said aloud. "You will be married in another year."

"Oh no!" said Vere with a glance of alarm.

"You unnatural child! How on earth would you like to live if you don't want to be married?"

"With the Fräulein in the country."

"All your life! And die an old maid?"

"I should not mind."

Lady Dolly laughed, but it was with a sort of shock and shudder, as an orthodox person laughs when they hear what is amusing but irreverent.

"Why do you say such things?" she said impatiently. "They are nonsense and you don't mean them."

"I mean them—quite."

"Nonsense!" said Lady Dolly, who never discussed with anybody, finding asseveration answer all purposes very much better; as, indeed, it does in most cases. "Well, good-bye my love; you want to rest, and you can't go out till you have something to wear, and I have an immense deal to do. Good-bye; you are very pretty!"

"Who was that gentleman I saw?" asked Vere, as her mother rose and kissed her once more on her silky fair hair. "Is he any relation of papa's? He was very kind."

Lady Dolly coloured ever so little.

"Oh! that's Jack. Surely you remember seeing Jack three years ago at Homburg, when you came out to meet me there?"

"Is he a relation of ours?"

"No; not a relation exactly; only a friend."

"And has he no name but Jack?"

"Of course. Don't say silly things. He is Lord Jura, Lord Shetland's son. He is in the Guards.[1] A very old acquaintance, dear—recollects you as a baby."

"A friend of my father's then?"

"Well, no dear, not quite. Not quite so far back as that. Certainly he may have fagged for poor Vere at Eton perhaps,[2] but I doubt it. Good-bye, darling. I will send you Adrienne. You may put yourself in her hands blindly. She has perfect taste."

Then Lady Dolly opened the door, and escaped.

---

1 A Life Guardsman, members of the military were regular guests at Ouida's dinner parties.

2 At schools like Eton, younger boys were required to do menial chores (i.e., "fag") for older pupils.

Vere Herbert was left to herself. She was not tired; she was strong and healthful, for all the white rose paleness of her fair skin; and a twelve hours' tossing on the sea, and a day or two's rumbling on the rail, had no power to fatigue her. Her grandmother, though a humdrum and a cat, according to Lady Dolly, had sundry old-fashioned notions from which the girl had benefited both in body and mind, and the fresh strong air of Bulmer Chase—a breezy old forest place on the Northumberland seashore, where the morose old duchess found a dower house to her taste—had braced her physically, as study and the absence of any sort of excitement had done mentally, and made her as unlike her mother as anything female could have been. The Duchess of Mull was miserly, cross-tempered, and old-fashioned in her ways and in her prejudices, but she was an upright woman, a gentlewoman, and no fool, as she would say herself. She had been harsh with the girl, but she had loved her and been just to her, and Vere had spent her life at Bulmer Chase not unhappily, varied only by an occasional visit to Lady Dolly, who had always seemed to the child something too bright and fair to be mortal, and to have an enchanted existence, where caramels and cosaques rained, and music was always heard, and the sun shone all day long.

She was all alone. The Fräulein was asleep in the next room. The maid did not come. The girl kneeled down by the window-seat and looked out through one of the chinks of the blinds. It was late afternoon by the sun; the human butterflies were beginning to come out again. Looking up and down she saw the whole sunshiny coast, and the dancing water that was boisterous enough to be pretty and to swell the canvas of the yachts standing off the shore.

"How bright it all looks!" she thought, with a little sigh; the salt fresh smell did her good, and Bulmer, amidst its slowly budding woods and dreary moors, and long dark winters, had been anything but bright. Yet she felt very unhappy and lonely. Her mother seemed a great deal farther away than she had done when Vere had sat dreaming about her on the side of the rough heathered hills, with the herons calling across from one marshy pool to another.

She leaned against the green blind and ceased to see the sea and the sky, the beach and the butterflies, for a little while, her tears were so full under her lashes, and she did her best to keep them back. She was full of pain because her mother did not care for her; but, indeed, why should she care? said Vere to herself; they had been so little together.

She looked, almost without seeing it at first, at the picture underneath her; the stream, which gradually swelled and grew larger, beautifully-dressed fairy-like women, whose laughter every now and then echoed up to her. It was one unbroken current of harmonious colour, rolled out like a brilliant riband on the fawn-coloured sand against the azure sea.

"And have they all nothing to do but to enjoy themselves?" thought Vere. It seemed so. If Black Care were anywhere at Trouville, as it was everywhere else in the world, it took pains to wear a face like the rest and read its "Figaro."

She heard the door underneath unclose, and from underneath the green verandah she saw her mother saunter out. Three other ladies were with her and half a dozen men. They were talking and laughing all at once, no one waiting to be listened to or seeming to expect it; they walked across the beach and sat down. They put up gorgeous sunshades and out-spread huge fans: they were all twitter, laughter, colour, mirth.

All this going to and fro of gay people, the patter of feet and flutter of petticoats, amused the girl to watch almost as much as if she had been amidst it. There were such a sparkle of sea, such a radiance of sunshine, such a rainbow of colour, that though it would have composed ill for a landscape, it made a pretty panorama.

Vere watched it, conjecturing in a youthful fanciful ignorant way all kinds of things about the persons who seemed so happy there. When she had gazed for about twenty minutes, making her eyes ache and getting tired, one of them especially attracted her attention by the way in which people all turned after him, as he passed, and the delight that his greeting appeared to cause those with whom he lingered. He was a man of such remarkable personal beauty that this alone might have been reason enough for the eager welcome of the listless ladies; but there was even a greater charm in his perfect grace of movement and vivacity and airy ease: he stayed little time with any one; but wherever he loitered a moment appeared to be the centre of all smiles. She did not know that he was her admirer of the noonday, who had looked at her as he had sauntered along in his bathing shroud and his white shoes; but she watched the easy graceful attitudes of him with interest as he cast himself down on the sand, leaning on his elbow, by a group of fair women.

"Can you tell me who that gentleman is?" she asked of her mother's head-maid, the inimitable Adrienne.

Adrienne looked and smiled,

"Oh! that is M. de Corrèze."

"Corrèze!" Vere's eyes opened in a blaze of eager wonder, and the colour rose in her pale cheeks. "Corrèze! Are you sure?"

"But yes: I am quite sure," laughed Adrienne. "Does mademoiselle feel emotion at the sight of him? She is only like all others of her sex. Ah! *le beau*[1] *Corrèze.*"

"I have never heard him sing," said Vere, very low, as if she spoke of some religious thing; "but I would give anything, anything, to do so. And the music he composes himself is beautiful. There is one 'Messe de Minuit—'"

"Mademoiselle will hear him often enough when she is once in the world," said Adrienne, good-naturedly. "Ah! when she shall see him in 'Faust' that will be an era in her life. But it is not his singing that makes the great ladies rave of him; it is his charm. Oh, *quel philtre d'amour!*"[2]

And Adrienne quite sighed with despair, and then laughed.

Vere coloured a little; Keziah did not discourse about men being love-philtres.

"Measure me for my clothes; I am tired," she said with a childish coldness and dignity, turning away from the window.

"I am entirely at mademoiselle's service," said Adrienne with answering dignity. "Whoever has had the honour to clothe mademoiselle has been strangely neglectful of her highest interests."

"My clothes my highest interest! I never think about them!"

"That is very sad. They are really barbaric. If Mademoiselle could behold herself—"

"They are useful," said Vere coldly; "that is all that is necessary."

Adrienne was respectfully silent, but she shuddered as if she had heard a blasphemy. She could not comprehend how the young barbarian could have been brought up by a duchess. Adrienne had never been to Bulmer, and had never seen Her Grace of Mull, with her silver spectacles, her leather boots, her tweed clothes, her farm-ledgers, her studbooks, and her ever-open Bible.

"Measure me quickly," said Vere. She had lowered the green jalousies, and would not look out any more. Yet she felt happier. She missed dark, old, misty Bulmer with its oakwoods by the ocean; yet this little gay room, with its pretty cretonne, cream-coloured, with pale pink roses, its gilded mirrors, its rose china, its white muslin, was certainly brighter and sunnier, and who could tell but what her mother would grow to love her some day?

At nine o'clock Lady Dolly, considering herself a martyr to maternity, ran into the little room where Vere was at tea with her gov-

---

1 The handsome.
2 "What a love potion!"

erness; Lady Dolly was arrayed for the evening *sauterie*[1] at the Casino, and was in great haste to be gone.

"Have you everything you like, darling?" she asked, pulling on her pearl-hued *crispens*. "Did you have a nice little dinner? Yes? Quite sure? Has Adrienne been to you? An excellent creature; perfect tastes. Dear me, what a pity!—you might have come and, jumped about to-night if you had had only something to wear. Of course you like dancing?"

"I dislike it very much."

"Dear me! Ah well! you won't say so after a cotillon or two. You shall have a cotillon that Zouroff leads: there is nobody better. Good night, my sweet Vera. Mind, I shall always call you Vera. It sounds so Russian and nice, and is much prettier than Vere."

"I do not think so, mother, and I am not Russian."

"You are very contradictory and opinionated; much too opinionated for a girl. It is horrid in a girl to have opinions. Fräulein, how could you let her have opinions? Good night, dear. I shall hardly see you to-morrow, if at all. We shall be cruising about in Jack's yacht, and we shall start very early. The Grand Duchess will go out with us. She is great fun, only she does get in such a rage when she loses at play, that it is horrible to see. So sorry you must be shut up, my poor Vera!"

"May I not go out just for a walk?"

"Well, I don't know—yes, really, I think you might; if it's very early mind, and you keep out of everybody's sight. Pray take care not a soul sees you."

"Is not this better, then?" murmured the offender, glancing down on a white serge frock, which she had put on in the hope that it might please. It was a simple braided dress with a plain silver belt, and was really unobjectionable.

Lady Dolly scanned the garment with a critical air and a *parti pris*.[2] Certainly it might have done for the morrow's yachting, but then she did not want the wearer of it on the yacht. The girl would have to be every-where very soon, of course, but Lady Dolly put off the evil day as long as she could.

"It is the *cut*," she said, dropping her glass with a sigh. It can't be Morgan's?"

---

1 Dance.
2 Set purpose.

"Who is Morgan?" asked the child, so benighted that she had not ever heard of the great Worth[1] of nautical costume.

"Morgan is the only creature possible for serge," sighed Lady Dolly. "You don't seem to understand darling. Material is nothing, Make is everything. Look at our *camelot* and *percale* gowns that Worth sends us; and look at the satins and velvets of a *bourgeoise* from Asnières or a wine-merchant's wife from Clapham! Oh, my dear child! cut your gown out of your dog's towel or your horses' cloths if you like, but mind Who cuts it: that is the one golden rule! But good-night, my sweetest. Sleep well."

Lady Dolly brushed her daughter's cheek with the diamond end of her earring, and took herself off in a maze of pale yellow and deep scarlet as mysteriously and perfectly blended as the sunset colours of an Italian night.

"She is really very pretty," she said to her counsellor as he put her cloak round her and pocketed her fan. "Really very handsome, like Burne-Jones's things and all that, don't you know."

"A long sight prettier and healthier than any of 'em," said the counsellor lighting his cigar; for he had small respect for the High Art of his period.

They went forth into the moonlit night to the Casino, and left Vere to the sleep into which she sobbed herself like a child as she still was, soothed at last by the sound of the incoming tide and the muttering of the good Fräulein's prayers.

CHAPTER III.

Vera was awoke at five o'clock by tumultuous laughter, gay shrill outcries, and a sudden smell of cigar smoke. It was her mother returning home. Doors banged; then all grew still. Vere got up, looked at the sea and remembered that permission to go out had been given her.

In another hour she was abroad in the soft cool sunshine of early morning, the channel before her, and behind her the stout form of Northumbrian Keziah.

Trouvilain,[2] as somebody has wittily called it, is not lovely. Were it

---

1 It is unclear who Morgan is. Charles Frederick Worth (1825-95) was the Father of Haute Couture. Ouida purchased most of her dresses from him, as did royalty and other celebrities.

2 "Trou" can be translated as a hole or a pit. "Vilain" means naughty or mischievous; together they suggest that the resort town is unattractive and that loose "naughty" behavior is characteristic of the inhabitants.

not so celebrated, undoubtedly it would be called commonplace; but, in the very first light of morning, every spot on earth, except a manufacturing city, has some loveliness, and Trouvilain at day break had some for Vere. There were yachts with slender trim lines beautiful against the clear sky. There were here and there provision boats pulling out with sailors in dark blue jerseys, and red capped. There were fleecy white clouds, and there were cool sands; cool now, if soon they would be no better than powder and dust. Along the poor planks that are the treadmill of fashion, Vere's buoyant young feet bore her with swiftness and pleasure till she reached the Corniche des Roches Noires[1] and got out into the charming green country.

She glanced at the water and longed to run into the shallows and wade and spread her limbs out, and float and swim, beating the sea with her slender arms and rosy toes as she had done most mornings in the cold, wind-swept, steel-grey northern tides of her old home.

But her bathing-costume had been forbidden, had even been carried away in bitter contempt by one of the French maids, and never would she go into the sea in this public place in one of those sleeveless, legless, circus-rider's tunics: no, never, she said to herself; and her resolves were apt to be very resolute ones. Her old guardian at Bulmer Chase had always said to her: "Never say 'no' rashly, nor 'yes' either; but when you have said them, stand to them as a soldier to his guns."

She did not at all know her way, but she had thought if she kept along by the water she would some time or other surely get out of the sight of all those gay houses, which, shut as all their persiennes[2] were, and invisible as were all their occupants, yet had fashion and frivolity so plainly written on their coquettish awnings, their balconies, their doorways, their red geraniums and golden calceolarias blazing before their blinds. At five o'clock there was nobody to trouble her certainly; yet within sight of all those windows she had felt as if she were still before the staring eyes and eyeglasses of the cruel crowd of that terrible yesterday.

She went on quickly with the elastic step which had been used to cover so easily mile after mile of the heathered moors of Bulmer, and the firm yellow sands by the northern ocean. Before the cloudless sun of the August daybreak was much above the waters of the east with the smoke of the first steamer from Havre towering grey and dark

---

1   Cornice of the Black Rocks.
2   Shutters.

against the radiant rose of the sky,Vere had left Trouville, and its sleeping beauties and yawning dandies in their beds, far behind her, and was nearly a third of the way to Villerville. She did not know anything at all about Lecamus *fils*, Jules David, Challamel, and Figaro with his cabin, who had made Villerville famous,[1] but she went onward because the sea was blue, the sand was yellow, the air was sweet and wholesome, and the solitude was complete.

Her spirits rose; light, and air, and liberty of movement were necessary to her, for, in the old woods and on the rough moors of Bulmer, her grandmother had let her roam as she chose, on foot or on her pony. It had been a stern rule in other things, but as regarded air and exercise she had enjoyed the most perfect freedom.

"Are you tired, Keziah?" she cried at last, noticing that the patient waiting-woman lagged behind. The stout Northumbrian admitted that she was. She had never been so in her life before; but that frightful sea journey from Southampton had left her stomach "orkard."

Vere was touched to compunction.

"You poor creature! and I brought you out without your breakfast, and we have walked—oh! ever so many miles," she said in poignant self-reproach. "Keziah, look here, there is a nice smooth stone. Sit down on it and rest, and I will run about. Yes; do not make any objection; sit down."

Keziah, who adored her very shadow as it fell on sward or sand, demurred faintly, but the flesh was weak, and the good woman dropped down on the stone with a heavy thud, as of a sack falling to earth, and sat there in plaid shawl and homespun gown, with her hands on her knees, the homely sober figure that had seemed to Lady Dolly to have come out of the ark like the indigo bathing-dress.

Vere left her on that madreporic[2] throne, and strayed onward herself along by the edge of the sea.

---

1 Villerville, like other resort towns on the Normandy coast, attracted many artists and intellectuals. Lecamus *fils* is probably a reference to the French artist, Pierre Duval-Lecamus (1790-1854); Jules David (1808-92) was a fashion illustrator; Jean Baptiste Marius Augustin Challamel (1818-94) was a popular French historian, whose works were enhanced by his numerous illustrations; Figaro is probably a reference to Alphonse Karr (1808-90), editor of the French newspaper *Le Figaro* and a famous satirical journalist. Delighted with a rural village near Villerville, Karr bought a house and invited many writers to visit him. The beach scenes, the ladies in crinolines and bathing attire, were the subject of many paintings by the Impressionists.

2 Coral.

On one side of her was a dark bastion of rock, above that, out of sight, were green pastures and golden corn fields; on the other was the Channel, placid, sunny, very unlike the surging turbulent gigantic waves of her old home.

"Can you ever be rough? Can you ever look like salt water?" she said with a little contempt to it, not knowing anything about the appalling chopping seas and formidable swell of the Channel which the boldest mariners detest more than all the grand furies of Baltic or Atlantic. But it was bright blue water fretted with little curls of foam, and the low waves rolled up lazily, and lapped the sand at her feet; and she felt happy and playful, as was natural to her age; and that she was quite alone mattered nothing to her, for she had never had any young companions, and never played except with the dogs.

She wandered about, and ran here and there, and found some sandpipers' empty nests, and gathered some gorse and stuck it in the riband of her old sailor's hat, and was gay and careless, and sang little soft low songs to herself, as the swallows sing when they sit on the roof in mid-summer. She had taken off her hat, the wind lifted the weighty gold of her straight cut hair, and blew the old brown holland skirt away from her slender ankles. She began to look longingly at the water, spreading away from her so far and so far, and lying in delicious little cool shallows amongst the stones. She could not bathe, but she thought she might wade and paddle. She took off her shoes and stockings, and waded in. The rock pools were rather deep, and the water rose above her ankles; those pretty roses, and lilacs, and feathery hyacinths of the sea that science calls *actiniae*,[1] uncurled their tufts of feathers, and spread out their starry crowns, and lifted their tiny bells around her; broad riband weeds floated, crabs waddled, little live shells sailed here and there, and all manner of *algae*, brown and red, were curling about the big stones. She was in paradise.

She had been reared on the edge of the sea—the cold dark stern sea of the north, indeed, but still the sea. This was only a quiet sunny nook of the French coast of the Channel, but it was charming from the silence, the sunshine, and the sweet liberty of the waters. She thought she was miles away from everyone, and therefore was duly obeying her mother's sole command. There was not even a sail in sight: quite far off was a cloud of dark boats, which were the fishing cobles of Honfleur; there was nothing else near, nothing but a score of gulls, spreading their white wings, and diving to catch the fish as they rose.

---

1   Sea-anemones.

She waded on and on: filling an old creel with seaweeds and seashells, for she was no more than a child in a great many things. The anemones she would not take, because she had no means of keeping them in comfort. She contented herself with standing nearly knee-deep, and gazing down on all their glories seen through the glass of the still sparkling water. She sprang from stone to stone, from pool to pool, forgetting Keziah seated on her rock. Neither did she see a pretty little dingy that was fastened to a stake amongst the boulders.

The air was perfectly still; there was only one sound, that of the incoming tide running up and rippling over the pebbles.

Suddenly a voice from the waves, as it seemed, began to chaunt parts of the Requiem of Mozart.[1] It was a voice pure as a lark's, rich as an organ's swell, tender as love's first embrace, marvellously melodious, in a word, that rarity which the earth is seldom blessed enough to hear from more than one mortal throat in any century: it was a perfectly beautiful tenor voice.

Vere was standing in the water, struck dumb and motionless; her eyes dilated, she scarcely breathed, every fibre of her being, everything in her, body and soul, seemed to listen. She did not once wonder whence it came; the surpassing beauty and melody of it held her too entranced.

Whether it were in the air, in the water, in the sky, she never asked—one would have seemed as natural to her as the other.

From the Requiem it passed with scarce a pause to the impassioned songs of Gounod's Romeo. Whatever the future may say of Gounod,[2] this it will never be able to deny, that he is the supreme master of the utterances of Love. The passionate music rose into the air, bursting upon the silence and into the sunlight, and seeming to pierce the very heavens, then sinking low and sweet and soft as any lover's sigh of joy, breaking off at last abruptly and leaving nothing but the murmur of the sea.

The girl drew a great breathless cry, as if something beautiful were dead, and stood quite still, her figure mirrored in the shallows.

The singer came round from the projecting ledge of the brown cliffs, uncovered his head and bowed low, with apology for unwitting intrusion on her solitude.

It was he whom Adrienne had called *le philtre d'amour*.

Then the girl, who had been in heaven, dropped to earth; and

---

1   Wolfgang Amadeus Mozart (1756-91) was an Austrian composer.
2   Charles Gounod (1818-93) was a French composer, whose most famous operas are *Faust* and *Romeo and Juliet*.

remembered her wet and naked feet, and glanced down on them with shame, and coloured as rosy-red as the sea-flowers in the pool.

She threw an eager glance over the sands. Alas! she had forgotten her shoes and stockings, and the place where they had been knew them no more—the waves had rippled over them and were tossing them, heaven could tell how near or far away.

The "sad leaden humanity," which drags us all to earth,[1] brought her from the trance of ecstasy to the very humblest prose of shame and need.

"I have lost them," she murmured; and then felt herself grow from rose to scarlet, as the singer stood on the other side of the pool gazing at her and seeing her dilemma with amusement.

"Your shoes and stockings, mademoiselle?"

He was so used to seeing pretty nude feet at Trouville that it was impossible for him to measure the awful character of the calamity in the eyes of Vere.

"Yes, I took them off; and I never dreamt that anyone was here."

"Perhaps you have only forgotten where you put them. Let me have the honour to look for your lost treasures."

Vere stood in her shallow, amongst the riband weed, with her head hung down, and the colour burning in her face. All her pride, of which she had much, could not avail her here. She was nervously ashamed and unhappy.

The new-comer searched ardently and indefatigably, leaving no nook of rock or little deposit of sea-water unexamined. He waded in many places, and turned over the weed in all, but it was in vain. The sea was many an inch deeper over the shore than when she had first come, and her shoes and hose were doubtless drifting loose upon the waves: there was no trace of them.

Unconscious of this tragedy enacting, Keziah sat in the calm distance, a grey and brown figure, facing the horizon.

Vere stood all the while motionless; the sweet singing seeming still to throb and thrill through the air around, and the sunny daylight seeming to go round her in an amber mist through which she only saw her own two naked feet, still covered in some sort with the water and the weeds.

"They are gone, mademoiselle!" said the singer, coming to her

---

1 Ouida might have been thinking of the following passage from Milton's "Il Penseroso": "Forget thy self to Marble, till / With a sad Leaden downward cast, / Thou fix them on the earth as fast." (42-44) and "The still sad music of humanity" from Wordsworth's "Tintern Abbey" (77).

with eyes that he made most tender and persuasive. They were beautiful eyes, that lent themselves with willingness to this familiar office.

"They must have been washed away by the tide; it is coming higher each moment. Indeed, you must not remain where you are or you will be surrounded very soon, and carried off yourself. These channel tides are treacherous and uncertain."

"I will go to my maid," murmured Vere, with a fawn-like spring from her stones to others, forgetting in her shame to even thank him for his services.

"To that admirable person enthroned yonder?" said the singer of the songs. "But, mademoiselle, there is the deep sea between you and her already. Look!"

Indeed, so rapidly had the tide run in, and the waters swelled up, that she was divided from her attendant by a broad sheet of blue shallows. Keziah, tired and sleepy from her journeyings, was nodding unconsciously on her throne of rocks.

"And she will be drowned!" said Vere with a piercing cry, and she began wading knee-deep into the sea before her companion knew what she was about. In a moment he had caught her and lifted her back on to the firm sand.

"Your good woman is in no danger, but you cannot reach her so, and you will only risk your own life, mademoiselle," he said gently. "There is nothing to be alarmed about. Shout to your attendant to take the path up the cliffs—perhaps she would not understand me— and we will take this road; so we shall meet on the top of this tableland that is now above our heads. That is all. Shout loudly to her."

Vere was trembling, but she obeyed—she had learned the too oft-forgotten art of obedience at Bulmer Chase, and she shouted loudly till she aroused Keziah who awoke, rubbing her eyes, and dreaming, no doubt, that she was in the servants' hall at Bulmer.

When she understood what had happened and what she was bidden to do, the stout north country-woman tucked up her petticoats, and began to climb up the steep path with a will, once assured that her young mistress was out of all danger. The face of the cliff soon hid her figure from sight, and Vere felt her heart sink strangely.

But she had no time to reflect, for the stranger propelled her gently towards the worn ridge in the rocks near them, a path which the fisher-people had made in coming up and down.

"Let us mount quickly, mademoiselle. I did not notice myself that the tide was so high. Alas! I fear the rocks will hurt your feet. When we reach the first ledge you must wind some grass round them. Come!"

Vere began to climb. The stones, and the sand, and the rough dry weeds cut her feet terribly, but these did not hurt her so much as the idea that he saw her without shoes and stockings. Reaching a ledge of stone he bade her sit down, and tore up some broad grasses and brought them to her.

"Bind these about your feet," he said kindly, and turned his back to her. "Ah! why will you mind so much? Madame, your lovely mother, dances about so for two or three hours in the water-carnival every noonday!"

"Do you know my mother?" said Vere, lifting her face, very hot and troubled from winding the grass about her soles and insteps.

"I have had that honour for many years in Paris. You will have heard of me, perhaps. I am a singer."

Vere, for the first time, looked in his face, and saw that it was the face whose beauty had attracted her in the sunlight on the shore, and whom Adrienne had called the *philtre d'amour*.

"It was you who were singing, then?" she said timidly, and thinking how beautiful and how wonderful he was, this great artist, who stood before her clothed in white, with the sun shining in his luminous eyes.

"Yes. I came here to bathe and to swim, and then run over some of the scores of a new opera, that we shall have in Paris this winter, of Ambroise Thomas's.[1] One cannot study in peace for ten minutes in Trouville. You love music, mademoiselle? Oh! you need not speak: one always knows."

"I never went to any opera," said Vere under her breath, resuming her climb up the rock.

"Never! May I sing to you then in the first opera you hear! Take care; this path is steep. Do not look back; and catch at the piles where the *guindeaux*[2] hang. You need fear nothing. I am behind you."

Vere climbed on in silence; the thick bands of grass protected her feet in a measure, yet, it was hard and rough work. Young and strong though she was, she was glad when they reached the short grass on the head of the cliffs and sank down on it, field-fares and several birds of all kinds wheeling about her in the grey clear air.

"You are not faint?" he asked anxiously.

"Oh no! Only tired."

"Will you rest here ten minutes, and I will come back to you?"

---

1 Charles Louis Ambroise Thomas (1811-96) was one of the leading
   French opera composers of the nineteenth century.
2 Windlasses.

"If you wish me."

He smiled at the childish docility of the answer and left her, whilst she leaned down on the turf of the table-land, and gazed at the sea far down below, and at the horizon where many a white sail shone, and here and there streamed the dark trail of a steamer's smoke. She had forgotten Keziah for the moment; she was only hearing in memory those wonderful tones, clear as a lark's song, rich as an organ's swell, ringing over the waters in the silence.

In less than ten minutes he was back at her side with a pair of little new wooden shoes in his hand.

"I thought these might save you from the stones and dust a little, Mademoiselle Herbert," he said, "and it is impossible to procure any better kind in this village. Will you try them?"

She was grateful; the little shoes were a child's size and fitted as if they had been the glass slipper of Cinderella.

"You are very good," she said timidly. "And how can you tell what my name is?"

"I witnessed your arrival yesterday. Besides, who has not heard of lovely Madame Dolly's daughter?"

Vere was silent. She vaguely wondered why her mother was called Dolly by all men whatever.

Suddenly, with a pang of conscience, she remembered Keziah, and sprang up on her *sabots*.[1] Corrèze divined her impulse and her thought.

"Your good woman is quite safe," he said; "the peasants have seen her on the top of the rocks, but she seems to have taken a wrong path, and so it may be half-an-hour before we overtake her. But do not be afraid or anxious. I will see you safely homeward."

Vere grew very pale. "But mother made me promise to see no one."

"Why?"

"Because my dress is all wrong. And poor Keziah!—oh, how frightened she will be!"

"Not very. We shall soon overtake her. Or, better still, I will send a lad after her while we rest a little. Come and see my village, if you can walk in your *sabots*. It is a village that I have discovered, so I have the rights of Selkirk. Come, if you are not too tired. Brava!"

He cried "brava!" because she walked so well in her wooden shoes; and he saw that to please him she was overcoming the timidity which the solitude of her situation awoke in her.

---

1 Wooden shoes.

"How can she be the daughter of that little impudent *fine mouche?*"[1] he thought.

Vere was shy but brave. Lady Dolly and her sisterhood were audacious but cowardly.

He led her across the broad hard head of the cliffs, mottled black and grey where the rock broke through the grass, and thence across a sort of rambling down with low furze-bushes growing on it, further by a cart-track, where cart-wheels had cut deep into the soil, to a little cluster of houses, lying sheltered from the sea winds by the broad bluff of the cliffs which rose above them, and gathered under the shelter of apple and cherry trees, with one great walnut growing in the midst.

It was a poor little village enough, with a smell of tar from the fishing-nets and sails spread out to dry, and shingle roofs held down with stones, and little dusky close-shut pigeon-holes for windows: but, in the memory of Vere for ever afterwards, that little village seemed even as Arcadia.[2]

He had two wooden chairs brought out, and a wooden table, and set them under the cherry-trees, all reddened then with fruit. He had a wooden bowl of milk, and honey, and brown bread, and cherries, brought out too. There were lavender and a few homely stocks and wallflowers growing in the poor soil about the fences of the houses; bees hummed and swallows cleft the air.

"You are thirsty and hungry, I am sure," he said, and Vere, who had not learned to be ashamed of such things, said with a smile, "I am."

He had reassured her as to Keziah, after whom he had sent a fisher-boy. That the fisher-boy would ever find Keziah he did not in the least see any reason to believe; but he did not see any reason either why he should tell Vere so, to make her anxious and disturbed. The girl had such a lovely face, and her innocence and seriousness pleased him.

"Are you sure the boy will soon find my woman?" she asked him wistfully.

"Quite sure," he answered. "He saw her himself a little while ago on the top of the cliff yonder. Do not be dismayed about that, and find some appetite for this homely fare. I have made requisitions like any Prussian, but the result is poorer than I hoped it might be. Try some cherries."

---

1 Artful minx.
2 In Greek mythology Arcadia is a sanctuary on the Acropolis in Athens and the home of Pan. It became a symbol of pastoral simplicity.

The cherries were fine biggaroons, scarlet and white, and Vere was still a child. She drank her milk and ate them with keen relish. The morning was growing warm as the sun clomb higher in the heavens. She took off her hat, and the wind lifted the thick hair falling over her forehead; exertion and excitement had brought a flush of colour in her cheeks; the light and shade of the walnut leaves was above her head; little curly-headed children peeped behind the furze fence and the sweetbriar hedge; white-capped old women looked on, nodding and smiling; the sea was out of sight, but the sound and the scent of it came there.

"It is an idyl," thought her companion; idyls were not in his life, which was one of unending triumphs, passions, and festivals, dizzily mingled in a world which adored him. Meanwhile it pleased him, if only by force of novelty, and no incident on earth could ever have found him unready.

"You love music?" he cried to her. "Ah! now if we were but in Italy in that dark little cottage there would sure to be a *chitarra*,[1] and I would give you a serenade to your cherries; perhaps without one— why not, if you like it? But first, Mademoiselle Herbert, I ought to tell you who I am."

"Oh! I know," said Vere, and lifted her soft eyes to him with a cherry against her lips.

"Indeed?"

"Yes, I saw you on the *plage*[2] yesterday, and Adrienne told me. You are Corrèze."

She said the name tenderly and reverently, for his fame had reached her in her childhood, and she had often thought to herself, "If only I could hear Corrèze once!"

He smiled caressingly.

"I am glad that you cared to ask. Yes, I am Corrèze, that is certain; and perhaps Corrèze would be the name of a greater artist if the world had not spoilt him—your mamma's world, mademoiselle. Well, my life is very happy, and very gay and glad, and after all the fame of the singer can never be but a breath, a sound through a reed. When our lips are once shut there is on us for ever eternal silence. Who can remember a summer-breeze when it has passed by, or tell in any after-time how a laugh or a sigh sounded?"

His face grew for the moment sad and overcast—that beautiful

---

1 A guitar (Italian).
2 Beach.

face which had fascinated the eyes of the girl as it had done the gaze of multitudes in burning nights of enthusiasm from Neva to Tagus, from Danube to Seine.[1]

Vere looked at him and did not speak. The gaze of Corrèze had a magic for all women, and she vaguely felt that magic as she met those eyes that were the eyes of Romeo and of Faust.

"What a lovely life it must be, your life," she said timidly. "It must be like a perpetual poem, I think."

Corrèze smiled.

"An artist's life is far off what you fancy it, I fear; but yet at the least it is full of colour and of change. I am in the snows of Russia one day, in the suns of Madrid another. I know the life of the palaces, I have known the life of the poor. When I forget the latter may heaven forget me! Some day when we are older friends, Mademoiselle Herbert, I will tell you my story."

"Tell me now," said Vere softly, with her gaze beginning to grow intent and eager under the halo of her hair, and letting her cherries lie unheeded on her lap.

Corrèze laughed.

"Oh, you will be disappointed. I have not much of one, and it is no secret. I am Raphael de Corrèze; I am the Marquis de Corrèze[2] if it were of any use to be so; but I prefer to be Corrèze the singer. It is much simpler, and yet much more uncommon. There are so many marquises, so few tenors. My race was great amongst the old noblesse de Savoie, but it was beggared in the Terror,[3] and their lands were confiscated and most of their lives were taken. I was born in a cabin; my grandfather had been born in a castle; it did not matter. He was a philosopher and a scholar, and he had taken to the mountains and loved them. My father married a peasant girl, and lived as simply as a shepherd. My mother died early. I ran about barefoot and saw to the goats. We were on the Valais side of the Pennine Alps. I used to drive the goats up higher, higher, higher, as the summer drew on, and the grass was eaten down. In the winter an old priest, who lived with us, and my father, when he had leisure, taught me. We were very poor and often hungry, but they were happy times. I think of them when

---

1 The Neva is an inlet of the Balkan Sea in Russia; the Tagus is a river that flows through the mountains in Spain; the Danube is a river in Vienna; the Seine is a river in Paris.

2 A Marquis is a nobleman ranking next below a Duke and above an Earl or a Count.

3 The Reign of Terror during the French Revolution.

I go across the Alps wrapped up in my black sables that the Empress of Russia has given me. I think I was warmer in the old days with the snow ten feet deep all around! Can you understand that snow may be warmer than sables? Yes? Well, there is little to tell. One day, when it was summer, and travellers were coming up into the Pennine valleys, some one heard me sing, and said my voice was a fortune. I was singing to myself and the goats among the gentian, the beautiful blue gentian—you know it? No, you do not know it, unless you have roamed the Alps in May. Other persons came after him and said the same thing, and wanted me to go with them; but I would not leave my father. Who could stack wood for him, and cut paths through the snow, and rake up the chestnuts and store them? I did all that. I would not go. When I was fifteen he died. "Do not forget you are the last Marquis de Corrèze," he said to me with his last breath. He had never forgotten it, and he had lived and died in the shadow of the Alps an honest man and a gentleman in his mountain hut. I passed the winter in great pain and trouble: it had been in the autumn that he had died. I could not resolve whether it would displease him in his grave under the snow that a Corrèze should be a singer; yet a singer I longed to be. With the spring I said to myself that after all one could be as loyal a gentleman as a singer as a soldier; why not? I rose up and walked down to the bottom of our ravine, where twice a week the diligences for Paris run; I found one going on the road; I went by it, and went on and on until I entered Paris. Ah! that entry into Paris of the boy with an artist's ambition and a child's faith in destiny! Why have they never written a poem on it? Once in Paris my path was easy; my voice made me friends. I went to Italy, I studied, I was heard, I returned to my dear Paris and triumphed. Well, I have been happy ever since. It is very much to say; and yet sometimes I long for the old winter nights, roasting the chestnuts, with the wall of snow outside!"

Vere had listened with eloquent dim eyes, and a fast beating heart; her cherries lying still uneaten on her lap. She gave a little quiet sigh as his voice ceased.

"You feel so about it because your father is dead," she said very low, and under her breath. "If he were here to know all your triumphs—"

Corrèze bent down and touched her hand, as it hung forward over her knee, with his lips. It was a mere habitual action of graceful courtesy with him, but it gave the child a strange thrill. She had never seen those tender easy ceremonies of the South. He saw that he had troubled her, and was sorry.

"Eat your cherries, Mademoiselle Herbert, and I will sing you a song," he said gaily, dropping a cherry into his own mouth, and he began to hum in his perfect melodious notes odds and ends of some of the greatest music of the world.

Then he sang with a voice only raised to one tenth of its power, the last song of Fernando,[1] his lips scarcely parting as he sang, and his eyes looking away to the yellow gorse and the sheep-cropped grass, and the drifting clouds; giving to the air and sea what he often refused to princes.

For the great tenor Corrèze was a prince himself in his caprices.

The perfect melody that held multitudes enthralled, and moved whole cities to ecstasies, that dissolved queens in tears and made women weep like little children, was heard on the still sunny silence of the cliffs with only a few babies tumbling in the sandy grass, and an old woman or two sitting spinning at her door. Down in gay Trouville all his worshippers could not woo from him a note; the entreaties that were commands found him obdurate and left him indifferent; and he sang here to the lark that was singing over his head, because a girl of sixteen had lost her shoes and stockings, and he wished to console her.

When once the voice left his lips, he sang on, much as the lark did, softly and almost unconsciously; the old familiar melodies following one another unbidden, as in his childhood he had used to sing to the goats with the flush of the Alpine roses about his feet, and the snow above his head.

The lark dropped, as though owning itself vanquished, into the hollow, where its consort's lowly nest was made. Corrèze ceased suddenly to sing, and looked at his companion. Vere was crying.

"Ah! my beautiful angel!" said an old peasant woman to him, standing close against the furze fence to listen; "do you come out of paradise to tell us we are not quite forgot there?"

Vere said nothing; she only turned on him her great soft eyes whilst the tears were falling unchecked down her cheeks.

"Mademoiselle," said Corrèze, "I have had flattery in my time, and more than has been good for me; but who ever gave me such sweet flattery as yours?"

"Flattery!" murmured Vere. "I did not mean—oh! how can you say that? The woman is right—it is as if it came from the angels!"

"By a servant of angels most unworthy, then, said Corrèze, with a

---

1 Tenor role in Mozart's opera *Cosi Fan Tutte* (1790).

smile and sigh. "As for the woman—good mother, here is a gold piece that carries Paradise in it; or at least men think so. But I am afraid, myself, that by the time we have found the gold pieces we have most of us forgotten the way to Paradise."

Vere was silent. She was still very pale; the tears stood on her lashes as the rain stands on the fringes of the dark passion-flower after a storm.

"Tell me your name, my angel," said the old woman, with her hand on the coin.

"Raphael."

"I will pray to St. Raphael[1] for you; if indeed you be not he?"

"Nay; I am not he. Pray always, good soul; it is pleasant to think that some one prays for us. Those cries cannot all be lost."

"Have you none to love you?" said the old woman. "That is odd, for you are beautiful."

"I have many to love me—in a way. But none to pray that I know of—that is another affair. Mother, did you see that lark that sang on against me, and dropped to its nest at last?"

"I saw it."

"Then have a heed that the boys do not stone, and the trappers net it."

"I will. What is your fancy?"

"It is a little brother."

The peasant woman did not understand, but she nodded three times. "The lark shall be safe as a king in his court. The plot he is in is mine. When you want a thing say to women you wish it—you do not want to say anything else."

Corrèze laughed, and pulled down a rose from behind the sweet-briar. He held it out to Vere.

"If there were only a single rose here and there upon earth, men and women would pass their years on their knees before its beauty. I wonder sometimes if human ingratitude for beauty ever hurts God? One might fancy even Deity wounded by neglected gifts. What do you say?"

He plucked a little lavender and some sea-pinks, and wound them together with the rose.

"When the fools throw me flowers they hurt me; it is barbarous," he said. "To throw laurel has more sense; there is a bitter smell in it, and it carries a sound allegory; but flowers!—flowers thrown in the

---

1 Archangel whose name means "God has healed."

dust, and dying in the gas-glare! The little live birds thrown at Carnival are only one shade worse.[1] Ah! here is the lad that I sent to find your waiting-woman."

The rose, the song, the magical charm seemed all dissolved before Vere as by the speaking of some disenchanter's spell: the hardness and fearfulness of prosaic fact faced her.

The fisher-lad explained that he had been miles in search of the good woman, but he had not found her. Men he had lately met had told him they had seen such a figure running hard back to the town.

"What shall I do?" she murmured aloud. "I have been forgetting all the trouble that I have been to you. Show me the way back—only that—I can find it—I can go alone. Indeed I can, M. de Corrèze."

"Indeed, you will do nothing of the kind," said Corrèze. "Your woman is quite safe, you see, so you need fear nothing for her. No doubt she thinks you have gone that way home. Mademoiselle Herbert, if you will listen to me, you will not distress yourself, but let me take you in my little boat that is down there to Trouville. It is impossible that you should walk in those wooden shoes, and carriage or even cart there is none here. Come, it is half-past nine only now. The sun is still temperate; the sea is smooth. Come, I will row you home in an hour."

"But I have been such a trouble to you."

"May I never have worse burdens!"

"And my mother will be so angry."

"Will she? Madame Dolly, a mother and angry! I cannot picture it; and I thought I knew her in every phase. My child, do not be so troubled about nothing. We will drift back slowly and pleasantly, and you shall be in your mother's house before noon strikes. And everyone knows me. That is one of the uses of notoreity; it has many drawbacks, so it need have some compensations. Come. I rowed myself out here. I studied music a year in Venice when I was a lad, and learned rowing on the Lido[2] from the fruit-girls. Come."

She did not resist much more; she thought that he must know best. With the grey lavender and the rose at her throat, she went away from under the cherry trees; the old woman in her blue gown gave them her blessing; the lark left his nest and began to sing again; the sunny hour was over, the black steep head of the cliffs was soon between them and the little hamlet.

1　As noted in the Introduction (p. 10), Ouida threw flowers to Mario, the prototype of Corrèze, with a gift and a note inside; he never acknowledged the gift or her note.

2　A beach resort in Venice.

They walked down by an easier way to the shore. The little boat was rocking on a high tide.

"Can you steer?" said Corrèze.

"O, yes," said Vere, who was learned in all sailing and boating, after a childhood passed by the rough grey waters of an iron coast.

He took the oars, and she the ropes. The sea was smooth, and there was no wind, not even a ruffle in the air; the boat glided slowly and evenly along.

He talked and laughed, he amused and beguiled her; he told her stories; now and then he sang low sweet snatches of Venetian boat-songs and rowing chaunts of the Lombard lakes and of the Riveria gulfs and bays; the sun was still cool; the sea looked blue to her eyes which had never beheld the Mediterranean. There were many craft in sight, pleasure and fishing vessels, and farther away large ships; but nothing drew near them save one old coble going in to Etretat from the night's dredging. It was an enchanted voyage to Vere, as the hamlet on the cliffs, and the homely lavender, and the cabbage rose, had all been enchanted things. She was in a dream. She wondered if she were really living. As she had never read but great and noble books, she thought vaguely of the Faerie Queen and of the Fata Morgana.[1] And through the sunlight against the sea, she saw as in a golden halo the beautiful dreamy face of Corrèze.

At last the voyage was done.

The little boat grated against the sands of Trouville, and against the side of a yacht's gig waiting there with smart sailors in white jerseys and scarlet caps, with "Ephemeris" in large blue letters woven on their shirts.

It was still early, earlier than it was usual for the fashionable idleness of the place to be upon the shore; and Corrèze had hoped to run his boat in on land unnoticed. But, as the crankiness of fate would have it, several people had been wakened before their usual hour. The yachts of a great channel race, after having been all night out towards the open ocean, had hove in sight on their homeward tack, and were objects of interest, as heavy bets were on them. Corrèze, to his annoyance, saw several skiffs and canoes already out upon the water round him, and several poppy-coloured and turquoise-coloured stripes adorning the bodies of human beings, and moving to and fro, some on the sand, some in the surf, some in the deeper sea.

---

1   *The Faerie Queen* (1590, 1596) is by Edmund Spenser; *Fata Morgana* is probably an Italian poemetta written by Piedmonte and published in 1797; Bulwer-Lytton, however, also published a poem entitled *Fata Morgana* in 1869.

There was no help for it, he saw, but to run the boat in, and trust to chance to take his companion unnoticed across the few hundred yards that separated the shore from the little house of Lady Dolly. But chance chose otherwise.

As he steered through the still shallow water, and ran the boat up on the sand, there were some human figures, like gaily painted peg-tops, immediately swarming down towards him, and amongst them Lady Dolly herself; Lady Dolly with a penthouse-like erection of straw above her head to keep the sun off, and her body tightly encased in black and yellow stripes, till she looked like a wasp—if a wasp had ever possessed snowy arms quite bare and bare white legs.

Corrèze gave his hand to Vere to alight, and she set her little wood-en shoes upon the dusty shore, and did not look up. The golden clouds seemed all about her still, and she was wondering what she could ever say to him to thank him enough for all his care.

A peal of shrill laughter pierced her ear and broke her musing.

"Corrèze, what nymph or naiad have you found? A mermaid in *sabots*! Oh! oh! oh!"

The laughter pealed and shrieked, as fashionable ladies' laughter will, more often than is pretty; and then, through the laughter she heard her mother's voice.

"Ah—ha! Corrèze! So this is why you steal away from supper when the daylight comes?"

Corrèze, surrounded by the swarming and parti-coloured pegtops, lifted his head, comprehended the situation, and bowed to the ground.

"I have had the honour and happiness, madame, to be of a slight service to Mademoiselle Herbert."

The group of pegtops was composed of Lady Dolly, the Princesse Hélène, a Princess Zephine, three other ladies, and several gentlemen, just come to the edge of the sea to bathe.

Vere gave one amazed glance at her mother and blushed scarlet. The glance and the blush were not for the shame of her own misdo-ing; they were for the shame of her mother's attire. Vere, who had been overwhelmed with confusion at the loss of her shoes, was very far from comprehending the state of feeling which adopts a fashion-able swimming costume as perfect propriety, and skips about in the surf hand in hand with a male swimmer, the cynosure of five hun-dred eye-glasses and *lorgnons*.[1]

---

1   Eyeglasses clipped to the bridge of the nose.

She had seen the bathing-dress indeed, but though she had perceived that it was legless and armless, she had imagined that something must be worn with it to supplement those deficiencies, and she had not in any way reckoned the full enormity of it as it had hung limp over the back of a chair.

But her mother!

As the group of living human pegtops swarmed before her on the edge of the sea, and she realised that it was actually her mother, actually her dead father's wife, who was before her, with those black and yellow stripes for all her covering, Vere felt her cheeks and brow burn all over as with fire. They thought she was blushing with shame at herself, but she was blushing for shame for them, and those tight-drawn rainbow-coloured stripes that showed every line of the form more than the kilted skirts and scant rags of the fisher-girls ever showed theirs. If it were right to come down to dance about in the water with half-a-dozen men around, how could that which she had done herself be so very wrong? The sea and the sands and the sky seemed to go round with her. She was only conscious of the anger sparkling from her mother's eyes; she did not heed the tittering and the teasing with which the other ladies surrounded her companion.

"Vere!"—Lady Dolly for the moment said nothing more. She stood blankly staring at her daughter, at the sunburnt hat, the tumbled hair, the wooden shoes; and at the figure of Corrèze against the sun.

"You—with Corrèze!" she cried at length; and Corrèze, studying her pretty little face, thought how evil pretty women could sometimes look.

"Mademoiselle Herbert had lost her maid, and her road, and her shoes," he hastened to say with his most charming grace; "I have been happy enough to be of a little—too little—service to her. The fault was none of hers, but all of the tide; and, save the loss of the shoes, there is no mischief done."

"M. Corrèze has wasted his morning for me, and has been so very kind," said Vere. Her voice was very low, but it was steady. She did not think she had done any wrong, but she felt bewildered, and was not quite sure.

Her mother laughed very irritably.

"Corrèze is always too kind, and always a *preux chevalier*.[1] What on earth have you been doing, darling? and where are your women? and however could you be so quite too dreadfully foolish. I suppose you

---

1 Valiant knight.

think life is like Alice in Wonderland? Jack, see her home, will you? and join us at the yacht and lock her up in her room, and the German with her. How good of you, dear Corrèze, to bore yourself with a troublesome child. If it were anybody else except you who had come ashore like this with my Vera I should feel really too anxious and angry. But, with you—"

"Madame! I am too fortunate! If you deem me to be of any use, however, let me claim as a guerdon,[1] permission to attend mademoiselle your daughter to her home."

"Jack, see her home, pray. Do you hear me," said Lady Dolly again, sharply. "No—not you, Corrèze—you are quite too charming to be trusted. Jack's like an old woman."

The Princesse Hélène smiled at the Princess Zephine.

If old women are thirty years old, handsome in a fair bold breezy fashion, and six feet three in height, then was Lord Jura like them. He had come ashore from the "Ephemeris," and was the only one of the party decently clad.

"Why should she go home?" muttered Jura, "why may she not come with us—eh?"

"Out of the question," said Lady Dolly, very sharply.

He was a silent man; he said nothing now; he strode off silently to Vere's side, lifting his straw hat a little, in sign of his acceptance of his devoir.[2]

Vere made an inclination to her mother and the other ladies, with the somewhat stately deference that had been imposed on her at Bulmer Chase, and began to move toward the Châlet Ludoff, whose green blinds and gilded scroll balconies were visible in the distance. Corrèze bowed very low with his own matchless grace and ease, and began to follow them.

"No; not you Corrèze; I cannot permit it. You are too fascinating—infinitely too fascinating—to play chaperon," cried Lady Dolly once more. "Vera, when you get home go to your room, and stay there till I come. You have had enough liberty to-day, and have abused it shamefully."

Having screamed that admonition on the air, Lady Dolly turned to her friends the feminine pegtops, and entreated them not to think too badly of her naughty little puss—she was so young!

In a few moments all the pegtops had jumped into the water, and

---

1 Reward.
2 Duty.

the young Duc de Dinant was teaching Lady Dolly to execute in the waves a new dance just introduced in an operetta of Messieurs Meilhac and Hervé;[1] a dance that required prodigious leaps and produced boisterous laughter. Vere did not look back once; she felt very ashamed still, but not of herself.

Jura did not address a word to her, except when they had approached the steps of the Châlet Ludoff; then he said, somewhat sheepishly,—"I say—if she's nasty don't you mind. She can be; but it soon blows over—"

Vere was silent.

"Won't you come out to-day," he pursued. "I do so wish you would. It's my tub, you know, and you would like it. Do come?"

"Where?"

"On my yacht. We are going to picnic at Villiers. The Grand Duchess is coming, and she is great fun, when she aren't too drunk. Why shouldn't you come? It seems to me you are shut up like a nun. It's not fair."

"My mother does not wish me to come anywhere," said Vere dreamily, heeding him very little. "There is the house. Go back to them, Lord Jura. Thanks."

Jura went back; but not until he had sent her up a pretty little breakfast, and the most innocent of his many French novels.

"It is a beastly shame," he said, as he walked towards the swimmers over the sands.

Corrèze meanwhile, who had resisted all entreaties to bathe, and all invitations to pass the day on the "Ephemeris," wended his way slowly towards his hotel.

"She has claws, that pretty cat," he said to himself, thinking of Lady Dolly. He had never very much liked her, and he detested her now in a petulant impetuous way that now and then broke up the sunny softness of his temper.

"How sweet she is now; sweet as the sweetbriar, and as healthy," he thought to himself. "How clear the soul, how clear the eyes! If only that would last! But one little year in the world, and it will be all altered. She will have gained some *chic*, no doubt, and some talent and tact; she will wear high-heeled shoes, and she will have drawn in

---

1 Henri Meilhac (1830-97) and Ludovic Halévy (1834-1908) collaborated in writing librettos for a number of operettas, often with French composer Jacques Offenbach (1819-80).

her waist, and learned how to *porter le sein en offrande,*[1] and learned how to make those grand grey eyes look languid, and lustrous, and terrible. Oh, yes, she will have learned all that. But then, alas! alas! she will have learned so much too. She will have learned what the sickly sarcasms mean, and the wrapt-up pruriencies intend, and what women and men are worth, and how politics are knavish tricks, and the value of a thing is just as much as it will bring, and all the rest of the dreary gospel of self. What a pity! what a pity! But it is always so. I dare say she will never stoop to folly as her pretty mother does; but the bloom will go. She will be surprised, shocked, pained; then, little by little, she will get used to it all—they all do—and then the world will have her, body and soul, and perhaps will put a bit of ice where that tender heart now beats. She will be a great lady, I dare say—a very great lady—nothing worse, very likely; but, all the same, my sweetbriar will be withered, and my white wild rose will be dead— and what will it matter to me? I dare say I shall be a musical box with a broken spring, lying in a dust of dried myrtle and musty laurels!"

Lady Dolly danced, floated, bobbed like a cork, drifted languidly with her arms above her head, dived, and disappeared with only the rosy soles of her feet visible—did everything that a pretty woman and a good swimmer can do in shallow smooth water, with no breeze to mar her comfort. But she was in a very bad temper all the time.

Jura did not improve it, when she came out of the water, by asking her, again, to let her daughter go with them in the "Ephemeris."

"*Au grand jamais!*"[2] said Lady Dolly, quite furiously. "After such an exhibition of herself with a singer! Are you mad?"

She went home furious; changed her wet stripes for a yachting dress in sullen silence; refused to see the German governess, or to allow Vere's door to be opened till she should return in the evening, and went down to the yacht in a state of great irritation, with a charming costume, all white serge and navy blue satin, with anchor buttons in silver, and a Norwegian belt hung with everything that the mind of man could imagine as going on to a girdle.

The "Ephemeris" was one of the best yachts on the high seas; and had a good cook, wonderful wines, a piano, a library, a cabin of rosewood and azure, and deck hammocks of silk. Nevertheless, everything seemed to go wrong on board of her that day—at least to Lady Dolly. They got becalmed, and stuck stupidly still, while the steam yachts

---

1 To carry her bosom as an offering; to make men worship her.
2 To all eternity; (never; not ever).

were tearing ahead in a cruel and jeering manner; then the sea got rough all in a moment; the lobster salad disagreed with her, or something did; a spiteful stiff wind rose; and the Grand Duchess borrowed her cigarette case and never returned it, and of course could not be asked for it, and it contained the only verbena-scented *papelitos* that there were on board. Then Jura was too attentive to the comfort of another woman, or she fancied, at any rate, that he was; and none of her especial pets were there, so she could not make reprisals as she wished; and Corrèze had obstinately and obdurately refused to come at all. Not that she cared a straw about Corrèze, but she hated being refused.

"What a wax[1] you're in, Dolly!" said Lord Jura, bringing her some iced drinks and peaches.

"When I've had three mad people sent to me!" she cried in a rage. "And I'll be obliged to you, Jack, not to use slang to *me*."

Lord Jura whistled and went aft.

"What a boor he grows!" thought Lady Dolly; and the "Ephemeris" was pitching, and she hated pitching, and the little Duc de Dinant was not on board because Jack wouldn't have him; and she felt ill-used, furious, wretched, and hated the cook for making the lobster salad, and Vere for having been born.

"A boy wouldn't have been half so bad," she thought. "He'd have been always away, and they'd have put him in the army. But a girl! It's all very easy to say *marry* her, but she hasn't any money, and the Mull people won't give her any, and my own people can't, and as for Mr. Vanderdecken, one might as well try to get blood out of a flint; and they may say what they like, but all men want money when they marry nowadays, even when they've got heaps more than they know what to do with themselves. What a horrid woman the Grand Duchess is. She's drunk already, and it isn't three o'clock!"

"She's going splendidly now," said Jura, meaning the "Ephemeris," that plunged and reared as if she were a mare instead of a schooner; and the fresh sou'easter that had risen sent her farther and farther westward towards the haze of distant seas.

"I believe we're going straight to America! what idiocy is yachting!" said Lady Dolly savagely, as the wind tore at her tiny multitudinous curls.

Meanwhile, Vere, in religious obedience, had gone to the little chamber that was called by courtesy at the Châlet Ludoff a study, and

---

1 Fit of anger.

submitting to be locked in, remained happy in the morning's golden dream of sunshine, of song, of the sea, of the summer. She had found her lost Northumbrian safe, but in agonies of terror and self-reproach, and the amiable German for once very seriously angry. But Vere was not to be ruffled or troubled; she smiled at all reproof, scarcely hearing it, and put her cabbage rose and her sprigs of lavender in water. Then she fell fast asleep on a couch, from fatigue and the warmth of the Norman sun, and dreamed of the blue gentian of the Alps that she had never seen, and of the music of the voice of Corrèze.

When she awoke some hours had passed—the clock told her it was two. She never thought of moving from her prison. The ricketty white and gold door would have given way at a push, but to her it was inviolate. She had been reared to give obedience in the spirit as well as the letter.

She thought no one had ever had so beautiful a day as this morning of hers. She would have believed it a dream, only there were her rose and the homely heads of the lavender.

The German brought Euclid and Sophocles into the prison-chamber, but Vere put them gently away.

"I cannot study to-day," she said. It was the first time in her life that she had ever said so.

The Fräulein went away weeping, and believing that the heavens would fall. Vere, with her hands clasped behind her head, leaned back and watched the white clouds come and go above the sea, and fancied the air was still full of that marvellous and matchless voice which had told her at last all that music could be.

"He is the angel Raphael?" she said to herself. It seemed to her that he could not be mere mortal man.

Her couch was close to the glass doors of the room, and they opened into one of the scroll-work balconies which embroidered the fantastic front of the Châlet Ludoff. The room was nominally upstairs, but literally it was scarcely eight feet above the ground without.

It was in the full hot sunshine of early afternoon when the voice she dreamed of said softly, "Mademoiselle Herbert!"

Vere roused herself with a start, and saw the arm of Corrèze leaning on the balcony and his eyes looking at her; he was standing on the stone *perron*[1] below.

"I came to bid you farewell," he said softly. "I go to Germany

---

1 Flight of steps.

to-night. You are a captive, I know, so I dared to speak to you thus."

"You go away!"

To the girl it seemed as if darkness fell over the sea and shore.

"Ah! we princes of art are but slaves of the ring after all. Yes, my engagements have been made many months ago: to Baden, to Vienna, to Moscow, to Petersburg; then Paris and London once more. It may be long ere we meet, if ever we do, and I dare to call myself your friend, though you never saw my face until this morning."

"You have been so good to me," murmured Vere; and then stopped, not knowing what ailed her in the sudden sense of sorrow, loss, and pain, which came over her as she listened.

"Oh *altro!*"[1] laughed Corrèze, lifting himself a little higher, and leaning more easily on the iron of the balcony. "I found you a pair of wooden shoes, a cup of milk, and a cabbage rose. Sorry things to offer to an enchanted princess who had missed her road! My dear, few men will not be willing to be as good to you as you will let them be. You are a child. You do not know your power. I wonder what teachers you will have? I wish you could go untaught, but there is no hope of that."

Vere was silent. She did not understand what he meant. She understood only that he was going far away—this brilliant and beautiful stranger who had come to her with the morning sun.

"Mademoiselle Herbert," continued Corrèze, "I shall sound like a preacher, and I am but a graceless singer, but try and keep yourself 'unspotted from the world.'[2] Those are holy words, and I am not a holy speaker, but try and remember them. This world you will be launched in does no woman good. It is a world of moths. Half the moths are burning themselves in feverish frailty, the other half are corroding and consuming all that they touch. Do not become of either kind. You are made for something better than a moth. You will be tempted; you will be laughed at; you will be surrounded with the most insidious sort of evil example, namely, that which does not look like evil one whit more than the belladonna berry looks like death. The women of your time are not, perhaps, the worst the world has seen, but they are certainly the most contemptible. They have dethroned grace; they have driven out honour; they have succeeded in making men ashamed of the sex of their mothers; and they have

---

1 On the contrary.
2 James 1:27.

set up nothing in the stead of all they have destroyed except a feverish frenzy for amusement and an idiotic imitation of vice. You cannot understand now, but you will see it—too soon. They will try to make you like them. Do not let them succeed. You have truth, innocence, and serenity—treasure them. The women of your day will ridicule you, and tell you it is an old-fashioned triad, out of date like the Graces;[1] but do not listen. It is a triad without which no woman is truly beautiful, and without which no man's love for her can be pure. I would fain say more to you, but I am afraid to tell you what you do not know; and woe to those by whom such knowledge first comes! *Mon enfant*,[2] adieu."

He had laid a bouquet of stephanotis and orchids on the sill of the window at her feet, and had dropped out of sight before she had realized his farewell.

When she strained her eyes to look for him, he had already disappeared. Tears blinded her sight, and fell on the rare blossoms of his gift.

"I will try—I will try to be what he wishes," she murmured to the flowers. "If only I knew better what he meant."

The time soon came when she knew too well what he meant. Now she sat with the flowers in her lap and wondered wearily, and sobbed silently, as if her heart would break.

Corrèze was gone.

CHAPTER IV.

At sunset Lady Dolly returned, out of temper. They had been becalmed again for two hours, the sea all of sudden becoming like oil, just to spite her, and they had played to wile away the time, and the Grand Duchess had won a great deal of her money, besides smoking every one of her cigarettes and letting the case fall through the hatchway.

"I will never go out with that odious Russian again—never! The manners of a *cantinière*[3] and the claws of a *croupier*!"[4] she said in immeasurable disgust of the august lady whom she had idolised in the morning; and she looked in at the little study, when she reached home, to allay her rage with making someone uncomfortable.

---

1 In classical mythology the Graces are three goddesses who bestow beauty and charm and are the embodiment of both.

2 My child.

3 A woman who serves food to soldiers in a military canteen.

4 Attendant at a gaming table who collects and pays bets.

"Are you sufficiently ashamed of yourself, Vera?" she said as she entered.

Vere rose, rather uneasily, and with soft sad dewy eyes.

"Why should I be ashamed, mother?" she said simply.

"Why? why? you ask why? after compromising yourself, as you did this morning?"

"Compromise?"

Vere had never heard the word. Women who were compromised were things that had never been heard of at Bulmer.

"Do not repeat what I say. It is the rudest thing you can do," said her mother sharply. "Yes, compromised, hideously compromised—and with Corrèze of all persons in the world! You must have been mad!"

Vere looked at her stephanotis and orchids, and her young face grew almost stern. "If you mean I did anything wrong, I did no wrong. It was all accident, and no one could have been so kind as—he—was."

The ear of Lady Dolly, quick at such signs, caught the little pause before the pronoun.

"The world never believes in accidents," she said chillily. "You had better understand that for the future. To be seen coming home in a boat early in the morning all alone with such a man as Corrèze would be enough to ruin any girl at the outset of her life—to *ruin* her!"

Vere's eyes opened in bewildered surprise. She could not follow her mother's thoughts at all, nor could she see where she had been in any error.

"Corrèze, of all men upon earth!" echoed her mother. "Good heavens! do you know he is a singer?"

"Yes," said Vere softly; hearing all around her as she spoke the sweet liquid melody of that perfect voice which had called the skylark "a little brother."

"A great singer, I grant; the greatest, if you like, but still a singer, and a man with a hundred love affairs in every capital he enters! And to come home *alone* with such a man after hours *spent alone* with him. It was madness, Vera; and it was worse, it was forward, impudent, unmaidenly!"

The girl's pale face flushed; she lifted her head with a certain indignant pride.

"You must say what you will, mother," she said quietly. "But that is very untrue."

"Don't dare to answer *me*," said Lady Dolly, "I tell you it was disgraceful, disgraceful, and goodness knows how ever I shall explain it away. Hélène has been telling the story to everybody, and given it seven-leagued boots already. True! who cares what is true or what is not true—it is what a thing *looks!* I believe everybody says you had come from Havre with Corrèze!"

Vere stood silent and passive, her eyes on her stephanotis and orchids.

"Where did you get those extravagant flowers? Surely Jack never—" said Lady Dolly suspiciously.

"He brought them," answered Vere.

"Corrèze? Whilst I was away?"

"Yes. He spoke to me at the balcony."

"Well, my dear, you do Bulmer credit! No Spanish or Italian heroine out of his own operas could conduct herself more audaciously on the first day of her liberty. It is certainly what I always thought would come of your grandmother's mode of education. Well, go upstairs in your bedroom and do not leave it until I send for you. No, you can't take flowers upstairs; they are very unwholesome—as unwholesome as the kindness of Corrèze."

Vere went, wistfully regarding her treasures; but she had kept the faded rose and the lavender in her hand unnoticed.

"After all, I care most for these," she thought; the homely seaborn things that had been gathered after the songs.

When the door had closed on her Lady Dolly rang for her *maître d'hôtel*.[1]

"Pay the Fräulein Schroder three months' salary, and send her away by the first steamer; and pay the English servant whatever she wants and send her by the first steamer. Mind they are both gone when I wake. And I shall go to Deauville[2] the day after tomorrow; probably I shall never come back here."

The official bowed, obedient.

As she passed through her drawing-rooms Lady Dolly took up the bouquet of Corrèze and went to her own chamber.

"Pick me out the best of those flowers," she said to her maid, "and stick them about all over me; here and there, you know."

She was going to dine with the Duchesse de Sonnaz at Deauville.

---

1 Steward; butler.
2 Deauville is more exclusive than its twin resort of Trouville. The two are joined by a bridge over the estuary of the river Torques. It was created by the Duke de Morny, half-brother of Napoleon III, during the Second Empire.

As she went to her carriage the hapless German, quivering and sobbing, threw herself in her path.

"Oh, miladi miladi!" she moaned. "It cannot be true? You send me not away thus from the child of my heart? Ten years have I striven to write the will of God, and the learning that is better than gold, on that crystal pure mind, and my life, and my brain, and my soul I do give—"

"You should have done your duty," said Lady Dolly, wrapping herself up and hastening on. "And you can't complain, my good Schroder; you have got three months' in excess of your wages," and she drew her swan's-down about her and got into her carriage.

"Now, on my soul, that was downright vulgar," muttered John Jura. "Hang it all! it was vulgar!"

But he sighed as he said it to himself, for his experience had taught him that highborn ladies could be very vulgar when they were moved to be ill-natured.

Corrèze was at the villa.

She saw him a moment before dinner, and gave him her prettiest smile.

"Oh, Corrèze! what flowers! I stole some of them, you see. You would turn my child's head. I am glad you are going to Baden!"

He laughed, and said something graceful and novel, turned on the old *mater pulchra, filia pulchrior.*[1]

The dinner was not too long, and was very gay. After it everybody wandered out into the gardens, which were hung with coloured lamps and had musicians hidden in shrubberies, discoursing sweet sounds to rival the nightingales. The light was subdued, the air delicious, the sea glimmered phosphorescent and starlit at the end of dusky alleys and rose-hung walks. Lady Dolly wandered about with Sergius Zouroff and others, and felt quite romantic, whilst John Jura yawned and sulked; she never allowed him to do anything else while she was amusing herself.

Corrèze joined her and her Russians in a little path between walls of the quatre-saison[2] rose and a carpet of velvety turf. The stars sparkled through the rose-leaves, the sound of the sea stole up the silent little alley. Lady Dolly looked very pretty in a dress of dead white, with the red roses above her and their dropped leaves at her feet. She was smoking, which was a pity—the cigarette did not agree with the roses.

---

1 Mother beautiful, daughter more beautiful.
2 Year round.

"Madame," cried Corrèze, as he sauntered on and disengaged her a little from the others, "I have never seen anything so exquisite as your young daughter. Will you believe that I mean no compliment when I say so?"

"My dear Corrèze! She is only a child!"

"She is not a child. What would you say, madame, if I told you that for a full five minutes I had the madness to think to-day that I would pay my forfeit to Baden and Vienna for the sake of staying here?"

"Heaven forbid you should do any such thing! You would turn her head in a week!"

"What would you say, madame," he continued with a little laugh, disregarding her interruption, "what would you say if I told you that I, Corrèze, had actually had the folly to fancy for five minutes that a vagabond nightingale might make his nest for good in one virgin heart? What would you say, miladi?"

"My dear Corrèze, if you were by any kind of possibility talking seriously"—

"I am talking quite seriously—or let us suppose that I am. What would you say, miladi?"

"I should say, my dear Corrèze, that you are too entirely captivating to be allowed to say such things even in an idle jest, and that you would be always most perfectly charming in every capacity but one."

"And that one is?"

"As a husband for anybody!"

"I suppose you are right," said Corrèze with a little sigh. "Will you let me light my cigarette at yours?"

An hour later he was on his way to Baden in the middle hours of the starry fragrant summer night.

CHAPTER V.

Raphael de Corrèze had said no more than the truth of himself that morning by the sweetbriar hedge on the edge of the Norman cliffs.

All the papers and old documents that were needful to prove him the lineal descendant of the great Savoy family of Corrèze were safe in his bureau in Paris, but he spoke no more of them than he spoke of the many love-letters and imprudent avowals that were also locked away in caskets and cabinets in the only place that in a way could be called his home, his apartment in the Avenue Marigny. What was the use? All Marquis and Peer of Savoy though he was by descent he was none the less only a tenor singer, and in his heart of hearts he was too keenly proud to drag his old descent into the notice of men merely that he might look like a frivolous boaster, an impudent teller of empty tales. *Noblesse oblige*,[1] he had often said to himself, resisting temptation in his oft-tempted career, but no one ever heard him say aloud that paternoster of princes. His remembrance of his race had been always within him like a talisman, but he wore it like a talisman, secretly, and shy even of having his faith in it known.

Corrèze, with all his negligence and gaiety, and spoilt child of the world though he was, appraised very justly the worth of the world and his place in it.

He knew very well that if a rain-storm on a windy night were to quench his voice in his throat for ever, all his troops of lovers and friends would fall away from him, and his name drop down into darkness like any shooting star on an August night. He never deceived himself.

"I am only the world's favourite plaything," he would say to himself. "If I lost my voice, I should be served like the nightingale in Hans Andersen's story.[2] Oh! I do not blame the world—things are always so; only it is well to remember it. It serves, like Yorick's skull,[3] or Philip's slave,[4] to remind one that one is mortal."

The remembrance gave him force, but it also gave him a tinge of bitterness, so far as any bitterness is ever possible to a sunny, generous, and careless nature, and it made him before everything an artist.

When he was very insolent to grand people—which he often was in the caprice of celebrity—those people said to one another "Ah! that is because he thinks himself Marquis de Corrèze." But they were wrong. It was because he knew himself a great artist.

The scorn of genius is the most boundless and the most arrogant of all scorn, and he had it in him very strongly. The world said he was extravagantly vain; the world was wrong; yet if he had been, it would have been excusable. Women had thrown themselves into his arms from his earliest youth for sake of his beautiful face, before his voice had been heard; and when his voice had captured Europe there was

---

1 Rank has its obligations.
2 In Hans Christian Andersen's "The Nightingale" (1844), the real nightingale is banished from the country after the emperor receives a gift of a jeweled, artificial nightingale.
3 In the graveyard scene in *Hamlet* (V.i), Hamlet finds the skull of his court jester Yorick.
4 Philip II of Macedonia, who ruled as king from 359 to 336 B.C., required one of his slaves to whisper in his ear words to remind him of his mortality to keep him from thinking he was godlike.

scarcely any folly, any madness, any delirium, any shame that women had not been ready to rush into for his sake, or for the mere sight of him and mere echo of his song.

There is no fame on earth so intoxicating, so universal, so enervating, as the fame of a great singer; as it is the most uncertain and unstable of all, the most evanescent and most fugitive, so by compensation it is the most delightful and the most gorgeous; rouses the multitude to a height of rapture as no other art can do, and makes the dull and vapid crowds of modern life hang breathless on one voice, as in Greece, under the violet skies, men hearkened to the voice of Pindar or of Sappho.[1]

The world has grown apathetic and purblind. Critics still rave and quarrel before a canvas, but the nations do not care; quarries of marble are hewn into various shapes, and the throngs gape before them and are indifferent; writers are so many that their writings blend in the public mind in a confused phantasmagoria where the colours have run into one another and the lines are all waved and indistinct; the singer alone still keeps the old magic power, "the beauty that was Athens' and the glory that was Rome's,"[2] still holds the divine caduceus,[3] still sways the vast thronged auditorium, till the myriads hold their breath like little children in delight and awe. The great singer alone has the old magic sway of fame; and if he close his lips "the gaiety of nations is eclipsed,"[4] and the world seems empty and silent like a wood in which the birds are all dead.

It is a supreme power, and may well intoxicate a man.

Corrèze had been as little delirious as any who have drunk of the philtre of a universal fame, although at times it had been too strong for him, and had made him audacious, capricous, inconstant, and guilty of some follies; but his life was pure from any dark reproach.

"*Soyez gentilhomme*,"[5] his father had said to him in the little hut on the Pennine Alps, with the snow-fields severing them from all other life than their own, and had said it never thinking that his boy would

---

1   Pindar (522-446 B.C.) and Sappho (613-570 B.C.) were early Greek lyric poets.

2   From Edgar Allan Poe's "To Helen" (1831).

3   In mythology the divine caduceus was the staff of Mercury (Hermes), the messenger of the gods.

4   From James Boswell's *Life of Johnson* (1791). Learning of the death of actor David Garrick, Johnson wrote: "I am disappointed by that stroke of death, which has eclipsed the gaiety of nations."

5   Be a gentleman.

be more than at best a village priest or teacher; the bidding had sunk into the mind of the child, and the man had not forgotten it now that Europe was at his feet, and its princes but servants who had to wait his time; and he liked to make them wait. "Perhaps that is not *gentilhomme*,"[1] he would say in reproach to himself, but it diverted him and he did it very often; most often when he thought angrily that he was but like Hans Andersen's nightingale, the jewelled one, that was thrown aside and despised when once its spring was snapped and broken. If he were only that, he was now at the moment when emperor and court thought nothing in heaven or on earth worth hearing but the jewelled nightingale, and "the crowds in the streets hummed his song." Yet as the night train bore him through the level meadows, and cornfields glistening in the moonlight, and the hush of a sleeping world, his eyes were dim and his heart was heavy, and on the soft cushions of the travelling bed they had given him he could not find rest.

"The moths will corrupt her," he thought, sadly and wistfully. "The moths will eat all that fine delicate feeling away, little by little; the moths of the world will eat the unselfishness first, and then the innocence, and then the honesty, and then the decency; no one will see them eating, no one will see the havoc being wrought; but little by little the fine fabric will go, and in its place will be dust. Ah, the pity of it! The pity of it! The webs come out of the great weaver's loom lovely enough, but the moths of the world eat them all. One weeps for the death of children, but perhaps the change of them into callous men and worldly women is a sadder thing to see after all."

His heart was heavy.

Was it love? No; he fancied not; it could not be. Love with him—an Almaviva[2] as much off the stage as on it—had been a charming, tumultuous, victorious thing; a concession rather to the weakness of the women who sought him than to his own; the chief, indeed, but only one amongst many other distractions and triumphs.

It was not love that made his heart go out to that fair-haired child, with the thoughtful questioning eyes. It was rather pity, tenderness, reverence for innocence, rage against the world which would so soon change her;—poor little moth, dreaming of flying up to heaven's light, and born to sink into earth's commonest fires!

Corrèze did not esteem women highly. They had caressed him

---

1 Gentlemanly.

2 Almaviva is the hero of Rossini's comic opera, *The Barber of Seville* (1816). Disguised as a student, Almaviva courts and finally marries the heroine Rosina.

into satiety, and wooed him till his gratitude was more than half contempt; but in his innermost heart, where his old faiths dwelt unseen by even his best friends, there was the fancy of what a woman should be, might be, unspotted by the world, and innocent in thought, as well as deed.

Such a woman had seemed to him to be in the girl whom he had found by the sea, as the grand glory of the full white rose lies folded in the blush-rose bud.

It was too absurd!

Her mother had been right, quite right. The little frivolous, artificial woman, with her *perruque* and her *papelitos*, had said all that society would say. She had been wise, and he, in a passing moment of sentiment, a fool. He had scarcely really considered the full meaning of his own words, and where they would have led him had they been taken seriously.

He thought now of all the letters lying in those cabinets and caskets at Paris.

"What a burnt-sacrifice of notepaper I should have had to make!" he said to himself, and smoked a little, and tried to ridicule himself.

Was he, Corrèze, the lover of great rulers of society, the hero of a hundred and a thousand intrigues and romances, in love with a mere child, because she had serious eyes and no shoes and stockings? bewitched by a young girl who had sat half an hour beside him by a sweetbriar hedge on a cliff by the sea? It was too absurd.

From Baden there had come an impatient summons from a dark-haired duchess of the Second Empire,[1] who fancied that she reigned over his life because he reigned over hers like a fatality, an imperious and proud woman whom the lamps in the Avenue Marigny had shone on as she stole on foot, muffled and veiled, to hide her burning face on his breast; he thought of where she was waiting for him, and a little shudder of disgust went over him.

He threw open the window of his bed carriage, and leaned his head out, to meet the midnight wind.

The train was passing a little village, a few cottages, a pond, a mill, a group of willows silvery in the starlight. From the little green gardens there came a scent of sweetbriar and hedge roses.

"Shall I smell that smell all my life?" he thought impatiently.

---

1 See Introduction (pp. 18–19).

CHAPTER VI.

Lady Dolly had a very dear friend. Of course she had five hundred dear friends, but this one she was really fond of; that is to say, she never said anything bad of her, and only laughed at her goodnaturedly when she had left a room; and this abstinence is as strong a mark of sincerity nowadays, as dying for another used to be in the old days of strong feelings and the foolish expression of them.

This dear friend was her dear Adine, otherwise Lady Stoat of Stitchley, who had just won the honour of the past year's season by marrying her daughter (a beauty) to a young marquis, who, with the small exceptions of being a drunkard, a fool, and a brute, was everything that a mother's soul could desire; and all the mothers' souls in the world had accordingly burned for him passionately, and Lady Stoat had won him.

Lady Stoat was as much revered as a maternal model of excellence in her time as the mother of the Gracchi[1] in hers. She was a gentle-looking woman, with a very soft voice, which she never raised under any provocation. She had a will of steel, but she made it look like a blossoming and pliant reed; she was very religious and strongly ritualistic.

When Lady Dolly awoke the next morning, with the vague remembrance of something very unpleasant having happened to her, it was to this friend that she fled for advice as soon as she was dressed; having for that purpose to drive over to Deauville, where Lady Stoat, who thought Trouville vulgar, had a charming little place, castellated, coquettish, Gothic, Chinese, Moorish, all kinds of things, in a pretty pellmell of bonbon-box architecture, set in a frame of green turf and laurel hedges and round-headed acacias, and with blazing geranium beds underneath its gilded balconies and marqueterie[2] doors. Lady Dolly had herself driven over in the Duc de Dinant's *panier*[3] with his four ponies, and while he went to find out some friends and arrange the coming races, she took her own road to the Maison Perle.

"Adine always knows," she thought. She was really fond of her Adine, who was many years older than herself. But for her Adine, certain little bits of nonsense and imprudence in Lady Dolly's feverish little life might have made people talk, and given trouble to

---

1 Tiberius Sempronius Gracchus (163-133 B.C.) and Gaius Sempronius Gracchus (158-122 B.C.) were Roman reformers and orators. They were raised by their mother with great care.

2 Inlaid wood.

3 A go cart.

Mr. Vanderdecken, absorbed as he might be in Java, Japan, or Jupiter.

Lady Stoat of Stitchley was one of those invaluable characters who love to do good for good's own sake, and to set things straight for the mere pleasure of being occupied. As some persons of an old-maidish or old-bachelor turn of mind will go far out of their way to smoothe a crease or remove a crumb, though neither be marring their own property, so would Lady Stoat go far out of her way to prevent a scandal, reconcile two enemies, or clear a tangled path. It was her way of amusing herself. She had a genius for management. She was a clever tactician, and her tactics interested her, and employed her time agreeably. If anyone in her world wanted a marriage arranged, a folly prevented, a disgrace concealed, or a refractory child brought to reason, Lady Stoat of Stitchley would do it in the very best possible manner.

"It is only my duty," she would say in her hushed melodious monotonous voice, and nearly everybody thought Lady Stoat the modern substitute of a saint on earth.

To this saint now went Lady Dolly with her troubles and her tale.

"What *can* I do with her, dearest?" she cried plaintively, in the pretty little morning room, whose windows looked over the geranium beds to the grey sea.

Lady Stoat was doing crewel work; a pale, slight, gracefully made woman with small straight features, and the very sweetest and saddest of smiles.

"What young men are there?" said Lady Stoat, now in response, still intent on her crewel work. "I have not thought about them at all since the happiness of my own treasure was secured. By the bye, I heard from Gwen this morning; she tells me she has hopes—Our Mother in heaven has heard my prayers. Imagine, love, my becoming a grandmama! It is what I long so for!—just a silly old grandmama spoiling all her pets! I feel I was born to be a grandmama!"

"I am so glad, how very charming!" murmured Lady Dolly, vaguely and quite indifferent. "I am so terribly afraid Vere won't please, and I am so afraid of this affair with Corrèze."

"What affair? with whom?" asked Lady Stoat of Stitchley, waking from her dreams of being a grandmama.

Whereon she told it, making it look very odd and very bad indeed, in the unconscious exaggeration which accompanied Lady Dolly's talk, as inevitably as a great streak of foam precedes and follows the track of a steamer.

Lady Stoat was rather amused than shocked.

"It is very like Corrèze, and he is the most dangerous man in the world; everybody is in love with him; Gwendolen was, but all that is nothing, it is not as if he were one of us."

"He is one of us! He goes everywhere!"

"Oh! goes!—well; that is because people like to ask him—society is a pigstye—but all that does not alter his being a singer."

"He is a marquis, you know, they say!"

"All singers are marquises, if you like to believe them. My dear Dolly, you cannot be serious in being afraid of Corrèze? If you are, all the more reason to marry her at once."

"She is not the style that anybody likes at all nowadays," replied Lady Dolly, in a sort of despair. "She is not the style of the day at all, you know. She had great natural distinction, but I don't think people care for that, and they like *chien*.[1] She will always look like a gentle-woman, and they like us best when we don't. I have a conviction that men will be afraid of her. Is there anything more fatal? Vere will never look like a *belle petite*,[2] in a tea-gown, and smoke, never! She has gone a hundred years back, being brought up by that horrid old woman. You could fancy her going to be guillotined in old lace like Marie-Antoinette.[3] What can I do?"

"Keep her with you six months, dear," said the friend, who was a woman of some humour. "And I don't think poor Marie-Antoinette had any lace left to wear."

"Of course I must keep her with me," said Lady Dolly with exasperation, who was not a woman of humour, and who did not see the jest.

Lady Stoat reflected a moment. She liked arranging things, whether they closely concerned her or not.

"There is the Chambrée's son?" she said hesitatingly.

"I know! But they will want such a dower, and Vere has nothing—nothing!"

"But if she be a beauty?"

"She will be beautiful; she won't be a beauty; not in the way men like now. She will always look cold."

"Do they dislike that? Not in their wives I think; my Gwen looks very cold," said her friend; then added with an innocent impassive-ness, "You might marry her to Jura."

---

1   Sexually attractive (although not beautiful); to have "it."
2   Frivolous (trifling) beauty; later Zouroff uses this expression to refer to his mistresses.
3   Marie-Antoinette (1755-93) was the wife of Louis XVI and was Queen of France from 1755 to 1793. She was beheaded during the French Revolution.

Lady Dolly laughed and coloured.

"Poor Jack! He hates the very idea of marriage; I don't think he will ever——"

"They all hate it," said Lady Stoat tranquilly. "But they do it when they are men of position; Jura will do it like the rest. What do you think of Serge Zouroff?"

Lady Dolly this time did not laugh; she turned white underneath Piver's[1] bloom; her pretty sparkling eyes glanced uneasily.

"Zouroff!" she repeated vaguely, "Zouroff!"

"I think I should try," answered Lady Stoat calmly. "Yes; I do think I should try. By the way, take her to Félicité; you are going there, are you not? It would be a great thing for you, dear, to marry her this year; you would find it such a bore in the season; don't *I* know what it is! And for you, so young as you are, to go to balls with a *demoiselle à marier!*[2]—my poor little puss, you would die of it."

"I am sure I shall as it is!" said Lady Dolly; and her nerves gave way, and she cried.

"Make Zouroff marry her," said Lady Stoat soothingly, as if she were pouring out drops of chloral for a fretful child.

"Make Zouroff!" echoed Lady Dolly, with a certain intonation that led Lady Stoat to look at her quickly.

"Has she done naughty things that she has not told me," thought her confidante. "No, I do not fancy so. Poor little pussy! she is too silly not to be transparent."

Aloud, she said merely:

"Zouroff is middle-aged now; Nadine would be glad to see him take any one; she would not oppose it. He must marry some time, and I don't know anybody else so good as he."

"Good!" ejaculated Lady Dolly faintly. She was still startled and agitated, and strove to hide that she was so. "Vere would never," she murmured; "you don't know her; she is the most dreadful child——"

"You must bring her to me," said Lady Stoat.

She was very successful with girls. She never scolded them; she never ridiculed them; she only influenced them in a gentle, imperceptible, sure way that, little by little, made them feel that love and honour were silly things, and that all that really mattered was to have rank and to be rich, and to be envied by others.

---

1 Piver's was a large French make-up and perfume company, which sold gloves, trinkets, almond soap, powders for the face, and pomades and pastes to bleach the skin.

2 Marriageable daughter.

Lady Stoat never said this; never said, indeed, anything approaching it, but all girls that she took any pains with learned it by heart, nevertheless, as the gospel of their generation.

It was her own religion; she only taught what she honestly believed.

A little comforted, Lady Dolly left her calming presence; met her little duke and breakfasted with him merrily at a hotel, and drove back to her own *châlet* to dress for a dinner at the Maison Normande.

The doors of Félicité would not open until the first day of September, and there were still some dozen days of August yet to pass, and on those days Vere was to be seen occasionally by her mother's side on the beach, and in the villas, and at the races at Deauville, and was clad by the clever directions of Adrienne in charming, youthful dresses as simple as they were elegant. She was taken to the Casino, where the highborn young girls of her own age read, or worked, or played with the *petits chevaux*;[1] she was made to walk up and down the planks, where her innocence brushed the shoulders of Casse-une-croûte,[2] the last new villany out in woman, and her fair cheeks felt the same sunbeams and breeze that fell on all the faded *pêches à quinze sous*.[3] She was taken to the *bal des bébés*,[4] and felt a pang that was older than her years at seeing those little frizzed and furbelowed flirts of five, and those vain little simpering dandies of three.

"Oh, the poor, poor little children!" she thought, "they will never know what it is to be young!"

She, even in monastic old Bulmer, had been left a free, open-air, natural, honest child's life. Her own heart here was oppressed and lonely. She missed her faithful old friends; she took no pleasure in the romp and racket that was round her; she understood very little of all that she saw, but the mere sight of it hurt her. Society, to this untutored child of the Northumbrian moors, looked so grotesque and so vulgar. This Trouville mob of fine ladies and adventuresses, princes and blacklegs,[5] ministers and dentists, reigning sovereigns and queens of the theatres, seemed to her a Saturnalia[6] of Folly, and its laugh hurt her more than a blow would have done.

---

1 Ponies.
2 Literally *casse-croûte* means a snack or a light meal, suggestive of her occupation as a prostitute.
3 Literally this means old peaches that sell for fifteen cents; cheap—referring to prostitutes.
4 Childrens' party.
5 Swindlers.
6 Orgy.

Her mother took her out but little, and the less that she went the less troubled she was. That great mass of varicoloured, noisy life, so pretty as a spectacle, but so deplorable as humanity, dismayed and offended her. She heard that these ladies of Deauville, with their painted brows, their high voices, their shrill laughter, their rickety heels, were some of the greatest ladies of Europe; but, to the proud temper and delicate taste of the child, they seemed loathsome.

"You are utterly unsympathetic!" said her mother, disgusted, "frightfully unsympathetic! You are *guindée*,[1] positive, puritan! You have not a grain of adaptability. I read the other day somewhere that Madame Récamier,[2] who was always called the greatest beauty of our great-grandmothers' times, was really nothing at all to look at— quite ordinary; but she did smile so in everybody's face, and listen so to all the bores, that the world pronounced her a second Helen.[3] As for you—handsome though you are, and you really are quite beautiful they say—you look so scornful of everything, and so indignant at any little nonsense, that I should not wonder in the least if you never even got called a beauty at all."

Lady Dolly paused to see the effect of the most terrible prediction that it was in female power to utter. Vere was quite unmoved; she scarcely heard.

She was thinking of that voice, clear as the ring of gold, which had said to her:

"Keep yourself unspotted from the world."

"If the world is nothing better than this, it must be very easy to resist it," she thought in her ignorance.

She did not know that from these swamps of flattery, intrigue, envy, rivalry, and emulation there rises a miasma which scarcely the healthiest lungs can withstand. She did not know that though many may be indifferent to the tempting of men, few indeed are impenetrable to the sneer and the smile of women; that to live your own life in the midst of the world is a harder thing than it was of old to withdraw to the Thebaid;[4] that to risk "looking strange" requires a

---

1 Stiff; stilted.
2 Madame Récamier (1777-1849) was a famous Frenchwoman in literary and political circles. Portraits of her in galleries such as the Louvre indicate that she was, in fact, beautiful.
3 Helen of Troy was so beautiful that she caused the Trojan war after Paris abducted her.
4 An ancient region surrounding Thebes in Egypt where many monasteries are located.

courage perhaps cooler and higher than the soldier's or the saint's; and that to stand away from the contact and the custom of your "set" is a harder and a sterner work than it was of old to go into the sanctuary of La Trappe or Port Royal.[1]

Autres temps, autres mœurs[2]—but we too have our martyrs.

Félicité was a seaside château of the Princes Zouroff, which they had bought from an old decayed French family, and had transformed into a veritable castle of fairy-land. They came to it for about three months in as many years; but for beauty and loveliness it had no equal, even amongst the many summer holiday-houses scattered up and down the green coast, from Etretat to the Rochers de Calvados. This year it was full of people: the Princess Nadine Nelaguine was keeping open house there for her brother Sergius Zouroff. White-sailed yachts anchored in its bay; chasseurs[3] in green and gold beat its woods; riding parties and driving parties made its avenues bright with colour and movement; groups like Watteau[4] pictures wandered in its gardens; there was a little troupe of actors from Paris for its theatre; life went like a song; and Serge Zouroff would have infinitely preferred to be alone with some handsome Tschigan[5] women and many flagons of brandy.

Madame Nelaguine was a little woman, who wore a wig that had little pretence about it; and smoked all day long, and read *saletés*[6] with zest, and often talked about them; yet Madame Nelaguine could be a power in politics when she chose, could cover herself with diamonds and old laces, and put such dignity into her tiny person that she once crushed into utter nervousness a new-made empress, whom she considered varnish. She was wonderfully clever, wonderfully learned; she was cunning, and she could be cruel, yet she had in her own way a kind heart; she was a great musician and a great mathematician; she had been an ambassadress, and had distinguished herself at great courts. She had had many intrigues of all kinds, but had never been compromised by any one of them. She was considerably older than her brother and seldom approved of him.

---

1 Cistercian monasteries in France and Germany.
2 Manners change with the times.
3 Hunters.
4 Jean-Antoine Watteau (1684-1721) was a French painter who influenced fashion and garden design in the eighteenth century.
5 Gypsy.
6 Licentious reading materials.

"*On peut se débaucher, mais on doit se débaucher avec de l'esprit,*"[1] she would say: and the modern ways of vice seemed to her void of wit. "You are not even amused," she would add. "If you were amused one could comprehend, but you are not. You spend your fortunes on creatures that you do not even like; you spend your nights in gambling that does not even excite you; you commit vulgarities that do not even divert you, only because everybody else does the same; you caricature monstrous vices so that you make even those no longer terrible, but ridiculous; and if you fight a duel you manage to make it look absurd, you take a surgeon with you! You have no passions. It is a passion that dignifies life, and you do not know anything about it, any of you; you know only infamy. And infamy is always so dull; it is never educated. Why do you copy Vitellius? Because you have not the wit to be either Horace or Caesar."[2]

But Sergius Zouroff did not pay any heed to his cleverer sister. His Uraline mines, his vast plains of wheat, his forests and farms, his salt and his copper, and all that he owned, were treasures well-nigh inexhaustible, and although prodigal he was shrewd. He was not a man to be easily ruined, and, as long as his great wealth and his great position gave him a place that was almost royal in the society of Europe, he knew very well that he could copy Vitellius as he chose without drawing any chastisement on him. In a cold and heavy way he had talent, and with that talent he contrived to indulge all excesses in any vice that tempted him, yet remain without that social stigma that has marked before now princes wholly royal.[3]

"Everywhere they are glad to see me, and everybody would marry me to-morrow," he would say, with a shrug of his shoulders, when his sister rebuked him.

To Félicité drove Lady Dolly with Vere by her side. Vere had been given a white dress and a broad hat with white drooping feathers; she looked very pale, her mother supposed it was with excitement.

She thought it the moment to offer a little maternal advice. "Now,

---

1   One can be dissipated; but one must be dissipated with wit.
2   Aulus Vitellius (A.D. 15-69) was a Roman emperor who was known for his extravagance, debauchery, and incompetence; Horace (65-8 B.C.) was a lyric poet who satirized Roman society; Julius Caesar (100-44 B.C.) was a Roman leader who was renowned for his military genius, good judgment, and personal devotion to his men.
3   The title "Prince" did not necessarily mean that the noble was related to the Czar; it indicated that the bearer of the title was a descendent of Rurick, Russia's first ruler

dear, this will be quite going into the world for you. Do remember one or two things. Do try to look less grave; men hate a serious woman. And if you want to ask anything, don't come to me, because I'm always busy; ask Adrienne or Lady Stoat. You have seen what a sweet dear motherly creature she is. She won't mind telling you anything. There is a charming girl there, too, an American heiress, Fuschia Leach; a horrible name, but a lovely creature, and *very* clever. Watch her and learn all you can from her. *Tout Paris*[1] lost its head after her utterly this last winter. She'll marry anybody she chooses. Pray don't make me ashamed of you. Don't be sensational, don't be stupid, don't be pedantic; and, for mercy's sake, don't make any scenes. Never look surprised; never show a dislike to anybody; never seemed shocked, if you feel so. Be civil all round, it's the safest way in society; and pray don't talk about mathematics and the Bible. I don't know that there's anything more I can tell you: you must find it all out for yourself. The world is like whist, reading can't teach it. Try not to blunder, that's all, and—do watch Fuschia Leach."

"Is she so very beautiful and good?"

"Good?" echoed Lady Dolly, *désorientée*[2] and impatient. "I don't know, I am sure. No, I shouldn't think she was, by any means. She doesn't go in for that. She is a wonderful social success, and men rave about her. That is what I meant. If you watch her she will do you more good than I could if I had patience to talk to you for ever. You will see what the girl of your time must be if she want to please."

Vere's beautiful mouth curled contemptuously.

"I do not want to please."

"That is an insane remark," said Lady Dolly coldly. "If you don't, what do you live for?"

Vere was silent. At dark old Bulmer she had been taught that there were many other things to live for, but she was afraid to say so, lest she should be "pedantic" again.

"That is just the sort of silly thing I *hate* to hear a girl say, or a woman either. Americans never say such things," said Lady Dolly with vivacious scorn. "It's just like your father, who always would go out in the rain when dinner was ready, or read to somebody who had the scarlet fever, or give the best claret to a ploughboy with a sore throat. It is silly; it is unnatural. You *should* want to please. Why were we put in this world?"

---

1 Fashionable Paris society.
2 Disconcerted.

"To make others happier," Vere suggested timidly, her eyes growing dim at her father's name.

"Did it make *me* happier to have the scarlet fever brought home to me?" said Lady Dolly, irrelevantly and angrily. "That is just like poor Vere's sort of illogical reasonings; I remember them so well. You are exactly like him. I despair of you, I quite despair of you, unless Fuschia Leach can convert you."

"Is she my age?"

"A year or two older, I think; she is perfect now; at five-and-twenty she will be hideous, but she will dress so well it won't matter. I know for a fact, that she refused your cousin, Mull, last month. She was very right; he is awfully poor. Still, she'd have been a duchess, and her father kept a bar; so it shows you what she can do."[1]

"What is a bar?"

"Oh! pray don't keep asking me questions like that. You make my head whirl. A bar is where they sell things to drink, and her brothers have a great pig-killing place 'down west,' wherever that is."

"And she refused my cousin!"

"Dear, yes! This is the charming topsy-turvy world we live in— you will get used to it, my dear. They made a fuss because a tailor got to court last year. I am sure I don't know why they did; if he'd been an American tailor nobody'd have said anything; they wouldn't even have thought it odd. All the world over you meet them; they get in the swim somehow; they have such heaps of money, and their women know how to wear things. They always look like—what they shouldn't look like—to be sure; but so most of us do, and men prefer it."

Vere understood not at all; but she did not venture again to ask for an explanation.

Her mother yawned and brushed the flies away pettishly, and called to Lord Jura, who was riding beside their carriage, and had lagged a trifle behind in the narrow sandy road that ran level between green hedges. The high metal roof and gilded vanes of Félicité were already shining above the low rounded masses of distant woods. It stood on the sea-coast, a little way from Villers-sur-Mer.

Vere did not understand why Lord Jura always went with them as naturally as the maids did and the dressing-boxes; but he was kind, if a little rough. She liked him. Only why did her mother call him Jack, and quarrel with him so, and yet want him always with her?

---

1 There was an abundance of *nouveau riche* (newly rich) American heiresses who traveled about Europe in the 1880s, intent on marrying aristocrats.

Vere thought about it dimly, vaguely, perplexedly, especially when she saw the frank, blue eyes of Jura looking at herself, hard, and long, with a certain sadness and impatience in the gaze, as if he pitied her.

The reception at Félicité seemed to Vere to be a whirl of bright hues, pretty faces, and amiable words. The Princess Nadine Nelaguine was out on the terrace with her guests, and the Princess kissed her with effusion, and told her she was like a Gainsborough[1] picture. The Princess herself was a fairy-like little woman, with a bright odd Calmuck[2] face and two little brown eyes as bright as a marmoset's. Vere was presented to so many people that she could not tell one from another, and she was glad to be left in her room while her mother, having got into a wonderful gold-embroidered Watteau sacque[3] that she called a tea-gown, went to rejoin the other ladies amongst the roses and the perfumes, and the late afternoon light.

When Vere herself, three hours later, was dressed for dinner, and told to tap at her mother's door, she did not feel nervous, because it was not in her nature to be easily made so, but she felt oppressed and yet curious.

She was going into the world.

And the counsels of Corrèze haunted her.

Lady Dolly said sharply, "Come in!" and Vere entering, beheld her mother for the first time in full war-paint and panoply.

Lady Dolly looked sixteen herself. She was exquisitely painted; she had a gown cut *en coeur*[4] which was as indecent as the heart of woman could desire; jewels sparkled all over her; she was a triumph of art, and looked as exactly like Colifichet of the Bouffes[5] in her last new piece, as even her own soul could aspire to do.

"What are you staring at, child?" she asked of Vere, who had turned rather pale. "Don't you think I look well? What is the matter?"

"Nothing," said Vere, who could not answer that it hurt her to see so much of her mother's anatomy unveiled.

"You look as if you saw a ghost," said Lady Dolly impatiently; "you have such a horrid way of staring. Come!"

Vere went silently by her side down the wide staircase, lighted by

---

1 Thomas Gainsborough (1727-88) was an English portrait painter, celebrated for the elegance, vivacity, and refinement of his portraits.
2 Russian.
3 A loose, full back of a woman's gown formed by wide box pleats hanging from a high shoulder yoke and extending to the hem.
4 To her breast.
5 An actress in a comic opera.

black marble negroes holding golden torches. After the silence, the stillness, the gloom, of her Northumbrian home, with the old servants moving slowly through the dim oak-pannelled passages, the brilliance, the luxury, the glittering lustre, the *va-et-vient*[1] of Félicité seemed like a gorgeous spectacle. She would have liked to have stood on that grand staircase, amongst the hothouse flowers, and looked on it all as on a pageant. But her mother swept on into the drawing-rooms, and Vere heard a little murmur of admiration, which she did not dream was for herself.

Lady Dolly in her way was an artist, and she had known the right thing to do when she had had Vere clad in white cachemire, with an old silver girdle of German work, and in the coils of her hair a single silver arrow.

Vere was perfect in her stately, serious, yet childlike grace; and the women watching her felt a pang of envy.

Sergius Zouroff, her host, advancing, murmured a "*divinement belle!*"[2] and Lady Stoat, watching from a distant sofa, thought to herself, "What a lovely creature! really it is trying for poor little pussy."

Vere went in to her first great dinner. She said little or nothing. She listened and wondered. Where she sat she could not see her mother nor anyone she knew. The young French diplomatist who took her in tried to make himself agreeable to her, but she replied by monosyllables. He thought how stupid these lovely *ingénues*[3] always were. He had not the open sesame of Corrèze to the young mute soul.

Dinner over, Lady Stoat took possession of her in the charming motherly affectionate way for which she was celebrated with young girls. But even Lady Stoat did not make much way with her; Vere's large serious eyes were calmly watching everything.

"Will you show me which is Miss Leach?" she said suddenly. Lady Stoat laughed and pointed discreetly with a fan.

"Who has told you about Fuschia Leach?" she said amusedly. "I will make you known to her presently; she may be of use to you."

Vere's eyes, grave as a child's awakened out of sleep into the glare of gas, fastened where her fan had pointed, and studied Miss Leach. She saw a very lovely person of transparent colouring, of very small features, of very slight form, with a skin like delicate porcelain, an artistic tangle of artistically coloured red gold hair, a tiny impertinent nose, and a wonderful expression of mingled impudence, shrewdness,

---

1 Coming and going.
2 Exquisite beauty.
3 Simple, artless girls.

audacity and resolution. This person had her feet on an ottoman, her hands behind her head, a rosebud in her mouth, and a male group around her.

"I shall not like her; I do not wish to know her," said Vere slowly.

"My dear, do not say so," said Lady Stoat. "It will sound like jealousy, you know—one pretty girl of another—"

"She is not a lady," said Vere once more.

"There you are right," said Lady Stoat. "Very few people are, my love, nowadays. But that is just the sort of thing you must *not* say. It will get quoted against you, and make you, make you—oh! such enemies, my love!"

"Does it matter?" said Vere dreamily. She was wondering what Corrèze would have thought or did think of Miss Fuschia Leach.

"Does it matter to have enemies!" echoed Lady Stoat. "Oh, my sweet Vere! does it matter whether there is a pin sticking into one all day? A pin is a very little thing, no doubt, but it makes all the difference between comfort and discomfort."

"She is not a lady," said Vere again with a passing frown on her pretty brows.

"Oh, my dear! if you wait for that!" Lady Stoat's smile expressed that if she did wait for that she would be more exacting than society. "As for not knowing her—nonsense—you must not object to anybody who is in the same house-party with yourself."

"She is extremely pretty," added Lady Stoat. "Those American girls so very often are; but they are all like the *poupées de modiste*.[1] The very best of them are only very perfect likenesses of the young ladies that try the confections on for us at Pingat's or Worth's,[2] and the dress has always a sort of look of being the first toilette they ever had. I don't know why, for I hear they dress extremely well over there, and should be used to it, but it *has* that look, and they never get rid of it. No, my dear, no; you are right. Those new people are not gentlewomen any more than men's modern manners are like the *Broad Stone of Honour*.[3] But do not say so. They will repeat it, and it will not sound kind, and unless you can say what is kind, never say anything."

"I would rather have anyone I did not respect for an enemy than for a friend," said Vere with a child's obstinacy. Lady Stoat smiled.

"Phrases my love!—phrases! you have so much to learn, my child, as yet."

---

1 Mannequins.
2 European dress designers.
3 A book dealing with the practice of chivalry.

"I will not learn of Miss Leach."

"Well, I do not admire her very much myself. But then I belong to an old school, you know. I am an old woman, and have prejudices," said Lady Stoat sweetly. "Miss Leach has the world at her foot, and it amuses her to kick it about like a tennis ball, and show her ankles. I daresay you will do the same, love, in another six months, only you will not show your ankles. All the difference will be there."

And then Lady Stoat, who though she called herself an old woman would have been extremely angry if anybody else had called her so, thought she had done enough for once for poor little Pussy's daughter, and turned to her own little mild flirtations with a bald and beribboned ambassador.

Vere was left alone, to look and muse.

Men glanced at her and said what a lovely child she was; but they kept aloof from her. They were afraid of an *ingénue*, and there was Fuschia Leach, whose laughter was ringing up to the chandeliers and out to the conservatories—Fuschia Leach, who had never been an *ingénue*, but a coquette at three years old, and a woman of the world at six.

Jura alone came up and seated himself by Vere.

"How do you like it?" he said with an odd little smile.

"It is very pretty to look at," answered Vere.

"Ah, to be sure. As good as a play when you're new to it, and awfully like a treadmill when you're not. What do you think of Fuschia Leach?"

Vere remembered Lady Stoat's warning, and answered merely:

"I think she is handsome."

"I believe you; she threw over your cousin Mull, as if he were dirty boots; so she does heaps of them. I don't know what it is myself; I think it is her cheek.[1] I always tell Dolly so—I beg your pardon—I mean your mother."

Vere had heard him say "Dolly" very often, and did not know why he apologised.

"My mother admires her?" she said with a little interrogation in her voice. Jura laughed.

"Or says she does. Women always say they admire a reigning beauty. It looks well, you know. They all swear Mrs. Dawtry is divine, and I'm sure in their hearts they think her rather ugly than otherwise."

"Who is Mrs. Dawtry?"

"Don't you know? Good heavens! But, of course, you don't know

---

1   Arrogance; self-confidence.

anything of our world. It's a pity you ever should. Touch pitch[1]—
what is it the old saw says?"

It was the regret of Corrèze, differently worded.

"But the world, as you call it, means men and women? It must be
what they make it. They might make it good if they wished," said Vere
with the seriousness that her mother detested.

"But they don't wish, you see. That is it," said Jura with a sigh. "I
don't know how it is, when once you are in the swim you can't alter
things; you must just go along with the rest. One does heaps of things
one hates only because others do them."

"That is very contemptible," said Vere, with the disdain that
became her very well coming on her pretty proud mouth.

"I think we are contemptible," said Jura moodily; and to so frank
a confession there was no reply or retort possible, Vere thought.

"It is strange; he said much the same," she murmured, half aloud.
"Only he said it like a poet, and you—speak in such an odd way."

"How do I speak?" asked Jura amused.

"You speak as if words cost too much, and you were obliged to
use as few and choose as bald ones as you could find; English is such
a beautiful language, if you read Milton or Jeremy Taylor, or Beau-
mont and Fletcher, or any of the old divines and dramatists—"[2]

She stopped, because Jura laughed.

"Divines and dramatists! My dear child, we know nothing about
such things; we have St. Albans and French adaptations; they're our
reading of divinity and the drama.[3] Who was 'he' that talked like a
poet while I talk like a sweep?"

"I did not say you talked like a sweep[4]—and I meant the Marquis
de Corrèze."

"Oh! your singer? Don't call him a Marquis. He is the prince of
tenors, that's all."

"He is a Marquis," said Vere, with a certain coldness. "They were a

---

1   "They that touch pitch will be defiled."—British statesman Benjamin
    Disraeli (1804-81); i.e., become corrupted by society.
2   John Milton (1608-74), British poet; Jeremy Taylor (1613-67), British
    theologian; Francis Beaumont (1584-1616) and John Fletcher (1579-
    1625), British playwrights who collaborated from 1606 to 1616.
3   It is not clear what St. Albans has to do with divines and dramatists. The
    first Duke of St. Albans (Charles Beauclerk) (1680-1726) was a courtier
    during the reign of Charles I of England. He was well known as a gam-
    bler and a glutton.
4   Chimney sweep.

very great race. You can see all about it in the 'Livre d'Or' of Savoy;[1] they were like the Marquises Costa de Beauregard, who lost everything in 'ninety-two. You must have read M. de Beauregard's[2] beautiful book, *Un homme d'autrefois?*"[3]

"Never heard of it. Did the tenor tell you all that rubbish?"

"Where is mamma, Lord Jura?" said Vere. "I am tired of sitting here."

"That's a facer,"[4] thought Jura. "And, by Jove, very well given for such a baby. I beg your pardon," he said aloud. "Corrèze shall be a prince of the blood, if you wish. Your mother is over there; but I doubt if she'll thank you to go to her; she's in the thick of it with them; look."

He meant that Lady Dolly was flirting very desperately, and enjoying herself very thoroughly, having nearly as many men about her as Miss Fuschia Leach.

Vere looked, and her eyes clouded.

"Then I think I may go to bed. She will not miss me. Goodnight."

"No, she won't miss you. Perhaps other people will."

"There is no one I know, so how can they?" said Vere innocently, and rose to go; but Sergius Zouroff, who had approached in the last moment, barred her passage with a smiling deference.

"Your host will, Mademoiselle Herbert. Does my poor house weary you, that you think of your own room at ten o'clock."

"I always go to bed at ten, monsieur," said Vere. "It is nothing new for me."

"Let me show you my flowers first," at last said Prince Zouroff. "You know we Russians, born amidst snow and ice, have a passion for tropical houses; will you not come?"

He held out his arm as he spoke. Would it be rude to refuse? Vere did not know. She was afraid it would, as he was her host.

She laid her fingers hesitatingly on his offered arm, and was led through the rooms by Prince Zouroff.

---

1 The register book of all the family members of an aristocratic house—in this case, the château of Villard (Savoy).

2 Costa de Beauregard (1752-1824), the Marquis de Saint-Genis, was born in the château of Villard. He was in the military, but he also had literary and artistic interests. She is referring to 1792, during the French Revolution.

3 A man of times past.

4 Unexpected blow.

Fuschia Leach took her hands from behind her head, and stared; Lady Dolly would have turned pale, if she had not been so well painted; Lady Stoat put her eye-glass up, and smiled.

Prince Zouroff had a horror of unmarried women, and never had been known to pay any sort of attention to one, not even to his sister's guest, Fuschia Leach the irresistible.

Prince Zouroff was a tall large man of seven and thirty; loosely built, and plain of feature. He had all the vices, and had them all in excess, but he was a very polished gentleman when he chose; and he was one of the richest men in Europe, and his family, of which he was the head, was very near the throne, in rank and influence; for twenty years, ever since he had left the imperial Corps de Pages,[1] and shown himself in Paris, driving his team of black Orlofs, he had been the idolatry, the aspiration, and the despair of all the mothers of maidens.

Vere's passage through his drawing-rooms on his arm was a spectacle so astonishing, that there was a general lull for a moment in the conversation of all his guests. It was a triumph, but Vere was wholly unconscious of it; which made her charming in the eyes of the giver of it.

"I think that's a case!" said Miss Fuschia Leach to her admirers. She did not care herself. She did not want Zouroff, high, and mighty, and rich, and of great fashion though he was; she meant to die an English duchess, and she had only thrown over the unhappy Mull because she had found out he was poor. "And what's the use of being a duchess, if you don't make a splash?" she said very sensibly to his mother, when they talked it over. She had flirted with Mull shamelessly, but so she did with scores of them; it was her way. She had brought the way from America. She had young men about her as naturally as a rat-catcher has ferrets and terriers; but she meant to take her time before choosing one of them for good and all.

"What a beautiful child she is," thought Prince Zouroff, "and so indifferent! Can she possibly be naughty Dolly's daughter?"

He was interested, and he, being skilled in such ways, easily learned the little there was to know about her, whilst he took her through his conservatories, and showed her Japan lilies, Chinese blossoms that changed colour thrice a day, and orchids of all climes and colours.

The conservatories were really rare, and pleased her; but Prince Zouroff did not. His eyes were bold and cold, at once; they were red

---

1 A military-educational institution of a very high standard, which provided pages for duty at the Russian Court. Generally the pages were personally appointed by the Czar.

too, and there was an odour of brandy on his breath that came to her through all the scent of the flowers. She did not like him. She was grave and silent. She answered what he asked, but she did not care to stay there, and looked round for a chance of escape. It charmed Zouroff, who was so used to see women throw themsélves in his path that he found no pleasure in their pursuit.

"Decidedly she has been not at all with naughty Dolly!" he said to himself, and looked at her with so much undisguised admiration in his gaze, that Vere, looking up from the golden blossoms of an Odontoglossum, blushed to the eyes, and felt angry, she could not very well have told why.

"Your flowers are magnificent, and I thank you, monsieur; but I am tired, and I will say good night," she said quickly, with a little haughtiness of accent and glance which pleased Zouroff more than anything had done for years.

"I would not detain you unwillingly, mademoiselle, one moment," he said, with a low bow—a bow which had some real respect in it. "Pardon me, this is your nearest way. I will say to miladi that you were tired. To-morrow, if there be anything you wish, only tell me, it shall be yours."

He opened a door that led out of the last conservatory on to the foot of the great staircase; and Vere, not knowing whether she were not breaking all the rules of politeness and etiquette, bent her head to him and darted like a swallow up the stairs.

Sergius Zouroff smiled, and strolled back alone through his drawing-rooms, and went up to Lady Dolly, and cast himself into a long, low chair by her side.

"*Ma chère*,[1] your lovely daughter did not appreciate my flowers or myself. She told me to tell you she was tired, and has gone to her room. She is beautiful, very beautiful; but I cannot say that she is complimentary."

"She is only a child," said Lady Dolly hurriedly; she was half relieved, half frightened. "She *is* rude!" she added regretfully. "It is the way she has been brought up. You must forgive her, she is so young."

"Forgive her! *Mais de boncœur!*[2] Anything feminine that runs away is only too delightful in these times," said the Prince coolly. "Do not change her. Do not tease her. Do not try to make her like yourself. I prefer her as she is."

---

1 My dear.
2 But happily.

Lady Dolly looked at him quickly. Was it possible that already—?

Sergius Zouroff was lying back in his chair with his eyes closed. He was laughing a little silently, in an unpleasant way that he had; he had spoken insolently, and Lady Dolly could not resent his insolence.

"You are very kind, Prince," she said as negligently as she could behind her fan. "Very kind, to treat a child's *boutades*[1] as a girl's charm. She has really seen nothing, you know, shut up in that old northern house by the sea; and she is as eccentric as if she were eighty years old. Quite odd in her notions, quite!"

"Shall we play?" said Zouroff.

They began to play, most of them, at a little roulette table. Musicians were interpreting, divinely, themes of Beethoven's and Schumann's;[2] the great glass halls and marble courts of the flowers were open with all their array of bloom; the green gardens and gay terraces were without in the brilliancy of moonlight; the sea was not a score of yards away, sparkling with phosphorus and star-rays; but they were indifferent to all these things. They began to play, and heeded nothing else. The music sounded on deaf ears; the flowers breathed out odours on closed nostrils; the summer night spread its loveliness in vain; and the waters of salt wave and fresh fountain murmured on unheeded. Play held them.

Sergius Zouroff lost plenty of money to Lady Dolly, who went to bed at two o'clock, worried and yet pleased, anxious and yet exultant.

Vere's room was placed next to hers.

She looked in before passing on to her own. The girl lay sound asleep in the sweet dreamless sleep of her lingering childhood, her hair scattered like gold on the pillows, her limbs in the lovely grace of a serene and unconscious repose.

Lady Dolly looked at her as she slept, and an uneasy pang shot through her.

"If he do mean that," she thought, "I suppose it would be horrible. And how much too pretty and too innocent she would be for him—the beast!"

Then she turned away, and went to her own chamber, and began the toilsome martyrdom of having her *perruque* unfastened, and her night's preparations for the morning's enamel begun.

To women like Lady Dolly life is a comedy, no doubt, played on

---

1 Whims.

2 Ludwig van Beethoven (1770-1827) and Robert Schumann (1810-56) were German composers.

great stages and to brilliant audiences, and very amusing and charming, and all that; but alas! it has two dread passages in each short twenty-four hours; they are, the bore of being "done up," and the bore of being "undone!"

It is a martyrdom, but they bear it heroically, knowing that without it they would be nowhere; would be yellow, pallid, wrinkled, even perhaps would be flirtationless, unenvied, unregarded, worse than dead!

If Lady Dolly had said any prayers she would have said, "Thank God for Piver!"

CHAPTER VII.

It was a very pretty life at Félicité.

The riding parties meeting under the old avenue of Spanish chestnuts and dispersing down the flowering lanes; the shooting parties, which were not serious and engrossing as in England, but animated and picturesque in the deep old Norman woods; the stately dinner at nine o'clock every night, like a royal banquet; the music which was so worthy of more attentive hearers than it ever got; the theatre, pretty and *pimpant*[1] as a coquette of the last century; the laughter; the brilliancy; the personal beauty of the women assembled there; all made the life at Félicité charming to the eye and the ear. Yet amidst it all Vere felt very lonely, and the only friends she made were in the Irish horse that they gave her to ride, and in the big Russian hound that belonged to Prince Zouroff.

The men thought her lovely, but they could not get on with her; the women disliked her as much as they adored, or professed to adore, Fuschia Leach.

To Vere, who at Bulmer had been accustomed to see life held a serious, and even solemn thing—who had been accustomed to the gravity of age and the melancholy of a seafaring poor, and the northern tillers of a thankless soil—nothing seemed so wonderful as the perpetual gaiety and levity around her. Was there any sorrow in the world? Was life only one long laugh? Was it right to forget the woes of others as utterly as they were forgotten here? She was always wondering, and there was no one to ask.

"You are horribly in earnest, Vere," said her mother pettishly. "You should go and live with Mr. Gladstone."[2]

---

1 Stylish.

2 William Gladstone (1809-98) was a British statesman and Prime Minister.

But to Vere it seemed more horrible to be always laughing—and laughing at nothing. "When there are all the poor," she thought, "and all the animals that suffer so." She did not understand that, when these pretty women had sold china and flowers at a fancy fair for a hospital, or subscribed to the Society for Prevention of Cruelty, they had really done all that they thought was required of them, and could dismiss all human and animal pain from their mind, and bring their riding-horses home saddle-galled and spur-torn without any compunction.

To the complete innocence and honesty of the girl's nature the discovery of what store the world set on all things which she had been taught to hold sacred, left a sickening sense of solitude and depression behind it. Those who are little children now will have little left to learn when they reach womanhood. The little children that are about us at afternoon tea and at lawn tennis, that are petted by house-parties and romped with at pigeon-shooting, will have little left to discover. They are miniature women already; they know the meaning of many a dubious phrase; they know the relative value of social positions; they know much of the science of flirtation which society has substituted for passion; they understand very thoroughly the shades of intimacy, the suggestions of a smile, the degrees of hot and cold, that may be marked by a bow or emphasised with a good-day. All the subtle science of society is learned by them instinctively and unconsciously, as they learn French and German from their maids. When they are women they will at least never have Eve's excuse for sin; they will know everything that any tempter could tell them. Perhaps their knowledge may prove their safeguard, perhaps not; perhaps without its bloom the fruit to men's taste may seem prematurely withered. Another ten years will tell. At any rate those we pet to-day will be spared the pang of disillusion when they shall be fairly out in a world that they already know with cynical thoroughness—baby La Bruyères and girl Rochefoucaulds[1] in frills and sashes.

To Vere Herbert, on the contrary, reared as she had been upon grave studies and in country loneliness, the shocks her faiths and her fancies received was very cruel. Sometimes she thought bitterly she would have minded nothing if only her mother had been a thing she could have reverenced, a creature she could have gone to for support and sympathy.

---

1 Jean de La Bruyère (1645-96) was a French writer who had strong moral views on the economy, widespread poverty, and the idle life of the nobility; François de La Rochefoucauld (1613-80) was the author of the sardonic aphorisms and maxims in *Réflexions* (1665).

But her mother was the most frivolous of the whole sea of froth around her—of the whole frivolous womanhood about her the very emptiest bubble.

Vere, who herself had been cast by nature in the mould to be a noble mother of children, had antique sacred fancies that went with the name of mother. The mother of the Gracchi, the mother of Bonaparte, the mother of Garibaldi,[1] the many noble maternal figures of history and romance, were for ever in her thoughts; the time-honoured word embodied to her all sacrifice, all nobility, all holiness. And her mother was this pretty foolish painted toy, with false curls in a sunny circlet, above her kohl[2]-washed eyes, with her heart set on a cotillon, and her name in the mouths of the clubs; whose god was her tailor, and whose gospel was Zola;[3] whose life was an opera-bouffe, and who, when she costumed for her part in it, took "*la moindre excuse pour paraître nue!*"[4] The thought of her mother, thus, hurt her, as in revolutions it hurts those who believe in Mary to see a Madonna spat upon by a mob.

Lady Stoat saw this, and tried, in her fashion, to console her for it.

"My dear, your mother is young still. She must divert herself. It would be very hard on her not to be allowed. You must not think she is not fond of you because she still likes to waltz."

Vere's eyes were very sombre as she heard.

"I do not like to waltz. I never do."

"No, love? Well, temperaments differ. But surely you wouldn't be so cruel as to condemn your mother only to have your inclinations, would you? Dolly was always full of fun. I think you have not fun enough in you, perhaps."

"But my father is dead."

"My dear, Queen Anne is dead![5] *Henri Quatre est sur le Pont-Neuf.*[6]

---

1 Napoléon Bonaparte (1769-1821) was a general and then emperor of France; Giuseppe Garibaldi (1807-82) was an Italian patriot and general.

2 Eye shadow.

3 Émile Zola (1840-1902) was a French novelist, whose works were attacked and banned for their frankness and sordid details. One of his main subjects was French life during the reign of Napoleon III.

4 The least excuse to show off her body (bare skin).

5 Queen Anne (1665-1714) was the daughter of James II; she was Queen of England from 1702 to 1714.

6 Henry IV is on the New Bridge. There is a statue of Henry IV (1553-1610), the first Bourbon King of France from 1589 to 1610, riding horseback on the *Pont Neuf* in Paris.

What other news will you tell us? I am not saying, dear, that you should think less of your father's memory. It is too sweet of you to feel so much, and very, very rare, alas! for nowadays our children are so forgetful, and we are so little to them. But still you know your mama is young, and so pretty as she is, too, no one can expect her to shut herself up as a recluse. Perhaps, had you been always with her, things would have been different, but she has always been so much admired and so petted by everyone that it was only natural—only natural that—"

"She should not want me," said Vere, as Lady Stoat paused for a word that should adequately express Lady Dolly's excuses whilst preserving Lady Dolly's dignity before her daughter. "Oh, my dear, I never meant that," she said hastily, whilst thinking, "*Quel enfant terrible!*"[1]

★ ★ ★ ★ ★

The brilliant Fuschia was inclined to be very amiable and cordial to the young daughter of Lady Dorothy Vanderdecken, but Vere repelled her overtures with a chilling courtesy that made the bright American "feel foolish."

But Pick-me-up, as she was usually called in the great world, was not a person to be deterred by one slight, or by fifty. To never risk a rebuff is a golden rule for self-respect; but it is not the rule by which new people achieve success.

Fuschia Leach was delighted with her social success, but she never deceived herself about it.

In America her people were "new people"—that is to say, her father had made his pile selling cigars and drugs in a wild country, and her brothers were making a bigger pile killing pigs on a gigantic scale down west. In New York she and hers were deemed "shoddy"— the very shoddiest of shoddy—and were looked coldly on, and were left unvisited. But boldly springing over to less sensitive Europe, they found themselves without effort received at courts and in embassies, and had become fashionable people almost as soon as they had had time to buy high-stepping horses and ask great tailors to clothe them. It seemed very funny; it seemed quite unaccountable, and it bewildered them a little; but Fushia Leach did not lose her head.

"I surmise I'd best eat the curds while they're sweet," she said to herself, and she did eat them. She dressed, she danced, she made all

---

1 What a dreadful child.

her young men fetch and carry for her, she flirted, she caught up the ways and words and habits and graces of the great world, and adapted herself to her new sphere with versatile cleverness, but all the same she "prospected" with a keen eye all the land that lay around her, and never deceived herself.

"I look cunning, and I'm spry, and I cheek him, and say outrageous things, and he likes it, and so they all go mad on me after him," she said to herself; meaning by her pronoun the great personage[1] who had first made her the fashion. But she knew very well that whenever anything prettier, odder, or more "outrageous" than herself should appear she would lose her prestige in a day, and fall back into the ranks of the ten thousand American girls who overrun Europe.

"I like you," she said to Vere unasked one day, when she found her alone on the lawn.

"You are very good," said Vere with the coldness of an empress of sixty years old.

"I like you," reiterated Miss Leach. "I like you because you treat 'em like dirt under your feet. That's our way; but these Europeans go after men as the squir'ls[2] jump after the cobs. You are the only one I have seen that don't."

"You are very amiable to praise me," said Vere coldly.

The lovely Fuschia continued her reflections aloud.

"We're just as bad when the Englishmen go over to us; that's a fact. But with our own men we ain't; we just make shoeblacks and scallyrags of them; they fetch and carry, and do as they're told. What a sharp woman your mother is, and as lively as a katy-did.[3] Now on our side, you know, the old folks never get at play like that; they've given over."

"My mother is young," said Vere, more coldly still.

Miss Leach tilted her chair on end.

"That's just what's so queer. They are young on into any age over here. Your mother's over thirty, I suppose? Don't you call that old? It's Methuselah[4] with us. But here your grandmothers look as cunning as can be, and they're as skittish as spring-lambs; it's the climate I surmise?"

---

1 Albert Edward, the Prince of Wales (1841-1910), had flirtations with a number of American heiresses.
2 Squirrels.
3 An insect similar to a cricket or a grasshopper.
4 Methuselah was one of the Hebrew patriarchs in Genesis 5. Because he lived for nine hundred and sixty-five years, his name has become synonymous with longevity.

Vere did not reply, and Miss Fuschia Leach, undaunted, continued her meditations aloud.

"You haven't had many affairs, I think? You're not really out are you?"

"No—affairs?"

"Heart affairs, you know. Dear me! why before I was your age, I was engaged to James Fluke Dyson, down Boston way."

"Are you to marry him then?"

"*Me*? No—thanks! I never meant to marry him. He did to go about with, and it made Victoria Boker right mad. Then mother came to Europe: he and I vowed constancy and exchanged rings and hair and all that, and we did write to each other each mail, till I got to Paris; then I got more slack, and I disremembered to ask when the mails went out; soon after we heard he had burst up; wasn't it a piece of luck?"

"I do not understand."

"Piece of luck we came to Europe. I might have taken him over there. He was a fine young man, only he hadn't the way your men have; not their cheek either. His father'd always been thought one of the biggest note-shavers[1] in N'York City. They say it was the fall in silver broke him; any way, poor James he's a clerk in a tea-store now."

Vere looked at her in speechless surprise, Pick-me-up laughed all the more.

"Oh they are always at seesaw like that in our country. He'll make another pile I daresay by next year, and they'll all get on their legs again. Your people, when they are bowled over lie down; ours jump up; I surmise it's the climate. I like your men best, though; they look such swells, even when they're in blanket coats and battered old hats, such as your cousin Mull wears."

"Is it true that Frank wished to succeed Mr. James Fluke Dyson?" Vere asked after a sore struggle with her disgust.

"Who's Frank?"

"My cousin, Mull?"

"Is he Frank? Dear life! I always thought dukes were dukes, even in the bosom of their families. Yes; he was that soft on me—there, they all are, but he's the worst I ever saw. I said no, but I could whistle him back. I'm most sorry I did say no. Dukes don't grow on every apple-bough; only, he's poor they say—"

---

1 A person who buys notes at a discount greater than the legal rate of interest; a loan shark.

"He is poor," said Vere coldly, her disgust conquering all amusement.

"When I came across the Pond," said Miss Leach, continuing her own reflections, "I said to mother 'I'll take nothing but a duke.' I always had a kind o' fancy for a duke. There's such a few of them. I saw an old print once in the Broadway, of a Duchess of Northumberland, holding her coronet out in both hands. I said to myself then, that was how I'd be taken someday—"

"Do you think duchesses hold their coronets in their hands, then?"

"Well, no; I see they don't; but I suppose one would in a picture?"

"I think it would look very odd, even in a picture."

"What's the use of having one, then? There aren't coronations every day. They tell me your cousin might be rolling if he liked. Is it true he'd have five hundred pounds sterling a day if he bored for coal? One could live on that."

"He would never permit the forest to be touched to save his life!" said Vere, indignantly with a frown and a flush. "The forests are as old as the days of Hengist and Horsa;[1] the wild bulls are in them and the red deer; men crept there to die after Otterbourne;[2] under one of the oaks, King James saw Johnie Armstrong."[3]

Fuschia Leach showed all her pretty teeth. "Very touchin', but the coal was under them before that, I guess! That's much more to the point. I come from a business-country. If he'll hear reason about that coal, I'm not sure I won't think twice about your cousin."

Vere, without ceremony, turned away. She felt angry tears swell her throat and rise into her eyes.

"Oh! you turn up your nose!" said Fuschia Leach vivaciously. "You think it atrocious that new folks should carry off your brothers, and

---

1 The names of two brothers who led the Jutish invasion of Britain and founded Kent.

2 Land at Otterbourne was part of the Hundred Hides of Chilcomb granted to the church in the seventh century. It is listed in the Domesday Book. James, Second Earl of Douglas, and Sir Hugh Montgomery, his nephew, fought and defeated Henry "Hotspur" Percy on the field at Otterbourne in 1388.

3 Johnie Armstrong was from a Scottish clan of notorious border raiders who invaded villages, stealing and pillaging. In 1530, he was persuaded to attend a meeting at Carlingrigg with King James V, who wanted to get rid of the rebellious "Borderers." Armstrong and his followers were ambushed and then hanged.

cousins, and friends. Well, I'd like to know where's it worse than all your big nobility going down at our feet for our dollars? I don't say your English do it so much, but they do do it, your younger sons, and all that small fry; and abroad we can buy the biggest and best titles in all Europe for a few hundred thousand dollars a year. *That's* real mean! *That's* blacking boots, if you please. Men with a whole row of crusaders at their backs, men as count their forefathers right away into Julius Caesar's times, men that had uncles in the Ark with Noah, they're at a Yankee pile like flies around molasses. Wal, now," said the pretty American, with her eyes lighting fiercely and with sparks of scorn flashing out from them, "Wal, now, you're all of you that proud that you beat Lucifer, but as far as I see there aren't much to be proud of. We're shoddy over there. If we went to Boston we wouldn't get a drink, outside an hotel, for our lives. N'York, neither, don't think because a man's struck ile[1] he'll go to heaven with Paris thrown in; but look at all your big folk! Pray what do *they* do the minute shoddy comes their way over the pickle-field? Why they just eat it! Kiss it and eat it! Do you guess we're such fools we don't see that? Why your Norman blood and Domesday Book[2] and all the rest of it—pray hasn't it married Lily Peart, whose father kept the steamboat hotel in Jersey City, and made his pile selling soothers to the heathen Chinee? Who was your Marchioness of Snowdon if she weren't the daughter of old Sam Salmon the note-shaver? Who was your Duchesse de Dagobert, if she weren't Aurelia Twine, with seventy million dollars made in two years out of oil? Who was your Princess Buondelmare, if not Lotty Miller, who was born in Nevada, and baptized with gin in a miner's pannikin? *We* know 'em all? And Blue Blood's taken 'em because they had cash. That's about it! Wal, to my fancy, there aren't much to be proud of anyhow, and it aren't only us that need be laughed at."

"It is not," said Vere, who had listened in bewilderment. "There is very much to be ashamed of on both sides."

"Shame's a big thing—a four-horse concern," said the other with some demur. "But if any child need be ashamed it is not this child. There's a woman in Rome, Anastasia W. Crash; her father's a coloured person. After the war he turned note-shaver and made a pile; Anastasia aren't coloured to signify; she looks like a Creole, and she's handsome. It got wind in Rome that she was going there, and had six

---

1 Oil.
2 Describes the land holding and resources of late eleventh-century England.

million dollars a year safe; and she has that; it's no lie. Well, in, a week she could pick and choose amongst the Roman princes as if they were bilberries in a hedge, and she's taken one that's got a name a thousand years old; a name that every school-girl reads out in her history-books when she reads about the popes! There! And Anastasia W. Crash is a coloured person with us; with us we would not go in the same car with her, nor eat at the same table with her. What do you think of that?"

"I think your country is very liberal; and that your 'coloured person' has revenged all the crimes of the Borgias."[1]

The pretty American looked at her suspiciously.

"I guess I don't understand you," she said a little sulkily. "I guess you're very deep, aren't you?"

"Pardon me," said Vere, weary of the conversation; "if you will excuse me I will leave you now, we are going to ride—"

"Ride? Ah! That's a thing I don't cotton to anyhow," said Miss Fuschia Leach, who had found that her talent did not lie that way, and could never bring herself to comprehend how princesses and duchesses could find any pleasure in tearing over bleak fields and jumping scratching hedges. A *calorifère*[2] at eighty degrees always, a *sacque* from Sirandin's, an easy chair, and a dozen young men in various stages of admiration around her, that was her idea of comfort. Every thing out of doors made her chilly.

She watched Vere pass away, and laughed, and yet felt sorry. She herself was the rage because she was a great beauty and a great flirt; because she had been signalled for honour by a prince whose word was law; because she was made for the age she lived in, with a vulgarity that was *chic*, and an audacity that was unrivalled, and a delightful mingling of utter ignorance and intense shrewdness, of slavish submission to fashion and daring eccentricity in expression, that made her to the jaded palate of the world a social caviare, a moral absinthe. Exquisitely pretty, perfectly dressed, as dainty to look at as porcelain, and as common to talk to as a camp follower, she, like many of her nation, had found herself, to her own surprise, an object of adoration to that great world of which she had known nothing, except from the imaginative columns of "own correspondents." But Fuschia Leach was no fool, as she said often herself, and she felt, as her eyes followed

---

1 Italian Renaissance family who were brilliant patrons of the arts, but who were evil, ruthless, and treacherous.
2 Hot air stove; radiator.

Vere, that this calm cold child with her great contemptuous eyes and her tranquil voice, had something she had not; something that not all the art of Mr. Worth[1] could send with his confections to herself.

"My word! I think I'll take Mull just to rile her!" she thought to herself; and thought, too, for she was good natured and less vain than she looked: "Perhaps she'd like me a little bit then—and then, again, perhaps she wouldn't."

"That girl's worth five hundred of me, and yet they don't see it!" she mused now, as she pursued Vere's shadow with her eyes across the lawn. She knew very well that with some combination of scarlet and orange, or sage and maize upon her, in some miracle of velvet and silk, with a cigarette in her mouth, a thousand little curls on her forehead, the last slang on her lips, and the last news on her ear, her own generation would find her adorable while it would leave Vere Herbert in the shade. And yet she would sooner have been Vere Herbert; yet she would sooner have had that subtle, nameless, unattainable "something" which no combination of scarlet and orange, of sage and of maize, was able to give, no imitation or effort for half a lifetime would teach.

"We don't raise that sort somehow our way," she reflected wistfully.

She let the riding party go out with a sigh of envy—the slender figure of Vere foremost on a mare that few cared to mount—and went herself to drive in a little basket-carriage with the Princess Nelaguine, accompanied by an escort of her own more intimate adorers, to call at two or three of the *maisonettes*[2] scattered along the line of the shore between Félicité and Villers.

"Strikes me I'll have to take that duke after all," she thought to herself; he would come to her sign she knew, as a hawk to the lure.

That day Prince Zouroff rode by Vere's side, and paid her many compliments on her riding and other things; but she scarcely heard them. She knew she could ride anything, as she told him; and she thought everyone could who loved horses; and then she barely heard the rest of his pretty speeches. She was thinking, with a bewildered disgust, of the woman whom Francis Herbert, Duke of Mull and Cantire, was willing to make her cousin.

She had not comprehended one tithe of Pick-me-up's jargon, but she had understood the menace to the grand, old, sombre border forests about Castle Herbert, which she loved with a love only second to that she felt for the moors and woods of Bulmer.

---

1 Worth gowns were "necessities of life" for American heiresses.
2 Cottages.

"I would sooner see Francis dead than see him touch those trees!" she thought, with what her mother called her terrible earnestness. And she was so absorbed in thinking of the shame of such a wife for a Herbert of Mull, that she never noticed the glances Zouroff gave her, or dreamed that the ladies who rode with her were saying to each other, "Is it possible? Can he be serious?"

Vere had been accustomed to rise at six and go to bed at ten, to spend her time in serious studies or open-air exercise. She was bewildered by a day which began at one or two o'clock in the afternoon, and ended at cockcrow or later. She was harassed by the sense of being perpetually exhibited and unceasingly criticised. Speaking little herself, she listened, and observed, and began to understand all that Corrèze had vaguely warned her against; to see the rancour underlying the honeyed words; the enmity concealed by the cordial smile; the hate expressed in praise; the effort masked in ease; the endless strife and calumny, and cruelty, and small conspiracies which make up the daily life of men and women in society. Most of it was still a mystery to her; but much she saw, and grew heartsick at it. Light and vain temperaments find their congenial atmosphere in the world of fashion, but hers was neither light nor vain, and the falseness of it all oppressed her.

"You are a little Puritan, my dear!" said Lady Stoat, smiling at her.

"Pray be anything else rather than that!" said Lady Dolly pettishly. "Everybody hates it. It makes you look priggish and conceited, and nobody believes in it even. That ever a child of mine should have such ideas!"

"Yes. It *is* very funny!" said her dear Adine quietly. "You neglected her education, pussy. She is certainly a little Puritan. But we should not laugh at her. In these days it is really very interesting to see a girl who can blush, and who does not understand the French of the *Petits Journaux*,[1] though she knows the French of Marmontel and of Massillon."[2]

"Who cares for Marmontel and Massillon?" said Lady Dolly in disgust.

She was flattered by the success of Vere as a beauty, and irritated by her failure as a companionable creature. She was triumphant to see the impression made by the girl's blending of sculptural calm and

---

1 Cheap newspapers.

2 Jean-François Marmontel (1723-99) was a French historian, philosopher, and writer and Jean-Baptiste Massillon (1663-1742) was a celebrated French preacher and bishop.

childlike loveliness. She was infuriated a hundred times a day by Vere's obduracy, coldness, and unwise directness of speech.

"It is almost imbecility," thought Lady Dolly, obliged to apologise continually for some misplaced sincerity or obtuse negligence with which her daughter had offended people.

"You should never *froisser*[1] other people; never, never!" said Lady Dolly. "If Nero, and what—was—her name that began with an M,[2] were to come in your world, you should be civil to them; you should be charming to them, so long as they were people that were received. Nobody is to judge for themselves, never. If society is with you, then you are all right. Besides, it looks so much prettier to be nice and charitable and all that; and besides, what do you know, you chit?"

Vere was always silent under these instructions; they were but little understood by her. When she did *froisser* people it was generally because their consciences gave a sting to her simple frank words of which the young speaker herself was quite unconscious.

"Am I a Puritan?" Vere thought, with anxious self-examination. In history she detested the Puritans; all her sympathies were with the other side. Yet she began now to think that, if the Stuart court ever resembled Félicité, the Puritans had not perhaps been so very far wrong.[3]

Félicité was nothing more or worse than a very fashionable house of the period; but it was the world in little, and it hurt her, bewildered her, and in many ways disgusted her.

If she had been stupid, as her mother thought her, she would have been amused or indifferent; but she was not stupid, and she was oppressed and saddened. At Bulmer she had been reared to think truth the first law of life, modesty as natural to a gentlewoman as cleanliness, delicacy and reserve the attributes of all good breeding, and sincerity indispensable to self respect. At Félicité, who seemed to care for any one of these things?

Lady Stoat gave them lip-service indeed, but, with that exception, no one took the trouble even to render them that questionable homage which hypocrisy pays to virtue.

---

1 Offend.

2 Nero (A.D. 37-68) was the wanton, sinful, murderous, dissolute emperor of Rome. Lady Dolly may be referring to Statilia Messalina, his third wife.

3 The Puritans were a radical Protestant group who wanted to "purify" the Anglican Church and pare down church ritual; the Stuarts remained faithful to the Church of England.

In a world that was the really great world, so far as fashion went and rank (for the house-party at Félicité was composed of people of the purest blood and highest station, people very exclusive, very prominent and very illustrious), Vere found things that seemed passing strange to her. When she heard of professional beauties, whose portraits were sold for a shilling, and whose names were as cheap as red herrings, yet who were received at court and envied by princesses; when she saw that men were the wooed, not the wooers, and that the art of flirtation was reduced to a tournament of effrontery; when she saw a great duchess go out with the guns, carrying her own chokebore by Purdy[1] and showing her slender limbs in gaiters; when she saw married women not much older than herself spending hour after hour in the fever of *chemin de fer*, when she learned that they were very greedy for their winnings to be paid, but never dreamt of being asked to pay their losses; when she saw these women with babies in their nurseries, making unblushing love to other women's husbands, and saw everyone looking on the pastime as a matter of course quite goodnaturedly; when she saw one of these ladies take a flea from her person and cry, *Qui m'aime l'avale*,[2] and a prince of semi-royal blood swallow the flea in a glass of water, when to these things, and a hundred others like them, the young student from the Northumbrian moors was the silent and amazed listener and spectator, she felt indeed lost in a strange and terrible world; and something that was very like disgust shone from her clear eyes and closed her proud mouth.

Society as it was filled her with a very weariness of disgust, a cold and dreary disenchantment, like the track of grey mire that in the mountains is left by the descent of the glacier. But her mother was more terrible to her than all. At the thought of her mother Vere, even in solitude, felt her cheek burn with an intolerable shame. When she came to know something of the meaning of those friendships that society condones—of those jests which society whispers between a cup of tea and a cigarette—of those hints which are enjoyed like a bonbon, yet contain all the enormities that appalled Juvenal,[3]—then the heart of Vere grew sick, and she began slowly to realise what manner of woman this was that had given her birth.

---

1   A shotgun with a bore that narrows toward the muzzle to prevent the shots from scattering.

2   He who loves me will swallow it.

3   First to second century (A.D.) satirical Roman poet. His verse established a model for the satire of indignation.

"My dear, your pretty daughter seems to sit in judgment on us all! I am sadly afraid she finds us wanting," said the great lady who had signalised herself with utilising a flea.

"Oh, she has a dreadful look, I know," said Lady Dolly distractedly. "But you see she has been always with that odious old woman. She has seen nothing. She is a baby."

The other smiled:

"When she has been married a year, all that will change. She will leave it behind her with her maiden sashes and shoes. But I am not sure that she will marry quickly, lovely as she is. She frightens people, and, if you don't mind my saying so, she is rude. The other night when we had that little bit of fun about the flea she rose and walked away, turned her back positively, as if she were a scandalised dowager. Now, you know, that doesn't do nowadays. The age of saints is gone by—"

"If there ever were one," said Lady Dolly, who occasionally forgot that she was very high church in her doctrines.

"Vera would make a beautiful St. Ursula,"[1] said Lady Stoat, joining them. "There is war as well as patience in her countenance; she will resist actively as well as endure passively."

"What a dreadful thing to say!" sighed Lady Dolly.

The heroine of the flea erotic laughed at her.

"Marry her, my dear. That is what she wants."

She herself was only one and twenty, and had been married four years, had some little flaxen bundles in nurses' arms that she seldom saw, was deeply in debt, had as many adorers as she had pearls and diamonds, and was a very popular and admired personage.

"Why can't you get on with people?" Lady Dolly said to Vere irritably, that day.

"I do not think they like me," said Vere very humbly; and her mother answered very sharply and sensibly:

"Everybody is liked as much as they wish to be. If you show people you like them, they like you. It is perfectly simple. You get what you give my dear in this world. But the sad truth is, Vere, that you are unamiable."

Was she in truth unamiable?

She felt the tears gather in her eyes. She put her hand on the

---

1 St. Ursula was the daughter of a Christian king. In A.D. 383, she was supposedly killed with 11,000 other virgins by a group of Huns who captured them during a pilgrimage.

hound Loris's collar, and went away with him into the gardens; the exquisite gardens with the gleam of the sea between the festoons of their roses that no one hardly ever noticed except herself. In a deserted spot where a marble Antinous[1] reigned over a world of bigonias, she sat down on a rustic chair and put her arm round the dog's neck, and cried like the child that she was.

She thought of the sweetbriar bush on the edge of the white cliff—oh! if only Corrèze had been here to tell her what to do!

The dog kissed her in his own way, and was sorrowful for her sorrow; the sea wind stirred the flowers; the waves were near enough at hand for their murmuring to reach her; the quietness and sweetness of the place soothed her.

She would surely see Corrèze again, she thought; perhaps in Paris, this very winter, if her mother took her there. He would tell her if she were right or wrong in having no sympathy with all these people; and the tears still fell down her cheeks as she sat there and fancied she heard that wondrous voice rise once more above the sound of the sea.

"Mademoiselle Vera, are you unhappy? and in Félicité!"[2] said a voice that was very unlike that unforgotten music—the voice of Sergius Zouroff.

Vere looked up startled, with her tears still wet, like dew.

Zouroff had been kindness itself to her, but her first disgust for him had never changed. She was alarmed and vexed to be found by him, so, alone.

"What frets you?" he said, with more gentleness than often came into his tones. "It is a regret to me as your host that you should know any regret in Félicité. If there be anything I can do, command me."

"You are very good, monsieur," said Vere hesitatingly. "It is nothing—very little, at least; my mother is vexed with me."

"Indeed! Your charming mother, then, for once, must be in the wrong. What is it?"

"Because people do not like me."

"Who is barbarian enough not to like you? I am a barbarian but—"

His cold eyes grew eloquent, but she did not see their gaze, for she was looking dreamily at the far-off sea.

---

1 He was the chief suitor of Penelope, who Ulysses killed when he finally returned to Ithaca from the Trojan War.
2 Félicité is French for bliss.

"No one likes me," said Vere wearily, "and my mother thinks it is my fault. No doubt it is. I do not care for what they care for; but then they do not care for what I love—the gardens, the woods, the sea, the dogs."

She drew Loris close as she spoke, and rose to go. She did not wish to be with her host. But Zouroff paced by her side.

"Loris pleases you? Will you give him the happiness of being called yours?"

Vere for once raised a bright and grateful face to him, a flush of pleasure drying her tears.

"Mine? Loris? Oh that would be delightful!—if mamma will let me."

"Your mother will let you," said Zouroff, with an odd smile. "Loris is a fortunate beast, to have power to win your fancy."

"But I like all dogs—"

"And no men?"

"I do not think about them."

It was the simple truth.

"I wish I were a dog!" said Serge Zouroff.

Vere laughed for a moment—a child's sudden laugh at a droll idea; then her brows contracted a little.

"Dogs do not flatter me," she said curtly.

"Nor do I—*foi d'honneur!*[1] But tell me, is it really the fact that cruel Lady Dolly made you weep? In my house too!—I am very angry. I wish to make it Félicité to you, beyond any other of my guests."

"Mamma was no doubt right, monsieur," said Vere coldly. "She said that I do not like people, and I do not."

"*Dame!*[2] You have excellent taste then," said Zouroff with a laugh. "I will not quarrel with your coldness, Mademoiselle Vera, if you will only make an exception for me?"

Vere was silent.

Zouroff's eyes grew impatient and fiery.

"Will you not even like me a little for Loris's sake?"

Vere stood still in the rose-path, and looked at him with serious serene eyes.

"It was kind of you to give me Loris, that I know, and I am grateful for that; but I will not tell you what is false, monsieur; it would be a very bad return."

---

1 Word of honor.
2 Indeed.

"Is she the wiliest coquette by instinct, or only the strangest child that ever breathed?" thought Zouroff as he said aloud, "Why do you not like me, *mon enfant?*"[1]

Vere hesitated a moment.

"I do not think you are a good man."

"And why am I so unfortunate as to give you that opinion of me?"

"It is the way you talk; and you kicked Loris one day last week."

Serge Zouroff laughed aloud, but he swore a heavy oath under his breath.

"Your name in Russian means Faith. You are well named, Mademoiselle Vera," he said carelessly, as he continued to walk by her side. "But I shall hope to make you think better things of me yet, and I can never kick Loris again, as he is now yours, without your permission."

"You will never have that," said Vere, with a little smile, as she thought, with a pang of compunction, that she had been very rude to a host who was courteous and generous.

Zouroff moved on beside her, gloomy and silent.

"Take my arm, mademoiselle," he said suddenly, as they were approaching the château. Vere put her hand on his arm in timid compliance; she felt that she must have seemed rude and thankless. They crossed the smooth lawns that stretched underneath the terraces of Félicité.

It was near sunset, about seven o'clock; some ladies were out on the terrace, amidst them Lady Dolly and the heroine of the flea. They saw Zouroff cross the turf, with the girl in her white Gainsborough dress beside him, and the hound beside her.

Lady Dolly's heart gave a sudden leap, then stopped its beats in suspense.

"Positively—I do—think—" murmured the lady of the flea; and then fell back in her chair in a fit of uncontrollable laughter.

Vere loosened her hand from her host's arm as they ascended the terrace steps, and came straight to her mother.

"Monsieur Zouroff has given me Loris!" she cried breathlessly, for the dog was to her an exceeding joy. "You will let me have Loris, mamma?"

"Let her have Loris," said Zouroff, with a smile that Lady Dolly understood.

"Certainly, since you are so kind, Prince," she said charmingly. "But a dog! It is such a disagreeable thing; when one travels especial-

---

1 My child.

ly. Still, since you are so good to that naughty child, who gives all her heart to the brutes—"

"I am happy that she thinks me a brute too," said Zouroff, with a grim smile.

The ladies laughed.

Vere did not hear or heed. She was caressing her new treasure.

"I shall not feel alone now with Loris," she was saying to herself. The dull fierce eyes of Serge Zouroff were fastened on her, but she did not think of him, nor of why the women laughed.

Lady Dolly was vaguely perplexed.

"The girl was crying half an hour ago," she thought. "Perhaps she is deeper than one thinks. Perhaps she means to draw him on that way. Anyhow, her way appears to answer—but it hardly seems possible—when one thinks what he has had thrown at his head and never looked at! And Vere! such a rude creature, and such a simpleton!"

Yet a sullen respect began to enter into her for her daughter: the respect that women of the world only give to a shrewd talent for *finesse*.[1] If she were capable at sixteen of "drawing on" the master of Félicité thus ably, Lady Dolly felt that her daughter might yet prove worthy of her; might still become a being with whom she could have sympathy and community of sentiment. And yet Lady Dolly felt a sort of sickness steal over her as she saw the look in his eyes which Vere did not see.

"It will be horrible! horrible!" she said to herself. "Why did Adine ever tell me to come here?"

For Lady Dolly was never in her own eyes the victim of her own follies, but always that of someone else's bad counsels.

Lady Dolly was frightened when she thought that it was possible that this scorner of unmarried women would be won by her own child. But she was yet more terrified when the probable hopelessness of any such project flashed on her.

The gift of the dog might mean everything, and might mean nothing.

"What a constant misery she is!" she mused. "Oh, why wasn't she a boy? They go to Eton, and if they get into trouble men manage it all; and they are useful to go about with if you want stalls at a theatre, or an escort that don't compromise you. But a daughter!..."

She could have cried, dressed though she was for dinner, in a combination of orange and deadleaf, that would have consoled any woman under any affliction.

---

1 Artfulness.

"Do you think he means it," she whispered to Lady Stoat, who answered cautiously,—

"I think he might be made to mean it."

Dolly sighed, and looked nervous.

Two days later Loris had a silver collar on his neck that had just come from Paris. It had the inscription on it of the Troubadour's[1] motto for his mistress's falcon:

"Quiconque me trouvera, qu'il me mène à ma maîtresse: pour récompense il la verra."[2]

Vere looked doubtfully at the collar; she preferred Loris without it.

"He does mean it," said Lady Dolly to herself, and her pulses fluttered strangely.

"I'd have given you a dog if I'd known you wished for one," said John Jura moodily that evening to Vere. She smiled and thanked him.

"I had so many dogs about me at Bulmer I feel lost without one, and Loris is very beautiful—"

Jura looked at her with close scrutiny.

"How do you like the giver of Loris?"

Vere met his gaze unmoved. "I do not like him at all," she said in a low tone. "But perhaps it is not sincere to say so. He is very kind and we are in his house."

"My dear! That we are in his house or that he is in ours is the very reason to abuse a man like a thief! You don't seem to understand modern ethics," said the heroine of the flea epic, as she passed near with a little laugh, on her way to play *chemin de fer* in the next drawing-room.

"Don't listen to them," said Jura hastily. "They will do you no good; they are all a bad lot here."

"But they are all gentle-people?" said Vere in some astonishment. "They are all gentlemen and gentlewomen born."

"Oh, *born!*" said Jura, with immeasurable contempt. "Oh yes! they're all in the swim for that matter; but they are about as bad a set as there is in Europe; not but what it is much the same everywhere. They say the Second Empire did it. I don't know if it's that, but I do know that 'gentlewomen,' as you call it, are things one never sees nowadays anywhere in Paris or London. You have got the old grace,

---

1 Medieval poets who wrote songs and poems chiefly on themes of courtly love.

2 Whoever finds me, return me to my mistress: his reward will be to see her.

but how long will you keep it? They will corrupt you; and if they can't, they'll ruin you."

"Is it so easy to be corrupted or to be ruined?"

"Easy as blacking your glove," said Jura moodily.

Vere gave a little sigh. Life seemed to her very difficult.

"I do not think they will change me," she said, after a few moments' thought.

"I don't think they will; but they will make you pay for it. If they say nothing worse of you than that you are 'odd' you will be lucky. How did you become what you were? You, Dolly's daughter!"

Vere coloured at the unconscious contempt with which he spoke the last two words.

"I try to be what my father would have wished," she said under her breath.

Jura was touched. His blue eyes grew dim and reverential.

"I wish to heaven your father may watch over you!" he said in a husky voice. "In *our* world, my dear, you will want some good angel—bitterly. Perhaps you will be your own, though. I hope so."

His hand sought hers and caught it closely for an instant, and he grew very pale. Vere looked up in a little surprise.

"You are very kind to think of me," she said with a certain emotion.

"Who would not think of you?" muttered Jura, with a darkness on his frank, fair, bold face. "Don't be so astonished that I do," he said, with a little laugh, whose irony she did not understand. "You know I am such a friend of your mother's."

"Yes," said Vere gravely.

She was perplexed. He took up her fan and unfurled it.

"Who gave you this thing? It is an old one of Dolly's, I bought it in the Passage Choiseul myself; it's not half good enough for you now. I bought one at Christie's[1] last winter, that belonged to Maria Theresa;[2] it has her monogram in opals; it was painted by Fragonard,[3] or one of those beggars; I will send for it for you if you will please me by taking it."

"You are very kind," said Vere.

"That is what you say of Serge Zouroff!"

---

1   The Passage Choiseul is an area in Paris where several large art galleries are located; Christies's is a fashionable art auction gallery in London.

2   Maria Theresa (1717-80) was the Archduchess of Hungary and Bohemia, mother of Marie Antoinette.

3   Jean-Honoré Fragonard (1732-1806) was a French painter.

She laughed a little.

"I like you better than Monsieur Zouroff."

Jura's face flushed to the roots of his fair crisp curls.

"And as well as your favoured singer?"

"Ah no!—"Vere spoke quickly, and with a frown on her pretty brows. She was annoyed at the mention of Corrèze.

Lady Dolly approached at that moment—an apparition of white lace and *nénuphars*,[1] with some wonderful old cameos as ornaments.

"Take me to the tea-room, Jack," she said sharply. "Clementine de Vrille is winning everything again; it is sickening; I believe she marks the aces!"

Jura gave her his arm.

Vere, left alone, sat lost in thought. It was a strange world. No one seemed happy in it, or sincere. Lord Jura, whom her mother treated like a brother, seemed to despise her more than anyone; and her mother seemed to say that another friend, who was a French Duchess, descended from a Valois,[2] was guilty of cheating at cards!

Jura took the white lace and *nénuphars* into the tea-room. He was silent and preoccupied. Lady Dolly wanted pretty attentions, but their day was over with him.

"Is it true," he said abruptly to her, "that Zouroff wants your daughter?"

Lady Dolly smiled vaguely.

"Oh! I don't know; they say many things, you know. No; I should-n't suppose he means anything, should you?"

"I can't say," he answered curtly. "You wish it."

"Of course I wish anything for her happiness."

He laughed aloud.

"What damned hypocrites all you women are!"

"My dear Jura, *pray*: you are not in a guard-room or a club-room!" said Lady Dolly very seriously shocked indeed.

Lord Jura got her off his hands at length, and bestowed her on a young dandy, who had become famous by winning the Grand Prix in that summer. Then he walked away by himself into the smoking-room, which at that hour was quite deserted. He threw himself down on one of the couches, and thought—moodily, impatiently, bitterly.

"What cursed fools we are!" he mused. What a fool he had been ever to fancy that he loved the bloom of Piver's powders, the slim shape of a white satin corset, the falsehoods of a dozen seasons, the

---

1 Water lilies.
2 A member of a ruling French family that reigned from 1328 to 1589.

debts of a little gamester, the smiles of a calculating coquette, and the five hundred things of like value, that made up the human entity, known as Lady Dolly.

He could see her, as he had seen her first; a little gossamer figure under the old elms, down by the waterside at Hurlingham,[1] when Hurlingham had been in its earliest natal days of glory. There had been a dinner-party for a Sunday evening; he remembered carrying her tea, and picking her out the big strawberries under the cedar. They had met a thousand times before that, but had never spoken. He thought her the prettiest creature he had ever seen. She had told him to call on her at Chesham place; she was always at home at four. He remembered their coming upon a dead pigeon amongst the gardenias, and how she had laughed, and told him to write its elegy, and he had said that he would if he could only spell, but he had never been able to spell in his life. All the nonsense, all the trifles, came back to his memory in a hateful clearness. That was five years ago, and she was as pretty as ever: Piver is the true *fontaine de jouvence*.[2] She was not changed, but he—he wished that he had been dead like the blue-rock amongst the gardenias.

He thought of a serious sweet face, a noble mouth, a low broad brow, with the fair hair lying thickly above it.

"Good God!" he thought, "who would ever have dreamt that she could have had such a daughter!"

And his heart was sick, and his meditation was bitter. He was of a loyal, faithful, dog-like temper; yet in that moment he turned in revolt against the captivity that had once seemed sweet, and he hated the mother of Vere.

A little later Lord Jura told his host that he was very sorry, regretted infinitely, and all that, but he was obliged to go up to Scotland. His father had a great house-party there, and would have no denial.

Alone, Lady Dolly said to him, "What does this mean? what is this for? You know you *never* go to Camelot; you know that you go to every other house in the kingdom sooner. What did you say it for? And how dare you say it without seeing if it suit me? It doesn't suit me."

"I put it on Camelot because it sounds more decent; and I mean to go," said Lord Jura, plunging his hands in his pockets. "The truth is, Dolly, I don't care to be in this blackguard's house. He is a blackguard, and you're wanting to get him."

---

1 Hurlingham was a polo club in London.
2 Fountain of youth.

Lady Dolly turned pale and sick.

"What language! How is he any more a—what you say—than you are, or anybody else? And pray for what do I want him?"

The broad frank brows of Lord Jura grew stormy as he frowned.

"The man is a blackguard. There are things one can't say to women. Everybody knows it. You don't care; you want to get him for the child."

"Vera? Good gracious! What is Vera to you if it be what you fancy?"

"Nothing!" said Lord Jura, and his lips were pressed close together, and he did not look at his companion.

"Then why—I should think she isn't, indeed!—but why, in the name of goodness—"

"Look here, Dolly," said the young man sternly. "Look here. I'm death on sport, and I've killed most things, from stripes in the jungle to the red rover in the furrows; I don't affect to be a feeling fellow, or to go in for that sort of sentiment, but there was one thing I never could stand seeing, and that was a little innocent wild rabbit caught in a gin-trap. My keepers daren't set one for their lives. I can't catch you by the throat, or trottle Zouroff as I should a keeper if I caught him at it, so I go to Camelot. That's all. Don't make a fuss. You're going to do a wicked thing, if you can do it, and I won't look on; that's all."

Lady Dolly was very frightened.

"What do you know about Zouroff?" she murmured hurriedly.

"Only what all Paris knows; that is quite enough."

Lady Dolly was relieved, and instantly allowed herself to grow angry.

"All Paris! Such stuff! As if men were not all alike. Really one would fancy you were in love with Vera yourself!"

"Stop that!" said Lord Jura sternly; and she was subdued, and said no more. "I shall go to-morrow," he added carelessly; "and you may as well give me a book or a note or something for the women at Camelot; it will stay their tongues here."

"I have a tapestry pattern to send to your sisters," said Lady Dolly, submissive but infuriated. "What do you know about Sergius Zouroff, Jack? I wish you would tell me."

"I think you know it all very well," said Lord Jura. "I think you women know all about all the vices under the sun, only you don't mind. There are always bookcases locked in every library; I don't know why we lock 'em; women know everything. But if the man's rich it don't matter. If the fellows we used to read about in

Suetonius[1] were alive now, you'd marry your girls to them and never ask any questions—except about settlements. It's no use my saying anything; you don't care. But I tell you all the same that if you give your daughter when she's scarce sixteen to that brute, you might just as well strip her naked and set her up to auction like the girl in *La Coupe ou La Femme!*"[2]

"You grow very coarse," said Lady Dolly, coldly.

Lord Jura left the room, and, in the morning, left the house.

As the "Ephemeris" went slowly, in a languid wind, across the channel in the grey twilight, he sat on deck and smoked, and grew heavy-hearted. He was not a book-learned man, and seldom read anything beyond the sporting papers, or a French romance; but some old verse, about the Fates making out of our pleasant vices whips to scourge us[3] crossed his mind, as the woods and towers of Félicité receded from his sight.

He was young; he was his own master; he was Earl of Jura, and would be Marquis of Shetland. He could have looked into those grand grey eyes of Vere Herbert's with a frank and honest love; he could have been happy, only—only—only!

The Maria Theresa fan came from Camelot, but Jura never returned.

That night there was a performance in the little theatre; there was usually one every other night. The actors enjoyed themselves much more than the guests at Félicité. They all lived in a little *maisonette* in the park, idled through their days as they liked, and played when they were told. When his house-party bored him beyond endurance, Sergius Zouroff wandered away to that *maisonette* in his park at midnight.

That evening the piece on the programme was one that was very light. Zouroff stooped his head to Lady Dolly as they were about to move to the theatre.

"Send your daughter to her bed; that piece is not fit for her ears."

Lady Dolly stared and bit her lip. But she obeyed. She went back and touched Vere's cheek with her fan and caressed her.

---

1   Suetonius (A.D. 69–c. 140) was a Roman writer who exposed scandalous events and the immoral lifestyles of Roman aristocrats and emperors.

2   The Cup or the Woman.

3   This may be a reference to Richard Niccols' *Furies With Vertues Encomium* (1614): "Of wanton vice, The Furies she [the Muse] doth raise / With snakie whips to scourge such idle apes" and "That in their pride of Rage, all eyes may see / Justice hath whips to scourge impiety."

"My sweet one, you look pale. Go to your room; you do not care much for acting, and your health is so precious—"

"He must mean it," she thought, as they went into the pretty theatre, and the lights went round with her. The jests fell on deaf ears so far as she was concerned; the dazzling little scenes danced before her sight; she could only see the heavy form of Zouroff cast down in his velvet chair, with his eyes half shut, and his thick eyebrows drawn together in a frown that did not relax.

"He must mean it," she thought. "But how odd! Good heavens! that he should care—that he should think—of what is fit or unfit!"

And it made her laugh convulsively, in a sort of spasm of mirth, for which the gestures and jokes of the scene gave excuse.

Yet she had never felt so nearly wretched, never so nearly understood, what shame and repentance meant.

In the *entr'acte*[1] Zouroff changed his place, and took a vacant chair by Lady Dolly, and took up her fan and played with it.

"Miladi, we have always been friends, good friends, have we not?" he said with the smile that she hated. "You know me well, and can judge me without flattery. What will you say if I tell you that I seek the honour of your daughter's hand?"

He folded and unfolded the fan as he spoke. The orchestra played at that moment loudly. Lady Dolly was silent. There was a contraction at the corners of her pretty rosebud-like mouth.

"Any mother could have but one answer to you," she replied with an effort. "You are too good and I am too happy!"

"I may speak to her, then, to-morrow, with your consent?" he added.

"Let me speak to her first," she said hurriedly; "she is so young."

"As you will, madame! Place myself and all I have at her feet."

"What can you have seen in her! Good heavens!" she cried in an impulse of amaze.

"She has avoided me!" said Serge Zouroff, and spoke the truth: then added in his best manner, "And is she not your child?"

The violins chirped softly as waking birds at dawn; the satin curtain drew up; the little glittering scene shone again in the wax-light. Lady Dolly gasped a little for breath.

"It is very warm here," she murmured. "Don't you think if a window were opened. And then you have astonished me so—"

She shook double her usual drops of chloral out into her glass that night, but they did not give her sleep.

---

1 Intermission.

"I shall never persuade her!" she thought; gazing with dry, hot eyes at the light swinging before her mirror. The eyes of Vere seemed to look at her in their innocent, scornful serenity, and the eyes of Vere's father too.

"Do the dead ever come back?" she thought; "some people say they do."

And Lady Dolly, between her soft sheets, shivered, and felt frightened and old.

She was on the edge of a crime, and she had a conscience, though it was a very small and feeble one, and seldom spoke.

CHAPTER VIII.

Vere had been up with the sunrise, and out with Loris. She had had the pretty green park and the dewy gardens to herself; she had filled her hands with more flowers than she could carry; her hair and her clothes were fragrant with the smell of mown grass and pressed thyme; she stole back on tiptoe through the long corridors, through the still house, for it was only nine o'clock, and she knew that all the guests of Félicité were still sleeping.

To her surprise her mother's door opened, and her mother's voice called her.

Vere went in, fresh and bright as was the summer morning itself, with the dew upon her hair and the smell of the blossoms entering with her, into the warm oppressive air that was laden with the smells of anodynes and perfumes.

Her mother had already been made pretty for the day, and a lovely turquoise-blue dressing-robe enveloped her. She opened her arms, and folded the child in them, and touched her forehead with a kiss.

"My darling, my sweet child," she murmured, "I have some wonderful news for you; news that makes me very happy, Vera—"

"Yes?" said Vere, standing with wide-opened expectant eyes, the flowers falling about her, the dew sparkling on her hair.

"Yes, too happy, my Vera, since it secures your happiness," murmured her mother. "But perhaps you can guess, dear, though you are so very young, and you do not even know what love means. Vera, my sweetest, my old friend Prince Zouroff has sought you from me in marriage!"

"Mother!" Vere stepped backward, then stood still again; a speechless amaze, an utter incredulity, an unutterable disgust, all speaking in her face.

"Are you startled, darling," said Lady Dolly, in her blandest voice.

"Of course you are, you are such a child. But if you think a moment, Vera, you will see the extreme compliment it is to you; the greatness it offers you; the security that the devotion of a—"

"Mother!" she cried again; and this time the word was a cry of horror—a protest of indignation and outrage.

"Don't call me 'mother' like that. You know I hate it!" said Lady Dolly, lapsing into the tone most natural to her. "'Mother! mother!' as if I were beating you with a poker, like the people in the police reports. You are so silly, my dear; I cannot think what he can have seen in you, but seen something he has, enough to make him wish to marry you. You are a baby, but I suppose you can understand that. It is a very great and good marriage, Vera; no one could desire anything better. You are exceedingly young, indeed, according to English notions, but they never were my notions, and I think a girl cannot anyhow be safer than properly married to a person desirable in every way—"

Lady Dolly paused a moment to take breath; she felt a little excited, a little exhausted, and there was that in the colourless face of her daughter which frightened her, as she had been frightened in her bed, wondering if the dead came back on earth.

She made a little forward caressing movement, and would have kissed her again, but Vere moved away, her eyes were darkened with anger, and her lips were tremulous.

"Prince Zouroff is a coward," said the girl, very low, but very bitterly. "He knows that I loathe him, and that I think him a bad man. How dare he—how dare he—insult me so!"

"Insult you!" echoed Lady Dolly, with almost a scream. "Are you mad? Insult you! A man that all Europe has been wild to marry these fifteen years past! Insult you! A man who offers you an alliance that will send you out of a room before everybody except actually princesses of the blood? Insult you! When was ever an offer of marriage thought an insult in society?"

"I think it can be the greatest one," said Vere, still under her breath.

"You think! Who are you to think? Pray have no thoughts at all unless they are wiser than that. You are startled, my dear; that is, perhaps natural. You did not see he was in love with you, though everyone else did."

"Oh, do not say such horrible words!"

The blood rushed to the child's face, and she covered her eyes with her hands. She was hurt, deeply, passionately—hurt and humiliated, in a way that her mother could no more have understood than she could have understood the paths travelled by the invisible stars.

"Really you are too ridiculous," she said impatiently. "Even you, I should think, must know what love means. I believe even at Bulmer you read 'Waverley.'[1] You have charmed Sergius Zouroff, and it is a very great victory, and if all this surprise and disgust at it is not a mere piece of acting, you must be absolutely brainless, absolutely idiotic! You cannot seriously mean that a man insults you when he offers you a position that has been coveted by half Europe."

"When he knows that I cannot endure him," said Vere with flashing eyes; "it is an insult; tell him so from me. Oh mother! mother! that you could even call me to hear such a thing.... I do not want to marry anyone; I do not wish ever to marry. Let me go back to Bulmer. I am not made for the world, nor it for me."

"You are not, indeed!" said her mother in exasperation and disgust, feeling her own rage and anxiety like two strangling hands at her throat. "Nevertheless, into the world you will go as Princess Zouroff. The alliance suits me, and I am not easily dissuaded from what I wish. Your heroics count for nothing. All girls of sixteen are gushing and silly. I was too. It is an immense thing that you have such a stroke of good fortune. I quite despaired of you. You are very lovely, but you are old-fashioned, pedantic, unpleasant. You have no *chic*. You have no malleability. You are handsome, and that is all. It is a wonderful thing that you should have made such a *coup*[2] as this before you are even out. You are quite penniless; quite, did you understand that? You have no claim on Mr. Vanderdecken, and I am not at all sure that he will not make a great piece of work when I leave him to pay for your *trousseau*, as I must do, for I can't pay for it, and none of the Herberts will; they are all poor and proud as church mice and though Zouroff will of course send you a *corbeille*,[3] all the rest must come from me, and must be perfect and abundant, and from all the best houses."

Vere struck her foot on the floor. It was the first gesture of passion that she had ever given way to since her birth.

"That is enough, mother!" she said aloud and very firmly. "Put it in what words you like to Prince Zouroff, but tell him from me that I will not marry him. I will not. That is enough."

Then, before her mother could speak again, she gathered up the dew-wet flowers in her hand and left the room.

---

1 A historical romance by Sir Walter Scott published in 1814.
2 Accomplishment.
3 Wedding present given by the groom.

Lady Dolly shrugged her shoulders, and swore a naughty little oath, as if she had lost fifty pounds at bezique.[1] She was pale and excited, offended and very angry, but she was not afraid. Girls were always like that, she thought. Only, for the immediate moment it was difficult.

She sat and meditated awhile, then made up her mind. She had nerved herself in the night that was just past to put her child in the brazen hands of Moloch[2] because it suited her, because it served her, because she had let her little weak conscience sink utterly, and down in the deeps; and having once made up her mind she resolved to have her will. Like all weak people, she could be cruel, and she was cruel now.

When the midday chimes rang with music from the clock-tower, Lady Dolly went out of her own room downstairs. It was the habit at Félicité for the guests to meet at one o'clock breakfast—being in the country they thought it well to rise early. Serge Zouroff, as he met her, smiled.

"*Eh bien?*"[3] he asked.

The smile made Lady Dolly feel sick and cold, but she looked softly into his eyes.

"Dear friend, do not be in haste. My child is *such* a child—she is flattered—deeply moved—but startled. She has no thought of any such ideas, you know; she can scarcely understand. Leave her to me for a day or two. Do not hurry her. This morning if you will lend me a pony carriage, I will drive over with her to Le Caprice and stay a night or so. I shall talk to her, and then—"

Zouroff laughed grimly.

"*Ma belle,*[4] your daughter detests me; but I do not mind that. You may say it out; it will make no difference—to us."

"You are wrong there," said Lady Dolly so blandly and serenely that even he was deceived, and believed her for once to be speaking the truth. "She neither likes you nor dislikes you, because her mind is in its chrysalis state—isn't it a chrysalis, the thing that is rolled up in a shell asleep?—and of love and marriage my Vera is as unconscious as those china children yonder holding up the breakfast bouquets. She is cold, you know; that you see for yourself—"

---

1   A card game.
2   Moloch was a divinity worshiped by the idolatrous Israelites. The chief feature of their worship was the sacrifice of children.
3   "Well?"
4   My dear.

"*Un beau défaut!*"[1]

"*Un beau défaut* in a girl," assented Lady Dolly. "Yes. I would not have her otherwise, my poor fatherless darling, nor would you, I know. But it makes it difficult to bring her to say 'yes,' you see; not because she has any feeling *against* you, but simply because she has no feeling at all as yet. Unless girls are precocious it is always so—hush—don't let them overhear us. We don't want it talked about at present, do we?"

"As you like," said Zouroff moodily.

He was offended, and yet he was pleased; offended because he was used to instantaneous victory, pleased because this grey-eyed maiden proved of the stuff that he had fancied her. For a moment he thought he would take the task of persuasion out of her mother's hands and into his own, but he was an indolent man, and effort was disagreeable to him, and he was worried at that moment by the pretensions of one of the actresses at the *maisonette* a mile off across the park.

"My Vera is not very well this morning. She has got a little chill," volunteered Lady Dolly to Madame Nelaguine, and the table generally.

"I saw Miss Herbert in the gardens as I went to bed at sunrise," said Fuschia Leach in her high far-reaching voice. "I surmise morning dew is bad for the health."

People laughed. It was felt there was "something" about Vere and her absence, and the women were inclined to think that, despite Loris and the silver collar, their host had not come to the point, and Lady Dolly was about to retreat.

"After all, it would be preposterous," they argued. "A child, not even out, and one of those Mull Herberts without a penny."

"Won't you come down?" said Lady Dolly sharply to Vere a little later.

"I will come down if I may say the truth to Prince Zouroff."

"Until you accept him you will say nothing to him. It is impossible to keep you here *boudant*[2] like this. It becomes ridiculous. What will all those women say!... I will drive you over to Laure's. We will stay there a few days, and you will hear reason."

"I will not marry Prince Zouroff," said Vere.

After her first disgust and anger that subject scarcely troubled her. They could not marry her against her will. She had only to be firm, she thought; and her nature was firm almost to stubbornness.

---

1 A noble shortcoming!
2 Sulking.

"We will see," said her mother drily. "Get ready to go with me in an hour."

Vere, left to herself, undid the collar of Loris, made it in a packet, and wrote a little note, which said:—

"I thank you very much, Monsieur, for the honour that I hear from my mother you do me, in your wish that I should marry you. Yet I wonder that you do wish it, because you know well that I have not that feeling for you which could make me care for or respect you. Please to take back this beautiful collar, which is too heavy for Loris. Loris I will always keep, and I am very fond of him. I should be glad if you would tell my mother that you have had this letter and I beg you to believe me, Monsieur, yours gratefully,

"VERE HERBERT."

She read the note several times, and thought that it would do. She did not like to write more coldly, lest she should seem heartless, and though her first impulse had been to look on the offer as an insult, perhaps he did not mean it so, she reflected; perhaps he did not understand how she disliked him. She directed her packet, and sealed it, and called her maid.

"Will you take that to Monsieur Zouroff at once," she said. "Give it to him into his own hands."

The maid took the packet to her superior, Adrienne; Adrienne the wise took it to her mistress; Lady Dolly glanced at it and put it carelessly aside.

"Ah! the dog's collar to go to Paris to be enlarged? very well; leave it there; it is of no consequence just now."

Adrienne the wise understood very well.

"If Mademoiselle ask you," she instructed her underling, "you will say that Monsieur le Prince had the packet quite safe."

But Vere did not even ask, because she had not lived long enough in the world to doubt the good faith even of a waiting-maid. At Bulmer the servants were old-fashioned, like the place, and the Waverley novels. They told the truth, as they wore boots that wanted blacking.

If the little note had found its way to Serge Zouroff it might have touched his heart; it would have touched his pride, and Vere would have been left free. As it was, the packet reposed amidst Lady Dolly's pocket-handkerchiefs and perfumes till it was burnt with a pastille[1] in the body of a Japanese dragon.

---

1 An aromatic substance like incense.

Vere, quite tranquil, went to Le Caprice in the sunny afternoon with her mother, never doubting that Prince Zouroff had had it.

She did not see him, and thought that it was because he had read her message and resented it. In point of fact she did not see him because he was in the *maisonette* in the park, where the feminine portion of the troop had grown so quarrelsome and so exacting that they were threatening to make him a scene up at the château.

"What are your great ladies better than we?" they cried in revolt. He granted that they were no better; nevertheless, the prejudices of society were so constituted that château and *maisonette* could not meet, and he bade their director bundle them all back to Paris, like a cage of dangerous animals that might at any moment escape.

"You will be here for the ball for the Prince de Galles?"[1] said Princess Nelaguine to Lady Dolly; who nodded and laughed.

"To be sure; thanks; I only go for a few days, love."

"Are we coming back?" said Vere, aghast.

"Certainly," said her mother sharply, striking her ponies; and the child's heart sank.

"But he will have had my letter," she thought, "and then he will let me alone."

Le Caprice was a charming house, with a charming *châtelaine*,[2] and charming people were gathered in it for the sea and the shooting; but Vere began to hate the pretty picturesque women, the sound of the laughter, the babble of society, the elegance and the luxury, and all the graceful nothings that make up the habits and pleasures of a grand house. She felt very lonely in it all, and when, for sake of her beauty, men gathered about her, she seemed stupid because she was filled with a shy terror of them; perhaps they would want to marry her too, she thought; and her fair low brow got a little frown on it that made her look sullen.

"Your daughter is lovely, *ma chère*, but she is not sweet-tempered like you," said the hostess to Lady Dolly, who sighed.

"Ah no!" she answered, "she is cross, poor pet, sometimes, and hard to please. Now, I am never out of temper, and any little thing amuses me that my friends are kind enough to do. I don't know where Vera got her character; from some dead and gone Herbert, I suppose, who must have been very disagreeable in his generation."

And that night and every night she said the same thing to Vere:

---

1 The Prince of Wales.
2 Hostess.

"You must marry Serge Zouroff;" and Vere every night replied, "I have told him I will not. I will not."

Lady Dolly never let her know that her letter had been burned.

"Your letter?" she had said when Vere spoke of it. "No; he never told me anything of it. But whatever you might say, he wouldn't mind it, my dear. You take his fancy, and he means to marry you."

"Then he is no gentleman," said the girl.

"Oh, about that, I don't know," said Lady Dolly. "Your idea of a gentleman, I believe, is a man who makes himself up as Faust or Romeo, and screams for so many guineas a night. We won't discuss that."

Vere's face burned, but she was mute. It seemed to her that her mother had grown coarse as well as cruel. There was a hardness in her mother that she had never felt before. That her letter should have been read by Serge Zouroff, yet make no impression on him, seemed to her so dastardly that it left her no hope to move him; no hope anywhere except in her own resistance.

Three days later, Prince Zouroff drove over to Le Caprice, and saw Lady Dolly alone.

Vere was not asked for, and was thankful. Her eyes wistfully questioned her mother's when they met, but Lady Dolly's were unrevealing and did not meet her gaze.

The house was full of movement and of mirth; there were *sauteries* every evening, and distractions of all kinds. Lady Dolly was always flirting, laughing, dancing, amusing herself; Vere was silent, grave, and cold.

"You are much younger than your daughter, Madame Dolly," said an old admirer; and Lady Dolly ruffled those pretty curls which had cost her fifty francs a lock.

"Ah! Youth is a thing of temperament more than of years. That I *do* think. My Vera is so hard to please, and I—everything amuses *me*, and everyone to *me* seems charming."

But this sunny, smiling little visage changed when, every evening before dinner, she came to her daughter's room, and urged, and argued, and abused, and railed, and entreated, and sobbed, and said her sermon again, and again, and again; all in vain.

Vere said but few words, but they were always of the same meaning.

"I will not marry Prince Zouroff," she said always. "It is of no use to ask me. I will not."

And the little frown deepened between her eyes, and the smile that Corrèze had seen upon her classic mouth now never came there. She grew harassed and anxious.

Since her letter had made no impression on him how could she escape this weariness?

One evening she heard some people in the drawing-rooms talking of Corrèze.

They said that he had been singing in the "Fidelio,"[1] and surpassing himself, and that a young and beautiful Grand Duchess had made herself conspicuous by her idolatry of him; so conspicuous that he had been requested to leave Germany, and had refused, placing the authorities in the difficult position of either receding ridiculously or being obliged to use illegal force; there would be terrible scandal in high places, but Corrèze was always *accapareur des femmes!*[2]

Vere moved away with a beating heart and a burning cheek; through the murmur of the conversation around her she seemed to hear the exquisite notes of that one divine voice which had dropped and deepened to so simple and tender a solemnity as it had bidden her keep herself unspotted from the world.

"What would he say if he knew what they want me to do!" she thought. "If he knew that my mother even—my mother—!"

For, not even though her mother was Lady Dolly, could Vere quite abandon the fancy that motherhood was a sweet and sacred altar on which the young could seek shelter and safety from all evils and ills.

The week at Le Caprice came to an end, and the four days at Abbaye aux Bois also, and, in the last hours of their two days at the Abbaye, Lady Dolly said to her daughter:

"To-morrow is the Princes' ball at Félicité, I suppose you remember?"

Vere gave a sign of assent.

"That is the loveliest frock La Ferrière has sent you for it; if you had any heart you would kiss me for such a gown, but you have none, you never will have any."

Vere was silent.

"I must speak to you seriously and for the last time here," said her mother. "We go back to Félicité, and Sergius will want his answer. I can put him off no longer."

"He has had it."

"How?" said Lady Dolly, forgetting for the moment the letter she had burned. "Oh, your letter? Of course he regarded it as a baby's *boutade*; I am sure it was badly worded enough."

---

1   An opera by Beethoven (1805).
2   A monopolizer of women.

"He showed it you then?"

"Yes; he showed it me. It hurt him, of course; but it did not change him," said her mother, a little hurriedly. "Men of his age are not so easily changed. I tell you once for all, Vere, that I shall come to you to-night for the last time for your final word, and I tell you that you must be seen at that ball to-morrow night as the *fiancée* of Zouroff. I am quite resolute, and I will have no more shillyshallying or hesitation."

Vere's face grew warm, and she threw back her head with an eager gesture.

"Hesitation! I have never hesitated for an instant. I tell you, mother, and I have told you a hundred times, I will *not* marry Prince Zouroff."

"You will wear the new gown and you shall have my pearls," pursued her mother, as though she had not heard; "and I shall take care that when you are presented to his Royal Highness he shall know that you are already betrothed to Zouroff; it will be the best way to announce it *nettement*[1] to the world. You will not wear my pearls again, for Zouroff has already ordered yours."

Vere started to her feet.

"And I will stamp them to pieces if he give them to me; and if you tell the Prince of Wales such a thing of me I will tell him the truth and ask his help; he is always kind and good."

"The pearls are ordered," said her mother unmoved: "and you really are too silly for anything. The idea of making the poor Prince a scene!—you have such a passion for scenes, and there is nothing such bad form. I shall come to you to-night after dinner, and let me find you more reasonable."

With that Lady Dolly went out of the room, and out of the house, and went on the sea with her adorers, laughing lightly and singing naughty little chansons[2] not ill. But her heart was not as light as her laugh, and, bold little woman as she was when she had nerved herself to do wrong, her nerves troubled her as she thought the morrow was the last, the very last, day on which she could any longer procrastinate and dally with Serge Zouroff.

"I will go and talk to her," said Lady Stoat, who had driven over from Félicité, when she had been wearied by her dear Dolly's lamentations, until she felt that even her friendship could not bear them much longer.

---

1 Clearly.
2 Songs.

"But she hates him," cried Lady Dolly, for the twentieth time.

"They always *say* that, dear," answered Lady Stoat tranquilly. "They mean it, too, poor little things. It is just as they hated their lessons, yet they did their lessons, dear, and are all the better for having done them. You seem to me to attach sadly too much importance to a child's *boutades*."

"If it were only *boutades*! But you do not know Vere."

"I cannot think, dear, that your child can be so very extraordinarily unlike the rest of the human species," said her friend with her pleasant smile. "Well, I will go and see this young monster. She has always seemed to me a little Puritan, nothing worse, and that you should have been prepared for, leaving her all her life at Bulmer Chase."

Lady Stoat then went upstairs and knocked at the door of Vere's chamber, and entered with the soft, silent charm of movement which was one of the especial graces of that graceful gentlewoman. She kissed the girl tenderly, regardless that Vere drew herself away somewhat rudely, and then sank down in a chair.

"My child, do you know I am come to talk to you quite frankly and affectionately," she said in her gentle, slow voice. "You know what friendship has always existed between your dear mother and myself, and you will believe that your welfare is dear to me for her sake— very dear."

Vere looked at her, but did not speak.

"An uncomfortable girl," thought Lady Stoat, a little discomfited, but she resumed blandly, "Your mamma has brought me some news that it is very pleasant to hear, and gives me sincere happiness, because, by it your happiness, and through yours hers, is secured. My own dear daughter is only two years older than you are, Vere, and she is married, as you know, and ah! so happy!"

"Happy with the Duke of Birkenhead?" said Vere abruptly.

Lady Stoat was, for the moment, a little staggered.

"What a *very* unpleasant child," she thought; "and who would think she knew anything about poor Birk!"

"Very happy," she continued aloud, "and I am charmed to think, my dear, that you have the chance of being equally so. Your mamma tells me, love, that you are a little—a little—bewildered at so brilliant a proposal of marriage as Prince Zouroff's. That is a very natural feeling; of course you had never thought about any such thing."

"I had not thought about it," said Vere bluntly. "I have thought now; but I do not understand why he can want such a thing. He knows very well that I do not like him. If you will tell him for me that I do not I shall be glad; my mother will never tell him plainly enough."

"My sweet Vere!" said Lady Stoat smilingly. "Pray do not give me the mission of breaking my host's heart; I would as soon break his china! Of course your mamma will not tell him anything of the kind. She is charmed, my dear girl, charmed! What better future could she hope for, for you? The Zouroffs are one of the greatest families in Europe, and I am quite sure your sentiments, your jewels, your everything, will be worthy of the exalted place you will fit."

Vere's face grew very cold.

"My mother has sent you?" she said, more rudely than her companion had ever been addressed in all her serene existence. "Then will you kindly go back to her, Lady Stoat, and tell her it is of no use; I will not marry Prince Zouroff."

"That is not very prettily said, my dear. If I am come to talk to you it is certainly in your own interests only. I have seen young girls like you throw all their lives away for mere want of a little reflection."

"I have reflected."

"Reflected as much as sixteen can!—oh yes. But that is not quite what I mean. I want you to reflect, looking through the glasses of my experience and affection, and your mother's. You are very young, Vere."

"Charlotte Corday[1] was almost as young as I am, and Jeanne d'Arc."[2]

Lady Stoat stared, then laughed.

"I don't know where they come, either of them, in our argument, but if they had been married at sixteen it would have been a very good thing for both of them! You are a little girl now, my child, though you are nearly six feet high! You are a *demoiselle à marier*. You can only wear pearls, and you are not even presented. You are no one; nothing. Society has hundreds like you. If you do not marry, people will fancy you are old whilst you are still twenty; people will say of you 'She is getting *passée*;[3] she was out years and years ago.' Yes, they will say it even if you are handsomer than ever, and, what will be worse, you will *begin to feel it*."

Vere was silent, and Lady Stoat thought that she had made some impression.

---

1 During the French Revolution, Charlotte Corday (1768-93) murdered Jean-Paul Marat, leader of the Paris Commune and Jacobin party. She was subsequently beheaded on the guillotine.

2 Joan of Arc (1412-31) sparked the survival of French forces in the Hundred Years War. She was captured by the English and burned at the stake.

3 Faded.

"You will begin to feel it; then you will be glad to marry anybody, and there is nothing more terrible than that. You will take a younger son of a baronet, or a secretary of legation that is going to Hong Kong or Chili—anything, anybody, to get out of yourself, and not to see your own face in the ball-room mirrors. Now, if you marry early, and marry brilliantly—and this marriage is most brilliant—no such terrors will await you; you can wear diamonds, and, oh Vere! till you wear diamonds you do not know what life is!—you can go where you like, as you like, your own mistress; you are *posée*;[1] you have made yourself a power while your contemporaries are still *débutantes*[2] in white frocks; you will have your children, and find all serious interests in them, if you like; you will have all that is best in life, in fact, and have it before you are twenty; you will be painted by Millais[3] and clothed by Worth; you will be a politician if you like, or a fashionable beauty if you like, or only a great lady—perhaps the simplest and best thing of all; and you will be this, and have all this, merely because you married early and married well. My dear, such a marriage is to a girl like being sent on the battle-field to a boy in the army; it is the baptism of fire[4] with every decoration as its rewards!"

"The Cross too?" said Vere.[5]

Lady Stoat, who had spoken eloquently, and, in her own light, sincerely, was taken aback by the irony of the accent and the enigma of the smile. "A most strange child," she thought; "no wonder she worries poor flighty little Pussy!"

"The Cross? Oh, yes," she said. "What answers to the boy's Iron Cross,[6] I suppose, is to dance in the Quadrille d'Honneur[7] at Court. Princesse Zouroff would always be in the Quadrille d'Honneur."

"Princesse Zouroff may be so. I shall not. And it was of the Cross you wear, and profess to worship, that I thought."

Lady Stoat felt a little embarrassed. She bowed her head, and touched the Iona cross in jewels that hung at her throat.

---

1 Established.

2 Young women appearing in society for the first time.

3 John Everett Millais (1829-96) was a British painter of the Pre-Raphaelite School.

4 A soldier's first experience of combat.

5 Reacting to the word "baptism" and her own fear of becoming a martyr if she is "sold" to Zouroff, Vere is referring to Christ's martyrdom.

6 Confused what Vere means by the cross, Lady Stoat continues with her simile of marriage as a battle-field. She is referring to the Cross of the Legion of Honour for heroism in battle.

7 The first dance at a Court ball.

"Darling, those are serious and solemn words. A great marriage may be made subservient, like any other action of our lives, to God's service."

"But surely one ought to love to marry?"

"My dear child, that is an idea; love is an idea; it doesn't last, you know; it is fancy; what is needful is solid esteem—"

Lady Stoat paused; even to her it was difficult to speak of solid esteem for Sergius Zouroff. She took up another and safer line of argument.

"You must learn to understand, my sweet Vere, that life is prose, not poetry; Heaven forbid that I should be one to urge you to any sort of worldliness; but still, truth is everything; truth compels me to point out to you that, in the age we live in, a great position means vast power and ability of doing good, and that is not a thing to be slighted by any wise woman who would make her life beautiful and useful. Prince Zouroff adores you; he can give you one of the first positions in Europe; your mother, who loves you tenderly, though she may seem negligent, desires such a marriage for you beyond all others. Opposition on your part is foolishness, my child, foolishness, blindness, and rebellion."

The face of Vere as she listened lost its childish softness, and grew very cold.

"I understand; my mother does not want me, Mr. Vanderdecken does not want me; this Russian prince is the first who asks for me,—so I am to be sold because he is rich. I will not be sold!"

"What exaggerated language, my love. Pray do not exaggerate; no one uses inflated language now; even on the stage they don't, it has gone out. Who speaks of your being sold, as if you were a slave? *Quelle idée!*[1] A brilliant, a magnificent, alliance is open to you, that is all; every unmarried woman in society will envy you. I assure you if Prince Zouroff had solicited the hand of my own daughter, I would have given it to him with content and joy."

"I have no doubt you would," said the girl curtly.

Lady Stoat's sweet temper rose a little under the words. "You are very beautiful, my dear, but your manners leave very much to be desired," she said almost sharply. "If you were not poor little Dolly's child I should not trouble myself to reason with you, but let you destroy yourself like an obstinate baby as you are. What can be your objection to Prince Sergius? Now be reasonable for once; tell me."

---

1 What a notion!

"I am sure he is a bad man."

"My love! What should you know about bad men, or good ones either?"

"I am sure he is bad—and cruel."

"What nonsense! I am sure he has been charming to you, and you are very ungrateful. What can have given you such an impression of your devoted adorer?"

Vere shuddered a little with disgust.

"*I hate him!*" she said under her breath.

Lady Stoat for a moment was startled.

"Where could she get her melodrama from?" she wondered. "Dolly was never melodramatic; nor any of the Herbert people; it really makes one fancy poor Pussy must have had a *petite faute* [1] with a tragic actor!"

Aloud she answered gently:

"You have a sad habit, my Vere, of using very strong words; it is not nice; and you do not mean one-tenth that you say in your haste. No Christian ever hates, and in a girl such a feeling would be horrible—if you meant it—but you do not mean it."

Vere shut her proud lips closer, but there was a meaning upon them that made her companion hesitate, and feel uncomfortable, and at a loss for words.

"How wonderful that Pussy should ever have had a daughter like this!" she thought, and then smiled in a sweet, mild way.

"Poor Serge! That he should have been the desired of all Europe, only to be rejected by a child of sixteen! Really it is like—who was it?—winning a hundred battles and then dying of a cherry-stone! There is nothing he couldn't give you, nothing he wouldn't give you, you thankless little creature!"

Vere, standing very slender and tall, with her face averted and her fair head in the glow of the sunset light, made no reply; but her attitude and her silence were all eloquent.

Lady Stoat thought to herself, "Dear, dear! what a charming Iphigenia [2] she would look in a theatre; but there is no use for all that in real life. How to convince her?"

---

1 Little affair.

2 In Greek mythology Iphigenia is the tragic daughter of Agamemnon and Clytemnestra. Agamemnon has to sacrifice his daughter to appease Artemis so that a wind would take the Greek ships to Troy. Under the pretence that Iphigenia is to be married to Achilles, Agamemnon summons her to Aulis where she is killed. In other versions, when the sacrifice is about to be made Iphigenia is transported to a city on the Black Sea and an animal is sent in her place.

Even Lady Stoat was perplexed.

She began to talk vaguely and gorgeously of the great place of the Zouroff family in the world; of their enormous estates, of their Uraline mines, of their Imperial favour, of their right to sit covered at certain courts,[1] of their magnificence in Paris, their munificence in Petersburg, their power, their fashion, and their pomp.

Vere waited, till the long discursive descriptions ended of themselves, exhausted by their own oratory. Then she said very simply and very coldly:

"Do you believe in God, Lady Stoat?"

"In God?" echoed Lady Stoat, shocked and amazed.

"Do you or not?"

"My dear! Goodness! Pray do not say such things to me. As if I were an infidel!—*I*!"

"Then how can you bid me take His name in vain, and marry Prince Zouroff?"

"I do not see the connection," began Lady Stoat vaguely, and very wearily.

"I have read the marriage service," said Vere, with a passing heat upon her pale cheeks for a moment.

Lady Stoat for once was silent.

She was very nearly going to reply that the marriage service was of old date and of an exaggerated style; that it was not in good taste, and in no degree to be interpreted literally; but such an avowal was impossible to a woman who revered the ritual of her Church, and was bound to accept it unquestioned. So she was silent and vanquished—so far.

"May I go now?" said Vere.

"Certainly, love, if you wish, but you must let me talk to you again. I am sure you will change and please your mother—your lovely little mother!—whom you ought to *live* for, you naughty child, so sweet and so dear as she is."

"She has never lived for me," thought Vere, but she did not say so; she merely made the deep curtsey she had learned at Bulmer Chase, which had the serene and stately grace in it of another century than her own, and, without another word, passed out of the room.

"*Quel enfant terrible!*" murmured Lady Stoat, with a shiver and a sigh.

---

1   Only certain people could appear in court before a king or queen with a hat on. Appearing "covered" in court indicated that the person was asserting the ancient privilege of his or her family.

Lady Stoat was quite in earnest, and meant well. She knew perfectly that Sergius Zouroff was a man whose vices were such as the world does not care even to name, and that his temper was that of a savage bull-dog allied to the petulant exactions of a spoilt child. She knew that perfectly, but she had known as bad things of her own son-in-law, and had not stayed her own daughter's marriage on that account.

Position was everything, Lady Stoat thought, the man himself nothing. Men were all sadly much alike, she believed. Being a woman of refined taste and pure life, she did not even think about such ugly things as male vice.

Lady Stoat was one of those happy people who only see just so much as they wish to see. It is the most comfortable of all myopisms. She had had, herself, a husband far from virtuous, but she had always turned a deaf ear to all who would have told her of his failings. "I do my own duty; that is enough for me," she would answer sweetly; and, naturally, she wondered why other women could not be similarly content with doing theirs—when they had a Position. Without a position she could imagine, good woman though she was, that things were very trying; and that people worried more. As for herself, she had never worried, and she had no sympathy with worry in any shape. So that when Lady Dolly came to her weeping, excited, furious, hopeless, over her daughter's wicked obstinacy, Lady Stoat only laughed at her in a gentle rallying way.

"You little goose! As if girls were not always like that! She has got Corrèze in her head still, and she is a difficult sort of nature, I grant. What does it matter after all? You only have to be firm. She will come to reason."

"But I never, never could be firm," sobbed Lady Dolly. "The Herberts are, I am not. And Vere is just like her father; when I asked him to have a stole and a rochet[1] and look nice, nothing would induce him, because he said something about his bishop—"

Lady Stoat, in her superior wisdom, smiled once more.

"Was poor Vere so very *low* in the matter of vestments? How curious; the Herberts were Catholic until James the First's time. But why do you fret so? The child is a beauty, really a beauty. Even if she persist in her hatred of Zouroff she will marry well, I am sure; and she must not persist in it. You must have common sense."

"But what can one do?" said Lady Dolly in desperation. "It is all very easy to talk, but it is not such a little thing to force a girl's will

---

1 A vestment of linen resembling a surplice worn by bishops and abbots.

in these days; she can make a fuss, and then society abuses you, and I think the police can even interfere, and the Lord Chancellor if she have no father."

And Lady Dolly sobbed afresh.

"Dear little goose!" said Lady Stoat consolingly, but rather wearied. "Of course nobody uses *force*; but there are a thousand pleasant ways—children never know what is best for them. We, who are their nearest and dearest, must take care of their tender, foolish, ignorant, young lives, committed to us for guidance. Gwendolen even was reluctant—but now in every letter she sends me she says, 'Oh, mamma, how right you were!' That is what your Vera will say to you, darling, a year hence, when she will have been Princess Zouroff long enough to have got used to him."

Lady Dolly shivered a little at all that the words implied.

Her friend glanced at her.

"If Zouroff cause you apprehension for any reason I am unaware of," she said softly; "there are others; though, to be sure, as your pretty child is portionless, it may be difficult—"

"No, it must be Zouroff," said Lady Dolly, nervously and quickly. "She has no money, as you say; and everyone wants money nowadays."

"Except a Russian," said Lady Stoat, with a smile. "Then, since you wish for him, take him now he is to be had. But I would advise you not to dawdle, love. Men like him, if they are denied one fancy soon change to another; and he has all the world to console him for Vere's loss."

"I have told him he should have her answer in a day or two. I said she was shy, timid, too surprised; he seems to like that."

"Of course he likes it. Men always like it in women they mean to make their wives. Then, in a day or two, you must convince her; that is all. I do not say it will be easy with her very obstinate and peculiar temperament. But it will be possible."

Lady Dolly was mute.

She envied her dear Adine that hand of steel under the glove of velvet. She herself had it not. Lady Dolly was of that pliant temper, which, according to the temperature it dwells in, becomes either harmless or worthless. She had nothing of the *maîtresse femme*[1] about her. She was always doing things that she wished were undone, and knotting entanglements that she could not unravel. She was no ruler

---

1 A very capable woman.

of others, except in a coquettish, petulant fashion, of "Jack—and the rest."

And she had that terrible drawback to comfort and impediment to success—a conscience, that was sluggish and fitful, sleepy and feeble, but not wholly dead. Only this conscience, unhappily, was like a very tiny, weak, swimmer stemming a very strong opposing tide.

In a moment or two the swimmer gave over, and the opposing tide had all its own way.

After dinner that evening, whilst the rest were dancing, Vere slipped away unnoticed to her own room, a little tiny turret-room, of which the window almost overhung the sea. She opened the lattice, and leaned out into the cool fragrant night. The sky was cloudless, the sea silvery in the moonlight; from the gardens below there arose the scent of datura and tuberose. It was all so peaceful and so sweet, the girl could not understand why, amidst it all, she must be so unhappy.

Since Zouroff had had her letter there was no longer any hope of changing his resolve by telling him the truth, and a sombre hatred began to grow up in her against this man, who seemed to her her tormentor and her tyrant.

What hurt her most was that her own mother should urge this horror upon her.

She could see no key to the mystery of such a wish except in the fact that her mother cruelly desired to be rid of her at all cost; and she had written a letter to her grandmother at Bulmer Chase—a letter that lay by her on the table ready to go down to the post-bag in the morning.

"Grandmama loves me in her own harsh way," the child thought. "She will take me back for a little time at least, and then, if she do not like to keep me, perhaps I could keep myself in some way; I think I could if they would let me. I might go to the Fräulein in her own country and study music at Baireuth,[1] and make a career of it. There would be no shame in that."

And the thought of Corrèze came softly over her as the memory of fair music will come in a day dream.

Not as any thought of love. She had read no romances save dear Sir Walter's, which alone, of all the erring tribe of fiction, held a place on the dark oak-shelves of the library at Bulmer.

Corrèze was to her like a beautiful fancy rather than a living

---

1 Richard Wagner moved to Bayreuth, Germany, in the 1870s. He had an opera house constructed there for the performance of his operas.

being,—a star that shot across a summer sky and passed unseen to brighter worlds than ours.

He was a saint to the child—he who to himself was a sad sinner—and his word dwelt in her heart like a talisman against all evil.

She sat all alone, and dreamt innocently of going into the mystic German land and learning music in all its heights and depths, and living nobly, and being never wedded ("Oh, never, never!" she said to herself with a burning face and a shrinking heart); and some day meeting Corrèze, the wonder of the world, and looking at him without shame and saying, "I have done as you told me; I have never been burnt in the flame as you feared. Are you glad?"

It did not, as yet, seem hard to her to do so. The world was to her personified in the great vague horror of Serge Zouroff's name, and it cost her no more to repulse it than it costs a child to flee from some painted monster that gapes at it from a wall.

This night, after Lady Stoat's ineffectual efforts at conversion, Lady Dolly herself once more sought her daughter, and renewed the argument with more asperity and more callousness than she had previously shown.

Vere was still in her own chamber, trying to read, but, in truth, always thinking of the bidding of Corrèze, "Keep yourself unspotted from the world."

Dreaming so, with her hands buried in the golden clustering hair, and her lids drooped over her eyes, she started at the voice of her mother; and, with pain and impatience, listened with unwilling ear to the string of reproaches, entreaties, and censure that had lately become as much the burden of her day as the morning-prayer at Bulmer had been, droned by the duchess's dull voice to the sleepy household.

Vere raised herself and listened, with that dutifulness of the old fashion which contrasted so strangely in her, her mother thought, with her rebellion and self-willed character. But she grew very weary.

Lady Dolly, less delicate in her diplomacy than her friend had been, did not use euphuisms[1] at all, nor attempt to take any high moral point. Broadly and unhesitatingly she painted all that Sergius Zouroff had it in his power to bestow, and the text of her endless sermon was, that to reject such gifts was wickedness.

At the close she grew passionate.

"You think of love," she said. "Oh, it is of no use your saying you

---

1 Affected, elegant language.

don't; you do. All girls do. I did. I married your father. We were as much in love as any creatures in a poem. When I had lived a month in that wretched parsonage by the sea, I knew what a little fool I had been. I had had such wedding presents!—*such* presents! The queen had sent me a cachemire for poor papa's sake; yet, down in that horrid place, we had to eat pork, and there was only a metal teapot! Oh, you smile! it is nothing to smile at. Vere used to smile just as you do. He would have taken the cachemire to wrap an old woman up in, very probably; and he wouldn't have known whether he ate a peach or a pig. I knew; and whenever they put that tea in the metal teapot, I knew the cost of young love. Respect your father's memory? Stuff! I am not saying anything against him, poor dear fellow; he was very good—in his way, excellent; but he had made a mistake, and I too. I told him so twenty times a day, and he only sighed and went out to his old women. I tell you this only to show you I know what I am talking about. Love and marriage are two totally different things; they ought never to be named together; they are cat and dog; one kills the other. Pray do not stare so; you make me nervous."

"It is not wicked to love?" said Vere slowly.

"Wicked? no; what nonsense! It amuses one; it doesn't last."

"A great love must last, till death, and after it," said the child, with solemn eyes.

"After it?" echoed Lady Dolly with a little laugh. "I'm afraid that would make a very naughty sort of place of Heaven. Don't look so shocked, child. You know nothing about it. Believe me, dear, where two lovers go on year after year, it is only for Pont de Veyle's reason to Madame de Deffand: "Nous sommes si mortellement ennuyes l'un de l'autre que nous ne pouvons plus nous quitter!"[1]

Vere was silent. Her world of dreams was turned upside down, and shaken rudely.

"You have no heart, Vere; positively none," said her mother bitterly, resuming all the old argument. "I can scarcely think you are my child. You see me wearing myself to a shadow for your sake, and yet you have no pity. What in heaven's name can you want? You are only sixteen, and one of the first marriages in Europe opens to you. You ought to go on your knees in thankfulness, and yet you hesitate?"

---

1 "We are so mortally bored with one another that we can no longer leave each other." Madame Chamroud de Deffand (Marie de Vichy) (1697–1780) was a woman of letters and a scandalous figure in French society. She left her husband and became the mistress of many men. Pont de Veyle was one of her lovers.

"I do not hesitate at all," said Vere quickly. "I refuse!"

She rose as she spoke, and looked older by ten years. There was a haughty resolve in her attitude that cowed her mother for an instant. "I refuse," she said again. "And, if you will not tell Monsieur Zouroff so yourself, I will tell him tomorrow. Listen, mother, I have written to Bulmer, and I will go back there. Grandmama will not refuse to take me in. I shall be a trouble and care to you no longer. I am not made for your world nor it for me. I will go. I have some talent, they have always said, and at least I have perseverance. I will find some way of maintaining myself. I want so little, and I know enough of music to teach it; and so at least I shall be free and no burden upon anyone."

She paused, startled by her mother's laughter; such laughter as she, in a later day, heard from Croizette when Croizette was acting her own deathbed on the stage of the Français.[1]

Lady Dolly's shrill, unnatural, ghastly laughter echoed through the room.

"Is that your scheme? To teach music? And Corrèze to teach you, I suppose? *O la belle idée!*[2] You little fool! you little idiot! how dare you? Because you are mad, do you think we are mad too? Go to Bulmer *now*? Never! I am your mother, and you shall do what I choose. What I choose is that you shall marry Zouroff."

"I will not."

"Will not? will not? I say you shall!"

"And I say that I will not."

They confronted one another; the girl's face pale, clear and cold in its fresh and perfect beauty, the woman's grown haggard, fevered, and fierce in its artificial prettiness.

"I will not," repeated Vere with her teeth closed. "And my dead father would say I was right; and I will tell this man to-morrow that I loathe him; and, since surely he must have some pride to be stung, he will ask for me no more then."

"Vere! you kill me!" screamed her mother; and, in truth, she fainted, her pretty curly perruque twisting off her head, her face deathly pallid save for the unchanging bloom of cheek and mouth.

It was but a passing swoon, and her maid soon restored her to semi-consciousness and then bore her to her room.

"What a cold creature is that child," thought Adrienne, of Vere.

---

1 Sophie Alexandrine Croizette (1847-1901) appeared often on the stage of the Theatre Français in Paris.

2 Oh, what a beautiful notion!

"She sees miladi insensible, and stands there with never a tear, or a kiss, or a cry. What it is to have been brought up in England!"

Vere left alone, sat awhile lost in thought, leaning her head on her hands. Then she rang and bade them post the letter to Bulmer; the dark and drearsome, but safe and familiar home of her lost childhood.

The letter gone, she undressed and went to bed. It was midnight. She soon was asleep.

Innocent unhappiness soon finds this rest; it is the sinful sorrow of later years that stares, with eyes that will not close, into the hateful emptiness of night.

She slept deeply and dreamlessly, the moonbeams through the high window finding her out where she lay, her slender limbs, supple as willow wands, in calm repose, and her long lashes lying on her cheeks.

Suddenly she woke, startled and alarmed. A light fell on her eyes; a hand touched her; she was no longer alone.

She raised herself in her bed, and gazed with a dazzled sight and vague terror into the yellow rays of the lamp.

"Vere! It is I! it is I!" cried her mother with a sob in her voice. And Lady Dolly dropped on her knees beside the bed; her real hair dishevelled on her shoulders, her face without false bloom and haggard as the face of a woman of twice her own years.

"Vere, Vere! you can save me," she muttered with her hands clasped tight on the girl's. "Oh, my dear, I never thought to tell you; but, since you will hear no reason, what can I do? Vere, wake up—listen. I am a guilty, silly woman; guiltier, sillier, than you can dream. You are my child after all, and owe me some obedience; and you can save me. Vere, Vere! do not be cruel; do not misjudge me, but listen. You *must* marry Sergius Zouroff."

It was dawn when Lady Dolly crept away from her daughter's chamber; shivering, ashamed, contrite, in so far as humiliation and regret make up contrition; hiding her blanched face with the hood of her wrapper as though the faint, white rays of daybreak were spectators and witnesses against her.

Vere lay quite still, as she had fallen, upon her bed, her face upturned, her hands clenched, her shut lips blue as with great cold. She had promised what her mother had asked.

CHAPTER IX.

On the morrow it was known to all the guests of the house at which they were staying that the head of the Princes Zouroff was to marry the daughter of the Lady Dorothy Vanderdecken.

On the morrow Lady Dolly drove back to Félicité, with her daughter beside her.

She was victorious.

The sun was strong, and the east wind cold; she was glad they were so. The eyes of her daughter were heavy with dark circles beneath them, and her face was blanched to a deadly pallor, which changed to a cruel crimson flush as the turrets and belfries of the château of the Zouroffs came in sight above the woods of its park.

They had driven the eight miles from Le Caprice in unbroken silence.

"If she would only speak!" thought Lady Dolly; and yet she felt that she could not have borne it if her companion had spoken.

They drove round to a *petit entré*[1] at the back of the house, and were met by no one but some bowing servants. She had begged in a little note that it might be so, making some pretty plea for Vere of maiden shyness. They were shown straight to their rooms. It was early; noonday. The château was quite still. At night the great ball was to be given to the English princes, but the household was too well trained to make any disturbance with their preparations. Down the steps of the great terrace there was stretched scarlet cloth, and all the face of the building was hung with globes and cressets of oil, to be lit at dark. These were the only outward signs that anything more brilliant than usual was about to take place.

"You will come to breakfast?" said Lady Dolly, pausing at the threshold of her room.

It was the first word she had said to Vere since the dawn, when they had parted, and her own voice sounded strange to her.

Vere shuddered as with cold.

"I cannot. Make some excuse."

"What is the use of putting off?" said her mother fretfully. "You will be ill; you are ill. If you should be ill to-night, what will every-one say? what will he think? what shall I do?"

Vere went into her chamber and locked her door. She locked out even her maid; flung her hat aside, and threw herself forward on the bed, face downward, and there lay.

Lady Dolly went into her chamber, and glanced at her own face with horror. Though made up, as well as usual for the day, she looked yellow, worn, old.

"*I* must go down!" she thought—how selfish youth was, and how

---

1 Small entrance hall.

hard a thing was motherhood! She had herself dressed beautifully and took some ether.

She had sunk her drowned conscience fathoms deep, and begun once more to pity herself for the obstinacy and oddness of the child to whom she had given birth. Why could not the girl be like any others?

The ether began to move in her veins and swim in her head; her eyes grew brighter. She went out of her room and along the corridor to the staircase, fastening an autumn rose or two in her breast, taken from the bouquet of her dressing-table. As she glanced down the staircase into the hall where the servants in the canary-coloured liveries of the house were going to and fro, she thought of all the rank and riches of which Félicité was only one trifling portion and symbol, and thought to herself that—after all—any mother would have done as she had done; and no maiden surely could need a higher reward for the gift of her innocence to the minotaur[1] of a loveless marriage.

"If I had been married like that!" she thought; and felt that she had been cruelly wronged by destiny; if she had been married like that, how easy it would have been to become a good woman! What could Vere complain of?—the marriage was perfect in a worldly sense, and in any other sense—did it matter what it was?

So the ether whispered to her.

She began to taste the sweets of her victory and to forget the bitter, as the ether brought its consoling haze over all painful memories, and lent its stimulating brightness to all personal vanities.

After all it was very delightful to go down those stairs, knowing that when she met all those dear female friends whom she detested, and who detested her, no one could pity her and everyone must envy her. She had betrothed her daughter to one of the richest and best born men in all Europe. Was it not the crown of maternity, as maternity is understood in society?

So down she went, and crossed the great vestibule, looking young, fair, bewitching with the roses in her bosom, and an admirably chosen expression on her face, half glad and half plaintive, and with a flush under her paint that made her look prettier than ever; her eyes sparkled, her smile was all sunshine and sweetness, she pressed the

---

1 In classical mythology the minotaur is a monster that has the head of a bull and the body of a man. He lives in the labyrinth and feeds on human flesh; the word also refers to any person or thing that devours or destroys. Zouroff is later referred to as *the* Minotaur.

hands of her most intimate friends with an eloquent tenderness, she was exquisitely arrayed with cascades of old Mechlin[1] falling from her throat to her feet.

"A mother only lives to be young again in her child!" she said softly—and knew that she looked herself no more than twenty years old as she said it.

Sergius Zouroff, profuse in delicate compliment to her aloud, said to himself:

"*Brava*, naughty Dolly! *Bis-bis!*[2] Will she ever be like you, I wonder? Perhaps. The world makes you all alike after a little while."

He was ready to pay a high price for innocence, because it was a new toy that pleased him. But he never thought that it would last, any more than the bloom lasts on the peach. He had no illusions. Since it would be agreeable to brush it off himself, he was ready to purchase it.

There was a sense of excitement and of disappointment in the whole house party; and Princesse Nelaguine ran from one to another, with her little bright Tartar[3] eyes all aglow, murmuring, "*Charmée, charmée, charmée!*"[4] to impatient ears.

"Such a beast as he is!" said the men who smoked his cigars and rode his horses.

"And she who looked all ice and innocence!" said the women, already in arms against her.

Vere did not come down to taste the first-fruits of her triumph.

At the great midday breakfast, where most people assembled, she was absent. Zouroff himself laid another bouquet of orchids by her plate, but she was not there to receive the delicate homage.

"Mademoiselle Vera has not risen?" he asked now, with an angry contraction of his low brows, as no one came where the orchids were lying.

"Vera had a headache," said Lady Dolly serenely aloud. "Or said so," she murmured to his ear alone. "Don't be annoyed. She was shy. She is a little *farouche*,[5] you know, my poor darling."

Zouroff nodded, and took his caviare.

"What did I predict, love!" murmured Lady Stoat, of Stichley, taking her friend aside after breakfast. "But how quickly you succeeded!

---

1 French lace.
2 Here. Here!
3 Russian.
4 Delightful!
5 Unsociable.

Last evening only you were in despair! Was the resistance only a feint? Or what persuasions did you bring to bear?"

"I threatened to send her to Bulmer Chase!" said Lady Dolly with a little gay laugh. Lady Stoat laughed also.

"I wonder what you did do," she reflected, however, as she laughed. "Oh, naughty little Pussy—foolish, foolish little Pussy!—to have any secrets from *me*!"

The day wore away and Vere Herbert remained unseen in Félicité.

The guests grew surprised, and the host angered.

Princesse Nelaguine herself had ascended to the girl's room, and had been denied.

People began to murmur that it was odd.

"Go and fetch her," said Zouroff in a fierce whisper. "It is time that I at least should see her—unless you have told me a lie."

"Unless she be really ill, I suppose you mean, you cruel creature!" said her mother reproachfully; but she obeyed him and went.

"Girls are so fond of tragedy!" reflected Lady Stoat, recalling episodes in the betrothal of her own daughter, and passages that had preceded it.

It was now five o'clock. The day had been chilly, as it is at times along the channel shores, even in summer. Several persons were in the blue-room, so called because of its turquoise silk walls and its quantities of Delf, Nankin, Savona, and other blue china ranged there. It was the room for afternoon tea. Several of the ladies were there in tea-gowns of the quaintest and prettiest, that allowed them to lie about in the most gracefully tired attitudes. The strong summer sun found its way only dimly there, and the sweet smells of the flowers and of the sea were overborne by the scent of the pastilles burning in the bodies of blue china monsters.

Zouroff, who at times was very negligent of his guests, was pacing up and down the long dim chamber impatiently, and every now and then he glanced at the door. He did not look once at the pretty groups, like eighteenth century pictures tinged with the languor of odalisques,[1] that were sipping tea out of tiny cups in an alcove lined with celadon and crackling.[2] The tinkle of the tea-cups and the ripple of the talk ceased as the door at the farther end opened, and Vere entered, led by her mother.

---

1 Concubines in a harem were a favorite subject of nineteenth-century European artists. J.A.D. Ingres (1780-1867) and Henri Matisse (1869-1954) painted several odalisques.
2 Pottery.

She was white, and cold, and still; she did not raise her eyelids.

Zouroff approached with eager steps, and bowed before her with the dignity that he could very well assume when he chose.

"Mademoiselle," he said softly, "is it true that you consent to make the most unworthy of men the most happy?"

He saw a slight shudder pass over her as if some cold wind had smitten her.

She did not lift her eyes.

"Since you wish, monsieur—" she answered very low, and then paused.

"The adoration of a life shall repay you," he murmured in the conventional phrase, and kissed her hand.

In his own thoughts he said: "Your mother had made you do this, and you hate me. Never mind."

Then he drew her hand on his arm, and led her to the Princess Nelaguine.

"My sister, embrace your sister. I shall have two angels henceforth, instead of one, to watch and pray for my erring soul!"

Princess Nelaguine did not smile. She kissed the cold cheek of the girl with a glisten of tears in her eyes.

"What a sacrifice! what martyrdom!" she thought. "Ah, the poor child!—but perhaps he will *ranger*[1]—let us hope."

All the while Vera might have been made of marble, she was so calm and so irresponsive, and she never once lifted her eyes.

"Will you not look at me once?" he entreated. She raised her lids and gave him one fleeting hunted glance. Cruel though he was and hardened, Sergius Zouroff felt that look go to his soul.

"Bah! how she loathes me!" he said in his teeth. But the compassion in him died out almost as it was born, and the base appetites in him were only whetted and made keener by this knowledge.

Lady Stoat glided towards them and lifted her lips to Vera's cheek.

"My sweet child! so charmed, so delighted," she whispered. "Did I not say how it would be when your first shyness had time to fold its tents, as the poem says, and steal away?"[2]

"You are always a prophetess of good—and my mother's friend," said Vere. They were almost the first words she had spoken, and they chilled even the worldly breast of her mother's friend.

There was an accent in them which told of a childhood perished

---

1 Settle down.

2 From "The Day is Done," (1845) by Henry Wadsworth Longfellow:
   "And the nights shall be filled with music, / And the cares that infest the day / Shall fold their tents like the Arabs, / And as silently steal away."

in a night; of an innocence and a faith stabbed, and stricken, and buried for ever more.

"You are only sixteen, and you will never be young any more!" thought Princess Nelaguine, hearing the cold and bitter accent of those pregnant words.

But the ladies that made the eighteenth century picture had broken up and issued from the alcove, and were offering congratulations and compliments in honeyed phrases; and no one heeded or had time for serious thought.

Only Lady Dolly, in a passionate murmur, cried, unheeded by any, to her daughter's ear:

"For heaven's sake smile, blush, seem happy! What will they say of you to look at you like this?—they will say that I coerce you!"

"I do my best," answered Vere coldly.

"My lovely mother-in-law," muttered Prince Zouroff, bending to Lady Dolly, as he brought her a cup of tea, "certainly you did not lie to me this morning when you told me that your Vera would marry me; but did you not lie—just a little lie, a little white one—when you said she would love me?"

"Love comes in time," murmured Lady Dolly hurriedly.

Serge Zouroff laughed grimly.

"Does it? I fear that experience tells one rather that with time— it goes."

"Yours may; hers will come—the woman's always comes last."

"*Ma chère!* your new theories are astounding. Nevertheless, as your son-in-law, I will give my adhesion to them. Henceforth all the sex of your Vera—and yourself—is purity and perfection in my sight!"

Lady Dolly smiled sweetly in his face.

"It is never too late to be converted to the truth," she said playfully, whilst she thought, "Oh you beast! If I could strangle you!"

Meanwhile, Princess Nelaguine was saying with kindness in her tone and gaze:

"My sweet child, you look chilly and pale. Were you wise to leave your room out of goodness to us?"

"I am cold," murmured Vere faintly. "I should be glad if I might go away—for a little."

"Impossible," said the Princess; and added. "Dear, reflect; it will look so strange to people. My brother—"

"I will stay then," said Vere wearily, and she sat down and received the homage of one and the felicitations of another, still with her eyes always cast downward, still with her young face passionless, and chill as a mask of marble.

"An hour's martyrdom more or less—did it matter?" she said to herself. All her life would be a martyrdom, a long mute martyrdom, now.

A few hours later her maid dressed her for the ball. She had no need of her mother's pearls, for those which had been ordered from Paris jewellers were there; the largest and purest pearls that ever Indian diver plunged for into the deep sea. When they were clasped about her they seemed to her in no way different, save in their beauty, to the chains locked on slave-girls bought for the harem. But that was because she had been taught such strange ideas.

She was quite passive.

She resisted nothing; having given way in the one great thing, why should she dispute or rebel for trifles? A sense of unreality had come upon her, as it comes on people in the first approach of fever.

She walked, sat, spoke, heard, all as in a dream. It seemed to her as if she were already dead: only the pain was alive in her, the horrible sickening pain that would never be stilled, but only grow sharper and deeper with each succeeding hour.

She sat through the banquet, and felt all eyes upon her, and was indifferent. Let them stare as they would, as they would stare at the sold slave-girl.

She has too much self-possession for such a child, said the women there, and they thought that Sergius Zouroff would not find in her the young saint that he fancied he had won.

Her beauty was only greater for her extreme pallor and the darkness beneath her eyes. But it was no longer the beauty of an innocent unconscious child; it was that of a woman.

Now and then she glanced at her mother, at that pretty coquettish little figure, semi-nude, as fashion allowed, and with diamonds sparkling everywhere on her snow-white skin; with a perpetual laugh on cherubic lips, and gaiety and grace in each movement. And whenever she glanced there, a sombre scornful fire came into her own gaze, an unutterable contempt and disgust watched wearily from the fair windows of her soul.

She was thinking to herself as she looked: Honour thy father and thy mother. That was the old law! Were there such women then as she was now? Or was that law too a dead letter, as the Marriage Sacrament was?

"She is exquisitely lovely," said the great personage in whose honour the banquet and the ball were being given. "In a year or two there will be nothing so beautiful as she will be in all Europe. But—is she well—is she happy? Forgive the question."

"Oh, sir, she is but made nervous by the honour of your praise," said her mother, who was the person addressed. "Your Royal Highness is too kind to think of her health, it is perfect; indeed I may say, without exaggeration, that neither morally nor physically has my sweet child given me one hour's anxiety since her birth."

The Prince bowed, and said some pleasant gracious words; but his conviction remained unchanged by Lady Dolly's assurance of her daughter's peace and joy.

Vere was led out by Prince Zouroff to join the Quadrille d'Honneur.

"This is the Iron Cross!" she thought, and a faint bitter smile parted her lips.

She never once lifted her eyes to meet his.

"Cannot you tell me you are happy, *mon enfant*," he murmured once. She did not look at him, and her lips scarcely moved as she answered him.

"I obey my mother, monsieur. Do not ask more."

Zouroff was silent. The dusky red of his face grew paler; he felt a momentary instinct to tear his pearls off her, and bid her to be free; then the personal loveliness of her awoke too fiercely that mere appetite which is all that most men and many women know of love; and his hands clenched close on hers in the slow figure of the dance.

A stronger admiration than he had ever felt for her rose in him, too. He knew the bitterness and the revolt that were in her, yet he saw her serene, cold, mistress of herself. It was not the childlike simplicity that he had once fancied that he loved her for, but it was a courage he respected, a quality he understood. "One might send her to Siberia and she would change to ice; she would not bend," he thought, and the thought whetted his passion to new fierceness and tenacity.

The ball was gorgeous; the surprises were brilliant and novel; the gardens were illumined to the edge of the sea till the fishers out in the starry night thought the shore was all on fire. The great persons in whose honour it was, were gratified and amused—the grace and grandeur of the scene were like old days of Versailles or of Venice.

The child moved amidst it, with the great pearls lying on her throat and encircling her arms, and her eyes had a blind unconscious look in them like those of eyes that have recently lost their sight, and are not yet used to the eternal darkness.

But she spoke simply and well, if seldom; she moved with correct grace in the square dance; she made her perfect courtesy with the eighteenth century stateliness in it; all men looked, and wondered, and praised her, and women said with a sigh of envy, "Only sixteen!"

Only sixteen; and she might have said as the young emperor[1] said, when he took his crown, "O my youth, O my youth! farewell!"

Once her mother had the imprudence to speak to her; she whispered in her ear:

"Are you not rewarded, love? Are you not content?"

Vere looked at her.

"I have paid your debt. Be satisfied."

A great terror passed like a cold wind, over the little selfish, cruel, foolish woman, and she trembled.

The next morning a message came to her from her old Northumbrian home.

"My house must always be open for my dead son's child, and my protection, such as it is, will always be hers."

It was signed Sarah Mull and Cantire.

Vere read it, sitting before her glass in the light of the full day, whilst her woman undid the long ropes of pearls that were twisted about her fair hair. Two slow tears ran down her cheeks and fell on the rough paper of the telegram.

"She loves me!" she thought, "and what a foolish, fickle, sinning creature I shall for ever seem to her!"

Then, lest with a moment's longer thought her firmness should fail her, she wrote back in answer: "You are so good, and I am grateful. But I see that it is best that I should marry as my mother wished. Pray for me."

The message winged its way fleeter than a bird, over the grey sea to where the northern ocean beat the black Northumbrian rocks; and an old woman's heart was broken with the last pang of a sad old age.

A day or two later the house-party of Félicité broke up, and the château by the Norman sea was left to its usual solitude. Lady Stoat went to stay with her daughter, the Lady Birkenhead, who was at Biarritz, and would go thence to half-a-dozen great French and English houses. Prince Zouroff and his sister went to Tsarsko Selo,[2] as it was necessary for him to see his emperor, and Lady Dolly took her daughter straight to Paris.

Paris, in the commencement of autumn was a desert, but she had

---

1 Franz Joseph [Ouida's note]. Franz Joseph I (1830-1916) became Emperor of Austria in 1848, when he was 18 years old.

2 A city south of Leningrad where one of the main summer palaces of the Russian royal family was located.

a pretty apartment in the Avenue Joséphine. The marriage was fixed to take place in November, and two months was not too much for all the preparations which she needed to make. Besides, Lady Dolly preferred that her daughter should see as few persons as possible. What was she afraid of?—she scarcely knew. She was vaguely afraid of everything. She was so used to breaking her words that a child's promise seemed to her a thing as slight as a spider's gossamer shining in the dew.

It was safest, she fancied, for Vere to see no one, and to a member of the great world there is no solitude so complete as a city out of its season. So she shut Vere in her gilded, and silvered, and over-decorated, and over-filled, rooms in the Avenue Joséphine, and kept her there stifled and weary, like a woodland bird hung in a cage in a boudoir; and never let the girl take a breath of air save by her side in her victoria out in the Bois in the still, close evenings. Vere made no opposition to anything. When St. Agnes gave her young body and her fair soul up to torment, did she think of the shape of the executioner's sword?[1]

Lady Dolly was at this time much worried too about her own immediate affairs. Jura was gone to India on a hunting and shooting tour with two officers of his old regiment, and he had written very briefly to say so to her, not mentioning any period for his return. He meant to break it all off, thought Lady Dolly, with an irritated humiliation rankling in her. Two years before she would have been *Didone infuriata*;[2] but time tempers everything, and there were always consolations. The young dandy who had won the Grand Prix was devoted and amusing; it could not be said that Jura had been either of late. She had got used to him, and she had not felt it necessary to be always *en beauté*[3] for him, which was convenient. Besides there were heaps of things he had got into the way of doing for her, and he knew all her habits and tastes; losing him was like losing a careful and familiar servant. Still she was not inconsolable. He had grown boorish and stupid in the last few months; and, though he knew thousands of her secrets, he was a gentleman—they were safe with him, as safe as the letters she had written him.

---

1 At age 12, St. Agnes, a Christian convert, refused marriage. She would have no spouse but Jesus Christ. She died for her faith during the reign of Diocletian (A.D. 284–305).
2 Dido raging. Dido, Queen of Carthage, grieves passionately after Aeneas abandoned her.
3 Look her best.

But her vanity was wounded.

"Just because of that child's great grey eyes!—" she thought angrily.

Classic Clytemnestra, when murdered by her son, makes a grander figure certainly, but she is not perhaps more deeply wounded than fashionable Faustina when eclipsed by her daughter.[1]

"You look quite worn, poor Pussy!" said Lady Stoat tenderly, as she met her one day in Paris. "When you ought to be so pleased and so proud!"

Lady Stoat, who was very ingenious and very penetrating, left no means untried by which to fathom the reasons of the sudden change of Vere. Lady Stoat read characters too well not to know that neither caprice nor malleability were the cause of it.

"She has been coerced; but how?" she thought; and brought her microscope of delicate investigation and shrewd observation to bear upon the subject. But she could make nothing of it.

"I do what my mother wishes," Vere answered her, and answered her nothing more.

"If you keep your secrets as well when you are married," thought Lady Stoat, "you will be no little trouble to your husband, my dear."

Aloud, of course she said only:

"*So* right, darling, so very right. Your dear little mother has had a great deal of worry in her life; it is only just that she should find full compensation in you. And I am quite sure you will be happy, Vere. You are so clever and serious; you will have a *salon*,[2] I dare say, and get all the politicians about you. That will suit you better than frivolity, and give you an aim in society. Without an aim, love, society is sadly like playing cards for counters.[3] One wants a lover to meet, a daughter to chaperone, a cause to advance, a something beside the mere pleasure of showing oneself. You will never have the lover I am sure, and you cannot have the daughter just yet; so, if I were you, I would take the cause—it does not matter what cause in the least— say England against Russia or Russia against England; but throw yourself into it, and it will amuse you, and it will be a safeguard to you from the dangers that beset every beautiful young wife in the world. It is a melancholy thing to confess, and a humiliating one, but

---

1   In Greek mythology Orestes avenges his father's death (who is murdered by his mother Clytemnestra and her lover) by killing Clytemnestra.
    Faustina the Younger, wife of Marcus Aurelius, was apparently slightly more beautiful than her mother, Faustina the Elder.

2   A gathering of people of social or intellectual distinction.

3   Imitation coins.

all human beings are so made that they never can go on playing only for counters!"

And Lady Stoat, smiling her sweetest, went away from Vere with more respect than she had ever felt before for feather-headed little Pussy, since Pussy had been able to do a clever thing unaided, and had a secret that her friend did not know.

"Foolish Pussy!" thought her friend Adine. "Oh, foolish Pussy, to have a secret from *me*. And it takes such a wise head and such a long head to have a secret! It is as dangerous as a packet of dynamite to most persons."

Aloud to Lady Dolly she said only:

"So glad, dear love, oh *so* glad! I was quite sure with a little reflection the dear child would see the wisdom of the step we wished her to take. It is such an anxiety off your mind; a girl with you in the season would have harassed you terribly. Really I do not know which is the more wearing: an heiress that one is afraid every moment will be got at by some spendthrift, or a dear little penniless creature that one is afraid will never marry at all; and, with Vere's peculiar manners and notions, it might have been very difficult. Happily, Zouroff has only admired her lovely classic head, and has never troubled himself about what is inside it. I think she will be an astonishment to him—rather. But, to be sure, after six months in the world, she will change as they all do."

"Vere will never change," said Lady Dolly irritably, and with a confused guilty little glance at her friend. "Vere will always be half an angel and half an imbecile as long as ever she lives."

"Imbeciles are popular people," said Lady Stoat with a smile. "As for angels, no one cares for them much about modern houses, except in terra cotta."[1]

"It is not *you* who should say so," returned Lady Dolly tenderly.

"Oh, my dear!" answered her friend with a modest sigh of deprecation. "I have no pretensions—I am only a poor, weak, and very imperfect creature. But one thing I may really say of myself, and that is, that I honestly love young girls and do my best for them; and I think not a few have owed their life's happiness to me. May your Vere be of the number!"

"I don't think she will ever be happy," said Lady Dolly impatiently, with a little confused look of guilt. "She doesn't care a bit about dress."

---

1 Hand-fired clay sculptures.

"That is a terrible *lacune*[1] certainly," assented Lady Stoat with a smile. "Perhaps, instead, she will take to politics—those serious girls often do—or perhaps she will care about her children."

Lady Dolly gave a little shudder. What was her daughter but a child? It seemed only the other day that the little fair baby had tumbled about among the daisies on the vicarage lawn, and poor dead Vere in his mellow gentle voice had recited, as he looked at her, the glorious lines to his child of Coleridge.[2] How wretched she had been then!—how impatient of the straitened means, the narrow purse, the country home, the calm religious life! How wretched she would have been now could she have gone back to it! Yet, with the contradiction of her sex and character, Lady Dolly for a moment wished with all her soul that she had never left that narrow home, and that the child were now among the daisies.

One day, when they were driving down the Avenue Marigny, her mother pointed out to Vere a row of lofty windows *au premier*,[3] with their shutters shut, but with gorgeous autumn flowers hanging over their gilded balconies; the liveried *suisse*[4] was yawning in the doorway.

"That is where your Faust-Romeo lives," said Lady Dolly, who could never bring herself to remember the proverb, let sleeping dogs lie. "It is full of all kinds of beautiful things, and queer ancient things too; he is a connoisseur in his way, and everybody gives him such wonderful presents. He is making terrible scandal just now with the young Grand-Duchess. Only to think of what you risked that day boating with him makes one shudder! You might have been compromised for life!"

Vere's proud mouth grew very scornful, but she made no reply.

Her mother looked at her and saw the scorn.

"Oh, you don't believe me?" she said irritably; "ask anybody! an hour or two alone with a man like that ruins a girl's name for ever. Of course it was morning, and open air, but still Corrèze is one of those persons a woman *can't* be *seen* with, even!"

Vere turned her head and looked back at the bright balconies with their hanging flowers; then she said with her teeth shut and her lips turning white:

"I do not speak to you of Prince Zouroff's character. Will you be so good as not to speak to me of that of M. de Corrèze."

---

1 Deficiency.
2 "Frost at Midnight." See lines 44–75.
3 On the second floor.
4 Hall porter.

Her mother was startled and subdued. She wished she had not woke the sleeping dog.

"If she be like that at sixteen what will she be at six-and-twenty?" she thought. "She puts them in opposition already!"

Nevertheless, she never again felt safe, and whenever she drove along the Avenue Marigny she looked up at the house with the gilded balconies and hanging flowers to be sure that it gave no sign of life.

It did not occur to her that whatever Vere might be at six-and-twenty would be the result of her own teaching, actions, and example. Lady Dolly had reasoned with herself that she had done right after all; she had secured a magnificent position for her daughter, was it not the first duty of a mother?

If Vere could not be content with that position, and all its compensations, if she offended heaven and the world by any obstinate passions or imprudent guilt, if she, in a word, with virtue made so easy and so gilded, should not after all be virtuous, it would be the fault of Bulmer, the fault of society, the fault of Zouroff, the fault of Corrèze, or of some other man, perhaps,—never the fault of her mother.

When gardeners plant and graft, they know very well what will be the issue of their work; they do not expect the rose from a bulb of garlic, or look for the fragrant olive from a slip of briar; but the culturers of human nature are less wise, and they sow poison, yet rave in reproaches when it breeds and brings forth its like. "The rosebud garden of girls"[1] is a favourite theme for poets, and the maiden, in her likeness to a half-opened blossom, is as near purity and sweetness as a human creature can be, yet what does the world do with its opening buds?—it thrusts them in the forcing house amidst the ordure, and then, if they perish prematurely, never blames itself. The streets absorb the girls of the poor; society absorbs the daughters of the rich; and not seldom one form of prostitution, like the other, keeps its captives "bound in the dungeon of their own corruption."[2]

---

1 In Tennyson's "Maud," (1855) the speaker refers to Maud as "Queen rose of the rosebud garden of girls" as he waits for her to join him in the garden (Part I, XXII, 902).

2 From John Ruskin's *The Two Paths*, Lecture 1, January 1858. He is referring to Indian art, which, "never represents a natural fact.... Over the whole spectacle of creation they have thrown a veil in which there is no rent. For them no star peeps through the blanket of the dark—for them neither their heaven shines nor their mountains rise—for them the flowers do not blossom—for them the creatures of field and forest do not live. They lie bound in the dungeon of their own corruption...."

CHAPTER X.

It was snowing in Vienna. Snow lay heavy on all the plains and roads around, and the Danube was freezing fast.

"It will be barely colder in Moscow," said Corrèze, with a shiver, as he threw his furs about him and left the opera-house amidst the frantic cheers and adoring outcries of the crowd without, after his last appearance in *Romeo e Giulietta*.[1] In the bitter glittering frosty night a rain of hothouse flowers fell about him; he hated to see them fall; but his worshippers did not know that, and would not have heeded it if they had. Roses and violets, hyacinth and white lilac, dropped at his feet, lined his path and carpeted his carriage as if it were April in the south, instead of November in Austria.

His hand had just been pressed by an emperor's, a ring of brilliants beyond price had just been slid on his finger by an empress; the haughtiest aristocracy of the world had caressed him and flattered him and courted him; he was at the supreme height of fame, and influence, and fashion, and genius; yet, as he felt the roses and the lilies fall about him he said restlessly to himself:

"When I am old and nobody heeds me, I shall look back to this night, and such nights as this, as to a lost heaven; why, in heaven's name, cannot I enjoy it now?"

But enjoyment is not to be gained by reflecting that to enjoy is our duty, and neither the diamonds nor the roses did he care for, nor did he care for the cheers of the multitude that stood out under the chill brilliant skies for the chance of seeing him pass down the streets. It is a rare and splendid royalty, too, that of a great singer; but he did not care for its crowns. The roses made him think of a little hedge-rose gathered by a sweetbriar bush on a cliff by a grey quiet sea.

With such odd caprices does Fate often smite genius.

He drove to the supper-table of a very great lady, beautiful as the morning; and he was the idol of the festivity which was in his honour; and the sweet eyes of its mistress told him that no audacity on his part would be deemed presumption—yet it all left him careless and almost cold. She had learned Juliet's part by heart, but he had forgotten Romeo's—had left it behind him in the opera-house with his old Venetian velvets and lace.

---

1 *Romeo and Juliet* (1867) is an opera by Charles François Gounod. Corrèze sang a song from it in Chapter III. In the mid-nineteenth century, operas were performed in Italian despite the language of the world première performance, in this case, French.

From that great lady's, whom he left alone with a chill heart, empty and aching, he went with his comrades to the ball of the Elysium[1] down in the subterranean vaults of the city, where again and again in many winters he had found contagion in the elastic mirth and the buoyant spirit of the clean-limbed, bright-eyed children of the populace, dancing and whirling and leaping far down under the streets to the Styrian[2] music. But it did not amuse him this night; nor did the dancers tempt him; the whirl and the glow and the noise and the mirth seemed to him tedious and stupid.

"Decidedly that opera tires me," he said to himself, and thought that his weariness came from slaying Tybalt and himself on the boards of the great theatre. He told his friends and adorers with petulance to let him be still, he wanted to sleep, and the dawn was very cold. He went home to his gorgeous rooms in a gorgeous hôtel, and lit his cigar and felt tired. The chambers were strewn with bouquets, wreaths, presents, notes; and amidst the litter was a great gold vase, a fresh gift from the emperor, with its two *rilievi*, telling the two stories of Orpheus and of Amphion.[3]

But Corrèze did not look twice at it. He looked instead at a French journal, which he had thrown on his chair when his servant had roused him at seven that evening, saying that it was the hour to drive to the theatre. He had crushed the paper in his hand then and thrown it down; he took it up now, and looked again in a corner of it in which there was announced the approaching marriage of Prince Zouroff.

"To give her to that brute!" he murmured as he read it over once more. "Mothers were better and kinder in the days of Moloch!"

Then he crushed the journal up again, and flung it into the wood-fire burning in the gilded tower of the stove.

It was not slaying Tybalt that had tired him that night.

"What is the child to me!" he said to himself as he threw himself on his bed. "She never could have been anything, and yet—"

Yet the scent of the hothouse bouquets and the forced flowers seemed sickly to him; he remembered the smell of the little rose plucked from the sweetbriar hedge on the cliff above the sea.

---

1 In Greek mythology Elysium is a dwelling place assigned to happy souls after death; a place or condition of ideal happiness.

2 Austrian.

3 Reliefs: projected pictures of two mythological musicians. After Orpheus plays his lyre, Hades conditionally agrees to allow his wife Eurydice to return to earth. Amphion builds the walls of Thebes (with his twin brother), charming the stones into place with his lyre.

The following noon he left Vienna for Moscow, where he had an engagement for twenty nights previous to his engagement at St. Petersburg for the first weeks of the Russian New Year.

From Moscow he wrote to Lady Dolly. When that letter reached Lady Dolly it made her cry; it gave her a *crise des nerfs*.[1] When she read what he wrote she turned pale and shuddered a little; but she burnt what he wrote; that was all.

She shivered a little whenever she thought of the letter for days and weeks afterwards; but it changed her purpose in no way, and she never for one moment thought of acting upon it.

"I shall not answer him," she said to herself. "He will think I have never had it, and I shall send him a *faire part*[2] like anybody else. He will say nothing when the marriage is over. Absurd as it is, Corrèze is a gentleman; I suppose that comes from his living so much amongst us."

Amongst the many gifts that were sent to swell the magnificence of the Zouroff bridal, there was one that came anonymously, and of which none knew the donor. It gave rise to many conjectures and much comment, for there was not even the name of the jeweller that had made it. It was an opal necklace of exquisite workmanship and great value, and, as its medallion, there hung a single rose diamond cut as a star; beneath the star was a moth of sapphire and pearls, and beneath the moth was a flame of rubies. They were so hung that the moth now touched the star, now sank to the flame. It needed no word with it for Vere to know whence it came.

But she kept silence.

"A strange jewel," said Prince Zouroff, and his face grew dark: he thought some meaning or some memory came with it.

It was the only gift amidst them all that felt the kisses and tears of Vere.

"I must sink to the flame!" she thought, "and he will never know that the fault is not mine; he will never know that I have not forgotten the star!"

But she only wept in secret.

All her life henceforth was to be one of silence and repression. They are the *sepolte vive*[3] in which society immures its martyrs.

Some grow to like their prison walls, and to prefer them to light and freedom: others loathe them in anguish till death come.

---

1 Attack of nerves.
2 Announcement.
3 Vaults to bury one alive.

The gift of that strange medallion annoyed Zouroff, because it perplexed him. He never spoke to Vere concerning it, for he believed that no woman ever told the truth; but he tried to discover the donor by means of his many servants and agents. He failed, not because Corrèze had taken any especial means to ensure secresy, but from simple accident.

Corrèze had bought the stones himself of a Persian merchant many years before, had drawn the design himself, and had given it to a young worker in gems of Galicia whom he had once befriended at the fair of Novgorod;[1] and the work was only complete in all its beauty and sent to him when the Galician died of that terrible form of typhus which is like a plague in Russia. Therefore Zouroff's inquiries in Paris were all futile, and he gradually ceased to think about the jewel.

Another thing came to her at that time that hurt her, as the knife hurt Iphigenia. It was when the crabbed clear handwriting she knew so well brought her from Bulmer Chase a bitter letter.

"You are your mother's child, I see," wrote the harsh old woman, who had yet loved her so tenderly. "You are foolish, and fickle, and vain, and won over to the world, like her. You have nothing of my dead boy in you, or you would not sell yourself to the first rich man that asks. Do not write to me; do not expect to hear from me; you are for me as if you had never lived, and if, in your miserable marriage, you ever come to lose name and fame—as you may do, for loveless marriages are an affront to heaven, and mostly end in further sin—remember that you ask nothing at my hands. At your cry I was ready to open my hand to you and my heart, but I will never do so now, let you want it as you may. I pity you, and I despise you; for when you give yourself to a man whom you cannot honour or love, you are no better than the shameless women that a few weeks ago I would no more have named to you than I would have struck you a buffet on your cheek."

Vere read the letter with the hot brazen glow of the Paris sun streaming through the rose silk of the blinds upon her, and each word stood out before her as if it were on fire, and her cheek grew scarlet as if a blow were struck on it.

"She is right! Oh, how right!" she thought, in a sort of agony. "And I cannot tell her the truth! I must never tell her the truth!"

Sin and shame, and all the horror of base passions had been things

---

1   A city in Russia.

as unintelligible to her, as unknown, as the vile, miserable, frail women that a few roods off her in this city were raving and yelling in the wards of Ste. Pélagie.[1] And now, all in a moment, they seemed to have entered her life, to swarm about her, to become part and parcel of her—and from no fault of hers.

"O mother, spare me! Let me take back my word!" she cried, unconsciously, as she started to her feet with a stab of awful pain in her heart that frightened her; it felt like death.

But in the rose-bright room all around her was silence.

Her grandmother's letter lay at her feet, and a ray of the sun shone on the words that compared her to the hapless creatures whose very shame she even yet did not comprehend.

The door unclosed and Lady Dolly came in; very voluble, indifferent to suffering or humiliation, not believing, indeed, that she ever caused either.

Living with her daughter, and finding that no reproach or recrimination escaped Vere against her, Lady Dolly had begun to grow herself again. She was at times very nervous with Vere, and never, if she could help it, met her eyes, but she was successful, she was contented, she was triumphant, and the sense of shame that haunted her was thrust far into the background. All the vulgar triumphs of the alliance were sweet to her, and she did her best to forget its heavy cost. Women of her calibre soon forget; the only effort they have ever to make is, on the contrary, to remember. Lady Dolly had earnestly tried to forget, and had almost thoroughly succeeded.

She came now into the room, a pretty pearl grey figure; fresh from lengthened and close council with famous tailors.

"Vera, my sweet Vera, your sables are come; such sables! Nobody's except the grand-duchesses' will equal them. And he has sent bags of turquoises with them, literally *sacks*, as if they were oats or green peas! You will have all your toilette things set with them, and your inkstands, and all that, won't you? And they are very pretty, you know, set flat, very thick, in broad bands; *very* broad bands for the waist and the throat; but myself, I prefer—Who's been writing to you? Oh, the old woman from Bulmer. I suppose she is very angry, and writes a great deal of nonsense. She was always horrid. The only thing she gave me when I married poor Vere was a black Bible. I wonder what she will send to you? Another black Bible, perhaps. I believe she gets Bibles cheap because she subscribes to the men that go out to read Leviticus and Deuteronomy to the negro babies!"

---

1   A Paris prison.

Vere bent and raised the letter in silence. The burning colour had gone from her cheeks; she tore the letter up into many small pieces and let them float out into the golden dust of the sunlight of Paris. Her word had been given, and she was its slave.

She looked at her mother, whom she had never called mother since that last night at the château of Abbaye aux Bois.

"Will you, if you please, spare me all those details?" she said simply. "Arrange everything as you like best, it will satisfy me. But let me hear nothing about it. That is all."

"You strange, dear creature! Any other girl,—" began Lady Dolly, with a smile that was distorted, and eyes that looked away.

"I am not as other girls are. I hope there is no other girl in all the world like me."

Her mother made no answer.

Through the stillness of the chambers there came the sounds of Paris, the vague, confused, loud murmur of traffic and music, and pleasure and pain; the sounds of the world, the world to which Vere was sold.

The words of the old recluse of Bulmer were very severe, but they were very true, and it was because of their truth that they seared the delicate nerves of the girl like a hot iron. She did not well know what shame was, but she felt that her own marriage was shame; and as she rolled home from the Bois de Boulogne that night through the bright streets of Paris, past the Hôtel Zouroff that was to be her prison-house, she looked at the girls of the populace who were hurrying homeward from their workshops—flower-makers, glove-makers, clear-starchers, teachers of children, workers in factories—and she envied them, and followed them in fancy to their humble homes, and thought to herself: "How happy I would be to work, if only I had a mother that loved me, a mother that was honest and good!"

The very touch of her mother's hand, the very sound of her laugh, and sight of her smile, hurt her; she had known nothing about the follies and vices of the world, until suddenly, in one moment, she had seen them all incarnated in her mother, whose pretty graces and gaieties became terrible to her for ever, as the pink and white loveliness of a woman becomes to the eyes that have seen in its veiled breast a cancer.

Vere had seen the moral cancer. And she could not forget it, never could she forget it.

"When she was once beloved by my father—!" she thought; and she let her Bible lie unopened, lest, turning its leaves, she should see the old divine imprecations, the old bitter laws that were in it against such women as this woman, her mother, was.

One day in November her betrothed husband arrived from Russia. The magnificence of his gifts to her was the theme of Paris. The girl was passive and silent always.

When he kissed her hands only she trembled from head to foot.

"Are you afraid of me?" he murmured.

"No; I am not afraid."

She could not tell him that she felt disgust—disgust so great, so terrible, that she could have sprung from the balcony and dashed herself to death upon the stones.

"Cannot you say that you like me ever so little now?" he persisted, thinking that all his generosity might have borne some fruit.

"No—I cannot."

He laughed grimly and bitterly.

"And yet I dare take you, even as you are, you beautiful cold child!"

"I cannot tell you a falsehood."

"Will you never tell me one?"

"No; never."

"I do not believe you; every woman lies."

Vere did not answer in words, but her eyes shone for a moment with a scorn so noble that Sergius Zouroff bent his head before her.

"I beg your pardon," he said; "I think you will not lie. But then, you are not a maiden only; you are a young saint."

Vere stood aloof from him. The sunshine shone on her fair head and the long, straight folds of her white dress; her hands were clasped in front of her, and the sadness in her face gave it greater gravity and beauty.

"I am a beast to hold her to her word!" he thought; but the beast in him was stronger than aught else and conquered him, and made him ruthless to her.

She was looking away from him into the blue sky. She was thinking of the words, "keep yourself unspotted from the world." She was thinking that she would be always true to this man whom she loathed; always true; that was his right.

"And perhaps God will let me die soon," she thought, with her childish fancy that God was near and Death an angel.

Serge Zouroff looked at her, hesitated, bowed low, and left the room.

"I am not fit for her; no fitter than the sewer of the street for a pearl!" he thought, and he felt ashamed.

Yet he went to his usual companions and spent the night in drink and play, and saw the sun rise with hot red eyes; he could not change because she was a saint.

Only a generation or two back his forefathers had bought beautiful Persian women by heaping up the scales of barter with strings of pearls and sequins, and had borne off Circassian slaves in forays with simple payment of a lance left in the lifeless breasts of the men who had owned them: his wooing was of the same rude sort. Only being a man of the world, and his ravishing being legalised by society, he went to the great shops of Paris for his gems, and employed great notaries to write down the terms of barter.

The shrinking coldness, the undisguised aversion of his betrothed only whetted his passion to quicker ardour, as the shrieks of the Circassian captives, or the quivering limbs of the Persian slaves, had done that of his forefathers in Ukraine; and besides, after all, he thought, she had chosen to give herself, hating him, for sake of what he was and of all he could give. After all, her mother could not have driven her so far unless ambition had made her in a manner malleable.

Zouroff, in whose mind all women were alike, had almost been brought to believe in the honesty and steadfastness of the girl to whom he had given Loris, and he was at times disposed to be bitterly enraged against her because she had fallen in his sight by her abrupt submission; she seemed at heart no better than the rest. She abhorred him; yet she accepted him. No mere obedience could account for that acceptance without some weakness or some cupidity of nature. It hardened him against her; it spoilt her lovely, pure childhood in his eyes; it made her shudder from him seem half hypocrisy. After all, he said to himself, where was she so very much higher than Casse-une-Croûte? It was only the price that was altered.

When she came to know what Casse-une-Croûte was, she said the same thing to herself.

"Do you believe in wicked people, miladi?" he said the next evening to Lady Dolly, as they sat together in a box at the Bouffes.

"Wicked people? Oh dear no—at least—yes," said Lady Dolly vaguely. "Yes, I suppose I do. I am afraid one must. One sees dreadful things in the papers; in society everybody is very much like everybody else—no?"

Zouroff laughed; the little, short, hard laugh that was characteristic of him.

"I think one need not go to the papers. I think you and I are both doing evil enough to satisfy the devil—if a devil there be. But, if you do not mind it, I need not."

Lady Dolly was startled, then smiled.

"What droll things you say! And do not talk so of the——. It doesn't sound well. It's an old-fashioned belief, I know, and not probable they say now, but still—one never can tell—"

And Lady Dolly, quite satisfied with herself, laughed her last laugh at the fun of the *Belle Hélène*,[1] and had her cloak folded round her, and went out on the arm of her future son-in-law.

Such few great ladies as were already in Paris, passing through from the channel coast to the Riviera, or from one château to another, all envied her, she knew; and if anybody had ever said anything—that was not quite nice—nobody could say anything now when in another fortnight her daughter would be Princess Zouroff.

"Really, I never fancied at all I was clever, but I begin to think that I am," she said in her self-complacency to herself.

The idea that she could be wicked seemed quite preposterous to her when she thought it over. "Harmless little me!" she said to herself. True, she had felt wicked when she had met her daughter's eye, but that was nonsense; the qualm had always gone away when she had taken her champagne at dinner or her ether in her bedroom.

A fortnight later the marriage of the head of the house of Zouroff was solemnised at the chapel of the English Embassy and the Russian church in Paris.

Nothing was forgotten that could add to the splendour and pomp of the long ceremonies and sacraments; all that was greatest in the great world was assembled in honour of the event. The gifts were magnificent, and the extravagance unbridled. The story of the *corbeille* read like a milliner's dream of heaven; the jewels given by the bridegroom were estimated at a money value of millions of roubles, and with them were given the title-deeds of a French estate called Félicité, a free gift of love above and outside all the superb donations contained in the settlements. All these things and many more were set forth at length in all the journals of society, and the marriage was one of the great events of the closing year. The only details that the papers did not chronicle were that when the mother, with her tender eyes moist with tears, kissed her daughter, the daughter put her aside without an answering caress, and that when the last words of the sacrament were spoken, she, who had now become the Princess Zouroff, fell forward on the altar in a dead swoon, from which for some time she could not be awakened.

"So they have thrown an English maiden to our Tartar minotaur! Oh, what a chaste people they are, those English," said a Russian

---

1 A comic operetta (1864) by Halévy, Meilhac, and Offenbach.

Colonel of the Guard to Corrèze, as their sledge flew over the snow on the Newski Prospect.[1]

Corrèze gave a shudder of disgust; he said nothing.

Critics in music at the opera-house that night declared then, and long after, that for the first time in all his career he was guilty of more than one artistic error as he sang in the great part of John of Leyden.[2]

When the opera was over, and he sat at a supper, in a room filled with hothouse flowers and lovely ladies, while the breath froze on the beards of the sentinels on guard in the white still night without, Corrèze heard little of the laughter, saw little of the beauty round him. He was thinking all the while:

"The heaviest sorrow of my life will always be, not to have saved that child from her mother."

CHAPTER XI.

Between the Gulf of Villafranca and that of Eza[3] there was a white shining sunlit house, with gardens that were in the dreariest month of the year rich and red with roses, golden with orange fruit, and made stately by palms of long growth, through whose stems the blue sea shone. To these gardens there was a long terrace of white marble stretching along the edge of the cliff, with the waves beating far down below; to the terrace there were marble seats and marble steps, and copies of the Loves and Fauns of the Vatican and of the Capitol, with the glow of geraniums flamelike about their feet.

Up and down the length of this stately place a woman moved with a step that was slow and weary, and yet very restless; the step of a thing that is chained. The woman was very young and very pale; her skirts of olive velvet swept the white stone; her fair hair was coiled loosely with a golden arrow run through it; round her throat there were strings of pearls, the jewels of morning. All women envied her the riches of which those pearls were emblem. She was Vera, Princess Zouroff.

Vera always, now.

She moved up and down, up and down, fatiguing herself, and unconscious of fatigue; the sunny world was quiet about her; the greyhound paced beside her, keeping step with hers. She was alone,

---

1   A road in St. Petersburg.
2   From Giacomo Meyerbeer's *Le Prophète* (1849). John of Leydon (1509-36) was a Dutch Anabaptist leader.
3   The gulfs are on the French Riviera near Nice.

and there was no one to look upon her face and see its pain, its weariness, its disgust.

Only a week ago, she thought; only a week since she had fallen in a swoon at the altar of the Russian church; only a week since she had been the girl Vere Herbert. Only a week!—and it seemed to her that thousands of years had come and gone, parting her by ages from that old sweet season of ignorance, of innocence, of peace, of youth.

She was only sixteen still, but she was no more young. Her girlhood had been killed in her as a spring blossom is crushed by a rough hot hand that, meaning to caress it, kills it.

A great disgust filled her, and seemed to suffocate her with its loathing and its shame. Everything else in her seemed dead, except that one bitter sense of intolerable revulsion. All the revolted pride in her was like a living thing buried under a weight of sand, and speechless, but aghast and burning.

"How could she? how could she?" she thought every hour of the day; and the crime of her mother against her seemed the vilest the earth could hold.

She herself had not known what she had done when she had consented to give herself in marriage, but her mother had known.

She did not reason now. She only felt.

An unutterable depression and repugnance weighed on her always; she felt ashamed of the sun when it rose, of her own eyes when they looked at her from the mirror. To herself she seemed fallen so low, sunk to such deep degradation, that the basest of creatures would have had full right to strike her cheek, and spit in her face, and call her sister.

Poets in all time have poured out their pity on the woman who wakes to a loveless dishonour: what can the few words of a priest, or the envy of a world, do to lighten that shame to sacrificed innocence?—nothing.

Her life had changed as suddenly as a flower changes when the hot sirocco[1] blows over it, and fills it with sand instead of dew. Nothing could help her. Nothing could undo what had been done. Nothing could make her ever more the clear-eyed, fair-souled child that had not even known the meaning of any shame.

"God himself could not help me!" she thought with a bitterness of resignation that was more hopeless than that of the martyrs of old; and she paced up and down the marble road of the terrace, wondering how long her life would last like this.

---

1 A dry, dust-laden wind.

All the magnificence that surrounded her was hateful; all the gifts that were heaped on her were like insult; all the congratulations that were poured out on her were like the mockeries of apes, like the crackling of dead leaves. In her own sight, and without sin of her own, she had become vile.

And it was only a week ago!

Society would have laughed.

Society had set its seal of approval upon this union, and upon all such unions, and so deemed them sanctified. Year after year, one on another, the pretty, rosy, golden-curled daughters of fair mothers were carefully tended and cultured and reared up to grace the proud races from which they sprang, and were brought out into the great world in their first bloom like half-opened roses, with no other end or aim set before them as the one ambition of their lives than to make such a marriage as this. Whosoever achieved such was blessed.

Pollution? Prostitution? Society would have closed its ears to such words, knowing nothing of such things, not choosing to know anything.

Shame? What shame could there be when he was her husband? Strange fanciful exaggeration!—society would have stared and smiled.

The grim old woman who studied her Bible on the iron-bound Northumbrian shores; the frivolous, dreamy, fantastic singer, who had played the part of Romeo till all life seemed to him a rose-garden, moonlit and made for serenades; these two might perhaps think with her, and understand this intense revolt, this passionate repugnance, this ceaseless sense of unendurable, indelible reproach. But those were all. Society would have given her no sympathy. Society would have simpered and sneered. To marry well; that was the first duty of a woman.

She had fulfilled it; she had been fortunate; how could she fail to be content?

A heavy step trod the marble terrace, and a heavy shadow fell across the sunlight; her husband approached her.

"You are out without any shade; you will spoil your skin," he said, as his eyes fell gloomily on her, for he noticed the shudder that passed over her as he drew near.

She moved without speaking, where no sun fell, where the armless Cupid of the Vatican, copied in marble, stood amongst the rose of a hundred leaves.

"How pale you are. That gown is too heavy for you. Do you like this place?"

"I?"

She said the word with an unconscious sound in it, that had the wonder of despair; despair which asked what was there left in all the world to like or love?

"Do you like it, I say," he repeated. "Most women rave about it. You seem as if it were a prison-house. Will you be always like that?"

"The place is beautiful," she said in a low tone. "Have I complained?"

"No; you never complain. That is what annoys me. If you ever fretted like other women—but you are as mute as that marble armless thing. Sometimes you make me afraid—afraid—that I shall forget myself, and strike you."

She was silent.

"Would that you did strike sooner than embrace me!" she thought; and he read the unuttered thought in her eyes.

"I do love you," he said sullenly, with some emotion. "You must know that; I have left no means untried to show it you."

"You have been very generous, monsieur!"

"Monsieur! always monsieur!—it is ridiculous. I am your husband, and you must give me some tenderer word than that. After all, why cannot you be happy? You have all you want or wish for, and if you have a wish still unfulfilled, be it the maddest or most impossible, it shall be gratified if gold can do it, for I love you—you frozen child!"

He bent his lips to hers; she shuddered, and was still.

He kept his hand about her throat, and gathered one of the roses of a hundred leaves, and set it against the pearls and her white skin; then he flung it away into the sea roughly.

"Roses do not become you; you are not a *belle jardiniere*;[1] you are a statue. This place is dull, one tires of it; we will go to Russia."

"As you please."

"As I please! Will you say nothing else all your life? There is no pleasure in doing what one pleases unless there is some opposition to the doing it. If you would say you hated snow and ice, now, I would swear to you that snow and ice were paradise beside these sickly palms and tawdry flowers. Is there nothing you like? Who sent you that strange necklace of the moth?"

"I do not know."

"But you imagine?"

She was silent.

---

1 Pretty gardener.

"What is the meaning of it?"

"I think the meaning is that one may rise to great ends, or sink to base ones."

"Has it no love-token, then; no message?"

"No."

The red colour rose over her pale face, but she looked at him with unflinching gaze. He was but half satisfied.

"And do you mean to rise or sink?" he said, in a tone of banter. "Pray tell me."

"I have sunk."

The words stung him, and his pride, which was arrogant and vain, smarted under them.

"By God!" he said with his short hard laugh. "Did it never occur to you, my beautiful Vera, that you would do wiser not to insult me if you want to enjoy your life? I am your master, and I can be a bad master."

She looked at him without flinching, very coldly, very wearily.

"Why will you ask me questions? The truth displeases you, and I will not tell you other than the truth. I meant no insult—unless it were to insult myself."

He was silent. He walked to and fro awhile, pulling the roses from their stems and flinging them into the gulf below. Then he spoke abruptly, changing the subject.

"We will go to Russia. You shall see a ball in the Salle des Palmiers.[1] The world is best. Solitude is sweet for lovers, but not when one of them is a statue—or an angel. Besides, that sort of thing never lasts a week. The world is best. You would make me hate you— or adore you—if we stayed on alone, and I wish to do neither. If you were not my wife it might be worth while; but as it is—"

He threw another rose into the sea, as if in a metaphor of indifference.

"Come to breakfast," he said carelessly. "We will leave for Russia to-night."

As they passed down the terrace and entered the house, she moved wearily beside him with her face averted and her lips very pale.

The Salle des Palmiers had no charm for her. She was thinking of the nightingale that was then singing in the Russian snows.

If she saw Corrèze what could she say? The truth she could not tell him, and he must be left to think the moth had dropped into the earthly fires of venal ambitions and of base desires.

---

1 Hall of the palm trees.

"Could you not leave me here?" she said wistfully and a little timidly as she sat at the breakfast-table.

He answered with his curt and caustic laugh.

"I thank you for the compliment! No, my dear, one does not go through all the weariness and folly of marriage ceremonies to leave the loveliness one has purchased so hardly in a week! Have patience! I shall be tired of you soon, maybe. But not until you have shown your diamonds at an Imperial ball. Do not get too pale. The court will rally me upon my tyranny. You *are* too pale. A touch of your mother's rouge will be advisable unless you get some colour of your own."

Vere was silent.

Her throat seemed to contract and choke her. She set her glass down untouched.

This was her master!—this man who would tire of her soon, and bade her rouge whilst she was yet sixteen years old!

Yet his tyranny was less horrible to her than his tenderness.

That night they left for Russia.

A few days later the gossip of St. Petersburg, in court and café, talked only of two things—the approaching arrival of the new beauty, Princess Zouroff, with the opening of the long closed Zouroff Palace on the Newski Prospect; and of the immense penalty paid in forfeit by the great tenor, Corrèze, to escape the last twenty nights of his engagement in that city.

"I had better forfeit half my engagement than lose my voice altogether," said Corrèze impatiently, in explanation. "The thousands of francs I can soon make again; but if the mechanical nightingale in my throat give way—I must go and break stones for my bread. No! in this atmosphere I can breathe no longer. I pay—and I go to the south."

He paid and went; and St. Petersburg was half consoled for his departure by the entry on the following day of the Prince Zouroff, and of her whom all the world called now, and would call henceforward, Princess Vera.

END OF VOLUME I

VOLUME 2

CHAPTER I.

Again in the month of November, exactly one year after her marriage, a tall slender figure clothed in white, with white furs, moved to and fro very wearily under the palms of the Villa Nelaguine on the Gulf of Villafranca, and her sister-in-law, looking wistfully at her, thought:

"I hope he is not cruel—I hope not. Perhaps it is only the death of the child that has saddened her."

Vere read her thoughts and looked her in the eyes.

"I am glad that the child died," she said simply.

The Princess Nelaguine shuddered a little.

"Oh, my dear," she murmured, "that cannot be. Do not say that; women find solace in their children when they are unhappy in all else. You have a tender fond heart, you would have—"

"I think my heart is a stone," said the girl in a low voice; then she added: "In the poem of 'Aurora Leigh'[1] the woman loves the child that is born of her ruin; I am not like that. Perhaps I am wicked; can you understand?"

"Yes, yes; I understand," said the Princess Nelaguine hurriedly, and, though she was accounted in her generation a false and heartless little woman of the world, her eyes became dim and her hands pressed Vere's with a genuine pity. Long, long years before Nadine Zouroff had herself been given to a loveless marriage, when all her life seemed to her to be lying dead in a soldier's unmarked grave in the mountains of the Caucasus.

"That feeling will change, though, be assured," she said soothingly. "When we are very young all our sorrow is despair; but it does not kill us, and we live to be consoled. Once I felt like you—yes—but now I have many interests, many ties, many occupations, and my sons and daughters are dear to me, though they were not *his*; so will be yours, to you, in time."

Vere shuddered.

"People are different," she said simply; "to me it will always be the same."

She pulled a cluster of white roses, and ruffled them in her hands, and threw them down, almost cruelly.

---

1 By Elizabeth Barrett Browning, published in 1857. In the poem a young seamstress is trapped in a brothel.

"Will those roses bloom again?" she said. "What I did to them your brother has done to me. I cannot be altered now. Forget that I have said anything; I will not again."

One year had gone by since Vere had been given, with the blessing of her mother and the benison of society, to the Minotaur of a loveless marriage. To herself she seemed so utterly changed that nothing of her old self was left in her, body or soul. To the world she only seemed to have grown lovelier, as was natural with maturer womanhood, and to have become a great lady in lieu of a graceful child.

She was little more than seventeen now, but, herself, she felt as if centuries had rolled over her head.

After her winter at the Imperial Court, she had been so changed that she would at times wonder if she had ever been the glad and thoughtful child who had watched the North Sea break itself in foam in the red twilight of Northumbrian dawns.

She had a horror of herself.

She had a horror of the world.

But from the world and from herself there was now no escape.

She was the Princess Zouroff.

An immense disgust possessed her, and pervaded all her life; falling on her as the thick grey fog falls on a sunny landscape— heavy, dull, and nauseous.

The loveliest and youngest beauty in the Salle des Palmiers, with the stars of her diamonds shining on her like the planets of a summer night, she was the saddest of all earthly creatures.

The girl who had gone to bed with the sun and risen with it; who had spent her tranquil days in study and open-air exercise; who had thought it pleasure enough to find the first primrose, and triumph enough to write the three letters at the foot of a hard problem; who had gone by her grandmother's side to the old dusky church, where noble and simple had knelt together for a thousand years, and who had known no more of the evil and lasciviousness of the world at large than the white ox-eye opening under the oak glades; the girl who had been Vere Herbert on those dark chill Northumbrian shores was now the Princess Vera, and was for ever in the glare, the unrest, the fever, and the splendour, of a great society.

Night was turned into day; pleasure, as the world construed it, filled each hour; life became a spectacle; and she, as a part of the spectacle, was ceaselessly adorned, arrayed, flattered, censured, and posed—as a model is posed for the painter. All around her was grand, gorgeous, restless, and insincere; there was no leisure, though there was endless ennui; and no time for reflection, though there were monotony and a satiety of sensation. Sin she heard of for the first time, and it was smiled at; vice became bare to her, but no one shunned it; the rapacity of an ignoble passion let loose and called "marriage" tore down all her childish ignorance and threw it to the winds, destroyed her self-respect, and laughed at her, trampled on all her modest shame, and ridiculed her innocence.

In early autumn she had given birth to a son, who had lived a few hours, and then died. She had not sorrowed for its loss—it was the child of Sergius Zouroff. She thought it better dead. She had felt a strange emotion as she had looked on its little body, lying lifeless; but it was neither maternal love nor maternal regret; it was rather remorse.

She had been then at Svir,[1] on the shores of the Baltic, one of the chief estates of the Princes of Zouroff, which all the summer long had been the scene of festivities, barbaric in their pomp and costliness; festivities with which her husband strove to wile away the year which Imperial command had bade him pass, after marriage, on his hereditary lands.

"Do not allow my mother to come to me!" she had said once with a passionate cry when the birth of the child had drawn near. It was the first time she had ever appealed in any way to her husband. He laughed a little grimly, and his face flushed.

"Your mother shall not come," he said hastily. "Do you suppose she would wish to be shut up in a sick room? Perhaps she might, though, it is true; miladi always remembers what will look well. One must do her the justice to say she always remembers that, at least. But no; she shall not come."

So it came to pass that her mother in her little octagon boudoir in Chesham Place, lined with old fans of the Beau Siècle,[2] and draped with Spanish lace, could only weep a little with her bosom friends, and murmur, "My sweet child!—such a trial!—in this horrible weather by the Baltic—so cruel of the Emperor—and to think my health will not let me go to her!"

Zouroff, who passionately desired a legitimate son, because he hated with a deadly hatred his next brother Vladimir, took the loss of the male child to heart with a bitterness which was only wounded pride and baffled enmity, but looked like tenderness beside the marble-like coldness, and passive indifference of his wife.

---

1 A town near St. Petersburg.
2 Literally beautiful century; the name for the Second Empire of France.

Physicians, who always are too clever not to have a thousand reasons for everything, alleged that the change of climate and temperature had affected the health of the Princess Vera; and her husband, who hated Russia with all his might, urged this plea of her health to obtain a reduction of the time he had been ordered to remain on his own lands; and obtaining what he wished from the Tsar, returned in November to the French Riviera.

He had purchased the villa of his sister from her, although it was called still the Villa Nelaguine. He had bought it in a mood of captious irritation with his wife, knowing that to Vere, reared in the cold, grey days and under the cloudy skies, and by the sombre seas of the dark north, the southern seaboard was oppressive in its languor and its light. Sometimes he liked to hurt her in any way he could; if her child had lived he would have made it into a whip of scorpions for her. Yet he always lavished on her so much money, and so many jewels, and kept her so perpetually in the front of the greatest of great worlds, that everybody who knew him said that he made a good husband after all; much better than anyone would have anticipated.

He intended to stay at the villa on the Mediterranean for three months, and thither came, self-invited because she was so near—only at Paris—the Lady Dolly.

Neither Zouroff nor his sister ever invited her to their houses, but pretty Lady Dolly was not a woman to be deterred by so mere a trifle as that.

"I pine to see my sweet treasure!" she wrote; and Sergius Zouroff, knitting his heavy brows, said "Let her come," and Vere said nothing.

"What an actress was lost in your mother," he added with his rough laugh; but he confused the talent of the comedian of society with that of the comedian of the stage, and they are very dissimilar. The latter almost always forgets herself in her part; the former never.

So one fine, sunlit, balmy day towards Christmas, Lady Dolly drove up through the myrtle wood that led to the Villa Nelaguine.

It was noonday. The house guests were straying down from upstairs to breakfast in the pretty Pompeiian room, with its inlaid marble walls, and its fountains, and its sculpture, and its banks of hothouse flowers, which opened on to the white terrace, that fronted the rippling blue sea. On this terrace Zouroff was standing.

He saw the carriage approaching in the distance through the myrtles.

"*C'est madame mère*,"[1] he said, turning on his heel, and looking

---

1 "It is madam mother."

into the breakfast chamber. He laughed a little grimly as he said it.

Vere was conversing with Madame Nelaguine, who saw a strange look come into her eyes; aversion, repugnance, contempt, pain, and shame all commingled. "What is there that I do not know?" thought the Princess Nadine. She remembered how Vera had not returned her mother's embrace at the marriage ceremony.

Sergius Zouroff was still watching the carriage's approach, with that hard smile upon his face which had all the brutality and cynicism of his temper in it, and under which delicate women and courageous men had often winced as under the lash.

"*C'est madame mère*," he said again, with a spray of gardenia between his teeth; and then, being a grand gentleman sometimes, when the eyes of society were on him, though sometimes being rough as a boor, he straightened his loose heavy figure, put the gardenia in his button-hole, and went down the steps, with the dignity of Louis Quatorze going to meet a Queen of Spain, and received his guest as she alighted with punctilious politeness and an exquisite courtesy.

Lady Dolly ascended the steps on his arm.

She was dressed perfectly for the occasion; all a soft dove-hue, with soft dove-coloured feather trimmings, and silvery furs with a knot of black here and there to heighten the chastened effect, and show her grief for the child that had breathed but an hour. On her belt hung many articles, but chief among them was a small silver-bound prayer-book, and she had a large silver cross at her throat.

"She will finish with religion," thought Zouroff; "they always take it last."

Lady Dolly was seldom startled, and seldom nervous; but, as her daughter came forward on to the terrace to meet her, she was both startled and nervous.

Vera was in a white morning dress with a white mantilla of old Spanish lace about her head and throat; she moved with serene and rather languid grace; her form had developed into the richness of womanhood; her face was very cold. Her mother could see nothing left in this wonderfully beautiful and stately person of the child of eighteen months before.

"Is that Vere?" she cried involuntarily, as she looked upward to the terrace above.

"That is Vera," said Sergius Zouroff drily. All the difference lay there.

Then Lady Dolly recovered herself.

"My sweet child! Ah the sorrow!—the joy!" murmured Lady Dolly, meeting her with flying feet and outstretched arms, upon the white and black chequers of the marble terrace.

Vere stood passive, and let her cold cheeks be brushed by those softly-tinted lips. Her eyes met her mother's once, and Lady Dolly trembled.

"Oh this terrible *bise!*"[1] she cried, with a shiver; "you can have nothing worse in Russia! Ah, my dear, precious Vera! I was so shocked, so grieved!—to think that poor little angel was lost to us!"

"We will not speak of that," said Vere in a low voice, that was very cold and weary. "You are standing in the worst of the wind; will you not come into the house? Yes; I think one feels the cold more here than in Russia. People say so."

"Yes; because one has sunshades here, and one sees those ridiculous palms, and it ought to be warm if it isn't," answered Lady Dolly; but her laugh was nervous and her lips trembled and contracted as she thus met her daughter once more.

"She is so unnatural!" she sighed to Princess Nelaguine; "so unnatural! Not a word, even to *me*, of her poor dear little dead child. Not a word! It is really too painful."

The Princess Nelaguine answered drily: "Your daughter is not very happy. My brother is not an angel. But then, you knew very well, *chère madame,*[2] that he never was one."

"I am sure he seems very good," said Lady Dolly piteously, and with fretfulness. She honestly thought it.

Vere had enormous jewels, constant amusement, and a bottomless purse; the mind of Lady Dolly was honestly impotent to conceive any state of existence more enviable than this.

"To think what I am content with!" she thought to herself; she who had to worry her husband every time she wanted a cheque; who had more debts for dress and pretty trifles than she would pay if she lived to be a hundred; and who constantly had to borrow half-a-crown for a cup of tea at Hurlingham, or a rouleau[3] of gold to play with at Monaco.

Those were trials indeed!

"I hope you realise that you are my mother-in-law," said Zouroff, as Lady Dolly sat on his right hand, and he gave her some grapes at breakfast.

---

1 North wind.
2 Dear lady.
3 Roll.

He laughed as he said it. Lady Dolly tried to laugh, but did not succeed.

"You are bound to detest me," she said with an exaggerated little smile, "by all precedents of fiction and of fact."

"Oh no!" said Zouroff gallantly; "never in fiction or in fact had any man so bewitching and youthful a mother-in-law. On my life, you look no older than Vera."

"Oh-h!" said Lady Dolly, pleased but deprecatory. "Vera is in a grand style, you know. Women like her look older than they are at twenty, but at forty they look much younger than they are. That is the use of height and straight features, and Greek brows. When one is a little doll, like me, one must be resigned to looking insignificant always."

"Is the Venus de Medici insignificant?[1] she is very small," said Zouroff still most gallantly; and he added, in a lower key, "You were always pretty, Dolly; you always will be. I am sorry to see that prayer-book; it looks as if you felt growing old, and you will be wretched if you once get that idea into your head."

"I *feel* young," said Lady Dolly sentimentally. "But it would sound ridiculous to pretend to be so."

Her glance went to the graceful and dignified presence of her daughter.

"Vere is very handsome, very beautiful," she continued hesitatingly. "But—but—surely she is not looking very well?"

"She is scarcely recovered," said Zouroff roughly, and the speech annoyed him. He knew that his young wife was unhappy, but he did not choose for anyone to pity her, and for her mother, of all people, to do so!—

"Ah! to be sure, no!" sighed Lady Dolly. "It was so sad—poor little angel! But did Vera care much? I think not."

"I think there is nothing she cares for," said Zouroff savagely. "Who could tell *your* daughter would be a piece of ice, a *femme de marbre*?[2] It is too droll."

"Pray do not call me Dolly," she murmured piteously. "People will hear."

"Very well, *madame mère!*" said Zouroff, and he laughed this time aloud.

---

1 A statue of the mythological goddess of love and beauty. It is attributed to Praxitelles (fourth century B.C.).

2 Marble woman.

She was frightened—half at her own work, half at the change wrought in Vere.

"Who could tell she would alter so soon," she thought, in wonder at the cold and proud woman who looked like a statue and moved like a goddess.

"To think she is only seventeen!" said Lady Dolly aloud, in bewilderment.

"To be married to me is a liberal education," said her son-in-law, with his short sardonic laugh.

"I am sure you are very kind to her," murmured poor little Lady Dolly, yet feeling herself turn pale under her false bloom. "The beast!" she said to herself with a shudder. "The Centaurs must have been just like him."[1]

She meant the Satyrs.[2]

"Sergius," said Princess Nelaguine to her brother that night, "Vera does not look well."

"No?" he answered carelessly. "She is always too pale. I tell her always to rouge. If she do not rouge in Paris, she will scarcely tell in a ball, handsome though she is."

"Rouge at seventeen! You cannot be serious. She only wants to be—happy. I do not think you make her so. Do you try?"

He stared and yawned.

"It is not my *métier*[3] to make women happy. They can be so if they like. I do not prevent them. She has ten thousand francs a month by her settlements to spend on her caprices—if it is not enough she can have more. You may tell her so. I never refuse money."

"You speak like a *bourgeois*,"[4] said his sister, with some contempt. "Do you think that money is everything? It is nothing to a girl like that. She gives it all to the poor; it is no pleasure to her."

"Then she is very unlike her mother," said the Prince Zouroff with a smile.

"She is unlike her, indeed! you should be thankful to think how entirely unlike. Your honour will be safe with her as long as she lives; but to be happy—she will want more than you give her at present, but the want is not one that money will supply."

---

1 Centaurs are mythological monsters with heads, trunks, and arms of a man and legs of a horse.

2 Satyrs are woodland deities, sometimes part horse or goat. They are attendants of Bacchus, the mythological god of wine and revelry, and noted for unrestrained revelry and lasciviousness.

3 Job.

4 Member of the middle class.

"She has been complaining?" said her brother, with a sudden frown.

Madame Nelaguine added with a ready lie: "Not a word; not a syllable. But one has eyes—and I do so wish you to be kind to her."

"Kind to her?" he repeated, with some surprise. "I am not unkind that I know of; she has impossible ideas; they make me impatient. She must take me and the world as she finds us; but I am certainly not unkind. One does not treat one's wife like a saint. Perhaps you can make her comprehend that. Were she sensible, like others, she would be happy like them."

He laughed, and rose and drank some absinthe.

His sister sighed and set her teeth angrily on the cigarette that she was smoking.

"Perhaps she *will* in time be happy and sensible like them," she said to herself; "and then your lessons will bear their proper fruits, and you will be deceived like other husbands, and punished as you merit. If it were not for the honour of the Zouroffs I should pray for it!"

The Villa Nelaguine was full of people staying there, and was also but five miles distant from Monte Carlo.

Vere was never alone with her mother during the time that Lady Dolly graced the Riviera with her presence, carried her red umbrella under the palm-trees, and laid her borrowed napoléons on the colour.

No word of reproach, no word of complaint escaped her lips in her mother's presence, yet Lady Dolly felt vaguely frightened, and longed to escape from her presence, as a prisoner longs to escape from the dock.

She stayed this December weather at Villafranca, where December meant blue sea, golden sunshine, and red roses, because she thought it was the right thing to do. If there had been people who had said—well, not quite nice things—it was better to stay with her daughter immediately on the return from Russia. So she did stay, and even had herself visited for a day or two by Mr. Vanderdecken on one of his perpetual voyages from London to Java, Japan, or Jupiter.

Her visit was politic and useful; but it cost her some pain, some fretfulness, and some apprehension.

The house was full of pleasant people, for Zouroff never could endure a day of even comparative solitude; and amidst them was a very handsome Italian noble, who was more agreeable to her than the Duc de Dinant had of late grown, and who was about to go to England to be attached to the embassy there, and who had the eyes of Othello[1] with the manners of Chesterfield,[2] and whom she made her husband cordially invite to Chesham Place. She could play as high as she liked, and she could drive over to Monaco when she pleased, and no life suited her better then this life; where she could, whenever she chose, saunter through the aloes and palms to those magic halls where her favourite fever was always at its height, yet where everything looked so pretty, and appearances were always so well preserved, and she could say to everybody, "They do have such good music—one can't help liking Monte Carlo!"

The place suited her in every way, and yet she felt stifled in it, and afraid.

Afraid of what? There was nothing on earth to be afraid of, she knew that.

Yet, when she saw the cold, weary, listless life of Vere and met the deep scorn of her eyes, and realised the absolute impotency of rank, and riches, and pleasure, and all her own adored gods, to console or even to pacify this young wounded soul, Lady Dolly was vaguely frightened, as the frivolous are always frightened at any strength or depth of nature, or any glimpse of sheer despair.

Not to be consoled!

What can seem more strange to the shallow? What can seem more obstinate to the weak? Not to be consoled is to offend all swiftly forgetting humanity, most of whose memories are writ on water.

"It is very strange, she seems to one to enjoy nothing!" said Lady Dolly, one morning to Madame Nelaguine, when Prince Zouroff had announced at the noonday breakfast that he had purchased for his wife a famous historical diamond known in Memoirs and in European courts as the "Roc's egg."[3] and Vere, with a brief word of thanks acknowledged the tidings, her mother thought indignantly, as

---

1 The jealous Moor in Shakespeare's play of that name.
2 Philip Dormer Stanhope, Fourth Earl of Chesterfield (1694–1773) was a British statesman and wit. He is chiefly remembered for his *Letters to His Son* and *Letters to His Grandson*, guides to manners and the art of pleasure.
3 In Arabic legends, the roc is a gigantic bird with two horns on its head and four humps. It appears in *The Arabian Nights* in "The Second Voyage of Sinbad the Seaman." In the tale Sinbad finds a roc sitting on her egg. He ties himself to the roc, hoping that when it flies away, it will take him to a city. He is dropped off where the soil is "of diamond." He learns that vultures and rocs carry parts of slaughtered beasts (traps which diamond

though he had brought her a twopenny bunch of primroses.

"It is very strange!" repeated Lady Dolly. "The idea of hearing that she had got the biggest diamond in all the world, except five, and receiving the news like that! Your brother looked disappointed, I think, annoyed,—didn't you?"

"If he want ecstasies over a diamond he can give it to Noisette," said Madame Nelaguine, with her little cold smile. "I think he ought not to be annoyed that his wife is superior to Noisette."

"Was Vera always as cold as that at St. Petersburg before her child's death?" pursued Lady Dolly, who never liked Madame Nelaguine's smiles.

"Yes; always the same."

"Doesn't society amuse her in the least?"

"Not in the least. I quite understand why it does not do so. Without coquetry or ambition it is impossible to enjoy society much. Every pretty woman should be a flirt, every clever woman a politician; the aim, the animus, the intrigue, the rivalry that accompany each of those pursuits are the salt without which the great dinner were tasteless. A good many brainless creatures do, it is true, flutter through society all their lives for the mere pleasure of fluttering; but that is poor work after all," added Madame Nelaguine, ignoring the pretty flutterer to whom she was speaking. "One needs an aim, just as an angler must have fish in the stream or he grows weary of whipping it. Now your Vera will never be a coquette because her temperament forbids it. She is too proud, and also men have the misfortune not to interest her. And I think she will never be a politician; at least, she is interested in great questions, but the small means by which men strive to accomplish their aims disgust her, and she will never be a diplomatist. In the first week she was in Russia she compromised Sergius seriously at the Imperial Court by praising a Nihilist[1] novelist to the Empress!"

"Oh, I know!" said Lady Dolly, desperately. "She has not two grains of sense. She is beautiful and distinguished looking. When you have said that you have said everything that is to be said. The educa-

---

merchants have set) onto the mountain to eat. Diamonds from the soil are stuck to the carcasses. Sinbad fills his pockets and his unrolled turban with the choicest diamonds. Sir Richard Francis Burton, who regularly attended Ouida's dinner parties, translated the tale.

1 The Nihilists were Russian revolutionaries active in the latter half of the nineteenth century. They wanted to destroy existing social and political institutions. See also p. 319, note 2.

tion she had with her grandmother made her hopelessly stupid, actually *stupid!*"

"She is very far from stupid, pardon me," said Madame Nelaguine, with a delicate little smile. "But she has not your adaptability, *chère madame.* It is her misfortune."

"A misfortune, indeed," said Lady Dolly, a little sharply, feeling that her superiority was being despised. "It is always a misfortune to be unnatural, and she is unnatural. She takes no pleasure in anything that delights everyone else; she hardly knows serge from sicilienne; she has no tact because she does not think it worth while to have any. She will offend a king as indifferently as she will change her dress; every kind of amusement bores her, she is made like that. When everybody is laughing round her she looks grave, and stares like an owl with her great eyes. Oh, dear me; to think she should be my daughter! Nothing odder ever could be than that Vera should be my child."

"Except that she should be my brother's wife," said Madame Nelaguine, drily. Lady Dolly was silent.

The next day Lady Dolly took advantage of her husband's escort to leave the Villa Nelaguine for England; she went with reluctance, yet with relief. She was envious of her daughter, and she was impatient with her, and, though she told herself again and again that Vere's destiny had fallen in a golden paradise, the east wind, that she hated,[1] moaning through the palms seemed to send after her homeward a long-drawn despairing sigh—the sigh of a young life ruined.

Prince Zouroff stayed on in the south, detained by the seduction of the gaming-tables, until the Christmas season was passed; then, having won very largely, as very rich men often do, he left the Riviera for his handsome hôtel in the Avenue du Bois de Boulogne; and Madame Nelaguine left it also.

Like many of their country people they were true children of Paris, and were seldom thoroughly content unless they were within sight of the dome of the Invalides.[2]

He felt he would breathe more freely when from the windows of the railway carriage he should see the zinc roofs and shining gilt cupolas of his one heaven upon earth.

"Another year with only her face to look at, with its eyes of unending reproach, and I should have gone mad, or cut her throat,"

---

1 Earlier in the chapter she complains about the north wind.
2 The Hôtel des Invalides is the final burial place of Napoleon.

he said in a moment of confidence to one of his confidants and parasites.

They had never been alone one day, indeed; troops of guests had always been about them; but it had not been Paris, Paris with its consolations, its charm, and its crowds.

In Paris he could forget completely that he had ever married, save when it might please his pride to hear the world tell him that he had the most beautiful woman in Europe for his wife.

"Can you not sleep? do not stare so with your great eyes!" said Prince Zouroff angrily to his wife, as the night train rushed through the heart of France, and Vere gazed out over the snow-whitened moonlit country, as the land and the sky seemed to fly past her.

In another carriage behind her was her great jewel box, set between two servants, whose whole duty was to guard it.

But she never thought of her jewels; she was thinking of the moth and the star; she was thinking of the summer morning on the white cliff of the sea. For she knew that Corrèze was in Paris.

It was not any sort of love that moved her, beyond such lingering charmed fancy as remained from those few hours' fascination. But a great reluctance to see him, a great fear of seeing him, was in her. What could he think of her marriage! And she could never tell him why she had married thus. He would think her sold like the rest, and he must be left to think so.

The express train rushed on through the cold calm night. With every moment she drew nearer to him—the man who had bidden her keep herself "unspotted from the world."

"And what is my life," she thought, "except one long pollution!"

She leaned her white cheek and her fair head against the window, and gazed out at the dark flying masses of the clouds; her eyes were full of pain, wide opened, lustrous; and, waking suddenly and seeing her thus opposite him, her husband called to her roughly and irritably with an oath: "Can you not sleep?"

It seemed to her as if she never slept now. What served her as sleep seemed but a troubled feverish dull trance, disturbed by hateful dreams.

It was seven o'clock on the following evening when they arrived in Paris. Their carriage was waiting, and she and Madame Nelaguine drove homeward together, leaving Zouroff to follow them. There was a faint light of an aurora borealis[1] in the sky, and the lamps of

---

1 Northern lights.

the streets were sparkling in millions; the weather was very cold. Their coachman took his way past the opera-house. There were immense crowds and long lines of equipages.[1]

In large letters in the strong gaslight it was easy to read upon the placards.

Faust.... CORRÈZE

The opera was about to commence.

Vere shrank back into the depths of the carriage. Her companion leaned forward and looked out into the night.

"Paris is so fickle; but there is one sovereign she never tires of—it is Corrèze," said Madame Nelaguine, with a little laugh, and wondered to see the colourless cheek of her young sister-in-law flush suddenly and then grow white again.

"Have you ever heard Corrèze sing?" she asked quickly. Vere hesitated.

"Never in the opera. No."

"Ah! to be sure, he left Russia suddenly last winter; left as you entered it," said Madame Nelaguine, musing, and with a quick side-glance.

Vere was silent.

The carriage rolled on, and passed into the courtyard of the Hôtel Zouroff between the gilded iron gates, at the instant when the applause of Paris welcomed upon the stage of its opera its public favourite.

The house was grand, gorgeous, brilliant; adorned in the taste of the Second Empire, to which it belonged; glittering and over-laden, superb yet meretricious. The lines of servants were bowing low; the gilded gaseliers were glowing with light, there were masses of camellias and azaleas, beautiful and scentless, and heavy odours of burnt pastilles on the heated air.

Vere passed up the wide staircase slowly, and the hues of its scarlet carpeting seemed like fire to her tired eyes.

She changed her prison-house often, and each one had been made more splendid than the last, but each in its turn was no less a prison; and its gilding made it but the more dreary and the more oppressive to her.

"You will excuse me, I am tired," she murmured to her sister-in-

---

1 Carriages.

law, who was to be her guest, and she went into her own bed-chamber and shut herself in, shutting out even her maid from her solitude.

Through the curtained windows there came a low muffled sound; the sound of the great night-world of that Paris to which she had come, heralded for her beauty by a thousand tongues.

Why could she not be happy?

She dropped on her knees by her bed of white satin, embroidered with garlanded roses, and let her head fall on her arms, and wept bitterly.

In the opera-house the curtain had risen, and the realisation of all he had lost was dawning upon the vision of Faust.

The voice of her husband came to her through the door.

"Make your toilette rapidly," he said; "we will dine quickly; there will be time to show yourself at the opera."

Vere started and rose to her feet.

"I am very tired; the journey was long."

"We will not stay," answered Prince Zouroff. "But you will show yourself. Dress quickly."

"Would not another night—"

"*Ma chère*, do not dispute. I am not used to it."

The words were slight, but the accent gave them a cold and hard command, to which she had grown accustomed.

She said nothing more, but let her maid enter by an inner door.

The tears were wet on her lashes, and her mouth still quivered. The woman saw and pitied her, but with some contempt.

"Why do you lament like that?" the woman thought; "why not amuse yourself?"

Her maids were used to the caprices of Prince Zouroff, which made his wife's toilette a thing which must be accomplished to perfection in almost a moment of time. A very young and lovely woman, also, can be more easily adorned than one who needs a thousand artificial aids. They dressed her very rapidly in white velvet, setting some sapphires and diamonds in her bright hair.

"Give me that necklace," she said, pointing to one of the partitions in one of the open jewel cases; it was the necklace of the moth and the star.

In ten minutes she descended to dinner. She and her husband were alone. Madame Nelaguine had gone to bed fatigued.

He ate little, but drank much, though one of the finest artists of the Paris kitchens had done his best to tempt his taste with the rarest and most delicate combination.

"You do not seem to have much appetite," he said, after a little while. "We may as well go. You look very well now."

He looked at her narrowly.

Fatigue conquered, and emotion subdued, had given an unusual brilliancy to her eyes, an unusual flush to her cheeks. The white velvet was scarcely whiter than her skin; about her beautiful throat the moth trembled between the flame and the star.

"Have you followed my advice and put some rouge?" he asked suddenly.

Vere answered simply, "No."

"Paris will say that you are handsomer than any of the others," he said carelessly. "Let us go."

Vere's cheeks flushed more deeply as she rose in obedience. She knew he was thinking of all the other women whom Paris had associated with his name.

She drew about her a cloak of white feathers, and went to her carriage. Her heart was sick, yet it beat fast. She had learned to be quite still, and to show nothing that she felt under all pain; and this emotion was scarcely pain, this sense that so soon the voice of Corrèze would reach her ear.

She was very tired; all the night before she had not slept; the fatigue and feverishness of the long unbroken journey were upon her, making her temples throb, her head swim, her limbs feel light as air. But the excitement of one idea sustained her, and made her pulses quicken with fictitious strength: so soon she would hear the voice of Corrèze.

A vague dread, a sense of apprehension that she could not have explained, were upon her; yet a delighted expectation came over her also, and was sweeter than any feeling that had ever been possible to her since her marriage.

As their carriage passed through the streets, her husband smoked a cigarette, and did not speak at all. She was thankful for the silence, though she fancied in it he must hear the loud fast beating of her heart.

It was ten o'clock when they reached the opera-house. Her husband gave her his arm, and they passed through the vestibule and passage, and up the staircase[1] to that door which at the commencement of the season had been allotted to the name of Prince Zouroff.

---

1 The Grand Staircase was built as another sort of stage, which allowed the audience to gaze upon ticket holders as they ascended to their boxes.

The house was hushed; the music, which has all the ecstasy and the mystery of human passion in it, thrilled through the stillness. Her husband took her through the corridor into their box, which was next that which had once been the empress's. The vast circle of light seemed to whirl before her eyes.

Vere entered as though she were walking in her sleep, and sat down.

On the stage there were standing alone Margherita and Faust. The lights fell full upon the classic profile of Corrèze, and his eyelids were drooped, as he stood gazing on the maiden who knelt at his feet. The costume he wore showed his graceful form to its greatest advantage, and the melancholy of wistful passion that was expressed on his face at that moment made his beauty of feature more impressive. His voice was silent at the moment when she saw him thus once more, but his attitude was a poem, his face was the face she had seen by the sunlight where the sweetbriar sheltered the thrush.

Not for her was he Faust, not for her was he the public idol of Paris. He was the Saint Raphael of the Norman seashore. She sat like one spellbound gazing at the stage.

Then Corrèze raised his head, his lips parted, and uttered the

Tu vuoi, ahime!
Che t'abbandoni.[1]

It thrilled though the house, that exquisite and mysterious music of the human voice, seeming to bring with it the echo of a heaven for ever lost.

Women, indifferent to all else, would weep when they heard the voice of Corrèze.

Vere's heart stood still; then seemed to leap in her breast as with a throb of new warm life. Unforgotten, unchanged, unlike any other ever heard on earth, this perfect voice fell on her ear again, and held her entranced with its harmony. The ear has its ecstasy as have other senses, and this ecstasy for the moment held in suspense all other emotion, all other memory.

She sat quite motionless, leaning her cheek upon her hand. When he sang, she only then seemed herself to live; when his voice ceased, she seemed to lose hold upon existence, and the great world of light around her seemed empty and mute.

---

1 Do you want, my love, for me to abandon you (Italian).

Many eyes were turning on her, many tongues were whispering of her, but she was unconscious of them. Her husband, glancing at her, thought that no other woman would have been so indifferent to the stare of Paris as she was; he did not know that she was insensible of it; he only saw that she had grown very pale again, and was annoyed, fearing that her entry would not be the brilliant success that he desired it to be.

"Perhaps she was too tired to come here," he thought with some impatience.

But Paris was looking at her in her white velvet, which was like the snows she had quitted, and was finding her lovely beyond compare, and worthy of the wild rumours of adoration that had come before her from the north.

The opera, meanwhile, went on its course; the scenes changed, the third act ended, the curtain fell, the theatre resounded with the polite applause of a cultured city.

She seemed to awake as from a dream. The door had opened, and her husband was presenting some great persons to her.

"You have eclipsed even Corrèze, Princess," said one of these. "In looking at you, Paris forgot for once to listen to its nightingale. It was fortunate for him, since he sung half a note false."

"Since you are so tired we will go," said her husband, when the fourth act was over; when a score of great men had bowed themselves in and out of her box, and the glasses of the whole house had been levelled at the Russian beauty, as they termed her.

"I am not so very tired now!" she said wistfully.

She longed to hear that voice of Faust as she had never longed for anything.

"If you are not tired you are capricious, *ma chère*," said her husband, with a laugh. "I brought you here that they might see you; they have seen you; now I am going to the club. Come."

He wrapped her white feathery mantle round her, as though it were snow that covered her, and took her away from the theatre as the curtain rose.

He left her to go homeward alone, and went himself to the Rue Scribe.

She was thankful.

"You sang false, Corrèze!" said mocking voices of women gaily round him in the *foyer*.[1] He was so eminent, so perfect, so felicitous-

---

1 An elaborately decorated room where the public could circulate during intervals.

ly at the apex of his triumph and art, that a momentary failure could be made a jest of without fear.

"Pardieu!"[1] said Corrèze, with a shrug of his shoulders. "Pardieu! do you suppose I did not know it. A fly flew in my throat. I suppose it will be in all the papers to-morrow. That is the sweet side of fame."

He shook himself free of his tormentors, and went to his brougham as soon as his dress was changed. It was only one o'clock, and he had all Paris ready to amuse him.

But he felt out of tone and out of temper with all Paris; another half-note false and Paris would hiss him—even him.

He went home to his house in the Avenue Marigny, and sent his coachman away.

"The beast!" he said to himself, as he entered his chamber; he was thinking of Sergius Zouroff. He threw himself down in an easy chair, and sat alone lost in thought; whilst a score of supper-tables were the duller for his absence, and more than one woman's heart ached, or passion fretted, at it.

"Who would have thought the sight of her would have moved me so!" he said to himself in self-scorn. "A false note!—I!"

CHAPTER II.

In the bitter February weather all aristocratic Paris felt the gayer, because the vast Hôtel Zouroff, in the Avenue du Bois de Boulogne, had its scarlet-clad *suisse* leaning on his gold-headed staff at its portals, and its tribes of liveried and unliveried lacqueys languishing in its halls and ante-rooms; since these signs showed that the Prince and Princess were *en ville*,[2] and that the renowned beauty of the Winter Palace had brought her loveliness and her diamonds to the capital of the world.

The Hôtel Zouroff, under Nadine Nelaguine, had been always one of those grand foreign houses at which all great people meet; a noble *terra nullius*[3] in which all political differences were obliterated, and all that was either well born or well received met, and the Empire touched the Faubourg, and the Orléans princes brushed the marshals of the Republic. The Hôtel Zouroff had never been very exclusive, but it had always been very brilliant. Under the young Princess, Paris saw that it was likely to be much more exclusive, and perhaps in proportion less entertaining. There was that in the serene

---

1 Indeed!
2 In town.
3 Neutral ground.

simplicity, the proud serious grace of the new mistress of it, which rallied to her the old régime and scared away the new.

"You should have been born a hundred years ago," said her husband with some impatience to her. "You would make the house the Hôtel Rambouillet."[1]

"I do not care for the stories of 'Figaro,' at my dinner-table, and I do not care to see the romp of the cotillon in my ball-room; but it is your house, it must be ordered as you please," she answered him; and she let Madame Nelaguine take the reins of social government, and held herself aloof.

But though she effaced herself as much as possible, that tall slender proud figure, with the grave colourless face that was so cold and yet so innocent, had an effect that was not to be defined, yet not to be resisted, as she received the guests of the Hôtel Zouroff; and the entertainments there, though they gained in simplicity and dignity, lost in *entrain*.[2] Vere was not suited to her century.

Houses take their atmosphere from those who live in them, and even the Hôtel Zouroff, despite its traditions and its epoch, despite its excess of magnificence and its follies of expenditure, yet had a fresher and a purer air since the life of its new princess had come into it.

"You have married a young saint, and the house feels already like a sacristy," said the Duchesse de Sonnaz to Sergius Zouroff, "*Ça nous obsède, mon vieux!*"[3]

That was the feeling of society.

She was exquisitely lovely; she had a great distinction, she knew a great deal and though she spoke seldom, spoke well, but she was *obsédante*;[4] she made them feel as if they were in church.

Yet Paris spoke of nothing for the moment but of the Princess Zouroff. Reigning beauties were for the moment all dethroned, and, as Paris had for years talked of his racers, his mistresses, his play, and his vices, so it now talked of Sergius Zouroff's wife.

That fair, grave, colourless face, so innocent yet so proud, so child-like yet so thoughtful, with its musing eyes and its arched mouth,

---

1 Catherine de Vivonne Marquise de Rambouillet (1588-1665) found the coarseness and intrigue of the French court distasteful. She established the Hôtel de Rambouillet, where she kept a salon devoted to literary and cultural conversations. There nobles and men of letters mingled.
2 Liveliness.
3 That worries me, old friend.
4 Troublesome.

became the theme of artists, the adoration of dandies, the despair of women. As a maiden she would have been called lovely, but too cold, and passed over. Married, she had that position which adorns as diamonds adorn, and that charm as of forbidden fruit, which piques the sated palate of mankind.

She was the event of the year.

Her husband was not surprised either at her fame or her failure. He had foreseen both after the first week of his marriage. "She will be the rage for a season, for her face and her form," he said to himself. "Then they will find her *entêtée*[1] and stupid, and turn to some one else." He honestly thought her stupid.

She knew Greek and Latin and all that, but of the things that make a woman brilliant she knew nothing.

Life seemed to Vere noisy, tedious, glaring, beyond conception; she seemed, to herself, always to be *en scène*;[2] always to be being dressed and being undressed for some fresh spectacle; always to be surrounded with flatterers, and to be destitute of friends, never to be alone. It seemed to her wonderful that people who could rule their own lives chose incessant fatigue and called it pleasure. She understood it in nothing. That her mother, after twenty years of it, could yet pursue this life with excitement and preference seemed to her so strange that it made her shudder. There was not an hour for thought, scarcely a moment for prayer. She was very young, and she rose early while the world was still sleeping, and tried to gain some little time for her old habits, her old tastes, her old studies, but it was very difficult; she seemed to grow dizzy, tired, useless. "It was what I was sold to be," she used to think bitterly. Her husband was fastidious as to her appearance, and inexorable as to her perpetual display of herself; for the rest he said nothing to her, unless it were to sharply reprove her for some oblivion of some trifle in etiquette, some unconscious transgression of the innumerable unwritten laws of society.

In the midst of the most brilliant circle of Europe, Vere was as lonely as any captured bird. She would have been glad of a friend, but she was shy and proud; women were envious of her, and men were afraid of her. She was not like her world or her time. She was beautiful, but no one would have ever dreamed of classing her with "the beauties" made by princely praise and public portraiture. She

---

1 Obstinate.
2 On stage.

was as unlike them as the beauty of perfect statuary is unlike the Lilith[1] and the Vivienne[2] of modern painting.

Sometimes her husband was proud of that, sometimes he was annoyed at it. Soon he felt neither pride nor annoyance, but grew indifferent.

Society noticed that she seldom smiled. When a smile did come upon her face, it was as cold as the moonbeam that flits bright and brief across a landscape on a cloudy night. Very close observers saw that it was not coldness, but a melancholy too profound for her years that had robbed the light from her thoughtful eyes; but close observers in society are not numerous, and her world in general believed her incapable of any emotion, or any sentiment, save that of a great pride.

They did not know that in the stead of any pride what weighed on her night and day was the bitterness of humiliation—humiliation they would never have understood—with which no one would have sympathised; a shame that made her say to herself, when she went to her tribune at Chantilly, to see her husband's horses run, "My place should be apart there with those lost women; what am I better than they?"

All the horror of the sin of the world had fallen suddenly on her ignorance and innocence as an avalanche may fall on a young chamois; the knowledge of it oppressed her, and made a great disgust stay always with her as her hourly burden.

She despised herself, and there is no shame more bitter to endure.

"You are unreasonable, my child," said her sister-in-law, who, in a cold way, was attached to her, and did pity her. "Any other woman as young as yourself would be happy. My brother is not your ideal. No; that was not to be expected or hoped for; but he leaves you your

---

1   According to a Hebrew legend, Lilith was Adam's first wife. She was cre-
    ated, like Adam, from dust and insisted immediately that she was his
    equal. When he tried to force her to submit, she left him to reside with
    demons. She became a monster who preyed on newborn babies. She
    appears in Dante Gabriel Rossetti's "Demon Bower" (1871) as a serpent
    woman ("not a drop of her blood was human" 3). She also appears ser-
    pent-like in nineteenth century paintings and sculpture and, at the end
    of the century, in George MacDonald's *Lilith* (1895).
2   Ouida is probably referring to the seductive serpent-woman Vivien of
    Tennyson's "Merlin and Vivien" in *The Idylls of the King* (1859), who
    causes Merlin's downfall. She also was the subject of many nineteenth-
    century paintings.

own way; he is not a tyrant, he lets you enjoy yourself as you may please to do; he never controls your purse or your caprice. Believe me, my love, that, as the world goes, this is as nearly happiness as can be found in marriage—to have plenty of money and to be let alone. You want happiness, I know, but I doubt very much if happiness is really existent anywhere on earth, unless you can get it out of social success and the discomfiture of rivals, as most fortunate women do. I think you are unreasonable. You are not offended? No?"

"Perhaps I am unreasonable," assented Vere.

She never spoke of herself. Her lips had been shut on the day that she had accepted the hand of Sergius Zouroff, and she kept them closed.

She would have seemed unreasonable to everyone, as to Princess Nelaguine, had she done so.

Why could she not be happy?

With youth, a lovely face and form, the great world her own, and her riches boundless, why could she not be happy, or, at the least, amused and flattered?

Amusement and flattery console most women, but they had failed as yet to console her. By example or by precept everyone about her made her feel that they should do so. Upon the danger of the teaching neither her husband nor society ever reflected.

Young lives are tossed upon the stream of the world, like rose-leaves on a fast-running river, and the rose-leaves are blamed if the river be too strong and too swift for them, and they perish. It is the fault of the rose-leaves.

When she thought that this life must endure all her life, she felt a despair that numbed her, as frost kills a flower. To the very young, life looks so long.

To Sergius Zouroff innocence was nothing more than the virgin bloom of a slave had been to his father—a thing to be destroyed for an owner's diversion.

It amused him to lower her, morally and physically, and he cast all the naked truths of human vices before her shrinking mind, as he made her body tremble at his touch. It was a diversion, whilst the effect was novel. Like many another man, he never asked himself how the fidelity and the chastity that he still expected to have preserved for him, would survive his own work of destruction. He never remembered that as you sow so you may reap. Nor if he had remembered would he have cared. *Toute femme triche*[1] was engraved

---

1 All wives cheat.

on his conviction as a certain doctrine. The purity and the simplicity, and the serious sense of right and wrong that he discovered in Vere bewildered him, and half-awed, half-irritated him. But that these would last after contact with the world, he never for a moment believed, and he quickly ceased to regard or to respect them.

He knew very well that his wife and his *belles petites*[1] were creatures so dissimilar that it seemed scarcely possible that the same laws of nature had created and sustained them, the same humanity claimed them. He knew that they were as unlike as the dove and the snake, as the rose and the nightshade, but he treated them both the same.

There was a woman who was seen on the Bois who drove with white Spanish mules hung about with Spanish trappings, and had a little mulatto boy behind her dressed in scarlet. This eccentric person was speedily celebrated in Paris. She was handsome in a very dark, full-lipped, almond-eyed, mulattress fashion; she got the name of Casse-une-Croûte, and no one ever heard or cared whether she ever had had any other. Casse-une-Croûte, who was a mustang from over the seas, had made her début modestly with a banker, but she had soon blazed into that splendour in which bankers, unless they are Rothschilds, are despised. Prince Zouroff had seen the white mules, and been struck with them. Casse-une-Croûte had an apotheosis.

There was an actress who was called Noisette; she was very handsome too, in a red and white way, like Reubens's[2] women; she too drove herself, but drove a mail-phaeton[3] and very high-stepping English horses; she drank only Burgundy, but plenty of it; she had a *hôtel entre cour et jardin*;[4] on the stage she was very vulgar but she had *du chien*[5] and wonderful drolleries of expression. Prince Zouroff did not care even to look at her, but she was the fashion, and he had taken her away from his most intimate friend; so, for years, he let her eat his roubles as a mouse eats rice, and never could prevail on his vanity to break with her, lest men should think she had broken with him.

In that unexplainable, instinctive way in which women of quick perceptions come to know things that no one ever tells them, and which is never definitely put before them in words, Princess Zouroff

---

1 Mistresses.
2 Peter Paul Rubens (1577-1640) was a Flemish Baroque painter who is famous for his sensual paintings of voluptuous women.
3 An open four-wheeled carriage.
4 Townhouse between a courtyard and a garden.
5 Sex appeal.

became gradually aware that Noisette and Casse-une-Croûte were both the property of her husband. The white mules or the mail-phaeton crossed her own carriage-horses a dozen times a week in the Champs Elysées, and she looked away not to see those women, and said in the bitter humiliation of her heart, "What am I better than either of them!" When either of them saw her, Casse-une-Croûte said, "*V'là la petite!*"[1] contemptuously. Noisette said, "*Je mangerai même ses diamants à elle.*"[2]

"Sergius," said Nadine Nelaguine one night, "in that wife that you neglect for your creatures you have a pearl of price."

"And I am one of the swine, and best live with my kind," said her brother savagely, because he was ashamed of himself, and angered with all his ways of life, yet knew that he would no more change them than will swine change theirs.

"You have married a young saint. It is infinitely droll!" said the Duchesse de Sonnaz, who was always called by her society Madame Jeanne, one day to Sergius Zouroff, as he sat with her in her boudoir that was full of *chinoiseries*,[3] and Indian wares, and Persian potteries.

Jeanne de Sonnaz was a woman of thirty-three years old, and had been one of the few really great ladies who had condescended to accept the Second Empire. Born of the splendid Maison de Meril-hac, and married to the head of the scarce less ancient Maison de Sonnaz, she belonged, root and branch, to the *vieille souche*, and her people all went annually to bow the knee at Frohsdorf.[4] But Mdme. Jeanne, wedded at sixteen to a man who was wax in her hands, had no fancy for sacrifice and seclusion for the sake of a shadow and a lily. She was a woman who loved admiration and who loved display. She had condescended to accept the Second Empire, because it was the millennium of these her twin passions. She had known that it would not last, but she had enjoyed it while it did. "*C'est un obus qui va s'eclater,*"[5] she had always said cheerfully, but meanwhile she had danced on the shell till it exploded, and now danced on its débris.

The Duchesse de Sonnaz dressed better than any living being; was charming, without having a good feature in her face except her

---

1 There is the child.
2 I will eat even *her* diamonds.
3 Chinese curios.
4 A castle in Austria, which was the residence of the Count de Chambord, grandson of Charles X. Louis Philippe recognized him as head of the monarchal party in France.
5 It is a shell that is going to explode.

eyes, and was admired where Helen or Venus might have been over-looked. She was not very clever, but she was very malicious, which is more successful with society, and very violent, which is more successful with lovers. She had the power of being very agreeable. To the young Princess Zouroff she made herself even unusually so.

Vere did not notice that even a polite society could not help a smile when it saw them together.

"You have married a young saint; it is very droll," the duchesse now said for the twentieth time to Zouroff. "But do you know that I like her? Is not that very droll too?"

"It is very fortunate for me," said Zouroff drily, wondering if she were telling him a lie, and, if so, why she told one.

She was not lying; though, when she had first heard of his intend-ed marriage, she had been beside herself with rage, and had even rung violently for them to send her husband to her that she might cry aloud to him, "you never revenge yourself, but you must and you shall revenge me." Fortunately for the peace of Europe her husband was at the club, and by the time he had returned thence she had thought the better of it.

"What will you do with a saint?" she continued now. "It is not a thing for you. It must be like that White Swan in 'Lohengrin.'"[1]

"She is stupid," said Zouroff; "but she is very honest."

"How amusing a combination!"

"I do not see much of her," Zouroff added with an air of fatigue. "I think she will be always the same. She does not adapt herself. It is a pity her children should not live. She is the sort of woman to be a devoted mother."

"*Quel beau rôle!*[2] and she is not eighteen yet," said Madame de Sonnaz with amusement.

"It is what we marry good women for," he said somewhat gloomily. "They never divert one; every one knows that. *Elles ne savent pas s'encanailler.*"[3]

Jeanne de Sonnaz laughed again, but her face had an angry irony in it.

"Yes: *nous nous encanaillons;*[4] that is our charm. A beautiful com-

---

1 An opera (1850) by Richard Wagner. The hero first appears in a boat drawn by a swan. At the end the magical swan disappears.
2 What a beautiful role!
3 They don't know how to keep company with men—how to 'enter-tain'—to act like a harlot.
4 We know how to entertain men.

pliment. But it is true. It is the charm of our novels, of our theatres, of our epoch. *Le temps nous enfante.*[1] Things manage themselves drolly. A man like you gets a young angel; and an honest, stupid, innocent soul like my poor Paul gets—me."

Zouroff offered her no compliment and no contradiction; he was sitting gloomily amidst the *chinoiseries* and porcelains, but their intercourse had long passed the stage at which flattery is needful. He was glad for sake of peace that she was not an enemy of Vere's; but he was annoyed to hear her praise his wife. Why did everyone regard the girl as sacrificed? It offended and annoyed him. She had everything that she could want. Hundreds of women would have asked no more admirable fate than was hers.

"She is of the old type; the old type pure are proud," his friend pursued, unheeding his silence. "We want to see it now and then. She would go grandly to the guillotine, but she will never understand her own times, and she will always have a contempt for them. She has dignity; we have not a scrap, we have forgotten what it was like; we go into a passion at the amount of our bills; we play and never pay; we smoke and we wrangle; we have café-singers who teach us slang songs; we laugh loud, much too loud; we intrigue vulgarly, and, when we are found out, we scuffle, which is more vulgar still; we inspire nothing unless now and then a bad war or a disastrous speculation; we live showily, noisily, meanly, gaudily. You have said, '*On sait s'encanailler.*' Well, your wife is not like us. You should be thankful."

"All the same," said Zouroff, with a shrug of his shoulders; "she is not amusing."

"Oh, that is another affair. Even if she were, I do not believe you would go to your wife to be amused. I think you are simply discontented with her because she is not somebody else's wife. If she were fast and frivolous you would be angry at that."

"She is certainly not fast or frivolous!"

"Perhaps my friend—after all—it is only that she is not happy."

It was the one little poison-tipped arrow that she could not help speeding against the man whose marriage had been an insult to a "friendship" of many years' duration.

"If she were not a fool she would be perfectly happy," he answered petulantly, and with a frown.

"Or if she understood compensations as we understood them,"

---

1 We are begotten of our time.

said Mdme. de Sonnaz, lighting a cigarette. "Perhaps she never will understand them. Or, perhaps, on the other hand, some day she will."

"*Vous plaisantez, madame*,"[1] said Sergius Zouroff with a growl, as the duchess laughed.

A sullen resentment rose in him against Vere. He had meant to forget her, once married to her. The marriage had been a caprice; he had been moved to a sudden passion that had been heightened by her aversion and her reluctance; she did as well as another to bear children and grace his name; he had never meant to make a burden of her, and now everyone had agreed to speak of her as a martyr to her position.

Her position! he thought; what woman in Europe would not have been happy in it?

Vere herself might have fanciful regrets and fantastic sentiments; that he could admit; she was a child, and had odd thoughts and tastes; but he resented the pity for her—pity for her as being his—that spoke by the cynical lips of his sister and Jeanne de Sonnaz.

He began almost to wish that she would be brought to understand the necessity of *de s'encanailler*.[2] There are times when the very purity of a woman annoys and oppresses a man—even when she is his wife; perhaps most of all when she is so.

If she had disobeyed him or had any fault against him, he could still have found some pleasure in tyranny over her; but she never rebelled, she never opposed him. Obedience was all she had to give him, and she gave it in all loyalty; her grandmother had reared her in old-world ideas of duty that she found utterly out of place in the day she lived in, yet she clung to them as she clung to her belief in heaven.

Her whole nature recoiled from the man to whom she owed obedience, yet she knew obedience was his due, and she gave it. Although he would have borne with nothing less, yet this passive submission had begun to irritate him; his commands were caprices, wilful, changeable, and unreasonable. But as they were always obeyed, it ceased to be any amusement to impose them.

He began to think that she was merely stupid.

He would have believed that she was quite stupid, and nothing else, but for a certain look in her eyes now and then when she spoke, a certain gesture that occasionally escaped her of utter contempt and weariness. Then he caught sight for a moment of depths in Vere's

---

1 You jest, my lady.
2 Lowering herself.

nature that he did not fathom, of possibilities in her character that he did not take into consideration.

Had she been any other man's wife, the contradiction would have attracted him, and he would have studied her temper and her tastes. As it was he only felt some irritation, and some ennui[1] because his wife was not like his world.

"She is not amusing, and she is not grateful," he would say; and each day he saw less of her and left her to shape her own life as she chose.

CHAPTER III.

In the chilly spring weather, Lady Dolly, sitting on one chair with her pretty little feet on another chair, was at Hurlingham watching the opening match of the year and saying to her friend Lady Stoat of Stichley; "Oh my dear, yes, it is so sad, but you know my sweet child never was quite like other people; never will be I am afraid. And she never did care for me. It was all that horrid old woman, who brought her up so strangely, and divided entirely from me in every way, and made a perfect Methodist of her, really a Methodist! If Vere were not so exquisitely pretty she would be too ridiculous. As she is so handsome, men don't abuse her so much as they would if she were only just nice-looking. But she is very *very* odd; and it is so horrible to be odd! I would really sooner have her ugly. She is so odd. Never would speak to me even of the birth and death of her baby. Could you believe it? Not a word! not a word! what would you feel if Gwendolin ... Goodness! the Duke and Fred have tied. Is it true, Colonel Rochfort? Yes? Thanks. A pencil, one moment; thanks. Ah, you never bet, Adine, do you? But, really, pigeon-shooting's very stupid if you don't. Talking of bets, Colonel Rochfort, try and get 'two monkeys'[2] for me on Tambour-Battant to-morrow, will you? I've been told a thing about his trainer; it will be quite safe, quite. As I was saying, dear, she never would speak to me about that poor little lost cherub. Was it not sad—terrible? Of course she will have plenty of others; but still, never to sorrow for it at all—so unnatural! Zouroff felt it much more; he has grown very nice, really very nice. Ah! that bird has got away; the Lords will lose

---

1 Boredom.
2 A monkey is five hundred pounds. She is asking him to bet on a horse for her.

I am afraid, after all. Ah, my dear Lesterel, how are you? What are they saying of my child in Paris?"

The Marquis de Lesterel, secretary of legation, bowed smiling.

"Madame la Princesse has turned the head of 'tout Paris.' It was too cruel of you, madame; had you not already done mischief enough to men that you must distract them with such loveliness in your daughter?"

"All that is charming, and goes for nothing," said Lady Dolly good-humouredly. "I know Vera is handsome, but does she take? Est-ce qu'elle a du charme?[1] That is much more."

"But certainly!" rejoined the French marquis with much emphasis; "she is very cold, it is true, which leaves us all lamenting; and nothing, or very little at least, seems to interest her."

"Precisely what I expected!" said Lady Dolly despairingly. "Then she has not du charme.[2] Nobody has who is not amused easily and amused often."

"Pardon!" said the marquis. "There is charme and charme. There is that of the easily accessible and of the inaccessible, of the rosebud and of the edelweiss."[3]

"Does she make many friends there?" she continued, pursuing her inquiries, curiosity masked as maternal instinct. "Many women-friends, I mean; I am so afraid Vera does not like women much, and there is nothing that looks so unamiable."

"It would be impossible to suspect the Princess of unamiability," said the marquis quickly. "One look at that serene and noble countenance"—

"Very nice, very pretty; but Vere can be unamiable," said her mother tartly. "Do tell me, is there any woman she takes to at all? Anyone she seems to like much?"

("Anybody she is likely to tell about me?" she was thinking in the apprehension of her heart.)

"Madame Nelaguine"—began the young man.

"Oh her sister-in-law!" said Lady Dolly. "Yes, I believe she does like that horrid woman. I always hated Nadine myself—such an ordering sharp creature, and such a tongue! Of course I know the Nelaguine is never out of their house; but is there anybody else?"

A little smile came on the face of the Parisian.

---

1 Does she have the ability to captivate?
2 Sexual attraction; enchantment.
3 A white flower that grows high on the Alps.

"The Princess is often with Madame de Sonnaz. Madame Jeanne admires her very much."

Lady Dolly stared a minute, and then laughed; and Lady Stoat even smiled discreetly.

"I wonder what that is *for*," murmured Lady Dolly vaguely, and, in a whisper to Lady Stoat, she added, "She must mean mischief; she always means mischief; she took his marriage too quietly not to avenge herself."

"People forget nowadays; I don't think they revenge," said Lady Stoat consolingly.

"When did you see my poor darling last?" asked Lady Dolly aloud.

"At three o'clock last night, madame, at the Elysée.[1] She looked like a Greek poet's dream draped by Worth."

"How very imaginative!" said Lady Dolly, a little jealously. "How could poor dear Worth dress a dream? That would tax even his powers! I hope she goes down to Surennes[2] and chats with him quietly; that is the only way to get him to give his mind to anything really good. But she never cares about that sort of thing; never!"

"The Princess Zouroff knows well," said the Marquis de Lesterel, with some malice and more ardour, "that let her drape herself in what she might, were it sackcloth and ashes, she would be lovelier in it than any other woman ever was on earth—except her mother," he added with a chivalrous bow.

"What a horrid thing it is to be anybody's mother! and how old it makes one feel—'shunt'[3] it as one may!" thought Lady Dolly as she laughed and answered, "You are actually in love with her, marquis! Pray remember that I *am* her mother, and that she has not been married much more than a year. I am very delighted that she does please in Paris. It is her home, really her home. They will go to Petersburg once in ten years, but Paris will see them every year of their lives; Zouroff can be scarcely said to exist out of it. I am so very sorry the boy died; it just lived to breathe and be baptized, you know; named after the Tsar. So sad!—oh, so sad! Who is that shooting now? Regy? Ah-h-h? The bird is inside the palings, isn't it? Oh! that is superb! Just inside!—only just!"

And Lady Dolly scribbled again in a tiny betting-book, bound in oxydised silver, that had cost fifty guineas in Bond Street.

---

1 The palace of the President.
2 Worth owned a villa in Surennes, a town near Paris.
3 Avoid.

Lady Dolly was very fond of betting. As she practised it, it was both simple and agreeable. She was always paid, and never paid.

The ladies who pursue the art on these simplified principles are numerous, and find it profitable.

When Colonel Rochfort, a handsome young man in the Rifles, tried the next day to get her five hundred "on," at Newmarket, the Ring[1] was prudent; it would take it in his name, not in hers.

But the men of her world could not be as prudent—and as rude—as the Ring was. Besides, Lady Dorothy Vanderdecken was still a very pretty woman, with charming little tricks of manner and a cultured sagacious coquetry that was hard to resist; and she was very good company too at a little dinner at the Orleans Club,[2] when the nightingales sang, or *tête-à-tête*[3] in her fan-lined octagon boudoir.

Lady Dolly did not see much of her daughter. Lady Dolly had taken seriously to London. London had got so much nicer, she said, so much less starchy; so much more amusing; it was quite wonderful how London had improved since polo and pigeon-shooting had opened its mind. Sundays were great fun in London now, and all that old nonsense about being so very particular[4] had gone quite out. London people, the very best of them, always seemed, somehow or other—what should one say?—provincial, after Paris. Yes, provincial; but still London was very nice, and Lady Dorothy Vanderdecken was quite a great person in it; she had always managed so well that nobody ever had talked about her.

"It is so horrid to be talked about, you know," she used to say; "and, after all, so silly to *get* talked about. You can do just as you like if you are only careful to do the right things at the right time and be seen about with the right people. I am always so angry with those stupid women that are compromised; it is quite too dreadfully foolish of them, because, you know, *really*, nobody need be. People are always nice if one is nice to them."

So, from New Year to Midsummer she was in the house in Chesham Place, which she made quite charming with all sorts of old Italian things and the sombre and stately Cinque Cento,[5] effectively, if barbarously, mixed up with all the extravagancies of modern upholstery.

1   Newmarket was a horse-race course, and the Ring was a bookmaker.
2   The Orleans Club was a plush men's club. Members were allowed to bring ladies to the private-dining rooms.
3   Alone together.
4   About women's improprieties; i.e., extra-marital sexual liaisons.
5   Sixteenth-century Italian art.

Lady Dolly's house, under the combination of millinery and mediævalism, was too perfect, everybody said; and she had a new friend in her Sicilian attached to the Italian Legation,[1] who helped her a great deal with his good taste, and sent her things over from his grim old castles in the Taormina;[2] and it was a new toy and amused her; and her fancy-dress frisks, and her musical breakfasts, were great successes; and, on the whole, Lady Dolly had grown very popular. As for Mr. Vanderdecken, he was always stingy and a bear, but he knew how to behave. He represented a remote and peaceful borough,[3] which he had bought as his wife bought a poodle or a piece of *pâte tendre*;[4] he snored decorously on the benches of St. Stephens,[5] and went to ministerial dinners, and did other duties of a rich man's life; and, for the rest of his time, was absorbed in those foreign speculations and gigantic loans which constituted his business, and took him to Java, or Japan, or Jupiter so often. He was large, ugly, solemn, but he did extremely well in his place, which was an unobtrusive one, like the great Japanese bonze[6] who sat cross-legged in the hall. What he thought no one knew; he was as mute on the subject of his opinions as the bonze was. In the new order of fashionable marriage a silence that must never be broken is the part allotted to the husband; and the only part he is expected to take.

On the whole Lady Dolly was very contented. Now and then Jura would give her a sombre glance, or Zouroff a grim smile, that recalled a time to her when she had been on the very brink of the precipice, on the very edge of the outer darkness, and the recollection made her quite sick for the moment. But the qualm soon passed. She was quite safe now, and she had learned wisdom. She knew how to be "so naughty and so nice" in the way that society in London likes, and never punishes. She had been very silly sometimes, but she was never silly now, and meant to never be silly any more. She tempered roulette with ritualism, and always went to St. Margaret's church in the morning of a Sunday, if she dined down at the Orleans or at old Skindle's[7] in the evening. She had had a great "scare," and the peril and the fright of it had sobered her and shown her the way she should go.

---

1 Embassy.
2 A city in Sicily.
3 A town represented by a Member of Parliament.
4 Delicate pastry.
5 A club in London.
6 A statue of a Buddhist monk.
7 The Skindles Hotel hosted royalty and celebrities daily.

For Lady Dolly was always careful of appearances; she had no patience with people who were not. "It is such very bad form to make people talk," she would always say; "and it is so easy to stop their mouths."

Lady Dolly liked to go to court, to be intimate with the best people, to dine at royal tables, and to "be in the swim" altogether. Everybody knew she was a naughty little woman, but she had never been on the debateable land; she had never been one of the "*paniers à quinze sous;*"[1] she had never been coldly looked on by anybody. She had never let "Jack," or anybody who preceded or succeeded "Jack," get her into trouble. She liked to go everywhere, and she knew that, if people once begin to talk, you may very soon go nowhere.

She was not very wise in anything else, but she was very wise in knowing her own interests. Frightened and sobered, she had said to herself that it was a horrible thing to get any scandal about you; to fall out of society; to have to content yourself with third-rate drawing-rooms; to have to take your gaieties in obscure continental towns; to reign still, but only reign over a lot of shady dubious *déclassé*[2] people, some with titles and some without, but all "nowhere" in the great race. It was a horrible thing; and she vowed to herself that never, never, never, should it be her fate.

So she took seriously to the big house in Chesham Place, and her religion became one of the prettiest trifles in all the town.

With her brougham full of hothouse flowers, going to the Children's Hospital, or shutting herself up and wearing black all Holy Week, she was a most edifying study. She maintained some orphans at the Princess Mary's pet home, and she was never absent if Stafford House[3] had a new charitable craze. She did not go into extremes, for she had very good taste; but only said very innocently, "Oh, all these things are second nature to me, you know; you know my poor Vere was a clergyman."

If she did sing naughty little songs after dinner on the lawn at the Orleans; if the Sicilian *attaché* were always rearranging pictures or tapestries in her drawing-rooms; if she did bet and lose and never pay; if she did go to fancy frisks in a few yards of gossamer and her jewels, nobody

---

1 A cheap, loose woman; literally—fifteen-cent baskets.
2 "Ruined"; no longer received by fashionable society.
3 Stafford House was regarded as the greatest town house in London. The Duchess of Stafford was a good friend of Queen Victoria, who was often a guest there. The Duchess worked for prison reform, for the lot of miners, and for the poor in workhouses.

ever said anything, except that she was such a dear little woman. It is such a sensible thing to "pull yourself together" and be wise in time.

Lord Jura, who was leading his old life, with Lady Dolly left out of it, stupidly and joylessly, because he had got into the groove of it, and could not get out, and who had become gloomy, taciturn, and inclined to drink more than was good for him, used to watch the comedy of Lady Dolly's better-ordered life with a cynical savage diversion. When he had come back from his Asiatic hunting tour, which had lasted eighteen months, he had met her as men and women do meet in society, no matter what tragedies divide or hatreds rage in them; but she had seen very well that "Jack" was lost to her for ever. She did not even try to get him back; and when she heard men say that Jura was not the good fellow he used to be, and played too high and drank too deep for the great name he bore, she was pleased, because he had had no earthly right to go off in that rough way, or say the things he had said.

"I never see very much of Jura now," she would say to her friends. "He is become so very *farouche* since that eastern trip; perhaps some woman—I said so to his dear old father last week—poor Jack is so good and so weak, he is just the man to fall a prey to a bad woman."

The ladies to whom she said this laughed a little amongst themselves when they had left her, but they liked her all the better for ridding herself of an old embarrassment so prettily; it formed a very good precedent. Jura of course said nothing, except to his very intimate friends, who rallied him. To them he said, "Well I went to India, you know, and she didn't like it, and when I came back she had got the Sicilian fellow with her. So I don't bore her any more; she is a dear little woman; yes."

For honour makes a lie our social life's chief necessity, and Jura, having thus lied for honour's sake, would think of the Princess Zouroff in Paris, and swear round oaths to himself, and go upstairs where they were playing baccarat, and signing fortunes and estates away with the scrawl of a watch-chain's pencil.

"I think I could have made her happy if it hadn't been impossible," he would think sometimes. "She would always have been miles beyond me, and no man that ever lived would have been good enough for her; but I think I could have made her happy; I would have served her and followed her like a dog—anyway, I would have been true to her, and kept my life decent and clean; not like that brute's."

Then he would curse Sergius Zouroff, as he went home alone down St. James's Street in the grey fog of early morning, sick of pleasure, weary of play, dull with brandy, but not consoled by it; knowing that he might have been a better man, seeing the better ways too late; loathing the senseless routine of his life, but too listless to shake off habit and custom, and find out any different or higher life.

He was Earl of Jura; he had a vast inheritance; he had good health and good looks; he was sound in wind and limb; he had a fair share of intelligence, if his mind was slow; in a few years, when he should succeed to his father, he would have a thousand pounds a day as his income. Yet he had got as utterly into a groove that he hated as any ploughman that rises every day to tread the same fields behind the same cattle; and habit made him as powerless to get out of it as his poverty makes the ploughman.

"London is the first city in the world, they say," he thought, as he went down St. James's in the mists that made a summer morning cheerless as winter, and as colourless. "Well, it may be, for aught I know; but, damn it all, if I don't think the Sioux in the big swamps, or the hill tribes in the Cashgar passes, are more like men than we are. And we are all so used to it, we never see what fools we are."

CHAPTER IV.

One morning the young Duke of Mull and Cantire arrived in Paris, where he was seldom seen, and chanced to find his cousin alone in her morning room at the Hôtel Zouroff.

He was a good-looking young man, with a stupid honest face; he dressed shabbily and roughly, yet always looked like a gentleman. He had no talents, but, to compensate, he had no vices; he was very simple, very loyal, and very trustful. He was fond of Vere, and had been dismayed at the marriage so rapidly arranged; but he had seen her at St. Petersburg, and was deceived by her coldness and calm into thinking her consoled by ambition.

"I am about to marry too," he said with a shamefaced laugh, a little while after his entrance. "I have asked her again and she says 'Yes.' I ran down to Paris to tell you this."

Vere looked at him with dismay.

"You do not mean Fuschia Leach?" she said quickly.

The young duke nodded.

"She's quite too awfully pretty, you know; a fellow can't help it."

"She is pretty, certainly."

"Oh, hang it, Vere, that's worse than abusing her. You hate her, I can see. Of course I know she isn't our form, but—but—I am very fond of her; dreadfully fond of her; and you will see, in a year or two, how fast she will pick it all up—"

Vere sat silent.

She was deeply angered; her chief fault was pride, an incurable pride of birth with all its prejudices, strong as the prejudices of youth alone can be.

"Won't you say something kind?" faltered her cousin.

"I cannot pretend what I do not feel," she said coldly. "I think such a marriage a great unworthiness, a great disgrace. This—this—person is not a gentlewoman, and never will be one, and I think that you will repent giving your name to her—if you do ever give it."

"I give it most certainly," said the young lover hotly and sullenly; "and if you and I are to be friends, dear, in the future, you must welcome her as a friend too."

"I shall not ever do that," said Vere simply; but the words, though they were so calm, gave him a chill.

"I suppose you will turn the forests into coal-mines now?" she added, after a moment's pause. The young man reddened.

"Poor grandmamma!" said Vere wistfully, and her eyes filled with tears.

The stern old woman loved her grand-children well, and had done her best by them, and all they were fated to bring her in her old age were pain and humiliation.

Would the old duchess ever force herself to touch the flower-like cheek of Fuschia Leach with a kiss of greeting? Never, thought Vere; never, never!

"When all is said and done," muttered the young duke angrily, "what is the utmost you can bring against my poor love? That she is not our form? That she doesn't talk in our way, but says 'cunning' where we say 'nice'? Is that a great crime? She is exquisitely pretty. She is as clever as anything—a prince of the blood might be proud of her. She has a foot for Cinderella's slipper. She never tried to catch me, not she; she sent me about my business twice; laughed at me because I wear such old hats; she's as frank as sunlight! God bless her!"

"I think we will not speak of her," said Vere coldly. "Of course you do as you please. I used to think Herbert of Mull a great name, but perhaps I was mistaken. I was only a child. I am almost glad it has ceased to be mine, since so soon she will own it. Will you not stay to dinner, Monsieur Zouroff will be most happy to see you?"

"I will see your husband before I leave Paris," said the young man, a little moodily, "and I am very sorry you take it like that, Vere, because you and I were always good friends at old Bulmer."

"I think you will find that everyone will take it like that—who cares for you or your honour."

"Honour!—Vere, I should be so sorry to quarrel. We won't discuss this thing. It is no use."

"No. It is no use."

But she sighed as she spoke; it was a link the more added to the heavy chain that she dragged with her now. Everyone seemed failing her, and all old faiths seemed changing. He was the head of her family, and she knew his uprightness, his excellence, his stainless honour—and he was about to marry Fuschia Leach.

The visit of her cousin brought back to her, poignantly and freshly, the pain of the letter written to her on her own marriage from Bulmer. A great longing for that old innocent life, all dull and sombre though it had been, came on her as she sat in solitude after he had left her, and thought of the dark wet woods, the rough grey seas, the long gallops on forest ponies, the keen force of the north wind beating and bending the gnarled storm-shaven trees.

What she would have given to have been Vere Herbert once again! never to have known this weary, gilded, perfumed, decorated, restless and insincere world to which she had been sold!

"Really I don't know what to say," said Lady Dolly, when, in her turn, she heard the tidings in London. "No, really I don't. Of course you ought to marry money, Frank; an immensity of money; and most of these Americans have such heaps. It is a very bad marriage for you, very; and yet she is so very much the fashion, I really don't know what to say. And it will drive your grandmother wild, which will be delightful; and these American women always get on somehow; they have a way of getting on; I dare say she will be Mistress of the Robes[1] some day, and all sorts of things. She is horribly bad form; you don't mind me saying so, because you must see it for yourself. But then it goes down, and it pleases better than anything; so, after all, I am not sure that it matters. And, besides, she will change wonderfully when she is Duchess of Mull. All those wild little republicans get as starchy as possible once they get a European title. They are just like those scatter-brained princes in history, that turn out such stern good-goody sort of despots, when once the crown is on their heads. Really, I don't know what to say. I knew quite well she meant to get you when she went to Stagholme this October after you. Oh, you thought it was accident, did you? How innocent of you, and how nice! You ought to have married more money; and it is horrible to

---

1 A lady who enjoys the highest rank of the ladies in the service of the Queen and who is supposed to have the care of her robes.

have a wife who never had a grandfather; but still, I don't know, she will make your place very lively, and she won't let you wear old hats. Yes—yes—you might have done worse. You might have married out of a music-hall or a circus. Some of them do. And, after all, Fuschia Leach is a person everybody can *know*."

The young lover did not feel much comforted by this form of congratulation, but it was the best that any of his own family and friends had given him, and Lady Dolly quite meant to be kind.

She was rather glad herself that the American would be Duchess of Mull. She had hated all the Herberts for many a long year, and she knew that, one and all, they would sooner have seen the young chief of their race in his grave. Lady Dolly felt that in large things and in little, Providence, after treating her very badly, was at last giving her her own way.

The young Duke of Mull a month later had *his* way, and married his brilliant Fuschia in the teeth of the stiffest opposition and blackest anathemas from his family. Not one of them deigned to be present at the ceremony of his sacrifice except his aunt, Lady Dorothy Vanderdecken, who said to her friends:—

"I hate the thing quite as much as they all do, but I can't be ill-natured, and poor Frank feels it so; and, after all, you know, he might have married out of a music-hall or a circus. So many of them do."

People said what a dear little amiable woman she was; so different from her daughter, and, on the whole, the marriage, with choral service at the Abbey,[1] and the breakfast at a monster hotel where Mrs. Leach had a whole half of the first floor, was a very magnificent affair, and was adorned with great names despite the ominous absence of the Herberts of Mull.

"I'm glad that girl put my monkey up about the coal, and made me whistle him back," thought the brilliant Fuschia to herself as the choir sang her epithalamium.[2] "It's a whole suit and all the buttons on; after all, a duchess is always a four-horse concern when she's an English one; and they do think it some pumpkins at home. I'm afraid the money's whittled away a good deal, but we'll dig for that coal before the year's out. Duchess of Mull and Cantire! After all it's a big thing, and sounds smart."

And the bells, as they rang, seemed to her fancy to ring that and that only all over London. "Duchess of Mull! Duchess of Mull!"

---

1 Westminster Abbey.
2 A song in honor of the bride and bridegroom.

It was a raw, dark, rainy day, in the middle of March, as unpleasant as London weather could possibly be; but the shining eyes of the lovely Fuschia, and her jewels, and her smiles, seemed to change the sooty, murky, mists to tropic sunshine.

"How will you quarter the arms, Frank?" whispered Lady Dolly, as she bade her nephew adieu. "A pig *gules* with a knife in its throat, and a bottle *argent* of pick-me-up?—how nice the new blazonries will look!"[1]

But the young duke had no ears for her.

Very uselessly, but very feverishly, the obligation to call Fuschia Leach cousin irritated the Princess Zouroff into an unceasing pain and anger. To her own cousin on the marriage she sent a malachite cabinet and some grand jade vases, and there ended her acknowledgment of it. She was offended, and did not conceal it.

When the world who had adored Pick-me-up as a maiden, found Pick-me-up as Duchess of Mull and Cantire as adorable as another generation had found Georgina Duchess of Devonshire,[2] Vere's proud mouth smiled with ineffable contempt.

"What will you, my love?" said Madame Nelaguine. "She is frightfully vulgar, but it is a piquante vulgarity. It takes."

Vere frowned and her lips set close.

"She has made him sink coal shafts in the forest already; *our* forest!"

Madame Nelaguine shrugged her shoulders.

"It is a pity, for the forests. But we dig for salt; it is cleaner, prettier, but I am not sure that is more princely, salt than coal."

"No Herbert of Mull has ever done it," said Vere with darkening flashing eyes. "Not one in all the centuries that we have been on the Northumbrian seaboard, for we were there in the days of Otterbourne and Flodden.[3] No man of them would ever do it. Oh, if you

---

1 Lady Dolly is referring to Mull's coat of arms (blazonries). Tinctures are the colors used on the coat of arms. Gules is red—the most honorable heraldic color. The royal livery of England is red. But in French *gueules* means the mouth or the throat of an animal. She is mocking Fuschia's brothers' occupation by suggesting that the red pig (with the knife in the throat) would be in the center of the coat of arms. Argent is silver or white, and staffs, or moon-shaped images would traditionally be the border around the coat of arms. Lady Dolly is again insulting Fuschia's family—in this case her father who sells liquor—by suggesting that bottles would surround the pig.

2 The fifth Duchess of Devonshire (1757-1806) was a leader of Regency society and a great beauty.

3 Invading Scottish warriors were defeated there by the British in 1513.

had seen that forest! and soon now it will be a blackened, smoking, reeking treeless waste. It is shameful of my cousin Francis."

"He is in love still, and does what she tells him. My dear, our sex is divided into two sorts of women—those who always get their own way and those who never get it. Pick-me-up, as they call your cousin's wife in London, is of the fortunate first sort. She is vulgar, ignorant, audacious, uneducated, but she takes, and in her way she is *maîtresse femme*. You have a thousand times more mind, and ten thousand times more character, yet you do not get your own way; you never will get it."

"I would have lived on beechmast and acorns from the forest trees sooner than have sunk a shaft under one of them," said Vere unheeding, only thinking of the grand old glades, the deep, still greenery, the mossy haunts of buck and doe, the uplands and the yellow gorze, that were to be delivered over now to the smoke-fiend.

"That I quite believe," said her sister-in-law. "But it is just that kind of sentiment in you which will for ever prevent your having influence. You are too lofty; you do not stoop and see the threads in the dust that guide men."

"For thirteen centuries the forest has been untouched," answered Vere.

It was an outrage she could not forgive.

When she first met the Duchess of Mull after her marriage, Fuschia Leach, translated into Her Grace, said across a drawing-room, "Vera, I am going to dig for that coal. I guess we'll live to make a pile that way." Vere deigned to give no answer, unless a quick, angry flush, and the instant turning of her back on the new duchess could be called one. The young duke sat between them, awed, awkward, and ashamed.

"I will never forgive it," his cousin said to him later. "I will never forgive it. She knows no better because she was born so—but you!"

He muttered a commonplace about waste of mineral wealth, and felt a poor creature.

"I think you're quite right to dig," said Lady Dolly in his ear to console him. "Quite right to dig; why not? I dare say your wife will make your fortune, and I am sure she ought if she can, to compensate for her papa, who helps people to 'liquor up,' and her brothers, who are in the pig-killing trade, pig-killing by machinery; I've seen a picture of it in the papers; the pigs go down a gangway, as we do on to the Channel steamers, and they come up hams and sausages. Won't you have the pig-killers over? They would be quite *dans le métier*[1] at

---

1 In the trade.

Hurlingham. Of course she tells you to dig, and you do it. Good husbands always do what they're told."

For Lady Dolly detested all the Herberts, and had no mercy whatever on any one of them; and, in her way, she was a haughty little woman, and though she was shrewd enough to see that in her day aristocracy to be popular must pretend to be democratic, she did not relish any more than any other member of that great family, the connection of its head with the pig-killing brothers down west.

Yet, on the whole, she made herself pleasant to the new duchess, discerning that the lovely Fuschia possessed in reserve an immense retaliating power of being "nasty" were she displeased, so that sensible Lady Dolly even went the length of doing what all the rest of the Mull family flatly refused to do—she presented her niece "on her marriage."

And Her Grace, who, on her first girlish presentation, when she had first come over "the pickle-field," had confessed herself "flustered," was, on this second occasion perfectly equal to it; carrying her feathers as if she had been born with them on her head, and bending her bright cheeks over a bouquet in such a manner that all London dropped at her feet. "If Sam and Saul could see me," thought the American beauty, hiding a grin with her roses; her memory reverting to the big brothers, at that moment standing above a great tank of pigs' blood, counting the "dead 'uns" as they were cast in the caldrons.

"It is so very extraordinary. I suppose it is because she is so dreadfully odd," said Lady Dolly of her daughter to Lady Stoat that spring, on her return from spending Easter in Paris. "But when we think she has everything she can possibly wish for, that when she goes down the Bois really nobody else is looked at, that he has actually bought the Roc's egg for her—really, really, it is flying in the face of Providence for her not to be happier than she is. I am sure if at her age I might have spent ten thousand pounds a season on my gowns, I should have been in heaven if they had married me to a Caffre."[1]

"I never think you did your dear child justice," said Lady Stoat gently. "No, I must say you never did. She is very steadfast, you know, and quite out of the common, and not in the least vulgar. Now, if you won't mind me saying it,—because I am sure you do enjoy yourself, but then you are such a dear, _enjouée_,[2] good-natured little creature that you accommodate yourself to anything—to enjoy the present

---

1 An offensive term for any black African.
2 Sprightly.

generation one must be a little vulgar. I am an old woman, you know, and look on and see things, and the whole note of this thing is vulgar even when it is at its very best. It has been so ever since the Second Empire."

"The *dear* Second Empire; you never were just to it," said Lady Dolly, with the tears almost rising to her eyes at the thought of all she had used to enjoy in it.

"It was the apotheosis of the vulgar; of the sort of *blague*[1] and shamelessness which made De Morny put an Hortensia on his carriage panels,"[2] said Lady Stoat calmly. "To have that sort of epoch in an age is like having skunk fur on your clothes; the taint never goes away, and it even gets on to your lace and your cachemires. I am afraid our grand-children will smell the Second Empire far away into the twentieth century, and be the worse for it."

"I daresay there will have been a Fourth and a Fifth by then."[3]

"Collapsed windbags, I dare say. The richest soil always bears the rankest mushrooms. France is always bearing mushrooms. It is a pity. But what I meant was that your Vere has not got the taint of it at all; I fancy she scarcely cares at all about that famous diamond unless it be for its historical associations. I am quite sure she doesn't enjoy being stared at; and I think she very heartily dislikes having her beauty written about in newspapers, as if she were a mare of Lord Falmouth's or a cow of Lady Pigott's; she is not Second Empire, that's all."

"Then you mean to say I am vulgar!" said Lady Dolly, with some tartness.

Lady Stoat smiled, a deprecating smile, that disarmed all sufferers, who without it might have resented her honeyed cruelties.

"My dear! I never say rude things; but, if you wish me to be sincere, I confess I think everybody is a little vulgar now, except old women like me, who adhered to the Faubourg[4] while you all were

---

1 Humbug.
2 Charles Auguste Louis Joseph, The Duc de Morny (1811-65) was a French political and social leader. He was the illegitimate son of Hortense de Beauharnais, estranged wife of Louis Napoleon Bonaparte. He was involved in the *coup d'état* which resulted in his half-brother becoming emperor Napoleon III. Morny's coat of arms featured a hydrangea (in French *l'hortensia*), and he became known as "the Comte Hortensia."
3 The Third Republic went from 1870-1946; the Fourth, 1946-57; the Fifth, 1958-present.
4 A district lying outside the original city limits of Paris.

dancing and changing your dresses seven times a day at St. Cloud.[1] There is a sort of vulgarity in the air; it is difficult to escape imbibing it; there is too little reticence, there is too much tearing about; men are not well-mannered, and women are too solicitous to please, and too indifferent how far they stoop in pleasing. It may be the fault of steam; it may be the fault of smoking; it may come from that flood of new people of whom 'L'Étrangère,'[2] is the scarcely exaggerated sample; but, whatever it comes from, there it is—a vulgarity that taints everything, courts and cabinets as well as society. Your daughter somehow or other has escaped it, and so you find her odd, and the world thinks her stiff. She is neither; but no dignified long-descended point-lace, you know, will ever let itself be twisted and whirled into a cascade and a *fouillis*[3] like your Bretonne lace that is just the fashion of the hour, and worth nothing. I admire your Vera very greatly; she always makes me think of those dear old stately hôtels with their grand gardens in which I saw, in my girlhood, the women, who, in theirs, had known France before '30. Those hotels and their gardens are gone, most of them, and there are stucco and gilt paint in their places. And there are people who think that a gain. I am not one of them."

"My sweetest Adine," said Vere's mother pettishly, "if you admire my child so much, why did you persuade her to marry Sergius Zouroff?"

"To please you, dear," said Lady Stoat with a glance that cowed Lady Dolly. "I thought she would adorn the position; she does adorn it. It is good to see a gentlewoman of the old type in a high place, especially when she is young. When we are older, they don't listen much; they throw against us the *laudator temporis acti*,[4]—they think we are disappointed or embittered. It is good to see a young woman to whom men still have to bow, as they bow to queens, and before whom they do not dare to talk the *langue verte*.[5] She ought to have a great deal of influence."

"She has none; none whatever. She never will have any," said Lady Dolly, with a sort of triumph, and added, with the sagacity that some-

---

1 A large château on the Left Bank of the Seine, a few miles from Paris. The Imperial Court spent part of the summer there, where they often entertained foreign royalty.
2 The Stranger.
3 Hodgepodge.
4 Praisers of time past (from Horace's *Arts Poetica*).
5 Slang.

times shines out in silly people—"You never influence people if you don't like the things they like; you always look what the boys call a prig. Women hate Vere, perfectly *hate* her, and yet I am quite sure she never did anything to any one of them; for, in her cold way, she is very good-natured. But then she spoils her kind things; the way she does them annoys people. Last winter, while she was at Nice, Olga Zwetchine—you know her, the handsome one, her husband was in the embassy over here some time ago—utterly ruined herself at play, pledged everything she possessed, and was desperate; she had borrowed heaven knows what, and lost it all. She went and told Vera. Vera gave her a heap of money *sans se faire prier*,[1] and then ran her pen through the Zwetchine's name on her visiting list. Zouroff was furious. 'Let the woman be ruined,' he said, 'what was it to you; but go on receiving her; she is an ex-ambassadress; she will hate you all your life.' Now what do you call that?"

"My friends of the old Faubourg would have done the same," said Lady Stoat, "only they would have done it without giving the money."

"I can't imagine why she did give it," said lady Dolly. "I believe she would give to anybody—to Noisette herself, if the creature were in want."

"She probably knows nothing at all about Noisette."

"Oh yes, she does. For the Zwetchine, as soon as she had got the money safe, wrote all about that woman to her, and every other horrid thing she could think of too, to show her gratitude, she said. Gratitude is always such an unpleasant quality, you know; there is always a grudge behind it."

"And what did she say, or do about Noisette?"

"Nothing; nothing at all. I should never have heard of it, only she tore the Zwetchine letters up, and her maid collected them and pieced them together, and told my maid; you know what maids are. I never have any confidence from Vera. I should never dare to say a syllable to her."

"Very wise of her; very dignified, not to make a scene. So unlike people now-a-days, too, when they all seem to think it a positive pleasure to get into the law-courts and newspapers."

"No; she didn't do anything. And now I come to think of it," said Lady Dolly, with a sudden inspiration towards truthfulness, "she struck off the Zwetchine's name *after* that letter, very likely; and I dare

---

1 Willingly.

say she never told Zouroff she had had it, for she is very proud, and very silent, dreadfully so."

"She seems to me very sensible," said Lady Stoat. "I wish my Gwendolen were like her. It is all I can do to keep her from rushing to the lawyers about Birk."

"Vera is ice," said Lady Dolly.

"And how desirable that is; how *safe!*" said Lady Stoat, with a sigh of envy and self-pity, for her daughter, Lady Birkenhead, gave her trouble despite the perfect education that daughter had received.

"Certainly safe, so long as it lasts, but not at all popular," said Lady Dolly, with some impatience. "They call her the Edelweiss in Paris. Of course it means that she is quite inaccessible. If she were inaccessible in the *right* way, it might all be very well, though the time's gone by for it, and it's always stiff, and nobody is stiff now-a-days; still, it might answer if she were only exclusive and not—not—so very rude all around."

"She is never rude; she is cold."

"It comes to the same thing," said Lady Dolly, who hated to be contradicted. "Everybody sees that they bore her, and people hate you if they think you bore you; it isn't that they care about you, but they fancy you find them stupid. Now, isn't the most popular woman in all Europe that creature I detest, Fuschia Mull? Will you tell me anybody so praised, so petted, so sought after, so raved about? Because she's a duchess? O, my love, no! You may be a duchess, and you may be a nobody outside your own county, just as that horrid old cat up at Bulmer has always been. Oh, that has nothing to do with it. She is so popular because everybody delights her, and everything is fun to her. She's as sharp as a needle, but she's as gay as a lark. I hate her, but you can't be dull where she is. You know the prince always calls her 'Pick-me-up.' At that fancy fair for the poor Wallacks—whoever the poor Wallacks may be—the whole world was there. Vera had a stall, she loaded it with beautiful things, things much too good, and sat by it, looking like a very grand portrait of Mignard's.[1] She was superb, exquisite, and she had a bower of orchids, and a carved ivory chair from Hindostan. People flocked up by the hundreds, called out about her beauty, and—went away. She looked so still, so tired, so contemptuous. A very little way off was Fuschia Mull, selling vile tea and tea-cakes, and two-penny cigarettes. My dear, the whole world surged

---

1 Pierre Mignard (1612-95) was a French painter known for his court portraits.

round that stall as if it were mad. Certainly she had a lovely Louis Treize hat on, and a delicious dress, gold brocade with a violet velvet long waistcoat. Her execrable tea sold for a sovereign a cup, and when she kissed her cigarettes they went for five pounds each! Zouroff went up and told his wife: 'A brioche[1] there fetches more than your Saxe, and your Sèvres,[2] and your orchids,' he said. 'You don't tempt the people, you frighten them.' Then Vera looked at him with that way—she has such a freezing way—and only said: 'Would you wish me to kiss the orchids?' Zouroff laughed. 'Well, no; you don't do for this thing, I see; you don't know how to make yourself cheap.' Now I think he hit exactly on what I mean. To be liked now-a-days you must make yourself cheap. If you want to sell your cigar you must kiss it."

"But suppose she has no cigars she wants to sell?"

"You mean she has a great position, and need care for nobody? That is all very well. But if she ever come to grief, see how they will turn and take it out of her!"

"I never said she was wise not to be polite," pleaded Lady Stoat. "But as to 'coming to grief,' as you say, that is impossible. She will always sit in that ivory chair."

"I dare say; but one never knows, and she is odd. If any day she get very angry with Zouroff, she is the sort of temper to go out of his house in her shift, and leave everything behind her."

"What a picture!" said Lady Stoat, with a shudder. Nothing appalled Lady Stoat like the idea of anyone being wrought upon to do anything violent. She would never admit that there could be any reason for it, or excuse.

She had been an admirable wife to a bad husband herself, and she could not conceive any woman not considering her position before all such pettier matters as emotions and wrongs.

When her daughter, who was of an impetuous disposition, which even the perfect training she had received had not subdued, would come to her in rage and tears because of the drunkenness or because of the open infidelities of the titled Tony Lumpkin[3] that she had wedded, Lady Stoat soothed her, but hardly sympathised. "Lead your own life, my love, and don't worry," she would say. "Nothing can unmake your position, and no one, except yourself." When her daughter passionately protested that position was not all that a woman wanted at twenty years old and with a heart not all trained out of her, Lady Stoat

---

1 Pastry.
2 Pewter and porcelain.
3 The boorish son in Oliver Goldsmith's play, *She Stoops to Conquer* (1773).

would feel seriously annoyed and injured. "You forget your position," she would reply. "Pray, pray do not jeopardise your position. Let your husband go to music-halls and creatures if he must; it is very sad, certainly, very sad. But it only hurts him; it cannot affect your position." Farther than that the light she possessed could not take her.

She would not have been disposed to quarrel with the Princess Zouroff, as her own mother did, for not playing the fool at fancy fairs, but she would have thought it horrible, inexcusable, if, under the pressure of any wrong, the affront of infidelity, she had—in Lady Dolly's figure of speech—left her husband's house in her shift.

"Never lose your position," would have been the text that Lady Stoat would have written in letters of gold, for all young wives to read, and it was the text on which all her sermons were preached.

Position was the only thing that, like old wine or oak furniture, improved with years. If you had a good position at twenty, at forty you might be a power in the land. What else would wear like that? Not love, certainly, which indeed at all times Lady Stoat was disposed to regard as a malady; a green sickness, inevitable, but, to onlookers, very irritating in its delirious nonsense.

It was neither mere rank nor mere riches that Lady Stoat considered a great position. It was the combination of both, with a power—inalienable except by your own act—to give the tone to those around you; to exclude all who did not accord with your own notions; to be unattainable, untroubled, unruffled; to be a great example to society; metaphorically to move through life with carpet always unrolled before your steps. When you had a position that gave you all this, if you had tact and talent enough to avail yourself of it, what could you by any possibility need more?

Yet her own daughter, and her friend's daughter, had this and both were dissatisfied.

Her own daughter, to her anguish unspeakable, revolted openly and grew vulgar; even grew vulgar; went on the boxes of the four-in-hand-men's coaches,[1] shot and hunted, played in amateur performances before London audiences far from choice; had even been seen at the Crystal Palace;[2] had "loud" costumes with wonderful waist-

---

1 The Four-in-Hand was a men's coaching club. Members met in their large, four-horse coaches, had competitions, and drove to various elegant places for lunch.

2 The large glass building was built for the Great Exhibition of 1851 in London. After the Exhibition closed, the Crystal Palace was moved to Sydenham Hill in South London and reconstructed in what was, in effect, a two hundred acre Victorian theme park.

coats; and had always a crowd of young men wherever she went. Lady Stoat honestly would sooner have seen her in her grave.

The Princess Zouroff, who had the very perfection of manner even if she offended people, who knew of her husband's infidelities and said nothing, went coldly and serenely through the world, taking no pleasure in it perhaps, but giving it no power to breathe a breath against her.

"Why was she not my child!" sighed Lady Stoat sadly.

If Lady Stoat could have seen into the soul of Vere, she would have found as little there with which she could have sympathised as she found in her own daughter's tastes for the stage, the drag,[1] and the loud waistcoats.

She could not imagine the price at which Vere's composure was attained; the cost at which that perfect manner, which she admired, was kept unruffled by a sigh or frown. She could not tell that this young life was one of perpetual suffering, of exhausting effort to keep hold on the old faiths and the old principles of childhood amidst a world which has cast out faith as old-fashioned and foolish, and regards a principle as an affront and an ill-nature. Her own society found the young Princess Vera very cold, unsympathetic, strange; she was chill about fashionable good works, and her grand eyes had a look in them, stern in its sadness, which frightened away both courtiers and enemies. The verdict upon her was that she was unamiable.

The world did not understand her.

"The poor you always have with you,"[2] had been an injunction that, in the days of her childhood, she had been taught to hold sacred.

"The poor you always have with you," she said to a bevy of great ladies once. "Christ said so. You profess to follow Christ. How have you the poor with you? The back of their garret, the roof of their hovel, touches the wall of your palace, and the wall is thick. You have dissipations, spectacles, diversions that you call charities; you have a tombola[3] for a famine; you have a dramatic performance for a flood, you have a concert for a fire, you have a fancy fair for a leprosy. Do you never think how horrible it is, that mockery of woe? Do you ever wonder at revolutions? Why do you not say honestly that you care nothing? You do care nothing. The poor might forgive the

---

1 The four-horse coach.
2 "You will always have the poor among you, but you will not always have me" (John 12:8).
3 A lottery in which tickets are drawn from a revolving drum.

avowal of indifference; they will never forgive the insult of affected pity."

Then the ladies who heard were scandalised, and went to their priests and were comforted, and would not have this young saint preach to them as Chrysostom preached to the ladies of Constantinople.[1]

But Vere had been reared in tender thoughtfulness for the poor. Her grandmother, stern to all others, to the poor was tender.

"Put your second frock on for the Queen if you like," she would say to the child; "but to the poor go in your best clothes or they will feel hurt." Vere never forgot what was meant in that bidding. Charity in various guises is an intruder the poor see often; but courtesy and delicacy are visitants with which they are seldom honoured.

It is very difficult for a woman who is young and very rich not to be deceived very often, and many an impostor, no doubt, played his tricks upon her. But she was clear-sighted and much in earnest, and found many whose needs were terrible, and whose lives were noble. The poor of Paris are suspicious, resentful, and apt to be sullen in their independence; but they are often also serious and intelligent, tender of heart, and gay of spirit. Some of them she grew to care for very much, and many of them forgave her for being an aristocrat and welcomed her for her loveliness and her sympathy. As for herself, she sometimes felt that the only reality life had for her was when she went up to those damp chill attics in the metal roofs, and spoke with those whose bread was bitterness and whose cup was sorrow. Her husband, with some contempt, told her she grew like Saint Elizabeth of Thuringia,[2] but he did not forbid her doing as she pleased. If she were present to drive in the Bois, or ride there before sunset, and afterwards went to dinner, or ball, or reception, as the engagements of the night might require, he did not exact any more account of her time or ask how her mornings were spent.

---

1 St. John Chrysostom (347-407 B.C.) was Bishop of Constantinople and called "golden mouth" because of his eloquence in speech.

2 Saint Elizabeth, Princess of Hungary (1207-31) was betrothed in infancy to Louis IV of Thuringia (also Louis of Hungary), at whose court she was raised. The marriage was ideal, but brief. Louis died of plague on the way to the Sixth Crusade. She joined the Third Order of St. Francis and built a hospice for the poor and sick, to whose service she devoted the rest of her life. There was a legend, often depicted in paintings, of Elizabeth unexpectedly meeting her husband on one of her charitable visits. The loaves she was carrying miraculously turned to roses.

"You leave Vera too much alone, terribly too much," said his sister to him once.

He stared, then laughed.

"Alone? a woman of her rank is never alone. Not a whit more than queens are!"

"I mean you are not with her; you never ask what she does all the day."

"I suppose her early hours are given to her tailor and her milliner, and the later ones to morning visits," he answered with a yawn. "It does not matter what she does. She is a fool in many things, but she will not abuse liberty."

For, though he had never believed in any woman, he did believe in his wife.

"She will not abuse it yet; no," thought Madame Nelaguine. "No, not yet, whilst she is still under the influence of her childish faiths and her fear of God. But after?—after five, six, seven years of the world, of this world into which you have cast her without any armour of love to protect her—how will it be then? It will not be men's fault if she misuse her liberty; and assuredly it will not be women's. We corrupt each other more than men corrupt us."

Aloud the Princess Nelaguine merely said, "You allow her to be friends with Jeanne de Sonnaz?"

Zouroff laughed again and frowned.

"All women in the same set see one another day and night. Who is to help that?"

"But—"

"Be reasonable," he said roughly. "How can I say to my wife, 'Do not receive the Duchesse de Sonnaz.' All Paris would be convulsed, and Jeanne herself a demoniac. Good heavens! Where do you get all these new scruples? Is it your contact with Vera?"

"Your contact with her does not teach them to you," said his sister coldly. "Oh, our world is vile enough, that I know well, but somewhere or other I think it might keep a little conscience, for exceptional circumstances, and so might you."

"Do not talk nonsense. I cannot tell Jeanne not to know my wife, or my wife not to know Jeanne. They must take their chance; there is nothing exceptional; every man does the same."

"Yes; we are very indecent," said Madame Nelaguine quietly. "We do not admit it, but we are."

Her brother shrugged his shoulders to express at once acquiescence and indifference.

In one of the visits that her charities led his wife to make she heard one day a thing that touched her deeply. Her horses knocked down a girl of fifteen who was crossing the Avenue du Bois de Boulogne. The girl was not hurt, though frightened. She was taken into the Hôtel Zouroff, and Vere returned to the house to attend her. As it proved, the child, when the faintness of her terror had passed, declared herself only a little bruised, smiled and thanked her, and said she would go home; she wanted nothing. She was a freckled, ugly, bright-looking little thing and was carrying some of those artificial flowers with which so many girls of Paris gain their daily bread. Her name was Félicie Martin, and she was the only child of her father, and her mother was dead.

The following day the quiet little *coupé*[1] that took Vere on her morning errands, found its way into a narrow but decent street in the Batignolles, and the Princess Zouroff inquired for the Sieur[2] Martin.

Vere bade her men wait below, and went up the stairs to the third floor. The house was neat, and was let to respectable people of the higher class of workers. In her own world she was very proud, but it was not the pride that offends the working classes, because it is dignity and not arrogance, and is simple and natural, thinking nothing of rank though much of race, and far more still of character.

"May I come in?" she said in her clear voice, which had always so sad an accent in it, but for the poor was never cold. "Will you allow me to make myself quite sure that your daughter is none the worse for that accident, and tell you myself how very sorry I was? Russian coachmen are always so reckless!"

"But, madame, it is too much honour!" said a little, fair man who rose on her entrance, but did not move forward. "Forgive me, madame, you are as beautiful as you are good; so I have heard from my child, but alas! I cannot have the joy to see such sunlight in my room. Madame will pardon me—I am blind."

"Blind?"—the word always strikes a chill to those who hear it; it is not a very rare calamity, but it is the one of all others which most touches bystanders, and is most quickly realised. He was a happy-looking little man, nevertheless, though his blue eyes were without light in them gazing into space unconsciously; the room was clean, and gay, and sweet-smelling, with some pretty vases and prints and other simple ornaments, and in the casement some geraniums and heliotrope.

"Yes, I am blind," he said cheerfully. "Will Madame la Princesse kindly be seated? My child is at her workshop. She will be so glad and

1 Carriage.
2 Mr.

proud. She has talked of nothing but madame ever since yesterday. Madame's beauty, madame's goodness;—ah yes, the mercy of it! I am always afraid for my child in the streets, but she is not afraid for herself; she is little, but she is brave. It is too much kindness for Madame la Princesse to have come up all this height, but madame is good; one hears it in her voice. Yes, my child makes flowers for the great Maison Justine. Our angel did that for us. She is my only child, yes. Her dear mother died at her birth. I was fourth clarionet at the Opéra Comique at that time."

"But can you play still?"

"Ah no, madame. My right arm is paralysed. It was one day in the forest at Vincennes. Félicie was ten years old. I thought to give her a Sunday in the wood. It was May. We were very happy, she and I running after one another, and pulling the hawthorn when no one looked. All in a moment a great storm came up and burst over us where we were in the midst of the great trees. The lightning struck my eyes and my right shoulder. Ah the poor, poor child!... But madame must excuse me; I am tiresome—"

"It interests me; go on."

"I fell into great misery, madame. That is all. No hospital could help me. The sight was gone, and my power to use my right arm was gone too. I could not even play my clarionet in the streets as blind men do. I had saved a little, but not much. Musicians do not save, any more than painters. I had never earned very much either. I grew very very poor. I began to despair. I had to leave my lodging, my pretty little rooms where the child was born and where my wife had died; I went lower and lower, I grew more and more wretched; a blind, useless man with a little daughter. And I had no friends; no one; because, myself, I came from Alsace, and the brother I had there was dead, and our parents too had been dead long, long before; they had been farmers. Madame, I saw no hope at all. I had not a hope on earth, and Félicie was such a little thing she could do nothing. But I fatigue madame?"

"Indeed no. Pray go on, and tell me how it is that you are so tranquil now."

"I am more than tranquil; I am happy, Princess. That is his doing. My old employers all forgot me. They had so much to think of; it was natural. I was nobody. There were hundreds and thousands could play as well as I had ever played. One day when I was standing in the cold, hungry, with my little girl hungry too, I heard them saying how the young singer Corrèze had been engaged at fifty thousand francs a night for the season. I went home and I made the child write a letter to the young man. I told him what had happened to me, and I said, 'You are young and famous, and gold rains on you like dew in midsummer; will you remember that we are very wretched? If you said a word to my old directors—you—they would think of me.' I sent the letter. I had often played in the orchestra when the young man was first turning the heads of all Paris. I knew he was gay and careless; I had not much hope."

"Well?" Her voice had grown soft and eager; the man was blind, and could not see the flush upon her face.

"Well, a day or two went by, and I thought the letter was gone in the dust. Then he came to me, he himself, Corrèze. I knew his perfect voice as I heard it on the stairs. You can never forget it once you have heard. He had a secretary even then, but he had not left my letter to the secretary. He came like the angel Raphael whose name he bears."

Vere's eyes filled; she thought of the white cliffs by the sea, of the sweetbriar hedge, and the song of the thrush.

"But I tire madame," said the blind man. "He came like an angel. There is no more to be said. He made believe to get me a pension from the opera, but I have always thought that it is his own money, though he will not own to it; and as my child had a talent for flower-making he had her taught the trade, and got her employed later on by the Maison Justine. He sent me that china, and he sends me those flowers, and he comes sometimes himself. He has sung here—*here!*—only just to make my darkness lighter. And I am not the only one, madame. There are many, many, many who if they ever say their prayers, should never forget Corrèze."

Vere was silent, because her voice failed her.

"You have heard Corrèze, madame, of course, many times?" asked the blind man. "Ah, they say he has no religion and is careless as the butterflies are; to me he has been as the angels. I should have been in Bicêtre[1] or in my grave but for him."

The girl at that moment entered.

"Félicie," said the Sieur Martin, "give the Princess a piece of heliotrope. Oh, she has forests of heliotrope in her conservatories, that I am sure, but she will accept it; it is the flower of Corrèze."

Vere took it and put it amidst the old lace at her breast.

"You have Félicie Martin amongst your girls I think?" said Vere to the head of the Maison Justine a little later.

---

1 A prison. During the Second Empire condemned men were incarcerated there.

The principal of the fashionable house, a handsome and clever woman, assented.

"Then let her make some flowers for me," added Vere. "Any flowers will do. Only will you permit me to pay her through you very well for them; much better for them than they are worth?"

"Madame la Princesse," said the other with a smile, "the little Martin cannot make such flowers as you would wear. I employ her, but I never use her flowers, never. I have to deceive her; it would break her heart if she knew that I burn them all. The poor child is willing, but she is very clumsy. She cannot help it. Madame will understand it is a secret of my house; a very little harmless secret, like a little mouse. Corrèze, madame knows whom I mean, the great singer?—Corrèze came to me one day with his wonderful smile, and he said, 'There is a blind man and he has a little girl who wants to make flowers. Will you have her taught, madame, and allow me to pay for her lessons?' I allowed him. Six months afterwards I said, 'M. Corrèze, it is all of no use. The child is clumsy. When once they have fingers like hers it is of no use.' Then he laughed. 'It ought to be difficult to make artificial flowers. I wish it were impossible. It is a blasphemy. But I want to make the girl believe she earns money. Will you employ her, burn the flowers, and draw the money from my account at Rothschild's?' And I did it to please him and I do it still; poor little clumsy ugly thing that she is, she fancies that she works for the Maison Justine! It is compromising to me. I said so to M. Corrèze. He laughed and said to me, 'Ma chère, when it is a question of a blind man and a child we must even be compromised, which, no doubt, is very terrible.' He is always so gay, M. Corrèze, and so good. If the child were Venus he would never take advantage of maintaining her, never, madame. Ah, he is an angel, that beautiful Corrèze. And he can laugh like a boy; it does one good to hear his laugh. It is so sweet. My poor Justine used to say to me, 'Marie, hypocrites weep, and you cannot tell their tears from those of saints; but no bad man ever laughed sweetly yet.' And it is true, very true; Madame la Princesse will forgive my garrulity."

When she went down to her carriage the world did not seem so dark.

There was beauty in it, as there were those flowers blooming in that common street. The little picture of the father and daughter, serene and joyous in their humble chamber, in the midst of the gay, wild, ferocious riot of Paris, seemed like a little root of daisies blooming white amidst a battle-field.

That night she went to her box at the Grand Opéra, and sat as far in the shadow as she could and listened to Corrèze in the part of Gennaro.[1]

"He does not forget that blind man," she thought. "Does he ever remember me?"

For she could never tell.

From the time she had entered Paris she had longed, yet dreaded to meet, face to face, Corrèze.

She saw him constantly in the street, in the Bois, in society, but he never approached her; she never once could be even sure that he recognised or remembered her. She heard people say that Corrèze was more difficult of access, more disinclined to accept the worship of society, than he had been before, but she could not tell what his motive might be; she could not believe that she had any share in his thoughts. His eyes never once met hers but what they glanced away again rapidly, and without any gleam of recognition. Again and again in those great salons where he was a petted idol, she was close beside him, but she could never tell that he remembered her. Perhaps his life was so full, she thought; after all, what was one summer morning that he should cherish its memory?

Often in the conversations that went on around her, she heard his successes, his inconstancies, his passions of the past, slight or great, alluded to, laughed over, or begrudged. Often, also, she heard of other things; of some great generosity to a rival, some great aid to an aspirant of his art, some magnificent gift to a college made by the famous singer. Or, on the other hand, of some captiousness as of a too spoilt child, some wayward caprice shown to the powers of the State by the powers of genius, some brilliant lavishness of entertainment or of fancy. When she heard these things her heart would beat, her colour would change; they hurt her, she could not have told why.

Meantime that one solace of her life was to see his genius and its triumphs, its plenitude and its perfect flower. Her box at the Grand Opéra was the only one of the privileges of her position which gave her pleasure. Her knowledge of music was deep and had been carefully cultured, and her well-known love for it made her devotion to the opera pass unremarked. Seldom could the many engagements made for her let her hear any one opera from its overture to its close. But few nights passed without her being in her place, sitting as far in the shadow as she could, to hear at least one act or more of "Fidelio,"

---

1 Character in *Lucrezia Borgia* (1838) by Gaetano Donizetti.

of "Lucia," of the "Prophète," of the "Zauberflöte," of "Faust," or of the "Il Trovatore."[1] She never knew or guessed that the singer watched for her fair-haired head amidst the crowded house, as a lover watches for the rising of the evening planet that shall light him to his love.

She saw him in the distance a dozen times a week, she saw him, not seldom, at the receptions of great houses, but she never was near enough to him to be sure whether he had really forgotten her, or whether he had only affected oblivion.

Corrèze, for his own part, avoided society as much as he could, and alleged that to sing twice or three times a week was as much as his strength would allow him to do, if he wished to be honest and give his best to his impresario. But he was too popular, too much missed when absent, and too great a favourite with great ladies to find retirement in the midst of Paris possible. So that, again and again, it was his fortune to see the child he had sung to on the Norman cliffs announced to the titled crowds as Madame la Princesse Zouroff. It always hurt him. On the other hand he was always glad when, half-hidden behind some huge fan or gigantic bouquet, he could see the fair head of Vere in the opera-house.

When he sang, he sang to her.

"How is it you do not know Princess Vera?" said many of his friends to him; for he never asked to be presented to her.

"I think she would not care to know an artist," he would say. "Why should she? She is at the height of fame and fortune, and charm and beauty; what would she want with the homage of a singing-mime? She is very exquisite; but you know I have my pride; *la probité des pauvres, et la grandeur des rois;*[2] I never risk a rebuff."

And he said it so lightly that his friends believed him, and believed that he had a fit of that reserve which very often made him haughtier and more difficult to persuade than any Roi Soleil[3] of the lyric stage had ever been.

"I am very shy," he would say sometimes, and everybody would laugh at him. Yet, in a way, it was true; he had many sensitive fancies, and all in his temperament that was tender, spiritual, and romantic

---

1 *Fidelio* or *Conjugal Love* (1805) is Beethoven's only opera; *Lucia di Lammermoor* (1835) is by Gaetano Donizetti; *Le Prophète* (1849) is by Giacomo Meyerbeer; *Die Zauberflöte* (1791) is by Wolfgang Amadeus Mozart; *Il Trovatore* (1853) is by Guiseppi Verdi.

2 The integrity of the poor and the nobility of kings.

3 Sun King.

had centred itself in that innocent emotion which had never been love, which was as fantastic as Dante's, and almost as baseless as Keats's,[1] and was therefore all the more dear to him because so unlike the too easy and too material passions which had been his portion in youth.

"It can do her no harm," he would think, "and it goes with me like the angel that the poets write of, that keeps the door of the soul."

It was a phantasy, he told himself, but then the natural food of artists was phantasies of all kinds; and so this tenderness, this regret, went with him always through the gay motley of his changeful days, as the golden curl of some lost love, or some dead child, may lie next the heart of a man all the while that he laughs and talks, and dines, and drives, and jests, and yawns in the midst of the world.

"It can do her no harm," he said, and so he never let his eyes meet hers, and she could never tell whether he ever remembered that Vera Zouroff had once been Vere Herbert.

And the weeks and the months rolled on their course, and Corrèze was always the Roi Soleil of his time, and Vere became yet of greater beauty, as her face and form reached their full perfection. Her portraits by great painters, her busts by great sculptors, her costumes by great artists, were the themes of the public press; the streets were filled to see her go by in the pleasure-capital of the world; amongst her diamonds the famous jewel of tragic memories and historic repute that was called the roc's egg shone on her white breast as if she had plucked a planet from the skies. No day passed but fresh treasures in old jewels, old wares, old gold and silver from the sales of the Hôtel Drouot, were poured into her rooms with all the delicate charm about them that comes from history and tradition. Had she any whim, she could indulge it; any taste, she could gratify it; any fancy, she could execute it; and yet one day when she saw a picture in the Salon[2] of a slave-girl standing with rope-bound wrists and fettered ankles, amidst the lustrous stuffs and gems of the harem, surrounded by the open coffers and glittering stones and chains of gold in which her captors were about to array her nude and trembling limbs, she looked long at it, and said to the master of oriental art who had painted it, "Did you need to go to the East for *that*?"

---

1 Dante's (Alighieri) (1265-1321) unrequited love for Beatrice is celebrated in his *Divina Commedia*. John Keats (1795-1817) met and fell in love with Fanny Brawne and remained in love with her until he died of tuberculosis three years later.

2 The Hôtel Drouot is a famous auction house, offering art, antiques, etc. The Salon is where the pieces to be auctioned are displayed.

She bought the picture, and had it hung in her bed-chamber in Paris; where it looked strange and startling against the pink taffetas, and the silver embroideries of the wall.

"That is not in your usual good taste," said her husband, finding that the painting ill agreed with the decorations of the room.

Vere looked at him, and answered: "It suits any one of my rooms."

He did not think enough of the matter to understand; the picture hung there amidst the silver Cupids, and the embroidered apple-blossoms of the wall.

"A painful picture, a horrible picture, like all Gérôme's,"[1] said her mother before it once.

A very cold smile came on Vere's mouth.

"Yes," she said simply, "we have no degradation like that in Europe, have we?"

Lady Dolly coloured, turned away, and asked if Fantin[2] had designed those charming wreaths of apple-blossoms and amorini.

But it was very seldom that the bitterness, and scorn, and shame, that were in her found any such expression as in the purchase of the "Slave of the Harem." She was almost always quite tranquil, and very patient under the heavy burden of her days.

All the bitterness and humiliation of her heart she choked down into silence, and she continued to live as she had done hitherto, without sympathy and in an utter mental isolation. She felt that all she had been taught to respect was ridiculous in the eyes of those who surrounded her; she saw all that she had been accustomed to hold in horror as sin made subject for jest and for intrigue; she saw that all around her, whilst too polite to deride the belief and the principles that guided her, yet regarded them as the cobwebs and chimeræ[3] of childhood; she saw that the women of her world, though they clung to priests, and in a way, feared an offended heaven—when they recollected it—yet were as absolutely without moral fibre and mental cleanliness as any naked creatures of Pacific isles sacrificing to their obscene gods. All that she saw; but it did not change her.

She was faithful, not because his merit claimed it, but because her duty made such faith the only purity left to her. She was loyal, not because his falseness was ever worthy of it, but because her nature would not let her be other than loyal to the meanest thing that lived.

---

1 Jean-Léon Gérôme (1824-1904) was a French painter and sculptor.
2 Henri Fantin-Latour (1836-1904) was a French painter and lithographer.
3 Idle dreams.

Chastity was to her as honour to the gentleman, as courage to the soldier. It was not a robe embroidered and worn for mere parade, and therefore easy to be lifted in the dark by the first audacious hand that ruffled it.

"*On se console toujours*,[1] we know," her sister-in-law thought, who watched her keenly. "Still, there is an exception now and then to that rule as to any other, and she is one of those exceptions. It is strange, generally the great world is like æther,[2] or any other dram-drinking; tasted once, it is sought for more and more eagerly every time, and ends in becoming an indispensable intoxication. But nothing intoxicates her, and so nothing consoles her. I believe she does not care in the least for being one of the very few perfectly lovely women in Europe. I believe her beauty is almost distasteful and despicable to her, because it brought about her bondage; and although it is an exaggerated way of looking at such things, she is right; she was bought, quite as barbarously as Gérôme's slave. Only were she anybody else she would be reconciled by now—or be revenged. The only time I ever see her look in the least happy is at the opera, and there she seems as if she were dreaming; and once, at Svir, when we were driving over the plains in the snow, and they said the wolves were behind us—then she looked for the moment all brilliancy and courage; one would have said she was willing to feel the wolves' breath on her throat. But in the world she is never like that. What other women find excitement to her is monotony. Pleasure does not please her, vanity does not exist in her, and intrigue does not attract her; some day love will."

And then Madame Nelaguine would pull the little curls of her perruque angrily and light her cigar, and sit down to the piano and compose her nerves with Chopin.

"As for Sergius he deserves nothing," she would mutter, as she followed the dreamy intricate melodies of the great master.

But then it was not for her to admit that to anyone, and much less was it for her to admit it to his wife. Like most great ladies, she thought little of a sin, but she had a keen horror of a scandal, and she was afraid of the future, very afraid of it.

"If she were not a pearl what vengeance she would take!" she thought again and again, when the excesses and indecencies of her brother's career reached her ears.

---

1 People always console themselves.
2 Ether.

For she forgot that she understood those as the one most outraged by them was very slow to do.

Vere still dwelt within the citadel of her own innocence, as within the ivory walls of an enchanted fortress. Little by little the corruption of life flowed in to her and surrounded her like a fœtid[1] moat, but, though it approached her it did not touch her, and often she did not even know that it was near. What she did perceive filled her with a great disgust, and her husband laughed at her.

In these short months of her life in Paris she felt as though she had lived through centuries. Ten years in the old grey solitude of Bulmer would not have aged her morally and mentally as these brief months of the riot of society had done. She had drunk of the cup of knowledge of good and evil, and, though she had drunk with sinless lips, she could not entirely escape the poison the cup held.

She hated the sin of the world, she hated the sensuality, the intrigue, the folly, the insincerity, the callousness of the life of society, yet the knowledge of it was always with her like a bitter taste in the mouth.

It hurt her unceasingly; it aged her like the passing of many years.

In the beginning of the time she had tried to get some threads of guidance, some words of counsel, from the man who was her husband, and who knew the world so well. The answers of Sergius Zouroff left her with a heavier heart and a more bitter taste. The chill cynicism, the brutal grossness, of his experiences tore and hurt the delicate fibres of her moral being, as the poisons and the knife of the vivisector tear and burn the sensitive nerves of the living organism that they mutilate.

He did not intend to hurt her, but it seemed to him that her ignorance made her ridiculous. He pulled down the veils and mufflers in which the vices of society mask themselves, and was amused to see her shrink from the nude deformity.

His rough, bold temper had only one weakness in it; he had a nervous dread of being made to look absurd. He thought the innocence and coldness of Vere made him look so.

"They will take me for a *mari amoureux*,"[2] he thought; and Madame de Sonnaz laughed, and told him the same thing fifty times a week. He began to grow impatient of his wife's unconsciousness of all that went on around her, and enlightened her without scruple.

---

1 Fetid.
2 A husband in love (with his own wife).

He sat by her, and laughed at Judic and at Théo,[1] and was angry with her that she looked grave and did not laugh; he threw the last new sensation in realistic literature on to her table, and bade her read it, or she would look like a fool when others talked. When a royal prince praised her too warmly, and she resented it, he was annoyed with her. "You do not know how to take the world," he said impatiently. "It is myself that you make ridiculous; I do not aspire to be thought the jealous husband of the theatres, running about with a candle and crying *aux voleurs!*"[2]

When she came to know of the vices of certain great ladies who led the fashion and the world, she asked him if what was said were true.

He laughed.

"Quite true, and a great deal that is never said, and that is worse, is as true too."

"And you wish me to know them? to be friends with them?" she asked in her ignorance.

He swore a little, and gave her a contemptuous caress, as to a dog that is importuning.

"Know them? Of course; you must always know them. They are the leaders of society. What is their life to you or anybody? It is their husbands' affair. You must be careful as to women's position, but you need not trouble yourself about their character."

"Then nothing that anyone does, matters?"

He shrugged his shoulders. "It depends on how the world takes it. You have a proverb in English about the man who may steal a horse and the man who must not look at the halter. The world is very capricious; it often says nothing to the horse-stealer, it often pillories the person that looks at the halter. You are not in it to redress its caprices. All you need be careful about is to know the right persons."

"The people that may steal the horses?" said Vere with the faint, fine smile that had no mirth in it, and was too old for her years; the smile that alone had ever come on her lips since her marriage.

"The people that may steal the horses," said Zouroff with a short laugh, not heeding her smile nor what seed his advice might sow.

When he had left her that day she went into her bed-chamber and sat down before Gerôme's "Slave of the Harem."

"The men of the east are better than these," she thought. "The men of the east do veil their women and guard them."

---

1 Cabaret singers.
2 Stop thieves.

What could he say, what reproach could he make, if she learned her lesson from his teaching, and learned it too well for his honour?

A note was lying on her table from a great prince whom all the world of women loved to praise, and languished to be praised by; a note written by himself, the first initiatory phrases of an adoration that only asked one smile from her to become passion. Such power of vengeance lay for her in it as there lies power of destruction in the slender, jewel-like head of the snake.

She only had to write a word—name an hour—and Sergius Zouroff would taste the fruit of his counsels.

The thought, which was not temptation because it was too cold, glided into her mind, and, for the moment, looked almost sweet to her because it seemed so just—that sad, wild justice which is all that any revenge can be at its best.

She took the note and let it lie on her lap; the note that compromised a future king. She felt as if all her youth were dying in her; as if she were growing hard, and cruel, and soulless. What use were honour, and cleanliness, and dignity? Her husband laughed at them; the world laughed at them. Nothing mattered. No one cared.

The voice of one of her maids roused her, asking, "Is there any answer from Madame to Monseigneur?"

Vere lifted her eyes, like one who wakes from a feverish sleep. She pushed her hair back with a quick gesture and rose.

"No; none," she answered curtly; and she took the note, and lighted a match, and burned it.

The slight cold smile came on her face.

"After all," she thought, "there is no merit in virtue, when sin would disgust one. I suppose the world is right to be capricious in its award. Since it is only a matter of temperament it is nothing very great to be guiltless. If one like one's soul clean, like one's hands, it is only a question of personal taste. There is no right and no wrong—so they say."

And her eyes filled, and her heart was heavy; for, to the young and noble, there is no desert so dreary to traverse as the vast waste of the world's indifference. They would be strong to combat, they would be brave to resist, but in that sickly sea of sand they can only faint and sink and cease to struggle.

It is harder to keep true to high laws and pure instincts in modern society than it was in days of martyrdom. There is nothing in the whole range of life so dispiriting and so unnerving as a monotony of indifference. Active persecution and fierce chastisement are tonics to the nerves; but the mere weary conviction that no one cares, that no one notices, that there is no humanity that honours, and no deity that pities, is more destructive of all higher effort than any conflict with tyranny or with barbarism.

Vere saw very well that if she stooped and touched the brink of vice—if she lent her ear to amorous compliment that veiled dishonour—if she brought herself to the level of the world she lived in, women would love her better, and her husband honour her none the less.

What would he care?

Perhaps he would not have accepted absolute dishonour, but all the temptations that led to it he let strew her path in all the various guises of the times.

That night there was a great costume ball at one of the legations. It had been talked of for months, and was to be the most brilliant thing of this kind that Paris had seen for many seasons. All the tailors of fashion, and all the famous painters of the day, had alike been pressed into the service of designing the most correct dresses of past epochs, and many dusty chronicles and miniatures in vellum in old châteaux in the country, and old libraries in the city, had been disturbed, to yield information and to decide disputes.

The Prince and Princess Zouroff were among the latest to arrive. He wore the dress of his ancestor in the time of Ivan II,[1] a mass of sables and of jewels. She, by a whim of his own, was called the Ice-spirit, and diamonds and rock crystals shone all over her from head to foot. Her entrance was the sensation of the evening; and as he heard the exclamations that awarded her the supreme place of beauty where half the loveliness of Europe had been assembled, that vanity of possession which is the basest side of passion revived in him, and made his sluggish pulses beat at once with the miser's and the spendthrift's pleasure.

"Yes, you are right; she is really very beautiful," whispered Jeanne de Sonnaz in his ear. "To represent Ice it is not necessarily to have *chien*."

Zouroff frowned; he was never pleased with being reminded of things that he said himself.

---

1 Ivan II ("the Meek"), Ivanovich Krasnii (1326-59), was grand prince of Moscow and grand prince of Vladimir (1353-59). During his brief reign, he was unable to achieve the changes in the authority of princes he desired. He contributed little to the expansion of Moscow's territory. He was called Ivan the Meek because of his demeanor. It is ironic that Zouroff chose to dress as that particular ineffectual ancestor.

The duchesse herself had *chien* enough for twenty women. She called herself a Sorceress, and was all in red, a brilliant, poppy-like, flame-like, Mephistophelian[1] red, with her famous rubies, and many another jewel, winking like wicked little eyes all over her, while a narrow Venetian mask of black hid her ugliest features, and let her blazing eyes destroy their worlds.

As a pageant the great ball was gorgeous and beautiful; as a triumph few women ever knew one greater than that night was to Vere. Yet the hours were tiresome to her. When her eyes had once rested on the pretty picture that the splendid crowd composed, she would willingly have gone away. She felt what the easterns call an asp at her heart. The barrenness and loneliness of her life weighed on her; and it was not in her nature to find solace in levity and consolation in homage. Others might do so and did do so; she could not.

"Madame, what can you want to be content?" said an old wit to her. "You have rendered every man envious and every woman unhappy. Surely that is a paradise for you, from which you can look down smiling in scorn at our tears?"

Vere smiled, but not with scorn.

"I should be sorry to think I made anyone unhappy. As for my success, as you call it, they stare at the diamonds, I think. There are too many, perhaps."

"Madame, no one looks at your diamonds," said the old beau. "There are diamonds enough elsewhere in the rooms to cover an Indian temple. You are willfully cruel. But ice never moved yet for mortals."

"Am I really ice?" thought Vere, as she sat amidst the changing groups that bent before her, and hung on her words. She did not care for any of them.

They found her unusually beautiful, and thronged around her. Another year it would be some one else; some one probably utterly unlike her. What was the worth of that?

There are tempers which turn restive before admiration, to which flattery is tiresome, and to which a stare seems impertinence. This was her temper, and the great world did not change it.

She moved slowly through the rooms with the roc's egg gleaming above her breast, and all the lesser stones seeming to flash sunrays from snow as she moved, while she held a fan of white ostrich feathers between her and her worshippers, and her train was

---

1 Mephistopheles was one of the seven chief devils and tempter of Faust.

upheld by two little De Sonnaz boys dressed as the pole star and the frost.

Her very silence, her defect usually to society, suited her beauty and her name that night; she seemed to have the stillness, the mystery, the ethereality of the Arctic night.

"One grows cold as you pass, madame," whispered the great prince whom she had not answered that day; "cold with despair."

She made him a deep curtsey. She scarcely heard. Her eyes had a misty brilliancy in them; she had forgotten his letter. She was wondering if her life would be always like this ball, a costly and empty pageant—and nothing more.

Into the crowd there came at that moment a Venetian figure with a lute. His clothes were copied from those of the famous fresco of Battista Zelotti; he looked like Giorgione[1] living once more. Some great ladies, safe in the defence of their masks, were pelting him with blossoms and bon-bons. He was laughing, and defending himself with a gold caduceus that he had stolen from a friend who was a Mercury. He was surrounded by a maze of colours and flowers and white arms. He was hurrying onward, but a personage too great to be gainsaid or avoided called out to him as he passed: "My friend, what use is your lute since its chords are silent?"

"Monseigneur," answered the Joueur-du-luth,[2] "like the singer who bears it, it has a voice never dumb for you."

They were in a long gallery away from the ball-room; the windows opened on the lamplit garden; the walls were tapestried; figures of archers and pages and ladies worked in all the bright fair colours of the Gobelin looms;[3] there was a gilded estrade that opened on to a marble terrace, that in its turn led to lawns, cedar-circled, and with little fountains springing up in the light and shadow.

The Venetian lute-player moved a little backward, and leaned against the gild railing, with his back to the garden and the sky. He touched a chord or two, sweet and far-reaching, seeming to bring on their sigh all the sweet dead loves of the old dead ages. Then he sang to a wild melody that came from the Tchiganes, and that he had learnt round their camp-fires on Hungarian plains at night, while the troops of young horses had scoured by through the gloom, affright-

---

1 Battista Zelotti (1526-78) and Giorgione (1477-1510) were Italian painters who painted largely for the aristocracy.
2 Lute player.
3 Fifteenth-century tapestries.

ed by the flame and song. He sang the short verse of Heine,[1] that has all the woe of two lives in eight lines:

Ein Fichtenbaum steht einsam
Im Norden auf kahler Höh':
Ihn schläfert; mit weisser Decke
Umhüllen ihn Eis und Schnee.

Er träumt von einer Palme,
Die fern im Morgenland
Einsam und schweigend trauert
Auf brennender Felsenwand.[2]

As the first notes touched the air, Vere looked for the first time at the lute-player—she saw in him Corrèze. As for himself, he had seen her all night; had seen nothing else even while he had laughed, and jested, and paid his court to others.

He too had felt chill as she passed.

And he sang the song of Heine; of the love of the palm and the pine. The royal prince had, with his own hands, silently pushed a low chair towards Vere. She sat there and listened, with her face to the singer and the illumined night.

It was a picture of Venice.

The lute-player leaned against the golden balustrade; the silver of falling water and shining clouds were behind him; around against the hues of the Gobelins stood the groups of maskers, gorgeous and sombre as figures of the Renaissance. The distant music of the ball-room sounded like the echoes of a far-off chorus, and did not disturb the melody of the song, that hushed all laughter and all whispers, and held the idlest and the noisiest in its charm.

"Give us more, O nightingale;" said the great prince. "Son of Procris![3] I wish we were in the old times of tyranny that I

1 Heinrich Heine (1797-1856) was a German lyric poet.
2 A fir tree stands alone / In the North upon a barren height: / It slumbers; ice and snow / Cover it over with a white blanket. / It dreams of a palm tree, / Which, far in the East / Alone and silent mourns / Upon a burning cliff wall.
3 In mythology, Procris is the wife of Cephalus, an avid hunter. After a passerby hears Cephalus addressing the wind, asking it to cool him, he tells Procris that her husband has a lover. She follows Cephalus, hears him speak, and sobs, believing he is making love to a woman. Cephalus hears her. Mistaking her sob for that of an animal, he throws his javelin (a former gift of Procris) killing his beloved wife.

could imprison you close to me all your life in a golden cage."

"In a cage I should sing not a note, monseigneur. They are but bastard nightingales that sing imprisoned," said Corrèze.

All the while he did not look at Vere directly once, yet he saw nothing except that fair, cold, grave face, and the cold lustre of the diamonds that were like light all over her.

"Sing once more or recite," said the prince carelessly. "Sing once more and I will reward you; I will bring you into the light of the midnight sun, and after that you will never bear the glare of the common day."

"Is that reward, monseigneur? To be made to regret all one's life?" said Corrèze.

And where he still leaned against the rail, with the moonlit and lamplit gardens behind him, he struck a chord or two lingeringly on his lute as Stradella[1] might have struck them under the shadow of St. Mark, and recited the "Nuit de Mai"[2] of Alfred de Musset:[3]

Poète, prends ton luth ...
Le printemps naît ce soir ...[4]

The "Nuit d'Octobre"[5] is more famous because it has been more often recited by great actors; but the "Nuit de Mai" is perhaps still finer, and is more true to the temper and the destiny of poets.

All the sweet intoxication of the spring-tide at evening, when "*le vin de la jeunesse fermente cette nuit dans les veines de Dieu*"[6] is but the prelude to the terrible struggle that has its symbol in the bleeding bird dying before the empty ocean and the desert shore, having rent its breast and spent its blood in vain.

The superb peroration,[7] which closes one of the noblest and most sustained flights of imagery that any poet of any nation has ever produced, rolled through the silence of the room in the magnificent

---

1 Alessandro Stradella (1642–82) was an Italian composer, violinist, and singer.
2 "May Night."
3 Alfred de Musset (1810–57) was a French Romantic poet and playwright.
4 Poet take your lute ... / Spring is born this evening.
5 "October Night."
6 The wine of youth ferments this night in the veins (inspiration) of God.
7 Lengthy speech.

melody of a voice, tuned alike by nature and by art to the highest expression of human feeling and of human eloquence.

Then his voice dropped low and stole, like a sigh of exhaustion, through the hush around him, in the answer of the poet; the answer that the heart of every artist gives soon or late to Fate.

O muse, spectre insatiable,
Ne m'en demande pas si long,
L'homme n'écrit rien sur le sable
A l'heure où passe l'aquilon.
J'ai vu le temps où ma jeunesse
Sur vos lèvres était sans cesse,
Prête à chanter comme un oiseau;
Mais j'ai souffert un dur martyre.
Et le moins que j'en pourrais dire,
Si je l'essayais sur ma lyre,
La briserait comme un roseau.[1]

When the words sank into silence, the silence remained unbroken. The careless, the frivolous, the happy, the cynical, were all alike smitten into a sudden pain, a vague regret, and, for that passing moment, felt the pang the poet feels, always, till death comes to him.

Two great tears rolled down the cheeks of the loveliest woman there, and fell on the great diamonds. When the prince, who had shaded his eyes with his hand, looked up, the lute-player bowed low to him and glided through the crowd.

"And I was just about to present him to the Princess Zouroff," said the royal personage, slightly annoyed and astonished. "Well, one must pardon his caprices, for we have no other like him; and perhaps his judgment is true. One who can move us like that should not, immediately on our emotion, speak to us as a mere mortal in compliment or commonplace. The artist, like the god, should dwell unseen sometimes. But I envy him if I forgive him."

For he looked at the dimmed eyes of Vere.

---

1 Oh, muse, insatiable spectre / Don't question me of this at length, / Man does not write anything on the sand / When the north wind passes. / I saw the time when my youth / Was constantly upon your lips, / Ready to sing like a bird; / But I suffered a hard martyrdom. / And the least I would be able to say about it, / If I tried it on my lyre, / Would break it like a reed.

CHAPTER V.

On the day following Corrèze left Paris to fulfil his London engagements; it was the beginning of May.

When his name disappeared from the announcements, and his person from the scenes of the Grand Opéra, then, and then alone, Vere began to realise all that those nights at the lyric theatre had been in her life.

When she ceased to hear that one perfect voice, the whole world seemed mute. Those few hours in each week had gone so far to solace her for the weariness, the haste, the barren magnificence, and the tiresome adulation of her world; had done so much to give her some glimpse of the ideal life, some echo of lost dreams, some strength to bear disillusion and disgust.

The utter absences of vanity in her made her incapable of dreaming that Corrèze avoided her because he remembered only too well. She fully thought he had forgotten her. What was a morning by the sea, with a child, in the over-full life of a man foremost in art and in pleasure, consecrated at once to the Muses and the world? She was quite sure he had forgotten her. Even as he had recited the "Nuit de Mai" his eyes had had no recognition in them. So she thought.

This error made her memory of him tender, innocent, and wistful as a memory of the dead, and softened away all alarm for her from the emotion that possessed her.

He was nothing to her—nothing—except a memory; and she was not even that to him.

Paris became very oppressive to her.

That summer Prince Zouroff, by Imperial command, returned to his estate in Russia, to complete the twelve months' residence which had been commanded him.

They were surrounded by a large house party wherever they resided, and were never alone. Vere fulfilled the social duties of her high station with grace and courtesy, but he found her too cold and too negligent in society, and reproached her continually for some indifference to punctilio, some oblivion of precedence.

Neither her mind nor her heart was with these things. All of them seemed to her so trivial and so useless; she had been born with her mind and her heart both framed for greater force and richer interest than the pomp of etiquette and ceremonial, the victories of precedence and prestige.

They had made her a great lady, a woman of the world, a court beauty, but they could not destroy in her the temper of the studious and tender-hearted child who had read Greek with her dogs about her under the old trees of Bulmer Chase. She had ceased to study because she was too weary, and she strove to steel and chill her heart because its tenderness could bring her no good; yet she could not change her nature. The world was always so little to her; her God and the truth were so much. She had been reared in the old fashion and she remained of it.

In the gorgeous routine of her life in Russia she always heard in memory the echo of the "Nuit de Mai."

A great lassitude and hopelessness came over her, which there was no one to rouse and no one to dispel. Marriage could never bring her aught better than it brought her already—a luxurious and ornamented slavery; and maternity could bring her no consolation, for she knew very well that her children would be dealt with as tyrannically as was her life.

They remained that winter in Russia. The Duke and Duchesse de Sonnaz came there for a little time, and the Duchesse Jeanne wore out her silver skates at the midnight fêtes[1] upon the ice, a miracle of daring and agility, in her favorite crimson colours, with her sparkling and ugly face beaming under a hood of fur.

"Why does one never tire of *you?*" Zouroff muttered, as he waltzed with her over the Neva in one of the most gorgeous fêtes of the winter season.

Madame Jeanne laughed.

"Because I am ugly, perhaps, or because, as you said once, because, *j'ai le talent de m'encanailler.* But then, so many have that."

He said nothing, but as he felt her wheel and dart with the swiftness of a swallow, elastic and untiring as though her hips where swung on springs of steel, he thought to himself that it was because she never tired herself. "*Elle se grise si bien,*"[2] he said of her when he had resigned her to an officer of the guard, that night. To *se griser*[3] with drink, or with play, or with folly, or with politics, is the talent of the moment that is most popular. To be temperate is to be stupid.

His wife, in her ermine folds, which clothed her as in snow from head to foot, and without any point of colour on her anywhere, with her grave proud eyes that looked like arctic stars, and her slow, silent, undulating movement, might have the admiration of the court and city, but had no charm for him. She was his own; he had paid a price

1 Festivities.
2 She is so delightful when intoxicated.
3 Get intoxicated.

for her that he at times begrudged, and she had humiliated him. In a sense she was a perpetual humiliation to him, for he was a man of intellect enough to know her moral worth, and to know that he had never been worthy to pass the threshold of her chamber, to touch the hem of her garment. At the bottom of his heart there was always a sullen reverence for her, an unwilling veneration for her sinlessness and her honour, which only alienated him farther from her with each day.

"Why would you marry a young saint?" said his friend, the Duchesse Jeanne, always to him in derisive condolence.

Did he wish her a sinner instead? There were times when he almost felt that he did; when he almost felt that even at the price of his own loss he would like to see her head drop and her eyes droop under some consciousness of evil; would like to be able once to cast at her some bitter name of shame.

There were times when he almost hated her, hated her for the transparent purity of her regard, for the noble scorn of her nature, for the silence and the patience with which she endured his many outrages. "After all," he thought to himself, "what right has she to be so far above us all? She gave herself to me for my rank, as the others gave themselves for my gold."

That cold glittering winter passed like a pageant, and in the midst of it there came a sorrow to her that had in it something of remorse. The old Dowager Duchess at Bulmer died after a day's illness; died in solitude, except for the faithful servants about her, and was buried under the weird bent oaks by the moors, by the northern sea. Vere lamented bitterly. "And she died without knowing the truth of me!" she thought with bitter pain; and there was no message of pardon, no sign of remembrance from the dead to console her. "We are an unforgiving race," thought Vere, wearily. "I, too, cannot forgive. I can endure, but I cannot pardon."

This loss, and the state of her own health, gave her reason and excuse for leaving the world a little while. She remained absent while her husband waltzed with the Duchesse Jeanne at Imperial balls and winter fêtes, and gave suppers in the cafés of which the rooms were bowers of palms and roses, and the drinkers drank deep till the red sunrise.

She remained in solitude in the vast, luxurious, carefully heated palace of the Zouroff princes, where never a breath of cold air penetrated. Her health suffered from that imprisonment in a hot-house, which was as unnatural to her as it would have been to one of the young oak trees of Bulmer Chase, or to one of its moor-born forest does.

Another child was born to her, and born dead; a frail, pale, little corpse, that never saw the light of the world. She was long ill, and even the tediousness and exhaustion of lengthened weakness were welcome to her since they released her from the court, from society, and from her husband.

When she was at length strong enough to breathe the outer air, the ice was broken up on the Neva, and even in Russia trees were budding, and grass pushing up its slender spears through the earth.

The Duchesse de Sonnaz had long before returned to Paris, and Prince Zouroff had gone there for business. By telegram he ordered his wife to join him as soon as she was able, and she also travelled there with Madame Nelaguine when all the lilac was coming into blossom in the Tuileries and the Luxembourg gardens, and behind the Hôtel Zouroff in the Avenue du Bois de Boulogne.

A year had gone by; she had never seen the face of Corrèze.

She had learned in midwinter by the public voice that he had refused all engagements in Russia, giving as the plea the injury to his throat from the climate in past seasons. She had seen by the public press that he had been singing in Madrid and Vienna, had been to Rome for his pleasure, and for months had been, as of old, the idol of Paris.

As she entered the city it was of him once more that she thought.

A flush of reviving life came into the paleness of her cheek, and a throb of eager expectation to her pulses as she thought that once more in the opera-house she would hear that perfect melody of the tones which had chanted the "Nuit de Mai." It was May now, she remembered, and it was also night with her, one long dark hopeless night.

"*Voilà la belle Princesse!*"[1] said a work-girl with a sigh of envy, as she chanced to stand by the great gilded gates of the Hôtel Zouroff, as Vere went through them in her carriage, lying back on the cushions of it with what was the lassitude of physical and mental fatigue, but to the work-girl looked like the haughty indolence and languor of a great lady. She was more beautiful than she had ever been, but she looked much older than she was; her youth was frozen in her, the ice seemed in her veins, in her brain, in her heart.

Prince Zouroff met her at the foot of the staircase. He had been in Paris two months.

"I hope you are not too tired?" he said politely, and gave her his arm to ascend the stairs. "You look terribly white," he added, when

---

1   There is the beautiful Princess!

they were alone, and had reached the drawing-room. "You will really have to rouge, believe me."

Then, as if remembering a duty, he kissed her carelessly.

"I hope you will feel well enough to go to Orloff's to-night," he added; "I have promised that you will, and Worth tells me that he has sent you some new miracle expressly for it. The party is made for the Grand Duke, you know."

"I dare say I shall be well enough," Vere answered him simply. "If you will excuse me, I will go to my room and lie down a little while."

She went to her bedchamber where the "Slave" of Gérôme hung on the wall.

"All these came this morning and yesterday for madame," said her maid, showing her a table full of letters, and notes, and invitation cards, and one large bouquet of roses amidst them.

Roses had been around her all winter in Petersburg, but these were very lovely unforced flowers; all the varieties of the tea-rose in their shades and sizes, with their delicate faint smell that is like the scent of old perfumed laces, but in the centre of all these roses of fashion and culture there was a ring of the fragrant homely dewy cabbage rose, and in the very centre of these, again, a little spray of sweet-briar.

Vere bent her face over their sweetness.

"Who sent these?" she asked; and before she asked she knew.

No one in the house did know. The bouquet had been left that morning for her. There was no name with it except her own name.

But the little branch of sweet-briar said to her that it was the welcome of Corrèze, who had not forgotten.

It touched and soothed her. It seemed very sweet and thoughtful beside the welcome of her husband, who bade her rouge and go to an embassy ball.

"I always thought he had forgotten!" she mused, and, tired though she was, with her own hands she set the roses in a great cream-coloured bowl of Pesaro pottery of Casali di Lodi's, and had them close beside her couch as she fell asleep.

She who had so much pride had no vanity. It seemed strange to her that in his brilliant and busy life, full of its triumphs and its changes, he should remember one summer morning by the sea with a child.

That night she went to the splendour of Prince Orloff's fête; she did not rouge, but Paris found her lovelier than she had ever been; beneath the diamonds on her breast she had put a little bit of sweet-briar that no one saw. It seemed to her like a little talisman come out to her from her old lost life, when she and the world had been strangers.

It was a great party in the Rue de Grenelle. Corrèze was there as a guest; he did not approach her.

The next night she was in her box in the opera-house. Corrèze sang in the Prophète. She met the gaze of his eyes across the house, and something in their regard throbbed through her with a thrill like pain, and haunted her. He had never been in grander force or more wondrous melody than he was that night. The Duchesse de Sonnaz, who accompanied Vere, broke her fan in the vehemence and enthusiasm of her applause.

"They say that there are two tenor voices, *la voix de clairon et la voix de clarinette*,"[1] she said. "The voice of Corrèze is the *voix du clairon* of an archangel."

Vere sighed, quickly and wearily.

Jeanne de Sonnaz looked at her with a sudden and close scrutiny.

"Was there not some story of her and Corrèze?" she thought.

The next evening Corrèze was free.

He dined at Bignon's with some friends before going to the receptions of the great world. As they left the café about ten o'clock they saw Prince Zouroff enter with a companion and pass on to one of the private rooms; he was laughing loudly.

"Who is with him to-night?" said one of the men who had dined with Corrèze. Another of them answered:

"Did you not see her black eyes and her mouth like a poppy? It is Casse-une-Croûte."

Corrèze said nothing; he bade his friends goodnight and walked down the Avenue de l'Opéra by himself, though rain was falling and strong winds blew.

If he had followed his impulse he would have gone back into Bignon's, forced open the door of the *cabinet particulier*,[2] and struck Sergius Zouroff. But he had no right!

He returned to his own rooms, dressed, and went to two or three great parties. The last house he went to was the hotel in the Faubourg St. Germain of the Duc and Duchesse de Sonnaz.

It was a great *soirée*[3] for foreign royalties; Vere was present; the last injunction of her husband had been, as he had risen from the dinner-table: "Go to Jeanne's by one o'clock to-night or she will be annoyed;

---

1 The trumpet voice and the clarinette voice.
2 Private room.
3 Evening party.

you will say I am engaged; there is a club-meeting at the Ganaches."

Vere never disobeyed his commands.

"I cannot love or honour you," she had said to him once, "but I can obey you," and she did so at all times.

The night was brilliant.

It recalled the best days of the perished Empire.

The Princess Zouroff came late; Corrèze saw her arrive, and the crowds part, to let her pass, as they part for sovereigns; she wore black velvet only, she was still in mourning; her white beauty looked as though it were made of snow.

"And he goes to a mulattress!" thought Corrèze.

Later in the evening she chanced to be seated where there stood a grand piano in one of the drawing-rooms. He saw her from afar off; the Duchesse Jeanne passing him hurriedly was saying to him at the time: "If only you had not the cruel selfish rule never to sing a note for your friends, what a charm of the *bel imprévu*[1] you might give to my poor little ball!"

Corrèze bowed before her. "Madame, my rules, like all laws of the universe, must yield to you!"

He crossed the drawing-room to the piano.

Corrèze had never consented to sing professionally in private houses.

"The theatre is a different affair, but I do not choose my friends to pay me money," he universally answered, and out of his theatre he was never heard, unless he sang for charity, or as an act of mere friendship. Even as a social kindness it was so rare that anyone could induce him to be heard at all, that when this night he approached the piano and struck a minor chord or two, the princely crowds hurried together to be near like the commonest mob in the world. Vere, only, did not move from where she sat on a low chair beneath some palms, and the four or five gentlemen about her remained still because she did so.

She was some little distance from the instrument, but she saw him as he moved towards it more nearly than she had done since the recital of the "Nuit de Mai."

She saw the beautiful and animated face that had fascinated her young eyes in the early morning light on the rocks of the Calvados shore. He had not changed in any way; something of the radiance and gaiety of its expression was gone—that was all.

He sat down and ran his hands softly over the keys in Schumann's "Adieu." She could no longer see him for the plumes of the palms and blossoms of the azaleas, that made a grove of foliage and flowers

1 Unexpected pleasure.

which concealed the piano, and there was a courtly crowd of gay people and grand people gathered around him in silence, waiting for the first sound of that voice which, because it was so rarely heard, was so eagerly desired. Hour after hour in his own rooms he would sing to the old man Auber, whom he loved, or in the rough studios in the village of Barbisant he would give his music all night long to artists whose art he cared for, but by the world of fashion he was never heard out of the opera-house.

He struck a few pathetic chords in B minor, and sang to a melody of his own a song of Heine:

In mein gar zu dunkles Leben,[1]

the song of the singer who is "like a child lost in the dark."

Had she understood that he had a tale to tell? Had the song of Heine, that bewailed a vanished vision, carried his secret to her? He could not know.

She sat quite still and did not lift her eyes. The crowd moved and screened her from his view.

"Will she understand?" he thought, as the applause of the people around him followed on the breathless stillness of delight with which they had listened. He heard nothing that they said to him. He was looking at her in the distance, where she sat with the great white fan dropped upon her knee and her eyelids drooped over her eyes. He was thinking as he looked:

"And that brute goes with a quadroon to a restaurant! And when she had a dead child born to her, he went all the while with Jeanne de Sonnaz to masked balls and court fêtes on the ice!"

Over his mobile face as he mused a dark shadow went; the shadow of passionate disgust and of futile wrath.

His hands strayed a little over the keys, toying with memories of Chopin, and Beethoven, and Palestrina.[2] Then to the air of a Salutaris Hostia[3] that he had composed and sung for a great mass in Notre Dame years before, he sang clear and low as a mavis's call at daybreak to its love the Prière[4] of a French poet.

---

1 In my altogether too dark life (German).

2 Giovanni Pierluigi da Palestrina (1525-94) was an Italian composer.

3 A hymn used at Benediction in the Holy Catholic Church in praise of Christ truly present in the Blessed Sacrament. The words mean "O saving Host."

4 "Prayer." The poet is Sully Prudhomme, a pen name for René François Armand Prudhomme (1839-1907). He won the Nobel Prize for literature in 1901.

She could not see him for the throngs of grand people and giddy people who surged about him in their decorations and their jewels, but the first notes of his voice came to her clear as a bird's call at daybreak to its love.

He sang to a melody in the minor of his own the simple pathetic verses of a young poet:

Prière

AH! si vous saviez comme on pleure
De vivre seul et sans foyers,
Quelquefois devant ma demeure
Vous passeriez.

Si vous saviez ce que fait naître
Dans l'âme triste un pur regard,
Vous regarderiez ma fenêtre,
Comme au hasard.

Si vous saviez quel baume apporte
Au cœur la présence d'un cœur,
Vous vous assoiriez sous my porte,
Comme une sœur.

Si vous saviez que je vous aime,
Surtout si vous saviez comment,
Vous entreriez peut-être même
Tout simplement.[1]

His voice sank to silence as softly as a rose-leaf falls to earth.

Then there arose, like the buzz of a thousand insects, the adoring applause of a polished society.

---

1 If you knew how much I mourn / From living alone and without a family / Sometimes in front of my house / You would pass.
If you knew what produces / In my sad spirit a pure, innocent gaze / You would look at my window, / As if by chance.
If you knew what sort of consolation brings / To my heart the nearness of another heart / You would sit at my doorway, / Like a sister.
If you knew that I love you / Above all if you knew how much, / You would even, perhaps, enter / Just like that.

Si vous saviez que je vous aime,
Surtout si vous saviez comment,
Vous entreriez peut-être même
Tout simplement!

The words had filled the room with their sweet ineffable melody, and had reached Vere and brought their confession to her.

Her heart leaped like a bound thing set free; then a burning warmth that seemed to her like fire itself seemed to flood her veins. In some way the great crowd had parted and she saw the face of Corrèze for a moment, and his eyes met hers.

He had told his tale in the language he knew best and loved the most.

The next he was lost in the midst of his worshippers, who vainly implored him to return and sing again.

Vere, tutored by the world she lived in, sat quite still, and let her broad fan of white feathers lie motionless in her hands.

"Am I vile to have told her? Surely she must know it so well!" said Corrèze to himself as he sent his horses away and walked through the streets of Paris in the chill mists that heralded daylight. "Am I vile to have told her? Will she ever look at me again? Will she hate me for ever? Will she understand? Perhaps not. I sing a thousand songs; why should one have more meaning than another? She sees me play a hundred passions on the stage. Why should she believe I can feel one? And yet—and yet I think she will know, and perhaps she will not forgive; I fear she will never forgive."

He reproached himself bitterly as he walked home after midnight through the throngs of the Boulevards. He said to himself that if he had not seen Sergius Zouroff entering Bignon's he would never so far have broken his resolution and failed in his honour. He reached his home, disturbed by apprehension and haunted with remorse. For an empire he would not have breathed a profane word in the ear of the woman who fulfilled his ideal of women, and he was afraid that he had insulted her.

He did not go to his bed at all; he walked up and down his long suite of rooms in the intense scent of the hothouse bouquets which as usual covered every table and console in the chambers.

For a lesser declaration than that, he had seen great ladies glide veiled through his doors; nay, they had come unasked.

But he knew very well that she would never come one step on the way to meet him, even if she understood.

And that she would even understand he doubted.

The morning rose and the sun broke the mists, but its rays could not pierce through the olive velvet of his closed curtains. He walked to and fro, restlessly, through the artificial light and fragrance of his rooms. If she had been like the others, if he had heard her step on the stair, if he had seen that proud head veiled in the mask of a shameful secrecy, what would he have felt?—he thought he would have felt the instant rapture, the endless despair, that men felt in the old days who sold their souls to hell; the rapture that lived an hour, the despair that endured an eternity.

When he threw back his shutters and saw the brightness of morning, he rang and ordered his horse and rode out into the Bois without breaking his fast; the rides were all moist with the night's rain; the boughs were all green with young leaf; birds were singing as though it were the heart of the provinces. He rode fast and recklessly: the air was clear and fresh with a west wind stirring in it; it refreshed him more than sleep.

As he returned two hours later he saw her walking in one of the *allées des piétons*;[1] she was in black, with some old white laces about her throat; before her were her dogs and behind her was a Russian servant. He checked his horse in the ride adjacent, and waited for her to pass by him.

She did pass, bowed without looking at him, and went onward between the stems of the leafless trees.

Then he thought to himself that she had understood, but he doubted that she ever would forgive.

When she was quite out of sight he dismounted, gathered a late violet in the grass where she had passed him, and rode home.

"She understood a little," he thought, "enough to alarm, enough to offend her. She is too far above us all to understand more. Even life spent by the side of that brute has not tainted her. They are right to call her the ice-flower. She dwells apart in higher air than we ever breathe."

And his heart sank, and his life seemed very empty. He loved a woman who was nothing to him, who could be nothing to him, and who, even if ever she loved him, he would no more drag down to the low level of base frailties than he would spit upon the cross his fathers worshipped.

The next night was the last of his engagement at the Grand Opéra. It was a night of such homage and triumph as even he had

---

1   Tree-lined pedestrian avenue.

hardly known. But to him it was blank; the box that was Prince Zouroff's was empty.

He left Paris at daybreak.

Vere did indeed, but imperfectly, understand. As the song had reached her ear a sudden flood of joy came to her with it; it had been to her as if the heavens had opened; she had for one moment realised all that her life might have been, and she saw that he would have loved her.

When she reached the solitude of her chamber at home, she reproached herself; she seemed to herself to have sinned, and it seemed to her a supreme vanity to have dreamed of a personal message in the evening song of an eloquent singer. Did he not sing every night of love—every night that the public applauded the sorcery of his matchless music?

That he might have loved her, she did believe. There was a look in his regard that told her so, whenever his eyes met hers across the opera-house, or in the crowds of the streets, or of society. But of more she did not, would not, think.

Perhaps some memory of that one summer morning haunted him as it haunted her, with the sad vision of a sweetness that might have been in life, and never would be now; perhaps a vague regret was really with him. So much she thought, but nothing more.

The world she lived in had taught her nothing of its vanities, of its laxities, of its intrigues. She kept the heart of her girlhood. She was still of the old fashion, and a faithless wife was to her a wanton. Marriage might be loveless, and joyless, and soulless, and outrage all that it brought; but its bond had been taken, and its obligations accepted; no sin of others could set her free.

Her husband could not have understood that, nor could her mother, nor could her world; but to Vere it was clear as the day, that, not to be utterly worthless in her own sight, not to be base as the sold creatures of the streets, she must give fidelity to the faithless, cleanliness to the unclean.

Even that caress she had given to the roses seemed to her treacherous and wrong.

CHAPTER VI.

Prince Zouroff stayed in Paris until the end of June. There was no place that he liked so well. Lady Dolly passed a few weeks at Meurice's, and told her daughter with a little malice and a little pleasure, that the son to whom the Duchess of Mull had recently given birth, to the joy of all the Northumbrian border, had been baptised with the name of Vere, with much pomp at Castle Herbert.

"My name and my father's!" said Vere with coldest indignation. "And *her* father sold drink and opium to miners!"

"And the brothers kill pigs—by machinery," said her mother. "Certainly it is very funny. If Columbus had never discovered America would all these queer things have happened to us? There is no doubt we do get 'mixed,' as the lovely Fuschia would say."

Pick-me-up, as Duchess of Mull, had become even a greater success, were that possible, than Fuschia Leach had been. No fancy frisk, no little dinner, no big ball was anything without that brilliantly tinted face of hers, with the little impertinent nose, and the big radiant audacious eyes that had the glance of the street-arab, and the surprise of the fawn. Francis of Mull, tender, stupid and shy, lived in a perpetual intoxication at the wonder of his own possession of so much beauty, so much mirth, and so much audacity, and no more dreamed of opposing her wishes than, excellent young man that he was, he had ever dreamed of opposing his tutors and guardians. He was under her charm in a blind, dazed, benighted way that diverted her, and yet made her heartily sick of him; and she took the reins of government into her own hands and kept them. Not a tree was felled, not a horse was bought, not a farm lease was signed, but what the young duchess knew the reason why.

"I'll stop all this beastly waste, and yet I'll do it much finer, and get a lot more for my money," she said to herself when she first went to the biggest house of all their houses, and she did so with that admirable combination of thrift and display of which the American mind alone has the secret.

The expenses of his household in six months had been diminished by seven thousand pounds, yet the Duke of Mull had entertained royalty for three days at Castle Herbert with a splendour that his county had never seen. She was not at all mean, except in charities, but she got her money's worth.

"My dear old donkey, your wife didn't go pricing sprats[1] all down Broadway without knowing what to give for a red herring," said Her Grace, in the familiar yet figurative language in which the great nation she had belonged to delights.

"Cooking accounts won't go down with her," said the bailiffs, and the butlers, the housekeepers, the stud-grooms, and the head

---

1 Small common herrings.

gardeners, to one another with a melancholy unanimity at all her houses.

"Do you know, Vere, she is a great success," said Lady Dolly one day. "Very, very great. There is nobody in all England one quarter so popular."

"I quite believe it," said Vere.

"Then why won't you be friends with her?"

"Why should I be?"

"Well, she is your cousin."

"She is a woman my cousin has married. There is no possible relation between her and me."

"But do you not think it is always as well to—to—be pleasant?"

"No, I do not. If no one else remember the oaks of the forests I do not forget them."

"Oh, the oaks," said Lady Dolly. "Yes, they are mining there; but they were nasty, damp, windy places, I don't see that it matters."

"What a terribly proud woman you are, Vera," added the Princess Nadine, who was every whit as proud herself, "and yet you think so little of rank."

"I think nothing of rank," said Vere, "but I do think very much of race; and I cannot understand how men, who are so careful of the descent of their horses and hounds, are so indifferent to the contamination of their own blood."

"If you had lived before '90 you would have gone very grandly to the guillotine,"[1] said her sister-in-law.

"I should have been in good company," said Vere; "it is difficult to live in it now-a-days."

"With what an air you say that," said Madame Nelaguine; "really sometimes one would think you were a marquise of a hundred years old, and in your childhood had seen your château burnt by the mob."

"All my châteaux were burnt long ago," said Vere, with a sigh that she stifled.

Madame Nelaguine understood.

Vere was glad when the warmth grew greater with the days of early summer, and her husband entering her morning-room, said abruptly:

"The Grand Prix is run to-morrow. You seem to have forgotten it. On Saturday we will go down to Félicité. You will invite Mdme. de Sonnaz and Mdme. de Merilhac, and anyone else that you please. Nadine will come, no doubt."

---

1 A reference to the French Revolution (1789-99).

A Zouroff horse won the Grand Prix, and Prince Zouroff was for once in a contented mood, which lasted all the next day. As the train ran through the level green country towards Calvados he said with good-humoured gallantry to his wife,

"You have not invited me, Vera. The place is yours. I have no business in it unless you wish for me."

"The place is always yours, and I am yours," she answered in a low tone.

From a woman who had loved him the words would have been tender; from her, they were but an acknowledgment of being purchased. His humour changed as he heard them; his face grew dark; he devoted himself to Mdme. Jeanne, who was travelling with them; she had refused to stay at Félicité, however, and had taken for herself the little Châlet Ludoff at Trouville.

"You are a bear; but she makes you dance, Sergius," whispered the duchess with malice.

Zouroff frowned.

"Bears do something besides dancing," he muttered.

"Yes; they eat honey," replied Mdme. de Sonnaz. "You have had more honey than was good for you all your days. Now you have got something that is not honey."

Vere, with her delicate straight profile against the light, sat looking at the green fields and the blue sky, and did not hear what was said.

"If she cared, or rather if she understood," thought the Duchesse Jeanne, as she glanced at her; "she would rule him instead of being ruled; she could do it; but she would have to keep the bear on hot plates—as I did."

Zouroff, screened behind "Figaro," looked from one woman to the other.

"How *grande dame*[1] she is," he thought. "Beside her Jeanne looks *bizarre*, ugly, almost vulgar. And yet Vera bores me when she does not enrage me, and enrages me when she does not bore me; while with the other, one is always on good terms with one's self."

"I know what you were thinking, my friend," whispered the duchess under cover of the noise and twilight of the Martainville tunnel. "But all the difference, I assure you, is that she is your wife and I am Paul's. If she were not your wife you would be furiously in love with her, and were I your wife you would find me a *chatte enragée*[2] with frightful green eyes."

---

1 Great lady.
2 Mad pussy-cat.

Zouroff laughed grimly. He did not tell her that his thoughts had been less complimentary than those she had attributed to him.

"I could find it in me to tell you your eyes were green when you spite me by not coming to Félicité," he murmured instead.

Mdme. Jeanne twisted the "Figaro" about, and said: "Chut! We shall meet more freely at the little Ludoff house."

Vere only heard the rustling of the "Figaro" sheet. She was looking at the clock-tower of St. Tourin, and the summer glory of the forest of Evreux.

Madame Jeanne stayed at Trouville. Vere, with her husband, drove in the panier, with four white ponies, that awaited them at the station, along the shady avenue that leads out of the valley of the Toucques toward Villiers. The sunshine was brilliant, the air sweet, the sea, when the rise of the road brought it into view, was blue as the sky, and the fishing fleets were on it. Vere closed her eyes as the bright marine picture came in sight, and felt the tears rise into them.

Only three years before she had been Vere Herbert, coming on the dusty sands below, with no more knowledge or idea of the world's pomps, and vanities, and sins, and vices, than any one of the brighteyed deer that were now living out their happy lives under the oak shadows of Bulmer Chase. Only three years before!

Zouroff, lying back in the little carriage, looked at her through his half-shut eyelids.

"*Ma chère!*" he said with his little rough laugh, "we ought to feel very sweet emotions, you and I, returning here. Tell me are you à *la hauteur de l'occasion?*[1] I fear I am not. Perhaps, after a glass of sherry, the proper emotion may visit me."

Vere made no reply. Her eyes, wide-opened now, were looking straight forward; she drove her ponies steadily.

"What do you feel?" he persisted. "It is an interesting return. Pray tell me."

"I have ceased to analyse what I feel," she answered, in her clear cold voice. "I prefer to stifle it."

"You are very courteous!"

"I think you have very often said yourself that courtesy is not one of the obligations of marriage. You ask me for the truth, I tell you the truth."

"In three years of the world have you not learned a pretty lie yet!"

"No. I shall not learn it in twenty years."

---

1 Up for the occasion.

"Do you know that there are times when you answer me so that I could beat you like a dog?"

"I dare say."

"Is that all you say?"

"What should I say? If you beat me, it would not hurt me much more than other things."

Zouroff was silent. He saw that she drove her ponies on tranquilly, and that her blush-rose cheek neither flushed nor paled. Master of her body and mind, present and future, though he was, he had a sullen sense of her escaping him always, and he had as sullen a respect for her courage and her calmness.

"She could be a mother of young lions!" he thought, as Lamartine[1] thought of Delphine Gay,[2] and he felt bitter against her that his sons had died.

They reached Félicité as the sun set over the sea, where the low shores by Caen were hidden in a golden mist. The dressing bell was ringing in the Gothic clock tower; the tribe of canary-hued lacqueys were bending to the ground in the beautiful cedar-wood hall, with its pointed arches, and its illuminated shields, which had captivated the young eyes of Vere Herbert.

Madame Nelaguine had arrived before them, and her welcome, wit, and careful tact saved them from the terrors and the tedium of a *tête-à-tête*.

"Are you glad to come here, Vera?" she asked.

"I am glad to see the sea," answered Vere. "But I am tired of moving from house to house. We have no home. We have only a number of hôtels."

"I think you will be happier than in Paris," said the Princess Nadine. "You will have the trouble of a house party, it is true; but your mornings you can spend in your garden, your hothouses, with your horses, or on the sea; you will be freer."

"Yes," assented Vera. She did not hear; she was looking through the great telescope on the terrace down along the line of the shore; she was trying to discern amongst the broken confused indentations of the rocky beach the place where Corrèze had sung to her and to the

---

1 Alphonse de Lamartine (1790-1869) was a French Romantic poet, historian, and statesman.

2 Delphine Gay de Girardin (1804-55) was a French author of comedies, stories, and sketches of Parisienne life. Her literary salon was noted for its brilliance. Lamartine compared her to Italian waterfalls and precipices, a statuesque but flawed beauty.

lark. But the sea and land were blent in one golden glow as the sun went down behind the black cliffs of western Calvados, and she could discern nothing that she knew.

The dressing-bell was ringing, and she hurried to her rooms. Her husband was intolerant of any excuses of fatigue or indisposition, and always expected to see her in full toilette whether there was no one, or whether there were fifty persons, at his table. Sometimes it seemed to her as if all her life were consumed in the mere acts of dressing and undressing; the paradise of other women was her purgatory.

They dined alone, only enlivened by the ironies of the Princess Nadine, who, when she chose could be exceedingly amusing, if very acid in her satires; when dinner was over they went out on to the terrace where the moonlight was brilliant. Some gentlemen from the Château Villiers had ridden over to congratulate Prince Zouroff on the achievement of his racer. They were old friends of his, heroes and disciples of "le sport." After a while they talked only of that idol. Vere sat looking at the moonlit Channel. Madame Nelaguine, within the room, was playing quaint mournful melodies of old German composers, and sad Russian folk-airs. Félicité was very peaceful, very lovely; on the morrow the glittering noisy feverish life of the great world would begin under its roof, with its house-party of Parisians and Russians.

"What a pity, what a pity! One has not time to breathe," thought Vere, as she leaned her head against the marble balustrade, and rested her eyes on the sea.

"What a pity!" she thought, "the loveliest things in all creation are the sunrise and the moonlight; and who has time in our stupid life, that is called pleasure, to see either of them?"

A full moon made the narrow sea a sheet of silver; a high tide had carried the beach up to the edge of the black rocks; in the white luminous space one little dark sail was slowly drifting before the wind, the sail of a fishing or dredging boat. The calmness, the silence, the lustre, the sweet, fresh, strong sea-scent, so familiar to her in her childhood, filled her with an infinite melancholy.

Only three years, and how changed she was! All her youth had been burnt up in her; all hope was as dead in her heart as if she were already old.

She sat and thought, as the dreamy music from within united with the murmur of the sea; she had said truly that she now strove to stifle thought, but her nature was meditative, and she could never wholly succeed.

"Perhaps I am not right, perhaps I do not do all that I might," she mused; and her conscience reproached her with harshness and hatred against the man whom she had sworn to honour.

"Honour!" she thought bitterly: what a world of mockery lay in that one little word.

Yet he was her husband; according to his light he had been generous to her; she would have to bear his children, and his name was her name for ever. It would be better if they could live in peace.

When his friends had ridden back to Villiers, and his sister was still dreamily wandering through many musical memories, Sergius Zouroff was standing on the terrace, looking seaward, and calculating how quickly his yacht would be able to come round on the morrow from Cherbourg. Midnight chimes were sounding softly from the Flemish carillon in the clock-tower of his château.

Vere looked at him, hesitated, then rose and approached him.

"Sergius," she said in a low voice, "I spoke wrongly to you to-day; I beg your pardon."

Zouroff started a little, and looked down in surprise at the proud delicate face of his wife as the moonlight fell on it.

"You are not going to make me a scene?" he said irritably and apprehensively.

On the lofty yet wistful mood of Vere the words fell like drops of ice. A momentary recollection had moved her to something like hope that her husband might make her duty less penance and less pain to her, by some sort of sympathy and comprehension. She had bent her temper to the concession of a humility very rare with her, and this was all her recompense. She checked the reply that rose to her lips, and kept her voice serene and low.

"I do not wish to annoy you in any way," she said simply; "I saw that I was wrong to-day; that I had failed in the respect I owe you: I thought I ought to confess it and beg your pardon."

Zouroff stared at her with his gloomy sullen eyes. She looked very fair to him, as she stood there with the silvery rays of the moon on her bent face and her white throat and breast; and yet she had lost almost all charm for him, whilst the ugliness of Jeanne de Sonnaz kept his sluggish passions alive through many years. He stared down on her, scarcely thinking at all of her words, thinking only as men do every hour and ever century, why it was that the pure woman wearies and palls, the impure strengthens her chains with every night that falls. It is a terrible truth, but it is a truth.

"How lovely she is!" he thought, "her mouth is a rose, her eyes are stars, her breasts are lilies, her breath is the fragrance of flowers; and—

I like Casse-une-Croûte better, who is the colour of copper, and smells of smoke and brandy as I do!"

That was what he was thinking.

Vere looked away from his face outward to the sea, and laid her hand for a moment on his arm.

"It is three years ago," she said wistfully, "I did not know very well what I did; I was only a child; now I do know—I would do otherwise. But there is no going back. I am your wife. Will you help me a little to do what is right? I try always—"

Her voice faltered slightly.

Her husband's mind came out from his thoughts of Casse-une-Croûte and Duchesse Jeanne, and realised that she was asking him for sympathy. He stared; then felt a passing heat of sullen shame; then thrust away the emotion and laughed.

"My dear," he said, with the cynical candour that was rather brutality than sincerity, "three years ago we both made a great mistake. Everyone who marries says the same. But we must make the best of it. I am a rich man, and an indulgent one, and that must content you. You are a lovely woman, and a cold one, and that must content me. If you bear me living sons you will do all a wife wants to do, and if I pay your bills and allow you to amuse yourself in your own way I do not see that you can complain of me. The less we are alone, the less likely are we to quarrel. That is a conjugal maxim. And do not make me serious scenes of this sort. They tire me, and I have no wish to be rude to you. Will you not go to your room? You look fatigued."

Vere turned away, and went into the house. Her husband remained on the terrace sending the smoke of his great cigar out on to the moonlit sea-scented air.

"She grows sentimental," he said to himself, "it is better stopped at once. Can she not be content with her chiffons and her jewels?"

The following day the Parisian contingent filled the château, and from morn till night, the mirth and movement of a gay house-party spoiled for the mistress of Félicité its woodland beauty and its seashore freshness.

Never to escape from the world grew as wearisome and as terrible to Vere as the dust of the factory to the tired worker, as the roar of the city streets to the heart-sick sempstress. Never to escape from it; never to be alone with the deep peace of nature, with the meditations of great dead poets, with the charm of lonely and noble landscape—this seemed to her as sad and as dreary as, to the women who surrounded her, it would have seemed to have been condemned to a year without lovers and rivals, to a solitude without excitement, and intrigue, and success. To have a moment alone was their terror; never to have a moment alone was her torture. The difference of feeling made a gulf between her and them that no equality of beauty, and accomplishment, and position could bridge. There was no sympathy possible between Vere and the pretty painted people of her world. She had no standing-point in common with them, except her social rank. Their jargon, their laughter, their rivalries, their pleasures, were all alike distasteful to her. When she drove over with them to Trouville at five o'clock, and sat amidst them, within a stone's throw of what the horrible pleasantry of society calls the *jolies impures*,[1] she thought the levée[2] that the proscribed sisterhood held on those sands was quite as good as the levée of the great ladies around her.

In return women hated her. "She is so *farouche*," they said. They only meant that she was chaste, with that perfect chastity of thought, as well as of act, which the whole tone and tenour of society destroys in its devotees, and ridicules in the few cases where it cannot be destroyed.

Only Jeanne de Sonnaz professed to admire, nay to love, her. But then everyone knew that Madame Jeanne was a clever woman, who said nothing, and did nothing, without a reason.

"Try to be amiable—if you know how to be amiable—with Madame de Sonnaz," had been the command of Zouroff to his wife on the first day that she and the French duchess had met; and Vere had been indebted to the brilliant Parisienne for many a word of social counsel, many an indication of social perils, where the stiff frivolities of etiquette were endangered, or a difficult acquaintance required tact to conciliate or rebuff it. Vere believed innocently and honestly that Jeanne de Sonnaz liked her, and was angered with and reproached herself for not being sufficiently grateful, and being unable fully to return the regard.

"I think she is not a good woman," she said once, hesitatingly, to her sister-in-law.

Madame Nelaguine smiled a little grimly, with a look that made her resemble her brother. "My dear, do not be too curious about goodness. If you inquire so much for it, it will lead you into as much trouble as the pursuit of the Sangréal[3] did the knights of old; and I am afraid you will not find it. As for Jeanne, she is always in her chair

---

1 Prostitutes.
2 Reception.
3 Holy Grail.

at the Messe des Paresseux[1] at St. Philippe, she turns a lottery wheel at fêtes for the poor, and her husband has always lived with her. What more can you want? Do not be too exacting."

Vere vaguely felt that Madame Nelaguine thought anything but well of her friend; but she got no more information, and Madame Jeanne came most days over to Félicité and said to all there, "How lovely is Vera!—odd, cold, inhuman, yes; but one adores her."

One morning Vere, risen several hours before her guests, felt a wistful fancy, that had often visited her, to try and find again that little nest of fishers' cottages where she had eaten the cherries, and heard Corrèze sing in rivalry to the lark. It was a wish so innocent and harmless that she saw no reason to resist it; she had her ponies ordered while the day was still young, and drove out of her own park-gates down to Deauville and Trouville, and through them, and along the road to Villerville. At Villerville she left her ponies, and walked with no escort except Loris through the sea of greenery that covers the summit of the table-land of Calvados, while the salt sea washes its base.

The name of this little village she had never known, but, guessing by the position it had been in above the sea, she knew that it must have been somewhere between Grand Bec and Villerville; and she followed various paths through orchards, and grass meadows, and cornfields divided by lines of poplars, and at last found the lonely place quite unchanged.

The old woman who had called him Saint Raphael was knitting by the fence of furze; the cherry trees were full of fruit; the cabbage-roses were pushing their dewy heads against the tiny roses of the sweet-briar; sun-burnt children were dragging nets over the short grass; the lark was singing against the sky. Nothing had changed except herself.

No one of them recognised her.

The old woman gave her a frank good-morrow, and the children stared, but no one of them thought that this great lady, with the gold-headed cane, and the old lace on her white skirts, was the child that had sat there three years before, and drunk the milk in its wooden bowl, and worn the wooden shoes. She asked for a little water, and sat down by the sweet-briar hedge; she was thinking of Corrèze. He was seldom absent from her thoughts; but he remained so pure, so lofty, so ideal a figure in her fancy, that his empire over her memory never alarmed her.

---

1 Mass for the idle.

He was never to her like other men.

She sat and listened, with divided attention, to the garrulity of the old white-capped woman, who went on knitting in the sun, against her wall of furze, and chattered cheerfully, needing no reply. They were hard times, she thought. People had said with the Republic[1] there would be no poor, but she could see no difference herself; she had lived through many of them—meaning governments—but they were each as bad as the other, she thought. Bread was always dear. The *moules*[2] were plentiful this year; the Republic had no hand in that; and the deep-sea fishing had been very fair too. Did madame see that lark? That little fool of a bird brought her in as much as the *moules*; a gentleman had taken such a fancy to it that he came and saw it was safe every summer, sometimes oftener; and he always left her five napoléons[3] or more. There were so many larks in the world, or would be if people did not eat them; she could not tell what there was about hers, but the gentleman always gave her money because she let it live in the grass. Perhaps madame had heard of him; he had a beautiful face; he was a singer, they said; and to hear him sing—she had heard him once herself—it was like heaven being opened.

Vere listened with undivided attention now, and her eyes grew soft and dim.

"Does he remember like that?" she thought; and it seemed to her so strange that he should never have sought to speak to her.

"Does he come for the lark only?" she asked.

"He says so," answered the old woman. "He always takes a rose and a bit of sweet-briar. The first day he was here there was a pretty girl with him, that he bought sabots for, because she had lost her shoes on the beach. Perhaps the girl may be dead. I have thought so sometimes; it cannot be only for the lark; and he sits here a long time, a long time—and he is sad. He was here a day in May—that was the last."

The warmth of a sudden blush came over her hearer's proud face. She did not know what she felt; she felt a thrill of alarm, a strange pleasure, a vague trouble. She rose at once, and left a little money in the lean hand, as she bade the old peasant goodday, called Loris from his chase of chickens, and began to retrace her way to Villerville.

The old woman looked after her along the flat path over the turf that went on under the apple trees, and through the wheatfields, till it joined the road to Grand Bec.

---

1   The Third Republic.
2   Mussels.
3   French gold coins.

"Now I think of it," she muttered to her knitting needles. "That great lady has the eyes of that tired child who had the wooden shoes. Perhaps she is the same—only dead that way—dead of being stuffed with gold, as so many of them are."

"Granny, that is the Russian Princess from Félicité," said a fisherman who was coming up over the edge of the rocks, hanging his nets on the poles; and saw the tall slender figure of Vere going through the tall green corn.

"Aye, aye!" said the old woman. "Well, she has given me a gold bit. Never was a bird that brought so much money from the clouds as my lark."

Her son laughed. "I saw your other lark in Trouville this morning; he had come by the Havre packet from England. He knew me, and asked for you all. He said he would only stay here an hour on his way to Paris, but would soon be back again, and then would come and see you. They took all my fish at the Roches Noires, just at a word from him to the porter in the hall!"

"Tiens!"[1] said the old woman thoughtfully, and she kept her thoughts to herself.

"Where have you been, O ma belle matinâle,"[2] said the Duchess Jeanne, as Vere went up the steps of the sea-terrace to enter the anteroom of Félicité, where the duchess, just downstairs at twelve o'clock, was breathing the morning air in the most charming of dressing gowns—a miracle of swan's down and old Mechlin, with a knot here and there of her favourite cardinal red. She had passed the night there after a ball.

Zouroff was with her; both were smoking.

"I have been a long drive," answered Vere; "you know I rise early."

"Where did you go?" asked Zouroff brusquely. "I object to those senseless, long drives in the country."

"I went as far as Villerville," she answered. "I went to see a few fisher-people that live on the coast near there."

The hour before she would have said it without any other thought than what her words expressed.

Now her remembrance of what the woman had said of Corrèze made her hesitate a little, and a certain colour came in her face, that both her husband and her guest noticed. It seemed to the exquisite and loyal truthfulness of her temper that she had been guilty of a thing even meaner than a falsehood—a reservation.

---

1 Well!
2 Oh, my beautiful morning riser.

"It was where I lost my way the first day I was with my mother," she said; and turned to her husband, as making the explanation only to him. "Perhaps you remember? Everyone laughed about it at the time."

"I think I remember," said Zouroff moodily. "It could scarcely be worth a pilgrimage."

"Unless she have a *carte tendre du pays*,"[1] said the duchess with a little laugh. "Oh, a million pardons, my sweet Vera; you never permit a jest, I know."

"I permit any jest if it be witty, and have no offence in it," said Vere very coldly. "If you and the Prince will allow me, I will go indoors; I am a little tired and dusty, and Loris is more than a little."

"You had no intention in what you said, Jeanne?" muttered Zouroff to his companion, when Vere had entered the house. "You cannot possibly mean—"

"Mean! Of your pearl of women, your white swan, your emblem of ice? What should I mean? It amused me to see her look angry; that is all. I assure you, if you made her angry much oftener, she would amuse you more. Do you know, do you know, *mon vieux*,[2] I should never be in the least surprised, if a few years later, you were to become a jealous husband! How funny it will be. But really, you looked quite oriental in your wrath just now. Be more angry more often. Believe me, your wife will entertain you much more. Especially as she will never deserve it."

Leaving that recipe behind her, fraught with all the peril it might bear, Madame Jeanne dragged her muslins and her Mechlin over the marbles of the terrace, and went also within doors to attend to the thousand and one exigencies of a great spectacle which she had conceived, and was about to give to the world.

It was a Kermesse[3] for the poor—always for the poor.

Madame Jeanne, who was a woman of energy, and did not mind trouble (she had been one of the leaders of a *régime*[4] that dressed seven times a day), was the head and front, the life and soul, of her forthcoming Kermesse, and was resolute to leave no pains untaken that should make it the most successful fancy fair of its season. She had

---

1 Literally map out the territory. *Tendre* (tender does not fit into the phrase). The Duchesse is insinuating that Vere might have an attraction to someone she visited and plans to see that person again.
2 My old one (friend).
3 Country fair.
4 Society.

already quantities of royalties promised her as visitors. Poor Citron had pledged herself to preside at a puppet show; "*toute la gomme*"[1] would be golden lambs to be shorn; and all the great ladies, and a few of the theatrical celebrities, were to be vendors, and wear the costumes and the jewellery of Flemish peasantry.

"I have written to beg Corrèze to come, but he will not," she said once in the hearing of Vere. "He used to be at Trouville every year, but he never comes now. I suppose some woman he cares about goes elsewhere."

She was very provoked, because she wanted to have a grand mass at Notre Dame des Victoires, and "quêter"[2] afterwards; and if Corrèze would have sung some Noël or some Salutaris Hostia, it would have brought hundreds more napoléons into her plate for the poor; so, angrily, she abandoned the idea of the mass, and confined herself to the glories of the Kermesse.

Vere, to whom the mingling of the poor with a fancy fair, and the confusion of almsgiving with diversion, always seemed as painful as it was grotesque, took no heed of all the preparations, and received in silence her husband's commands to take a place in it. He was peremptory, and she was always obedient. She wrote to her people in Paris to send her down all that was necessary, and after that ceased to occupy herself with a folly she secretly disapproved; a mockery of the misery of the world which made her heart ache.

The day before the first opening of this Kermesse, which was to eclipse every other show of the sort, Prince Zouroff, with his wife and sister, and most of their guests, drove over to Trouville to see the arrangements. Madame Jeanne had erected her pretty booths in the glades of the Comte d'Hautpoul, and had had that charming park conceded to her for her merry-go-rounds, her lotteries, her *diseurs de bonnes aventures*,[3] her merry-andrews,[4] and her other diversions. Madame Jeanne's taste was the taste of that Second Empire, under which the comet of her course had reached its perihelion;[5] but the effect of her taste in this little canvas city of pleasure was bright, brilliant, and picturesque, and the motley colours in which she delighted made a pretty spectacle under the green leaves of the trees. Every booth had the name of the lady who would officiate at it blazoned

---

1 All the smart (fashionable) people.
2 Take up a collection.
3 Fortune tellers.
4 Clowns.
5 The point of orbit when a comet is closest to the sun.

above; and, above the lottery-booth was written, "Madame de Sonnaz," with a scarlet flag that bore her arms and coronet fluttering against the blue sky. The next was the Marquise de Merilhac's, green and primrose, the next the Countess Schondorff's, amber and violet; the next, of pale blue, with a pale blue pennon,[1] and the arms and crown in silver, was the Princess Zouroff's.

"It is exceedingly pretty," said Vere, as she stood before the little pavilion.

There were about ten others, all in divers hues, with their pennons fluttering from tall Venetian masts. The pretty booths stood about in a semi-oval where the sward[2] was green and the trees were tall. Servants were bringing in all the fanciful merchandise that was to be for sale on the morrow; a few gendarmes had been sent to protect the fair during the night; some children, with flying hair and fluttering skirts, and some baby-sailors, were at play on the real wooden horses which the duchess had had down from St. Cloud.

"It is extremely pretty," said Vere courteously to the projectress and protectress of it all, and her eyes glanced round the semi-circle. Immediately facing hers was a booth of white stripes and rose-colour, looped up with great garlands of pink roses; the flag above had no arms, but, instead, had a device in gold, a squirrel cracking nuts, with the motto, "*Vivent le bracconniers!*"[3] It was a device known to *tout Paris*, except to Vere; but even she knew the name underneath, which she read in the glow of the late afternoon light,

"Mademoiselle Noisette."

She stood in the entrance of her own pavilion and saw it. Her face grew very white, and a haughty indignation blazed in her grand, grave eyes.

Madame Jeanne, standing by, and chattering volubly, with her eyeglasses up to her eyes, saw the look and rejoiced in her soul.

"It will be amusing," she said to herself. "How *very* angry quiet people can be!"

Vere, however, disappointed her. She made no scene; she remained still and tranquil, and, in a clear voice, gave a few directions to the servants who were arranging the contents of her own stalls.

Madame Jeanne felt the pang an archer knows when, at a great public fête, the arrow aimed for the heart of the gold, misses its mark, and strikes the dust.

---

1 Banner.
2 Turf.
3 Long live the poachers.

It was to be chagrined like this that she, Duchesse de Sonnaz, and daughter of the mighty Maison du Merilhac, had stretched her Second Empire laxities so far as to permit on the grounds of her own Kermesse the Free Lances[1] of the Paris Theatres!

Nothing was said; nothing was done; Madame Jeanne felt cheated, and her Kermesse seemed already shorn of its splendour.

Vere remained very calm, very still; she did not move outside the curtains of her own azure nest.

"Guilt hath pavilions and no secrecy," murmured the Princess Nadine, changing the well-known line by a monosyllable, as she glanced across at the pink and white booth with its peccant squirrel. But she murmured it only in the ear of a tried and trusty old friend, the Count Schondorff, who for more years than she would have cared to count had been her shadow and her slave, her major-domo and her souffredouleur.[2] "I am so glad Vera takes it well," she thought with relief.

A little later there came into the pink tent a handsome woman in a black dress, with knots of pink; she had a dome-like pile of glistening hair, gorgeous beauty, a splendid bust; she looked like a rose-hued rhododendron made human.

It was Noisette. She bustled and banged about rather noisily and laughed loudly with the men accompanying her, and scolded the servants unpacking her packages.

"V'là la petite!" said Noisette as she looked across the sward at the azure pavilion. She always said the same thing when she saw the Princess Zouroff.

In a good-natured scornful way Noisette pitied her.

The sunset hour wore away, and Vere had made no sign that she had seen the name beneath the golden squirrel and the woman whose badge the poaching-squirrel was.

Madame de Sonnaz was disappointed and perplexed. She had seen the look in Vere's eyes, and as she thought her cold, but not tame, she wondered that she bore the insult so passively. She drove homeward with them to dine at Félicité and pass the night there.

"Surely it will be a great success to-morrow," she cried gleefully. "O mon Dieu![3] how tired I am—and how much more tired I shall be!"

---

1 Artists who sell their services to employers without long term commitments.
2 Drudge; butt (object of ridicule).
3 Oh, my God!

"You are too good to the poor," said Vere with an intonation that the duchesse did not admire.

"She will be unbearable when she is a little older," she said to herself.

Vere reached her home, changed her dress for dinner, went down with the light on her opals and in her eyes—which had a dark stern look in them, new there—and bore herself throughout the dinner with that cold grace, that lofty simplicity, which had gained her the name of the Alpine flower.

"I suppose she accepts the thing with the rest," thought Madame Jeanne, as she sat on the right hand of Zouroff; and she felt bitterly angry with herself for having stooped to open the pavilions of her fancy-fair to the dramatic sisterhood, even though it were in the pure interests of charity.

After dinner when her people were scattered about—some playing cards, some merely flirting, some listening to the choral and orchestral music that the choice taste of Madame Nelaguine had always made a constant charm of the house-parties of Félicité—Sergius Zouroff, as he passed one moment from the card-room to the smoking-room, was stopped by his wife. She stood before him with her head erect, her hands crossed on a large fan of feathers.

"Monsieur," she said very calmly, though her voice was altogether unlike what it had been on the terrace the night of their return; "Monsieur, you desired me to take part in the so-called Kermesse tomorrow?"

"Certainly," said Zouroff, and he stared at her.

"Then," she said, very quietly still, "you will see that the pavilion of the actress, Mademoiselle Noisette, is taken down, or differently occupied. Otherwise, I do not go to mine."

Zouroff was silent from utter amazement. He stared at her blankly.

"What did you say?" he said savagely, after some moments' silence. "What did you say? Are you mad?"

"I think you heard very well what I said," replied Vere. "All I have to say is that if Mademoiselle Noisette be present I shall not be. That is for you to decide."

Then, without any more words, or even any look at him, she passed on into the music-room, and joined some other ladies.

Sergius Zouroff stood and stared after her. He felt much the same emotion as his ancestors might have felt when some serf, whom they had been long used to beat and torture, rose up and struck them in return. What did she know of Noisette? He supposed that she must know all, since she took no exception to the two other actresses, who were permitted to take part in the Kermesse of the *grandes dames*.

He did not care what she knew—or he thought he did not; but he cared bitterly that she should dare to affront him and defy him, dare to make him what he termed a scene, dare to erect her will in opposition to his own. And, amidst all the turbulence of anger, self-will, was a sullen sense of shame; a consciousness that his life was no more fit to be mated with hers than the lips of a drunkard are fit to touch an ivory chalice of consecrated wine.

He sought his sister.

"Nadine," he said sharply, "have you ever told Vera of Noisette?"

Madame Nelaguine glanced at him with some contempt.

"I? do I ever talk? do I ever do anything but what is rational?"

"Who has then?"

"Has anyone? Probably *le tout Paris*, everybody and nobody. What is the matter?"

"The matter! She has made me a scene. She declares that if Noisette be in her booth to-morrow, she will not go to her own. She is not the ignoramus that you think."

"After three years as your wife, Sergius, how should she be? I am sorry she has begun to observe these things. I will speak to her if you like. Unless you will withdraw Noisette."

"Withdraw Noisette! Do you suppose she ever listens to me? do you suppose I should not be the laughing-stock of all society if I quarrelled with her to please Vera's caprices?"

"If you annoyed your mistress to avoid insulting your wife, society would laugh at you? Yes, I suppose it would. What a nice world it is," thought the Princess Nadine, as she said aloud, "I will see Vera. But she is difficult to persuade. And you will pardon me, Sergius, but here I do think she is rather right. It is not good form to have Mademoiselle Noisette or Mademoiselle anybody else of the same—adventurous—reputation mixed up with *us* in any affair of this kind."

"Perhaps not," said Zouroff roughly. "But Jeanne chose to have it so. She thought they would attract. So they will, and it is no more than having their carriages next yours in the Bois."

"Or our lovers, and brothers, and husbands in their dressing-rooms," thought Madame Nelaguine. "You are not very just, Sergius," she said aloud. "Jeanne may have a will of her own, Noisette may have one, anybody; but not Vera."

"Vera is my wife," said Prince Zouroff.

To him it seemed as clear as day that all the difference between these women was thus expressed.

"You are quite resolved then," she said with some hesitation, "not to see any justice in this objection of Vera's, not to give in to it, not to contrive in some way to secure the absence of Mademoiselle Noisette to-morrow?"

"Nadine Nicolaivna!" cried her brother in wrath. "After forty years that we have been in this world, do you know me so little that you want to ask such a thing? After Vera's insolence I would drag Noisette to that pavilion to-morrow if she were dying!"

"Will you drag your wife?" said Madame Nadine, with a little disgust; but Zouroff had left her, and was on his way to the smoking-room.

"He is nothing but a spoiled child grown big and brutal," thought his sister, with a little shrug of her shoulders. "How I wish he had married a *diablesse*[1] like Jeanne."

An hour later, when the ladies all went to their rooms, Madame Nelaguine asked entrance for a moment at Vere's door, and, without beating about the bush, said simply:

"My dear, Sergius has asked me to speak to you about the Kermesse to-morrow. Now I think I know all that actuates you, and I will admit that my own feeling is quite with you; but it is too late now to alter anything; Sergius is obstinate, as you know; especially obstinate if he fancy his will is disputed. This objection of yours can only lead to scenes, to disputes, to differences, very trying, very useless, and— worst of all—very diverting to others. Will you not abandon the point? It is not you that the presence of this person at the fair will shame, but himself."

Vere heard quite patiently; her maid, who did not understand English, which Madame Nelaguine, like most Russians, spoke admirably, was brushing out her thick bright hair.

"It was my fault not to attend more to the details of the thing," she answered; "but I had heard nothing of Mademoiselle Noisette being permitted in the park. It is your brother's shame certainly, but if I submitted to so public an insult as that, I should be, I think, scarcely higher than Mademoiselle Noisette herself. We will not talk about it; it is of no use; only, unless you can tell me that her name and her flag are withdrawn from the pavilions, I do not stir from here to-morrow. That is all."

"Ah!" ejaculated Madame Nadine, very wearily. "My dear, have you any conception of what Sergius can be, can do, when he is

1 She-devil.

crossed? Believe me, I am not defending him for an instant—no one could; but I have seen twice as long a life as you have, Vera, and I have never seen any good come of the wife's indignation in these cases. Society may go with her for the moment, but it deserts her in the long run. Her husband is embittered by the exposure, and he has always a strength she has not. The world does not insist that a wife shall have Griselda's[1] virtue or Griselda's affection, but it does insist that she shall have Griselda's patience. Noisette, and a thousand Noisettes, if your husband forget himself for them, cannot hurt *you* in the eyes of the world; but one rash moment of indignation and rupture may be your ruin."

Vere lifted her face, with all its loosened hair like a golden cloud about it, and her face was very cold and contemptuous, and almost hard in its scorn.

"Dear Princess," she said very briefly and chillily, "I did not wish to trouble you on this subject. You are not to blame for your brother's vices, or for my marriage. Only, pray understand, since we do speak of it, that my mind is quite made up. If Mademoiselle Noisette be permitted to be present at the park to-morrow, I shall be absent. I was a child three years ago, but I am not a child now."

Madame Nelaguine sighed.

"Of course you know everything, dear; women always do, even when nobody says a syllable to them. You are wronged, wounded, insulted, all that I admit with sorrow. But what I want to persuade you is, that this method of avenging yourself will do no sort of good. You will only give a triumph to Noisette; you will only give a laugh to your friends and your enemies—for friends and enemies are so sadly alike in the way they look at one's misfortunes! My dear child, society has settled all these things; the *belles petites* are seen everywhere except just in our drawing-rooms; they will be soon there also, perhaps. The fiction of society is, that we know nothing of their existence; the fact of society is, that they are our most powerful and most successful rivals, and dispute each inch of ground with us. Now, wise women sustain the fiction and ignore the fact; like society. I want you to be one of these wise ones. It ought to be easy to you, because you have no love for Sergius."

A very bitter look came for the moment on Vere's face. She raised her head once more with a very proud gesture.

---

1 A patient, long suffering wife. (The subject of Chaucer's "Clerk's Tale" in *The Canterbury Tales*. The term originates from *The Decameron* [Day 10, Tale 10]).

"Let us say no more, Nadine. I have self-respect. I will not be a public spectacle *vis-à-vis*[1] with one of Prince Zouroff's mistresses. He can choose whether he sees her in her pavilion, or me in mine. He will not see both. Good-night."

Sorrowful, discomforted, baffled, but knowing that her sister-in-law had justice on her side, though not prudence, the Princess Nelaguine went to her own chamber.

"War has begun," she thought; and she shuddered, because she knew her brother's temper. When he was ten years old she had seen him strangle a pet monkey because the small creature disobeyed him in its tricks.

Madame Nelaguine awoke in the morning feverish with anxiety. She was not a good woman, but she had honour in her, and was capable of affection. She had begun to detest her brother, and to care much for his wife. The day was clear and warm, not too warm; and a strong soft wind was tossing the white foam of the sea, and would blow brightly on the pretty pennons of the Kermesse pavilions. Vere rose earlier than anyone, as her habit was, and walked out into the garden with Loris by her side. She was not in any way anxious; her mind was made up; and, of anything that her husband might say or might do, she had no fear.

"At the utmost he could but kill me," she thought with a little contemptuous derision; "and that would not matter very much. No Herbert of the Border was ever insulted yet."

She walked over the grass above the sea, where the rose thickets grew, and the whole coast could be seen from Honfleur to the Rochers de Calvados. It was rather a rampart than a terrace, and the waves beat and fretted the wall below.

It was only nine o'clock; no one except herself rose so early at Félicité.

As she walked a stone fell at her feet. A letter was tied to it. Instinctively she took it up, and on the note she read her own name. She hesitated a moment, then opened it. The writing she did not know. It was very brief, and only said:

"Mademoiselle Noisette was called to Paris last night. The Princess Zouroff is entreated by a humble well-wisher not to disturb herself any more on this matter. She can honour the Kermesse in safety."

Vere read it, and stood still in wonder. Could it be from the actress herself?

---

1 Face to face.

The writing was that of a man, elegant, free, and clear.

She leaned over the grey stone wall of the garden and searched the shore with her eyes. In a little skiff was a fisherman rowing hard. She called to him but he did not hear, or would not hear. She did not see his face, as it was bent over the oars. "He must have thrown me the letter," she thought.

She felt rather annoyed than relieved. She would have been glad to have had cause to strike the blow in public; she was weary of bearing patiently and in silence the faithless life of Zouroff.

"If it be true, I am sorry," she thought doubtfully, and then felt angered that anyone should resume so to address her, and tore the note in two and threw it in the sea below.

She went and paid her morning visit to her horses, to her hot-houses, to the rest of the gardens, and at eleven returned with neither haste nor interest to the house.

People were just downstairs; being a little earlier that day by reason of the Kermesse. The Duchesse Jeanne—already in her Flemish dress with wonderful gold ornaments that she had bought once of a Mechlin peasant, an exquisite high cap, and bright red stockings and real sabots—was very eagerly chattering, explaining, laughing, frowning, vociferating.

Zouroff stood behind her, his brows as dark as a thunder-cloud.

When his wife came in sight a silence fell upon the group about the wooden shoes of the duchess.

Madame Nelaguine, whose grace of tact never deserted her, turned and said easily and indifferently to Vere:

"There is a great revolution in our toy kingdom, Vera. Mademoiselle Noisette, the actress, was called to Paris by the first train this morning. The loss is irreparable, they say, for no one could act Punch[1] with a handkerchief and a penny whistle like this famous person."

Vere was silent; those who watched her countenance could see no change in it. She felt for the moment both anger and disappointment, but she showed neither.

Zouroff's face was very sullen. For the first time in his life he had been baffled.

"To whom do you accord the pavilion?" Vere said very quietly to the duchess, who shrugged her shoulders, and raised her eye-brows in a gesture of despair.

---

1   Reference to the popular Punch and Judy puppet show. With his club, Punch kills his wife Judy, the baby, a beadle, a doctor, a policeman, and the hangman. His final triumph is against the devil.

"The committee at Trouville will have arranged it," she answered. "There has been no time to consult us."

Vere said in a low tone to her sister-in-law: "This is true? Not a trick?"

"Quite true, thank heaven!" said Madame Nelaguine. "I have seen the telegram—you can see it; her director has a new *pensionnaire*[1] who is to play in her own great part, Julie Malmaison; she was beside herself they say; quite raving; nothing would keep her."

At that moment a note was taken to the Duchesse Jeanne, who read it and then leapt for joy in her red stockings and her wooden shoes. It was from one of her male committee, who wrote from the Union Club at Trouville.

"Corrèze has come," she shouted. "He was here an hour or two yesterday, and promised them to return for the fair, and he has returned, and they have got him to take Noisette's place! Oh dear! the pity that we did not have the Mass!—but he is inimitable at a fair, he always can sell any rubbish for millions, and as a *diseur de bonnes aventures* he is too perfect!"

A slight colour came into Vere's cheeks, which Madame de Sonnaz noticed, although no one else did. Vere understood now who had penned the letter; who had been the fisher rowing.

She was bewildered and astonished; yet life seemed a lovelier thing than it had seemed possible to her a few hours before that it ever could look in her sight.

Sergius Zouroff said nothing; he had been baffled, and he did not know with whom to quarrel for his defeat. He said nothing to his wife, but when his eyes glanced at her they were very savage, dull, and dark. He would have given half his fortune to have had Noisette still in Trouville.

"Dearest Princess," whispered Madame de Sonnaz to her, taking her aside; "now this woman is so providentially gone you will come, won't you? *Pray* do not make a scene; your husband is more than sufficiently annoyed as it is. It was all my fault. I ought to have objected more strongly to the permission to hold her pavilion, but you see the world is so indifferent nowadays, and indeed—indeed—I never fancied you *knew*."

A glow of impatient colour flushed Vere's face. She could bear her husband's infidelities, but she could not endure to hear them alluded to by another woman.

---

1 Actress at the Comédie Française.

"I will come," she said briefly, "if you think it will prevent any annoyance. The sole object of life seems to be to avoid what you all call 'scenes.'"

"Of course it is men's," said Madame Jeanne. "Women like scenes, but men hate them; probably because they are always in the wrong, and always get the worst of them. I felt entirely with you about Mademoiselle Noisette, but I don't think I should have done as you did, spoken as you spoke. It is never worth while. Believe me it never makes the smallest atom of difference."

"Who told you what I did, what I said?" asked Vere suddenly, looking her friend full in the eyes.

Madame de Sonnaz was, for the moment, a little disconcerted.

"Only two people knew," said Vere; "Nadine and her brother."

"It was not Nadine," said the duchesse, recovering her composure, and laughing a very little. "You ought to know by this time, Vera—I may call you Vera?—that your husband has very few secrets from me. Sergius and I have been friends, so long—so horribly long, it makes me feel quite old to count the years since I saw him first driving his Orloffs down the Bois. *O, le beau temps!*[1] Morny was not dead, Paris was not republican, hair was not worn flat, realism was not invented, and I was not twenty. *O, le beau temps!* Yes, Sergius told me all about the scene you had made him—he called it a scene; I told him it was proper feeling and a compliment to him, and he was extremely angry, and I was wretched at my own thoughtlessness. My dear, you are so young; you make mistakes; you should never let a man think you are jealous, if you are so."

"Jealous!" All the blood of the Herberts of the Border leaped to fire in Vere's veins. As she turned her face upon Madame de Sonnaz with unutterable scorn and indignation on it, the elder woman did that homage to her beauty which a rival renders so reluctantly, but which is truer testimony to its power than all a lover's praise. Madame Jeanne gave a little teasing laugh.

"Jealous, my fairest! why yes. If you were not jealous why should you have insisted on the woman's absence?"

"There can be no jealousy where there is only abhorrence," Vere said quickly, with her teeth shut. "You do not seem to understand; one resents insults for oneself. An insult like that is to a woman like the insult that a blow is to a man."

Madame Jeanne shrugged her shoulders.

---

1 Oh, the good times! (The Second Empire).

"My love! Then we are all black and blue *nous autres*.[1] Of course in theory you are quite right, but in practice no one feels in such a way; or, if anyone feels, she says nothing. But we will not discuss it. The woman is away. You must come now, because you said you would occupy your pavilion if hers were taken down. We do not take it down because there is not time; but we have given it to Corrèze. You know him—in society I mean? I think so?"

"Scarcely," said Vere; and she felt a glow of colour come over her face because she was sure that the note had come from him, and that the fisher pulling his boat had been one with the luteplayer of Venice.

"She has known him, and she does not want to say so," thought Madame Jeanne, swift to observe, swift to infer, and, like all experienced people, always apt to make the worst deductions.

But the bells of the horses, harnessed like Flemish teams to the breaks and other carriages, were jingling in the avenue, and the tasselled and ribboned postilions were cracking their whips. There was little time to be lost, and she reluctantly let Vere escape her. As she drove along with Sergius Zouroff in his mail phaeton to Trouville, she gave him her own version of Vere's conversation. She exaggerated some things and softened others; she gave him full cause to feel that his wife abhorred him, but she said nothing of Corrèze, because she was a prudent tactician, and never touched a fruit till it was ripe to fall.

"It was possibly merely my fancy," she reflected, as in all the whirl of her lottery, and all the pressure of her admiring throng, she found time to cast many glances at the tent of Corrèze, and saw that he was never beside his opposite neighbour. He was everywhere else—a miracle of persuasiveness, a king of caprice, the very perfection of a seller and a showman, dealing in children's toys with half the shops of the Palais Royal emptied into his booth, and always surrounded by a crowd of children, on whom he rained showers of sparkling sweetmeats—but he was never beside the Princess Zouroff. He had taken down the pennon of Noisette, and its stead was one with his own device; a Love whose wings were caught in a thorny rose-bush. He told fortunes, he made himself a clairvoyant, he mystified his clients, and made them happy. He was dressed like a Savoyard,[2] and carried an old ivory guitar, and sang strange, sweet, little ditties in a dulcet

---

1 All of us.
2 A native of Savoy, the area in France where Corrèze's aristocratic ancestors lived.

falsetto. He was the Haroun al Raschid[1] of the Trouville Kermesse, and poured gold into its treasuries by the magic of his name and his voice, the contagion of his laughter and his gaiety. But he never once approached the Princess Zouroff; and no one could tell that, as he roamed about, with his five-year-old adorers flocking after him, or prophesied from a bowl of water the destinies of fair women, in his heart he was always saying, "Oh, my wild white rose! Why did I not gather you and keep you while I could. You are a great lady, and they all envy you, and all the while you are outraged and desolate!"

Vere sat in her azure pavilion, and looked fitter to be a Lily of Astolat[2] presiding at a tournament of knights. She bought most of her own things herself, and gave them away to children.

The sun was strong, the heat was great, the chatter, the clamour, the many mingling and dissonant sounds, made her head ache, and the bright rainbow-like semicircle of tents, and the many colours of the changing multitude, often swam as in a mist before her eyes.

Could it, after all, have been he who had warned her? she began to doubt. It was too improbable. Why should he care? She told herself that she had been conjecturing a vain and baseless thing. Why should he care?

He was merely there, in the pavilion that was to have been Noisette's, because, no doubt, all artistes were his comrades; and he replaced the actress from the same good fellowship as he sold roses at Madame Lilas' stall, and ivory carvings at Cécile Challon's. It could have been nothing more.

He never approached her. She could see his graceful head and throat above the throng, as he sold his puppets and his playthings; she could hear the thrill of his guitar, the echo of his voice, the delighted shouts of his child-troop, the laughter with which women pelted him with flowers as in Carnival time; she could see him nearly all day long, as he stood under Noisette's rosy garlands, or wandered with jest and compliment through the fair. But to her he never came. At sunset he was missing. The flag, with the Love caught in the thorns of

---

1   A Caliph of Bagdad (A.D. 764-809); he became a legendary hero in *The Arabian Nights.*

2   Elaine Le Blank, the daughter of Sir Bernard of Astolat, appears in Malory's *Morte D'Arthur* and in Tennyson's "Lady of Shalott." In Tennyson's "Lancelot and Elaine" (*Idylls of the King*), she is referred to as "the lily maid of Astolat." She falls in love with Lancelot; and, after he rejects her, she dies for love of him. He does wear her favor on his helmet in a tournament at Camelot.

the roses, was down; a negro stood like a statue cut in ebony between the pink curtains of Noisette's tent. It was a slave of Soudan who had long been a free man in his service; a picturesque figure, well-known to Paris. He did not speak, but he had a scroll in his hands, a scroll that hung down, and on which was written, "*Désolé de vous quitter, mais un pauvre luthier n'est pas maître de soi-même.*"[1]

"It was charming of Corrèze," said Madame de Sonnaz. "Very charming of him. He had only twenty-four hours of his own between the last night at Covent Garden and the royal fêtes in Brussels. And he spent those twenty-four hours in answering my call and coming to help our Kermesse. He is gone to Belgium to-night. It was really charming. And the use he has been! the impetus he gave! the money he has got for us! I shall always be grateful to him."

Whilst she spoke, she thought nevertheless, "It is very eloquent that he should never have gone near her. They must understand each other very well, if at all. He never took all that trouble for nothing, and no mere accident could have been so perfectly à*propos.*"[2]

The house party and the host of Félicité dined at ten o'clock that night with her at the Châlet Ludoff.

Vere, pleading great fatigue, drove homeward in the pale moonlight, through the cool air, sweet with the scent of apple-orchards and the sea. Madame Nelaguine accompanied her: neither spoke.

In Paris at that hour Mademoiselle Noisette, arriving hot with the sun, enraged with the dust, furious at leaving Trouville, and ready for murder if she could not have vengeance, burst, as the hurricane and the storm burst over lake and mountain, into the peaceful retreat where the director of her theatre passed his leisure moments, and found that there was no new *pensionnaire* to play Julie Malmaison; that her greatness was on the same unapproachable pinnacle it had occupied ever since her *début*; that her director and her public alike were the most loyal and submissive of slaves; that, in a word, she had been hoaxed.

"*Qui donc a voulu me mystifier!*"[3] she screamed a thousand times, and plunged into abysses of suspicion, and was only pacified by promises of the Chef de Sûreté[4] and his myrmidons. But she stormed, raged, cursed, wept, foamed at the mouth for half and hour,

1 I'm sorry to have to leave you, but a poor musician is not his own master.
2 Appropriate.
3 Who then wanted to play a hoax on me?
4 The Chief of the French National Police.

and then—forgot the Préfet de Police, and let herself be taken down to Enghien-les-Bains in time for dinner by a German Margrave,[1] whom she pillaged from patriotism, and with whom she stayed a whole week.

The Duchess Jeanne, excruciatingly tired as she was the next morning, felt her spirits good, and her limbs elastic, as she got into her red and black stripes and a red cap—*vrai bonnet rouge*,[2] as she said—and displayed her skill in the waters of Trouville, and on them with her canoe. She had got a clue to follow; a mere misty, intangible thread at present, but still something on which to spin her web.

"Corrèze was the hero of the adventure of the lost shoes and stockings, and what adventure is ever so sweet in a woman's life as the first?" thought this experienced being, as she lay stretched out on the waves, or made her canoe shoot over them. "Corrèze comes for a few hours down here; that very day she drives off before we are up, and makes her pilgrimage to the place of the lost shoes; when we interrogate her she colours and grows angry; he takes Noisette's pavilion—Noisette's, whom he detests—I have heard artists say so a hundred times. He is charming, he is exquisite, he is adorable; and all within a few yards of Vere, to whom he nevertheless never speaks! Something there must be. The thing to do is to bring them near one another; then one would see, inevitably."

And, lying on her back on the sunny water, she resolved to do so. What did she want? She did not know precisely. She wanted to do what the moths do to ermine.

CHAPTER VII.

Pretty green Ischl[3] was growing dusky in the evening hours.

Ischl, like a young girl, is prettiest in the morning. Its morning light is radiant and sweet; of the sunset it sees little or nothing, and its evenings are sad-coloured; the moon seems a long time coming up over these heights of pine-forest, but, when it does come, it is very fair, shining on the ripple of the rapid Traun with the lights of the houses on the banks twinkling in the moss-green surface of the

---

1 Marquis.
2 A real red cap.
3 Known as Bad Ischl, Ischl is one of he oldest salt-water spas in Austria. The healing power of salt water baths was discovered at the beginning of the eighteenth century. Royalty took their cures in the remote salt village, and the whole region developed into a huge recreational landscape.

stream, with every now and then a gentle splash breaking the silence as the ferry-boat goes over from side to side, or a washing-barge is moored in closer to the shore.

Ischl is calm, and sedate, and simple, and decorous. Ischl is like some tender fair wholesome yet patrician beauty in a German picture, like the pretty aristocratic Charlotte in Kaulbach's picture,[1] who cuts the bread and butter, yet looks a patrician. Ischl has nothing of the *belle petite*,[2] like her sister of Baden, nothing of the titled *cocodette*[3] like her cousin of Monaco. Ischl does not gamble or riot or conduct herself madly in any way; she is a little old-fashioned still, in a courtly way; she has a little rusticity still in her elegant manners; she is homely whilst she is so visibly of the *fine fleur* of the *vieille souche*.[4]

She is like the noble dames of the past ages, who were so high of rank and so proud of habit, yet were not above the distilling-room and the spinning-wheel, who were quiet, serious, sweet, and smelt of the rose leaves with which they filled their big jars.

Ischl goes early to bed and early rises.

It was quite quiet on this August evening. It was very full, its throng was a polite and decorous one. Groups walked noiselessly up and down under the trees of the esplanade; music had long ago ceased from sounding; men and women sat out on the balconies with dimly-lit chambers behind them; but there was no louder sound than a dog's bark, or a girl's laughter, or the swish of an oar in the river.

From the road of the north-east, and over the grey bridge, with its canopied saint, there came suddenly, with a sound of trampling hoofs, whips cracking in air, and clanging post horns, that harshly broke the repose of the twilight hour, a travelling carriage with four horses, containing two ladies and a dog.

The carriage had come from Salzburg. It was open, for the night was mild, and, as a miracle of kindness, did not rain. A man, leaning in a casement of the Kaiserin Elizabeth, recognised both ladies and dog as the heavy landau rolled off the bridge across the road, then disappeared round the corner of the building. It was followed by another carriage full of servants. The host of the Kaiserin Elizabeth with all his officials small and great, precipitated themselves into the street, bowing bare-headed, as the fiery horses were pulled up before the door.

---

1 Wilhelm von Kaulbach (1805-74) was a German painter, illustrator, and muralist.
2 Prostitute.
3 Loose women.
4 Refined bloom (refinement) of the old school.

The quick twilight fell; the valleys from dusky grew dark; the Traunwater began to look like a shoal of emeralds under the sunrays; a white round moon began to show itself behind the hills; the forms of people walking on the banks became indistinct, though the murmur of their voices and laughter grew clearer; otherwise it was so still that he who leaned over his balcony and saw the carriage arrive, could hear the swish of the barge-ropes as the water moved them, and the sound of a big dog lapping in the river underneath him.

"It is destiny!" he said to himself. "For two whole years I have avoided her, and fate, taking the shape of our physicians, sends us here!"

He leaned over the balcony, and watched the water flow under the shadows of the houses and the trees.

"Is it Duchesse Jeanne's doing?" he thought, with that unreasoning instinct which in some men and women guides their fancy to true conclusions. "That is nonsense, though; what can she know? And yet I remember, at that ball, after the "Nuit de Mai," she seemed to suspect something. She laughed; she told me I alone could thaw ice—"

At that moment an Austrian march, stoutly brayed under the windows of the Kaiserin Elizabeth seemed to his ears to fill the night with discord.

He started to his feet with impatience and with suffering, as the sounds grated in his ears, and rapidly shut his windows, one after another, to exclude the sound.

"Where is Anatole?" he muttered irritably, as he paced the dull chambers allotted to him. He had arrived only twenty minutes earlier from Linz. He had not given his name, and for once found a spot where he was not known by sight to all. Instead of his servant, Anatole, one of the servants of the hotel tapped at the door, and, entering his chamber which he himself had only entered a few minutes before, presented him, with many apologies, a printed document to sign. It was the schedule and exordium with which, Ischl, in childlike faith in the integrity of humanity—or astute faith in its snobbery—requires from each of her visitors his declaration of rank and riches, and fines him that he may support her promenades and her trinkhalle[1] according to his social means and place.

He glanced at the paper absently, then took up his pen. Under the

---

1 The pump room, a building where guests could sample the healing waters.

head of residence, he wrote u*n peu partout;*[1] under that of rank he wrote *artiste,* and under that which required the declaration of his name he wrote, "*Corrèze.*"

Then he threw down five napoléons to pay his fees. "A droll document," he said, as he pushed it away. "It displays great astuteness; it never yet found, I am sure, anybody who sought immunity from its tax by declaring himself *d'un rang inférieur, et hors de société.*[2] Really, your tax-paper does credit to the municipal knowledge of human nature."

The waiter smiled and took up the gold.

"Monsieur gives this for the good of the town?"

"For the good of the town or the good of yourself," said Corrèze; "according as altruism or acquisitiveness prevails in your organisation."

The waiter, perplexed, bowed and pocketed the money.

"Wait a moment. Shall I hear this noise every evening?"

"The noise?" The waiter was perplexed.

"You call it music, perhaps," said Corrèze. "If I cannot have my windows open without hearing it I must go up into the mountains."

"Monsieur will hear it seldom," said the waiter. "It is the *chapelle de musique;*[3] it serenades royal personages; but monsieur will understand that such do not come every day."

"It is to be hoped not, if they have ears," said Corrèze. "Who is it that they are serenading now?"

"The Princess Zouroff has arrived."

"She is not royal."

"That is true, monsieur; but almost. The Prince Zouroff is so very rich, so very great."

"He is not here?"

"No, monsieur."

"What rooms do they give her?"

"Those immediately beneath monsieur. If they had not been engaged for the princess, monsieur should have had them," said the youth, feeling that this princely artist should be lodged like an ambassador.

"These do very well," said Corrèze. "I shall not change them. You may go now. Order my dinner for nine o'clock, and send me my own man."

---

1   A little everywhere.
2   Inferior rank and outside of society.
3   Choir.

Silence had come again, and the *chapelle de musique* had gone its way after its last burst of that melody which the great singer called noise. The stillness was only broken by the sound of a boat passing, and the murmur of voices from people sauntering underneath. Corrèze threw himself into a chair that stood in the centre of the room.

"I have honestly tried to avoid her," he said to himself. "It is Fate!"

His old and tried servant, Anatole, entered, and began to unpack his things. Corrèze raised his head.

"Put the guitar out," he said, "and then go down and see the cook, and preserve me from what ills you can; you know what it is to dine where German is spoken."

Anatole took out the guitar-case and placed it by his master, then went obediently.

He opened one of the casements and looked out; it had become almost dark; the tranquil pastoral loveliness was calm and dusky; lights twinkled on the opposite bank and up amongst the woods; the nearer casements were bright and ruddy above the stream; the murmur of voices came from under the indistinct leafy masses of the trees on the esplanade; the sound of oars in water made a pleasant ripple. It was a little too much like one of the scenes of his own theatres to please him perfectly; he preferred wilder scenery, more solitary places; at Ischl the glaciers and the ice-peaks, though really near, seem far away, and are seen but by glimpses. Yet it was so quiet, so innocent, so idyllic, it touched and soothed him.

"After all," he thought, "how much we lose in that hot-house we call the great world."

There was a balcony to his chamber. He leaned over it and looked down into the one beneath; there the dog, Loris, was lying, the starlight shining on his silver-grey hair; beside him on a chair there were a bouquet of Alpine roses and a large black fan.

Corrèze felt his pulse beat quicker.

"Kismet!"[1] he said to himself, and the dreamy charm of a romantic fatalism began to steal on him. Pure accident has the ruling of most of our hours, but, in concession to our weakness or to our pride, we call it destiny, and we like to think its caprices are commands.

"Now she shall have a serenade in truth; a better welcome than from the *chapelle de musique*," he said to himself, and withdrew into his own room and took the guitar out of its case—a large Spanish guitar

1 Fate, destiny.

that he never travelled without, considering its melody a far better accompaniment for the voice than any piano could ever be. The organ has all the music of the spheres, and the violin all the emotions of the human heart; the organ is prayer, the violin is sorrow. The guitar, though but a light thing, has passion in it; passion and tenderness and all the caress of love; and, to those who have grown to care for it under southern skies and summer stars, it speaks of love and sighs for it; it has told its tale so often where the fireflies flash amongst the lemon blossoms and the myrtle.

He took up his guitar, and blew out all the many wax candles lighted in his honour, and sat down in the darkness of his chamber.

Then he began to sing; such song as no bribe could get from his lips unless he were in the mood to give it.

Scarcely had the first notes of that incomparable voice rung out clear as a golden bell upon the silent night, than the people sauntering on the bridge and before the hotel, paused to listen, and turned to one another, wondering and entranced.

"Who is that?" they cried to one another, and some one answered, "They say Corrèze came to-night." Then they were quiet, listening, as in the north, where nightingales are few, people listen to them. Then several others from farther down and farther up the street joined them, and people came from under the trees, and from over the bridge; and soon a little crowd was gathered there, silent, delighted, and intent.

"It is Corrèze at his studies," the people said one to another; and his voice, rising in its wonderful diapason clearer and clearer, higher and higher, rang over the water, and held all its hearers spell-bound. As a boat passed down the river the rowers paused; and as a long raft pushed its slow way through the silver of the moonlit ripples, the steersman unbidden, checked it, and remained still, lest any sound of rope or of chain should break the charm.

The Princess Zouroff, wearily resting in the salon beneath him, started as the first notes reached her, and rose to her feet and listened, her heart beating fast.

There was no other such voice in all the world. She knew that he was here as well as though she had seen his face. She went to the balcony and stepped out into the moonlight where the dog was, and the roses and the fan were on the chair, and leaned against the balustrade—a slender white figure with ermine drawn about her, and the moon rays shedding their silver around.

He was singing the "Salve Dimara."[1]

---

1 Hail Dimara.

She grew very pale, and her fingers grasped the rail of the balcony till her rings hurt her skin.

Yet how happy she was!

The river ran by, with a sweet song of its own; the tranquil town seemed to sleep; the people gathered below were hushed and reverent; the fresh glad wind that lives in Alpine forests swept by, bringing the scent of the pine-wood with it.

He sang on, the chords of the guitar filling the pauses of the voice with a low dulcet sound, as if some answering echo sighed. The perfect melody was poured out as from some wild bird's throat, seeming to thrill through the darkness and make it living and beautiful like the shadows of a night that veils the ecstasies of Love. She listened with her head bent and her face very pale. It was her welcome, and she felt that it was for her: for her alone.

He sang the "Salve Dimara" of that living master, who, whatever his weakness or his fault, has in his music that echo of human passion and of mortal pain, which more faultless composers, with their purer science, have missed. Then scarcely pausing, he sang from the music of the "Fidelio" and the "Iphigenia,"[1] music familiar and beloved with him as any cradle-song to a child; and he let all his heart go out in his voice, that poured itself into the silence of the summer evening, as though, like the nightingales, he sang because his heart would break if he were silent. Then, last of all, he sang his favourite song of Heine: the song of the palm-tree and the pine.

Suddenly, with one deep plaintive chord of the guitar, as if its strings were breaking with that last sweet sigh, his voice ceased; as the nightingale's may cease all at once, when, amidst the roses, it tires of its very plenitude of power. There was the sound of a closing casement, then all was still.

The people, standing entranced below, were silent a moment or two, still in the trance of their wonder and delight; then, with one accord, they shouted his name with such a welcome as they never gave but to their own Kaiser.[2] The Kaiser was great, but even he could not command that voice at will; and they had had the sweetness and the splendour of it all to themselves here, by the quiet Traun water, as if it were a bird's song and no more.

They cheered him so loudly, and so loudly called on his name, that

---

1 A song by German composer Franz Schubert (1797-1828) and poet Johann Baptist Mayrhofer (1787-1836).

2 Austrian emperor.

he could do no less than advance on his balcony, and thank them in their own tongue. Then he bade them good-night, and once more closed his window.

Below, Vere stood quite still, leaning back in the low chair with her fan spread between her face and the upraised eyes of the people. She felt tears fall slowly down her cheeks. Yet she was almost happy.

The fresh forest wind, rising and blowing the green moonlit water into rippling silver, seemed to echo around her the song of Heine; the song of the palm-tree and the pine.

The gay brusque tones of Jeanne de Sonnaz roused her almost roughly; the duchesse came out on to the balcony, muffled in a cloak of golden feathers.

"*Ma chère*, how charming! Of course you recognised the voice? and, to make sure, I sent the servants to ask. Now we shall never be dull. No one is dull where Corrèze can be seen. It is too charming! And how divinely he sang. I suppose he was only studying; though he must know all those things by heart. Perhaps he has heard we are underneath him."

She spoke in apparent ignorance and surprise, heedlessly and gaily, but her quick eyes read a look that came into Vere's, and for which she was searching. When she had suggested Ischl in August to Zouroff for his wife, she had known from Vienna that Corrèze was to pass through there.

"I do believe it is as I thought," said Jeanne de Sonnaz to herself. "Is it possible that *le bon diable* has found the *petite entrée*[1] after all? It would be diverting—and why not?"

When all Ischl awoke the next morning, the day was brilliant; the green river sparkled; coffee-cups tinkled on all the balconies; the washing-barges were full of white linen, and of women who laughed as they worked; ladies, old and young, were borne down the walk in their chairs; the little red and white ferry-boat trailed along its rope, leaving a track of sunshine; dogs swam; children ran about; pretty women, with high heels and high canes, sauntered under the trees; green and grey huntsmen went by, going towards the hills to slay izard and roebuck. It was all sylvan, tranquil, picturesque, Watteau-like. That there could be anywhere a world full of revolution, speculation, poverty, socialism, haste and noise, seemed impossible.

---

1 The old devil has found the back door (to Vere's affection).

At Ischl life may be still a *voyage à Cythère*;[1] but not in the reckless and frivolous fashion of other places. All remains calm, placid and touched with the graceful decorum of another time than ours. The bright Viennese are gay indeed, as any butterflies can be; but Ischl is still Ischl, and not Trouville, not Monaco, not Biarritz. It is aristocratic, Austrian, and tranquil; and still belongs to an age in which Nihilism and the electric light were unknown.[2]

"A place to doze and dream in, and how good that is!" thought Corrèze, as he stood out on his balcony an hour after sunrise. "What will the world be like when there are no such places? Horrible! but I shall be out of it; that is a supreme comfort."

Yet, as he thought, so he did not realise that he would ever cease to be in the world—who does? Life was still young in him, was prodigal to him of good gifts, of enmity he only knew so much as made his triumph finer, and of love he had more than enough. His life was full—at times laborious—but always poetical and always victorious. He could not realise that the day of darkness would ever come for him, when neither woman nor man would delight him, when no roses would have fragrance for him, and no song any spell to rouse him. Genius gives immortality in another way than in the vulgar one of being praised by others after death; it gives elasticity, unwearied sympathy, and that sense of some essence stronger than death, of some spirit higher than the tomb, which nothing can destroy. It is in this sense that genius walks with the immortals.

Corrèze leaned over his balcony, and watched the emerald-hued Traun flow by, and the sun's rays touch the woods behind the watermill upon the left. His life was of the world and in it, but the mountaineer's love of nature remained with him. But it was not of the woods or the waters, or even of the pretty women who went by in their chairs to the Trinkhalle, that he was thinking now. He was look-

---

1 Watteau's painting, *Embarkation from Cytheria*, depicts lovers leaving the island of love, which supposedly had magical properties. In addition, one of the poems in Charles Baudelaire's *Les Fleurs du Mal* [the flowers of sickness and evil] (1861), is entitled, "Voyage to Cytheria." In the poem the speaker laments that the "blooming island full of flowers and festivals," has become an "island sad and black."

2 In Russia, nihilism was a revolutionary movement (c. 1860-1917) that rejected the authority of the state, church, and family. Nihilists believed that all values were baseless and nothing could be known or communicated. Thomas Edison invented the light bulb in 1879.

ing at the empty chair in the balcony underneath, and the fan that had lain there all night.

As he bent down and looked, a knot of edelweiss was flung upward, and fell at his feet, and a voice that he knew cried out to him, "Good morning, Corrèze! You serenaded us divinely last night. Come and breakfast with us at ten o'clock. We live by cock-crow here."

The voice was the voice of Jeanne de Sonnaz, who came out on to the balcony that he had been told was Vere's. Astonished, and not pleased, he returned some graceful compliment, and wondered how it was that she was there.

The duchesse looked up at him and laughed; her ugly face looked prettier than many women's. She was in a loose white gown that was all torrents and cascades of lace; she had a real moss-rose over her right ear, and at her bosom; she had little Chinese slippers on, all over pearls, with filagree butterflies that trembled above her toes.

"I cannot see you without craning my neck," she cried to him. "You will come to breakfast. You will meet Vera Zouroff. You know her. Doctors say she is ill. I cannot see it. There was only one big salon free, so she and I have shared it. A pretty place. Were you here before? A little too like your own *décor de scène*?[1] Well, perhaps, a valley with a river and châlets always has that look—Ems[2] has it. I think it is terribly dull. I am glad you are here. Come to us at ten. We are all alone. I shall expect you to amuse us."

Corrèze said some pretty nothings with that grace which charmed all women; they talked a little of people they knew, laughed a little, and were very agreeable. Then the duchesse went within, and Corrèze went for a stroll towards the Rettenbach mill.

"Now I shall see what there is between them," she said to herself; and he said to himself, "How can that brute let her be with Jeanne de Sonnaz?"

Vere, tired, and having had sweet strange disturbed dreams, had slept later than her wont, then had gone out to the bath and the draught prescribed her; she thought they were useless; she felt well.

Some one dressed in white linen passed her, and bowed low: it was Corrèze. There was a child selling mountain flowers; she bought them and carried them on her knee; the polite crowd looked after her chair and whispered her name.

---

1 Scenery; stage effects.
2 Bad Ems, a health resort in western Germany with mineral springs and a thermal spa.

The band was playing under the trees; she did not hear it; she heard only the song of Heine.

When she returned there was almost a colour in her cheeks; she had a gown of white wool stuff and a silver girdle of old German work that had a silver missal hung on it.

"You look like Nillson's Marguerite!"[1] said Jeanne de Sonnaz; "only you are too lovely and too haughty for that, my dear. By the way, I have secured Faust. He will come to breakfast."

"M. de Corrèze?" said Vere with the colour leaving her face. "Why? why?—why did you ask him?"

"I asked him because it pleased me, because he is charming, because he serenaded us exquisitely; there are a hundred 'becauses.' You need not be alarmed, my love; Corrèze goes everywhere. He is a gentleman, though he is a singer. We always treat him so."

Vere said nothing; she was angered with herself that she had seemed to slight him, and she was uncertain how to reply aught.

The sharp eyes of the Duchesse Jeanne watched her, and, as worldly-wise eyes are apt to do, saw very much that did not exist to be seen.

Vere stood mute, arranging her mountain flowers.

The servants announced Corrèze.

Vere was not conscious of the trouble, the gladness, the vague apprehension, and as vague hope that her face expressed; and which Jeanne de Sonnaz construed according to her own light, and Corrèze according to his.

"What will that *diablesse* think?" he said angrily to himself. "A hundred thousand things that are not, and never will be true!"

For his own part, the world had taught him very well how to conceal his feelings when he chose, and, in his caressing grace, that was much the same to all women, he had an impenetrable mask. But Vere had none. Vere was as transparent as only a perfectly innocent creature ever is; and the merciless eyes of Jeanne de Sonnaz were on them.

"You know the Princess Zouroff, I think?" said the latter negligently. "Was it Vera, or was it myself, that you serenaded so beautifully. An indiscreet question; but you know I am always indiscreet."

"Madame," said Corrèze whilst he bowed before Vere, and then turned to answer his tormentor, "truth is always costly, but it is always

---

1 Christine Nillson was a nineteenth-century opera singer and a contemporary of Mario. She played the role of Marguerite in Gounod's *Faust*.

best. At the risk of your displeasure I must confess that I sang on no other sentiment than perfect exasperation with the *chapelle de musique*. That I serenaded yourself and Princess Zouroff was an accidental honour that I scarcely deserved to enjoy."

"What a pretty falsehood, and how nicely turned," thought Madame de Sonnaz, as she pursued persistently: "Then Vera was right; she said you did not know we were here. Nevertheless, you and she are old friends, I think, surely?"

Corrèze had taken his seat between them; he was closer to the duchesse; there was a little distance between him and Vere, whose eyes were always on the flowers that employed her fingers.

"I knew Madame la Princesse a little, very little, when she was a child," he said with a smile. "Neither acquaintances nor court presentations before marriage count after it, I fear. Princess Vera at that time had a sailor hat and no shoes—you see it is a very long time ago."

Vere looked up a moment and smiled. Then the smile died away into a great sadness. It was long ago, indeed, so long that it seemed to her as though a whole lifetime severed her, the wife of Sergius Zouroff, from the happy child that had taken the rose from the hand of Corrèze.

"No shoes! This is interesting. I suppose they were dredging, and she had lost herself. Tell me all about it," said the high voice of Duchesse Jeanne; and Corrèze told her in his own airy graceful fashion, and made her laugh.

"If I did not tell her something, God knows what she would conjecture," he said to himself; and then he sat down to the breakfast-table beside the open windows, and made himself charming in a gay and witty way that made the duchess think to herself: "She is in love, but he is not."

Vere sat almost silent. She could not imitate his *insouciance*,[1] his gaiety, his abandonment to the immediate hour, the skill with which he made apparent frankness serve as entire concealment.

She sat in a sort of trance, only hearing the rich sweet cadence of the voice whose mere laughter was music, and whose mere murmur was a caress.

The sunshine and the green water glancing through the spaces of the blinds, the pretty quaint figures moving up and down under the trees on the opposite bank; the scent of the mountain strawberries and the Alpine flowers; the fragrance of the pine-woods filling the air; the

---

1 Carefree attitude.

voice of Corrèze, melodious even in its laughter, crossed by the clear harsh imperious tones of Jeanne de Sonnaz; all seemed to Vere like the scenes and the sounds of a dream, all blent together into a sweet confusion of sunshine and shade; of silver speech and golden silence. She had longed to meet him; she had dreaded to meet him. Month after month her heart had yearned and her courage had quailed; his eyes had said so much, and his lips had said nothing. They had been strangers so long, and now, all in a moment, he was sitting at her table in familiar intimacy, he who had sung the *Prière* of Sully Prudhomme.

Her eyes shone with unaccustomed light; her serious lips had a smile trembling on them; the coldness and the stillness which were not natural to her years, gradually changed and melted, as the snow before the sunbeam of summer; yet she felt restless and apprehensive. She wondered what he thought of her; if he condemned her in haste, as one amongst the many bought by a brilliant and loveless marriage; if he believed that the moth had forgotten the star and dropped to mere earthly fire?

She could not tell.

Corrèze was not the Saint Raphael who had given her the rose; he was the Corrèze of Paris, witty, brilliant, careless, worldly-wise, bent on amusing and disarming the Duchesse de Sonnaz.

Vere, who knew nothing of his motive, or of her peril, felt a chill of faint, intangible disappointment. She herself had no duality of nature; she had nothing of the flexible, changeful, many-sided temper of the artist; she was always Vere, whether she pleased or displeased, whether she were happy or unhappy; whether she were king or peasant she was always what she had been born; always Vere Herbert, never Vera Zouroff, though church and law had called her so.

"She is like a pearl," thought Corrèze, watching her; "she has nothing of the opal or the diamond; she does not depend on light; she never changes or borrows colour; she is like a pearl; nothing alters the pearl—till you throw it into the acid."

Meanwhile, as he thought so, he was making Jeanne de Sonnaz shed tears of inextinguishable laughter at stories of his friends of the Comédie Français; for in common with all great ladies, her appetite was insatiable for anecdotes of the women whom she would not have visited, yet whom she copied, studied, and, though she would not have confessed it, often envied.

"*Le diable est entré*,"[1] thought the Duchesse Jeanne, ruffling the moss-rose amidst her lace, amused.

1 The devil has entered.

"*Le diable n'entrera jamais*,"[1] thought Corrèze, who guessed very nearly what she was thinking.

Vere was almost always silent. Every now and then she found his soft, pensive eyes looking at her, and then she looked away, and her face grew warm.

What did he think of her? she was asking herself uneasily; he, who had bidden her keep herself unspotted from the world; he who had sent her the parable of the moth and the star, he, who filled her thoughts and absorbed her life more absolutely than she had any idea of, had said nothing to her since the day he had bade her farewell at Trouville.

Corrèze answered her in the same strain; and Vere listened, trying to detect in this gay and amiably cynical man of the world the saviour of Père Martin, the artist of the lyric drama, the hero of all her innocent memories and dreams. He was more kindred to her ideal when he grew more in earnest, and spoke of himself and his own art in answer to Jeanne de Sonnaz, who reproached him with apathy to the claims of Berlioz.[2]

"No!" he said with some warmth; "I refuse to recognise the divinity of noise; I utterly deny the majesty of monster choruses; clamour and clangour are the death-knell of music, as drapery and so-called realism (which means, if it mean aught, that the dress is more real than the form underneath it!) are the destruction of sculpture. It is very strange. Every day art in every other way becomes more natural and music more artificial. Every day I wake up expecting to hear myself *dénigré*[3] and denounced as old-fashioned, because I sing as my nature as well as my training teaches me to do. It is very odd; there is such a cry for naturalism[4] in other arts—we have Millet instead of Claude; we have Zola instead of George Sand; we have Dumas *fils* instead of Corneille; we have Mercié instead of Canova;[5] but in music we have

---

1   The devil will never enter.

2   Louis-Hector Berlioz (1803-69) was a French composer. He wrote a treatise on instrumentation and orchestration published in 1843-44 and reissued in 1855 in an enlarged version. It was a landmark in the history of symphony orchestra.

3   Disparaged, discredited.

4   Realism.

5   Jean-François Millet (1814-75) was a French painter. He was a realist who depicted peasant life in his paintings. Claude Lorrain (1600-82), known as "Claude," painted stylized landscapes that Ouida may be contrasting to Millet's more realistic country scenes. Emile Zola (1840-1902)

precisely the reverse, and we have the elephantine creations, the elaborate and pompous combinations of Baireuth,[1] and the Tone school,[2] instead of the old sweet strains of melody that went straight and clear to the ear and the heart of man. Sometimes my enemies write in their journals that I sing as if I were a Tuscan peasant strolling through his corn—how proud they make me! But they do not mean to do so. I will not twist and emphasize. I trust to melody. I was taught music in its own country, and I will not sin against the canons of the Italians. They are right. Rhetoric is one thing, and song is another. Why confuse the two? Simplicity is the soul of great music; as it is the mark of great passions. Ornament is out of place in melody which represents single emotions at their height, be they joy, or fear, or hate, or love, or shame, or vengeance, or whatsoever they will. Music is not a science any more than poetry is. It is a sublime instinct, like genius of all kinds. I sing as naturally as other men speak; let me remain natural—"

"But you are too strong for it to matter what they say!"

Corrèze shrugged his shoulders.

"I am indifferent. Indifference is always strength. Just now I do as I like, to be sure, and yet I have the world with me. But that is only because I am the fashion. There is so much more of fashion than of fame in our generation. Fame was a grand thing, serious and solemn;

---

was a French novelist. He was the founder of the naturalist movement in literature. George Sand (1804–76) was a French novelist of the Romantic school. Her pastoral novels present an idyllic view of peasant life. Alexander Dumas *fils* (the younger) (1824–95) was a French novelist and playwright who focused on illicit love, a subject with which he was obsessed. Pierre Corneille (1606–84) was a French playwright. Most critics call him the father of French tragedy. Marius-Jean-Antonin Mercié (1845–1916) was a French sculptor and painter. He was known for his realistic style. Antonio Canova (1757–1822) was a Neoclassical (order, symmetry, and simplicity of style) Italian sculptor.

1   Baireuth is a reference to Richard Wagner (1813–83), the father of German Romanticism. Wagner rejected the format of traditional opera, which consisted of relatively quiet recitatives, interspersed with arias accompanied by the full orchestra. He changed the concept of stage music by enormous productions in which recitative and aria blend into one another, constantly accompanied by the orchestra. He believed in the inherent equality of drama and symphonic accompaniment.

2   The Tone School promoted tone consciousness: concentrating on producing the ultimate vocal pitch. This consciousness, however, precludes spontaneity, and singing became a contrived calculated skill. It inhibited the development of free, natural vocal technique.

the people gave it—such people as ran before Correggio's[1] Madonna, as before a heaven-descended thing, and made Catherine of Sienna a living possibility in their midst. It was a grand guerdon,[2] given in grand times. It is too serious and too stern for us; we have only fashion; a light thing that you crown one day and depose the next; a marsh light born of bad gases that dances up to one moment, and dances away the next. Well, we have what we are worth; so much is certain."

"Do you think we always have the fate we merit?" said Vere in a low tone.

Corrèze looked up, and she thought his soft eyes grew stern.

"I have usually thought so, Princess;—yes."

"It is a cruel doctrine."

"And a false one? Well—perhaps. So many side-winds blow; so many diseases are in the air; so many wandering insects, here to-day and gone to-morrow, sting the plant and canker it—that is what you mean? To be sure. When the aphis eats the rose it is no fault of the rose."

"Zouroff is the aphis, I suppose," thought Jeanne de Sonnaz as she looked at Vere. "Do not speak in parables, Corrèze. It is detestable. A metaphor always halts somewhere, like an American paper I read last week, which said, 'Memphis is sitting in the ashes of woe and desolation, and our stock of groceries is running low!' So Vera complains of fate and you of fame?—what ingratitude!"

"Fame, duchesse!" cried Corrèze. "Pray do not use such a *gros mot*[3] to me. Michael Angelo has fame, and Cromwell, and Monsieur Edison,[4] but a singer!—we are the most ephemeral of all ephemeridæ. We are at best only a sound—just a sound! When we have passed away into 'the immemorial silences' there is nothing left

---

1   Antonio Allegri da Correggio (c. 1489-1534) was an Italian painter. His works are characterized by the soft play of light, color, and perspective. His Madonna is surrounded by saints resting on clouds and a multitude of playful, life-like cherubs. His St. Catherine has her head bent in an ecstatic rapture of love.

2   Reward.

3   Bad word.

4   Michelangelo (1475-1564) was an Italian sculptor, painter, architect, and poet. Oliver Cromwell (1599-1658) was an English general, Puritan statesman, and Lord Protector of England, Scotland, and Ireland. Thomas Edison (1847-1931) was an American inventor, especially of electrical devices.

of us, no more than of the wind that blew through Corydon's pipe."[1]

"Monsieur Edison will tell you that Corydon's pipe will be heard a thousand years hence through the skill of science."

"What horror!" said Corrèze. "I think I never should have courage to sing another note if I believed that I should echo through all the ages in that way."

"And yet you say that you want fame."

"I think I never said that, madame. I said fame is not a gift of our times; and if it were, a singer would have no title to it."

"You have something very like it at all events. When half a city drags your carriage like a chariot of victory—"

"Caprice, madame; pure caprice," said Corrèze. "I have happened for the moment to please them."

"And what do Cæsars, and Napoleons, and other rulers do?—happen for the moment to frighten them. Yours is the prettier part to play."

"A sugar-stick is prettier than a ramrod, but—"

"You do not deserve the Kaiserin's strawberries," said Jeanne de Sonnaz, tumbling the big berries nevertheless on to his plate.

"I never deserved anything, but I have had much," said Corrèze. "Even Madame de Sonnaz, while she scolds, smiles on me—like Fortune."

"Madame Vera neither smiles nor scolds," said the duchess. "Perhaps she thinks Fortune and I have spoiled you."

Vere broke biscuits for Loris, and seemed not to have heard. She felt herself colour; for, though she was a great lady, she was still very young. She could not follow his careless, easy banter, and its airy negligence hurt her. If he had sent her the jewelled metaphor of the moth and the star, how could he be altogether indifferent to her fate? She had felt that the song of Heine had been sung for her; yet now she began to doubt whether the meaning that she had given to it had not been her own delusion; whether the eloquence he had thrown into the German words had not been the mere counterfeit emotion of an artist, the emotion of his Gennaro, of his Edgardo,[2] of his Romeo. It is the doubt with which every artist is wronged by those

---

1 In Virgil's *Second Eclogue* (42 B.C.), Corydon is a shepherd in love with a beautiful young boy (Alexis). He wants the boy to hear his song and for him to pipe beside him with his pipe of hemlock made by Pan.

2 Gennaro is a character in Donizetti's *Lucrezia Borgia* (1838). Edgardo is a character in Donizetti's *Lucia di Lammermoor* (1835).

for whom he feels the most. Vere, as she doubted, felt wounded and disillusioned.

Breakfast ended, the duchesse made him sit out on the balcony under the awning; she made him smoke her cigarettes; she made him tell her more anecdotes of that artist life which she was convinced must be one long holiday, one untired carnival. Corrèze obeyed, and kept her amused. Vere sat within the window making lace, never caring to have her fingers quite idle.

Her heart had sunk; the shining river and the bright sunshine had grown dull; the old heavy burden of hopelessness and apathy had fallen on her again. She did not find her Saint Raphael, and she listened with pain as his laugh mingled with the shrill gay tones of the duchesse. Everyone seemed able to be happy, or at least light-hearted, except herself; it must be some fault in her, she thought.

Corrèze, even as his eyes seemed to glance out to the green river, or to fasten admiringly on the *fouillis*[1] and moss-roses of his companion, in reality never ceased to see that figure which sat so still inside the window; with its white gown, its silver girdle, its proud bent head, its slender hands weaving the thread lace.

"My pearl, that they set in a hog's drinking trough!" he thought bitterly. "Alas, no! not mine! never mine! If only she were at peace it would not matter, but she is not; she never will be; they cannot kill her soul in her, though they try hard."

"But do they ever really pay Felix for their dresses," the duchesse was crying; "Or do they not think, like Sheridan,[2] that to pay any debt is a waste of good money?"

At that moment some Austrians of the Court were announced— handsome young chamberlains and aides-de-camp—who came to pay their homage to the Princess Zouroff and her friend.

After a little while the duchesse monopolised them, as she had a talent for monopolising most things and most people; and Corrèze, as he took his leave, found himself for one moment alone before Vere's chair.

The duchesse and the Austrians were all out on the balcony, laughing rather noisily, and planning riding parties, dining parties, hunting, boating, and all other means of diversion that the simplicity of Ischl afforded.

---

1 Mass of foliage.
2 Richard Brinsley Sheridan (1751-1816) was an Irish dramatist and political leader. His last years were plagued with financial difficulties.

Corrèze hesitated a moment, then touched the lace-work on her cushion.

"Work for fairies, Princess," he said, as his fingers caressed the cobweb of thread.

"Very useless, I am afraid—as useless as the poor fairies are nowadays," she answered, without looking up from it.

"Useless? Surely not? Is not lace one of the industries of the world?"

"Not as I make it, I think. It is better than sitting with idle hands, that is all. When I have made a few mètres, then I give them to any poor girl I meet; she could make better herself, but she is generally good-natured enough to be pleased—"

Her voice trembled a little as she spoke. The artist had made so much of her mental and spiritual life all through the past months, that it almost hurt her to have the man before her; to her he was the lover, the poet, the king, the soldier, the prophet, the cavalier of the ideal worlds in which he had become familiar to her. It was an effort to speak tranquilly and indifferently to him as to any other drawing-room idler.

"It would not require much good-nature to be grateful for any thing you gave," said Corrèze with a smile. "I am rather learned in lace. I knew old women in Venice who even showed me the old forgotten *point italien*.[1] May I show it to you? It is almost a lost art."

His fingers, slender and agile, like the fingers of all artists, took up the threads and moved them in and out with skill.

"It is not man's work," he said, with a little low laugh, "but then you know I am an artist."

"You say that as Courcy used to say '*Je suis ni roi ni prince.*'"[2]

"Perhaps! No doubt *les rois et les princes*[3] laughed at Courcy."

"I do not think they did. Courcy's price always seemed to me so far above laughter."

"You do not look at my *point italien*, madame," said Corrèze.

Instead of looking down at his fingers with the threads on them she looked up and met his eyes. The blood flew into her fair face; she felt confused and bewildered; the frankness of her nature moved her lips.

---

1 Italian handmade lace.
2 I am neither king nor prince. "Courcy" is Enguerrand III of Coucy (1155-1242) "the builder," a Lord of Northern France. His motto was "King, nor Prince, nor Duke, nor Count either, I am the Lord of Coucy, Count de Roucy and of the Pole."
3 The kings and the princes.

"I have wanted to tell you always," she said hurriedly; "to thank you—you sent me that necklace of the moth and the star?"

Corrèze bowed his head over the lace.

"You forgive my temerity?" he murmured.

"What was there to forgive? It was beautiful, and—and—I understood. But it was not my fault that I sank."

Then she stopped suddenly; she remembered how much her words implied; she remembered all that they admitted of her marriage.

Corrèze gazed on her in silence. It had been a mystery to him always, a mystery of perplexity and pain, that the innocent, resolute, proud nature which he had discerned in Vere Herbert should have bent so easily and so rapidly under the teaching of her mother to the tempting of the world. Again and again he had said to himself that that child surely had a martyr's spirit and a heroine's courage in her; yet had she succumbed to the first hour of pressure, the first whisper of ambition, like the weakest and vainest creature ever born of woman. He had never understood, despite all his knowledge of Lady Dorothy, the sudden and unresisted sacrifice of her daughter. Her words now startled and bewildered him; and showed him a deeper deep than any of which he had dreamed.

More versed in the world's suspicions than she, he saw the keen glittering eyes of the Duchesse Jeanne studying them from the balcony, as she laughed and clattered with her chamberlains and soldiers. He released the threads of the lace, and replaced the pillow, and bowed very low.

"You do me too much honour, Princess," he murmured, too gently for them to reach the keen ears of the brilliant spy of the balcony. "To accept my allegory was condescension; to interpret it was sympathy; to forgive it is mercy. For all three I thank you. Allow me—"

He bowed over her hand, which he scarcely touched, bowed again to Madame de Sonnaz, and then left the chamber.

Vere took up her lace-work, and began afresh to entangle the threads.

Her heart was heavy.

She thought that he condemned her; he seemed to her cold and changed.

"How that stupid lace absorbs you, Vera!" cried Jeanne de Sonnaz. "The Empress has sent to us to ride with her at four, and there is a little *sauterie* in the evening up there. You cannot refuse."

CHAPTER VIII.

The next morning Corrèze, breakfasting at noon in the bay window of the bright Speiseaal[1] that looks on the three-cornered Platz, and the trees on the esplanade, said to himself, "I ought to go away." But he did not resolve to go.

The night before he also had been summoned to the Schloss.[2] He was famous for his captiousness to sovereigns, but he had been to this summons obedient, and had been welcomed by all, from their majesties to the big dog; and had taken his guitar, and sung, as he sang to please himself, and had been in his most brilliant and his most bewitching mood. In truth their majesties, charming and gracious and sympathetic though they were, had been of little account to him; what he had thought about, what he had sung to, was a tall slender form clothed in white, with waterlilies about her waist and throat, as though she were Undine.[3] He approached her little; he looked at her always. The knowledge that she was there gave him inspiration; when he sang he surpassed himself; when he went away and strolled on foot down through the pine glades into the little town, he sang half aloud still; and an old forester, going to his work in the grey dawn told his wife that he had heard a *Nix*,[4] with a voice like a nightingale, down in the heart of the woods.

He remained always a mountaineer at heart. The grey stillness and mist of the daybreak, the familiar smell of the pine-boughs, the innocent forest creatures that ran or flew before his feet, the gleam of snow on the peaks in the distance, the very moss at his feet bright with dew, all were delightful to him, and brought his boyhood back to him.

Yet his heart was heavy because he had seen the woman he could have loved; indeed, could no longer deny to himself that he did love her, and yet knew very well that she was as utterly lost to him as though she had been a wraith of the mountain snow that would vanish at the touch of the sunrise.

All things were well with him, and fortune spoiled him, as he had said.

As he sat at breakfast in the wide sunny window, and opened his "Figaro," he read of the affection of Paris for him, the regret of a

---

1 Restaurant.
2 Castle.
3 A female water sprite.
4 A water spirit that draws its victims into its underwater home (German folklore).

world which has, like a beautiful woman, so many to teach it forgetfulness, that any remembrance in absence is unusual homage. A
courtier brought him from the court a silver casket of old niello work
inlaid with precious stones, and having a miniature by Penicaudius[1]
in the lid, and what he cared for more, a bidding from the Kaiser to
hunt chamois amongst the ice-peaks of the Dachstein at daybreak on
the morrow. The post arriving brought him little scented letters which
told him, in language more or less welcome, that the universal regret
of the many was shared in deeper and tenderer sentiment by the few;
and some of these could not fail to charm his vanity, if they failed to
touch his heart. Yet he had not much vanity, and he was used to all
these favours of peoples, of sovereigns, of beauties. They rained on him
as rose-leaves rain on grass in mid-summer; and it was the height of
summer with him, and none of his rose-leaves were faded. Still—

"I ought to go," he thought, and that thought absorbed him. He
discerned the influence his presence had on Vere. He knew too well
his power on women to mistake its exercise. He saw what she had not
seen herself; he had long endeavoured to avoid her; he had long
feared for them both, the moment when the accidents of society
should bring them in contact. No vanity and no selfishness moved
him; but an infinite compassion stirred in him, and an infinite sorrow.

"If I let myself love her, my life will be ruined. She will never be
as others have been. There will be nothing between us ever except an
immense regret." So he thought as he sat looking out on the sunshine
that played on the silver and gold of the emperor's casket.

At that moment they brought him from Madame de Sonnaz a
note bidding him dine with her that night. Corrèze penned in reply
a graceful excuse, pleading that he was to set out for the Dachstein at
nightfall. "Who shall say that we need Nihilism," he wrote in conclusion, "when a public singer scales ice-peaks with a Kaiser?"

His answer despatched, he lit another cigar, and watched the Traun
water gleam under the old grey arches of the bridge.

"So she thinks I shall help her to her vengeance on Sergius
Zouroff," he thought. "*Vous êtes mal tombée, duchesse!*"[2]

August noontide is cool enough in the duchy of Salzburg; he did
not feel in the mood for the chatter of the casino and the humours
of the Trinkhalle; for the pretty women in their swinging chairs and

---

1   The Pénicaud family were the finest French enamelers in Limoges dur-
    ing the sixteenth century.
2   You are out of luck, duchess.

whist and *écarté*[1] in the river balconies; there were half a hundred people here who in another half hour would seize on him beyond escape, as they trooped back from their morning exercise and baths. He bethought himself of an offer of horses made him by a Grand Duke staying there, sent a line to the Duke's equerry,[2] and, before his acquaintances had returned from the Trinkhalle, was riding slowly out on a handsome Hungarian mare, taking his road by chance, as he paced out of the little town, following the ways of the Traun as it flowed along towards Styria, with the wood-clothed hills rising to right and left.

There is a noble road that runs through the Weissbach Thal to the lake of Attersee. It is sixteen miles or more of forest-roadway. The woods are grand, the trees are giants, moss-grown with age, and set in a wilderness of ferns and flowers; the Weissbach rushes through them white with perpetual foam; the great hills are half light, half gloom beyond the branches, and there is the grey of glaciers, the aerial blue of crevasses, for ever shining behind the forest foliage, where the clouds lie on the mountains, where summer lightnings flash and summer rains drift like mist. The place is full of birds, and all wild woodland creatures; there is scarcely a habitation from one end of the road to the other. Where any wood has been cleared, there are tracks of lilac heather, and of broom; here and there is a cross telling of some sudden death from flood, or frost, or woodman's misadventure; under the broad drooping branches of the Siberian pines, countless little streams rise and bubble through the grasses; and at the end of it all there is the blue bright lake, blue as a mouse-ear, bright as a child's eyes; the largest lake in all Austria; the Attersee.

War-worn Europe has little left that is more beautiful than that grand tranquil solitary forest-ride with that azure water for its goal and crown.

The Attersee is very lovely, blue as the Mediterranean; radiantly, wonderfully blue; sweeping away into the distance to the Schaffberg range, with white-sailed boats upon it, and here and there, alas! the trail of a steamer as the vessels go to and from Unterach and Stein-bach and Nussdorff.

At Weissbach the meadows go close down to the water, meadows of that rich long flower-filled grass that is the glory of Austria and grows all about the little white stone quays; the boats come up to the

---

1 Cards.
2 An officer charged with the care of the horses.

edge of the meadows, and the rowers, or those who sail in them, land in that knee-deep grass, under the shade of beech trees. There is a little summer inn on the shore, with balconies and hanging creepers; it is modest and does not greatly hurt the scene; the hills rise sheer and bold above it. A little higher yet are the mountains of the Hochlaken and Hoellen ranges, where you can shoot, if you will, the golden eagle and the vulture.

Corrèze, beguiled by the beauty of the road, followed it leisurely, till it led him to the Attersee in some two hours' time. There he dismounted and strolled about. It was not very often that he had leisure for long quiet hours in the open air, but he always enjoyed them; he felt angry with himself that in this pure atmosphere, in this serene loveliness, he remained dissatisfied and ill at ease—because he was alone.

Do what he would he could not forget the grand troubled eyes of Vere, and the accent of her voice when she had said, "It was not my fault that I sank!"

"Nothing could ever be her fault," he thought, "yet what could they do to her so quickly? what force could her mother use?"

He left the mare in the inn-stable for rest, and wandered up into the higher slopes of the hills, leaving the lake with its boats that came and went, its meadows, dotted with human butterflies, its little landing-place with flags flying. "The forest-road is grander," he said, and told his groom to lead the horse back after him when it was rested; he meant to return to Ischl on foot. Fifteen miles of woodland on a summer afternoon is more charming out of saddle than in it.

"With a horse one must go so terribly straight," he thought to himself; "it is the by-paths that are the charm of the forest; the turning to left or to right at one's whim; the resting by the way, the losing oneself even, and the chance of passing the night under the stars; the pleasure of being young again at our old *école buissonière*.[1] All that is inevitably lost when one rides."

So he turned his back on the blue Attersee, and walked home along the dale, that seemed a path of green and gold as the sunbeams of afternoon shone through the trees.

There is a part that is mere moorland, where the pines have been felled and the heather grows alone; the sandy road track runs between the lilac plumes, lying open to the light for a little while before it plunges again into the deep sweet shadows of the forest growth. On

---

1 Playing truant.

the crest of that more open part he saw two human figures and a dog; they were dark and colourless against the bright afternoon light, yet, in an instant, he recognised them—they were the figures of Vere and of a Russian servant.

In a few moments he could overtake them, for they moved slowly. He hesitated—doubted—said to himself that he would do best to turn back again whilst he was still unseen. At that moment Vere paused, looked behind her to see the sun going towards its setting above the mountains, and saw also himself.

He hesitated no more, but approached her.

He saw that delicate colour, that was like the hue of the wild rose he had once given her, come into her face; but she gave him her hand simply and cordially, and he bowed over it with his head uncovered.

"You have been to the lake, Princess? So have I; but the forest is better. The Attersee has too many people by it, and I saw a funnel in the distance—all illusion was destroyed."

"The steamers make the tour of it, unhappily. But this forest road is perfect. I send my ponies on to wait for me by the Chorynsky-clause—and you?"

"I have left my horse, or rather Duke Ludwig's horse, to follow me. She is a young mare, and needs one's attention, which spoils the pleasures of the wood. What a grand country it is! If it did not rain so often it would be Arcadia. Are you strong enough to walk so far, madame?"

The "madame" hurt him to say, and hurt her to hear. She answered, a little hurriedly, that she liked walking—it never hurt her—in Paris she could walk so little, that tired her far more. And Corrèze, unasked but unrepulsed, strolled on beside her; the grim white-bearded servant behind them.

She was dressed with perfect simplicity in something cream-hued and soft, but he thought that she looked lovelier than she had done even in her jewels and her nénuphars at night.

"*O gioventù, primavera della vita!*"[1] he thought. "Even a tyrant like the Muscovite[2] cannot altogether spoil its glories."

They had come now into the fragrant gloom of the forest, where the trees stood thick as bowmen in a fight in olden days, and the mountains rose behind them stern and blue like tempest-clouds, while the silence was full of the fresh sound of rushing waters.

---

1 Oh youth, the spring of life!
2 Russian.

Loris was darting hither and thither, chasing hares, scenting foxes, starting birds of all species, but never going very far afield from his mistress.

They walked on almost in silence—the woodland had that beauty amidst which idle speech seems a sort of profanation—and Corrèze was musing:

"Shall I tell her the truth, and frighten her and disgust her, and never see her face again, except across the gas-glare of the Grand Opéra? Or shall I keep silence, and try and deserve her trust, and try and be some shield between her and the world they have cast her into; and become in time, perhaps, of some aid and service to her? One way is selfish and easy; the other—"

He knew himself, and knew women, too well to be blind to any of the dangers that would befall both in the latter course; but an infinite compassion was in him for this young and beautiful woman; a deep tenderness was in him for her—mournful and wistful—quelling passion. He for ever reproached himself that he had not followed his impulse, and cast prudence to the winds, and stayed by the grey northern sea and saved her, whilst yet there had been time, from the world and from her mother.

They paced onward side by side.

The old man-servant followed with a frown on his brows. He knew Corrèze by sight, he had seen all Petersburg wild with adoration of their idol, running before his sledge, and strewing flowers and evergreens on the frozen earth in his honour; but he did not think it fitting for a mere foreign singer to walk side by side with the Princess Zouroff. Nevertheless, he kept respectfully his due distance behind them, marvelling only whether it would lie within his duty to tell his master of this strange summer day's stroll.

"Madame de Sonnaz is not with you to-day?" Corrèze was saying as he roused himself from his meditation.

Vere answered him: "No. She has many other friends in Ischl; she is with the Archduchess Sophie."

"Ah! You like Madame de Sonnaz? Of course you do, since you travel together."

"She offered to come with me. M. Zouroff accepted for me. It was very kind of her."

"Bah! And that is the way they trick you, and you never dream of their shame!" thought Corrèze, as he merely said aloud, "The duchesse is very witty, very charming; she must be an amusing companion—when she is in a good humour!"

"You do not like her? You seemed as if you did yesterday."

It was a little reproach that unconsciously escaped her. His gallantries and his *persiflage*[1] at the breakfast had hurt her too much for her to so soon forget them.

"I like her as I like all her world," said Corrèze. "I like her with my intelligence infinitely; with my heart, or what does duty for it, I abhor her."

"You separate intelligence and feeling then?"

"By five thousand leagues! Will M. Zouroff join you here?"

"He will meet us at Vienna; Madame de Sonnaz is going to stay with me at Svir."

"You will be long in Russia?"

"Oh, no; the two next months, perhaps."

"But so much long travel; does it not tire you, since you are not strong?"

"I think I am strong enough. It is not that; I am tired—but it is of being useless."

She would have said joyless and friendless too, but she knew that it was not well for any lamentation to escape her which could seem to cast blame upon her husband or ask pity for herself.

"I am as useless as the lace I make," she said more lightly, to take weight off her words. "There is so much routine in the life we lead; I cannot escape from it. The days are all swallowed up by small things. When I was a child, and read of the old etiquette of Versailles, of the *grand couvert* and the *petit couvert*, and the *très petit couvert*, and all the rest of the formal divisions of the hours, I used to think how terrible it must have been to be the king; but our lives are much the same, they are divided between *petits couverts* and *grand couverts*,[2] and there is no other time left."

"Yes, our great world is much like their great world—only with the dignity left out!" said Corrèze, as he thought:

---

1 Banter.

2 During Louis XIV's reign, the three terms referred to the formal meals served. The "*couvert*" represented the number of utensils, dishes, and services the king decided upon each day and the degree of formality required for the meals. *Très petit*—very small, presumably morning; *petit*—about one o'clock in the afternoon; *grand*—great, at ten o'clock in the evening. Actually, the Russian ambassador of the Czar introduced a less regimented mealtime protocol to Paris during the Second Empire. Fashionable society quickly adopted the Russian service, which, among other things, emphasized the gourmet quality of the food and reduced the time necessary for the meal.

No head but some world genius should rest
Above the treasures of that perfect breast.
　　　...Yet thou art bound—
O waste of nature!—to a shameless hound;
To shameless lust ... Athene to a Satyr! [1]

"And how did they make her take the Satyr?" he mused. "She is not a reed to be blown by any wind, nor yet a clay to be molded by any hand. What force did Miladi Dolly use?"

"It is very difficult to be of much use," Vere said once more as she walked on; "they say one does more harm than good by charity, and what else is there?"

"Your own peasantry? In those Russian villages there must be so much ignorance, so much superstition, so little comprehension of the value of freedom or morality—"

"My husband does not like me to interfere with the peasantry; and, besides, I am so rarely in that country. The little I can do, I do in Paris. Ah!" She interrupted herself with a sudden remembrance, and a smile beamed over her face, as she turned it to Corrèze. "I know Père Martin and his daughter; how they love you! They told me everything. What simple good creatures they are!"

Corrèze smiled too.

"They are like the public—they over-estimate me sadly, and their enthusiasm dowers me with excellencies that I never possessed. How came you to find that father and daughter out, Princess? I thought they lived like dormice."

She told him the little tale; and it drew them together, and made them more at ease one with another by its community of interest, as they moved slowly down the woodland road through the leafy dusky shadows. For in the heart of each there was a dread that made them nervous. She thought always: "If only he will spare me my husband's name." And he thought: "If only she would never speak to me of her husband!"

Memories were between them that held them together, as the thought of little dead children will sometimes hold those who have loved and parted for ever.

He longed to know what force, or what temptation, had brought her to this base and joyless marriage; but his lips were shut. He had saved her from the insult of Noisette, but he thought she did not

---

1　Charles Kingsley (1819-75), "Sonnet" from *Poems* (1856).

know it; he went yearly to hear the lark sing on the head of the cliff where he had gathered her rose, but he thought she knew nothing of that either. Yet the sense of these things was between them; and he dared not look at her as he went on down the mountain road.

She was thinking always of his bidding to her, when she had been a child, to keep unspotted from the world. She longed to tell him that she had not stooped to the guilt of base vanities when she had given herself to Sergius Zouroff, but her lips were shut.

"I must not blame my mother, nor my husband," she thought. Her cheeks burned as she felt, since he had saved her from the outrage of the Kermesse, that he must know the daily insults of her life. She was troubled, confused, oppressed; yet the charm of his presence held her like an incantation. She went slowly through the grand old wood, as Spenser's heroines through enchanted forests.[1]

"You said that you like Madame de Sonnaz?" he asked again abruptly.

"She is very agreeable," she said, hesitatingly; "and she is very good-natured to me; she reminds me of many things that I displease Prince Zouroff in; mere trifles of ceremonies and observances that I forget, for I am very forgetful, you know."

"Of little things, perhaps; thoughtful people often are. Big brains do not easily hold trifles. So Madame de Sonnaz plays the part of Mentor to you about these little packets of starch that the *beau monde*[2] thinks are the staff of life? That is kind of her, for I think no one ever more completely managed to throw the starch over their left shoulder than she has done!"

"You do not like her?"

"Oh! one always likes great ladies and pretty women. Not that she is pretty, but she has *du charme*,[3] which is perhaps more. All I intended to say was, that she is not invariably sincere, and it might be as well that you should remember that, if she be intimate enough with you to give you counsels—"

"My husband told me to always listen to, and follow what she said. He has, I believe, a great esteem for her."

Corrèze swore an oath, that only a foxglove heard, as he stooped to gather it. There was a great disgust on his mobile face, that she did not see, as he was bending down amongst the blossoms.

---

1 In the *Faerie Queene*.
2 Fashionable world.
3 Some attraction; charm.

"No doubt," he said briefly; "esteem is not exactly what the Duchesse Jeanne has inspired or sought to inspire; but M. Zouroff possibly knows her better than I can do—"

"But is she not a good woman?" Vere asked, with a little sternness coming on her delicate face.

Corrèze laughed a little; yet there was a great compassion in his eyes as he glanced at her.

"Good? Madame Jeanne? I am afraid she would laugh very much if she heard you. Yes; she is very good for five minutes after she has left the confessional—for she does go to confess, though I cannot imagine her telling truth there. It would be *trop bourgeoise*."[1]

"You speak as if she were indeed not good!"

"Good? bad? If there were only good and bad in this world it would not matter so much," said Corrèze a little recklessly and at random. "Life would not be such a disheartening affair as it is. Unfortunately the majority of people are neither one nor the other, and have little inclination for either crime or virtue. It would be almost as absurd to condemn them as to admire them. They are like tracks of shifting sand, in which nothing good or bad can take root. To me they are more despairing to contemplate than the darkest depth of evil; out of that may come such hope as comes of redemption and remorse, but in the vast, frivolous, featureless, mass of society there is no hope. It is like a feather bed, in which the finest steel must lose point and power!—"

"But is the Duchesse de Sonnaz characterless? Frivolous, perhaps, but surely not characterless?" said Vere, with that adherence to the simple point of argument and rejection of all discursiveness which had once made her the despair of her mother.

"See for yourself, Princess," said Corrèze suggestively. "What she has, or has not, of character may well become your study. When we are intimate with any person it is very needful to know them well; what one's mere acquaintances are matters little, one can no more count them than count the gnats on a summer day; but about our friends we cannot be too careful."

"She is not my friend; I have not any friend."

There was a loneliness and a melancholy in the simplicity of the words that was in pathetic contrast with that position which so many other women envied her.

Tender words, that once said could never have been withdrawn,

---

1 Too middle class.

and would have divided him from her for ever, rose to the lips of Corrèze, but he did not utter them; he answered her with equally simple seriousness:

"I can believe that you have not. You would find them perhaps in a world you are not allowed to know anything of; a world of narrow means but of wide thoughts and high ideals. In our world—I may say ours, for if you are one of its great ladies I am one of its pets and play-things, and so may claim a place in it—there is very little thought, and there is certainly no kind of ideal beyond winning the Grand Prix for one sex, and being better dressed than everybody, for the other. It is scarcely possible that you should find much sympathy in it; and, without sympathy there is no friendship. There are noble people in it still here and there, it is true, but the pity of modern life in society is that all its habits, its excitements, and its high pressure, make as effectual a disguise morally as our domino[1] in Carnival ball does physically. Everybody looks just like everybody else. Perhaps, as under the domino, so under the appearance, there may be great nobility as great deformity; but all look alike. Were Socrates[2] amongst us he would only look like a club-bore, and were there Messalina[3] she would only look—well—look much like our Duchesse Jeanne."

Vere glanced up at him quickly, then reddened slightly, and rose from the bench.

"What a baseness I am committing to speak ill of a woman who gave me her smiles and her strawberries," thought Corrèze. "Nevertheless, warned against Madame Jeanne she must be, even if she think me ever so treacherous to give the warning. She knows nothing; it would be as well she should know nothing; only, if she be not on her guard, Jeanne will hurt her—some way. The mistress of Zouroff will never forgive his wife, and Casse-une-Croûte would pardon her more readily than would the wife of Duc Paul. Oh God! what a world to throw her into! The white doe of Rylstone[4] cast into a vivi-sector's torture trough!"

---

1 A large hooded cloak with a mask covering the eyes, worn at masquerade balls.

2 Socrates (469-399 B.C.) was an Athenian philosopher.

3 Valeria Messalina (c. A.D. 22-48) was the third wife of the Roman Emperor Claudius I. In her husband's absence she married her lover and attempted to place him on the throne. When the plot failed, she was killed.

4 The title of William Wordsworth's (1770-1850) long narrative poem, a tale of feminine triumph over suffering.

And what could he say to her of it all? Nothing.

Midway in this dale of Weissbach there is a memorial cross, with a rude painting; the trees are majestic and gigantic there; there is a wooden bench; and a little way down, under the trees, there is the river broken up by rocks and stones into eddies and freshets of white foam.

"Rest here Princess," said Corrèze. "You have walked several miles by this, and that stick parasol of yours is no alpenstock to help you much. Look at those hills through the trees; one sees here, if nowhere else, what the poets' 'blue air' means.[1] Soon the sun will set, and the sapphire blue will be cold grey. But rest a few moments, and I will gather you some of that yellow gentian. You keep your old love of flowers, I am sure?"

Vere smiled a little sadly.

"Indeed, yes; but it is with flowers as with everything else, I think, in the world; one cannot enjoy them for the profusion and the waste of them everywhere. When one thinks of the millions that die at one ball!—and no one hardly looks at them. The most you hear anyone say is, 'the rooms look very well to-night.' And the flowers die for that."

"That comes of the pretentious prodigality we call civilisation," said Corrèze. "More prosaically it is just the same with food; at every grand dinner enough food is wasted to feed a whole street, and the number of dishes is so exaggerated that half of them go away untasted, and even the other half is too much for any mortal appetite. I do not know why we do it; no one enjoys it; Lazarus out of the alleys might, perhaps, by way of change, but then he is never invited."

"Everything in our life is so exaggerated," said Vere, with a sigh of fatigue, as she recalled the endless weariness of the state banquets, the court balls, the perpetual succession of entertainments, which in her world represented pleasure. "There is nothing but exaggeration everywhere; to me it always seems vulgarity. Our dress is overloaded like our dinners; our days are over-filled like our houses. Who is to blame? The leaders of society, I suppose."

"Leaders like Madame Jeanne," said Corrèze quickly.

She smiled a little.

"You are very angry with her!"

"Princess—frankly, I do not think she is a fit companion for you."

"My husband thinks that she is so."

---

1 The sky as viewed in daylight.

"Then there is no more to be said, no doubt," said Corrèze with his teeth shut. "For me to correct the judgment of M. Zouroff would be too great presumption."

"You may be quite right," said Vere. "But you see it is not for me to question; I have only to obey."

Corrèze choked an oath into silence, and wandered a little way towards the water to gather another foxglove.

Vere sat on the low bench under the crucifix on the great tree; she had taken off her hat; she had the flowers in her lap; her dress was white; she had no ornament of any sort; she looked very like the child who had sat with him by the sweet-briar hedge on Calvados. Taller, lovelier, with a different expression on her grave, proud, face, and all the questioning eagerness gone for ever from her eyes; yet, for the moment, very like—so like, that, but for the gleam of the diamond circlet that was her marriage ring, he would have forgotten.

He came and leaned against one of the great trees, and watched the shadows of the leaves flutter on her white skirts. He realised that he loved her more than he had ever loved anything on earth—and she was the wife of Sergius Zouroff. She was no more Vere, but the Princess Vera, and her world thought her so cold that it had called her the edelweiss.

He forced himself to speak of idle things.

"After all," he said aloud, "when all is said and done, I do believe the artistic life to be the happiest the earth holds. To be sure, there is a general feeling still that we do not deserve Christian burial, but that need not much trouble a living man. I think, despite all the shadows that envy and obtuseness, and the malevolence of the unsuccessful rival, and the absurdities of the incapable critic, cast upon its path, the artistic life is the finest, the truest, the most Greek, and so the really happiest. Artists see, and hear, and feel more than other people; when they are artists really, and not mere manufacturers, as too many are or become. My own art has a little too much smell of the footlights; I have too few hours alone with Beethoven and Mozart, and too many with the gaslit crowds before me. Yet it has many beautiful things in it; it is always picturesque, never mediocre. Think of my life beside a banker's in his parlour, beside a lawyer's in the courts, they are like spiders, shut up in their own dust. I am like a swallow, who always sees the sun because he goes where it is summer."

"It is always summer with you." There was a tinge of regret and of wistfulness in her voice of which she was not conscious.

"It will be winter henceforward," he thought as he answered: "Yes; it has been so. I have been singularly fortunate—perhaps as much in the temperament I was born with as in other things; for, if we escape any very great calamity, it is our own nature that makes it summer or makes it winter with us."

"But if you were in Siberia," said Vere with a faint smile; "could you make it summer there?"

"I would try," said Corrèze. "I suppose Nature would look grand there sometimes, and there would be one's fellow-creatures. But then, you know, it has been my good fortune always to be in the sun; I am no judge of darkness. I dread it. Sometimes I wake in the night and think if I lost my voice all suddenly, as I may any day, how should I bear it?—to be living and only a memory to the public, as if I were dead—scarcely a memory even; there is no written record of song, and its mere echo soon goes off the ear. How should I bear it—to be dumb? to be dethroned? I am afraid I should bear it ill. After all, one may be a coward without knowing it."

"Do not speak of it!" said Vere quickly, with a sense of pain. Mute! That voice which she thought had all the melody that poets dream of when they write of angels! It hurt her even to imagine it.

"It could not be worse than Siberia, and men live through that," said Corrèze. "Have you not seen, Princess, at a great ball, some one disappear quickly and quietly, and heard a whisper run through the dancers of 'Tomsk,'[1] and caught a look on some faces that told you a tarantass[2] was going out into the darkness, over the snow, full gallop, with a political prisoner between his guards? Ah! it is horrible! When one has seen it it makes one feel cold, even at noon in midsummer to remember it."

"Russia is always terrible," said Vere, with a little shudder. "Nowhere on earth are there such ghastly contrasts; you live in a hothouse with your palms, and the poor are all around you in the ice; everything is like that."

"And yet you are Russian;" said Corrèze a little cruelly and bitterly; for he had never forgiven her quick descent into her mother's toils, her quick acceptance of temptation. "You are certainly Russian. You are no longer Vere even; you are Princess Vera."

---

1   Russian regional administrative city from which prisoners were sent to Siberia. Over 1,000 people were condemned to hard labor each year. They were whipped and subjected to hard labor in silver, lead, copper, and gold mines. Many of them died from poisonous fumes; others were executed.

2   A horse-drawn Russian sleigh that could ride on any imaginable surface.

"I am always Vere," she said in a low tone. "They must call me what they will, but it alters nothing."

"And Vera is a good name, too," said Corrèze, bending his eyes almost sternly on hers. "It means Faith."

"Yes; it means that."

He glided into the grass at the foot of the tree, and sat there, leaning on his elbow, and looking towards her; it was the attitude in which she had seen him first upon the beach at Trouville.

He was always graceful in all he did; the soft afternoon light was upon his face; he had thrown his broad felt hat on the grass; a stray sunbeam wandered in the bright brown of his hair.

Vere glanced at him, and was about to speak; then hesitated—paused—at last unclosed her lips so long shut in silence.

"You remember that you bade me keep myself unspotted from the world?" she said suddenly. "I want to tell you, that I strive always to do so—yes, I do. I was never ruled by ambition and vanity—as you think. I cannot tell you more; but, if you understand me at all, you will understand that that is true."

"I knew it without your telling me."

He ceased to remember that ever he had suspected her, or ever reproached her. It was a mystery to him that this proud, strong, pure nature should have ever been brought low by any force; but he accepted the fact of it as men in their faith accept miracles.

"She was such a child; who can tell what they did or said?" he mused, as an infinite tenderness and compassion came over him. This woman was not twenty yet, and she had tasted all the deepest bitterness of life, and all its outrages of passion and of vice!

She was to him like one of the young saints of old, on whom tyrants and torturers spent all the filth and fury of their will, yet could not touch the soul or break the courage of the thing that they dishonoured.

Women had not taught him reverence. He had found them frail when he had not found them base; but, as great a reverence as ever moved Gawaine or Sintram,[1] moved him towards Vere now. He

---

1 Sir Gawaine is one of the knights of King Arthur's round table. In the English tradition he appears as the principal hero and an exemplar of chivalry and courtesy, as in *Sir Gawain and the Green Knight*. In French romances and in Malory's *Le Morte d'Arthur* (1485), however, he is not the hero, but his adventures parallel the hero's. Sintram is the Greek hero of Baron Friedrich de la Motte Fouqué's (1777-1843) German romance, *Sintram and His Companions* (1815).

feared to speak lest he should offend her; it was hard to give her sympathy, even to give her comprehension, without seeming to offer her insult. He knew that she was too loyal to the man whose name she bore to bear to hear him blamed, with whatsoever justice it might be.

He was silent, while leaning on his arm, and looking down upon the cups and sceptres of the green moss on which he rested. If he looked up at her face he feared his strength of self-control would fail him, and his lips be loosened.

Vere bound together his wild flowers one by one. She longed for him to believe her guiltless of the low ambitions of the world; she could not bear that he should fancy the low temptations of the world's wealth and rank had ever had power over her.

Yet she was the wife of Sergius Zouroff. What could she hope to make him think in face of that one fact?

Suddenly he looked up at her; his brilliant eyes were dim with tears, yet flashed darkly with a sombre indignation.

"I understand," he said at last, his old habit of quick and eloquent speech returning to him. "I think I have always understood without words; I think all the world does. And that is why one half of it at least has no forgiveness for you—Princess."

He added the title with a little effort; it was as a curb on his memory, on his impulse; he set it as a barrier between him and her.

"It is I who do not understand," said Vere, with a faint smile, and an accent of interrogation. She did not look away from the wood-flowers. His eyes fed themselves on the lines of her delicate and noble features; he breathed quickly; the colour came into his face.

"No; you do not understand," he said rapidly. "There is your danger. There is your weakness. Do you know what it costs to be an innocent woman in the world you live in?—the great world as it calls itself, God help us! To be chaste in mind and body, thought and deed, to be innocent in soul and substance, not merely with sufficient abstinence from evil not to endanger position, not merely with physical coldness that can deny the passions it is diverted to influence, but real chastity, real innocence, which recoils from the shadow of sin, and shrinks from the laughter of lust. Do you know what the cost of such are? I will tell you. Their cost is isolation—the sneer they are branded with is 'out of fashion'—no one will say it, perhaps, but all will make you feel it. If you be ashamed to go half clothed; if you be unwilling to laugh at innuendoes; if you be unable to understand an indecency in a song, or a gag at a theatre; if you do not find a charm in suggested filth; if you do not care to have loose women for your friends, however high may be their rank; if adultery look to you all the worse because it is a domestic pet and plaything; and if immorality seem to you but the more shameful because it is romped with at the children's hour, danced with at the Queen's ball, made a guest at the house-parties, and smuggled smilingly through the custom-officers of society—if you be so behind your time as this, you insult your generation; you are a reproach to it, and an *ennui*.[1] The union of society is a Camorra or a Mafia.[2] Those who are not of it must at least subscribe to it, and smile on it, or they are lost. There is your danger, my Princess of Faith. How can they forgive you, any one of them, the women who have not your loveliness and your mind, and to whom you are a perpetual, an unconscious, an inexorable rebuke? Clothed with innocence is metaphor and fact with you, and do you understand the women of your world so little yet as not to understand that they would pardon you the nakedness of vice much sooner than they ever will those stainless robes which you share with the children and the angels?"

He ceased; eloquence when he was moved was habitual as song had been to him in his childhood when he had gathered his sheep and goats on the green alp. He paused abruptly, because, had he spoken more, he would have uttered words that could never have been recalled, words that would have been set for ever between them like a gulf of flame.

Vere had listened; her face had flushed a little, then had grown paler than was even usual to her. She understood now well enough—too well; an intense sweetness and a vague shame came to her with his words; the one that he should read her soul so clearly, the other that he should know her path so dark, her fate so hateful.

She gathered the wood-flowers together and rose.

"I am far from the angels and you think too well of me," she said, with a tremor in her voice. "I think the sun is setting; it grows late."

Corrèze rose, with a sigh, to his feet, and raised her hat from the ground.

"Yes. It will soon be dark; very dark to me. Princess, will you think of what I said? will you be on your guard with your foes?"

"Who are they?"

"All women, most men. In a word, a world that is not fit for your footsteps."

---

1 Vexation, annoyance.
2 The Camorra was a secret Italian criminal association in Naples. The Mafia is a name given to a number of secret organized groups of Sicilian criminals.

Vere was silent, thinking.

"I have more courage than insight," she said, with a little smile, at last; "and it is easier to me to endure than to influence. I think I influence no one. It must be my fault. They say I am wanting in sympathy."

"Nay, the notes around you are too coarse to strike an echo from you—that is all. You have a perfect sympathy with all that is noble, but they never give you that."

"Let us move quickly, the sun is set," she said, as she took her hat from him, and walked on down the forest road.

Neither spoke. In a little time they had reached the sluices, where the imprisoned timbers lay awaiting the weekly rush of the waters. There a little low carriage with some mountain ponies, lent her by the Court, was awaiting her.

Keeping his wild blossoms of the forest in one hand, she gave him the other.

"I shall see you to-morrow?" she asked, with the frank simplicity and directness of her nature.

He hesitated a moment, then answered: "To-night I go up into the Thorstein ice-fields; we may be away some days; but when I come down from the mountains, yes; certainly yes, madame, I will have the honour of saluting you once more. And I will bring you some edelweiss. It is the flower they call you after in Paris."

"Do they? I did not know it. Adieu."

Her little postilion, a boy from the Imperial stables, with a silver horn and a ribboned and tasselled dress, cracked his whip, and the ponies went away at a trot down towards the valley, whilst beyond, the last brightness of daylight was shining above the grey-white sheet of the Carl Eisfeld that rose in view.

Corrèze stood on the edge of the wilderness of timber, lying in disorder in the dry bed of the river, awaiting the loosening of the White Brook floods to float them to the Traun. Some birds began singing in the wood; as the sun set behind the glacier.

"They are singing in my heart too," thought Corrèze, "but I must not listen to them. Heine knew the caprice and the tragedy of fate. He wrought no miracle to make the pine and the palm-tree meet."

The days that followed dragged slowly over the head of Vere.

Ischl, in its nook between the hills, has always a certain sadness about it, and to her it seemed grown grey and very dull. The glaciers of Dachstein and Thorstein gleamed whitely afar off, and her thoughts were with the hunters underneath those buttresses of ice in the haunts of the steinbock and the vulture.

The perpetual clatter of the duchesse's voluble tongue, and the chatter of society that was always about her—even here, in the heart of the Salzkammergut—wearied her and irritated her more than usual. She felt a painful longing for that soft deep voice of Corrèze, which to her never spoke a commonplace or a compliment, for the quick instinctive sympathy which he gave her without alarming her loyalty or wounding her pride.

"You are very dull, Vera," said the duchesse impatiently, at length.

"I am never very gay," said Vere coldly. "You knew that when you offered to accompany me."

"Your husband wished us to be together," said Madame Jeanne, a little angrily.

"You are very kind—to my husband—to so study his wishes," said Vere, with a certain challenge in her glance. But the duchesse did not take up the challenge.

"Corrèze has told her something," she thought.

To quarrel with Vere was the last thing she wished to do. She laughed carelessly, said something pleasant, and affected to be charmed with Ischl.

They went to the Imperial villa, rode a great deal, were courted by the notabilities as befitted one of the loveliest and one of the wittiest women of the time; and the five days slipped away, as the Traun water slid under its bridges and over its falls.

Vere began to listen wistfully for tidings of the return of the Kaiser's hunting party. One morning at breakfast she heard that the Emperor had come back at daybreak. But of Corrèze there was nothing said.

Had it been any other memory than that of Corrèze she would have been disgusted and angered with herself at his occupation of her thoughts; but he so long had been to her an ideal, an abstraction, an embodiment of all high and heroic things, a living poem, that his absorption of her mind and memory had no alarm for her. He was still an ideal figure; now, when he was lost in the midst of the ice-fields of the Dachstein, as in winter when before her in the creations of Beethoven, of Mozart, and of Meyerbeer.[1]

A little later that morning a jäger[2] brought to the Kaiserin hotel a grand golden eagle, shot so that it had died instantaneously, and been picked up upon the snow in all its beauty of plumage, without a

---

1 Giacomo Meyerbeer (1791-1864) was a German opera composer.
2 Hunter.

feather ruffled. He brought also a large cluster of edelweiss from the summit of Thorstein, and a letter. The letter was to Madame de Sonnaz from Corrèze.

She was sitting opposite to Vere on the balcony that fronted the bridge.

"From Der Freischütz!" she said with a laugh. "He has not shot his own arm off, like Roger, that is evident."[1]

Vere did not raise her head from her lace-work.

It had been written in the highest hut under the Dachsteinspitze, and was in pencil. After graceful opening compliments, in which no one knew better than himself how to make the commonplace triviality of formula seem spontaneous and fresh, he said:

"I have shot a nobler creature than myself—men generally do when they shoot at all. Emblematic of the Napoléonic[2] cause to which Madame la Duchesse has dedicated herself—inasmuch as it has lived on carrion, and though golden, it will be rotten in a day, or at best stuffed with straw—I desire to lay it at the feet of Madame Jeanne, where its murderer has ever longed, but never dared, to prostrate himself. I offer the edelweiss to Madame la Princesse Zouroff, as it is well known to be her emblem. It has no other value than that of representing her by living at an altitude where nothing but the snow and the star-rays presume to share its solitude."

He said, in conclusion, that his hunting trip having taken up the five days which he had allotted himself for Ischl, he feared he should see neither of them again until they met in Paris in winter, as his engagements took him at once to the Hague, thence to Dresden, where there were special performances in honour of one of the gods of his old faith—Glück.[3]

"Very pretty," reflected the Duchesse Jeanne as she read. "I suppose he reached the edelweiss himself, or he could scarcely have gathered it. I suppose Vera will understand that part of the 'emblem.'"

---

1 It is not clear what Ouida means here. *Der Freischütz* (the marksman) is an opera by the German composer, Carl Maria von Weber (1786-1826). The plot is based on a legend of magic bullets, six of which never miss their mark. The seventh belongs to the devil. It is set in a small village where hunting is the chief occupation, but there is no character named Roger and no one shoots off his arm.

2 The eagle was one of the symbols of The Second Empire.

3 Christoph Willibald von Glück (1714-87) was a German-born operatic composer. He revolutionized opera by establishing lyrical tragedy as a unified vital art form.

But though she thought so she did not say so; she was a courageous woman, but not quite courageous enough for that. She gave
the edelweiss and the note together to her companion, and only said,
with a little smile, "Corrèze always writes such pretty notes. It is an
accomplishment that has its dangers. There is scarcely a good-looking
woman in Paris who has not a bundle, more or less big, of his letters;
all with that tell-tale suggestive device of his—that silver Love, with
one wing caught in a thorn-bush of roses; he drew it himself. You saw
it on his flag at the Kermesse. Oh, of course it is not on this paper.
He scribbled this in some châlet of the Dachstein. I will have my
eagle stuffed, and it shall have real rubies for eyes; and I will put it in
my dining-room in Paris, and Corrèze for his sins shall sit underneath
it and pledge the Violet and the Bee.[1] Not that he ever will though;
if he have any political faith at all he is a Legitimist[2]—if he be not a
Communist. But I don't think he thinks about those things. He told
me once that nightingales do not build either in new stucco or in old
timber—that they only wanted a bush of rose-laurel. He is a *mortel
fantasque*,[3] you know, and people have spoiled him. He is very vain,
and he thinks himself a Sultan."

At the while the duchesse was studying narrowly her companion
as she spoke.

Vere, without any apparent attention to it, put her edelweiss in an
old hunting goblet, that she had bought that morning in one of the
little dark shops of Ischl; and the duchesse could tell nothing from her
face.

In her heart Vere felt a sense of irritation and disappointment. The
note seemed to her flippant, the homage of it insincere, and his
departure unnecessary and a slight. She did not know that he wanted to turn aside from her the suspicion of a woman in whom he foresaw a perilous foe for her; and that to disarm worldly perils he used
worldly weapons. Vere no more understood that than one of
Chaucer's heroines, with straight glaive and simple shield, would have
understood the tactics of a game of Kriegspiel.[4]

---

1 Napoleon III liked violets so much he adopted them as a symbol of his
   reign. The golden bee was also a symbol of the Second Empire.
2 The Legitimists favored a Bourbon restoration. They advocated rule by
   hereditary right as opposed to Communism, which advocated the direct
   and communal control of society for the benefit of all members.
3 Whimsical person.
4 A board game, a variant of chess, based on a military war game. Blocks
   and figures were used to simulate armies and equipment.

And why did he go?

She was far from dreaming that he went to avoid her. The song of Heine did not mean to her all that it meant to him. That she had some place in his memory, some hold on his interest, she thought—but nothing more; and even that she almost doubted now; how could he write of her to Jeanne de Sonnaz?

A cold and cruel fear that she had deceived herself in trusting him seized on her; she heard of him always as capricious, as unstable, as vain; who could tell, she thought? Perhaps she had only given him food for vanity and for laughter. Perhaps his seriousness and his sympathy had been but a mere passing mood, an emotion; no more real than those he assumed so perfectly upon his stage.

The doubt hurt her cruelly; and did not stay long with her, for her soul was too noble to harbour distrust. Yet, at her ear Jeanne de Sonnaz perpetually dropped slight words, little stories, shrewd hints, that all made him the centre of adventures as varied and as little noble as those of any hero of amorous comedy. Ever and again a chill sickening doubt touched her—that she, at once the proudest and the humblest woman in the world, had been the amusement of an hour to a brilliant but shallow *persifleur*.

She carried the gold goblet with the edelweiss of the Thorstein into her own chamber, and, when quite alone, she burst into tears.

She never shed tears now. It had seemed to her as if they were scorched up by the arid desolation of her life. They did her good like dew in drought. So much she owed Corrèze. Corrèze himself at that hour—having taken leave at daybreak of the imperial hunter and his courtly companions, who were returning into Ischl—was walking by his guide's side down the face of the Dachstein towards the green Rauris range, meaning to go across thence into the beautiful valley of Ens, and descend next day into the Maindling Pass between the Salzkammergut and Styria. He was still at a great elevation; still amidst snow and ice; and the Rauris lay below him like a green billowy sea. There was some edelweiss in his path, and he stooped and plucked a little piece, and put it in his wallet.

"O iceflower, you are not colder than my heart," he said to himself. "But it is best to go; best for her. I will dedicate myself to you, iceflower, and of the roses I will have no more; no, and no more of the 'lilies and languor.'[1] Edelweiss, you shall live with me and be my

---

1 From Algernon Charles Swinburne's (1837-1909) "Dolores": "Change in a trice / The lilies and languors of virtue / For the raptures and roses of vice."

amulet. You will wither and shrivel and be nothing, but you will remind me of my vow, and if others will rage, let them. To the ice-flower I will be true as far as a man in his weakness can be. Will that denial be love? In the old chivalrous days they read it so. They kept their faith though they never saw their lady's face. The Duchesse Jeanne would laugh—and others too."

And he went down over the rugged stony slope, with the snow deep on either side, and the green ice glistening at his feet, and the woods of the Rauris lifting themselves up from the clouds and the grey air below; and there on Dachstein, where never note of nightingale was heard since the world was made, this nightingale, that ladies loved and that roses entangled in their thorns, sang wearily to himself the song of Heine—the song of the palm-tree and the pine.

CHAPTER IX.

The days went on, and the duchesse made them gay enough, being one of those persons who cannot live without excitement, and make it germinate wherever they are. Carried in her *chaise-à-porteurs*,[1] playing *chemin de fer* on her balcony, waltzing at the little dances of the imperial court, making excursions in the pine-woods or down the lakes, she surrounded herself with officers and courtiers, and created around her that atmosphere of diversion, revelry, and intrigue, without which a woman of our world can no more live than a mocking-bird without a globe of water. But, all the while, she never relaxed in a vigilant observation of her companion; and the departure of Corrèze baffled and annoyed her.

She had had a suspicion, and it had gone out in smoke. She had spent much ingenuity in contriving to bring Vere to the Salzkammergut, after having disbursed much in discovering the projects for the summer sojourns of Corrèze; and, with his departure, all her carefully built house of cards fell to pieces. She did not understand it; she was completely bewildered, as he had intended her to be, by the airy indifference of his message to her companion, and his failure to return from the glaciers into the valley. She regretted that she had troubled herself to be buried for a month in this green tomb amongst the hills; but it was impossible to change her imprisonment. They had begun the routine of the waters, and she had to solace herself as best she might with the imperial courtesies, and with sending little notes

---

1   Sedan chair.

to her friends, the sparkle of which was like the brightness of an acid drink, and contrasted strongly with the few grave constrained lines that were penned by Vere.

One day, when they had but little more time to spend on the Traun banks, she got together a riding and driving party to Old Aussee.

Aussee is quaint, and ancient, and charming, where it stands on its three-branched river; its people are old-fashioned and simple; its encircling mountains and its dark waters are full of peace and solemnity. When the gay world breaks in on these quiet old towns, and deep lakes, and snow-girt hills, there seems a profanity in the invasion. It is only for a very little while. At the first breath of autumn the butterflies flee, and the fishermen and salt-workers, and timber-hewers and chamois-hunters are left alone with their waters and their hills.

The duchesse's driving party was very picturesque, very showy, very noisy—"good society" is always very noisy nowadays, and has forgotten that a loud laugh used to be "bad form." They were all people of very high degree, but they all smoked, they all chattered shrilly, and they all looked very much as if they had been cut out of the *Vie Parisienne*,[1] and put in motion. Old Aussee, with its legends, its homely Styrian towns-folk, and its grand circle of snowclad summits were nothing to them—they liked the Opern-ring, the Bois, or Pall-Mall.[2]

Vere got away from them, and went by herself to visit the Spitalkirche. The altar is pure old German work of the fourteenth century, and she had heard of it from Kaulbach. In these old Austrian towns the churches are always very reverent places; dark and tranquil; overladen indeed with ornament and images, but too full of shadow for these to much offend; there is the scent of centuries of incense; the ivories are yellow with the damp of ages. Mountain suzerains and bold ritters,[3] whose deeds are still sung of in twilight to the zither, sleep beneath the moss-grown pavement; their shields and crowns are worn flat to the stone they were embossed on by the passing feet of generations of worshippers. High above in the darkness there is always some colossal carved or molded Christ. Through the

---

1 A journal of humor and manners; also a comic opera by Jacques Offenbach (1866). The plot relies heavily on impersonation, concealed identity, and glittering Parisian life.
2 Fashionable boulevards in Vienna, Paris, and London.
3 Feudal lords and knights.

half-opened iron-studded door there is always the smell of pinewoods, the gleam of water, the greenness of Alpine grass; often, too, there is the silvery falling of rain, and the fresh smell of it comes through the church, by whose black benches and dim lamps there will be sure to be some old bent woman praying.

The little church was more congenial to Vere than the companionship of her friends, who were boating on the Traun, while their servants unpacked their luncheon and their wines. She managed to elude them, and began to sketch the wings of the altar. She sent her servant to wait outside. The place was dreary and dark; the pure Alpine air blew in from an open pane in a stained window, there was the tinkle of a cow-bell, and the sound of running water from without; a dog came and looked at her.

The altar was not an easy one to copy; the candles were not lighted before it, and the daylight, grey and subdued without, as it is so often here, was very faint within.

"After all, what is the use of my copying it," she thought, with a certain bitterness. "My husband would tell me, if I cared for such an old thing, to send some painter from Munich to do it for me; and perhaps he would be right. It is the only mission we have, to spend money."

It is a mission that most women think the highest and most blest on earth, but it did not satisfy Vere. She seemed to herself so useless, so stupidly, vapidly, frivolously useless; and her nature was one to want work, and noble work.

She sat still, with her hands resting on her knees, and the colour and oils lying on the stone floor beside her untouched. She looked at the dark bent figure of the old peasant near, who had set a little candle before a side altar, and was praying fervently. She was a grey-headed, brown, wrinkled creature, dressed in the old Styrian way, she looked rapt and peaceful as she prayed. When she rose Vere spoke to her, and the old woman answered willingly. Yes, she was very old; yes, she had always dwelt in Aussee; her husband had worked in the salt mines and been killed in them; her sons had both died, one at König-grätz, one in a snowstorm upon Dachstein, that was all long ago; she had some grandchildren, they were in the mines and on the timber rafts; one had broken his leg going down the Danube with wood; she had gone to him, he was only a boy; she could not get him home any other way, so she had rowed him back in a little flat boat, rowed and steered herself; it was winter, the Traun flood was strong, but they had come home safe; now he was well again, but he had seen the soldiers in Vienna, and a soldier he would be; there was no keeping him any more on the timber rafts. Vienna was very fine; yes, but herself she thought Aussee was finer; she had lighted that taper for her boy Ulrich; he was going to the army to-morrow; she had begged the saints to watch over him; the saints would let her see them all again one day. Had she much to live on? No; the young men gave her what they could, and she spun and knitted, and life was cheap at Aussee, and then one could always pray, that was so much, and the saints did answer, not always, of course, because there were so many people speaking to them all at once, but yet often; God was good.

Vere took her by the hand, the rough gnarled hand like a bit of old oak bough, that had rowed the boat all the way from Vienna, and, having no money with her, slipped into it some gold *porte-bonheurs*[1] off her wrist.

"If I stay I will come and see you. Tell me the way to find your house."

"I shall never see you again," said the old woman with swimming eyes. "One does not see Our Lady twice face to face till one gets up to heaven." And she went away wondering, feeling the gold circlets on her arm, and telling her gossips, as they knitted in the street, that she had seen either Our Lady or St. Elizabeth[2]—one of the two it must surely have been.

When she had gone leaving her little taper, like a glow-worm, behind her, Vere still sat on, forgetful of the gay people who were carrying their coquetries, their jealousies, and their charms, on to the Traun water. She had everything that in the world's esteem is worth having; the poor, looking at her, envied her, as one of those who walk on velvet, and never feel the stones. She had youth, she had beauty, she had a great position; yet, as she sat there, she herself envied the life of the poor. It was real; it was in earnest; it had the affections to sustain and solace it. What a noble figure that woman, rowing her sick boy down the river in the autumn rains, looked to her beside her own mother! Unconsciously she stretched out her arms into the vacant air; those slender beautiful white arms, that Paris said were sculpturally faultless, and that her husband liked to see bare to the shoulder at her balls, with a circle of diamonds clasping them; she felt they would have force in them to row through the rains and against the flood, if the boat bore a freight that she loved.

But love was impossible for her.

---

1 Good luck charms (bracelets).
2 St. Elizabeth of Thuringia.

At the outset of her life the world had given her all things except that one.

They had shut her in a golden cage; what matter if the bird starved within? It would be the bird's ingratitude to fate.

Even if her offspring lived—she shuddered as she thought of it—they would be his, they would have his passions and his cruelties; they would be taken away from her, reared in creeds and in ways alien to her, they would be Zouroff Princes whose baby tyrannies would find a hundred sycophants, not her little simple children to lead in her own hand up to God.

As she sat there the sound of the organ arose, and rolled softly through the church. It was a time-worn instrument, and of little volume and power, but the rise and fall of the notes sounded solemn and beautiful in this old mountain church. The player was playing the Requiem of Mozart.

When the last cords thrilled away into silence, of that triumph of a mortal over the summons of death, a voice rose alone and sang the *Minuit Chrétien* of Adam.[1]

She started and looked around into the gloom of the grey church. She saw no one; but the voice was that of Corrèze.

Then she sat motionless, following the beauty of the Noël as it rose higher and higher, as though angels were bearing the singer of it away from earth, as the angels of Orcagna[2] bear on their wings the disembodied souls.

For awhile the church was filled with the glory of rejoicing, with the rapture of the earth made the cradle of God—then all at once there was silence. His voice had not seemed to cease, but rather to float farther and farther above until it reached the clouds, and grew still from the fulness of an unimaginable joy, of an unutterable desire fulfilled. One or two minor chords of the organ, faint as sighs, followed, then they too were still.

Vere sat motionless.

Surprise, wonder, curiosity, were far away from her; all minor emotions were lost in that infinite sense of consolation and of immortality; even of him who sang she ceased for the moment to have any memory.

After a little while a lad came to her over the grey stones; a lad of

---

1 *Christian Midnight* ("Oh Holy Night") by Adolphe Charles Adam (1803–56), French composer of comic opera and ballet.
2 (Andrea di Cione) Orcagna (c. 1308-68) was a Florentine painter.

Aussee, flaxen-haired and blue-eyed, in the white shirt that served him as a chorister.

He brought her a great bouquet of Alpine roses, and in the midst of the roses was the rare dark-blue *Wolfinia Carinthiana* which grows upon the slopes of the Gartnerkögel, and nowhere else in all the world they say.

"The foreigner for whom I blew the organ-bellows bade me bring you this," said the boy. "He sends you his homage."

"Is he in the church?"

"Yes; he says—may he see you one moment?"

"Yes."

Vere took the Alpine bouquet in her hands. She was still in a sort of trance.

The Noël was still upon her ears.

She did not even wonder how or why he came there. Since she had heard the song of Heine, it seemed to her so natural to hear his voice.

She took her great bouquet in her hands and went slowly through the twilight of the church and towards the open doors. She was thinking of the little dog-rose gathered on the cliffs by the sea in Calvados.

In another moment Corrèze stood before her in the dusk. A stray sunbeam wandering through the dusty panes of the window fell on his bright uncovered head.

"I thought you were far way," she said, with effort—her heart was beating. "I thought you were at the Hague?"

He made a little gesture with his hand.

"I shall be there. But could you think I would leave Austria so abruptly when you were in it? Surely not!"

She was silent.

In his presence, with the sweetness of his voice on her ear, all her old pure and perfect faith in him was strong as in the childish hour when she had heard him call the lark his little brother.

"You wrote to Madame de Sonnaz—"

"I wrote to Madame de Sonnaz many things that I knew she would not believe," he rejoined quickly. "Oh, my Princess of Faith! one must fight the spirits of this world with worldly weapons, or be worsted. You are too true for that. Alas! how will the battle go with you in the end!"

He sighed impatiently. Vere was silent.

She but partly understood him.

"Have you been amongst the glaciers all this time?" she asked at length.

"No. I went to the Gitschthal in Carinthia. Do you know that yonder blue flower only grows there on the side of the Gartnerkögel, and nowhere else in all the breadth of Europe? I thought it was a fitter emblem for you than the edelweiss, which is bought and sold in every Alpine village. So I thought I would go and fetch it and bring it to you. The Gitschthal is very charming; it is quite lonely, and untrodden except by its own mountaineers. You would care for it. It made me a boy again."

"You went only for that?"

"Only for that. What can one give you? You have everything. Prince Zouroff bought you the roc's egg, but I think he would not care to climb for the Wolfinia. It is only a mountain flower."

Vere was silent.

It was only a mountain flower, but, as he spoke of it, he gave it the meaning of the flower of Oberon.[1]

Had she any right to hear him? The dusky shadows of the church seemed to swim before her sight; the beauty of the Noël seemed still to echo on her ear.

"How could you tell that I was here?" she murmured.

He smiled.

"That was very easy. I was in Ischl at daybreak. I would have sung a *réveil*[2] under your window while the east was red, only Madame Jeanne would have taken it to herself. You go to Russia?"

"In three days—yes."

Corrèze was silent.

A slight shudder passed over him, as if the cold of Russia touched him.

Suddenly he dropped on his knee before her.

"I am but a singer of songs," he murmured. "But I honour you as greater and graver men cannot do perhaps. More than I do, none can. They will speak idly of me to you, I dare say, and evil too, perhaps; but do not listen, do not believe. If you ever need a servant—or an avenger—call me. If I be living I will come. Alas! alas! Not I, nor any man, can save the ermine from the moths, the soul from the world; but you are in God's hands if God there be above us. Farewell."

Then he kissed the hem of her skirts and left her.

She kept the mountain flowers in her hand, and knew how her doubt had wronged him.

---

1 King of the fairies in Medieval folklore and in Shakespeare's *Midsummer Night's Dream*.

2 Song to awaken.

Ten minutes later she left the church, hearing the voices of her friends. At the entrance she was met by Madame de Sonnaz, whose high silver heels and tall ebony cane, and skirts of cardinal red, were followed by an amazed group of Styrian children and women with their distaffs.

"Where have you been, my dear?" asked Duchesse Jeanne. "We have missed you for hours. We have been on the river, and we are very hungry. I am dying for a quail and a peach. What is that dark blue flower; does that grow in the church?"

A grey-headed English ambassador, Lord Bangor, who was in the rear of the duchesse, and was a keen and learned botanist, bent his eye-glasses on the rare blue blossom.

"The Wolfinia!" he cried in delighted wonder. "The *Wolfinia Carinthiana*; that is the very phœnix of all flowers! Oh, Princess! if it be not too intrusive, may one beg to know wherever you got that treasure? Its only home is leagues away on the Gitschthal."

"It came from the Gitschthal; a boy brought it to me," answered Vere; yet, though the words were literally true, she felt herself colour as she spoke them, because she did not say quite all the truth.

Duchesse Jeanne looked at her quickly, and thought to herself, "Corrèze sent her those wild flowers, or brought them to her. I do not believe in La Haye."[1]

Vere, indifferent to them all, stood in the church porch, with the soft grey light shed on her, and the alpine roses in her hands, and the spell of the Noël was still with her. "Lift up my soul," prays the Psalmist—nothing will ever answer that prayer as music does.[2]

"What a beautiful creature she is," said the old ambassador incautiously to the Duchesse Jeanne, as he looked at her, with that soft light from sunless skies upon her face.

The Duchesse Jeanne cordially assented. "But," she added with a smile, "people say so because she is faultlessly made, face and form; they say so, and there is an end. It is like sculpture; people go mad about a bit of china, a length of lace, a little picture, but no one ever goes mad about marble. They praise—and pass."

"Not always," said the imprudent diplomatist, forgetful of diplomacy. "I think no one would pass here if they saw the slightest encouragement or permission to linger."

"But there is not the slightest. What I said—she is sculptural."

---

1 The Hague. In his note to Jeanne de Sonnaz, Corrèze wrote that he had an engagement there.

2 Psalm 25:1.

"How happy is Zouroff!"

"Ah! Call no man happy till he is dead. Who knows if she will be always marble."

"She will never be a woman of the period," said the old man with some asperity. "I think her portrait will never be sold in shops. So far she will for ever miss fame."

"It is amusing to see oneself in shops," said Madame de Sonnaz. "Now and then I see a little crowd before mine; and the other day I heard a boy say—a boy who had a tray full of pipes on his head—'Tiens! Celle-ci; elle est joliment laide, mais elle est crâne, la petite; v'là!'[1] That was at my portrait."

"It is popularity, madame," said the ambassador with a grave bow. "The boy with the pipes knew his period."

"And how much that is to know!" said the lady with vivacity. "It is better to be the boy with the pipes than Pygmalion.[2] To know your own times, and adapt yourself to them, is the secret of success in everything from governing to advertising. Now-a-days a statesman has no chance unless he is sensational; a musician none unless he is noisy; an artist none unless he is either diseased or gaudy; a government none unless it is feverish, startling, and extravagant. It is the same with a woman. To be merely faultlessly beautiful is nothing, or next to nothing; you must know how to display it, how to provoke with it, how to tint it here and touch it there, and make it, in a word, what my boy with the pipes called me. I have not a good feature in my face, you know, and I have a skin like a yellow plum, that Piver can do nothing to redeem, and yet ninety-nine of the whole world of men will look at that perfect beauty of Princess Zouroff, praise her, and leave her to come to me. The boy with the pipes is a type of mankind, I assure you. Will you tell me, pray, why it is?"

"Excuse me, madame," said the old man, with another low bow. "To explain the choice of Paris is always a most painful dilemma; the goddesses are all so admirable—"

"No phrases. You are old enough to tell me the truth; or, if you like, I will tell it to you."

"I should certainly prefer that."

"Well—"

"Well?"

---

1 Well, this one, she is extremely ugly, but she is the low (sensual) fashionable style (of the age). There it is.

2 King of Cyprus who carved and then fell in love with a statue of a woman, which Aphrodite brought to life as Galatea.

"I will tell you, then, in her own husband's words: *elle ne sait pas s'encanailler.*"

And the duchesse, with a cigarette in her mouth, laughed, and carried her cardinal red skirts, and her musical silver heels over the stones of Aussee to a raft on the river which the skill of her attendants had turned into a very pretty awning-shaded flower-decked barge, where their breakfast was spread in the soft grey air above the green water.

Such women as Duchesse Jeanne or Lady Dolly are never in the country; they take Paris and London with them wherever they go.

The old diplomatist sat silent through the gay and clamorous breakfast, looking often at Vere, beside whose plate lay the alpine roses, and in whose ruffled lace at her throat was the blue Wolfinia.

"Good God! what an age we live in!" he thought. "In which a husband makes it a reproach to his wife that she does not understand how to attract other men! I do believe that we have sunk lower than the Romans of the empire; they did draw a line between the wife and the concubine. We don't draw any. Perhaps, after all, the Nihilists are right, and we deserve cutting down root and branch in our corruption. The disease wants the knife."

He muttered something of his thoughts to his next neighbour, the young Prince Traoï.

The young man nodded, smiled, and answered, "Duchesse Jeanne is quite right. Princess Vera is as beautiful as a Titian;[1] but one gets tired of looking at a Titian that one knows will never come into the market. Or rather she is like a classic statue in one of the old patrician museums in Rome. You know nothing will ever get the statue into your collection; you admire and pass. The other day, at the Hôtel Drouot, there was a tobacco-pot in Karl Theodor porcelain,[2] that was disputed by half Europe, and went at a fabulous price; the woman we like resembles that tobacco-pot; it is exquisite, but it can be got at, and anybody's hand may go into it; and even in its beauty—for Karl Theodor *is* so beautiful—it is suggestive and redolent of a coarse pleasure."

"All that is very well," said Lord Bangor; "but though it may explain the modern version of Paris's choice, it does not explain why in marriage—"

---

1   Tiziano Vecellio Titian (c. 1485-1576) was considered the greatest painter of the Venetian school.

2   In the late eighteenth century, Prince Carl Theodor directed two German faience factories (glazed earthen pottery used as a substitute for porcelain).

"Yes, it does," said the younger man. "The Roman noble does not care a straw for the statues that ennoble his vestibule; if he saw them once being disputed in the Rue Drouot he would quicken into an owner's appreciation. Believe me, the only modern passion that is really alive is envy. How should any man care for what is passively and undisputably his? To please us a woman must be hung about with other men's desires, as a squaw with beads."

"Then you, too, would wish your wife to *savoir s'encanailler*?"

"Not my own wife," said the young man with a laugh. "But then I belong to an old school, though I am young; Austrians all do."

"Whilst Russians," said the old man savagely, "Russians are all Bussy Rabutins crossed with Timour Beg.[1] By all, I mean of course the five or seven thousand of 'personages' that are all one sees of any nation in society. The nation, I dare say, is well enough, for it has faith, if its faith takes many odd shapes, and it can be very patient."

The Duchesse Jeanne called aloud to him that he must not talk politics at breakfast.

Then the breakfast came to an end, with many fruits and sweet-meats and Vienna dainties left to be scrambled for by the Aussee water-babies; and the driving party of Madame de Sonnaz began their homeward way over the Potschen-Joch. The old ambassador contrived to saunter to the carriages beside Vere.

"If I were a score of years younger, madame," he said with a glance at the dark blue flower at her throat, "I would beg you to make me your knight and give me the *Wolfinia* for my badge. It is the only flower you ought to wear, for it is the only one really emblematic of you; the edelweiss, that they call you after in Paris, is too easily found—and too chilly. Have you liked the day; has it tired you very much?"

"It takes a great deal to tire me physically," said Vere. "I am stronger than they think."

"But mentally you tire soon, because the atmosphere you are in does not suit you; is it not so?"

"I suppose so. I do not care for the chatter of the salons amidst the mountains."

"No—

---

1 Roger de Rabutin, Count de Bussy (1618-93), was a seventeenth century French nobleman, soldier, and man of letters. He was imprisoned
for publishing a salacious book dealing with the love lives of four noble
ladies. Timour Beg (1336-1405) was a bloodthirsty Turkish soldier whose
mission was to convert the "pagans" or bad Muslims.

Le vent qui vient à travers les montagnes
Me rendra fou—[1]

is a fitter spirit in which to meet the glaciers face to face. I think people either have a love of the mountains that is a religion, that is unutterable, sacred, and intense; or else are quite indifferent to them—like our friends. I know a man in whom they remain a religion despite all the counter-influences of the very gayest of worlds and most intoxicating of lives. I do not know whether you ever met him—I mean the singer Corrèze."

"Yes; I know him."

"He is a very keen mountaineer; he has a passion for the heights, not that of the mere climber of so many thousand feet, but rather of the dweller on the hills, whom nature has made a poet too. I saw him first when he was a little lad in the hills above Sion. You know people always say that part of his story is not true, but it is quite true. I am not aware why people who have not genius invariably think that people of genius lie; but they do so. I suppose Mediocrity cannot comprehend Imagination failing to avail itself of its resources! Three-and-twenty years ago, Princesse, I was already an old man, but more active than I am now. After a long and arduous season at my post I was allowing myself the luxury of an incognito tour, leaving my secretaries and servants at Geneva. No one enjoys the privacy and ease of such holidays like an old harness-worn public servant, and there is no harness heavier than diplomacy, though they do give it bells and feathers. One of those short—too short—summer days I had overwalked myself amongst the green Alps of the Valais, and had to rest at a considerable elevation, from which I was not very certain how I should get down again. It was an exquisite day; such days as only the mountains can give one, with that exhilarating tonic in the air that does worried nerves more good than all the physicians. Almost unconsciously I repeated aloud in the fulness of my heart, with a boyishness that I ought perhaps to have been ashamed of, but was not, the Thalysia;[2] you will know it, Princesse; I have heard that you are a student that would have charmed Roger Ascham.[3] As I murmured it to myself I heard a voice

1 The wind that comes across the mountains will drive me mad.
2 A song from Theocrititus's 7th Idyll. Theocritus was a Greek poet (310-250 B.C.). His poems were called "Idylls" (little poems).
3 Roger Ascham (1515-68) was a scholar and man of letters who also taught Greek. His most famous student was Princess Elizabeth (Queen Elizabeth I).

take up the Idyl, and continue with the song of Lycidas;[1] a pretty childish voice, that had laughter in it, laughter no doubt at my surprise. I turned and saw a little fellow with a herd of goats; he was a beautiful child about nine or ten years old. His Greek was quite pure. I was very astonished, and questioned him. He told me he was called Raphael de Corrèze. As it was near evening he offered me to go down with him to his father's hut, and I did so; and, as he trotted by my side, he told me that his father had taught him all he knew. He kept goats, he said, but he studied too. I was belated, and should have fared ill but for the hospitality of that mountain hut. I cannot tell you how greatly his father interested me. He was a scholar, and had all the look and bearing of a man of birth. He told me briefly how *his* father had taken to the mountains when the revolution ruined the nobility of Savoy. He was then in feeble health; he was anxious for the future of his boy, who was all alive with genius, and mirth, and music, and sang to me, after the simple supper, in the sweetest boyish pipe that it has ever been my lot to hear. I left them my name, and begged them to use me as they chose; but I never heard anything from them after the bright morning walk, when the boy guided me down into the high road for Sion. I sent him some books and a silver flute from Geneva, but I never knew that he got them. My own busy life began again, and I am shocked to say that I forgot that hut in the Alps, though that tranquil homely interior was one of the prettiest pictures which life has ever shown me. Many years afterwards, in Berlin, one night after the opera, going on to the stage with some of the princes to congratulate a new singer, who had taken the world by storm, the singer looked hard at me for a moment and then smiled. 'I have the silver flute still, Excellency,' he said. 'I do hope you had the note I wrote you, to thank you for it, to Geneva.' And then, of course, in that brilliant young tenor I knew my little goat-boy, who had quoted Theocritus, and wondered how I could have been so stupid as not to have remembered his name when I heard it in the public mouth. So I, for one, know that is quite true that he is a mountaineer no less than he is an artist and a Marquis de Corrèze. They say he has been in Ischl; I wish I had known it, for I am always so glad to see him out of the whirl of cities, where both he and I, in our different ways, are too pressed for time to have much leisure for talk. He is a very charming companion, Corrèze. Forgive me, Princesse, for telling you such a long story. Prosiness is pardoned to age; and here are the carriages.''

---

1 Lycidas is the shepherd who is one of the speakers in the idyll.

Vere had listened with changing colour, all the dejection and indifference passing from her face, and a light of pleasure and surprise shining in her frank grave eyes.

"Do not apologise. You have interested me very much," she said simply.

And the astute old man noticed that, as she spoke, she unconsciously touched the blue mountain flower at her throat.

"Improbable as it seems," he thought to himself; "I would wager that it is Corrèze who gave her that Wolfinia. She is not as cold as they say. '*Elle ne sait pas s'encanailler.*' No; and she will never learn that modern science. But there are greater perils for great natures than the bath of mud, that they never will take though it is the fashion. The bath of mud breaks nothing, and mesdames come out of it when they like white as snow. But these people fall from the stars, and break everything as they fall, in them and under them. She is half marble still; she is not quite awake yet; but when she is—when she is, I would not wish to be Prince Sergius Zouroff!"

The party went homeward in the fresh mountain air, leaving the evening lights on Old Aussee lying amidst its many waters. Vere was very silent, her alpine roses lay in her lap, the *Minuit Chrétien* was on her ear. The sun had set when they descended into Ischl. Her servants came to meet her, and said that her husband had arrived.

"*Quel preux chevalier de mari!*"[1] cried the Duchesse Jeanne with her shrill laughter, that was like the clash of steel.

"*Quel preux chevalier de mari,*" repeated the Duchesse de Sonnaz to Prince Zouroff alone, as they stood on the balcony of the hôtel after dinner.

He laughed as he leaned over the balustrade smoking.

"*Je l'ai toujours été, pour toi,*"[2] he whispered.

The Duchesse de Sonnaz gave him a blow with her pretty fan, that Fantin had painted with some Loves playing blind-man's-buff.

Vere was inside the room; she was intent upon her lace-work. The shaded light of a lamp fell on the proud, mournful calmness of her face. She wore black velvet with a high ruff of old Flemish lace; she looked like a picture by Chardin.[3]

Prince Zouroff sauntered in from the balcony and approached his wife.

---

1 What a valiant husband-knight!
2 I have always been so, for you.
3 Jean-Baptiste-Siméon Chardin (1699-1779) was one of the greatest eighteenth-century French painters.

"Vera," he said suddenly to her, "they tell me you are great friends with that singing fellow Corrèze. Is it true?"

Vere looked up from her lace-work.

"Who say so?"

"Oh—people. Is it true?"

"I have seen M. de Corrèze little, but I feel to know him well."

She answered him the simple truth, as it seemed to be to herself.

"Ah!" said Prince Zouroff, "then write and tell him to come to Svir. We must have some grand music for the Tsarewitch,[1] and you can offer him five hundred more roubles a night than the Petersburg opera gives him; he can have his own suite of rooms, and his own table; I know those artists give themselves airs."

Vere looked at him for a moment in astonishment, then felt herself grow cold and pale, with what emotion she scarcely knew.

"You had better let Anton write if you wish it," she answered, after a little pause. Anton was his secretary. "But M. de Corrèze would not come; he has many engagements; and I believe he never goes to private houses unless he goes as a guest, and then, of course, there is no question of money."

Zouroff was looking at her closely through his half-closed eyelids. He laughed.

"Nonsense. If an artist cannot be hired the world is coming to an end. They have no right to prejudices, those people; and, in point of fact, they only assume them to heighten the price. I prefer you should write yourself; you can give him any sum you like; but he shall come to Svir."

Vere hesitated a moment, then said very calmly, "It is not for me to write; Anton always does your business; let him do this."

The forehead of Zouroff grew clouded with a heavy frown; she had never contradicted or disobeyed him before.

"I order you to write, madame," he said sternly. "There is an end."

Vere rose, curtsied, and passed before him to a writing-table. There she wrote:

"Monsieur,—My husband desires me to beg you to do us the honour of visiting us at Svir on the fifteenth of next month, when the Tsarewitch will have the condescension to be with us; I believe, however, that you will be unable to do us this gratification, as I think your time is already too fully occupied. All arrangements you may wish to

---

1 The eldest son of the Czar.

make in the event of your acceding to his desire you will kindly communicate to M. Zouroff. I beg you to assure you of my distinguished consideration.

> "Vera, Princess Zouroff"

She wrote rapidly, addressed the letter, and handed it to her husband.

"Pooh!" he said, as he read it, and tore it up. "You write to the fellow as if he were a prince himself. You must not write to a singer in that fashion. Say we will pay him anything he choose. It is a *question d'argent*;[1] there is no need for compliments and consideration."

"You will pardon me, monsieur, I will not write with less courtesy than that."

"You will write as I choose to dictate."

'No." She spoke very quietly and took up her lace-work.

"You venture to disobey me?"

"I will not disobey any absolute command of yours, but I will not insult a great artist because you wish me to do so."

There was a look of resolve and contempt on her face that was new to him. She had always obeyed his caprices with a passive, mute patience that had made him believe her incapable of having will or judgment of her own. It was as strange to him as if a statue had spoken, or a flower had frowned. He stared at her in surprise that was greater than his annoyance.

"*Pardieu!*[2] what has come to you?" he said fiercely. "Take up your pen and write what I have spoken."

"*Napoléon, tu t'oublies!*"[3] quoted Duchesse Jeanne, as she came to the rescue with laugh. "My dear Prince, pardon me, but your charming wife is altogether in the right. Corrèze is a great artist; emperors kneel before him; it will never do to send for him as if he were an organ-grinder, that is, at least, if you want him to come. Besides, Vera and he are old friends; they cannot be expected to deal with one another like *entrepreneur* and *employé*, in the sledge-hammer style of persuasion, which seems to be your idea of beguiling stars to shine for you. Believe me, your wife is right. Corrèze will never come to Svir at all unless—"

"Unless what?"

---

1 Question of money.
2 By God!
3 Napoleon, you forget yourself.

"Unless as her friend, and yours."

There was a little accent on the first pronoun that cast the meaning of many words into those few monosyllables.

Zouroff watched his wife from under his heavy eyelids.

Vere sat still, and composed, taking up the various threads of her lace-pillows. She had said what she had thought courage and courtesy required her to say; to the effect of what she had said she was indifferent, and she did not perceive the meaning in the duchess's words—a pure conscience is often a cause of blindness and deafness that are perilous.

"When I have spoken—" began her husband, for he had the childishness of the true tyrant in him.

Madame de Sonnaz puffed some cigarette-smoke into his face.

"Oh, Cæsar; when you have spoken, what then? You have no serfs now, even in Russia. You can have none of us knouted.[1] You can only bow and yield to a woman's will, like any other man. *Voyons!*[2] I will write to Corrèze. I have known him ever since he first set all Paris sighing as Edgardo, and I will insinuate to him gently that he will find a bouquet on his table each day with a million roubles about the stalks of it; that will be delicate enough perhaps to bring him. But do you really wish for him? That is what I doubt."

"Why should you doubt it?" said the prince, with his sombre eyes still fastened on his wife.

Duchess Jeanne looked at him and smiled; the smile said a great many things.

"Because it will cost a great deal," she said demurely, "and I never knew that the Tsarewitch cared especially for music. He is not Louis of Bavaria."[3]

Then she sat down and wrote a very pretty letter of invitation and cajolery and command, all combined. Vere never spoke; her husband paced up and down the room, angry at having been worsted, yet reluctant to oppose his friend Jeanne.

It was the first disobedience of Vere's since she had sworn him obedience at the altar. It gave him a strange sensation, half of rage, half

---

1 Flogged with a whip. Knouts were used to punish Russian serfs and criminals.
2 Just look!
3 Louis of Bavaria was Louis II (1845-86). He was an intimate friend of Richard Wagner. Possessed by the composer's music, the king became Wagner's patron and he conceived the idea of building the opera house at Bayreuth.

of respect; but the mingling of respect only served to heighten and strengthen the rage. He had been a youth when the emancipation was given by Alexander to his people;[1] and in his boyhood he had seen his servants and his villagers flogged, beaten with rods, driven out into the snow at midnight, turned adrift into the woods to meet the wolves, treated anyhow, as whim or temper dictated on the impulse of a moment's wrath. The instinct of dominion remained strong in him; it always seemed to him that a blow was the right answer to any restive creature, whether dog or horse, man or woman. He had seen women scourged very often, and going in droves from Poland to Siberia. He could have found it in his heart to throw his wife on her knees and strike her now. Only he was a man of the world and knew what the world thought of such violence as that; and, in his own coarse way, he was a gentleman.

Corrèze received the letter of Duchesse Jeanne one evening on the low sands of Schevening, where some of the noblest ladies of northern nobilities were spoiling and praising him, as women had done from the day of his début. Corrèze felt that he ought to have been content; he was seated luxuriously in one of the straw hive-like chairs, a lovely Prussian Fürstin[2] had lent him her huge fan, a Dutchwoman, handsome as Rubens' wife, was making him a cigarette, and a Danish ambassadress was reading him a poem of François Coppée;[3] the sea was rolling in, in big billows, and sending into the air a delicious crisp freshness and buoyancy; all along the flat and yellow dunes were pleasant people, clever people, handsome people, distinguished people.

He ought to have been content. But he was not. He was thinking of green, cool, dusky, fir-scented Ischl.

The Danish beauty stopped suddenly in her reading. "You are not listening, Corrèze!" she cried aloud in some dismay and discomfiture.

"Madame," said Corrèze gallantly, "Coppée is a charming poet, but I would defy anyone to think of what he writes when it is you who are the reader of it!"

"That is very pretty," said the lovely Dane; "it would be perfect indeed; only one sees that you suppress a yawn as you say it!"

"I never yawned, or wished to yawn, in my life," said he promptly. "I cannot understand people who do. Cut your throat, blow out

1 Alexander II freed the serfs in 1861.
2 Princess.
3 François Edouard Joachim Coppée (1842-1908) was a French poet, dramatist, and novelist.

your brains, drown yourself, any one of these—that is a conceivable impulse; but yawn! what a confession of internal nothingness! What a vapid and vacant windbag must be the man who collapses into a yawn!"

"Nevertheless, you were very near one then," said the Danish beauty, casting her Coppée aside on the sand. "Compliments aside, you are changed, do you know? You are serious, you are preoccupied."

At that moment his secretary brought him his letters. His ladies gave him permission to glance at them, for some were marked urgent. Amongst them was the letter of Madame de Sonnaz.

He read it with surprise and some anger. It was a temptation; and the writer had known very well that it was so.

He would not have touched the roubles of the master of Svir, and would not willingly even have broken his bread, yet he would have given everything he possessed to go, to be under the same roof with the wife of Zouroff; to see, to hear, to charm, to influence her; to sing his songs for her ear alone.

The rough great northern ocean came booming over the sands. Corrèze sat silent and with a shadow on his face.

Then he rose, wrote a line in a leaf of his notebook, gave it to his secretary to have telegraphed at once to Ischl. The line said merely:

"Mille remerciments. Très honoré. Impossible d'accepter à cause d'engagements. Tous mes hommages."[1]

The sea rolled in with a grand sound, like a chant on a great organ.

"It is very *bourgeois* to do right," thought Corrèze; "but one must do it sometimes. Madame Jeanne is too quick; she plays her cards coarsely. All those Second Empire women are conspirators, but they conspire too hurriedly to succeed. My beautiful edelweiss, do they think I should pluck you from your heights? Oh! the Goths![2] Madame," he said aloud, "do be merciful, and read me the harmonies of Coppée again. You will not? That is revengeful. Perhaps I did not attend enough to his charming verses. There is another verse running in my head. Do you know it? I think Sully Prudhomme wrote it. It is one of those things so true that they hurt one; and one carries the burden of them about like a sad memory.

---

1 A thousand thanks. Very honored. Impossible to accept because of engagements. All my respect.
2 Barbarians.

"Dans les verres épais du cabaret brutal,
Le vin bleu coule à flots, et sans trève à la ronde.
Dans le calice fin plus rarement abonde
Un vin dont la clarté soit digne du cristal.

Enfin, la coupe d'or du haut d'un piédestal
Attend, vide toujours, bien que large et profonde,
Un cru dont la noblesse à la sienne répond:
On tremble d'en souiller l'ouvrage et le métal."[1]

"Have your letters made you think of that poem?" asked his companion.

"Yes."

"And where is the golden cup?"

"At the banquet of a debauchee who prefers 'Les verres épais du cabaret brutal.'"

END OF VOL. II.

---

1 In the thick glasses of the brutish cabaret, / The blue wine flows in waves, in an incessant round. / In the fine chalice (Communion cup), rarely does there abound / A wine whose clarity is worthy of crystal. Finally, the golden goblet atop a pedestal / Awaits, still empty though wide and deep, / A vintage whose nobility can answer its own: / One trembles at the prospect of contaminating its craftsmanship and metal.

VOLUME 3

CHAPTER I.

A few weeks later they were at Svir.

Svir was one of the grandest summer palaces of the many palaces of the Princes Zouroff. It had been built by a French architect in the time of the great Catherine's[1] love of French art, and its appanages were less an estate than a province or principality that stretched far away to the horizon on every side save one, where the Baltic spread its ice-plains in the winter, and its blue waters to the brief summer sunshine. It was a very grand place; it had acres of palm-houses and glass-houses; it had vast stables full of horses; it had a theatre, with a stage as large as the Follies-Marigny's;[2] it had vast forests in which the bear and the boar and the wolf were hunted with the splendour and the barbarity of the royal hunts that Snyders[3] painted; it was a Muscovite Versailles, with hundreds of halls and chambers, and a staircase, up which fifty men might have walked abreast; it had many treasures, too, of the arts, and precious marbles, Greek and Roman; yet there was no place on earth which Vere hated as she hated Svir.

To her it was the symbol of despotism, of brutal power, of soulless magnificence; and the cruelties of the sport that filled all the days, and the oppression of the peasantry by the police-agents which she was impotent to redress, weighed on her with continual pain. She had been taught in her girlhood to think; she knew too much to accept the surface gloss of things as their truth; she could not be content with a life which was a perpetual pageantry, without any other aim than that of killing time.

So much did the life at Svir displease her, and so indifferent was she to her own position in it, that she never observed that she was less mistress of it than was the Duchesse de Sonnaz, who was there with the Duc Paul, a placid sweet-tempered man, who was devoted to entomology and other harmless sciences. It was not Vere, but Madame Jeanne who directed the amusements of each day and night. It was Madame Jeanne who scolded the manager of the operetta troup, who selected the pieces to be performed in the theatre, who organised the hunting parties and the cotillons, and the

---

1 Catherine II, "Catherine the Great" (1729-96). She was Empress of Russia from 1762 to 1796.
2 A Paris theater where many of Offenbach's operettas were produced.
3 Frans Snyders (1579-1657) was a Dutch painter.

sailing, and the riding. It was Madame Jeanne who, with her pistols in her belt, and her gold-tipped ivory hunting-horn, and her green tunic and trowsers, and her general *franc-tireur*[1] aspect, went out with Sergius Zouroff to see the bear's death-struggle, and give the last stroke in the wolf's throat.

Vere—to whom the moonlit *curée*[2] in the great court was a horrible sight, and who, though she had never blenched when the wolves had bayed after the sledge, would have turned sick and blind at sight of the dying beasts with the hunters' knives in their necks— was only glad that there was anyone who should take the task off her hands of amusing the large house-party and the morose humours of her husband. The words of Corrèze had failed to awaken any suspicion in her mind.

That the presence of Madame de Sonnaz at Svir was as great an insult to her as that of Noisette in the Kermesse pavilion never entered her thoughts. She only as yet knew very imperfectly her world.

"It is well she is beautiful, for she is only a bit of still life," said Prince Zouroff very contemptuously to some one who complimented him upon his wife's loveliness.

When she received their Imperial guests at the foot of her staircase, with a great bouquet of lilies of the valley and orchids in her hand, she was a perfect picture against the ebony and malachite of the balustrade—that he granted; but she might as well have been made of marble for aught of interest or animation that she showed.

It angered him bitterly that the luxury and extravagance with which she was surrounded did not impress her more. It was so very difficult to hurt a woman who cared for so little; her indifference seemed to remove her thousands of leagues away from him.

"You see it is of no use to be angry with her," he said to his confidant, Madame Jeanne. "You do not move her. She remains tranquil. She does not oppose you, but neither does she alter. She is like the snow, that is so white and still and soft; but the snow is stronger than you; it will not stop for you."

Madame Jeanne laughed a little.

"My poor Sergius! you *would* marry!"

Zouroff was silent; his eyebrows were drawn together in moody meditation.

---

1 Sharpshooter.
2 Quarry.

Why had he married? he wondered. Because a child's coldness, and a child's rudeness had made her loveliness greater for a moment in his sight than any other. Because, also, for Vere, base as his passion had been, it had been more nearly redeemed by tenderness than anything he had ever known.

"The snow is very still, it is true," said Madame Jeanne musingly; "but it can rise in a very wild *tourmente*[1] sometimes. You must have seen that a thousand times."

"And you mean—?" said Zouroff, turning his eyes on her.

"I mean that I think our sweet Vera is just the person to have a *coup de tête*,[2] and to forget everything in it."

"She will never forget what is due to me," said Zouroff angrily and roughly.

Madame de Sonnaz laughed.

"Do you fancy she cares about that? what she does think of is what is due to herself. I always told you she is the type of woman that one never sees now—the woman who is chaste out of self-respect. It is admirable, it is exquisite; but all the same it is invulnerable; because it is only a finer sort of egotism."

"She will never forget her duty," said her husband peremptorily, as though closing the discussion.

"Certainly not," assented his friend; "not as long as it appears duty to her. But her ideas of duty may change—who can say? And, *mon cher*, you do not very often remember yours to her!"

Zouroff blazed into a sullen passion, at which Madame de Sonnaz laughed, as was her wont, and turned her back on him, and lighted a cigar.

"After all," she said, "what silly words we use! Duty!—honour!—obligation! '*Tout cela est si purement géographique*,'[3] as was said at Marly long ago. I read the other day of Albania, in which it is duty to kill forty men for one, and of another country in which it is duty for a widow to marry all her brothers-in-law. Let us hope our Vera's views of geography will never change."

They were standing together in one of the long alleys of the forest, which was resounding with the baying of hounds and the shouting of beaters. For all reply Sergius Zouroff put his rifle to his shoulder; a bear was being driven down the drive.

---

1 Disturbance.
2 Act of desperation.
3 All that is purely geographical.

"*A moi!*"[1] cried Madame Jeanne. The great brown mass came thundering through the brushwood, and came into their sight; she raised her gun, and sent a bullet through its forehead, and snatched Zouroff's breech-loader from him, and fired again. The bear dropped; there was a quick convulsive movement of all its paws, then it was still for ever.

"I wish I could have married you!" cried Zouroff enthusiastically. "There is not another woman in Europe who could have done that at such a distance as we are!"

"*Mon vieux*, we should have loathed one another," said Madame Jeanne, in no way touched by the compliment. "In a conjugal capacity I much prefer my good Paul."

Zouroff laughed—restored to good humour—and drew his hunting-knife to give the customary stroke for surety to her victim. The day was beautiful in the deep green gloom and balmy solitude of the forest, which was chiefly of pines.

"Sport is very stupid," said Madame Jeanne, blowing her ivory horn to call the keepers. "Vera is employing her time much better, I am sure; she is reading metaphysics, or looking at her orchids, or studying Nihilism."

"Let me forget for a moment that Vera exists," said her husband, with his steel in the bear's throat.

Vere was studying Nihilism, or what has led to it, which comes to the same thing.

The only town near Svir was one of no great importance, a few miles inland, whose citizens were chiefly timber-traders, or owners of trading ships, that went to and from the Baltic. It had some churches, some schools, some war of sects, and it had of late been in evil odour with the government for suspected socialist doctrines. It had been warned, punished, purified, but of late was supposed to have sinned again; and the hand of the Third Section[2] had fallen heavily upon it.

Vere this day rode over to it, to visit one of its hospitals; her

---

1 Help!
2 The Third Section or Department was responsible for the surveillance of politically suspicious persons and their banishment to remote provinces in Russia. Such victims were often students suspected of subversive ideas and working men who spoke against authorities. A fourteen-year-old girl, for example, was exiled for shouting in a crowd that it was a shame to condemn people to death for nothing (P. Kropotkin, *In Russian and French Prisons* [1887]).

mother, and other ladies, drove there to purchase sables and marten skins.

Lady Dolly had been so near—at Carlsbad, a mere trifle of a few hundred miles—that she had been unable to resist the temptation of running over for a peep at Svir, which she was dying to see, so she averred. She was as pretty as ever. She had changed the colour of her curls, but that prevents monotony of expression, and, if well done, is always admired. She had to be a little more careful always to have her back to the light, and there was sometimes about her eyes lines which nothing would quite paint away; and her maid found her more pettish and peevish. That was all; twenty years hence, if Lady Dolly live, there will be hardly more difference than that.

Her Sicilian had been also on the banks of the Teple—only for his health, for he was not strong—but he had been too assiduous in carrying her shawls, in ordering her dinners, in walking beside her mule in the firwoods, and people began to talk; and Lady Dolly did not choose to imperil all that the flowers for the Children's Hospitals, and the early services at Knightsbridge,[1] had done for her, so she had summarily left the young man in the fir woods, and come to Svir.

"I always like to witness my dear child's happiness, you know, with my own eyes when I can; and in London and Paris both she and I are so terribly busy," she said to her friends at Carlsbad.

Herself, she always recoiled from meeting the grave eyes of Vere, and the smile of her son-in-law was occasionally grim and disagreeable, and made her shiver; but yet she thought it well to go to their houses, and she was really anxious to see the glories of Svir.

When she arrived there, she was enraptured. She adored novelty, and new things are hard to find for a person who has seen as much as she had. The Russian life was, in a measure, different to what she had known elsewhere, the local colour enchanted her, and the obeisances and humility of the people she declared were quite scriptural.

The grandeur, the vastness, the absolute dominion, the half-barbaric magnificence that prevailed in this, the grandest summer palace of the Zouroffs, delighted her; they appealed forcibly to her imagination, which had its vulgar side. They appeased her conscience, too; for, after all, she thought, what could Vere wish for more? Short of royalty, no alliance could have given her more wealth, more authority, and more rank.

---

1   In Volume 2, Chapter III, in an effort to protect her reputation, Lady Dolly became very charitable, and her new religious fervor was "one of the prettiest trifles in all the town."

These Baltic estates were a kingdom in themselves, and the prodigal, careless, endless luxury, that was the note of life there, was mingled with a despotism and a cynicism in all domestic relations that fascinated Lady Dolly.

"I should have been perfectly happy if I had married a great Russian," she often said to herself; and she thought that her daughter was both thankless to her fate and to her. Lady Dolly really began to bring herself to think so.

"Very few women," she mused, "would ever have effaced themselves as I did; very few would have put away every personal feeling and objection as I did. Of course she doesn't know—but I don't believe any woman living would have done as I did, because people are so selfish."

She had persuaded herself in all this time that she had been generous, self-sacrificing, even courageous, in marrying her daughter as she did; and when now and then a qualm passed over her, as she thought that the world might give all these great qualities very different and darker names, Lady Dolly took a little sherry or a little chloral, according to the time of day, and very soon was herself again.

To be able to do no wrong at all in one's own sight, is one of the secrets of personal comfort in this life. Lady Dolly never admitted, even to herself, that she did any. If anything looked a little wrong, it was only because she was the victim to unkindly circumstance over which she had no control.

People had always been so jealous of her, and so nasty to her about money.

"It is all very well to talk about the saints," she would say to herself, "but they never had any real trials. If the apostles had had bills due that they couldn't meet, or St. Helen and St. Ursula had had their curls come off just as they were being taken in to dinner, they might have talked. As it was, I am sure they enjoyed all their martyrdom, just as people scream about being libelled in 'Truth' or 'Figaro,' and delight in having their names in them."

Lady Dolly always thought herself an ill-used woman. If things had been in the least just, she would have been born with thirty thousand a year, and six inches more in stature.

Meanwhile she was even prettier than ever. She had undergone a slight transformation; her curls were of a richer ruddier hue, her eyelashes were darker and thicker, her mouth was like a little pomegranate bud. It was all Piver; but it was the very perfection of Piver. She had considered that the hues and style of the fashions of the coming year, which were always disclosed to her very early in secret conclave in the Rue de la Paix, required this slight deepening and heightening of her complexion.

"I do wish you would induce Vera to rouge a little, just a little. Dress this winter really will want it; the colours will all be dead ones," she had said this day at Svir to her son-in-law, who shrugged his shoulders.

"I have told her she would look better; but she is obstinate, you know."

"Oh-h-h!" assented Lady Dolly. "Obstinate is no word for it; she is *mulish*; of course, I understand that she is very proud of her skin, but it would look all the better if it were warmed up a little; it is *too* white, *too* fair, if one can say such a thing, don't you know? And, besides, even though she may look well now without it, a woman who never rouges has a frightful middle-age before her. Didn't Talleyrand say so?"[1]

"You are thinking of whist;[1] but the meaning is the same. Both are resources for autumn that it is better to take in summer," said Madame Nelaguine, with her little cynical smile.

"Vera is very fantastic," said the Duchesse Jeanne. "Besides, she is so handsome she is not afraid of growing older; she thinks she will defy Time."

"I believe you can if you are well enamelled," said Lady Dolly seriously.

"Vera will be like the woman under the Merovingian kings,"[2] said Madame Nelaguine. "The woman who went every dawn of her life out into the forests at day break to hear the birds sing, and so remained, by angels' blessing, perpetually young."

"I suppose there was no society in France in that time," said Lady Dolly; "or else the woman was out of it. In society everybody has always painted. I think they found all sorts of rouge-pots at Pompeii,[3] which is so touching, and brings all those poor dear creatures so near to us; and it just shows that human nature was always exactly the same."

---

1 Charles Maurice de Talleyrand-Périgord (1754-1838) was a French statesman and diplomat. Madame Nelaguine is referring to the following quotation: "You do not play then at whist, sir? Alas, what a sad old age you are preparing for yourself."

2 Merovia was a Frankish dynasty which reigned in Gaul and Germany from A.D. 476 to 751.

3 Pompeii was an ancient city in Italy on the bay of Naples. It was buried by an eruption of nearby Mount Vesuvius in A.D. 79.

"The Etruscan focolare,[1] I dare say, were trays of cosmetics," suggested Madame Nelaguine sympathetically.

"Yes?" said Lady Dolly, whose history was vague. "It is so interesting, I think, to feel that everybody was always just exactly alike, and that when they complain of us it is such nonsense, and mere spite. Vera, why will not you rouge a little, a very little?"

"I think it a disgusting practice," said her daughter, who had entered the room at that moment, dressed for riding.

"Well, I think so too," said Madame Nelaguine with a little laugh. "I think so too, though I do it; but my rouge is very honest; I am exactly like the wooden dolls, with a red dab on each cheek, that they sell for the babies at fairs. Vera would be a sublime wax doll, no doubt, if she rouged; but, as it is, she is a marble statue. Surely that is the finer work of art."

"The age of statues is past," murmured the Duchess Jeanne. "We are in the puppet and monkey epoch."

"It is all cant to be against painting," said Lady Dolly. "Who was it said that the spider is every bit as artificial as the weaver?"

"Joseph le Maistre,"[2] said Madame Nelaguine, "but he means—"

"He means, to be sure," said Lady Dolly with asperity, "that unless one goes without any clothes at all, like savages, one must be artificial; and one may just as well be becomingly so as frightfully so; only I know frights are always *thought* natural, as snubbing, snapping creatures are thought so sweetly sincere. But it doesn't follow one bit; the frights have most likely only gone to the wrong people to get done up."

"And the disagreeable snappers and snubbers and snarlers?"

"Got out of bed the wrong end upwards," said Lady Dolly, "or have forgotten to take their dinner-pills."

"I begin to think you are a philosopher, Lady Dolly."

"I hope I am nothing so disagreeable," said Lady Dolly. "But at least I have eyes, and my eyes tell me what a wretched, dull, pawky-looking creature a woman that doesn't do herself up looks like at a ball."

"Even at twenty years old?"

"Age has nothing to do with it," said Lady Dolly very angrily. "That is a man's idea. People don't paint because they're old; they

---

1 Sixth-century clay trays made in Etruria, an ancient Italian country.
2 Joseph-Marie, Comte de Maistre (1753-1821) was a French philosophical, political, and religious writer.

paint to vary themselves, to brighten themselves, to *clear* themselves. A natural skin may do very well in Arcadia, but it won't do where there are candles and gas. Besides, a natural skin's always the same; but when you paint, you make it just what goes best with the gown you have got on for the day; and as women grow older what are they to do? It is all very well to say 'bear it,' but who helps you to bear it? Not society, which shelves you; not men, who won't look at you; not women, who count your curls if they are false, and your grey hairs if they are real. It is all very well to talk poetry, but who likes *déchéance*.[1] It is all very well to rail about artificiality and *postiche*,[2] but who forced us to be artificial, and who made *postiche* a necessity? Society; society; society. Would it stand a woman who had lost all her teeth and who had a bald head? Of course not. Then whose is the fault if the woman goes to the dentist and the hair-dresser? She is quite right to go. But it is absurd to say that society does not make her go. All this cry about artificiality is cant, all cant. Who are admired in a ball-room? The handsome women who are not young but are dressed to perfection, painted to perfection, coiffed to perfection, and are perfect bits of colour. If they come out without their *postiche*[3] who would look at them? Mothers of boys and girls you say? Yes, of course they are; but that is their misfortune; it is no reason why they shouldn't look as well as they can look, and, besides, nowadays it is only married women that are looked at, and children in short frocks, which is disgusting."

Lady Dolly paused for breath, having talked herself into some confusion of ideas, and went away to dress and drive.

She forgot the wrongs of fate as she drove to Molv with the old ambassador Lord Bangor, who was staying there, and a charming young Russian of the Guard, whose golden head and fair beauty made her Sicilian seem to her in memory yellow and black as an olive; he had really had nothing good but his eyes, she reflected as she drove.

When she reached Molv she admired everything; the bearded priests, the churches, the bells, the pink and yellow houses, the Byzantine shrines. She was in a mood to praise. What was not interesting was so droll, and what was not droll was so interesting. If her companion of the Imperial Guard had not had a head like a Cir-

---

1 Degeneration.
2 In this context, falseness.
3 In this context, a wig.

cassian chief, and a form like Hercules,[1] she might perhaps have found out that Molv was ugly and very flat, dirty and very unsavoury, and so constituted that it became a pool of mud in winter, and in summer a shoal of sand. But she did not see these things, and she was charmed. She was still more charmed when she had bought her sealskins and sables at a price higher than she would have given in Regent Street; and, coming out opposite the gilded and painted frontage of the chief church, which was that of St. Vladimir, she saw a sad sight.

Nothing less than a score of young men and a few women being taken by a strong force of Cossacks to the fortress; the townspeople looking on, gathered in groups, quite silent, grieved but dumb, like poor beaten dogs.

"Dear me! how very interesting!" said Lady Dolly, and she put up her eye-glasses. "How very interesting! some of them quite nice-looking, too. What have they done?"

The Russian of the Guard explained to her that they were suspected of revolutionary conspiracies, had harboured suspected persons, or were suspected themselves: Nihilists, in a word.

"How very interesting!" said Lady Dolly again. "Now, one would never see such a sight as that in England, Lord Bangor?"

"No," said Lord Bangor seriously; "I don't think we should. There are defects in our constitution—"

"Poor things!" said Lady Dolly, a pretty figure in *feuillemorte*[2] and violet, with a jewelled ebony cane as high as her shoulder, surveying through her glass the chained, dusty, heart-sick prisoners. "But why couldn't they keep quiet? So stupid of them! I never understand those revolutionaries; they upset everything, and bore everybody, and think themselves martyrs! It will be such a pity if you do get those horrid principles here. Russia is too charming as it is; everybody so obedient and nice as they are at present, everybody kneeling and bowing, and doing what they're told—not like *us* with our horrid servants, who take themselves off the very day of a big party, or say they won't stay if they haven't pine-apples. I think the whole social system of Russia perfect—quite perfect; only it must have been nicer still before the Tsar was too kind, and let loose all those serfs, who, I am quite sure, haven't an idea what to do with themselves, and will be sure to shoot him for it some day."

---

1 Circassian natives were noted for their legendary beauty; Hercules is a
   mythological hero possessing exceptional physical strength.
2 Yellow-brown.

Lady Dolly paused in these discursive political utterances, and looked again at the little band of fettered youths and maidens, dusty, pale, jaded, who were being hustled along by the Cossacks through the silent scattered groups of the people. A local official had been wounded by a shot from a revolver, and they were all implicated, or the police wished to suppose them to be implicated, in the offence. They were being carried away beyond the Ourals; their parents, and brothers and sisters, and lovers knew very well that never more would their young feet tread the stones of their native town. A silence like that of the grave—which would perhaps be the silence of the grave—would soon engulf and close over them. Henceforth they would be mere memories to those who loved them: no more.

"They look very harmless," said Lady Dolly, disappointed that conspirators did not look a little as they do on the stage. "Really, you know, if it wasn't for these handcuffs, one might take them for a set of excursionists; really now, mightn't we? Just that sort of jaded, dusty, uncomfortable look—"

"Consequent on 'three shillings to Margate and back.' Yes; they have a Bank holiday look," said Lord Bangor. "But it will be a long Bank holiday for them; they are on their first stage to Siberia."

"How interesting!" said Lady Dolly.

At that moment an old white-haired woman, with a piercing cry broke through the ranks, and fell on the neck of a young man, clinging to him for all that the police could do, till the lances of the Cossacks parted the mother and son.

"It is a sad state of things for any country," said Lord Bangor; and the young captain of the Guard laughed.

"Well, why couldn't they keep quiet?" said Lady Dolly. "Dear me! with all this crowd, however shall we find the carriage. Where is Vere, I wonder? But she said we need not wait for her. Don't you think we had better go home? I shouldn't like to meet wolves."

"Wolves are not hungry in summer," said Lord Bangor. "It is only the prison's maw that is never full."

"Well, what are they to do if people won't keep quiet?" said Lady Dolly. "I'm sure those young men and women do not look like geniuses that would be able to set the world on fire. I suppose they are working people, most of them. They will do very well, I dare say, in Tomsk. Count Rostrow, here, tells me the exiles are beautifully treated, and quite happy; and all that is said about the quicksilver mines is all exaggeration; newspaper nonsense."[1]

"No doubt," said Lord Bangor. "To object to exile is a mere bad form of Chauvinism."

"Why couldn't they keep quiet if they don't like to go there?" she said again; and got into the carriage, and drove away out into the road over the plain, between the great green sea of billowy grasses, and the golden ocean of ripened grain; and, in time, bowled through the gilded gates of Svir; and ate her dinner with a good appetite; and laughed till she cried at the drolleries of a new operetta of Métra's,[2] which the French actors gave in the little opera-house.

"Life is so full of contrasts in Russia; it is quite delightful; one can't be dull," she said to Lord Bangor, who sat beside her.

"Life is full of contrasts everywhere, my dear lady," said he. "Only, as a rule, we never look on the other side of the wall. It bores us even to remember that there is another side."

Vere that night was paler and stiller even than it was her wont to be. She went about amongst her guests with that grace and courtesy which never changed, but she was absent in mind; and once or twice, as the laughter of the audience rippled in echo to the gay melodies of Métra, a shiver as of cold went over her.

"She must have heard something about Corrèze that has embarrassed her," thought Madame de Sonnaz, but she was wrong.

Vere had only seen the same sight that her mother had seen, in the little town of Molv.

That night, when the house party had broken up to go to their apartments, and she had gained the comparative peace of her own chamber, Vere, when her maids had passed a loose white gown over her and unloosed her hair, sent them away, and went into the little oratory that adjoined her dressing-room. She kneeled down, and leaned her arms on the rail of the little altar, and her head on her arms; but she could not pray. Life seemed to her too terrible; and who cared? who cared?

Riches had done their best to embellish the little sanctuary: the walls were inlaid with malachite and marbles; the crucifix was a wonderful work in ivory and silver; the *priedieu*[3] was embroidered in

---

1   Prisoners were actually subjected to abominable treatment in the mines. Enchained, they worked in darkness, while overseers whipped them. Prisoners died from poisonous gases, flogging, and scurvy.

2   Olivier Métra (1830–89) composed operettas. He also directed the orchestra at the Bal Mabille, where the cancan was performed.

3   Prayer stool.

silk and precious stones; there was a triptych of Luke von Cranach,[1] and Oriental candelabra in gold. It was a retreat that had been sacred to the dead Princess Mania, her husband's mother, a pious and melancholy woman.

Vere cared little for any of these things; but the place was really to her a sanctuary, as no one ever disturbed her there; even Zouroff never had presumed to enter it; and the painted casements, when they were opened, showed her the green plain, and, beyond the plain, the beautiful waters of the Baltic. Here she could be tranquil now and then, and try to give her thoughts to her old friends the Latin writers; or read the verse of George Herbert or the prose of Thomas à Kempis, and pray for force to bear the life she led.

But to-night she could not pray.

She was one of those who are less strong for the woes of others than for her own.

She leaned her face upon her arms, and only wondered—wondered—wondered—why men were so cruel, and God so deaf.

It was nearly two in the morning; through the painted panes the stars were shining; beyond the plain there was the silver of the dawn.

Suddenly a heavy step trod on the marbles of the pavement. For the first time since their marriage, her husband entered the place of prayer. She turned, and half rose in astonishment, and her heart grew sick; she was not safe from him even here. He marked the instinct of aversion, and hated her for it; the time was gone by when it allured and enchained him.

"Excuse me for my entrance here," he said with that courtesy to which the presence of his wife always compelled him, despite himself. "I am exceedingly annoyed, compromised, disgusted. You were in Molv to-day?"

"Yes; I rode there. I went to see your mother's hospital."

She had quite risen, and stood, with one hand on the altar rail, looking at him.

"I hear that you saw those prisoners; that you spoke to them; that you made a scene, a scandal; that you gave one of the women your handkerchief; that you promised them all kinds of impossible follies. Be so good as to tell me what happened."

"Who spies upon me?" said Vere, with the colour rising to her face.

---

1   Lucas von Cranach (1472-1553) was a German painter and graphic artist; his son, Lucas the Younger (1515-80), was also an artist.

"Spies! No one. If you choose to exhibit yourself in a public street, a hundred people may well see you. What did happen? Answer me."

"This happened. I met the prisoners. I do not believe any of them are guilty of the attempt to assassinate General Marcoloff. They are all very young, several were girls; one of the girls broke from the guards, and threw herself before me, sobbing and begging my help. Her arm was cut and bleeding, I suppose in fastening the chains; I took my handkerchief and bound it up; I promised her to support her mother, who is old and infirm. I spoke to them all and bade them try and bear their fate calmly. I wept with them, that I confess; but I was not alone—there were not many dry eyes in Molv. I believe all these young people to be quite innocent. I believe if the Emperor saw the things that are done in his name, he would not sanction them. That is all I have to tell you. It has haunted me all the evening. It is horrible that such tyrannies should be; and that we should dine, and laugh, and spend thousands of roubles in a night, and live as if no living creatures were being tortured near us. I cannot forget it; and I will do what I can to serve them."

She had never spoken at such a length to her husband in all the three years of her married life; but she felt strongly, and it seemed to her that here reticence would have been cowardice. She spoke quite tranquilly, but her voice had a depth in it that told how keenly she had been moved.

Zouroff heard her with a scowl upon his brows; then he laughed contemptuously and angrily.

"*You* believe!" he echoed. "What should you know, and why should you care? Will you learn to leave those things alone? A Princess Zouroff dismounting in the dust to bind up the wounds of a Nihilist convict! What a touching spectacle! But we will have no more of these scenes if you please; they are very unbecoming, and, more, they are very compromising. The Emperor knows me well, indeed, but enemies might carry such a tale to him; and he might see fit to suspect, to order me not to leave Russia, to imprison me on my estates. It is as likely as not that your theatrical vagaries may get bruited about at Court. I neither know nor care whether these creatures shot Marcoloff or abetted shooting at him; what I do care for is the dignity of my name."

Vere, standing beside the great ivory crucifix, with the draperies of plush and ermine falling about her, and her fair hair unbound and falling over her shoulders, turned her face more fully upon him. There was a faint smile upon her lips.

"The dignity of *your* name!" she said merely; and the accent said the rest.

The calm contempt pierced his vanity and his self-love, and made him wince and smart. The first sign she had given that the unworthiness of his life was known to her had been when she had ordered him to remove the pavilion of Noisette. He had always set her aside as a beautiful, blonde, ignorant, religious creature, and the shock was great to him to find in her a judge who censured and scorned him.

"The dignity of my name," he repeated sullenly and with greater insistence. "We were great nobles with the Dolgarouki, when the Romanoffs were nothing.[1] I do not choose my name to be dragged in the dust because you are headstrong enough, or childish enough, to fancy some incendiaries and assassins are martyrs. Have politics, if you like, in Paris in your drawing-room, but leave them alone here. They are dangerous here, and worse than dangerous. They are low. I deny you nothing else. You have money at your pleasure, amusement, jewels, anything you like; but I forbid you political vulgarities. I was disgusted when I heard of the spectacle of this morning; I was ashamed"—

"Is it not rather a matter for shame that we eat and drink, and laugh and talk, with all this frightful agony around us?" said Vere, with a vibration of rare passion in her voice. "The people may be wrong; they may be guilty; but their class have so much to avenge, and your class so much to expiate, that their offence cannot equal yours. You think I cannot understand these things? You are mistaken. There are suffering and injustice enough on your own lands of Svir alone to justify a revolution. I know it; I see it; I suffer under it; suffer because I am powerless to remedy it, and I am supposed to be acquiescent in it. If you allowed me to interest myself in your country, I would try not to feel every hour in it an exile; and the emptiness and nothingness of my life would cease to oppress and torment me—"

"Silence!" said Zouroff, with petulance. "You may come here for prayer, but I do not come here for sermons. The emptiness of your life! What do you mean? You are young, and you are beautiful; and you have in me a husband who asks nothing of you except to look well and to spend money. Cannot you be happy? Think of your new

---

1   The Romanoffs were a Russian Imperial dynasty that ruled from 1613 to 1917. The Dolgoruky (Ouida misspelled the name) family was a large and influential family which descended from Rurik, a ninth-century Dane.

cases from Worth's, and let political agitators keep the monopoly of their incendiary rubbish. You have been the beauty of Paris and Petersburg for three years. That should satisfy any woman."

"It merely insults me," she answered him. "Society comes and stares. So it stares at the actress Noisette, so it stares at that nameless woman whom you call Casse-une-Croûte. Is that a thing to be proud of? You may be so; I am not. Men make me compliments, or try to make them, that I esteem no better than insults. Your own friends are foremost. They talk of my portraits, of my busts, of my jewels, of my dresses. Another year it will be someone else that they will talk about, and they will cease to look at me. They find me cold, they find me stupid. I am glad that they do; if they did otherwise, I should have lived to despise myself."

"*Nom de Dieu!*" muttered Zouroff; and he stared at her, wondering if she had said the names of Noisette and Casse-une-Croûte by hazard, or if she knew? He began to think she knew. He had always thought her blind as a statue, ignorant as a nun; but, as she stood before him, for the first time letting loose the disdain and the weariness that consumed her heart into words, he began slowly to perceive that, though he had wedded a child, she was a child no longer; he began to perceive that, after three years in the great world, his wife had grown to womanhood with all that knowledge which the great world alone can give.

As she had said nothing to him, after the Kermesse, of the absence of Noisette, he had fancied her anger a mere *boutade*, due perhaps to pride, which he knew was very strong in her. Now he saw that his wife's silence had arisen not from ignorance but from submission to what she conceived to be her duty, or perhaps, more likely still, from scorn; a scorn too profound and too cold to stoop to reproach or to reproof.

"Why cannot you be like any other woman?" he muttered. "Why cannot you content yourself with your *chiffons*,[1] your conquests, your beauty? If you were an ugly woman one could understand your taking refuge in religion and politics; but, at your age, with your face and figure! Good heavens! it is too ridiculous!"

The eyes of Vere grew very stern.

"That is your advice to me? to content myself with my *chiffons* and my conquests?"

"Certainly; any other woman would. I know you are to be trusted; you will never let men go too far."

---

1 Trinkets.

"If I dragged your name in the dust throughout Europe you would deserve it," thought his wife; and a bitter retort rose to her lips. But she had been reared in other ways than mere obedience to every impulse of act or speech. She still believed, despite the world about her, that the word she had given in her marriage vow required her forbearance and her subjection to Sergius Zouroff—she was still of the "old fashion."

She controlled her anger and her disdain, and turned her face full on him with something pleading and wistful in the proud eyes that had still the darkness of just scorn.

"You prefer the society of Noisette and Casse-une-Croûte; why do you need mine too? Since they amuse you, and can content you, cannot you let me be free of all this gilded bondage, which is but a shade better than their gilded infamy? You bid me occupy myself with *chiffons* and conquests. I care for neither. Will you give me what I could care for? This feverish frivolous life of the great world has no charm for me. It suits me in nothing; neither in health nor taste, neither in mind nor body. I abhor it. I was reared in other ways, and with other thoughts. It is horrible to me to waste the year from one end to the other on mere display, mere dissipation—to call it amusement is absurd, for it amuses no one. It is a monotony, in its way, as tiresome as any other."

"It is the life we all lead," he interrupted her with some impatience. "There is intrigue enough in it to salt it, God knows!"

"Not for me," said Vere coldly, with an accent that made him feel ashamed. "You do not understand me—I suppose you never will; but, to speak practically, will you let me pass my time on one of your estates; if not here, in Poland, where the people suffer more, and where I might do good? I have more strengths of purpose than you fancy; I would educate the peasant children, and try and make your name beloved and honoured on your lands—not cursed, as it is now. Let me live that sort of life, for half the year at least; let me feel that all the time God gives me is not utterly wasted. I helped many in Paris; I could do more, so much more, here. I would make your people love me; and then, perhaps, peace at last would come to me. I am most unhappy now. You must have known it always, but I think you never cared."

The simplicity of the words, spoken as a child would have spoken them, had an intense pathos in them, uttered as they were by a woman scarcely twenty, who was supposed to have the world at her feet. For one moment they touched the cold heart of Zouroff, as once before at Félicité the uplifted eyes of Vere had touched him at their betrothal, and almost spurred him to renunciation of her and refusal of her sacrifice. And she looked so young, with her hair falling back over her shoulders, and behind her the white crucifix and the stars of the morning skies—and her child had died here at Svir.

For the moment his face softened, and he was moved to a vague remorse and a vague pity; for a moment Noisette and Casse-une-Croûte, and even Jeanne de Sonnaz, looked to him vulgar and common beside his wife; for a moment *les verres épais du cabaret brutal*[1] seemed tainted by the many lips that used them, and this pure golden cup seemed worthy of a god. But the moment passed, and the long habits and humours of a loose and selfish life resumed their sway within him; and he only saw a lovely woman whom he had bought as he bought the others, only with a higher price.

He took the loose gold of her hair in his hands with a sudden caress and drew her into his arms.

"*Pardieu!*" he said with a short laugh. "A very calm proposition for a separation! That is what you drive at, no doubt; a separation in which you should have all the honours as Princess Zouroff still! No, my lovely Vera, I am not disposed to gratify you,—so. You belong to me, and you must continue to belong to me, nilly-willy. You are too handsome to lose, and you should be grateful for your beauty; it made you mistress of Svir. Pshaw! how you shudder! You forget you must pay now and then for your diamonds."

There are many martyrdoms as there are many prostitutions that law legalises and the churches approve.

She never again prayed in her oratory. The ivory Christ had failed to protect her.

All the month long there was the pressure of social obligations upon her, the hot-house atmosphere of a Court about her, for imperial guests followed on those who had left a few days earlier, and there could be no hour of freedom for the mistress of Svir.

Her mother was radiantly content; Count Rostrow was charming; and a Grand Duke found her still a pretty woman; play was high most nights; and the Sicilian was forgotten. All that troubled her was that her daughter never looked at her if she could help it, never spoke to her except on the commonplace courtesies and trifles of the hour. Not that she cared, only she sometimes feared other people might notice it.

---

1 A refrain from the poem by Prudhomme that Corrèze recited at the end of Volume 2, Chapter IX (p. 372).

These days seemed to Vere the very longest in all her life. Her apathy had changed into bitterness, her indifference was growing into despair. She thought, with unutterable scorn, "If the world would only allow it, he would have Casse-une-Croûte here!"

She was nothing more in her husband's eyes than Casse-une-Croûte was.

All the pride of her temper, and all the purity of her nature, rose against him. As she wore his jewels, as she sat at his table, as she received his guests, as she answered to his name, all her soul was in revolt against him; such revolt as to the women of her world seemed the natural instinct of a woman towards her husband, a thing to be indulged in without scruple or stint, but which to her, in whom were all the old faiths and purities of a forgotten creed, seemed a sin.

A sin!—did the world know of such a thing? Hardly. Now and then, for sake of its traditions, the world took some hapless boy, or some still yet unhappier woman, and pilloried one of them, and drove them out under a shower of stones, selecting them by caprice, persecuting them without justice, slaying them because they were friendless. But this was all.

For the most part, sin was an obsolete thing; archaic and unheard of; public prints chronicled the sayings and the doings of Noisette and Casse-une-Croûte; society chirped and babbled merrily of all the filth that satirists scarce dare do more than hint at lest they fall under the law. There was no longer on her eyes the blindness of an innocent unconscious youth. She saw corruption all around her; a corruption so general, so insidious, so lightly judged, so popular, that it was nearly universal; and amidst it the few isolated souls, that it could not taint and claim and absorb, were lost as in a mist, and could not behold each other.

A dull hopelessness weighed upon her. Her husband had counselled her to lose herself in *chiffons* and in conquests!

She knew very well he would not care if she obeyed him; nay, that he would perhaps like her the better. As he had often bade her put red upon her cheeks, so he would have awakened to a quicker esteem of her if he had seen her leaving ballrooms in the light of morning, with the ribbons of the cotillons on her breast, smiling on her lovers above the feathers of her fan, provoking with effrontery the gaze of passion, answering its avowals with smiling reproof that meant forgiveness, and passing gaily through the masque of society with kohl around her eyes, and a jest upon her mouth, and hidden in her bosom or her bouquet some royal lover's note. He would have esteemed her more highly so. Perhaps, then, she might even have stood higher in his eyes than Casse-une-Croûte.

She thought this, as she sat in the evening at his table, with her imperial guests beside her, and, before her eyes, the glow of the gold plate with the Zouroff crown upon it. She was as white as alabaster; her eyes had a sombre indignation in them; she wore her Order of St. Catherine[1] and her necklace of the moth and the star.

"If one did not keep to honour, for honour's sake," she thought, "what would he not make me!—I should be viler than any one of them."

For, as she saw her husband's face above that broad gleam of gold, the longing for one instant came over her, with deadly temptation, to take such vengeance as a wife can always take, and teach him what fruit his own teachings brought, and make him the byword and mock of Europe.

The moment passed.

"He cannot make me vile," she thought. "No one can—save myself."

As her breast heaved quicker with the memory, the ever trembling moth of the medallion rose and touched the star.

"An allegory or a talisman?" said one of the imperial guests who sat on her right hand, looking at the jewel.

"Both, sir," answered Vere.

Later in the evening, when, after seeing a *Proverbe*[2] exquisitely acted, the princes were for the present hour absorbed in the card-room, Madame Nelaguine lingered for a moment by her sister-in-law. Vere had gone for an instant on to the terrace, which overlooked the sea, as did the terrace of Félicité.

"Are you well to-day, my Vera?"

"As well as usual."

"I think Ischl did you little good."

"Ischl? What should Ischl do for me? The Traun is no Lethe."[3]

"Will you never be content, never be resigned?"

---

1 The Order of Saint Catherine was founded by Peter the Great in 1711. It was created to commemorate his wife Catherine after she gave up her jewels to bribe the Turks. The Empress of Russia was the Sovereign Head of the Order. Grand Duchesses, Princesses, and other noble ladies were members of the Order. The insignia of the Order consisted of a star, an investment badge (an oval medallion showing St. Catherine holding an enamel cross and a small diamond cross), and a riband or sash.

2 A comedy illustrating a proverb.

3 The mythological river in Hades whose water causes forgetfulness of the past in those who drink it.

"I think not."

Madame Nelaguine sighed.

She had never been a good woman, nor a true one, in her world; but in her affection for her brother's wife she was sincere.

"Tell me," said Vere abruptly, "tell me—you are his sister, I may say so to you—tell me it does not make a woman's duty less, that her husband forgets his?"

"No, dear—at least—no—I suppose not. No, of course not," said Madame Nelaguine. She had been a very faithless wife herself, but of that Vere knew nothing.

"It does not change one's own obligation to him," said Vere wearily, with a feverish flush coming over her face. "No; that I feel. What one promised, one must abide by; that is quite certain. Whatever he does, one must not make that any excuse to leave him?"

She turned her clear and noble eyes full upon his sister's, and the eyes of Madame Nelaguine shunned the gaze and fell.

"My dear," she said evasively, "no, no; no wife must leave her husband; most certainly not. She must bear everything without avenging any insult; because the world is always ready to condemn the woman—it hardly ever will condemn the man. And a wife, however innocent, however deeply to be pitied, is always in a false position when she quits her husband's house. She is *déclassé* at once. However much other women feel for her, they will seldom receive her. Her place in the world is gone, and when she is young, above all, to break up her married life is social ruin. Pray, pray do not ever think of that. Sergius has grave faults, terrible faults, to you; but do not attempt to redress them yourself. You would only lose caste, lose sympathy, lose rank at once. Pray, pray, do not think of that."

Vere withdrew her hand from her sister-in-law's; a shadow of disappointment came on her face, and then altered to a sad disdain.

"I was not thinking of what I should lose," she said, recovering her tranquillity. "That would not weigh with me for a moment. I was thinking of what is right; of what a wife should be before God."

"You are sublime, my dear," said the Russian princess, a little irritably because her own consciousness of her own past smote her and smarted. "You are sublime. But you are many octaves higher than our concert pitch. No one now ever thinks in the sort of way that you do. You would have been a wife for Milton.[1] My brother is, alas! quite incapable of appreciating all that devotion."

---

1 John Milton's first wife left her husband and went back to live with her
   mother a few days after they were married. She returned to him four
   years later, a submissive wife.

"His power of appreciation is not the measure of my conduct," said Vere, with a contempt that would have been bitter if it had not been so weary.

"That is happy for him," said his sister drily. "But, in sad and sober truth, my Vera, your ideas are too high for the world we live in; you are a saint raising an oriflamme above a holy strife; and we are only a rabble of common maskers—who laugh."

"You can laugh."

"I do not laugh, heaven knows," said her sister-in-law, with a glisten of water in her shrewd, bright eyes, that could not bear the candid gaze of Vere. "I do not laugh. I understand you. If I never could have been like you, I revere you—yes. But it is of no use, my dear, no use, alas! to bring these true and high emotions into common life. They are too exalted; they are fit for higher air. Roughly and coarsely if you will, but truly, I will tell you there is nothing of nobility, nothing of duty, in marriage, as our world sees it; it is simply—a convenience, a somewhat clumsy contrivance to tide over a social difficulty. Do not think of it as anything else; if you do, one day disgust will seize you; your high and holy faiths will snap and break; and then—"

"And then?"

"Then you will be of all women most unhappy; for I think you could not endure your life if you despised yourself."

"I have endured it," said Vere in a low voice. "You think I have not despised myself every day, every night?"

"Not as I mean. The wrong has been done to you. You have done none. All the difference lies there—ah, such a difference, my dear! The difference between the glacier and the mud-torrent!"

Vere was silent. Then, with a shiver, she drew her wraps about her as the cold wind came over the sea.

"Shall we go in the house? It is chilly here," she said to her sister-in-law.

CHAPTER II.

The two shooting-months passed at Svir; brilliantly to all the guests, tediously and bitterly to the mistress of the place. Lady Dolly had early vanished to see the fair of Nijni Novgorod with a pleasant party, and Count Rostrow for their guide; and had vague thoughts of going down the river and seeing the spurs of the Caucasus, and meeting her husband in St. Petersburg, where, so enraptured was she with the country, she almost thought she would persuade him to live. Duc Paul and Duchesse Jeanne had gone on a round of visits to friends in Croatia, Courland, and Styria. Troops of guests in succession had arrived, stayed at, and departed from, the great Zouroff palace on the Baltic; and, when the first snows were falling, Sergius Zouroff travelled back to his villa on the Riviera with no more preparation or hesitation than he would have needed to drive from the Barrière de l'Étoile to the Rue Helder.

"What a waste it all is!" thought his wife, as she looked at the grand front of Svir, its magnificent forests and its exquisite gardens. For ten months out of the year Svir, like Félicité, was like a hundred thousand castles and palaces in Europe; it served only for the maintenance and pleasure of a disorderly and idle troop of hirelings, unjust stewards, and fattening thieves of all sorts.

"What would you do with it if you had your way?" asked Madame Nelaguine.

She answered, "I would live in it; or I would turn it into a Russian St. Cyr."[1]

"Always sublime, my love!" said Madame Nelaguine, with a touch of asperity and ridicule.

The towers of Svir faded from Vere's sight in the blue mists of evening; a few days and nights followed and then the crocketted pinnacles and metal roofs of the Riviera villa greeted her sight against the blue sky and the blue water of the gulf of Saint-Hospice.

"This is accounted the perfection of life," she thought. "To have half a dozen admirably appointed hôtels all your own, and among them all—no home!"

The married life of Vere had now begun to pass into that stage common enough in our day, when the husband and the wife are utter strangers one to another; their only exchange of words being when the presence of others compels it, and their only appearance together being when society necessitates it.

A sort of fear had fallen on Sergius Zouroff of her, and she was thankful to be left in peace. Thousands of men and women live thus in the world; never touch each other's hand, never seek each other's glance, never willingly spend five seconds alone, yet make no scandal and have no rupture, and go out into society together, and carry on the mocking semblance of union till death parts them.

Again and again Vere on her knees in her solitude tried to exam-

---

1 Saint-Cyr was a French national military academy founded in Fontainebleau by Napoleon Bonaparte.

ine the past and see what blame might rest on her for her failure to influence her husband and withhold him from vice, but she could see nothing that she might have done. Even had she been a woman who had loved him she could have done nothing. His feeling for her had been but a mere animal impulse; his habits were engrained in every fibre of his temper. If she had shown him any tenderness, he would have repulsed it with some cynical word; fidelity to his ear was a mere phrase, meaning nothing; honour in his creed was comprised in one thing only, never to shrink before a man. Even if she had been a woman who had cared for him she would have had no power to alter his ways of life. Innocent women seldom have any influence. Jeanne de Sonnaz could always influence Zouroff; Vere never could have done so, let her have essayed what she would. For be the fault where it may in our social system, the wife never has the power or the dominion that has the mistress.

A proud woman, moreover, will not stoop as low as it is necessary to do to seize the reins of tyranny over a fickle or sluggish tempered man; what is not faithful to her of its own will, a proud woman lets go where it may without effort, and with resignation, or with scorn, according as love or indifference move her to the faithless.

The first thing she saw on her table at Villafranca was a letter from her mother.

Lady Dolly had found the Caucasus quite stupidly like the Engadine; she thought St. Petersburg a huge barrack and hideous; the weather was horribly cold, and she was coming back to Paris as quickly as she could. She would just stay a day, passing, at the villa.

"Count Rostrow has not come up to her expectations of him," thought Madame Nelaguine.

Vere said nothing.

If she could have prayed for anything, she would have prayed never to be near her mother. Lady Dolly was a living pain, a living shame, to her, now, even as she had been on that first day when she had stepped on shore from the boat of Corrèze, and seen the figure of her mother in the black and yellow stripes of the bathing-dress out in the full sunshine of Trouville.

But Lady Dolly wanted to forget the slights of Count Rostrow; wanted to play at Monaco; wanted to be seen by her English friends with her daughter; and so Lady Dolly, who never studied any wishes but her own, and never missed a point in the game of self she always played, chose to come, and as she drove up between the laurel and myrtle hedges, and looked at the white walls and green verandas of the villa, rising above the palms, and magnolias, and Indian coniferæ of its grounds, said to herself: "With three such places on three seas, and two such houses in Paris and St. Petersburg as she has, what on earth *can* she want to be happy?"

Honestly, she could not understand it. It seemed to her very strange.

"But she is within a stone's throw of the tables, and she has oceans of money, and yet she never plays," she thought again; and this seemed to her yet more unnatural still.

"She is very odd in all ways," she thought in conclusion, as the carriage brushed the scent out of the bruised arbutus leaves as it passed.

Life for Vere was quieter on the Riviera than elsewhere. There were but few people in the house; these spent nearly the whole of their time at Monte Carlo; and she had many of her own hours free to do with as she chose.

Her husband never asked her to go to Monte Carlo. It was the one phase of the world that he spared her. In himself he felt that he did not care for those grand grave eyes to see him throwing away his gold, and getting drunk with the stupid intoxication of that idiotic passion, with his *belles petites* about him, and the unlovely crowd around. Vere lived within a few miles of the brilliant Hell under the Tête du Chien,[1] but she had never once set foot in it.

The change from the strong air of the Baltic to the hot and languid autumn weather of the south affected her strength; she felt feverish and unwell. She had been reared in the fierce fresh winds of the north, and these rose-scented breezes and fragrant orange alleys seemed to stifle her in "aromatic pain."

"Perhaps I grow fretful and fanciful," she thought, with a sudden alarm and anger at herself. "What use is it for me to blame each place I live in? The malady is in myself. If I could only work, be of use, care for something, I should be well enough. If I could be free—"

She paused with a shiver.

Freedom for her could mean only death for her husband. To the sensitive conscience of Vere it seemed like murder to wish for any liberty or release that could only be purchased at such a cost as that.

Jeanne de Sonnaz could calmly reckon up and compare her chances of loss and gain if her placid Paul should pass from the living world; but Vere could do nothing of the kind. Although Sergius

---

1 The Tête du Chien (literally, head of the dog) is a mountain surrounding Monaco, which provides an overhang on the city.

Zouroff outraged and insulted her in many ways, and was a daily and hourly horror to her, yet she remained loyal to him, even in her thoughts.

"I eat his bread, and wear his clothes, and spend his gold," she thought bitterly. "I owe him at least fidelity such as his servants give in exchange for food and shelter!"

There were times when she was passionately tempted to cast off everything that was his, and go out, alone and unaided, and work for her living, hidden in the obscurity of poverty, but free at least from the horrible incubus of an abhorred union. But the straight and simple rectitude in which she had been reared, the severe rendering of honour and of obligation in which she had been trained, were with her, too strongly engrained to let her be untrue to them.

"I must bide the brent," she told herself, in the old homely words of the Border people; and her delicate face grew colder and prouder every day. The iron was in her soul; the knotted cords were about her waist; but she bore a brave countenance serenely. She could not endure that her world should pity her.

Her world, indeed, never dreamed of doing so. Society does not pity a woman who is a great lady, who is young, and who could have lovers and courtiers by the crowd if only she smiled once.

Society only thought her—unamiable.

True, she never said an unkind thing, or did one; she never hurt man or woman; she was generous to a fault, and, to aid even people she despised, would give herself trouble unending. But these are serious simple qualities that do not show much, and are soon forgotten by those who benefit from them. Had she laughed more, danced more, taken more kindly to the fools and their follies, she might have been acid of tongue and niggard of sympathy: society would have thought her much more amiable than it did now.

Her charities were very large, and they were charities often done in secrecy to those of her own rank, who came to her in the desperation of their own needs, or their sons' or their brothers' debts of honour; but it would have served her in better stead with the world if she had stayed for the cotillons, or if she had laughed heartily when Madame Judic sang.

It would have been so much more natural.

"If she would listen to me!" thought her mother, in the superior wisdom of her popular little life. "If she would only kiss a few women in the morning, and flirt with a few men in the evening, it would set her all right with them in a month. It is no use doing good to anybody, they only hate you for it. You have seen them in their straits; it is like seeing them without their teeth or their wig; they never forgive it. But to be pleasant, always to be pleasant, that is the thing; and, after all, it costs nothing."

But to be pleasant in Lady Dolly's, and the world's, meaning of the words was not possible to Vere—Vere, with an aching heart, an outraged pride, and a barren future; Vere, haughty, grave, and delicate of taste, to whom the whole life she led seemed hardly better or wiser than sitting out the glittering absurdities of the Timbale d'Argent or Niniche.[1]

One warm day in December she had the unusual enjoyment of being alone from noon to night. All in the house were away at Monte Carlo, and Madame Nelaguine had gone for the day to San Remo to see her Empress. It was lovely weather, balmy and full of fragrance, cold enough to make furs needful at nightfall, but without wind, and with a brilliant sun.

Vere wandered about the gardens till she was tired; then, her eyes lighting on her own felucca moored with other pleasure-boats at the foot of the garden-quay, she looked over the blue tranquil sea, went down the stairs, and pushed the little vessel off from shore. She had never lost her childish skill at boating and sailing. She set the little sail, tied the tiller-rope to her foot, and, with one oar, sent herself quickly and lightly through the still water. There was nothing in sight; the shore was as deserted as the sea. It was only one o'clock. The orange-groves and pine woods shed their sweet smell for miles over the sea. She ceased to row, and let the boat drift with the slight movement of the buoyant air.

She was glad to be alone—absolutely alone; away from all the trifling interruptions which are to some natures as mosquitoes to the flesh.

She passed a fishing-felucca, and asked the fisherman in it if the weather would hold; he told her it would be fine like that till the new year. She let the boat go on. The orangeries and pine woods receded farther and farther, the turrets of the villa grew smaller and smaller in the distance.

Air and sea, space and solitude, were delightful to her. Almost for the moment, going through that sparkling water, she realised her youth, and felt that twenty years were still not on her head. As she

1 Anna Judic secured her popularity in *La Timbale d'Argent* (1872), a comic opera by Léon Vasseur (1844-1917). She also caused a sensation in the vaudeville play, *Niniche* (1878), when she appeared on the stage in a bathing suit.

lay back in the little vessel, her shoulders resting on its silken cushions, the oar being idle, her eyes gazing wistfully into the depths of
the azure sky, she did not see a canoe that, lying off the shore when
she had taken the water, had followed her at a little distance.

Suddenly, with a quick, arrow-like dart, it covered the space
dividing it from her; and came alongside of her boat.

"Princesse," said the voice of Corrèze, "the sea is kind to me,
whether it be in north or south. But are you quite wise to be so far
out on it all alone?"

He saw the face, that never changed for all the praise of princes
or the homage of courts, and always was so cold, grow warm and
lighten with surprise and welcome, wonder in the great grave eyes,
a smile on the proud mouth.

"You!" she said simply.

He had had much flattery and much honour in his life, but nothing that had ever seemed to him so sweet, so great, as that one word,
and the accent of it.

"I!" he said simply too, without compliment. "I am a stormy
petrel,[1] you know; never at rest. I could not help hovering near your
lonely sail in case of any sudden change of weather. These waters are
very treacherous."

"Are they?" said Vere without thinking. She grew confused; she
thought of the Wolfinea, of the Kermesse, of her husband's invitation
to Svir, of his last words in the Spitalkirche; of many things all at
once; and the gladness with which she saw him startled her—it
seemed so strange to be so glad at anything!

"The fisherman says this weather will last till the new year," she
said, feeling that her voice was not quite steady.

Corrèze had one hand on the side of her boat.

"The fisherman should know better than I, certainly," he
answered. "But they are over-sanguine sometimes; and there is a
white look in the south that I do not like, as if Africa were sending
us some squall. If I might venture to advise you, I would say turn
your helm homeward. You are very far off shore."

"You are as far."

"I followed you."

Vere was silent; she spent the next few moments in tacking and
bringing the head of her little vessel landward once more.

"I thank you," said Corrèze, as she obeyed him.

---

1 A sea bird.

She did not ask him why.

"There is no tide, the clever people tell us, in the Mediterranean," he continued. "But there is something that feels very unpleasantly like it sometimes, when a boat wants to go against the wind. You see a breeze has sprung up; that white cloud yonder will be black before very long."

"Are we really very far from the land?"

"A mile or two. It will take some stiff rowing to get there."

"But the sun is so bright—"

"Ah yes. I have seen the sun brilliant one moment, and the next the white squall was down in a fury of whirling mist and darkened air. Take your second oar."

The wind began to stir, as he had foreseen, the white in the south grew leaden-coloured, the swell in the sea grew heavy. Vere took in her sail, and the resistance of the water to the oars grew strong for her hands.

"With your permission," said Corrèze; and he balanced himself on his canoe, tied its prow to the stern of her boat, and leapt lightly into her little vessel.

"If it get rougher, that might have become harder to do," he said apologetically; "and, in the sea that we shall soon have, you will be unable to both steer and row. Will you allow me to take your oars?"

She gave them to him in silence, and took the tiller ropes into her hands.

She saw that he was right.

An angry wind had risen, shrill and chill. The foam of the tideless sea was blowing around them like white powder scattered by a great fan. There was a raw, hard feeling in the air, a moment before so sunny and laden only with the scent of orange and pinewood. The sky was overcast, and some sea-birds were screaming.

Neither he nor she spoke; he bent with a will to his oars, she steered straight for the shore. The wind chopped and changed, and came now from the west and now from the mountains—either way it was against them.

He had taken a waterproof from his canoe and put it about her. "Never trust the sun when you come seaward," he said with a smile. Without it, she would have been wet through from the spray, for her gown was only of ivory-white cashmere, and ill-fitted for rough weather.

Corrèze rowed on in silence, pulling hard against the heavy water.

Both thought of the morning on the sea in Calvados; and the memory was too present to both for either to speak of it.

"There is no real danger," he said once, as the boat was swept by the rush of white water.

"I am not afraid; do you think I am?" said Vere with a momentary smile.

"No, I do not. Fear is not in your temper," said Corrèze. "But most other women would be; the sea will soon stand up like a stone wall between us and the land."

"Yes?" said Vere absently; she was thinking very little of the sea; then she added, with a sudden recollection, and a pang of self-reproach, "I was very imprudent; I am sorry; it is I who have brought you into this danger—for danger I think there must be."

"Oh! as for that—" said Corrèze, and he laughed lightly. In his heart he thought, "To die with you—how sweet it would be! How right were the old poets!"

Peril, to a degree, there was, because it became very probable that the cockle-shell of a pleasure-boat might heel over in the wind and swell, and they might have to swim for their lives; and they were still a long way off the land. But neither of them thought much of it. He was only conscious that she was near him, and she was wondering why such deep peace, such sweet safety, always seemed to fall on her in his presence.

The sea rose, as he had said, and looked like a grey wall between them and the coast. Mists and blowing surf obscured the outlines of the land; but she held the head of the boat straight against the battling waves, and he rowed with the skill that he had learned of Venetians and Basque sea-folk in sudden storms; and, slowly but safely, at the last they made their way through the fog of foam, and whirling currents of variously driving winds, and brought the little vessel with the canoe rocking behind it, up on to the landing-stairs that she had left in the full flood of sunshine two hours before. There was no rain, but the sky was very dark, and the spray was being driven hither and thither in showers.

"Are you wet at all, Princesse?" he asked as they landed.

She turned on the steps and held out her hand.

"You have saved my life," she said in a low voice. He bowed low over her hand, but did not touch it with his lips.

"I am happy," he said briefly.

There was a crowd of servants and out-door men above on the head of the little garden-quay, Loris leaping and shouting in their midst, for all the household had discovered its mistress's absence and the absence of the boat, and had been greatly alarmed; for if her world disliked her, her servants adored her, even while they were a little afraid of her.

"She is like no one else; she is a saint," said the old Russian steward very often. "But if she be ever in wrath with you—ah, then it is as if St. Dorothea struck you with her roses and broke your back!"[1]

Even as they landed the clouds burst, the rain began to fall in torrents, the sea leaped madly against the sea-wall of the gardens.

"You will come in and wait at least till the storm passes?" she said to Corrèze. He hesitated.

"Into Prince Zouroff's house!" he said aloud, with a shadow on his face.

"Into my house," she said with a shade of rebuke in her tone.

"You are too good, madame; but, if you will permit me, I will seem ungrateful and leave you."

The servants were standing around on the strip of variegated marble pavement that separated the sea-wall from the house. He only uttered such words as they might hear.

Vere looked at him with a wistful look in the haughty eyes that he would not see.

"You have saved my life," she said again in a soft hushed voice.

"Nay, nay," said Corrèze, "you have too many angels surely ever about your steps to need a sorry mortal! Princesse—adieu."

"But you are staying near here?"

"A few days—a few hours. I am en route[2] from Milan to Paris. I like Paris best when I am not on an Alp. Life should be tout ou rien.[3] Either the boulevard or the hermitage."

He did not tell her that he had come by the Riviera for sake of seeing the turrets of her home above the sea, for sake of the chance of beholding her walk by him in the sun upon the terrace above.

"Will you not wait and see—my husband?" she said a little abruptly, with a certain effort.

---

1 Saint Dorothea was a virgin and martyr who suffered during the persecution of Diocletian, A.D. 311. She was brought before the prefect and was tried, tortured, and sentenced to death. On her way to her execution, a pagan lawyer taunted her: "Bride of Christ, send me some fruits from your bridegroom's garden." Before she was executed, she sent him her headdress which was filled with the heavenly fragrance of roses and fruits. The lawyer at once confessed himself a Christian and he was put on the rack and killed.

2 On the way.

3 All or nothing.

"I have not the honour to know Prince Zouroff."

"He will wish to thank you—" the words seemed to choke her; she could not finish them.

Corrèze bowed with his charming grace.

"Princesse! When shall I persuade you that I have done nothing for which to be thanked! If I may venture to remind you of so prosaic a thing, your dress must be damp, and mine is wet through. I beseech you to change yours at once."

"Ah! how thoughtless I am! But if you will not come in, will you accept a carriage or a horse?"

"Thanks, no; a quick walk will do me far more good. If you will give the canoe shelter I shall be very indebted; but for myself the shore in this wind is what will please me most. It will make me think of the old *tourmentes*[1] of my home mountains. Princesse, once more—adieu."

She gave him her hand; he bent over it; a mist came before her eyes that was not from the driving of the sea spray. When it cleared from her eyelids, Corrèze was gone.

"If I had entered the house with her I could not have answered for my silence. It was best to come away whilst I could," he thought, as he went on along the Corniche, with the winds and the rains beating him back at each step, and, below him and beyond, the sea mass of white and grey steam and froth.

When Prince Zouroff returned from Monte Carlo, he brought several guests with him to dinner. He had won largely, as very rich men often do; he was in a good humour because he had been well amused; and he had been driven home by his orders at so terrific a pace in the storm that one horse had dropped dead when it reached the stables. But this was not a very uncommon occurrence with him; a carriage-horse did not matter; if it had been one of his racers it would have been a different business. That was all he said about it.

Vere went up to him after dinner and took him aside one moment.

"I was on the sea in the beginning of the storm."

"What were you doing?"

"Rowing myself—all alone."

"A mad freak! But nothing happened. All is well that ends well."

"Yes." Vere's teeth were shut a little as she spoke, and her lips were pale. "It might not have ended so well—if it be well to live—had it

---

1 Storms.

not been for M. de Corrèze. He was in a canoe and warned me in time."

"The singer?"

"M. de Corrèze."

"Well, there is only one; you mean the singer? How came he near you?"

"I do not know."

"And what did he do?"

"He saved my life."

Sergius Zouroff looked wearied.

"You are always so emotional, *ma chère*. Do you mean he did anything I ought to acknowledge? Where is he to be found?"

"I do not know."

"Oh, I can hear at the Cercle.[1] But are you not talking in hyperboles?"

"I told you the fact. I thought you ought to know it."

"Ah, yes," said her husband, who was thinking of other things. "But he did not come to sing at Svir. I cannot forgive that. However, I will send him my card, and then you can ask him to dinner. Or send him a diamond ring—artists always like rings."

Vere turned away.

"I remember hearing once," said Lady Dorothy, approaching him, "that Corrèze had one thousand three hundred and seventy-six diamond rings, all given him by an adoring universe. You must think of something more original, Sergius."

"Ask him to dinner," said Prince Zouroff. "People do; though it is very absurd."

Then he went to the card-room for *écarté*, thinking no more of his wife than he thought of his dead horse.

"Corrèze and the sea seem quite inseparable—quite like Leander,"[2] said Lady Dolly, who had heard the whole story before dinner from her maid, when she too had returned from Monte Carlo. But she said it half under her breath, and did not dare speak of it to her daughter; she was haunted by the memory of the letter she had received from Moscow, the letter of Corrèze that she had burned and left unanswered.

"It is odd he should have been in that canoe just to-day, when we

---

1   Club.

2   Leander is a mythological Greek youth who swam the Hellespont every night to visit his lover Hero until he drowned in a storm.

were all away," she thought with the penetration of a woman who knew her world, and did not believe in accidents, as she had once said to her child. "And to say she does not know where he is—that is really too ridiculous. I am quite sure Vere never will do anything—anything—to make people talk, but I should not be in the least surprised if she were to insist on something obstinate and romantic about this man. She is so very emotional. Zouroff is right, she is always in the clouds. That comes of being brought up on those moors by that German, and Corrèze is precisely the person to answer these fancies—even in daylight at a concert he is so handsome, and even in dinner-dress he always looks like Romeo. It would really be too funny if she ever did get talked about—so cold, and so reserved, and so quite too dreadfully and awfully *good* as she is!"

And Lady Dolly looked down the drawing-rooms at her daughter in the distance, as Vere drew her white robes slowly through her salons; and she thought, after all, one never knew—

The next day Zouroff's secretary sent his master's card to the hotel where he learned that Corrèze was staying, and sent also an invitation to dinner at an early date. Corrèze sent his card in return, and a refusal of the invitation, based on the plea that he was leaving Nice.

When he had written his refusal, Corrèze walked out into the street. He met point-blank a victoria with very gaudy liveries, and, in the victoria, muffled in sables, sat a dark-skinned, ruby-lipped woman.

The brilliant and insouciant face of Corrèze grew dark, and he frowned.

The woman was Casse-une-Croûte.

"The brute," he muttered. "If I sat at his table I should be choked—or I should choke him."

As he went on he heard the gay people in the street laughing, and saw them look after the gaudy liveries and the quadroon.

"His wife is much more beautiful, and as white as a lily," one man said. "That black thing throws glasses and knives at him sometimes, they say."

"I protected her from Noisette. I cannot protect her here," thought Corrèze. "Perhaps she will not know it; God send her ignorance."

The talk of Nice was Casse-une-Croûte, who had arrived but a week or so before. She had a villa in the town, she had her carriage and horses from Paris, she spent about sixty napoléons a day, without counting what she lost at Monte Carlo; the city preferred her to any

English peeress or German princess of them all. When the correspondents of journals of society sent their budgets from Nice and Monaco, they spoke first of all of Casse-une-Croûte—the Princess Zouroff came far afterwards with other great ladies in their chronicles.

When Casse-une-Croûte after supper set fire to Prince Zouroff's beard, and shot away her chandelier with a saloon pistol, her feats were admiringly recorded in type. Vere did not read those papers, so she knew nothing; and the ignorance Corrèze prayed for her remained with her; she did not even know that Casse-une-Croûte was near her.

A little later in that day Corrèze met Lady Dolly at Monte Carlo. She greeted him with effusion; he was courteous, but a little cold. She felt it, but she would not notice it.

"So you saved my Vere's life yesterday, Corrèze?" she said with charming cordiality. "So like you! Always in some *beau rôle!*"[1]

"It would be a *beau rôle*, indeed, to have saved the Princess Zouroff from any danger; but it is not for me. I warned her of the change in the weather; that was all."

"You are too modest. True courage always is. I think you rowed her boat home for her, didn't you?"

"Part of the way—yes. The sea was heavy."

"She quite *thinks* you saved her life," said Lady Dolly. "My sweet Vera is always a little *exaltée*,[2] you know; you can see that if you look at her. One always rather expects to hear her speak in blank verse; don't you know what I mean?"

"Madame, I have heard so much blank verse in my life that I should as soon expect frogs to drop from her lips," answered Corrèze a little irritably. "No; I do not think I know what you mean, the Princess Vera seems to me to play a very difficult part in the world's play with an exquisite serenity, patience, and good taste."

"A difficult part! Goodness! My dear Corrèze, she has only to look beautiful, go to courts, and spend money!"

"And forgive infidelity, and bear with outrage."

His voice was low, but it was grave and even stern, as his face was.

Lady Dolly, who was going up towards the great Palace of Play, stopped, stared, and put up a scarlet sunshade, which made her look as if she blushed.

"My dear Corrèze! I suppose people of genius are privileged, but

---

1 Noble role; heroic part.
2 Over-imaginative; excitable.

otherwise—really—you have said such an extraordinary thing I ought not to answer you. The idea of judging between married people! The idea of supposing that Prince Zouroff is not everything he ought to be to his wife—"

Corrèze turned his clear lustrous eyes full on her.

"Miladi," he said curtly, "I wrote you some truths of Prince Zouroff from Moscow long ago. Did you read them?"

"Oh—stories! mere stories!" said Lady Dolly vaguely and nervously, "you know I never listen to rumours; people are so horridly uncharitable."

"You had my letter from Moscow then?"

"Oh yes, and answered it," said Lady Dolly with *aplomb*.[1] "I think you forgot to answer it," said Corrèze quietly; "your answer was a *faire part*[2] to the marriage."

"I am sure I answered it," said Lady Dolly once more, looking up into the scarlet dome of her umbrella.

"I told you and proved to you that the man to whom you wished to sacrifice your child was a mass of vice; of such vice as it is the fashion to pretend to believe shut up between the pages of Suetonius and Livy.[3] And I offered, if you would give me your young daughter, to settle a million of francs upon her and leave the stage for her sake. Your answer was the *faire part* of the Zouroff marriage."

"I answered you," said Lady Dolly obstinately, "oh dear yes, I did. I can't help it if you didn't get it; and I had told you at Trouville it was no use, that idea of yours; you never were meant to marry—so absurd!—you are far too charming; and, besides, you know you *are* an artist; you can't say you are not."

"I am an artist," said Corrèze, with a flash sombre and brilliant in his eyes that she could not front, "but I have never been a beast, and had I wedded your daughter I would not have been an adulterer."

"Hus-s-sh!" said Lady Dolly, scandalised. Such language was ter-

---

1 Self possession.

2 Announcement.

3 Suetonius (A.D. 69–c. 140) wrote about the lives of the first Roman emperors and their families. He focused on scandalous events and on the immoral and pleasure-seeking lifestyles of the aristocrats. Titus Livy (59 B.C.-A.D. 17) wrote a history of Rome and included legend and epic drama. He wanted his work to be heroic enough for the greatest empire on Earth at the time. Ouida may have confused Livy with Tacitus, who like Suetonius, exposed vice and scandal.

rible to her, though she did laugh at the Petit Duc[1] and Niniche. "Hus-s-sh, hush—*pray!*"

But Corrèze had bowed and had left her.

Lady Dolly went on between the cactus and the palms and the myrtles looking dreamily up into the scarlet glow of her sunshade, and thinking that when you let artists and people of that sort into your world they were quite certain to *froisser*[2] you sooner or later. "And I am sure he is in love with her still," she thought as she joined some pleasant people and went up to the great building to hear the music, only for that; the music at Monte Carlo is always so good.

"As if I would ever have given my child to a singer!" she thought in the disgust of mingled virtue and pride.

At the entrance of the hall she met her son-in-law, who was coming out, having won largely.

"I forgot my purse, Sergius; lend me the sinews of war," said Lady Dolly with a laugh.

He handed her some *rouleaux*.[3]

"Some one would plunder me before I got through the gardens," he said to himself as he sauntered on, "it may as well be Dolly as another."

Lady Dolly went on and staked her gold. At the same table with her were Aimée Pincée[4] of the Hippodrome,[5] and Casse-une-Croûte; but Lady Dolly was not hurt by that either in pride or virtue.

The real Commune is Monte Carlo.[6]

Meanwhile Corrèze did not approach Vere.

"If you ever need a servant or an avenger call me," he had said to her, but he had known that she never would call him. From afar off he had kept watch on her life, but that was all.

She knew that he was near her, and the knowledge changed the current of her days from a joyless routine to a sweet yet bitter unrest. When the sun rose she thought, "shall I see him?" When it set she

---

1 Le Petit Duc (1878) was an operetta by Charles Lecocq (1832-1914).
2 Clash with.
3 Rolls (probably with roulette chips).
4 Literally the name means Beloved Pinched.
5 Arena for equestrian and other spectacles. One of Louis-Napoleon's mistresses was a circus rider.
6 Note Ouida's irony. The Commune of Paris was an insurrection against the French government in 1871. It has been considered both as an expression of Parisian republicanism and patriotism and as the first organized uprising of the proletariat against capitalism.

thought, "will he come to-morrow?" The expectation gave a flush of colour and hope to her life which with all its outward magnificence was chill and pale as the life of a pauper because its youth was crushed under the burden of a loveless splendour.

For the first time this warm winter of the southern seaboard, with its languid air, its dancing sunbeams, its odours of roses and violets and orange-buds seemed lovely to her. She did not reason; she did not reflect; she only vaguely felt that the earth had grown beautiful.

Once while the air was still dark with the shadows of night, but the sky had the red of the dawn, she, lying wide awake upon her bed, heard a voice upon the sea beneath her windows singing the *stella virgine, madre pescatore!*[1] of the Italian fisherman, and knew that the voice was his.

At that hour Sergius Zouroff was drinking brandy in the rooms of Casse-une-Croûte, while the quadroon was shooting the glass drops off her chandelier.

One day she went to see the village priest about some poor of the place, and sought him at the church of the parish. It was a little whitewashed barn, no more, but it had thickets of roses about it and a belt of striped aloes, and two tall palms rose straight above it, and beyond its narrow door there shone the sea. She went toward the little sacristy to speak to the priest. Madame Nelaguine was with her. They met Corrèze on the threshold. Mass was just over. It was the day of St. Lucy.[2]

"Have you been to mass at our church and do not visit us?" cried Princess Nadine in reproach as she saw him; "that is not kind, monsieur, especially when we have so much for which to thank you; my brother would be very glad of an occasion to speak his gratitude."

"Prince Zouroff owes me none, madame," said Corrèze. Vere had been silent. "Is the little church yours?" he continued. "It is charming. It is almost as primitive as St. Augustine or St. Jerome[3] could wish it to be, and it is full of the smell of the sea and the scent of the roses.

"It is the church of our parish," said Madame Nelaguine; "we have our own chapel in the villa for our own priest, of course. Were you not coming to us? No? You are too *farouche*. Even to persons of

---

1 Virgin star, fishing mother. This suggests the Virgin Mary, who gave birth to Jesus, the fisher of souls. The star is probably the north star, which sets navigation and acts as a guide and savior for fishermen.

2 13 December.

3 Both St. Augustine (354-430) and St. Jerome (347-420) lived austerely.

your fame one cannot allow such willful isolation; and why come to this very gay seaboard if you want to be alone?"

"I came by way of going to Paris from Milano; indeed, in Paris I must be in a very few days; I have to see half a score of directors there. Which of the three seas that you honour with residence do you prefer, mesdames?"

"Why does Vere not speak to him, and why does he not look at her?" thought the Princess Nelaguine, as she answered aloud:

"Myself, I infinitely prefer the Mediterranean, but Vere persists in preferring the narrow colourless strip of the northern channel; it is not like her usual good taste."

"The climate of Calvados is most like that which the Princess knew in her childhood," Corrèze said with a little haste; "childhood goes with us like an echo always, a refrain to the ballad of our life. One always wants one's cradle-air. Were I to meet with such an accident as Roger did I would go to a goat-hut on my own Alps above Sion."

"You would? how charming that would be for the goats and their sennerins!" said Madame Nelaguine as she caught a glimpse of the priest's black *soutane*[1] behind the roses and chased it through the hedge of aloes and caught the good man, who was very shy of this keen, quick, sardonic Russian lady.

"You might have been dead in those seas the other day—for me," said Vere, in a low voice without looking at him as they stood alone.

"Ah! nothing so beautiful is in store for me, Princesse," he answered lightly; "indeed, you overrate my services; without me no doubt you would have brought your boat in very well; you are an accomplished sailor."

"I should have stayed out without noticing the storm," said Vere, "and then—Loris would have been sorry, perhaps."

Corrèze was silent.

He would not let his tongue utter the answer that rose to his lips.

"We are too afraid of death," he said; "that fear is the shame of Christianity."

"I do not fear it," said Vere in a low tone; her eyes gazed through the screen of roses to the sea.

"And you have not twenty years on your head yet!" said Corrèze bitterly, "and life should be to you one cloudless spring morning only full of blossom and of promise—"

---

1 Cassock.

"I have what I deserve, no doubt."

"You have nothing that you deserve."

Madame Nelaguine came back to them with the priest.

"Why did you not come to Svir?" she asked of Corrèze, as the curate made his obeisance to Vere.

"I had not the honour to know your brother."

"No; but I believe—"

"He offered to pay me? Oh yes. He was *dans son droit*[1] in doing that; but I too had my rights, and amongst them was the right to refuse, and I took it. No doubt he did not know that I never take payments out of the opera-house."

"I see! you are cruelly proud."

"Am I proud? Perhaps, I have my own idea of dignity, a 'poor thing, but my own.' When I go into society I like to be free, and so I do not take money from it. Many greater artists than I, no doubt, have thought differently. But it is my fancy."

"But other artists have not been Marquises de Corrèze," said Madame Nelaguine.

"Nay, I have no title, Madame," said Corrèze; "it was buried in another generation under the snows above Sion, and I have never dug it up; why should I?"

"Why should you, indeed? There is but one Corrèze, there are four thousand marquises to jostle each other in their struggles for precedence."

He laughed a little as he bowed to her. "Yes, I am Corrèze *tout court*;[2] I like to think that one word tells its own tale all over the world to the nations. No doubt this is only another shape of vanity, and not dignity at all. One never knows oneself. I do not care to set up my old *couronne*,[3] it would be out of place in the theatres. But I like to think that I have it, and if ever I need to cross swords with a noble, he cannot refuse on the score of my birth."

His face grew darker as he spoke, he pulled the roses from one another with an impatient action; the quick marmoset eyes of Madame Nelaguine saw that he was thinking of some personal foe.

"I suppose you have had duels before now?" she said indifferently.

"No," answered Corrèze. "No man ever insulted me yet, and I think no man ever will. I do not like brawling; it is a sort of weakness with my fraternity, who are an irritable genus. I have always

---

1 Within his right.
2 Simply.
3 Crown.

contrived to live in amity. But—there are offences for which there is no punishment except the old one of blood."

He was thinking of what he had seen that night; Sergius Zouroff against the shoulder of Casse-une-Croûte playing at the roulette table whilst his wife was left alone. Madame Nelaguine looked at him narrowly; Vere was standing a little apart listening to the good priest's rambling words.

"M. le Marquis," she said with a little smile, "you are very well known to be the gentlest and sunniest of mortals, as well as the sweetest singer that ever lived. But—do you know—I think you could be very terrible if you were very angry. I think it is quite as well that you do not fight duels."

"I may fight them yet," said Corrèze, "and do not give me that title, madame, or I shall think you laugh at me. I am only Corrèze!"

"Only! 'I am Arthur, said the King!'[1] Will you not be merciful in your greatness—and come and sing to us as a friend here, though you would not come as a guest to Svir?"

Corrèze was silent.

"Do come to-night, you would make me so proud; we have a few people," urged the Princess Nadine; "and you know," she added, "that to me your art is a religion."

"You make it difficult indeed to refuse," said Corrèze, "but I have not the honour to know Prince Zouroff."

"With what an accent he says that honour!" thought the sister of Zouroff, but she said aloud: "That is my brother's misfortune, not his fault. Vere, ask this *Roi Soleil* to shine on our house? He is obstinate to me. Perhaps he will not be so to you."

Vere did not lift her eyes, her face flushed a little as she turned towards him.

"We should be happy if you would break your rule—for us."

She spoke with effort; she could not forget what he had said on his knees before her in the little church at Old Aussee. Corrèze bowed.

"I will come for an hour, *mes princesses*, and I will sing for you both."

Then he made his adieu and went away.

Vere and her sister-in-law returned to the house. Madame Nelaguine was usually grave.

---

1 Legendary British king (with only one name) who appears in a cycle of medieval romances. He is the founder of the Round Table.

When they went home, they found the newspapers of the day; the lightest and wittiest of them contained a florid account of the rescue from a sea-storm of a Russian Princess by Corrèze. Without a name the Russian Princess was so described, that all her world could know beyond doubt who it was.

"Really position is a pillory nowadays," said Madame Nelaguine angrily; "sometimes they pelt one with rose-leaves, and sometimes with rotten eggs, but one is for ever in the pillory!"

When Sergius Zouroff read it he was very enraged.

"Patience!" said his sister drily, when his wife was out of hearing. "In to-morrow's number I daresay they will describe you and the quadroon."

Then she added, "Corrèze will come here this evening; he will come to sing for me; you must not offer him anything, not even a ring, or you will insult him."

"Pshaw!" said Zouroff roughly. "Why do you not get others to sing for you whom you can pay properly like artists? There are many."

"Many singers like Corrèze? I am afraid not. But I induced him to come, not only for his singing, but because when he has saved your wife's life, it is as well you should look thankful, even if you do not feel so."

"You grow as romantic as she is, in your old age, Nadine," said Zouroff, with a shrug of his shoulders.

"In old age, perhaps, one appreciates many things that one over-looks in one's youth," said the Princess unruffled, and with a little sigh. "Twenty years ago I should not have appreciated your wife per-haps much more than—you do."

"Do you find her amusing?" he said with a little laugh and a yawn.

Later that day Vere drove out alone. Madame Nelaguine was oth-erwise occupied and her mother was away spending a day or two with a friend who had a villa at La Condamine. She had never once driven down the Promenade des Anglais since she had been on the Riviera this year, but this day her coachman took his way along that famous road because the house to which she was going, a house taken by Vladimir Zouroff, and at which his wife, a pretty Galician woman, lay ill, could not so quickly or so easily be reached any other way. She drove alone, her only companion Loris stretched on the opposite cushions, beside a basket of violets and white lilacs which she was taking to Sophie Zouroff. The afternoon was brilliant; the snow-white palaces, the green gardens, and the azure sea sparkled in the sunlight; the black Orloffs flew over the ground tossing their silver head-pieces and flashing their fiery eyes; people looked after them and told one another "That is the Princess Vera: look, that is the great Russian's wife."

Vere leaning back with Loris at her feet, had a white covering of polar bear-skins cast over her; she had on her the black sables which had been in her marriage *corbeille*; the black and white in their strong contrast enhanced and heightened the beauty of her face and the fairness of her hair; she held on her lap a great cluster of lilies of the valley.

"That beautiful pale woman is Prince Zouroff's wife; he must have strange taste to leave her for a negress," said one man to another, as she passed.

There were many carriages out that day as usual before sunset; the black Russian horses dashed through the crowd at their usual headlong gallop, tossing their undocked manes and tails in restless pride. Close against them passed two bays at full trot; the bays were in a victoria;[1] in the victoria was a woman, swarthy and lustrous-eyed, who wore a Russian kaftan, and had black Russian sables thrown about her shoulders; she was smoking; she blew some smoke in the air and grinned from ear to ear as she went past the Zouroff carriage; in her own carriage, lying back in it, was Sergius Zouroff.

A slight flush, that went over Vere's face to her temples and then faded to leave her white as new fallen snow, was the only sign she gave that she had recognised her husband with the quadroon who was called Casse-une-Croûte. Another moment, and the black Orloffs, flying onward in a cloud of dust and flood of sunlight, had left the bays behind them. Vere bent her face over the lilies of the valley.

Half a mile further she checked their flight, and told the coachman to return home by another road instead of going onward to Sophie Zouroff's.

When she reached the villa it was twilight—the short twilight of a winter day on the Mediterranean. She went up to her bed-chamber, took off her sables, and with her own hands wrapped them altogether, rang for her maid, and gave the furs to her.

"When the Prince comes in take these to him," she said, in a calm voice; "tell him I have no farther use for them; he may have some."

---

1 Four-wheeled carriage with seats for two passengers and a perch in the front for the driver.

The woman, who was faithful to her, and knew much of the patience with which she bore her life, looked grave as she took them; she guessed what had happened.

It was six o'clock.

The Princess Nadine came for a cup of yellow tea in Vere's dressing-room. She found her gentle and serious as usual; as usual a good listener to the babble of pleasant cynicism and philosophic commentaries with which Madame Nelaguine always was ready to garnish and enliven the news of the hour.

Madame Nelaguine did not notice anything amiss.

An hour later, when Zouroff came home to dress for dinner, the waiting-woman, who loved her mistress and was very loyal to her, took him the sables and the message.

He stared, but said nothing. He understood.

The Prince of Monaco and other princes dined at the Zouroff villa that evening. There was a dinner party of forty people in all. He did not see his wife until the dinner hour. Vere was pale with the extreme pallor that had come on her face at sight of the quadroon; she wore white velvet and had a knot of white lilac at her breast, and her only ornaments were some great pearls given her by the Herberts on her marriage.

He stooped towards her a moment under pretext of raising a handkerchief she had dropped.

"Madame," he said in a harsh whisper, "I do not like *coups de théâtre*,[1] and with my actions you have nothing to do. You will wear your sables and drive on the Promenade des Anglais to-morrow. Do you hear?" he added, as she remained silent. Then she looked at him.

"I hear; but I shall not do it."

"You will not do it?"

"No."

Their guests entered. Vere received them with her usual cold and harmonious grace.

"Really she is a grand creature," thought Zouroff, with unwilling respect, "but I will break her will; I never thought she had any until this year; now she is as stubborn as a mule."

The long dinner went on its course, and was followed by an animated evening. Madame Nelaguine had always made the Zouroff entertainments more brilliant than most, from their surprises, their vivacity, and their *entrain*,[2] and this was no exception to the rest.

---

1 Dramatic turn of events.

2 Animation.

That Prince Zouroff himself was gloomy made no cause for remark; he never put any curb on his temper either for society or in private life, and the world was used to his fits of moroseness. "The Tsar sulks" his sister would always say, with a laugh, of him; and so covered his ill-humour with a jest. This night she did not jest: her fine instincts told her that there was a storm in the air.

About eleven o'clock everyone was in the white drawing-room, called so because it was hung with white silk, and had white china mirrors and chandeliers. Two clever musicians, violinist and pianist, had executed some pieces of Liszt[1] and Schumann; they were gone, and two actors from the Folies Dramatiques had glided in as Louis treize personages, played a witty little *revue*, written for the society of the hour, and had in turn vanished. Throughout the long white room—in which the only colour allowed came from banks and pyramids of rose-hued azaleas—there was on every side arising that animated babel of polite tongues which tells a hostess that her people are well amused with her and with themselves, and that the spectre of ennui is scornfully exorcised.

Suddenly the door opened, and the servants announced Corrèze.

"*Quel bonheur!*"[2] cried Madame Nelaguine; and muttered to her brother, "Say something cordial and graceful, Sergius; you can when you like."

Corrèze was bending before the mistress of the house; for the first time he saw the moth and the star at her throat.

"Present me to M. de Corrèze, Vera," said her husband, and she did so.

"I owe you much, and I am happy to be able in my own house to beg you to believe in my gratitude, and to command it when you will," said Zouroff, with courtesy and the admirable manner which he could assume with suavity and dignity when he chose.

"I was more weatherwise than a fisherman, monsieur; that is all the credit I can claim," said Corrèze, lightly and coldly: everyone had ceased their conversation, men had lost their interest in women's eyes, the princes present grew eager, and were thrown into the shade. Corrèze had come. Corrèze, with the light on his poetic face, his grace of attitude, his sweet, far-reaching voice, his past of conquest, his present of victory, his halo of fame, his sorcery of indifference.

---

1   Franz Liszt (1811-86) was a Hungarian composer and pianist. For Schumann see p. 125, note 2.
2   What good fortune!

Corrèze stood by the side of his hostess, and there was a gleam of challenge in his eyes, usually so dreamy, this night so luminous; he was just as pale as she.

"I came to sing some songs to mesdames, your sister, and your wife," said Corrèze, a little abruptly to Zouroff. "Is that your piano? You will permit me?"

He moved to it quickly.

"He knows why he is asked to come," thought Zouroff, "but he speaks oddly; one would think he were the prince and I the artist!"

"He is a rarer sort of prince than you," murmured Madame Nelaguine, who guessed his thoughts. "Do not touch him rudely, or the nightingale will take wing."

Corrèze struck one loud chord on the notes, and through the long white room there came a perfect silence.

Not thrice in twelve months was he ever heard out of his own opera-houses.

He paused with his hands on the keys; he looked down the drawing-room, all he saw of all that was around him were a sea of light, a bloom of rose-red flowers, a woman's figure in white velvet, holding a white fan of ostrich feathers in her hand, and with a knot of white lilac at her breast. He closed his eyelids rapidly one instant as a man does who is dazzled by flame or blinded with a mist of tears; then he looked steadily down the white room and sang a Noël of Felicien David's.[1]

Never in all his nights of triumph had he sung more superbly. He was still young, and his voice was in its perfection. He could do what he chose with it, and he chose to-night to hold that little crowd of tired great people hanging on his lips as though they were sheep that hearkened to Orpheus.

He chose to show her husband and her world what spell he could use, what power he could wield; a charm that their riches could not purchase, a sorcery their rank could not command. He was in the mood to sing, and he sang, as generously as in his childhood he had warbled his wood-notes wild to the winds of the mountains; as superbly, and with as exquisite a mastery and science as he had ever sung with to the crowded theatres of the great nations of the world.

The careless and fashionable crowd listened, and was electrified into emotion. It could not resist; men were dumb and women heard with glistening eyes and aching hearts; Sergius Zouroff, for whom

---

1 Félicien-César David (1810-76) was a French composer.

music rarely had any charm, as he heard that grand voice rise on the stillness, clear as a clarion that calls to war, and then sink and fall to a sweetness of scarcely mortal sound, owned its influence, and as he sat with his head downward, and his heavy eyelids closed, felt dully and vaguely that he was vile, and Deity perchance not all a fable; and shuddered a little, and felt his soul shrink before the singer's as Saul's in its madness before David.[1]

When Corrèze paused all were silent. To give him compliment or gratitude would have seemed almost as unworthy an insult as to give him gold.

Vere had not moved; she stood before the bank of azaleas quite motionless; she might have been of marble for any sign she gave.

Corrèze was silent; there was no sound in the white room except the murmur of the waves without against the sea-wall of the house.

Suddenly he looked up, and the brilliant flash of his gaze met Sergius Zouroff's clouded and sullen eyes.

"I will sing once more," said Corrèze, who had risen; and he sat down again to the piano. "I will sing once more, since you are not weary of me. I will sing you something that you never heard."

His hands strayed over the chords in that improvisation of music which comes to the great singer as the sudden sonnet to the poet, as the burst of wrath to the orator. Corrèze was no mere interpreter of other men's melody; he had melody in his brain, in his hands, in his soul.

He drew a strange pathetic music from the keys; a music sad as death, yet with a ring of defiance in it, such defiance as had looked from his eyes when he had entered, and had stood by the side of the wife of Zouroff.

He sang "La Coupe" of Sully Prudhomme; the "Coupe d'Or"[2] that he had quoted on the sands by the North Sea at Scheveming.

"Dans les verres épais du cabaret brutal
  Le vin bleu coule à flots, et sans trêve à la ronde.
Dans le calice fin plus rarement abonde,
  Un vin dont la clarté soit digne du cristal.

---

1 See 1 Samuel 18.
2 The Golden Cup. See the translation at the end of Volume 2, Chapter IX (p. 372).

Enfin, la coupe d'or haut d'un piédestal
Attend, vide toujours, bien que large et profonde,
Un cru dont la noblesse à la sienne réponde:
On tremble d'en souiller l'ouvrage et le métal."

He sang it to music of his own, eloquent, weird, almost terrible; music that seemed to search the soul as the rays of a lamp probe dark places.

The person he looked at while he sang was Sergius Zouroff.

Les verres épais du cabaret brutal!

The words rang down the silence that was around him with a scorn that was immeasurable, with a rebuke that was majestic.

Sergius Zouroff listened humbly as if held under a spell, his eyes could not detach their gaze from the burning scorn of the singer.

Les verres épais du cabaret brutal!

The line was thundered through the stillness with a challenge and a meaning that none who heard it could doubt, and with a passion of scorn that cut like a scourge and spared not.

Then his voice dropped low, and with the tenderness of an unutterable yearning recited the verse he had not spoken by the sea.

"Plus le vase est grossier de forme et de matière,
Mieux il trouve à combler sa contenance entière,
Aux plus beaux seulement il n'est point de liqueur."[1]

There was once more a great silence. Vere still stood quite motionless.

Sergius Zouroff leaned against the white wall with his head stooped and his eyes sullen and dull, with an unwilling shame.

Corrèze rose and closed the piano.

"I came to sing; I have sung; you will allow me to leave you now, for I must go away by daybreak to Paris."

And though many tried to keep him, none could do so, and he went.

Vere gave him her hand as he passed out of the white drawing-room.

"I thank you," she said very low.

The party broke up rapidly; there was a certain embarrassment and apprehension left on all the guests; there was not one there who had not understood the public rebuke given to Sergius Zouroff.

---

1 The more the vessel is coarse in shape and matter, / The better it manages to fill to its entire capacity, / Only to the most beautiful is there no liquor

He had understood it no less.

But for his pride's sake, which would not let him own he felt the disgrace of it, he would have struck the lips of the singer dumb. When the white room was empty, he paced to and fro with quick, uneven steps. His face was livid, his eyes were savage, his breath came and went rapidly and heavily; for the first time in all his years a man had rebuked him.

"You asked him here to insult me?" he cried, pausing suddenly before his wife. She looked him full in the face.

"No. There would be no insult in a poem unless your conscience made it seem one."

She waited a moment for his answer, but he was silent; he only stared at her with a stifled, bitter oath; she made a slight curtsey to him, and left his presence without another word.

"You should honour his courage, Sergius," said Madame Nelaguine, who remained beside him; "you must admit it was *very* courageous."

A terrible oath was his answer.

"Courageous!" he said savagely at last. "Courageous? The man knows well enough that it is impossible for me to resent a mere song; I should be ridiculous, *farceur*,[1] and he knows that I cannot fight him—he is a stage-singer—"

"He thinks himself your equal," she answered quietly; "but probably your wife is right, it is only your conscience makes you see an insult in a poem."

"My conscience!"—Sergius Zouroff laughed aloud; then he said suddenly, "Is he Vera's lover?"

"You are a fool," said the Princesse Nadine with tranquil scorn. "Your wife has never had any lover, and I think never will have one. And what lover would rebuke *you*? Lovers are like husbands—they condone."

"If he be not her lover why should he care?"

Madame Nelaguine shrugged her shoulders.

"My dear Sergius, people are different. Some feel angry at things that do not in the least concern them, and go out of their way to redress wrongs that have nothing to do with them; they are the *exaltés* members of the world. Corrèze is one of them. Have you not said he is an artist? Now, I am no artist, and never am *exaltée*, and yet I also do not like to see the golden cup cast aside for the *cabaret brutal*. Good night."

---

1 Joker, clown.

Then she too left him.

The next day Madame Nelaguine went up to her sister-in-law on the sea-terrace of the house. Vere was sitting by the statue of the wingless Love; she had a book in her hand, but she was not reading, her face was very calm, but there was a sleepless look in her eyes. The Princesse Nadine, who never in her life had known any mental or physical fear, felt afraid of her; she addressed her a little nervously.

"Have you slept well, love?"

"Not at all," said Vere, who did not speak falsely in little things or large.

"Ah!" sighed Madame Nelaguine, and added wistfully, "Vera, I want to ask you to be still patient, to do nothing in haste; in a word, to forgive still if you can. My dear, I am so pained, so shocked, so ashamed of all the insults my brother offers you, but he has had a lesson very grandly given,—it may profit him, it may not; but in any way, Vera, as a woman of the world who yet can love you, my love, I want to entreat you for all our sakes, and your own above all, not to separate yourself from my brother."

Vere, who had her eyes fixed on the distant snows of the mountains of Esterelle, turned and looked at her with a surprise and with something of a rebuke.

"You mean?—I do not think I understand you."

"I mean," murmured her sister-in-law almost nervously, "do not seek for a divorce."

"A divorce!"

Vere echoed the words in a sort of scorn.

"You do not know me much yet," she said calmly. "The woman who can wish for a divorce and drag her wrongs into public—such wrongs!—is already a wanton herself; at least I think so."

Madame Nelaguine breathed a little quickly with relief, yet with a new apprehension.

"You are beyond me, Vera, and in your own way you are terribly stern."

"What do you wish me to be?" said Vere tranquilly. "If I were of softer mold I should make your brother's name the shame of Europe. Be grateful to my coldness; it is his only shield."

"But you suffer—"

"That is nothing to anyone. When I married Prince Zouroff I knew very well that I should suffer always. It is not his fault; he cannot change his nature."

His sister stood beside her and pulled the yellow tea-roses absently.

"You are altogether beyond me," she said hurriedly, "and yet you are not a forgiving woman, Vera?"

"Forgiveness is a very vague word; it is used with very little thought. No, I do not forgive, certainly. But I do not avenge myself by giving my name to the mob, and telling the whole world things that I blush even to know!"

"Then you would never separate yourself from Sergius?"

"I may leave his roof if he try me too far, I have thought of it; but I will never ask the law to set me free from him. What could the law do for me? It cannot undo what is done. A woman who divorces her husband is a prostitute legalised by a form; that is all."[1]

"You think fidelity due to the faithless?"

"I think fidelity is the only form of chastity left to a woman who is a wife; the man's vices cannot affect the question. I abhor your brother, I could strike him as a brave man strikes a coward, but I have taken an oath to him and I will be true to it. What has the law to do with one's own honour?"

"It is happy for him that you have such unusual feeling," said Madame Nelaguine with a little acrimony, because she herself had been far from guiltless as a wife. "But your knight? your defender? your hero with the golden nightingale in his throat, are you as cold to him? Did you not see that while he sang his heart was breaking, and he would have been glad if his song had been a sword?"

They were imprudent words and she knew it, yet she could not resist the utterance of them; for even in her admiration of Vere a certain bitterness and a certain impatience moved her against a grandeur of principle that appeared to her strained and out of nature.

Vere, who was sitting leaning a little back against the sea-wall, raised herself and sat erect; a warmth of colour came upon her face, her eyes grew angered and luminous.

"I will not affect to misunderstand you," she said tranquilly, "but you misunderstand both him and me. Long, long ago I think he could have loved me, and I—could have loved him. But fate had it otherwise. He is my knight, you say—perhaps—but only as they were knights in days of old, without hope and without shame. I think you had no need to say this to me, and, perhaps, no right to say it."

---

1 Divorce was not possible without a public scandal. Vere would be forced publicly to expose Zouroff's sexual relations with his mistresses. In addition, divorce cases appeared in the daily newspapers, which would have violated all of her privacy.

The Princess Nadine touched her hand reverently. "No, I had no right, Vera. But I thank you for answering me so. Dear—you are not of our world. You live in it, but it does not touch you. Your future is dark, but you bear the lamp of honour in your hand. We think the light old-fashioned and dull, but it burns in dark places where we, without it, stumble and fall. Corrèze did not sing in vain; my brother, I think, will say no more to you of the sables and the Promenade des Anglais."

"It matters very little whether he does or no," said Vere, "I should not drive there, and he knows it. Will you be so good as not to speak to me again of these things? I think words only make them harder to bear, and seem to lower one to the level of the women who complain."

"But to speak is so natural—"

"Not to me."

It was three o'clock in the December day; the *mistral* was blowing, although in this sheltered nook of the bay of Villafranca it was but little felt, the sky was overcast, the waves were rolling in heavy with surf, little boats, going on their way to Sans Soupir or Saint Jean, ploughed through deep waters.

Vere moved towards the house.

Madame Nelaguine went down towards the garden to visit the young palms she was rearing for the palace in the Newski Prospect, where heated air was to replace the lost south to them, as the fever of society replaces the dreams of our youth.

Her husband met Vere in the entrance and stopped her there; his face was reddened and dark; his heavy jaw had the look of the bulldog's; his eyes had a furtive and ferocious glance; it was the first time they had met since she had curtsied to him her good-night. He barred her way into the entrance chamber.

"Madame, the horses are ready," he said curtly, "go in and put on your sables."

She lifted her eyes, and a great contempt spoke in them; with her lips she was silent.

"Do you hear me?" he repeated, "go in and put on your sables; I am waiting to drive with you."

"Along the Promenade des Anglais?" she said, very calmly.

"On the Promenade des Anglais," repeated Zouroff; "do you need twice telling?"

"Though you tell me a hundred times, I will not drive there."

He swore a great oath.

"I told you what you were to do last night. Last night you chose to have me insulted by an opera-singer; do you suppose that changed my resolve? When I say a thing it is done; go in and put on your sables."

"I will never put them on again; and I will not drive with you!"

Rage held him speechless for a moment. Then he swore a great oath.

"Go in and put on your sables, or I will teach you how a Russian can punish rebellion. You insulted me by the mouth of an opera-singer, who had your orders no doubt what to sing. You shall eat dust to-day; that I swear."

Vere gave a little gesture of disdain.

"Do you think you can terrify me?" she said tranquilly. "We had better not begin to measure insults. My account against you is too heavy to be evenly balanced on that score."

The calmness of her tone and of her attitude lashed him to fury.

"By God! I will beat you as my father did his serfs!" he muttered savagely, as he seized her by the arm.

"You can do so if you choose. The Tsar has not enfranchised *me*. But make me drive as you say, where you say, that is beyond your power."

She stood facing him on the terrace; the angry sea and clouded sky beyond her. Her simple dignity of attitude impressed him for an instant with shame and with respect; but his soul was set on enforcing his command. She had had him humiliated by the mouth of a singer; and he was resolved to avenge the humiliation; and having said this thing, though he was ashamed of it, he would not yield nor change.

He pulled her towards him by both hands, and made her stand before him.

"You shall learn all that my power means, madame. I am your master; do you deny me obedience?"

"In things that are right, no."

"Right—wrong! What imbecile's words are those? I bid you do what I choose. You insulted me by your singer's mouth last night; I will make you eat dust to-day."

Vere looked him full in the face.

"I said we had better not measure insults; I have had too many to count them, but at last they may pass one's patience—yours has passed mine."

"Body of Christ!" he cried savagely, "what were you? Did I not buy you? What better are you than that other woman who has my sables except that I bought you at a higher cost? Have you never thought of that? You high-born virgins who are offered up for gold, how are you so much nobler and higher than the *jolies impures*[1] whom you pretend to despise?"

"I have thought of it every day and night since I was made your wife. But you know very well that I did not marry you for either rank or riches, neither for any purpose of my own."

"No? For what did you then?"

Vere's voice sank very low, so low that the sound of the sea almost drowned it.

"To save my mother—you know that."

The face of her husband changed, and he let go his hold of her wrists.

"What did she tell you?" he muttered; "what did she tell you?"

"She told me she was in your debt; that she could not pay you; that you had letters of hers to some one—she did not say to whom—that placed her in your power; and you had threatened to use your power unless I—But you must know all that very well; better than I do. It seemed to me right to sacrifice myself; now I would not do it; but then I was such a child, and she prayed to me in my father's name—"

She paused suddenly, for Zouroff laughed aloud; a terrible jarring laugh that seemed to hurt the peace and silence around.

"What a liar! what a liar always!" he muttered, "and with it all how pretty, and empty-headed, and harmless she looks—my Lady Dolly!"

Then he laughed again.

"Was it not true?" said Vere.

A great cold and a great sickness came over her: the look upon her husband's face frightened her as his rage had had no power to do.

"True? was what true?"

"That she was in your power?"

His eyes did not meet hers.

"Yes—no. She had had plenty of my money, but that was no matter," he answered her in a strange forced voice, "she—she had paid me; there was no cause to frighten you, to coerce you."

Then he laughed again—a dissonant cruel laugh, that hurt his wife more than the bruise he had left upon her wrists.

"Was it not true?" she muttered again wearily; she trembled a little.

---

1 Unchaste women.

"Be quiet!" said her husband roughly, with the colour passing over his face again like a hot wind, "do not talk of it; do not think of it; she wished you to marry me, and she was—well, in a sense she was afraid, and wished to muzzle me. Ah! those dainty ladies! and they think to meet the *lionnes*[1] in the Passage des Anglais is pollution!"

Then he laughed yet again.

Vere felt a faintness steal over her, she felt terror—she knew not of what nor why.

"Then my mother deceived me!"

His eyes looked at her strangely in a fleeting glance.

"Yes, she deceived you!" he said briefly. "In a sense she was afraid of me; but not so—not so."

His dark brows frowned, and his face grew very troubled and full of a dusky red of shame. Vere was mute.

"It is of no use speaking of it now; your mother never could be true to anyone," he said, with an effort. "I am—sorry. You were misled—but it is of no use now—it is too late. Give the sables to the first beggar you meet. That damned singer was right last night; you are a cup of gold and I—like best the trough where the swine drink!"

Vere stood motionless and mute, a vague terror of some unknown thing unnerved her and paralysed her dauntless courage, her proud tranquillity; she felt that for her mother this man who was before her had a scorn as boundless as any he could feel for the basest creatures of the world: and for once she was a coward, for once she dared not ask the truth.

Zouroff stood still a moment, looked at her wistfully, then bowed to her with deep respect, and turned away in silence. A little while later he was driving rapidly through Eza to the Casino of Monte Carlo.

His sister came to Vere anxiously as she saw his horses drive away.

"I hope he was not violent, my dear?"

"No."

"And he did not speak of your driving on that road?"

"He did not enforce it."

Vere spoke feebly, her teeth chattered a little as with cold; she had sat down by the balustrade of the terrace and had a stupefied look like the look of some one who has had a blow or fall.

---

1 Bold impure women (lions).

"I am thankful my children died at their birth," she said after some moments, in a voice so low that it scarcely stirred the air.

Then she got up, drew a shawl about her and went once more towards the house; a great darkness was upon her; she felt as in the Greek tragedies which she had read in her childhood, those felt who were pursued, innocent, yet doomed by the Furies[1] for their mother's sins.

Meanwhile, her husband was driving against the hot south-east wind across the Place du Palais of Monaco.

He was thinking—"the quadroon is a beast of prey but she is honesty itself beside half the women in society, the delicate dainty dames that we flirt with in the ballroom alcoves, and lift our hats to as they go by in the parks!"

A little while later he went up the steps of the great temple of Hazard.[2] He met the mother of Vere coming out between the columns from the vestibule; it was sunset, she had been playing since three o'clock and had amused herself, she had won a thousand francs or so; she was going home to dinner contented and diverted. She was still staying with her friends at the villa of the Condamine. She looked like a little Dresden figure, she had a good deal of pale rose and golden brown in her dress, she had a knot of pink roses in her hand, and had above her head a large pink sunshade. Casse-une-Croûte had been playing very near her at the table, but Lady Dolly did not mind these accidents, she was not supposed to know Casse-une-Croûte by sight from any other unrecognisable person amongst the pilgrims of pleasure.

"The ponies are waiting for you, madame," said her son-in-law as he met her, and took her from her little attendant group of young men, and sauntered on by her side down by the marble stairs.

There was a gorgeous sunset over sea and sky, the thickets of camellias were all in gorgeous blossom, the odorous trees and shrubs filled the air with perfume, some music of Ambroise Thomas was floating on the air in sweet distant strains, throngs of gay people were passing up and down; the great glittering pile rose above them like a temple of Moorish art.

"I have won a thousand francs, *quel bonheur!*" cried Lady Dolly.

"*Quel bonheur,*" repeated Zouroff; "I suppose that sunshade did not cost much more?"

---

1 Mythological deities who punish crimes at the instigation of the victims.
2 Chance.

"Not half as much," said Lady Dolly seriously; "these stones in the handle are only Ceylon garnets."

Zouroff did not look at her, his face was flushed and gloomy. He turned a little aside at the foot of the steps into one of the winding walks and motioned to a marble bench: "Will you sit there a moment, the ponies can wait; I want to say a word to you that is better said here."

Lady Dolly put her bouquet of roses to her lips and felt annoyed. "When people want to speak to one, it is never to say anything agreeable," she thought to herself, "and he looks angry; perhaps it is because that Casse-une-Croûte was at my elbow—but I shall not say anything to Vere, I never make mischief; he must surely know that."

"Why did you induce your daughter to marry me by false representations?" said Zouroff abruptly.

"False what?" echoed Lady Dolly vaguely.

"You deceived me and you deceived her," said Zouroff.—Lady Dolly laughed nervously.

"Deceived! What a very low hysterical sort of word; and what nonsense!"

"You deceived her," he repeated, "and you cannot deny it; you told her nothing of the truth."

"The truth?" said Lady Dolly growing very pale and with a nervous contraction at the end corners of her mouth, "Who ever does tell the truth? I don't know anybody—"

"Of course you could not tell it her," said Zouroff, who also had grown pale, "but you forced her to your purpose with a lie—that was perhaps worse. You knew very well that I would not have had her driven to me so; you knew very well that I supposed her bought by ambition like any other; you did a vile thing—"

"You turned preacher!" said Lady Dolly, with a little shrill angry laugh, "that is really too funny, and you are speaking not too politely. You sought Vere's hand, I gave it you; I really do not know—"

"But I never bid you force her to me by a lie! You never feared me—*you*—you were no more in fear of me than of half a score of others; besides, you know very well that no man who is not a cur ever speaks—"

"I was afraid; I thought you would be furious unless she married you; when men are angry then they speak; how could I tell? You wished that thing, you had it; you are very ungrateful, and she too."

Lady Dolly had recovered herself; she had regained that effrontery which was her equivalent for courage; she had no conscience, and she did not see that she had done so much that was wrong. After all, what was a sin?—it was an idea. In her way she was very daring. She would kneel at the flower-services and weep at the Lenten ones, but she did not believe a word of all her prayers, and penance; they looked well, so she did them; that was all.

For the moment she had been frightened, but she was no longer frightened. What could he do, what could he say? When she could not be punished for it, guilt of any sort lay very lightly on her head. She knew that he was powerless, and she lost the fear with which the strong rough temper of Sergius Zouroff had often really moved her in an earlier time.

The contraction at the corners of her mouth still remained and quivered a little, but she recovered all her coolness and all that petulant impudence which was perhaps the most serviceable of all her qualities.

"You are very rude," she said, "and you are very thankless. You are a very faithless husband, and I know everything and I say nothing, and I come and stay in your house and you ought to thank me, yes, you ought to thank me. I do not know what you mean when you say I used force with my daughter; you could see very well she detested you and yet you chose to insist, whose fault was that? You have been generous, I do not deny that, but then you are just as much so to creatures—more so! I think you have spoken to me abominably; I am not used to that sort of language, I do not like being rebuked when I have always acted for the best if the results did not repay me my sacrifices. As for your imagining I wanted so very much to marry Vere to you, I can assure you I need not have done so, I could have married her at that very same time to Jura if I had chosen."

"To Jura?"

Zouroff looked at her, then burst into a bitter laughter that was more savage than any of his oaths.

"You are an extraordinary woman!" he said with a little short laugh.

"I don't know why you should say that," said Lady Dolly, "I don't know why you should say that; I am sure I am exactly like everybody else; I hate singularity, there is nothing on earth so vulgar; I do not know whatever I have done to deserve the insult of being called 'extraordinary.' I hate people who drive at things. I always detest conundrums and acrostics, perhaps I am too stupid for them; I would rather be stupid than extraordinary, it is less *voyant*."[1]

---

1 Showy, gaudy.

He stared down on her gloomily for awhile, while the laugh rattled in his throat with a cynical sound that hurt her nerves.

"You are a wonderful woman, Miladi, I never did you justice, I see," he said curtly; "Zola will want a lower deep before long, I suppose; he will do well to leave his cellars for the drawing-rooms."[1]

"What do you mean?" said Lady Dolly, opening innocent eyes of surprise.

Zouroff paced slowly by her side; he was silent for some moments, then he said abruptly,

"Pardon me if I do not ask you to return to my house, you and your daughter should not be sheltered by the same roof."

Lady Dolly's pretty teeth gnawed her under lip to keep in her fury; she could not rebuke, and she dared not resent it.

"We had better not quarrel," she said feebly, "people would talk so terribly."

"Of course we will not quarrel," said her son-in-law with his cynical smile, "whoever does quarrel in our world? Only—you understand that I mean what I say."

"I am sure I understand nothing that you mean to-day," said Lady Dolly, with a little feeble, flitting laugh.

Then in unbroken silence they went to where the ponies waited.

"You are too cruel to us not to return," said Zouroff publicly, for the sake of the world's wide-open ears, as she went to her carriage on his arm.

"I cannot stand your *mistral*," said Lady Dolly, also for the world, and, in his ear, added with an injured sweetness, "and I do not like reproaches, and I never deserve them."

Lady Dolly drove home to La Condamine, where she was staying with the Marquise Pichegru, and, when she was all alone, behind the ponies, shuddered a little, and turned sick, and felt for a moment as if the leaden hand of a dark guilt lay on her conscience; her nerves had been shaken, though she had kept so calm a front, so cool a smile; she had been a coward, and she had sacrificed the child of her dead husband, because in her cowardice she had feared the resurrection to her hurt of her own bygone sins, but she had never thought of herself as a wicked woman. In her frothy world there is no such thing as wickedness, there is only exposure; and the dread of it, which passes for virtue.

She lived, like all women of her stamp and her epoch in an

---

1 See Appendix A.4 (p. 550).

atmosphere of sugared sophisms; she never reflected, she never admitted, that she did wrong; in her world nothing mattered much unless, indeed, it were found out, and got into the public mouth.

Shifting as the sands, shallow as the rain-pools, drifting in all danger to a lie, incapable of loyalty, insatiably curious, still as a friend and ill as a foe, kissing like Judas, denying like Peter,[1] impure of thought, even where by physical bias or politic prudence, still pure in act, the woman of modern society is too often at once the feeblest and the foulest outcome of a false civilisation. Useless as a butterfly, corrupt as a canker, untrue to even lovers and friends because mentally incapable of comprehending what truth means, caring only for physical comfort and mental inclination, tired of living, but afraid of dying; believing some in priests, and some in physiologists, but none at all in virtue; sent to sleep by chloral, kept awake by strong waters and raw meat; bored at twenty, and exhausted at thirty, yet dying in the harness of pleasure rather than drop out of the race and live naturally; pricking their sated senses with the spur of lust, and fancying it love; taking their passions as they take absinthe before dinner; false in everything, from the swell of their breast to the curls at their throat;— beside them the guilty and tragic figures of old, the Medea, the Clytemnæstra, the Phædra,[2] look almost pure, seem almost noble.

When one thinks that they are the only shape of womanhood that comes hourly before so many men, one comprehends why the old Christianity which made womanhood sacred dies out day by day, and why the new Positivism,[3] which would make her divine, can find no lasting roost.

The faith of men can only live by the purity of women, and there is both impurity and feebleness at the core of the dolls of Worth, as the canker of the red phylloxera works at the root of the vine.

But there is "no harm" in them, that is the formula of society; there is "no harm" in them; they have never been found out, and they are altogether unconscious of any guilt.

---

1 See Matthew 26.
2 Medea is the mythological sorceress who helps Jason get the Golden Fleece. When Jason deserts her, she kills their children. Clytemnestra kills her husband Agamemnon and her son Orestes kills her and her lover. Phædra, wife of Theseus, falls in love with her stepson Hippolytus. After she causes his death, she hangs herself.
3 A philosophical movement founded by Auguste Comte (1798-1857). It was concerned with positive facts and phenomena, excluding speculation on ultimate causes or origins.

They believe they have a conscience as they know they have a liver, but the liver troubles them sometimes; the conscience is only a word.

Lady Dolly had been a very guilty woman, but she never thought so. Perhaps in real truth the shallow-hearted are never really guilty. "They know not what they do"[1] is a plea of mercy which they perchance deserve even no less than they need it.

A day or two later she made some excuse, and left the Riviera.

"After all," she thought to herself as the train ran into the heart of the rocks, and the palm trees of Monte Carlo ceased to lift their plumes against the sky, "after all it was quite true what I did tell her; I used to be horribly afraid of him, he can be such a brute. I never was really at ease till I saw my letters on the back of the fire; he can sulk, he can rage, he can quarrel with me if he choose, but he never can do me any harm. If he be ever so unpleasant about me, people will only laugh and say that a man always hates his wife's mother, and I really am Vere's mother, odd as it seems; I think I look quite as young as she does; it is such a mistake, she will never paint, she puts ten years on herself."

Then she took the little glass out of her travelling bag, and looked at her face; it was pretty, with soft curls touching the eyebrows under a black saucer of a hat with golden-coloured feathers; she had a yellow rose at her throat, linked into her racoon fur; she was satisfied with what she saw in the mirror; when she got into her train she found a charming young man that she knew a little going the same way, and she gave him a seat in her coupé, and flirted pleasantly all the way to Lyons.

"What a mistake it is to take life *au grand sérieux*,"[2] she thought; "now if poor Vere were not so tragic, I think she might be the happiest woman in the world—still."

But then Vere could not have flirted with a chance young man in a coupé, and given him a yellow rose with the whisper of a half-promised rendezvous as they parted; these are the capabilities that make happy women.

---

1 Jesus's words when he was dying on the cross, preceded by "Father, forgive them; for ..." (Luke 23:34).
2 Too seriously.

CHAPTER III.

In the house on the Gulf of Saint-Hospice a heavy gloom reigned.

Life ran the same course as usual, society came and went, people laughed and talked, guests were gathered and were dispersed, but there was a shadow in the house that even the ceremonies and frivolities of daily custom could not altogether hide or dissipate. Sergius Zouroff was taciturn and quarrelsome, and it taxed all the resources of his sister's tact and wit and worldly wisdom to repair the harm and cover the constraint produced by his captious and moody discourtesies. To his wife he said nothing.

Except the conventional phrase that society in the presence of servants necessitated, Zouroff preserved an unbroken silence to her; he was gloomy but taciturn, now and then under his bent brows his eyes watched her furtively. This forbearance was only a lull in the storm, such a peace as came over the gulf beneath her windows after storm, when the waves sank for an hour at noon to rise in redoubled fury and send the breakers over the quay at sunrise. As for her, the golden cup was now full, but was full with tears.

Would she have had it empty?

She was not sure.

The echo of that one song seemed always on her ear; in the dreams of her troubled sleep she murmured its words; the singer seemed to her transfigured, as to a woman bound in martyrdom, in days of old, seemed the saint with sword and palm that rode through fiery heats and living walls of steel to release her from the stake or wheel. "The woman in Calvados called him the Angel Raphael," she thought with dim eyes.

It was still midwinter when Sergius Zouroff, several weeks before his usual time, abruptly left the villa of Villafranca, and went with his wife and sister to his hotel in Paris. Zouroff had taken a bitter hatred to this place where the only reproof he had ever endured, the only challenge he had ever received, had been cast at him publicly and in suchwise that he could not resent nor avenge it. When he drove through the streets of Monaco or the streets of Nice, he thought he saw on every face a laugh; when he was saluted by his numerous acquaintances he heard in the simplest greeting a sound of ridicule; when a song was hummed in open air he fancied it was the song of the Coupe d'Or. In impatience and anger he took his household to Paris.

A great emotion, a sort of fear came upon Vere as she once more saw the walls of her house in Paris.

For in Paris was Corrèze.

To the honour and loyalty of her soul it seemed to her that she ought never to see his face or hear his voice again. She would have been willing could she have chosen to have gone far away from all the luxuries and homage of the world, to be buried in humility and obscurity, labouring for God and man, and bearing always in her memory that song which had been raised like a sword in her defence.

When at the end of the long cold journey—long and cold, despite all that wealth could do to abridge, and luxury to rob it of its terrors— she saw the pale January light of a Paris morning shine on the "Slave of Gérôme" in her bedchamber, on the table beneath the picture was a great bouquet of roses; with the roses was a little sprig of sweetbriar.

To be in leaf in the winter she knew that the little homely cottage plant must have had the care of hot-house science. She did not need to ask who had sent her that welcome once more.

She bent her face down on the roses and her eyes were wet. Then she put them away and fell on her knees and prayed the old simple prayer—simple and homely as the sweetbriar—to be delivered from evil.

At the same time her husband, who had driven not to his own house but straight to the Faubourg St. Germain, was standing amidst the gay *chinoiseries* of the Duchesse Jeanne's famous boudoir. The Duchesse was laughing and screaming; he was looking down with bent brows.

"Oh, can you think for a moment the story is not known to all Paris!" she was crying. "How could you—how could you—with a hundred people there to hear? My dear, it was only I who kept it out of 'Figaro'! Such a lovely story as it was, and of course they made it still better. My dear, how stupid you are, blind as a bat, as a mole! To be sure we are all dying now to see the first signs of your conversion. How will you begin? Will you go to church, will you drive your mother-in-law round the lake, will you take an oath never to enter a café? Do tell me how you mean to begin your reformation? It will be the drollest thing of the year!"

"*Il vous plaît de plaisanter,*"[1] said her visitor stiffly, between his shut teeth.

When he left the Hôtel de Sonnaz, the half-formed resolution which he had made to be less unworthy of his wife had faded away;

---

1 It pleases you to joke.

he felt galled, stung, infuriated. Casse-une-Croûte, and the other companions of his licentious hours, found him sullen, fierce, moody. When they rallied him he turned on them savagely, and made them feel that, though he had chosen to toy with them and let them stuff themselves with his gold, he was their master and their purchaser— a tyrant that it was dangerous to beard, a lion with whom it was death to play.

There was strength in his character, though it had been wasted in excesses of all kinds and in a life of utter selfishness and self-indulgence; and this strength left in him a certain manliness that even his modes of life and all his base habits could not utterly destroy; and that latent manliness made him yield a sullen respect to the courageousness and unselfishness of the woman who was his wife and his princess before the world, but in fact had been the victim of his tyrannies and the martyr of his lusts.

There were times when he would have liked to say to her, "forgive me, and pray for me." But his pride withheld him, and his cynical temper made him sneer at himself. He dreaded ridicule. It was the only dread that was on him. He could not endure that his world should laugh; so, uniting more display and effrontery than ever, he paraded his vices before that world, and all the while hated the panderers to them and the associates of them. He thought if he lived more decently, that the whole of Europe would make a mock of it, and say that he had been reformed by the rebukes of Corrèze. So he showed himself abroad with the *verres épais du cabaret brutal*, though they grew loathsome to him, and revenged himself on them by crushing their coarse frail worthlessness with savage harshness.

Vere could not tell the strange sort of remorse which moved him. She saw herself daily and hourly insulted, and bore it as she had done before. So long as he asked no public degradation of herself, like that which he had commanded on the Promenade des Anglais, she was passive and content, with that joyless and mournful contentment which is merely the absence of greater evils.

Although they only met in society there was a sort of timidity in the manner of Sergius Zouroff to his wife, a gentleness and a homage in his tone when he addressed her. Vere, who shrank from him rather more than less, did not perceive it, but all others did. "Will Zouroff end with being in love with his wife?" his friends said, with a laugh. The Duchesse Jeanne heard it said on all sides of her. "Will he be a good husband after all?" she thought angrily; and her vanity rose in alarm like the quills of the bruised porcupine.[1]

She attempted a jest or two with him, but they fell flat; there came an anxious sparkle in his gloomy eyes that warned her off such witticisms. She was perplexed and irritated. "After all, it will be very diverting if you should end as *le mari amoureux?*" she could not resist saying at hazard one day. Zouroff looked down, and his face was very grave.

"Let me alone. I can be dangerous; you know that. No, I am not in love with my wife; one is not in love with marble, however beautiful the lines of it. But I respect her. It is very odd for me to feel respect for any woman. It is new to me."

"It is a very creditable emotion," said the Duchesse, with a little sneer. "But it is rather a dull sentiment, is it not?"

"Perhaps," said Zouroff, gloomily.

A sort of uneasiness and anxiety was upon him. Something of the feeling that had touched him for the child Vere at Félicité moved him once more before his wife; not passion in any way, but more nearly tenderness than it had ever been in his nature to feel for any living thing. He had always thought that he had bought her as he had bought the others, only *par le chemin de la chapelle,*[2] and he had had a scorn for her that had spoiled and marred his thoughts of her. Now that he knew her to be the martyr of her mother's schemes, a pity that was full of honour rose up in him. After all, she was so innocent herself, and he had hurt her so grossly; hurt her with an injury that neither sophistry nor gold could make the less.

He was a coarse and brutal man; he had had his own will from childhood upon men and women, slaves and animals. He was cruel with the unthinking, unmeasured cruelty of long self-indulgence; but he was a gentleman in certain instincts, despite all, and the manhood in him made him feel a traitor before Vere. A kind of reverence that was almost fear came into him before her; he seemed to himself unworthy to cross the threshold of her room.

The leopard cannot change his spots, nor the Ethiopian his skin, nor could he abandon habits and vices engrained in all the fibre of his being; but he began to feel himself as unfit for his wife's young

---

1   In Shakespeare's *Hamlet*, when Hamlet describes his meeting with his father's ghost, he says that what the ghost told him would make hairs stand on end, "Like quills upon the fretful porcupine" (I.v.15).

2   By way of the church.

life as a murderer to touch the Eucharist.[1] She could not imagine anything of the thoughts and the remorse that moved him. She only saw that he left her alone and ceased to vent his tyrannies upon her. She was thankful. The hours and the weeks that passed without her seeing him were the most peaceful days of her life. When he addressed her with gentleness she was alarmed, she was more afraid of caresses than of his curses. He saw this fear in her, and a vague half sullen sadness began to enter into him. He began to understand that he owned this woman body and soul, and yet was further from her than any other creature, because no other had outraged her so deeply as he had done.

He was a man who heeded his sins not at all, and even of crime thought little. He had the absolute disbelief and the profound moral indifference of his century; but his offences against Vere he had been made to feel, and it rendered him in her presence also timid, and in her absence almost faithful. He had gathered the edelweiss and he knew that his love was only fit for the brambles and poison-berries.

The season passed away wearily to Vere; an intense pain and a vague terror were always with her. She went out into the world as usual, but it seemed to her more than ever the most monotonous, as it was the most costly, way of destroying time. She was in her tribune at Chantilly, in her carriage in the Bois, in her diamonds at Embassies, and she received that homage which a woman of her loveliness and her position is always surrounded by, however indifferent be her mood or unwilling her ear.

But the whole life seemed to her more than ever a disease, a fever, a strained and unwholesome folly. She strove more and more to escape from it and from herself by labour amidst the poor and tenderness for them.

"You should be canonized, Vera!" said her sister-in-law to her, with a little cynical impatience; to her brother, Madame Nelaguine said with moist eyes,

"Sergius, one day you will see the red and white roses of Paradise in your wife's lap as her husband did in St. Elizabeth's."

Zouroff was silent.

"Alas! alas! the age of miracles is past," thought his sister. "Good

---

1   The Eucharist is a ceremony during which symbolic or consecrated bread and wine are consumed to commemorate the last meal of Jesus Christ with his disciples. The murderer would be unfit to touch the bread or wine.

works bring their own fruits, to those capable of them, in peace of mind and innocence of soul, that I believe; but the world has ceased to adore; the very priests have ceased to believe; the ways of sin are not death but triumph; and the poor do not love the hand that feeds them; they snatch and tear, then snarl and bite, like a street cur. Alas! alas! *où sont les neiges d'antan!*"[1]

Meanwhile her mother Vere did not see at that time. She was thankful.

Lady Dolly was one of the five hundred leaders of English society, and could not leave her duties. She was more popular than ever before. Her balls were the prettiest of the year, and people could breathe at them; she was exclusive yet always amiable; she knew how to unite a social severity with a charming good-nature; she began to call herself old with the merriest little laugh in the world, and she began to doubt whether she still ought to dance. "A dear little woman," said the world; and everyone pitied her for having a daughter who was cold, who was austere, and who had so little affection for her.

"My Vere does not love me. It comes from my own fault, no doubt, in letting her be away from me in her childhood," said Lady Dolly softly, to her intimate friends; and her eyes were dim and her voice pathetic.

There were only two persons who did not believe in her in all her London world. These were a rough, gloomy, yet goodnatured man, who was no longer Lord Jura, but Lord Shetland; and Fushcia, Duchess of Mull.

"Guess she's all molasses," said her Grace, who in moments of ease returned to her vernacular, "but my word! ain't there wasps at the bottom."

"After all, poor little Pussy is not the simpleton I thought her," Lady Stoat of Stitchley, with a sigh of envy, for her own unerring wisdom and exquisite tact and prudence had not been able to avert exposure and scandal from her own daughter, who was living with a French actor in Italy, while Lord Berkhampstead was drinking himself to death on brandy.

A few days after their arrival, Corrèze had left Paris. For the first time in his life he had refused to play in Paris on his arrival from the south, and had signed a four months' engagement with Vienna and

---

1 Where are the snows of yester-year. From François Villon's *Ballade des Dames du Temps Jadis* (*The Ballad of the Olden Days*) (c. 1461).

Berlin. "They will say you are afraid to meet Prince Zouroff," said an old friend to him. "They may say it if they please," answered Corrèze, wearily, and with a movement of disdain.

He knew that his indignation and his disguise had carried him into an imprudence, an imprudence that he regretted now that the story of "La Coupe d'Or" had flown through society, regretted it lest it should annoy or compromise her; and for her sake he would not stay where she was.

He knew how the tongues of the world wagged with or without reason at a mere whisper, and he knew that there were so many who would rejoice to see the pure, cold, snow-white purity of Vere's name fall into the mud of calumny; rejoice out of sheer wantonness, mere purposeless malice, mere love of a new sensation. "Blessed are the pure of spirit"[1] says the Evangelist, but society says it not with him.

He loved her; but it was an emotion no more akin to the noble, tender, and self-denying love of other days than to the shallow sensualities of his own.

He had been satisfied with intrigue, surfeited with passion; underlying the capriciousness of a popular idol, and the ardour of an amorous temper, there were the patience and the loyalty of the mountaineer's heart in him. Whosoever has truly loved the Alpine heights in early youth, keeps something of their force and something of their freshness and their chastity in his soul always. Corrèze was an artist and a man of the world; but he had been first and was still, under all else, a child of nature; and he would utterly deny that nature was the foul thing that it is now painted by those who call themselves realists. He denied that a drunkard and a prostitute are all who are real in the world.

"When the soldier dies at his post, unhonoured and unpitied, and out of sheer duty, is that unreal because it is noble?" he said one night to his companions. "When the sister of charity hides her youth and her sex under a grey shroud, and gives up her whole life to woe and solitude, to sickness and pain, is that unreal because it is wonderful? A man paints a spluttering candle, a greasy cloth, a mouldy cheese, a pewter can; 'how real!' they cry. If he paint the spirituality of dawn, the light of the summer sea, the flame of arctic nights, of tropic woods, they are called unreal, though they exist no less than the candle and the cloth, the cheese and the can. Ruy

---

1 Matthew 5:3. It continues "for theirs is the Kingdom of Heaven."

Blas[1] is now condemned as unreal because the lovers kill themselves; the realists forget that there are lovers still to whom that death would be possible, would be preferable, to low intrigue and yet more lowering falsehood. They can only see the mouldy cheese, they cannot see the sunrise glory. All that is heroic, all that is sublime, impersonal, or glorious, is derided as unreal. It is a dreary creed. It will make a dreary world. Is not my Venetian glass with its iridescent hues of opal as real every whit as your pot of pewter? Yet the time is coming when everyone, morally and mentally at least, will be allowed no other than a pewter pot to drink out of, under pain of being 'writ down an ass'—or worse. It is a dreary prospect."[2]

And he would not be content with it. There were the Ruy Blas and the Romeo in him as there are in all men who are at once imaginative and ardent. He had the lover in him of southern lands, of older days. He would watch in long hours of cold midnight merely to see her image go by him; he would go down to the cliff on the northern coast only to gather a spray of sweetbriar on the spot where he had seen her first; he would row in rough seas at dark under her villa wall in the south for the sake of watching the light in her casement; his love for her was a religion with him, simple, intense, and noble; it was an unending suffering, but it was a suffering he loved better than all his previous joys. When he saw her husband in haunts of vicious pleasure, he could have strangled him for very shame that he was not worthier of her. When he saw him beside the dusky face of the quadroon, he could have dragged him from his carriage and hurled him under the feet of the wife he outraged.

In one of the few days before his departure he passed Sergius Zouroff on the Boulevard des Italiens. Corrèze stood still to let him speak if he would. Zouroff looked away and walked onward without any sign, except of anger, from the sudden sullen gleam in his half-shut eyes.

The arrogance of a man whose birth was higher, because his race

---

1 *Ruy Blas* (1838) is a verse drama by Victor Hugo (1802-85). In it Hugo makes a distinction between Romantic drama and real life. Ruy Blas, a common born valet, is involved in a plot in which a nobleman tries to get revenge on the Queen of Spain by expelling her from court for adultery. Ruy Blas saves the Queen, and they fall in love; but he commits suicide so that he would not taint her with his social inferiority. He dies of poison in her arms.

2 From Shakespeare's *Much Ado About Nothing*: "O that he were here to write me down an ass (IV.ii.80).

had been greater, than the Romanoffs', made it impossible for him to imagine that Corrèze could be his enemy or his rival.

He thought the singer had only sung what had been commanded him. He thought the rebuke to him had been his wife's, and Corrèze only its mouthpiece.

Still he hated him; he avoided him; he would have liked to wring the throat of that silver-voiced nightingale.

Corrèze suffered bitterly to do nothing, to go away, to go as if he were a coward; yet he did it lest the world should speak of her—the light and cruel world to which nothing is sacred, which makes a joke of man's dishonour and a jest of woman's pain.

He did it, and went and sang in the cities of the north with an aching heart. This is always the doom of the artist: the world has no pity. Its children must not pause to weep nor go aside to pray. They must be always in the front, always exerting all their force and all their skill before their public, or they pass from remembrance and perish. The artist, when he loves, has two mistresses, each as inexorable as the other.

Corrèze could not abandon his art; would not abandon it more than a yearling child will leave its mother. It was all he had. It was a delight to him, that empire of sound which came of a perfect mastery, that consciousness and clearness of genius. Without the listening crowds, the glittering houses, the nights of triumph, he might have been only dull and lonely; but without the delight of melody, the command of that song which had gone with him all his life, as a nightingale's goes with it till it dies, he would have been desolate.

Therefore in the keen cold of the northern winter and their tardy, niggard spring, he sang, as the nightingale sings, even while its lover lies shot under the leaves; and the multitudes and their leaders alike adored him. In Vienna the whole city saluted him as it salutes its Kaiser, and in the vast barrack of Berlin the blare of trumpets and the clash of arms were forgotten[1] for one soft voice that sang under Gretchen's cottage-window.

"After all, when one has known this, one has known human greatness surely," he thought wistfully, as he stood on his balcony in the keen starlight of northern skies, and saw vast throngs fill the square beneath him and all the streets around, and heard the mighty *hoch*,[2]

---

1   A reference, perhaps, to the Franco-German war (1870-71) or to the unification of all of Germany outside Austria (The Second Reich).

2   Hurrah.

that northern lungs give for their emperors and their armies ring, through the frosty air for him.

Yet a mist came over his eyes that obscured the torch-glare and the gathered multitudes, and the buildings that were so white and so vast in the moonlight. He thought that he would have given all his triumphs, all his joys—nay, his very voice itself—to undo the thing that had been done, and make the wife of Sergius Zouroff once more the child by the sweetbriar hedge on the cliff.

Though for all the world he was a magician, he had no sorcery for himself. He was but a man, like all the others, and to himself he seemed weaker than all the rest. The bonds of the world bound him—the bonds of its conventions, of its calumnies, of its common-places. He could not strike a blow for her honour that the world would not construe to her shame.

"And who knows but that if she knew that I loved her, she too might never forgive," he thought wearily; and the flowers flung to him through the frost seemed but weeds, the multitude fools, the rejoicing city a madhouse.

When Fame stands by us all alone, she is an angel clad in light and strength; but when Love touches her she drops her sword, and fades away, ghostlike and ashamed.

His sacrifice was of little use. There were too many women jealous of him, and envious of her, for the story of the "Coupe d'Or" not to be made the root and centre of a million false-hoods.

You may weep your eyes blind, you may shout your throat dry, you may deafen the ears of your world for half a lifetime, and you may never get a truth believed in, never have a simple fact accredit-ed. But the lie flies like the swallow, multiplies itself like the cater-pillar, is accepted everywhere, like the visits of a king; it is a royal guest for whom the gates fly open, the red carpet is unrolled, the trumpets sound, the crowds applaud.

Jeanne de Sonnaz laughed a little, shrugged her shoulders, then said very prettily that everyone knew there was nothing; Vere was a saint. And then the thing was done.

Who said it first of all no one ever knew. Who ever sees the snake-spawn, the plague-mist gather? The snake-brood grows and comes out into the light, the plague-mist spreads and slays its thou-sands—that is enough to see.

Who first whispered through the great world the names of the Princess Zouroff and the singer Corrèze together? No one could have told. All in a moment it seemed as if everyone in society were murmuring, hinting, smiling, with that damnable smile with which the world always greets the approach of a foul idea.

A cruel story runs on wheels, and every hand oils the wheels as they run.

"An old love, an early love," so they muttered; and the fans and the cigarettes made little breaks and waves in the air, as much as to say it was always so. You could say what you liked—they murmured—when people were so very cold, so very proud, so very proper; there was always some cause. An old love—ah? that was why she was so fond of music! Then society laughed; its inane cruel chirping laughter, when it smells a sin.

She had many foes. When those calm, deep, disdainful eyes had looked through the souls of others, those other souls—so often mean and shameless with paltry lusts or swollen with paltry forms of pride—had shrunk under that glance, and hated the one who all innocently gave it; when her serene simplicity and her grave grace had made the women around her look merely dolls of the Palais Royal toyshops, and the fantastic frivolity of her epoch seem the silliest and rankest growth of an age in nothing over wise—then, and for that alone, she had become beset by enemies unseen and unsuspected, but none the less perilous for their secrecy. When women had called her *farouche* in their drawing-room jargon, they had only meant that she was chaste, that she was grave, that folly did not charm her, and that she was a rebuke to themselves.

That under the snow there should be mud; that at the heart of the wildrose there should not be not one worm, but many; that the edelweiss should be rotten and worthless after all—what joy! The imagined joy of angels over one who repents can never be one-thousandth part so sweet and strong as the actual joy of sinners over one purity that falls.

So she had always been a falsehood like them all! So Correze had always been her lover! All the grand ladies and all the pretty ladies in the great world laughed gingerly, and tittered with that titter, which in Mary Jane and Louison one would call vulgar; and, in their nest of new knicknackery and old art, cooed together and soothed each others' ruffled plumage, and agreed that they were none of them surprised.

Meanwhile Vere knew nothing, and went on her way with calm, proud feet, unwitting that amongst the ermine of her mantle of innocence the moths of slander were at work. Who first said it? No one knew. Perhaps her mother engendered it by a sigh. Perhaps her husband's friend begot it by a smile. No one could ever tell. Only society talked. That was all. Society talked. It means as much as when in Borgia's days they said, "To-night the Pope sups with you."[1] Lady Dolly heard, as women like her hear everything. "Are they saying this? I always thought they would say it," she thought, and was vaguely disquieted, and yet not ill-pleased. When she had caught the first rumour of it one afternoon, in a whisper never meant for her ears, she had gone back to her dressing-room to get ready for a dinner at an embassy, and had been good-nature itself to her maid, easily pleased with her curls, and quite indifferent as to what jewels they gave her. "Anything looks well with white," she had said dreamily, and her maid thought she must have got another "affair" on the wind. But she was only feeling a sort of velvety content in the ultimate justice of things. "She has been so cruel to me," she thought, really, honestly thought it. "She has always been so cold and so grave, and so very unpleasant, and always looked really as if one were no better than one should be; it would be very funny if she gets a few 'nasty ones,' as the boys say, herself; it really will be no more than she deserves. And, besides, people don't like that sort of manner, that sort of way she has with her eyelids, as if one were something so very bad and queer if one just happen to say the least little thing that she fancies not quite correct; nobody does like it, it is so very unsympathetic; women are sure to pay her out if they get the least chance, and men will be quite as delighted to hear it. It is such a mistake not to make yourself pleasant, not to be like everybody else and always amiable. Such heaps of people will always take your part if you have been amiable. I wonder if it is true? No, of course it isn't true. I don't believe Corrèze ever kissed the back of her hand. But it will be very funny if she should get talked about; very sad, but so funny too!"

And Lady Dolly's mind drifted complacently and comfortably over a long series of years, in which she had skated on the very thinnest ice without ever getting a drenching, and had had all the four winds of heaven blowing "stories" about her like a scattered pack of cards, and yet had never been the worse for any one of them. "It is because I have always been so pleasant to them all," thought Lady Dolly complacently, and indeed she always had been.

She had said very ill-natured things when they were safe to be said; she had laughed at nearly everybody when their backs were turned; she had often amused herself with putting spokes in the

---

1 Cesare Borgia (1476-1507) was an Italian Cardinal, military leader, and Machiavellian politician. He was the son of Pope Alexander VI.

wheels of happy marriages, of promising courtships, of social ambitions, of youthful careers; but she had done it all merely as a squirrel steals nuts, and she had always been pleasant to women; always kissed them, always caressed them, always confided, or always seemed to confide, in them, and above all had always made them think her both silly and successful, a union of the two most popular social qualities. "Vere never would kiss any of them," she thought, with the contempt that an old diplomatist feels for an obstinate politician who will not understand that language is given to us to conceal our thoughts; and she drew her gloves up to the elbow and took her big fan and went to her party with a complacent feeling of superiority and expectation. "It would be very horrid, of course," she thought, "and of course it would be dreadful if there were any scene; and I am not very sure what the Russian laws are if it were to come to any *séparation du corps et de biens*;[1] but still if she were to get a fright one couldn't altogether be sorry. It would teach her that she was only made of the same stuff as other people."

For what with the many years of separation from her daughter, and the sense of shame that perpetually haunted her for the sacrifice she had made of Vere's fair life, Lady Dolly had almost grown to hate her. She was always envying, fearing, disliking the pale, cold, beautiful woman whose diamonds outshone her own as the sun outshines the lamps; Vere was not one tithe so much her dead husband's child as she was the Princess Zouroff, and there were many times when Lady Dolly caught herself, thinking of her only as the Princess Zouroff, as a social rival and a social superior, and, as such, hating her and forgetting, quite forgetting, that she had ever been a little flower-like baby that had owed life to herself. "Vere has been so cruel to me," she would think, "and so very unforgiving."

For Lady Dolly, true woman of the times, always thought that those whom she had wronged were cruel to her. Why would they not forget? She herself could always forget.

"It shows such a bad disposition to resent and remember so long," she would say to herself; life was too short for long memories. "Give me the art of oblivion," cried Themistocles;[2] Lady Dolly had learned the art, or rather had had the power born in her, and forgot,

---

1 A judicial separation.
2 Themistocles (c. 525–460 B.C.) was an Athenian politician and naval strategist. He was the creator of the Athenian sea power and the chief savior of Greece's subjection to the Persian Empire. During a period of intense political struggle, he, like other leaders, was ostracized.

as naturally as birds moult in autumn, her sins, her follies, her offences, and her friends.

Only one thing she never forgot, and that was a wound to her vanity—and no one ever looked at her when her daughter was nigh.

Zouroff, who did not know "society talked," still felt abashed before the presence of his wife; he felt as Louis of Hungary felt when he saw the celestial roses in the lap of that saintly queen to whom Madame Nelaguine compared Vere.

Since the day when her mother's name had been spoken between them, he had never seen his wife alone one moment, and never had fairly met her glance.

Yet when they were in the same room in society his eyes followed her as they had never done before, wistfully, sombrely, wonderingly. Jeanne de Sonnaz said to herself: "He will end as *le mari amoureux*," and so thinking spoke to him one morning early, when he was sitting in that little yellow boudoir, with all its Chinese idols, and Chinese work, which was so curiously unlike all the rest of the dark old hotel of the Renaissance, which a Duc de Sonnaz had built under Francis I. With all her cleverest tact she brought uppermost the name of Corrèze, and dropped little hints, little suggestions, harmless yet pregnant, as she leaned back in her low chair, smoking a cigarette with her cup of coffee.

Zouroff grew irritated at last, but he did not know how to express his irritation without appearing absurd in her sight, or provoking her laughter.

"My dear, you must be blind not to see that there is some sentiment between Vera and this lyric Bossuet,[1] who made your piano his pulpit," she continued, as he muttered something not very intelligible. "When he refused to come to Svir you might have known. What singer without a motive refuses a mountain of roubles? Besides, he was at Ischl. I did not tell you—why should I tell you—but he serenaded her adorably, he climbed to impossible altitudes to get her flowers; he went away in the oddest, most abrupt fashion. My dear Sergius, you are a brute, a bat, a mole—"

"Pshaw! the man is only a mime, a mime with a thrush's pipe," said Zouroff, with rough scorn. "Do you suppose she would descend—"

"*C'est convenu*,"[2] interrupted Madame Jeanne; "*Oh, c'est convenu.*

---

1 Jacques Bénigne Bossuet (1627-1704) was a French bishop, writer, and orator.
2 That's common knowledge.

Your wife is the pearl of her sex, she is a second Madame Saint Elizabeth, all the world knows that; when we see her at dinner we expect an angel to fill her glass with the wine of Paradise; oh yes, you cannot suppose I mean the slightest indiscretion in her. Vera is incapable of an indiscretion, so incapable, that in a less beautiful woman such extreme goodness would make her utterly uninteresting; but still, for that very reason she is just the sort of person to cling to an idea, to preserve a sentiment like a relic in a silver box; and I have always heard, if you have not, that Corrèze is her idea, is her relic."

Zouroff listened gloomily; he did not as yet believe her, yet a dark sense of jealousy began to burn in him as slow matches burn; a little spark slowly creeping that in time will fire a city. It was scarcely jealousy so much as it was offence, and irritated incredulity, and masterful possession stung by idea of invasion.

But as yet he believed nothing; he smiled a little moodily.

"Your imagination runs away with you," he said curtly. "Vera was sixteen years old when I married her; English girls, *ma chère*, do not have affairs at that age, even if, at the same hour in France, Cupid creep behind the lexicons and missals."

Jeanne de Sonnaz was angry in her turn. When she had been sixteen at her convent she had been very nearly causing a terrible scandal with a young lieutenant of Chasseurs,[1] whom her powerful family succeeded in having discreetly ordered to Africa; she had not thought that Sergius Zouroff knew aught of that silly old story.

"I did not speak of Cupid or of anything so demoralising and *démodé*,"[2] she said carelessly. "I know there was some story, I remember it very well, something romantic and graceful of Corrèze and your wife, when she was a girl—a very young girl; I think he saved her life, I am not sure; but I know that she thinks him a guardian angel. Pray did you know that it was his interposition that sent Noisette back to Paris that day of our fancy-fair?"

Zouroff swore a savage oath. "What accursed interference; what insolent audacity! Are you sure?"

"Corrèze is as insolent as if he were a prince of the blood. More so, for they must please to reign but he reigns to please—himself," said Madame Jeanne with a little laugh. "Did you never know that of Noisette? O how stupid men are! I guessed it and I found it out. Women always can, when they choose, find out anything. Corrèze is

---

1   Member of the French light cavalry.
2   Old fashioned.

always taking the part of knight to your wife; he kills the dragons and chases the robbers, and is always there when she wants him; did he not save her from the storm off Villafranca?"

Zouroff paced to and fro the room to the peril of the *brimborions*[1] and *bric-à-brac*. There was a heavy frown on his brows; he remembered the storm of Villafranca only too well since it had preceded the song of the "Golden Cup."

"I do not believe it," he said doggedly, for he did not.

"So much the better," said his friend drily.

"I always notice," she added after a little pause, "that very cynical and sceptical people (you are very sceptical and very cynical) never do believe in a simple truth that stares them in the face. I am not saying the least harm of your wife—where is the harm? She is of an exalted temperament; she takes life like a poem, like a tragedy; she is a religious woman who really believes in sins just as our peasantry in "la Bretange bretonnante"[2] believe in spirits and saints; she will never do any harm whatever. But for that very reason she shut her relic up in her silver box and worships it at home. Corrèze is always worshipped, though not always so spiritually. No one ever worships you, my dear, you are not of that order of men. Why do you look so angry? You should be thankful. It is very nice that your wife should admire a relic; she might, you know, be dragging your name across Europe at the coat tails of a dozen young dragoons, and though you could shoot them, no doubt, that is always very ridiculous. It is so impossible for husbands at any time not to look ridiculous. You must have looked very so when Corrèze was singing that song; oh, I shall regret to the last day of my life that I was not there!"

Madame Jeanne leaned back and laughed aloud, with her hands behind her head and her eyes shut.

Zouroff continued to pace to and fro the little pretty crowded chamber.

"You will break some of my idols," she said when she had done laughing. "I hope I have not broken one of your idols? How could one ever suppose you cared for your wife?"

"It is not that," said Zouroff roughly; he was shaken, disturbed, enraged; he did not know what to think, and the vanity and the

---

1 Knick-knacks.
2 Brittany is one of the historic provinces of France. A strong Celtic background distinguishes it from other regions of France; and as a result of the isolation of the region, the natives retained distinctive customs and language.

arrogance that served him in the stead of pride were up in arms.

"Of course, yes; it is that," said Madame Jeanne coolly; "I always wondered you were so indifferent to her; she is so handsome. And I always thought that if she ever loved anyone else you would be madly in love with her once more, or rather much more than you were at first."

Zouroff made a gesture so savage as he motioned her to silence, that even her tongue ceased for a moment its chatter.

"One must not say too much" she thought, "or he will go and do something premature."

"What does it matter," she said, consolingly; "a woman who is so much left to herself as Vera is, will be certain to find some compensation for all you deny her. You clumsy Baltic bear! you do not understand women. Believe me it is very dangerous to marry a mere girl, a child, hurl all her illusions and all her modesties away in one month, and then leave her all alone with the reflections you have inspired and the desires you have awakened. I am no moralist, *mon ami*, as you know, but that I do say. It is true ten thousand times in ten years—and ten thousand times the result is the same. Were the Princess Zouroff to have a lover, Corrèze or any other, you could not complain. It would simply be the natural sequence of your own initiations. As it is, you must be thankful that she is Madame Saint Elizabeth. You are not more ridiculous than the world is; mothers screen their daughters from every hint and every glimpse of impropriety, and then they marry them and think no harm can come of it. Can a bishop's blessing muzzle senses once *éveillés*,[1] passions once let loose? Vera is faithful to you *as yet*. But if she were not, could you blame her? Can you expect a woman of her years to live the life of a nun when you have treated her as if she were a *fille de joie*?[2] Be reasonable. You cannot tear the skin off a peach, and then complain that it does not retain its bloom. Yet that is what you and all men do. It is unutterably absurd. Some one will do it with my Berthe and my Claire, and I shall hate the some one; for I love my little girls. Yes, I do! While you know very well that she is—"

"You preach very eloquently!" said Zouroff, with his face flushed and his thick eyebrows drawn together.

"I preach what I know," said his friend; "what I have observed as

---

1 Awakened.
2 Whore.

I say a thousand times ten thousand times—men teach lubricity and expect chastity. It is really too ridiculous. But it is what we call the holiness of marriage. Now, will you please to go away? Paul has a 'fusion' breakfast of all the parties, and I want to dress."

"But—"

"Go away!" said Madame Jeanne, imperiously, with a little stamp of her slipper.

Zouroff, who even to his own autocratic master was seldom obedient, took his leave, and went. She had made his blood hot with rage, his head dull with suspicion. He threw himself into his carriage and drove through the streets of Paris in moody reflection. Uttered by a virtuous woman, the words he had heard would have made no more impression than any court sermon that he had to sit throughout and hear in an imperial chapel; but spoken by Jeanne de Sonnaz they smote him hardly.

A better emotion than was usual with her, had moved her in speaking them, a sense of justice towards the absent woman whom she had yet all the will in the world to destroy; and the bitterness of them was an unwilling witness from a *femme galante*[1] to which he could not attach either favouritism or prejudice, and so weighed on him and smote him heavily. A rebuke even from St. John of the Golden Mouth would have left him callous and scoffing, but a condemnation from the lips of one of the companions of his sins and follies—one of the worldliest of this world—made him wince under its justice; and he knew that his sins against his wife were heavier and grosser than even Jeanne de Sonnaz knew or guessed.

The sullen remorse that had brooded in him ever since the day on the terrace at Villafranca deepened and darkened over him. There was cruel and coarse blood in his veins, the blood of a race that through long centuries had passed their lives in passion, in tyranny, and in deeds of violence, denying no impulse, fearing no future. But there was manliness in him also, though weakened, depraved, and obscured; and this manliness made him feel a coward beside Vere.

A curious jealousy took possession of him, which was half hatred and half remorse. He felt like one of those princes who own a classic and world-renowned statue, and shut it in a cabinet, and never care to look at it, yet who being menaced with its loss, suddenly rise to fury, and feel beggared. Not because the classic marble was any joy

---

1 Courtesan; a so-called "respectable" married woman who is the mistress of another woman's husband. See Introduction (pp. 27-28).

or marvel to themselves, but because the world had envied it to them vainly, and it had made their treasure-house the desired of others. He suddenly realised that the loss of his wife would, like that of the statue, make him poor in the eyes of Europe, and leave his palaces without their chief ornament. He did not, as yet, believe himself menaced. Like most men of vicious lives, he was never deceived as to a woman's innocence. He knew his wife to be as innocent as the little dead children she had borne in her bosom. But how long would she be so?

And if she ceased to be so, truth, by those often untrue lips of Jeanne de Sonnaz, had told him that the fault would lie at his own door, that he would reap as he had sown.

As he drove through the streets amidst the noise of Paris, he saw nothing of the glitter and the movement round him—he saw Vere in her white childish loveliness, as he had seen her on her wedding night.

That evening, when he returned to make his toilette for a great dinner at the Russian Embassy, he was gloomy, perplexed, irresolute. It was towards the close of the season; the evening was hot; the smell of the lilacs in the garden filled all the air; over where ruined St. Cloud lay there was a mist that seemed full of rain and thunder.

For the first time for months he bade the women ask his wife if she could receive him in her room, and he entered it. Vere was standing beneath the picture of Gérôme; she was already dressed. She wore white velvet, a stuff which she preferred, and whose subtle shades of white it would have been the delight and the despair of Titian and Paul Veronese[1] to reproduce on canvas or on panel. She wore the great Russian Order of St. Catherine. About her throat she had coils of pearls, and under these hung the medallion of the moth and the star.

Zouroff approached her with a roughness that concealed an unusual nervousness. His eyes fell on the necklace, and his anger, that was half against himself and half against her, seized on the jewel as a scapegoat.

"Who gave you that?" he said, abruptly.

She answered:

"I think I ought not to say. When you asked me long ago I did not know."

"Your singer sent it you. Take it off."

---

1 Paolo Veronese (1528-88) was a Venetian painter.

She hesitated a moment, then unclasped it. She believed in the old forgotten duty of obedience still.

"Give it to me."

She gave it him.

Zouroff threw it on the ground, and set his heel on it, and stamped the delicate workmanship and the exquisite jewels out of all shape and into glittering dust.

Vere did not move a muscle. Only her face grew cold like a stone mask with unutterable scorn.

"A Princess Zouroff does not need to go to the properties of a theatre for her jewels," he said, in a thick, hoarse voice. "As I have treated that jewel, so I will treat the man, if ever you let him enter your presence again. You hear?"

"I hear."

All colour had gone from her lips, but her face remained cold and calm.

"Well?" said her husband, roughly, already, in a measure, ashamed of his violence, as the diamond star covered the carpet beneath his feet with sparkling atoms.

"What do you want me to say? I am your wife, and you can offend me in any way, and I cannot resent it. There is no use in saying what I think of that."

He was silent, and in a measure subdued. He knew very well that his violence had been cowardly and unworthy, that he had disgraced his name and place, that he had been a coward and no gentleman. His new-born sense of fear and veneration of her struggled with his incensed vanity and his irritated suspicions.

"Vera," he muttered, only half-aloud. "Before God, if you would let me, I could love you now!"

She shuddered.

"Spare me that, at least!"

He understood, and was silenced. He glanced at her longingly, sullenly, furtively. The shattered jewel lay at his feet.

"What is that singer to you?" he said, abruptly.

"A man who honours me. You do not."

"Were he only of my rank I would insult him, and shoot him dead."

Vere was silent.

"What do you say?" he muttered, impatient of her silence.

"He is of your rank, and he can defend himself. His hand is clean, and so also is his conscience."

"Will you swear he is no lover of yours?"

Her eyes flashed, but she took the book of prayer lying on her table, kissed it, and said:

"I swear that, certainly."

Then she laid the book down, and with an accent he had never heard from her, she turned suddenly on him, in a passion of indignation that transformed her coldness into fire.

"How dare you? how dare you?" she said, with a vibration in her voice that he had never heard there. "Now that you have done me the last insult that a man can pass upon his wife, be satisfied, and go."

Then she put her hand out, and pointed to the door.

He lingered, dazed and fascinated by that new power in her glance, that new meaning in her voice.

"Women change like that when they love," he said to her aloud. "Are you not of the new school, then? You know very well you have no fidelity from me. Why should you be faithful to me? They say you need not be."

She seemed to him transfigured and risen above him; her fair face had the glow of holy scorn of just wrath still on it.

"Are your sins the measure of my duty?" she said, with unutterable contempt. "Do you think if it were only for you, for *you*, that I were decent in my life and true to my obligation, I should not years ago have failed, and been the vilest thing that lives? You do not understand. Have you never heard of self-respect, of honour, and of God?"

The words touched him, and the look upon her face awed him for an instant into belief in her and belief in heaven; but against his instinct and against his faith the long habit of a brutal cynicism and a mocking doubt prevailed, and the devil in him, that had so long lived with the vile and the foolish of his world, drove him to answer her with a bitter sneer.

"Your words are grand," he said to her, "and I believe you mean them. Yes, you do not lie. But those fine things, my princess, may last so long as a woman is untempted. But so long only. You are all Eve's daughters!"

Then he bowed and left her. He hated himself for the thing he had said, but he could not have stayed the devil in him that uttered it. If his wife betrayed him that night he knew that he would have no title to condemn her; yet he thought, as he went from her presence, if she did—if she did—he would slit the throat of her singing-bird, or of any other man, if any other it were.

Vere stood erect, a sombre disgust and revolt in her eyes. Her husband had said to her, "thou fool! all sin alike; do thou likewise."

In a few moments she stooped and raised the fragments of the jewels and the twisted and broken goldsmith's work. It was all shattered except the sapphire moth.

She shut the moth and all the shining brilliant dust in a secret drawer of her jewel-case, then rang for her women. In another twenty minutes she entered her carriage, and drove in silence with her husband beside her to the Rue de Grénelle.

"Le Prince et la Princesse Zouroff!" shouted the lackeys, standing in a gorgeous line down the staircase of the Embassy.

CHAPTER IV.

It was an April night when the necklace of the moth and the star perished under the heel of Zouroff; there were two months more through which the life in Paris lasted, for Zouroff adored the boulevards, even in summer months; the asphalte had a power to charm him that even the grass of his forest drives never rivalled, and the warm nights of spring and early summer found him driving down the Champs Elysées to and fro his various haunts, his carriage lamps adding two stars the more to its long river of light.

Coming home in the full daylight from his pleasures he would at times meet his wife going out in the clear hours of the early forenoon. He asked her once roughly where she was going, and she told him, naming the poorest quarter on the other side of the Seine.

"Why do you go to such a place?" he asked her as she stood on the staircase.

"There are poor there, and great misery," she answered him reluctantly; she did not care to speak of these things at any time.

"And what good will you do? You will be cheated and robbed, and even if you are not, you should know that political science has found that private charity is the hotbed of all idleness."

"When political science has advanced enough to prevent poverty, it may have the right to prevent charity too," she answered him, with a contempt that showed thought on the theme was not new to her. "Perhaps charity—I dislike the word—may do no good; but friendship from the rich to the poor must do good; it must lessen class hatreds."

"Are you a socialist?"[1] said Zouroff with a little laugh, and drew

---

1 After the Paris Commune was defeated in 1871, socialists and workers continued to work for a Utopian republic. The working class, however, became more deeply alienated than before. It was not until the 1880s that socialism became a significant presence in France.

back and let her pass onward. They were the first words he had spoken to her alone since the night he had destroyed the necklace, and even now they were not unheard; for there were half a score of servants on the stairs and in the vestibule below. Vere went out to her little brougham in the fresh air of the warm lilac-scented morning as the clock struck ten.

Her husband took his way to his own set of rooms, rich with oriental stuffs and weapons, and heavy with the fumes of his tobacco. He thought of what his sister had said of St. Elizabeth and the roses of Paradise; he thought too of what Jeanne de Sonnaz had said. His wife was greatly changed.

She seemed to him to have aged ten years all suddenly; not in the fair beauty of her face, but in her regard, in her tone, in her look. Was she like the young royal saint of Hungary, or was she like all women, as he knew them? He had the careless, half-conscious, but profound belief in depravity that is the note of the century; he thought all women *coquines*.[1] That his wife was different to the rest he had believed; but that she was incapable of deceiving him he was in no way sure. Sooner or later they all went the same road, so he thought. He began to doubt that she told him the truth as to these errands of her morning hours; his sister believed in them indeed, but what should his sister know, who was never out of her bed till noon was past?

Vere had no physical fear, and at times she penetrated into the darkest and roughest quarters of Paris; the quarters that belch out those hidden multitudes that make revolution anarchy, and shatter in dust and blood the visions of patriots. But she was safe there, though once she heard one man say to another, "*Diantre!*[2] what a sight it would be, that lovely head on a scaffold." She turned and looked at him with a smile: "I think I should know how to die, my friend; are you quite sure that you would?"

As this worst form of suspicion, that of the tyrant who trembles, grew upon him, he did what he knew was low and vile and beneath him—he had her watched in these daily hours of absence. He excused his vigilance to those who had the task by the expression of his fears for her safety from the rude and ferocious classes amongst whom she went. They brought him the weekly report of all she did, minute by minute, in all its trifling details; the courage and the self-

---

1 Debauched.
2 The Deuce!

sacrifice of that thankless labour, the self-devotion and patience of that charity, were before him in a chronicle she would never have written herself. He was astonished; he was ashamed. The superstition that underlies the worldly wisdom of the aristocratic Russian, as it permeates the kindly stupidity of the Russian peasant, began to stir in him and trouble him. He began to think she was a holy creature. Though he had no faith, he had that vague religious fear, which often survives the death of all religious beliefs with those who have been educated in strict rituals, as he had been.

When June came they went to Félicité. It was the same thing every year. The world went with them. To her it seemed always as if they were perpetually on the stage before an audience; the audience varied, but the play was always the same.

She would have given ten years of her life for a few weeks' rest, silence, solitude, with "plain living and high thinking,"[1] and time to watch the clouds, the showers, the woodlands, the ways of birds and beasts, the loves of the bees and the flowers. But she never had one day even to herself. There was always on her ear the murmur of society; always, like the shadow on the sun-dial, some duty that was called pleasure, obscuring each hour as it came.

It was a bright Norman summer, the weather clear and buoyant, the country a sea of apple-blossoms. Once or twice she got away by herself, and went to the little cluster of cabins on the head of the cliffs beyond Villerville. The old woman was there—always knitting, always with a white cap and a blue linen gown, against the wall of furze.

"The lark is dead," she said, with a shake of the head. "It was no fault of mine, my Princesse; a boy with a stone one day—ah! ah!—how shall I tell the gentleman when he comes? He has not been yet this summer; he was here in midwinter—oh, quite midwinter—and he said he was going away into the north somewhere. Jesu-Maria! the heaps of cent-sous pieces he gave me to take care of that lark!"

The shrewd old woman under the white roof of her cap watched the face of her "Princesse." "I want to know if she cares too," she thought. "But that beautiful angel could not fail to be loved."

Vera went away slowly through the high grove, even under the shade of the apple-blossoms. How long ago,—it seemed long as a

---

1   From William Wordsworth's "Written in London, September 1802":
    "Plain living and high thinking are no more: / The homely beauty of
    the good old cause / Is gone; our peace, our fearful innocence, / And
    pure religion breathing household laws."

century—since she had been the child listening, with her heart in her eyes, to the song of the lark that was dead!

Her husband said to her sharply that day, after her return, "Where were you this morning? You were hours away."

"I drove to Villerville," she answered him.

"There is a shrine near there, I think?" added Madame Jeanne, with apparent simplicity.

The sombre thoughts of Zouroff caught her insinuation.

"I know of no remarkable shrine," replied Vere, who did not imagine any double meaning in the words. "There is none nearer than Val de Grâce."

Her husband was silent. The Duchesse rose, and hummed a little song then being sung by Jane Hading: *Vous voulez vous moquer de moi.*[1]

This year Madame Jeanne stayed at Félicité. Why not? She had her little girls Berthe and Claire with her, and her husband came now and then, and would come for a longer time when the bouquets of pheasants would begin to fall in the drives of the park.

"*Pourquoi pas?*"[2] she had said, when Zouroff had begged her to stay in his house, instead of taking a villa at Trouville.

"You would not last year," he said, with a man's stupidity.

"Last year was last year," said the Duchesse drily; and she came over and had all the south wing of the château for herself and her Berthe and Claire and their governesses. She was really fond of her children.

The papers of that day spoke of Corrèze. He was in Stockholm.

"That is far enough; she cannot have met him," thought the Duchesse. "Villerville must be a pilgrimage of remembrance. There are women who can live on memories. It must be like eating nothing but ices and wafers. A *bon bouillon*[3] and a little burgundy is better."

Vere had given her word to her husband and her oath; she never supposed that he could doubt either. If Corrèze had come before her in that time she would have said to him with loyal firmness, "I must not see you; my husband has forbidden me." She was steadfast rather than impassioned; honour was the first law of life to her; that love should stoop to tread in secret ways and hide in secret places seemed to her as shameful, nay grotesque, as for a sovereign to hide in a cel-

---

1 You want to make a fool of me. Jane Hading (1859–1933) was one of the leading French actresses and singers of the time (she acted in *Ruy Blas*).

2 Why not?

3 A good broth.

lar or flee in disguise. The intrigues she saw perpetually, in which her
world spent its time, as the spiders theirs in weaving webs, had no
savour, no sweetness, for her. Its roots were set in treachery or cowardice—in either, or in both. All the tenderness that was in her
nature Corrèze had touched; all her gratitude and all her imagination were awakened by him; she knew that the sorrow of a love that
might have been sweet and happy in their lives was with them both,
in sad and hopeless resignation. Yet if he had come before her now
she would have said to him, "I cannot see you, it would be disloyal."

For the old lovely quality of loyalty, which day by day is more and
more falling out from the creeds of men and women, was very
strong in her; and failure in it seemed to her like "shame, last of all
evils."

To Jeanne de Sonnaz this was very droll. So droll that it was
impossible for her to believe in it. She believed in realism, in the
mouldy cheese and the pewter can; she did not believe in Ruy Blas.
She watched Vere narrowly, but she failed to understand her.

"How the affair drags!" she thought, with some impatience. "Can
they really be the lovers of romance who separate themselves by a
thousand leagues, and only love the more the more they are divided? It is droll."

So she kept the snake of suspicion alive and warm in his bosom.

"You were wrong," said Zouroff with some triumph to her; "you
were wrong. The man is in Norway and Sweden."

"I may be," said the Duchesse meditatively. "But people come
back from Norway and Sweden, and I never said, you will remember, that he was more to your wife than her knight, her ideal, her
souvenir.[1] I never meant more than that. Wait until he shall return,
then you will see."

Then he told her how he had destroyed the necklace. For years
he had been in the habit of telling her such things, and now he sacrificed his wife to that habit of confidence in another woman.

"You see you were wrong," he added; "had she borne any sentiment towards him would she have seen his jewels destroyed? She is
not spiritless."

"No, she is not spiritless," said Madame Jeanne thoughtfully. "No,
certainly she is not that. But, in the old houses of the Faubourg,
Sergius, I meet a phantom of the past that we know nothing about;
a phantom that is made a deity and rules their lives like their love of

---

1 Memory.

Henri Cinq;[1] a mere ghost, but still potent to omnipotence, and we know nothing about it; they call it Principle. I suppose your wife may keep that old *démodé*[2] ghost by her too, and may be ruled by it. I have heard of such things. Oh, we have no principle, we have only convenience and impulse, and act either one or the other. But I assure you such a thing exists."

"Scarcely in a woman," said Zouroff with a contemptuous laugh.

"Sooner in a woman than a man, for that matter. But of course it will not last for ever. Your wife is human, and she will not pardon you that ruined locket."

"She said nothing, or very little."

"*Said!*" echoed Madame de Sonnaz with scorn, "you are used to *us*, and to your creatures. Do you think a woman of her temperament would scream as we, or swear as they do, would go into hysterics, or would tear your beard?"

"You seem to admire my wife," he said with irritation.

Jeanne de Sonnaz smiled. "You know I always did. I admire her as one admires Racine, as one admires the women of Port Royal, the paintings of Flandrin, the frescoes of Michael Angelo.[3] It is quite unattainable, quite unintelligible to me, but I admire dumbly and without comprehension. Only I told you that you never should have married a saint, and you never should. I am sorry you destroyed her medallion. It was brutal of you, and *bourgeois*."

"And she will remember it," she added, after a pause, as she gathered up her silks, with which she was working an altar screen for her parish church at Ruilhières, "be very sure of that. Vera is not a woman who forgets. I should box your ears, shake you, and laugh at it all next day, but she would be passive and yet never forget, nor forgive. Chut! There she is!"

Vera at that moment entered the room in which Madame Jeanne was working; her husband moved with a guilty consciousness away, but she had heard nothing.

---

1 Henry V (1387-1422) was the King of England whose victory at the Battle of Agincourt made England the strongest kingdom in Europe. He claimed a considerable amount of French territory and gained Normandy in 1420. He became heir to the French throne and Regent of France.

2 Old fashioned.

3 Jean Baptiste Racine (1639-99) was a French dramatist. He was educated at the convent of Port-Royal; Jean-Hippolyte Flandrin (1809-64) was a French painter. For Michael Angelo see p. 326, note 4.

"Princesse, tell me," said Madame de Sonnaz, "do you forgive easily? I think not."

"Forgive?" said Vera absently. "Is there any question of it? It is for those who offend to ask me that."

"Do you hear, Sergius?" said his friend with a little laugh. "I should like to hear your *mea culpa*."[1]

For the first time an angry doubt came into the mind of Vera, the doubt that her husband spoke of her with Jeanne de Sonnaz. She looked at them both quickly and haughtily, then said very clearly:

"If Monsieur Zouroff know anything that he desires me to pardon he can speak for himself without an ambassadress, and without a listener. I came to ask you to allow Berthe and Claire to come out with me on the sea."

"How good you are to those children, but you will inoculate them with your own sea phrenzy," answered the duchesse with a little laugh. "Of course they may go."

Zouroff had already gone from the room, angry with his friend, more angry with his wife. Madame Jeanne rose a little impetuously, dragging to the ground the artistic embroideries of the shield she was working.

"Vera," she said, with candour in her voice and honesty in her regard, "do not be angry. I am so old a friend of Sergius—he has told me how he tore off your locket and destroyed it. I am so sorry; so very sorry; so is he. But, alas! men are always the same; they are all brutes we know, and—Vera—he is very jealous of your singer."

Vera's face grew very stern.

"Has he commanded you to speak to me on his behalf?"

"No, my dear—not that; he would scarcely do that in plain words. But I am an old friend, and I am sorry. Of course it is too absurd; but he is very jealous. Be careful; men of his race have done mad and cruel things in their time. Do not provoke him. Do not see Corrèze."

"You mean well, madame," said Vera in tones of ice. "But you err in taste and wisdom, and I think your zeal outstrips your orders. I scarcely think even my husband can have charged you with his threats to me."

"Threats? who spoke of threats? A warning—"

"A warning then, but none the less an insult. You are in my house, so I can say nothing. Were I in yours I would leave it. Your children are waiting in impatience—excuse me."

---

1 Apology (my fault, Latin).

Madame Jeanne looked after her as she went through the glass doors on to the sea-terrace, where the pretty little figures of Berthe and Claire were dancing to and fro in the sunlight. Madame Jeanne drew her tapestry-frame towards her, and proceeded to fill in the lilies of St. Cunigonde. She smiled as she bent her head over the frame.

"If I have ever known my sex," she thought—"if I have ever known my sex, a word will go over the north sea, and Corrèze will come from his Norwegian summer to a Norman one, and then— and then—there will be droll things to see. It is like watching the curtain rise in the Ambigu[1]—there is sure to be melodrama."

Melodrama amused her; amused her more than comedy. She had no belief in quiet passion or quiet grief herself, no more than she had in quiet principles.

Vera went out to sea with the little children, and in the mellow sunshine and the sweet orchard-scented air her face was dark with anger and with disgust, and her heart heaved in a bitter rage and rebellion.

Her husband spoke of her to another woman—discussed her acts with another man's wife! "Oh the coward, the coward!" she said very low between her set teeth; it was the blackest word that her language held. That he should have broken her medallion and insulted her with doubt, was insult enough for a lifetime. But that he should relate the affront, and breathe the suspicion, to another woman seemed to her the very last baseness of life.

"If he were here!" she murmured, with a sudden newborn consciousness in her, as her eyes filled with scalding tears, and her heart heaved with indignation. For the first time an indefinite yearning rose in her to place her hand in the hand of Corrèze, and say "avenge me!" Yet had he even stood before her then she would not have said it, she would have bidden him go and leave her.

For what Madame Jeanne called a phantom was always beside her in her path—the phantom of old-world honour, the wraith of dead heroical days.

She leaned against the rail and watched the sea run by the vessel's side, and felt the quiet slow tears of a great anguish fill her eyes and wet her cheeks.

---

1 The Théâtre de l'Ambigu-Comique is located in Paris. Melodramas were often performed there. Zola's *L'Assommoir* premièred there on 18 January 1879.

"Do not cry: you are too pretty to cry," said little Claire, who was a soft and tender child; and Berthe, who was older and cleverer and harder, said, "You should not cry; it spoils the eyes." Then she added reflectively, "*Maman ne pleure jamais*."[1]

The small yacht they were in ran with the breeze through the sweet fresh air. It was a nautical toy, perfect in its way, that had been given to Vere by her husband when the estate of Félicité was settled upon her; the children had wanted to go to the Vaches Noires[2] and search for mussels, and the little ship skirted the coast as lightly as a sea-gull, the merry little girls scudding about its deck like kittens and climbing its cordage like squirrels, while their mother—their mother who never cried—remained in the garden of Félicité with a cigar in her teeth, her person stretched full length in a low-hung silk hammock, a circle of gentlemen around her, and amidst them her host, so charmed by the dexterity of her coquetteries, and so diverted by the maliciousness of her pleasantries, that the old passion, which a dozen years before she had awakened in him, perhaps the worst, as it was in a sense the strongest and most durable, he had ever known, revived in him sufficiently for jealousy, and held him by her side.

It was low water when they reached that part of the Vaches Noires which lies underneath what is called the desert. The strangely shaped rocks towered above, beyond, the sea was blue and smooth, the sand was wet, the children's *équille*[3] fishing promised well. A little boat took them off the yacht to the uncovered beach, and Berthe and Claire, with naked little legs, and their forks shaped like the real fisherfolk's, and their bright hair flying, forgot that they were little aristocrats and Parisiennes and became noisy, joyous, romping, riotous children, happy in their sport and the fine weather. At that part of the rough shore there was no one near except some peasants digging for their livelihood, as the little girls were digging for play, at the silvery hermits' holes in the sands. There were fêtes at Houlgate which kept the summer crowd that day from the distant rocks. Berthe and Claire, agile as they were, were no match for the agility of the lords of the soil, and the pastime absorbed and distracted them. Vere, seeing them so happy, left them in the care of her old skipper, who was teaching them the mysteries of the sport, and sat down under the sombre amphitheatre of the rocks.

---

1 Mama never cries.
2 Literally, "black cows" (a formation of rocks).
3 Sand-eel.

She was fond of the children, but this day their shouts and their smiles alike jarred on her; she had learned for the first time that it was with their mother that her husband discussed her acts and thoughts. She sat quite alone in a sheltered spot, where the slate of the lower formation had been hollowed by the winter waves at high tides into a sort of niche; she thought of the day when, older in years than these little children, but younger in heart than even they were now, she had come on these shores in her old brown holland skirts. It was just such weather as it had been then; clear, cloudless, with a sunlit sea, and an atmosphere so free from mist that the whole line of the far-reaching coast, now become so familiar to her sight, was visible in all its detail, from the mouth of Seine to the mouth of Orne.

Her heart was very weary.

The distant laughter of the little children borne to her ear by the wind, jarred on her. Where were the use of honour and good faith? They smelt sweet, like a wholesome herb, in her own hand, but in all her world none set any store on them. She was free to throw them aside if she chose. She would be more popular, find more sympathy, nay, to her husband himself would seem more human and more truthful if she did so. The sense of life's carelessness, impotency for good, and frightful potency for evil, weighed on her like a stone. Her husband had said to her that women were only loyal till they were tempted; was it so? Was honour so poor a thing? she thought. In dark old Bulmer the now dead woman had taught her to think honour a sword like Britomart's,[1] that in a maiden's hand might be as potent and as strong as in a knight's. What was the poor frail empty thing that bent at a touch and broke? She thought what they called honour must surely be no finer or better thing than a mere dread of censure, a mere subserviency to opinion; a thing without substance or soul, a mere time-service and cowardice.

A fisherman came by her with his load of mussels and little eels going on to Bougeval. He pointed up above her head and said, in his Froissart-like accent:[2]

---

1 Britomart is the powerful heroine in Book III of Spencer's *The Faerie Queene*. She is a female knight of chastity. The poet recounts her adventures in her quest for Artegall, the man she fell in love with from his image in a mirror.

2 Jean Froissart (c. 1337-1410) was a French historian. He writes in a peculiar fourteenth-century style, with syntax and spelling that are (by modern standards, of course) antiquated, even at times stilted. The fisherman's "Froissart-like accent" is probably a reference to its odd-sounding, even slang-like qualities, filled with regionalisms, etc.

"There will be a broken neck up yonder, unless our Lady interferes."

Vere, alarmed for the children, who were out of sight, looked upward; she saw a man coming down the precipitous cliffs from the country above.

Her heart stood still; her blood ran cold; she recognised Corrèze.

The fisherman stood staring upward; the descent was one which the people themselves would never have attempted; where the face of the dark stone was a sheer declivity, broken into sharp peaks and rough bastions, on which there seemed scarce a ledge for a sea-bird to perch on, Corrèze was descending with the sure foot that in his boyhood had let him chase the ibex and the boudequin of the Alps of Dauphiné and Savoy, and had let him in later years hunt the steinbock of Styria and Carinthia in its highest haunts. Vere, risen to her feet, stood like the fisherman gazing upward. She was like stone herself; she neither moved nor cried out; she scarcely breathed. She looked upward, and in those few moments all the horrors of death passed over her.

Was it an instant, or an hour? she never knew. One moment he was in the air, hanging as the birds hang to the face of the cliff, beneath him only the jagged points of a thousand pinnacles of rock: the next he stood before her, having dropped lightly and easily on the sands, while the peasant gasping, muttered his paternosters in incoherent awe.

Corrèze was very pale, and his lips trembled a little; but it was not the perilous descent of the rocks that had shaken him, it was the look which he saw on her face. If he had dared; nay, had she been any other woman, he would have said, "You cannot deny it now; you love me."

Their eyes met as they stood together on the same coast where they had first seen one another, when he was gay and without sorrow, and she was a child. They knew then that they loved each other, as they had not known it when he had sung in the Paris salon:

Si vous saviez que je vous aime,
Surtout si vous saviez comment—[1]

For between them there then had been doubt, hesitation, offence, uncertainty; but now the great truth was bare to them both, and neither dreamed of denying it.

---

1 If you knew that I love you / Above all if you knew how much.

Yet he only said as he uncovered his head, "Forgive me, Princesse; I fear I startled you."

"You startled me," she answered mechanically. "Why run such a frightful danger?"

"It is none to me; the rocks are safer than the ice-walls. I was above and I saw you: there was no other way."

The fisherman had shouldered his creel and was trudging homeward; he paused abruptly, he stood before her still bareheaded, he was very pale.

Without being conscious what she did she had seated herself again on the ledge of slate, the sea and the shore blended dizzily before her eyes.

Corrèze watched her anxiously, pitifully; his courage failed him, he was afraid of this woman whom he loved, he who had been always, in love, victorious.

"Have I displeased you?" he murmured humbly. "I have come straight from Norway; I thought I might take one hour on this coast before going to Paris; I heard that you were here. I have been an exile many months—"

She stopped him with a gesture.

"I will not affect to misunderstand, there is no good in affectation; but do not speak so to me. I cannot hear it. I thank you for your courage at Villafranca, I am not ungrateful; but we must not see each other—unless it be in the world."

"You did not say that at Villafranca."

"My husband had not then said it to me."

Corrèze moved and faltered a little, as if he had been struck a blow.

"You obey Prince Zouroff!" he exclaimed with disdain, and petulance, and passion.

"I obey the word I gave Prince Zouroff."

Silence fell between them.

Vere was very pale; she was still seated; there was sort of faintness on her; she had no time for thought or resolution, she only clung by instinct to one of the creeds of her childhood, the creed that a promise given was sacred.

Corrèze stood beside her checked, mortified, chafed, and humbled. He, the most eloquent, the most ardent, lover of his time, was mute and wounded, and could find no word at the instant that could speak for him. He was struck dumb, and all the vivid imagining, the fervent persuasiveness, the poetical fluency that nature had given to him and art had perfected, fled away from him as though they had never been his servants to command, and left him mute and help-less.

Vere looked away from him at the blue shining sea.

"If you think of me," she said slowly, "if you think of me as you thought when you sang the Coupe d'Or, you will go now."

"With no other word?"

"My life is hard enough," she murmured; "do not make it harder."

There was an unconscious appeal in the words that, from a woman so proud and so silent, touched him to the quick. All his passions longed to disobey her, but his tenderness, his chivalry, his veneration, obeyed.

"I told my husband not long ago that you honoured me," she added in a low voice. "Do not let me think that I deceived myself and him."

Corrèze bent his head.

"I will never deceive you," he said simply, "and at any cost I will obey you."

He looked at her once; her eyes were still gazing away from him at the sea. He lingered an instant, then he laid on her knee some for-get-me-nots he had gathered in the brooks above, and left her; across the wet sands and the disordered detritus[1] of the beach his light swift step bore him quickly to the edge of the murmuring sea. There was a boat there, an old brown rowing boat, and its owner was mending nets on its bench.

In another few moments the old boat was pushed in the water, the fisherman willingly bent to his oars—Corrèze also was rowing—with the helm set for Honfleur. When he was far away on the water he looked back, but then only: Vere sat motionless.

He had been beside her, he whom an hour earlier she had longed for as an avenger, and she had driven him away.

She had been true to the false, to the unfaithful faithful.

The man whose genius had been the one solace and pleasure of her life, whose beauty and whose sympathy and whose chivalry were as a sorcery to her, who would have put his whole fate in her hands as he had put the myosotis, had been there beside her to do with as she chose, and she had sent him from her.

Her husband had said, "women are true till they are tempted." she had been tempted and had been strong, strong enough not even to say to him, "Avenge me."

---

1 Broken rocks.

The sun had sunk low, the late day grew grey, the dusky sea ran swiftly and smoothly, soon the terraces and towers of Félicité rose in sight through the twilight mists. The little children, tired and sleeping, lay curled quietly on their cushions at her feet: she felt weak and weary as if from some long combat, and her heart ached—ached for the pain she caused, the pain she bore. She stretched her hand over the rails and dropped the forget-me-nots in the fast running sea.

She would not keep a flower of his now that she knew—

She saw the blue blossoms tossed for a moment on the water and then engulfed. "I do not want them," she thought, "I shall never forget; it will be he who will forget."

For she thought so, with that humility of a lonely soul which is deemed so proud only because it is so sad.

He would go into the world, be the world's idol, and forget. But she would remember till she died. And even at this consciousness a sense of guilt came over her, a sense of shame burned in her. She loved this man who was not her husband—she, a wife. To her conscience and her honour, both unworn and undulled, even so much as this seemed a treachery to her word and an uncleanliness. "Do I grow like the others?" she mused, with a sort of horror at herself; the others, the women of her world, who made intrigues their daily bread. "O my angel Raphael, you shall not fall nor I!" she murmured half aloud, as the sea swept on its foam the little blue blossoms, and her eyes grew blind and her heart grew faint.

Fall into the slough of abandoned passions, into the dishonesty of hidden loves, into the common coarse cowardice of an impure secrecy? ah, never, never! She felt cold, sick, weary, as she left the little road under the shadow of the walls of Félicité, and ascended the stone steps that mounted from the sea to the garden. But she moved firmly and with her head erect.

Honour is an old-world thing; but it smells sweet to those in whose hand it is strong.

It was nearly nine; the shadows were dark, a low pale yellow line where the sun had gone down was all that was left of day. The little girls, sound asleep, were carried away from the boat by their women. The first gong was sounding that summoned the guests of the house to dinner. She was dressed quickly, and went down to the drawing-rooms; there was a shade like a bruise under her eyes, and her lips were pale; otherwise she looked as usual.

Jeanne de Sonnaz, greeting her with effusion, kissed her and thanked her for the children's happy day.

Vere sat opposite her husband through the dinner, which was

always a banquet. Her eyes were tired, but there was a steady light in them; something heroic and invincible, that made the grave beauty of her face like that of a young warrior's. No one saw it. They only thought that she was tired, and so more silent than usual.

The evening wore on its way; to her it seemed endless; there were many people staying in the house; it was such an evening as the first that she passed at Félicité, when she had watched society with wondering gaze, as a bright comedy. Jeanne de Sonnaz, with a dress of red and gold, and some of her grand rubies on, sparkled like a jewel, till her ugly face seemed radiant and handsome. She sang songs of Theo and of Judic; she played impromptu a scene of Celine Chaumont's; she was brilliant and various as her manner was, and she sent a shower of mirth on the air that was to others as contagious as a laughing gas. "What a pity she tires herself so much by the sea or on it," she said of Vere to Sergius Zouroff. "It makes her so silent and so *morne*[1] in the evening."

He muttered something like a suppressed oath, and went to his wife.

"You look like a statue; you leave others to do all your duties for you; you sweep through the rooms like a ghost. Why cannot you rouse yourself, and laugh and dance?"

Vere made him no answer.

Laugh and dance in public, and in stealth betray him? To do that would have made him content, herself popular.

The night wore itself away in time; she never well knew how; it closed somewhat earlier than usual, for the morrow was the first day of shooting, and Madame Jeanne had bade them rise with the lark. Vere, instead of going to her room, went out into the gardens. The night was cool, fragrant, soundless, except for the murmur of the sea.

"To laugh and wear a false or a foolish face—that is all he asks of me!" she thought bitterly. If her husband could have seen her heart as it ached that night, if he could have known that only out of loyalty to him she had cast the myosotis from her hand into the sea, would he not only have told her she was an imbecile, and was too fond of tragedy, and he was no Othello to be jealous of a humble handkerchief?[2]

---

1 Mournful, dejected.

2 To get revenge on Othello in Shakespeare's play of the same name, Iago succeeds in making Othello believe that his wife Desdemona and Cassio are lovers. When Othello sees Cassio with the handkerchief he had given to his bride as a gift, he is prompted immediately to kill her.

Would he not have said, "Look around, and do like others."

It was between one and two o'clock; the stars were all at their brightest, except where clouds hung over the sea to the north, and obscured them; the château was quiet behind her; an irregular yet picturesque pile that grew sombre and fantastic in the shadows, while in its casements a few lights only gleamed here and there through the ivy.

Vere stood and looked at the waves of the channel without seeing them. The world seemed empty and silent. Never again would she hear the voice that had first come to her ear on those shores—never again—except in some crowded salon or across some public theatre.

She shuddered, and went within. The silence and the solitude were too like her destiny not to hurt her more than even the "vain laughter of fools."[1] It was the first time that the peace of nature and of night seemed a reproach to her. For though innocent of any act unworthy or disloyal to herself, she felt guilty, she felt as if some poison had fallen in that golden cup which she strove to keep pure. To her a thought, a desire, a regret, were forbidden things, since she was the wife of Sergius Zouroff.

One glass door was open, and some lamps were burning, for the servants had seen that she remained on the terrace, and two or three of them, yawning and sleepy, stood in the antechambers awaiting her entrance.

She went up the staircase, past those bronze negroes, with their golden torches, which had lighted her childish steps on her first night at Félicité.

There were two ways to her own chamber. One way, the usual and shortest one, was encumbered by some pictures and statues that were being moved to another corridor. She took the longer way, which led through the body of the house to the left wing of it, in which her own rooms were, by her choice, for sake of the view down the sea-coast and northward.

Going this way she passed the stately guest-chambers which had been allotted to the Duchesse de Sonnaz.

The lamps in the long gallery burned low; her footfall made no sound on the carpet; she passed on as silently as the ghost to which her husband impatiently likened her. She was thinking neither of

---

1 See Ecclesiastes 7:6: "For as the crackling of thorns under a pot, so is the laughter of the fool: this also is vanity."

him nor of her guests; she was thinking how long her life in all like-lihood would be since she was young, and how lonely. She was thinking, "he bade me keep myself unspotted from the world; it shall never be he who lowers me."

Suddenly a strong ray of light shone across her feet. She was pass-ing a half-opened door—a door that had been shut with a careless hand, and had reopened. The curtains within were parted a little; as she passed, she could not tell why, her eyes were drawn to the mel-low light shining between the tapestries.

It was the door of Jeanne de Sonnaz. Through the space Vera saw into the room, and saw her husband.

For a moment she made a step forward to enter and front them. The blood leaped into her face; all the pride in her, outraged and disgusted, sprang up in arms under that last and worst of insults. Then with a strong effort she thrust the door to, that others should not see what she had seen; that she should screen his dishonour, if he would not; and passed on unseen and unheard by those within to her own room. When she reached it she trembled from head to foot, but it was with rage.

She came of a bold race, who had never lightly brooked insult, though she had long borne its burden patiently, because duty was stronger with her than pride. She sat down and drew paper and pens to her, and wrote three lines:

"Either I or the Duchesse de Sonnaz leave Félicité to-morrow before noon.

(Signed)   "VERA, Princess ZOUROFF."

She sealed the note, and gave it to her woman for the Prince.

"You will give it to Ivan; he will give it to his master in the morn-ing," she said, as they were leaving the room. She was still careful of his dignity, as he was not. That night she did not sleep.

At sunrise they brought her a letter from her husband. It said only, "Do what you please. You cannot suppose I shall insult my friend for you.—ZOUROFF."

"His friend!" said Vere with a bitter smile. She recalled memories of her life in Paris and at Svir; recalled so many hints, so many glances, so many things that she had attached no meaning to, which now were quite clear as day. She remembered the warning of Corrèze.

"He too must have known!" she thought; and her face burned to think that the man who loved her should be aware of all the outrage passed on her by the man who owned her.

"The Prince asks an answer," they said, at her door.

"There is no answer," said Vere, and added, to her women, "bring me a little tea, and then leave me."

They thought she wished to sleep, and suspected nothing else. Left to herself she gathered up some needful things with her own hands, the first thing she had ever done for herself since the old simple days at Bulmer. She put together the jewels her own family had given her; shut the shattered necklace of the moth and the star up with them in a casket, and put on the plainest clothes she had. She was ready to leave his house now and for ever. She would take nothing with her that was his or that had been hers by his gift. Of the future she had no clear thought; all that she was resolute was, that no other night should find herself and Jeanne de Sonnaz under the same roof.

All the house was quiet. No one had risen except herself. She waited, because she did not choose to go out like one in hiding, or ashamed, from her own home. She intended to leave the place in full daylight and publicity. The world could say what it liked, but it could not then say she had left secretly, and the shame would be for those who merited it. Without and within all was still. The sea had scarce a sound, no breeze stirred in the trees, the silvery haze that heralded a hot day was over land and water. She stood at the window and looked out, and a quiet tranquility came over her. She was about to leave it all for ever, all the pomp and the splendour, all the monotony and the feverishness, all the burden of rank and the weariness of pleasure. She would soon be alone, and poor. She was not afraid. She would go into the dim, green German country, and live in some man-forgotten place, and get her bread in some way. She was not afraid. Only all the world should know where she went, and why. All the world should know she was alone.

She stood beside the open casement with the dog beside her; he would be her sole companion in the loneliness to which she would go. Corrèze—she thought of Corrèze, but, with the sternness which is apt to exist in very pure and very proud natures, she thought only, "if he come to me when I live alone he too will be a coward!"

And as a coward she would treat him, she thought; for her heart was but half awake still, and of passion she yet knew but little, and what she knew she feared as a thing unclean.

Suddenly her door was burst open; her husband entered; his eyes were bloodshot, his face was dark with fury.

"Are you mad?" he cried to her, as he saw her travelling jewel-case and the locked valise, and casket.

She looked at him with a grand dignity upon her face, as though she saw something leprous and loathsome.

"I gave you your choice," she said in a voice that vibrated with restrained wrath. "You took your choice."

She pointed to his letter that lay open on the table.

"And I tell you that neither you nor she shall go out of my house!" he swore with a great oath. "You shall receive her, smile on her, sit at the same table with her, please her in all things as I do. She is the only woman that I never tire of, the only woman that contents me—"

"Tell Paul de Sonnaz so; not me."

Her husband's face grew terrible and hideous in the convulsions of its rage.

"He! he is not a fool like you, he knows what the world is and women are. By Christ, how dare you?—how dare you speak to me of him or her? I am my own master, and I am yours. Sooner than let you insult my friends for one moment, I would fling you from this window in the sea."

"I know that. It is I who go, she who remains."

"As God lives, neither of you shall go. What! you think I shall allow such a scandal as my wife's departure from under my roof?—"

"I shall not allow such an outrage as for Madame de Sonnaz to be under your roof with me."

She spoke firmly and in a low tone and without violence. Something in her tone from its very calmness subdued and abashed him for an instant: but his hesitation scarcely lasted more than that. "Madame de Sonnaz is my guest—my honoured guest," he said passionately. "I will not have her affronted. I will not have a breath on her name. What, you will make a scene that will ring through all Europe—you will go out of my house when my friends are in it—you will make yourself and her and me the bye-words of society! Never, by heaven! You are my wife, and as my wife you stay."

Vere, who was very pale and as cold as though the summer morning were a winter's day, remained quite calm. By great effort she restrained her bitter rage, her boundless scorn. But he changed her resolve in nothing. "I stay, if Madame de Sonnaz go," she said between her teeth. "If she stay, I go. I told you to choose; you did choose."

Sergius Zouroff forgot that he was a gentleman, and all that was of manliness in him perished in his frenzy. He raised his arm and struck her. She staggered and fell against the marble of the console by which she stood, but no cry escaped her; she recovered herself and stood erect, a little stunned, but with no fear upon her face.

"You have all your rights now," he cried brutally, with a rough laugh that covered his shame at his own act. "You can divorce me, Madame, '*sous le toit conjugal*,' and '*violence personelle*,'[1] and all the rest; you have all your rights. The law will be with you."

"I shall not divorce you," said Vere, while the great pain of the blow, which had fallen on her breast, ached and throbbed through all her body. "I shall not divorce you, I do not take my wrongs into the shame of public courts; but—I go—or—she goes."

An exceeding faintness came over her, and she was forced to sit down lest she should fall again, and the air around her grew dark and seemed full of noise. Zouroff rang loudly for her woman.

"The Princess fell against the marble—an accident—she has fainted," he said hurriedly, and he escaped from the chamber. In a few moments he was with Jeanne de Sonnaz. In the utter weakness of his submission to the domination which she had obtained over him he had grown so used to seek her counsels in all things, and at all times, that he told her all now. Her rage extinguished his own as one fire swallows up another.

"Oh, imbecile!" she screamed at him. "If Paul hear—if the world know—I am lost for ever!"

He stared at her with gloomy amaze.

"Paul knows; society too—they always have known—"

"O madman!" she yelled at him, with her shining eyes all flame. "They have known certainly, but they could still seem *not* to know, and did so. Now if once it be a public scandal Paul will act, and the world will be with him! Good God! If your wife leave the house for me, I am ruined for ever!"

"I have given her what will keep her still."

"You are a brute, you were always a brute. That is nothing new. But your wife you do not know. She will get up though she be dying, and go—now she once knows, now she has once said that she will not stay where I am. Wait, wait, wait! you imbecile! Let me think; your wife must not go. For her sake? no! good heavens no!— for *mine*."

---

1   Adulterous relationships carried on in the marital bed (or literally, under the marital or conjugal roof) and personal (bodily) violence. Under the British Divorce Act of 1857, men were permitted to divorce on the grounds of adultery alone, women on the grounds of adultery and either physical cruelty, sodomy, incest, rape, bigamy, bestiality, or two years' desertion.

Sergius Zouroff stood passive and uncomplaining under the torrent of her abuse.

"A scandal, a story for the papers, a cause for the tribunals; good heavens! have you and I lived all these years only to fall into such helpless folly at the last?" she shrieked at him. "Why did you have me come here? Paul will take Berthe and Claire away, if he do no more. Oh you madman! why did you not show me your wife's note before you went to her? She is right, she is always right, and you were a brute to strike her; but she wants her divorce, of course, why not? she loves Corrèze, and she is a woman afraid of sin. But she shall not go—she must not go; I will go sooner—"

"You shall never go for her."

"I shall go for myself. You are a brute, you are an idiot; you understand nothing. I will be summoned—Paul can be ill, or Ruilhières on fire—something, anything, so that no one knows."

"You shall not go, you will humiliate me; she will think—"

"What do I care for your humiliation? I care to avert my own. Pshaw! Do you suppose I would stay an hour in this house if your wife were out of it? Do you suppose I would risk my good name, and make myself a scandal to the Faubourg? Good heavens! how little you know me after all these years. I shall obey your wife and go; she is the soul of honour in her own odd way. She will say nothing if I go. My name shall not serve her as a chisel to cut her fetters. Oh, what fools men are, what dolts, what mules! Why could you not bring her note to me, and ask me what to do? Instead, you must go and strike her! Do you suppose her women will not know? An accident! Who believes in accidents? All the house will know it before noon. Oh imbecile! You would marry a young saint, a creature from another world—it was sure to end like this. Go, go! or my women will see you, and it will be worse; go, and in a minute or two I shall send you word that Paul is dying. Go! Thank you? I?—no, why should I thank you? I never bade you be cruel to your wife or strike her; I always bade you treat her as a saint. She is one, though how long—"

"I struck her because she insulted you."

"She was right enough to insult me; she is more right still when she insults you. Now go!"

With sullen subjection he went; he learned what gratitude was from the women of his world. In half an hour's time there was some confusion in the well-ordered household of Félicité, for the Duchesse de Sonnaz, her children, their servants and her own, were departing in hot haste; it was said that M. le Duc was lying ill of sunstroke at their château of Ruilhières, in the department of Morbihan.[1]

Lying sick and blind on her bed, Vere heard the sound of the horses' feet.

"It is Madame la Duchesse who is leaving," said her maid, who from the other side of the closed door had heard all that had passed between Sergius Zouroff and his wife.

Vere said nothing.

It was the first day of shooting; there was a great breakfast, to which many sportsmen of the neighbourhood came; there were battues[2] on a large scale in the woods; there were noise and movement and the sound of many steps throughout the château, and out on the terrace, under her windows; now and then she heard her husband's voice; then after a while all was still; there was the echo of distant shots from the woods, that was all. The day wore away. Her women told the ladies of the house party that the Princess had a severe headache from a fall.

Towards evening she rose, and was dressed. The pain had lulled in a measure, and the faintness had passed away. She wished to avoid comment, to cover the departure of Jeanne de Sonnaz. Under the pale yellow roses of the bouquet at her bosom there was a broad black bruise. The evening passed as usual. The house party suspected nothing; Vere's women were discreet, and the surprise, the sorrow, the bewilderment of Jeanne de Sonnaz at what she had said were the sudden tidings from Ruilhières had been so natural, that the few people who had seen her at her departure had been deceived into believing those tidings true. The evening passed smoothly; a little operetta in the little theatre filled two of its hours, and if the mistress of Félicité looked pale and spoke little, she often did that. Zouroff never looked at his wife and never addressed her. But that also was not rare enough to be any matter for notice.

Vere underwent the fatigue of the night without faltering, though she was in physical pain, and at times a sickly sense of faintness came over her.

She was thankful when the men went to the smoking-room, the

---

1 Western France. France is divided into large departments or districts for administrative purposes.
2 Beaters to drive the game out from cover.

women to their bed-chambers, and she was free to be alone and rest. On the table in her own room there lay a letter. She shuddered a little, for she recognised the loose, rude handwriting of her husband. She was tired of pain and of insult, and she had little hope of any other thing.

She sat down and read it.

"You have had your own way," he wrote to her. "The only woman whom I care for has been driven away by you. Do not suppose you have gained any victory; you will pay the cost of the affront you have dared to pass on her. I shall not speak to you again if we meet here a thousand times. I wish to avoid a scandal for the present at least, not for your sake, but for hers. So I write to you now. You were about to leave this house. You will leave it. As soon as this circle of guests breaks up, the day after to-morrow, you will leave it. You will go to an estate of mine in Poland, Walrien and Ivan will accompany you, and you can take your women of course. There you will remain. If you wish to escape, you can sue me for a divorce. Whenever you do so, I shall not oppose it.

(Signed)

"SERGIUS NICOLAIVITCH, Prince ZOUROFF."

CHAPTER V.

In one of the most desolate parts of the country of Poland, there were vast estates of the Princes Zouroff, conferred on them at the time of the partition of that unhappy land between Christian sovereigns. They were vast, lonely districts, with villages few and scantily populated; immense plains of grain and grass, and swamps of reedy wildernesses, and dim, sandy forests of pines, straight, and colourless, and mournful.

In the heart of all these—whose yield made up no slight sum in the immense riches of the Russian Princes who owned them, and spent their produce on the pavement of Paris and St. Petersburg—there stood a large, lofty building, which had been once a fortified monastery, and had served for a century as the scarcely ever visited castle of the Zouroffs.

It was of immense extent. It had no architectural beauty; and, from its many narrow windows there was no outlook except on one side to the interminable woods of pine, and on the other over the plains and marshes, through which a sullen, yellow river crept. Within, it was decorated as it had been decorated by Ivan Zouroff at the time of the abdication of Stanislas Augustus;[1] Zouroff having hanged the peasants on the pine trees, and made the corn-lands red, before sunset and harvest-time, with blood, and in such wise pleased his imperial mistress.[2]

From the gay, gorgeous interior, and the sunlit gardens and sea terraces of the Norman château, Sergius Zouroff sent his wife to this place, amidst the desolation of a province, then bleeding afresh from the terrorism that strove to stamp out the Nihilists.

Vere left Félicité without protest. Félicité was hers by settlement, but she did not urge that fact. She accepted the commands of her husband, and travelled across Europe in almost unbroken silence, accompanied by the attendants he had selected, by her women, and by the dog Loris.

When she had read her husband's letter, her first impulse had been to refuse, and to disobey him; to go away with her own jewels, and no single thing of his, and gain her own bread in some way in solitude, as she had intended to do if Jeanne de Sonnaz had remained in her house. Then, on later and calmer thought, she accepted the banishment to Poland. Her pride made her willing to avoid all scandal, her principle made her deem it still right to obey her husband. She had asked him once to let her live on his estates, out of the world; she considered she had the request granted, though in a savage and bitter way. As to the condition that he made her return dependent on—she lifted her head, and drew herself erect, with the haughty resolve that she was capable of when stung and roused. Sooner than receive Jeanne de Sonnaz in her house, or ever salute her as a friend, she said to herself that she would live and die on the Polish plains. She did not answer; she did not protest or rebuke; she neither wrote nor spoke to her husband in the fortnight that followed; she entertained her guests with her usual calm, cold grace, and when the last of them had left, and the day of her departure

---

1 Stanislaw Leszczyski was elected King of Poland after the death of Augustus II in 1733. His opponents ousted him and forced the election of Augustus III. Stanislaw I was sent into exile in 1734. During the last years of the reign of Augustus III, Catherine the Great of Russia intervened in Polish affairs. Stanislaw II Augustus Poniatowski gained the crown of Poland in 1764, with the help of Russian troops. In the First Partition of Poland (1772), the country was divided by Russia, Prussia, and Austria.

2 Catherine the Great.

arrived, she went away tranquilly, as though she went of her own will, and in her own way, taking the dog Loris.

Zouroff had not been surprised.

Though he could ill appreciate her character, he did not misunderstand it. "She may break, she will never bend," he thought, as careful always of the outside observances of courtesy, he bade her a courtly farewell before his household.

"I am his prisoner!" she thought, as a week later she entered the austere gloom of Szarisla. But sooner than release herself on the terms he offered, she said in her heart that Poland should be her tomb, as it had been that of so many martyrs. Martyrs to an idea, the world said of those. It would have said the same of her.

To her mother, and her friends, and all society, Sergius Zouroff explained that his wife had long asked him to allow her to pass some months on his northern estates, to establish a school, and improve the moral condition of the peasantry, and at last he had consented; it was an insanity, he added, but an innocent one; she was a saint.

"Alas! alas! what has happened?" thought his sister, "what has happened? Oh, why was I not at Félicité!"

But she was the only one who feared or wondered—the Princess Vera had always been so strange; and she was a saint.

To Jeanne de Sonnaz alone Zouroff said, with his gloomy eyes full of sombre ferocity, "*Je vous venge.*"[1]

To her sister-in-law, and to the few to whom she ever wrote, Vera said always, in her brief letters, "I am tired of the world, as you know; I am glad of this retreat. It is desolate, and very dull, but it is peace."

Madame Nelaguine, with her eyes sparkling with rage, and all her little person erect in indignant dignity, reproached her brother in a torrent of rebuke and censure. "I imagine very well what happened," she said to him. "You would have Jeanne de Sonnaz under the same roof with Vere."

"Respect my friend's name," said Zouroff, with savage authority, "or you and I never meet again. Vere is a saint, you say. Well, she has her wish; she goes into retreat. Would it please you better if she were living with Corrèze?"

"Corrèze—he is nothing to her!" said Madame Nelaguine hotly.

Zouroff shrugged his shoulders. "Some think otherwise," he answered.

"You are a brute, and you are a coward—a malignant coward!"

---

1 I avenge you.

said his sister. "You outrage your wife in every way, and you must even dare to soil her innocence with suspicion."

"If it be suspicion only time will show," said Zouroff. "Go and live at Szarisla yourself, if you pity my wife so much."

But Madame Nelaguine, who loved the world, and could not live without its excitements and its intrigues, could not face that captivity in the Polish plain, though all the heart she had in her yearned towards her brother's wife.

"Will you imprison her all her life?" she cried.

Zouroff answered with impatience and fatigue, "She will remain there until she receives my friend with respect."

"You are a brute," said his sister once more.

"I protect Jeanne, and I avenge her," said Zouroff obstinately. He fancied that his honour was involved in the defence of his mistress.

"Jeanne!" echoed his sister with unutterable scorn. "You might as well defend and avenge your quadroon."

But she knew very well that she might as well seek to shake the Ural mountains at their base as change the obstinacy of her brother.

Jeanne de Sonnaz had gained the empire over him of a re-awakened passion; the empire of a strong woman over an indolent man; of a mistress once deserted, and so doubly tenacious of her hold. There was no beauty in her, and no youth; but she had the secret of dominion over men. She cowed this tyrant, she subdued this man, who, to the self-will of long self-indulgence, had the moral feebleness and inertness of the Slav temperament; she railed at him, jeered at him, commanded him, yet fascinated him. He knew her to be worthless, faithless, never wholly his, nor wholly any one's, yet she held him. "After all, she is the woman I have loved best," he said to himself; and believed it, because she had the gift of exciting all that was worst in him, and subduing his fierce impulses to her own will and whim.

When he had married, Jeanne de Sonnaz, who beyond all things valued her position, and loved the world, had kept her peace because she did not choose to jeopardize her name, or gain the ridicule of her society. But she had always said to herself, "*Je me vengerai.*"[1]

She kept her word.

Vere was in her captivity at Szarisla; and the Duchesse de Sonnaz—moving from one château to another, and entertaining circles of guests for the shooting at their own mighty place of Ruilhières—said easily in the ear of the two or three great ladies who were her most intimate associates, that there had been a scene at Félicité; she had tried to

1 I will get revenge.

mediate between her old friend and his wife, but vainly, so far as peace went; Zouroff had forbidden the Princess to receive Corrèze, and Corrèze had been found there at evening in the gardens; oh, there was nothing serious—Vera was a young saint—but all the same there had been a scene, and Zouroff had sent his wife to Szarisla.

Then the two or three whom she told told others, and so the tale ran, and grew as it ran, and was believed. The world was satisfied that the Princess Zouroff was in penitence in Poland.

"I think they were lovers many years ago. I remember, when she was a mere child, seeing her in a boat with Corrèze; she had come from Havre with him; her mother was distracted. I suppose Zouroff and the Nelaguine knew nothing of it," said the Princess Hélène Olgarousky, who made one of the brilliant autumn party at Ruilhières where Zouroff was not.

"Be sensible, mon ami," had said the Duchesse Jeanne; "now your wife is away I cannot receive you—it would not do. Oh, in winter, when we are all in Paris again, you may come and see Paul as usual. But stay at Ruilhières you will not; no—no—no. Three times, No!"

She had no beauty, and no youth, she had no heart, and no conscience; she had been his friend for fifteen years, and he usually tired of any woman in less than fifteen days. Yet Sergius Zouroff chafed at the interdiction to stay at Ruilhières, as though he were eighteen, and she seen but an hour before; and found himself waiting with impatience for the moment of his return to Paris, with a vague sense that without this woman life was stupid, empty, and purposeless.

He missed the goad to his senses and his temper with which she knew so well how to guide him, as the tamed elephant turned loose misses the prick of the mahout's[1] steel. But she, who knew that the elephant too long left to himself turns wild, and comes never again to his mahout's call, took care not to leave Zouroff too much to himself. When the first shooting-party broke up at Ruilhières, she left Duc Paul with some men to slay the pheasants, and went, for the sake of little Claire, who was not strong, to Arcachon and to Biarritz.[2]

There Zouroff went occasionally when she would allow him. He went alone. He would no more have dared to take the mulattress or any other newer toy within sight of Jeanne de Sonnaz now, than he would have dared to take them into his Tsarina's presence.

---

1 Elephant driver.
2 Resort areas in southwest France on La Côte d'Argent (The Silver Coast).

He had insulted his wife, but he dared not insult his mistress. She spoke to him often of his wife.

"You cannot keep Vera in Poland all winter," she said one day in the fragrant alleys of Arcachon while Berthe and Claire played before them with little silk balloons.

"I shall do so," he said gloomily.

"Impossible! They will call you a tyrant, an ogre, a fiend. You must have her in Paris."

"Not unless she receives you."

"Do not make me ridiculous, I beg of you," she said with some impatience. "You mean,—if she will consent not to receive Corrèze."

Zouroff was silent. He knew that he did not mean that. But it was the fiction which his ruler had set up between them.

"That is why you have sent her to Szarisla," continued Jeanne de Sonnaz. "All the world knows that, though of course we put a fair face on it. The idea of talking of her not receiving me. If she did not receive me, Paul would have to shoot you, which would have its inconveniences—for you and Paul."

She laughed a little, and impaled a blue butterfly on the sharp point of her tortoiseshell cone. Zouroff still said nothing; a sort of vague remorse touched him for a moment, as little Claire, whose balloon was entangled in a shrub, cried out, "Where is the princess? Why is she never with us now? She would get down my balloon. You are too cross."

Zouroff released the toy, and said roughly, "Run to your sister, Claire, you tease us."

"Madame Vera never said I teased," said the child sullenly, with a pout, as she obeyed, and joined her elder sister.

"Where is Corrèze?" said her mother.

"*Nom empesté!*"[1] swore Zouroff, "how should I know where a singer may be?"

"It is very easy to know where a great singer is. Comets are watched and chronicled. He was shooting in Styria, at Prince Hohenlohe's, last month. Why do you not know? Do you have no reports from Szarisla?"

"He is not there," said Zouroff angrily. He hated his wife, but he was jealous of her honour, even though it would, in a sense, have gratified him to be able to say to her, "You are no higher than the rest."

---

1 Accursed name.

"He may not be there," said the Duchesse de Sonnaz carelessly. "On the other hand, it is not very far from Styria to Poland, and he is singing nowhere in public this autumn. Are your reports to be trusted?"

"Ivan would tell me anything," said Zouroff moodily. "He writes me weekly of her health; he says nothing happens; no one goes—"

"Ivan is incorruptible, no doubt," said Jeanne de Sonnaz, a little drily.

"What do you mean?"

"You are always asking me what I mean? I am no Sphinx,[1] my dear friend, I am very transparent. I mean, that since your wife is there, it seems to me improbable that she does not, or will not, see Corrèze—"

Zouroff ground his heel on the turf with impatience, but he kept silent.

"I think it would be worth your while to make sure that she does not see Corrèze. I am quite aware that if they do meet, it will be merely a knight meeting a saint,—

Pauvres couples, à l'âme haute,
Qu'une noble horreur de la faute
Empêche seule d'être heureux.

and that he will—

Baise sa main sans la presser:
Comme un lis facile à blesser
Qui tremble à la moindre secousse—[2]

and all the rest. But still—if only as a moral phenomenon, it might be worth watching, and Ivan, on whom you depend, is, though a very superior servant, still only a servant."

---

1 Mythological monster having the head and torso of a woman, the hindquarters of a lion, and the wings of an eagle. She is seated on a rock outside of Thebes, where she proposes riddles to travelers. She kills those who give her the wrong answer. Metaphorically, a mysterious, inscrutable person who asks enigmatic questions or gives answers.
2 Poor couples elevated in soul / That a noble disgust of transgression / Alone keeps from being happy.
   Kiss her hand without squeezing it / Like a lily easy to bruise / Which trembles at the least jolt.

"What would you have me do? Go myself?"

"Yes, I think you should go yourself. It would prevent people saying unpleasant things or untrue ones. You must have your wife back in Paris, or you must be very certain of all that passes at Szarisla, or you may be made to play a foolish part—a part you would not like to play, when you have shut your wife up in it for her safety."

"Jeanne," said Zouroff gloomily, with his eyes fixed on the turf they were treading. "There is no one to hear, and we may speak as we mean; Vera does not return to me until she consents to receive you; there is no question of her honour; she will have that intact as if she were in a convent; she is made like that; she is no '*lis facile à blesser*,' she is made of steel. She knows everything, and she will no longer know you. To protect your name I exile her. She may live and die in Poland."

She heard him, knowing very well that he said the simple fact, yet her eyes grew angry, and her teeth shut tight.

"You are all imbeciles, you Russians," she said contemptuously. "You have only one remedy for all diseases—Siberia! It does not cure all diseases; Nihilism shows that. Corrèze is your best friend since you want to be free."

"If he set foot in Szarisla he shall be beaten with rods!"

Jeanne de Sonnaz, as they passed under the tamarisk trees, looked at him coldly, and crossed her hands lightly on her gold-headed cane as she leaned on it.

"On my word I do not understand you. Are you in love with your wife?"

"Jeanne!"

"I do not accept divided homage," said his friend with close-shut teeth; "and jealously is a form of homage. Perhaps the truer form."

"One may be jealous of one's honour—"

"You have none," said Jeanne de Sonnaz coolly. "Your wife told you so long ago. You have rank, but you have not honour. You do not know what it means. My poor Paul does, but then he is stupid and *arriéré*.[1] I think if I told Paul to kill you, it might perhaps arrange things—and then how happy they would be, these—

Purs amants sur terre égarés!"[2]

---

1 Backwards, slow.
2 Chaste lovers lost upon the earth!

Zouroff looked at her fixedly; his face grew anxious, sullen, and pale.

"Jeanne, say out; what is it you want me to do?"

"I want to reconcile your wife and you, of course," said Jeanne de Sonnaz, driving her cane through the yielding turf. "That, of course, first of all, if possible. If impossible, I would have you divorced from her. Things, as they are, are ridiculous; and," she added, in a lower breath, as the children and their balloons drew near, running against the wind, "and they may in time compromise me, which I do not choose to permit."

Zouroff understood what she required of him; and he felt a coward and a brute, as his sister had called him.

The lily might not be so easy to bruise, but it was easy to soil it.

"Corrèze is certainly in Styria," she added, as the children joined them.

Zouroff stood looking down on the green turf and the bright blossoms of the asters with moody eyes; he was thinking—what beast of prey was ever so hard of grip, so implacable in appetite, as a cruel woman? And yet this woman held him.

He dared not disobey, because he could not bear to lose her.

That autumn day, so sunny, balmy, and radiant in the sheltered gardens and forests of Arcachon, was winter at Szarisla. Sudden storms and heavy falls of snow had made the forests bare, the plains white; the winds were hurricanes, the thermometer was at zero, and the wolves ranged the lonely plateaux and moorlands in bands, hungered and rash. Szarisla in autumn was colder and drearier than Félicité could ever be in mid-winter, and the great, bare pile of the castle buildings rose black and sombre from out the unbroken world of whiteness.

There was an equally unchangeable melancholy around; it was in the midst of a district intensely and bitterly national; the Princes Zouroff were amongst the most accursed names of Poland, and the few, far-scattered nobles who dwelt in the province would no more have crossed the threshold of Szarisla than they would have kissed the cheek of Mouravieff, or the foot of the Gospodar.[1] Vere lived in

---

1 Mouravieff was the Governor-General of Eastern Siberia (1860-61), a
    Caucasian prince in the service of the Russian Government; the
    Gospodor is the title of the King of Moldova. The country, which bor-
    ders on Romania, became part of the Russian Empire in the late eigh-
    teenth and early nineteenth centuries.

absolute solitude, and knew that it was as virtually also a captivity as was ever that of Mary, or of Arabella, Stuart.[1]

Of course she was the Princess Vera, the mistress of Szarisla nominally and actually, but none the less she knew that every hour was watched, that every word was listened to, and that, whilst there was obsequious deference to all her commands, yet, had she expressed a wish to leave the place, she would have been reverentially entreated to await the wishes of the Prince, and would not have a found a man in her stables bold enough to harness her horses for her flight.

She had arrived there late one evening, and, despite the fires, the lights, the torches in the courts, the large household assembled in the entrance, a chill like that of the catacombs seemed around her, and she had felt that living she entered a grave.

Szarisla was an absolute solitude. The nearest town was a three days' journey of long, bad roads; and the town, when reached, was an obscure and miserable place. The peasantry were sullen and disaffected. The district was under the iron heel of a hated governor, and its scanty population was mute in useless and gloomy resentment. She had no friend, no society, no occupation save such as she chose to make for herself; she was waited upon with frigid ceremonial and etiquette, and she was conscious that she was watched incessantly. Many women would have lost their senses, their health, or both, in that bitter weariness of blank, chill, silent days.

Vere, whose childish training now stood her in fair stead and service, summoned all her courage, all her pride, and resisted the depression that was like a malady, the lassitude that might be the precursor of mental or bodily disease. She rode constantly, till the snow fell; when the snow came, and the frost, she had the wild young horses put in the sleigh, and drove for leagues through the pine woods, and over the moorlands. Air and movement were, she knew, the only true physicians. Little by little she made her way into the homes, and into the hearts of the suspicious and disaffected peas-

---

1 Mary, Queen of Scots (1542-87) was the Scottish Queen who was imprisoned for eighteen years and then put to death by her cousin Queen Elizabeth I. She was considered a threat to Elizabeth's throne; Arabella Stuart (1575-1616) was an English noblewoman, claimant to the throne of her cousin James I. James feared that her marriage might lead to a union with a foreign power. When she tried to leave England to wed an obscure Balkan prince, she was arrested and temporarily imprisoned. After she married William Seymour, she was again imprisoned in the Tower of London until she suffered a mental breakdown and died.

antry; it was slow work, and hard, and thankless, but she was not eas-ily discouraged or rebuffed. She could do little, for she was met at all times in her wishes for charity by the adamantine barrier of "the prince forbids it;" she had no more power, as she bitterly realised, than if she had been his serf. But all that personal influence could do, she did; and that was not little. She was the first living creature who had borne the name of Zouroff that had not been loathed and cursed at Szarisla.

Personal beauty is a rare sorcery, and when the fair face of the Princess Vera looked on them through the falling snow in the forests, or the dim light of their own wood cabins, the people could not altogether shut their hearts to her, though she bore the accursed name.

She was very unhappy; wearily and hopelessly so, because she saw no possibility of any other life than the captivity here, or the yet more arduous captivity of the great world, and in her memory she always heard the song,

Si vous saviez que je vous aime,
Surtout si vous saviez comment!

But she would not let her sorrow and her pain make slaves of her.

The wild and frequent storms of wind and snow tried her most hardly, because they mewed her in those gloomy rooms, and sunless corridors, which had seen so much human tyranny and human woe, and the long, black nights, when only the howl of the hurricane and the howl of the wolves were heard, were very terrible; she would walk up and down the panelled rooms through those midnight hours, that seemed like an eternity, and wondered if her husband had wished to drive her mad that he had sent her here. Her French women left her, unable to bear the cold, the dreariness, the loneli-ness; she had only Russians and Poles about her. At times in those lonely, ghastly nights, made hideous by the moans of the beasts and the roar of the winds, she thought of the Opera-house of Paris; she thought of the face of Faust. Then in that emptiness and darkness of her life she began to realise that she loved Corrèze; began to under-stand all that she cost to him in pain and vain regret.

If she would receive Jeanne de Sonnaz she could go back; go back to the splendour, the colour, the light of life; go back to the world where Corrèze reigned, where his voice was heard, where his eyes would answer hers. But it never once occurred to her to yield.

Now and then the truth came to her mind that Sergius Zouroff had sent her to this solitude not only as a vengeance, but as a temptation. Then all the strength in her repelled the very memory of Corrèze.

"Would my husband make me like Jeanne de Sonnaz," she thought with a shudder of disgust, "so that I may no longer have the right to scorn her?"

And she strove with all her might to keep her mind calm and clear, her body in health, her sympathies awake for other sorrows than her own.

She studied the dead languages, which she had half forgotten, with the old priest of Szarisla, and conjured away the visions that assailed her in those endless and horrible nights, with the sonorous cadence of the Greek poets; and in the daytime, when the frost had made the white world firm under foot, passed almost all the hours of light sending her fiery horses through the glittering and rarefied air.

So the months passed, and it was mid-winter. Letters and journals told her that the gay world went on its course, but to her it seemed as utterly alien as it could do to any worker in the depths of the salt or the quicksilver mines that supplied his wealth to Prince Zouroff. The world had already forgotten her. Society only said, "Princesse Vera is passing the winter in Poland; so eccentric; but she was always strange and a saint;" and then, with the usual little laugh, Society added, "There is something about Corrèze."

But the world does not long talk, even calumniously, of what is absent.

Prince Zouroff was on the boulevards; he gave his usual great dinners; he played as usual at his clubs; he entered his horses as usual for great races; the world did not concern itself largely about his wife.

She was in Poland.

She committed the heaviest sin against Society, the only one it never pardons. She was absent. No one had even the consolation to think that she had her lover with her.

Corrèze was singing in Berlin.

Madame Nelaguine, forcing herself to do what she loathed, went across Europe in the cold, wet weather as swiftly as she could travel, and visited Szarisla.

She strove to persuade her sister-in-law to accept the inevitable, and return to the Hôtel Zouroff and such consolations as the great world and its homage could contain.

"Be reasonable, Vera," she urged, with the tears standing in her keen, marmoset-like eyes. "My dear, society is made up of women like Jeanne de Sonnaz. Receive her, what does it matter? It is not as if you loved your husband, as if your heart were wounded. Receive her. What will it cost you? You need never even see her in intimacy. Go to her on her day, let her come to you on yours. Show yourself half an hour at her balls, let her show herself at yours. That is all. What does it amount to? what does it cost? Nothing."

"Little, no doubt," answered Vere. "Only—all one's self-respect."

And she was not changed or persuaded.

"I shall live and die here, very likely," she said at last, weary of resistance. "It is as well as any other place. It is better than Paris. Your brother has sent me here to coerce me. Go back and tell him that force will not succeed with me. I am not a coward."

Madame Nelaguine, grieved and yet impatient, shuddered, and left the bleakness and loneliness of Vere's prison-house with relief, and hurried home to the world and its ways, and said impetuously and bitterly to her brother, "Do not darken my doors, Sergius, while your wife is shut in that gaol of ice. Do not come to me, do not speak to me. You are a brute. Would to heaven Jeanne de Sonnaz were your wife; then you would be dealt with aright! Are you mad? do you wish to make her faithless? Can you think she will bear such a life as that? Can you leave a woman as young as she without friends, lovers, children, and expect her to change to snow, like the country you shut her in?—are you mad? If she shame herself there any way—any way— can you blame her? Can you take a girl, a child, and teach her what the passions of men are, and then bid her lead a nun's life just when she has reached the full splendour and force of her womanhood—?"

"She is a saint, you say," he answered with a smile; and he and his sister never spoke from that hour. In the boudoir of the Faubourg St. Germain his friend knew well how to surround him with an influence which little by little isolated him, and alienated him from all who had the courage to speak of his wife.

Jeanne de Sonnaz had one set purpose, the purpose which she had let him see in her at Arcachon; and until she should succeed in it she suffered no hand but her own to guide him.

The lily might have a stem of steel, and never be bent; but it could be broken.

Soilless though it might remain in its solitude amidst the snow, it should be broken; she had said it in her soul.

"*Ce que femme veut, l'homme veut*,"[1] was the proverb as her experience read it.

---

1 What woman desires, man desires.

All that there had been of manliness in Sergius Zouroff's nature resisted her still in this thing that she sought; he still had a faith in his wife that his anger against her did not change; in his eyes Vere was purity incarnate, and he could have laughed aloud in the face of suspicion. To ruin by open doubt and calumnious accusation a creature he knew to be sinless, seemed to him so vile that he could not bring himself to do an act so base.

He sent her into captivity, and he kept her there without mercy, but to hem her in with falsehood, to dishonour her by affected belief in her dishonour, was a lower deep than he could stoop to, even at the bidding of his mistress.

That her solitude was the sharpest and most terrible form of temptation he knew well, and he exposed her to it ruthlessly; willing she should fall, if to fall she chose. But whilst she was innocent, to assume and assert her guilty was what he would not do. Nay, there were even times, when the fatal drug of Jeanne de Sonnaz's presence was not on him, that he himself realised that he was a madman, who cast away the waters of life for a draught of poison, a jewel for a stone.

But he thrust aside the thought as it arose. He had surrendered himself to the will of his mistress. He had put his wife away for ever.

CHAPTER VI.

One day, when the snow was falling, a traveller reached the gates of Szarisla.

He was wrapped in fur from head to foot; he wished to see the Princesse Zouroff.

"No one sees her," answered the guardian of the gates; "it is the Prince's order."

"But I am a friend; will you not take my name to her?"

"I will not. No one enters; it is the Prince's order."

To the entreaties of the stranger, and to his gold, the custodian of the entrance-way was obdurate. In his boyhood he had felt the knout, and he dreaded his master.

The stranger went away.

The next day was the Immaculate Conception.[1] At Szarisla the Catholic religion was permitted by a special concession of a French princess Zouroff, and its functions were still allowed by her descendants.

---

1   December 8.

There was no other church for the peasants than that which was part of the great building, once the monastery of Szarisla. They all flocked to it upon holy days. It was sombre and ill lit, but gorgeous in Byzantine colour and taste from the piety of dead Zouroff princes.

The peasantry went over the snow through its doors; the stranger went with them; the mistress of Szarisla was at the midday mass, as well the household.

In the stillness, after the elevation of the host, a voice arose, and sang the Salutaris Hostia.

A warmth like the glow of summer ran through all the veins of Vere; she trembled; her face was lifted for one moment, then she dropped it once more on her hands.

The peasants and the household, awe-struck and amazed, listened with rapt wonder to what they thought was the song of angels; they could not see the singer. Kneeling as in prayer, with her face hidden, the mistress of Szarisla, who was also the captive of Szarisla, never moved.

The divine melody floated through the dimness and the stillness of the lonely Polish church; the priest stood motionless; the people were mute; some of them wept in ecstasy. When it ceased, they prostrated themselves on the earth. They believed that the angels of God were amongst them.

Vere arose slowly and stood pale and still, shrouded from head to foot in fur.

She looked towards the shadows behind the altar. There she saw Corrèze, as she had known that she would see him.

He came forward and bowed low. His eyes had a timidity and a fear in the wistfulness of their appeal to her.

They stood before each other, and were silent.

"Is this how you obey me?" her glance said to him without words.

"Forgive me," he murmured aloud.

By this time the people had arisen, and were gazing at him, amazed to find him but a mortal man.

Vere turned to the priest, and her voice trembled a little; "You are not angry, father? Will you not rather thank this—traveller?—he is known to me."

In Latin the priest spoke his admiration and his thanks, and in Latin the singer replied.

Vere looked at him, and said simply, "Come."

Corrèze obeyed her, and moved by her side. He dared not touch her hand, or speak any word that might offend her. He could see nothing of her face or form for the black furs that swept from her head to her feet. She passed into the sacristy with a passing word to the priest. She threw the heavy door close with her own hands, and let the furs fall off her in a heap upon the floor.

Then for the first time she looked at him.

"Why do you come? It is unworthy—"

He moved as if a blow had been struck him, his eyes, longing and passionate, burned like stars; he too cast his furs down; he stood before her with a proud humiliation in his attitude and his look.

"That is a harsh word," he said simply; "I have been in this district for weeks; I have seen you pass with your swift horses; I have been in your church before now; when you are imprisoned here do you think I could live elsewhere, do you think I could sing in gay cities? For some months I knew nothing; I heard that you were on your Russian estates, and nothing more; when I was in Styria five weeks ago, I heard for the first time that you were in Poland. A man who knew your husband spoke of Szarisla as no place for a woman. Then I came. Are you offended? Was I wrong? You cannot be here of your own will? It is a prison. When I rang at the gates they told me it was the Prince's order that you should see no one. It is a captivity!"

Vere was silent.

"You should not have come," she said with an effort; "I am alone here; it was ungenerous."

The blood mounted to his face.

"Cannot you make excuse?" he murmured. "I know what Russians are; I know what their tyrannies are; I trembled for you, I knew no rest night or day till I saw the walls of Szarisla, and then you passed by me in the woods in the snow, and I saw you were living and well; then I breathed again, then all the frozen earth seemed full of spring and sunshine. Forgive me;—how could I lead my life singing in cities, and laughing with the world, while I thought you were alone in this hotbed of disaffection, of hatred, of assassination, where men are no better than the wolves? For the love of heaven, tell me why you are here! Is it your husband's madness, or his vengeance?"

She was silent still. He looked at her and stooped, and said very low: "You learned the truth of Jeanne de Sonnaz. Was it that?"

She gave a gesture of assent. The hot colour came into her averted face.

Corrèze stifled a curse in his throat, "It is a vengeance then?"

"In a sense, perhaps," she answered with effort. "I will not receive her. I will never see her again."

"And your banishment is her work. But why imprison yourself? If you resisted, you would have all Europe with you."

"I obey my husband," said Vere simply, "and I am in peace here."

"In peace? In prison! We spoke once of Siberia; this is a second Siberia, and he consigns you to it in your innocence, to spare the guilty! Oh my God!"—

His emotion choked him as if a hand were at his throat; he gazed at her and could have fallen at her feet and kissed them.

"Noble people, and guiltless people, live in Siberia, and die there," said Vere with a faint smile. "It is not worse for me than for them, and the spring will come sometime; and the peasantry are learning not to hate me; it is a better life than that of Paris."

"But it is a captivity! You cannot leave it if you would; he does not give you the means to pass the frontier."

"He would prevent my doing so, no doubt."

"It is an infamy! It is an infamy. Why will you bear it, why will you not summon the help of the law against it?"

"If a man struck you, would you call in the aid of the law?"

"No. I should kill him."

"When I am struck, I am mute: that is a woman's courage; a man's courage is vengeance, but ours cannot be."

Corrèze sighed: a heavy, passionate, restless sigh, as under a weighty burden.

"A man may avenge you," he muttered.

"No man has any title," she said a little coldly. "I am the wife of Prince Zouroff."

A greater coldness than that of the ice world without, fell on the heart of her hearer. He did not speak for many moments. The snow fell; the wind moaned, the grey dull atmosphere seemed between him and the woman he loved, like a barrier of ice.

He said abruptly, almost in a whisper: "The world says you should divorce him; you have the right—"

"I have the right."

"Then you will use it?"

"No—no," she answered after a pause. "I will not take any public action against my husband."

"He wishes you to divorce him?"

"No doubt. I shall be here until I do so."

"And that will be—"

"Never."

"Never?"

She shook her head.

"I think," she said in a very low tone, "if you understand me at all, you understand that I would never do that. Those courts are only for shameless women."

He was silent. All that it was in his heart to urge, he dared not even hint. A great anguish seemed to stifle speech in him. He could have striven against every other form of opposition, but he could not strive against this which sprang from her very nature, from the inmost beauty and holiness of the soul that he adored.

The salt tears rose in his eyes.

"You have indeed kept yourself unspotted from the world!" he said wearily, and then there was silence.

It lasted long; suddenly he broke it, and all the floodgates of his eloquence were opened, and all the suffering and the worship that were in him broke up to light.

"Forgive me," he said passionately. "Nay, perhaps you will never forgive, and yet speak I must. What will you do with your life? Will you shut it here in ice, like an imprisoned thing, for sake of a guilty and heedless man, a coarse and thankless master? Will you let your years go by like beautiful flowers whose blossom no eyes behold? Will you live in solitude and joylessness for sake of a brute who finds his sport in shame? Your marriage was an error, a frightful sacrifice, a martyrdom, will you bear it always, will you never take your rights to liberty and light, will you never be young in your youth?"

"I am his wife," said Vere simply; "nothing can change that." She shuddered a little as she added: "God himself cannot undo what is done."

"And he leaves you for Jeanne de Sonnaz!"

"I rule my life by my own measure, not his. He forgets that he is my husband, but I do not forget that I am his wife."

"But why remember it? He has ceased to deserve the remembrance—he never deserved it—never in the first hour of your marriage to him."

Vere's face flushed.

"If I forgot it, what should I be better than the wife of Paul de Sonnaz?"

"You are cruel!"

"Cruel?"

"Cruel—to me."

He spoke so low that the words scarcely stirred the air, then he knelt down on the ground before her and kissed the hem of her gown.

"I dare not say to you what I would say; you are so far above all other women, but you know so well, you have known so long, that all my life is yours, to use or throw away as you choose. Long ago I sang to you, and you know so well, I think, all that the song said. I would serve you, I would worship you with the love that is religion, I would leave the stage and the world and art and fame, I would die to men, if I might live for you—"

She shook as she heard him, as a tall lily-stem shakes in a strong wind; she sighed wearily; she was quite silent. Was she insulted, angered, alienated? He could not tell. His ardent and eloquent eyes, now dim and feverish, in vain sought hers. She looked away always at the grey misty plain, the wide waste, treeless and sunless, swept with low driving clouds.

"You knew it always?" he muttered at length; "always, surely."

"Yes."

The single word came painfully and with hesitation from her lips; she put her hand on her heart to still its beating; for the first time in all her years she was afraid, and afraid of herself.

"Yes," she said once more. "I knew it lately—but I thought you never would speak of it to me. You should have been silent always—always; if I were indeed a religion to you, you would have been so. Men do not speak so of what they honour. Am I no better than my husband's mistresses in your eyes?"

She drew herself erect with a sudden anger, and drew the skirt of her gown from his hands; then a shiver as of cold passed over her, a sob rose in her throat; she stood motionless, her face covered with her hands.

He wished he had died a thousand deaths ere he had spoken. He rose to his feet and stood before her.

"Since the day by the sea that I gathered you the rose, I have loved you; where is the harm? All the years I have been silent. Had I seen you in peace and in honour I would have been silent to my grave. I have been a sinner often, but I would never have sinned against you. I would never have dared to ask you to stoop and hear my sorrow, to soil your hand to soothe my pain. I saw you outraged, injured, forsaken, and your rivals the base creatures that I could buy as well as he if I chose, and yet I said nothing; I waited, hoping your life might pass calmly by me, ready, if of any defence or any use I could be. What was the harm or the insult in that? You are the golden cup, holy to me; he drinks from the cabaret glasses; can you ask me, a man, and not old, and with life in my veins and not ice, to be patient and mute when I see that, and find you in solitude here?"

He spoke with the simplicity and the strength of intense but restrained emotion. All the passion in him was on fire, but he choked it into silence and stillness; he would not seem to insult her in her loneliness.

Vere never looked at him. All the colour had left her face, her hands were crossed upon her breast above the mark which her husband's blow had left there; she stood silent.

She remembered her husband's words: "All women are alike when tempted." For the first time in her pure and proud life temptation came to her assailing her with insidious force.

"What do you ask?" she said abruptly at last. "Do you know what you ask? You ask me to be no better a thing than Jeanne de Sonnaz! Go—my life was empty before; now it is full—full of shame. It is you who have filled it. Go!"

"These are bitter words—"

"They are bitter; they are true. What is the use of sophism?[1] You love me; yes; and what is it you would have me do? cheat the world with hidden intrigue, or brave it with guilty effrontery? One or the other; what else but one or the other could love be now for us?"

Then, with a sudden recollection of the only plea that would have power to persuade or force to move him, she added.

"To serve me best—go back to Paris; let Jeanne de Sonnaz hear you in all your glory there."

He understood.

He stood silent, while the large tears stood beneath his drooping eyelids.

"I would sooner you bade me die."

"It is so easy to die," she said, with a passing weary smile. "If—if you love me indeed—go."

"At once?"

She bent her head.

He looked at her long; he did not touch her; he did not speak to her; and he went. The door of the church closed with a heavy sound behind him.

His footsteps were lost upon the snow.

When the old priest entered the building he found the mistress of Szarisla kneeling before the altar.

She remained so long motionless that at length the old man was frightened and dared to touch her.

---

1 False arguments.

She was insensible.

Her household thought she had fainted from the cold.

CHAPTER VII.

Ten days later Corrèze sang in the midnight mass of Notre Dame. The face of the Duchesse de Sonnaz clouded. "*C'est une impasse*,"[1] she muttered.

The winter went on its course and the spring-time came.

Corrèze remained in Paris.

He sang, as of old, and his triumphs were many, and envy and detraction could only creep after him dully and dumbly. For the summer he took a little château in the old-world village of Marly-le-Roi;[2] and, there, gathered other artists about him. The world of women found him changed. He had grown cold and almost stern; amours he had none; to the seductions that had of old found him so easy a prey he was steeled.

In him, this indifference was no virtue. All women had become without charm to him. The dominion of a noble and undivided love was upon him; that love was nothing but pain; yet the pain was sacred to him. His lips would never touch the golden cup, but the memory of it forbade him to drink of any earthly wines of pleasure or of vanity.

His love, like all great love, was consecration.

"He will end in a monastery," said the neglected Delilahs;[3] and Sergius Zouroff heard them say it.

A sombre jealousy began to awaken on him as it had awakened at the sight of the necklace of the moth on the breast of Vere. What right had this singer to be faithful to the memory of his wife while he to his wife was faithless?

"Pur amant sur terre égaré!"

murmured Jeanne de Sonnaz again, with a little laugh, when she saw Corrèze passing out of the opera-house alone, and added in the ear of Zouroff: "How he shames *you*! Are you not ashamed?"

Zouroff grew sullen and suspicious. He began to hate the sight

---

1 It's a deadlock.

2 A small village on the Seine River about eleven miles west of Paris.

3 See Judges 16; Samson's mistress who betrays him to the Philistines; by analogy a seductive and treacherous woman.

of the face of Corrèze, or that of the letters of his name on the walls of Paris. It seemed to him that all the world was filled with this nightingale's voice. As the horses of Corrèze passed him on the Boulevards, as Corrèze entered the St. Arnaud or the Mirliton, when he was himself in either club; when the crowds gathered and waited in the streets, and he heard it was to see Corrèze pass by after some fresh success in his art, then Zouroff began to curse him bitterly.

There was a regard in the eyes of Corrèze when they glanced at his that seemed to him to say with a superb scorn: "I am faithful to your wife. And you?"

This hatred slumbered like a dull and sullen fire in him, but it was a living fire, and the lips of Jeanne de Sonnaz fanned it and kept it alive. With ridicule, with hint, with conjecture, with irony, one way or another she stung him a hundred times a week with the name of Corrèze.

"She is in Poland, he is in Paris; what can you pretend there can be between them?" he said to her once, in savage impatience. Then she smiled.

"Distance is favourable to those loves of the soul. Did I not quote you Sully Prudhomme's

Purs amants sur terre égarés!"

Once in that spring-time Zouroff wrote one line to his wife.

"If you are tired of Szarisla you know on what terms you can return to Paris."

He received no answer.

He was perplexed.

It seemed to him impossible that she could have courage, patience and strength, to remain in that solitude.

"It is obstinacy," he said. "It is stubbornness!"

"It is love," said Jeanne de Sonnaz, with a little smile.

Zouroff laughed also, but he chafed.

"Love! for the wolves or for the Poles?"

"It is love," said his friend. "It is the same love that makes Corrèze live like an anchorite in the midst of Paris, which makes your wife live like a saint at Szarisla. It is their idea of love, it is not mine or yours. It is the dissipation of the soul. Have you never heard of it?

Aux ivresses même impunies
Vous préférez un deuil plus beau,
Et vos lèvres même au tombeau
Attendent le droit d'être unies.[1]

When our poet wrote that he saw, or foresaw, the tragic and frigid loves of your wife and Corrèze. What can you do? It is of no use to swear. You cannot cite them *aux tribunaux*[2] for a merely spiritual attraction, for a docile and mournful passion that is *en deuil.*"

Then she laughed and made a little grimace at him.

"You cannot keep your wife in Poland all the same," she said, seriously. "It becomes ridiculous. It is not she and Corrèze who are so; it is you."

He knew that she meant what she had meant at Arcachon.

She was that day in his house; she had called there, she had little Claire with her whom she had sent to play in the garden under the budding lilacs; she was about to fetch Duc Paul from the Union, being a woman who was always careful to be seen often with her husband. Meanwhile she was in her friend's own suite of rooms in the Hôtel Zouroff; she was going about them, to and fro, as she talked.

"I must write a note to leave for Nadine," she said as she went to his bureau. "Why have you quarrelled with Nadine? It is so stupid to quarrel. If one has an enemy one should be more intimate with him, or her, than with anyone else, and your sister is your friend though she has an exaggerated adoration of Vera, sympathy through dissimilarity, the metaphysicians call it. *Ciel!*[3] what have you here? All women's letters! I will bet you the worth of your whole entries for Chantilly that the only woman whose letters are absent from this coffer is your wife!"

She had seen a large old casket of tortoise-shell and gilded bronze. The key was in the lock, it was full of notes and letters; she had pulled it towards her, turned the key, and was now tossing over its contents with much entertainment and equal recklessness.

---

1 To raptures even (if they go) unpunished / You prefer a more beautiful mourning (chastity), / And your lips even in the tomb / Await the right to be united.
2 In a Court of Justice.
3 Heavens!

"It is too scandalous," she cried, as she ran her eye over one here and there. "If there are not one-half of my acquaintances in this box! How imprudent of you to keep such things as these. I never wrote to you; I never write. None but mad women ever write to any man except their tailor. I shall take this box home—"

Zouroff, who only slowly awoke to the perception of what she was doing, strode to the bureau with a cry of remonstrance. "Jeanne! what are you about?" he said, as he strove to get the casket from her. "There is nothing that concerns you; they are all old letters, those, very old; you must not do that."

"Must not? Who knows that word? not I," said his friend. "I shall take the box away. It will amuse me while they put on my hair. Novels are dull; I will send you this thing back to-morrow."

"You cannot be serious!" stammered Zouroff, as he tried to wrest the box from her.

"I was never more serious," said his visitor, coolly. "Do not scream; do not swear. You know I do what I like. I want especially to see how my friends write to my friend. It is your own fault; I thought men always burnt letters. I wonder if Paul has a box like this. Adieu!"

She went away, with the coffer in her carriage, to fetch her husband on the Boulevard des Capucines, and Zouroff dared not arrest her; and the casket of letters went home to the Faubourg with her.

In the morning she said to him: "They were really too compromising, those letters. You had no business to keep them. I have burned them all, and Claire has got the coffer for her doll's trousseau. I never thought much of my sex at any time; I think nothing now. And, really, they should no more be trusted with ink than children with firearms. Pooh! why are you so furious? They were all old letters, from half a hundred different people; you have nothing to do with any one of the writers of them now; and of course I am as secret as the grave, as discreet as a *saint-père.*"[1]

With any other woman he would have let loose a torrent of abuse; with her he was sullen but apparently pacified.

After all they were old letters, and he could not very clearly remember whose letters had been shut away in that old tortoise-shell casket.

"I thought men always burnt these things," said Jeanne de Sonnaz. "But, indeed, if women are foolish enough to write them they

---

1 Holy father.

deserve to be unfortunate enough to have them kept. I never wrote to any man, except to Paul himself—and Worth."

"You are a model of virtue," said her companion, grimly.

"I am something better," said his friend. "I am a woman of sense. *Apropos*,[1] how long will this retreat in Poland last? It cannot go on; it becomes absurd. The world is already talking. The place of the Princess Zouroff is in the Hôtel Zouroff."

"It cannot be her place," said Zouroff, savagely. "She is—she is— obdurate still. I suppose she is content; the frost has broken, the weather is good even there."

Jeanne de Sonnaz looked him in the eyes.

"Weather is not all that a woman of twenty requires for her felicity. The whole affair is absurd; I shall not permit it to go on. I say again, what I said last year at Arcachon. It may end in compromising me, and that I will not have. You must take your wife back to your house here, and live with her later at Félicité, or you must prove to society that you are justified in separating from her; one or the other. As it is you are ridiculous, and I—I am suspected. *Faut en finir*."[2]

Zouroff turned away and walked gloomily to and fro the chamber.

"I will not take her back," he muttered. "Besides—probably—she would not come."

He dared not say to his companion that he could not insist on his wife's return without an open scandal, since she would for ever refuse to receive or to visit the Duchesse de Sonnaz, once her guest and her friend.

"Besides, probably, she would not come!" echoed Jeanne de Sonnaz, with a shrill laugh that made his sullenness rage. "My poor bear! is that all your growls and your teeth can do for you? You cannot master a woman of twenty, who has nothing in the world but what you gave her at your marriage. Frankly, it is too ridiculous. You must make a choice if you would not be the laughing stock of society; either you must have your wife here in Paris before all the world, and I will be the first to welcome her, or you must justify your separation from her; one of the two."

"I shall do neither!"

"Then, *mon ami*, I shall be very sorry indeed, because we have been friends so long, but unless you do one or the other, and that

---

1 By the way.
2 We must finish it.

speedily, I shall be obliged with infinite regret to side with your sister and all the House of Herbert against you. I shall be obliged to close my doors to you; I cannot know a man who is cruel to an innocent wife. There! you know I do what I say. I will give you a week, two weeks, to think of it. Afterwards I shall take my course according to yours. I shall be very sorry not to see you any more, my dear Sergius; but I should be more sorry if the world were to think I supported you in injustice and unkindness to Princess Zouroff. Please to go now; I have a million things to do, and a deputation about my *crèche*[1] is waiting for me downstairs."

Sergius Zouroff went out of her house in a towering passion; yet it never occurred to him to separate from his tormentor. She had an empire over him that he had long ceased to resist; he could no more have lived without seeing Jeanne de Sonnaz than he could live without his draughts of brandy, his nights of gambling. As there is love without dominion, so there is dominion without love.

He knew very well that she never wasted words; that she never made an empty menace. He knew that her calculations were always cool and keen, and that when she thought her own interests menaced, she was pitiless. She would keep her word; that he knew well. What could he do? It was impossible to recall his wife, since he knew that his wife would never receive Jeanne de Sonnaz. The presence of his wife in Paris could only complicate and increase the difficulties that surrounded him; had he not banished her to Poland for that very cause? He cursed the inconsistencies and insolences of women. The submission of his wife to his will and his command had softened his heart towards her; he had vague impulses of compassion and of pardon towards this woman who was so unyielding in her dignity, so obedient in her actions, so silent under her wrongs. As the year before, after he had found her the victim of her mother's falsehood, some better impulse, some tenderer instinct than was common with him had begun once more to move him towards that mute captive of his will at Szarisla. But Jeanne de Sonnaz had always been careful to smother those impulses at their birth under ridicule; to arouse in their stead anger, impatience, and the morbidness of a vague jealousy. Without the influence of Jeanne de Sonnaz Zouorff would have loved his wife; not nobly, because he was not noble, nor faithfully, because he could not be otherwise than inconstant; but still, with more honesty of affection, more indulgence, and more purity, than

---

1 Nativity scene.

he had ever had excited in him by any other creature. But perpetually, as that better impulse rose, she had been at hand to extinguish it by irony, by mockery, or by suggestion. He left her house, now, in bitter rage, which in justice should have fallen on her, but by habit fell instead upon his absent wife. Why could not Vere have been like any other of the many highborn maidens of whom he could have made a Princess Zouroff, and been indifferent and malleable, and wisely blind, and willing to kiss Jeanne de Sonnaz on the cheek, as great ladies salute each other all over the world, no matter what feuds may divide or rivalries may sting them? Why must she be a woman unfitted for her century, made only for those old legendary and saintly days when the bread had changed to roses in St. Elizabeth's hands?

A devilish wish that he was ashamed of, even as it rose up in him, came over him, without his being able to drive it away. He wished he could find his wife guilty. He knew her as innocent as children unborn; yet almost he wished he could find her weak and tempted like the rest.

His course would then be easy.

Throughout the adulation of the world she had remained untempted, and she remained so still, in that solitude, that dulness, that captivity which would have driven any other to summon a lover to her side before a month of that joyless existence had flown. But then she had no lover. He was certain she had none. Not all the mockery and insistence of his mistress could make him seriously credit any infidelity, even of thought or sentiment, in Vere. "And had she one I would strangle him to-morrow," he thought, with that vanity of possession which so sadly and cruelly survives the death of passion, the extinction of all love. Justify your separation from her, said his friend; but how; Sergius Zouroff was not yet low enough to accuse falsely a woman he believed from his soul to be innocent. He was perplexed, and bitterly angered against her, against himself, against all the world. He had meant to break her spirit and her will by her exile; he had never dreamed that she would bear it in patience and in silence; knowing women well, he had fully expected that the strength of her opposition would soon wear itself out, that she would soon see that to meet Jeanne de Sonnaz in society and exchange the commonplaces of courtesy and custom was preferable to a life in the snows of the north, with no one to admire her loveliness, no pleasure to beguile her days and nights; he had thought that one single week of the winter weather, with its lonely evenings in that deserted place, would banish all power of resistance in his wife. Instead of this, she remained there without a word, even of regret or of protest.

He was enraged that he had ever sent her into exile. He would not retreat from a step he had once taken; he would not withdraw from a position he had thought it for his dignity to assume. But he felt that he had committed the worst of all errors in his own sight; an error that would end in making him absurd in the eyes of the world. He could not keep his wife for ever at Szarisla; society would wonder, her family would murmur; even his Empress, perhaps, require explanation: and what excuse could he give? He could not say to any of these, "I separate from her because she has justly thought herself injured by Jeanne de Sonnaz."

As, lost in sullen meditation, he went down the Rue Scribe to go to his favourite club, he passed close by Corrèze.

Corrèze was walking with a German Margrave, who nodded to Zouroff with a little greeting, for they were friends; Corrèze looked him full in the face, and gave him no salutation.

The insolence (as it seemed to him) filled up the measure of his wrath.

"I will slit the throat of that nightingale," he muttered as they passed.

At that moment a friend stopped him in some agitation. "Good heavens, have you not heard? Paul de Sonnaz is dead; his horse has thrown him just before the door of the club. He fell with his head on the kerbstone; his neck is broken."

Zouroff, without a word, went into the Jockey Club and into the chamber upstairs, whither they had borne the senseless frame of the Duc de Sonnaz, who had died in an instant, without pain. Zouroff looked down on him, and his own face grew pale and his eyes clouded. Paul de Sonnaz had been a good, simple, unaffected man, *bon prince*[1] always, and unconscious of his wrongs; docile to his wife and blinded by her, cordial to his friends and trustful of them.

"Poor simpleton! he was very useful to me," muttered Zouroff, as he stood by the inanimate body of the man he had always deceived. It was of himself he thought, in the unchangeable egotism of a long life of self-indulgence.

When Zouroff went to his own house that day he found the usual weekly report from his faithful servant Ivan. Ivan affirmed that all things went on as usual and nothing happened, but ventured to add:

---

1 A good fellow.

"The climate does not seem to suit the princess. She rides a great deal, but she appears to lose strength, and the women say that she sleeps but little."

His sister came to him a little later in that day.

"It is of no use for us to quarrel, Sergius," she said to him. "I shall do Vera no good in that way. I am anxious; very anxious; she writes to me as of old, quite calmly; but Ivan writes, on the other hand, that she is ill and losing strength. Why do you not recall her? Paul de Sonnaz is dead; his wife must for some time be in retreat. Vera is your shield and safety now; without her, Jeanne would marry you."

Zouroff frowned.

"My wife can always return if she please," he said evasively.

Would she return?

He could not see the Duchesse de Sonnaz, who was surrounded by her family, and that of her husband, in the first hours of her bereavement; and without her counsels, her permission, he dared do nothing.

"I will write to Vera," he promised his sister; but she could not persuade him to write then and there. "Szarisla is healthy enough," he answered, impatient of her fears. "Besides, a woman who can ride for many hours a day cannot be very weak."

He knew Szarisla was a place that was trying to the health of the strongest by reason of its bitter cold springs and its scorching summers, with the noxious exhalation of it marshes. But he would not confess it.

"She could return if she chose," he added, to put an end to the remonstrances of the Princess Nelaguine. "As for her health, if you are disturbed about it send any physician you like that you employ to see her; she had never been so well as she was before the birth of that dead child in Russia."

"I shall not send a physician to her as if she were mad," answered his sister with anger.

"Send Corrèze," said Zouroff with a sardonic little laugh which he knew was vile.

"Would you had died yourself, Sergius, instead of that poor imbecile, whom you cheated every hour that he lived!"

Zouroff shrugged his shoulders. "I regret Paul—*pauvre garçon!*"[1] he said simply, and said the truth.

"Why do you not regret your own sins?"

---

1 Poor boy.

"They are the only things that have ever amused me," he replied with equal truth. "And I thought you were an *esprit fort*,[1] Nadine; I thought your new school of thinkers had all agreed that there is no such thing as sin any more; nothing but hereditary bias, for which no one is responsible. If we are not to quarrel again, pray make me no scenes."

"We will not quarrel; it is childish. But you promise me to recall your wife?"

"I promise you—yes."

"When I shall have seen Jeanne," he added in his own thoughts.

Nadine Nelaguine went to her own house angered, dissatisfied and anxious. She was a clever woman, and she was penetrated with the caution of the world, as a petrified branch with the lime that hardens it. She smiled cheerfully always when she spoke of her sister-in-law, and said tranquilly in society that she had not Vera's tastes, she could not dedicate herself to solitude and the Polish poor as Vera did. She kept her own counsel and did not call in others to witness her pain or her dilemma. She knew that the sympathy of society is chiefly curiosity, and that when it has any title to pity it is quite sure to sneer.

She held her peace and waited, but her often callous heart ached with heavy regret and anxiety.

"She has so much to endure!" she thought with hot tears in her sharp keen eyes. "So much, so much!—and it will pass her patience. She is young; she does not know that a woman must never resist. A woman should only—deceive. It is Jeanne's work, all her work; she has separated them; I knew well that she would. Oh, the fool that he is—the fool and the brute! If I, and Jeanne, and Lady Dorothy, and all the women that are like us, were eaten by dogs like Jezebel[2] the world would only be the better and the cleaner. But Vera, my lily, my pearl, my saint!—"

In Poland the slow cold spring was leaden-footed and grey of hue.

In the desolate plains that stretched around Szarisla the country slowly grew green with the verdure of budding corn and the yellow river outspread its banks, turbulent and swollen with the melted snows.

She knew what it was to be alive, yet not to live. If it had not been

---

1 Free-thinker.
2 See 1 Kings 21 and 2 Kings 9:10-37.

for the long gallops over the plains through the cold air which she forced herself to take for hours every day, she would scarcely have known she was even alive. Little by little as time went on and the household found that she remained there, and that her husband never visited her, the impression gained on all the people that she had been sent there either as captive or as mad; and a certain fear crept into them, and a certain dislike to be alone with her, and timidity when she spoke, came upon them. She saw that shrinking from her, and understood what their fancy about her was. It did not matter, she thought, only it hurt her when the little children began to grow afraid too, and flee from her.

"I suppose I am mad," she thought, with a weary smile. "The world would say so, too; I ought to go back to it and kiss Jeanne de Sonnaz on both cheeks."

But to do so never occurred to her for one moment as any temptation.

She was made to break, perhaps, but never to bend.

One day in the misty spring weather, which seemed to her more trying than all the ice and snow of winter, there came over the plains, now bright with springing grasses or growing wheat, a troika,[1] with hired horses, that was pulled up before the iron-bound doors of Szarisla.

From it there descended a very lovely woman, with an impertinent, delicate profile, radiant, audacious eyes, and a look that had the challenge of the stag with the malice of the marmoset.

When the servants on guard opposed her entrance with the habitual formula, "The Prince forbids it," she thrust into their faces a card signed Sergius Zouroff.

On the card was written, "Admit to Szarisla the Duchess of Mull."

The servants bowed to the ground, and ushered the bearer of that irresistible order into the presence of their mistress, without preparation or permission.

Vere was sitting at a great oak table in one of the high embrasured windows; the dog was at her feet; some Greek books were open before her; the white woollen gown she wore fell from her throat to her feet, like the robe of a nun; she had no ornament except her thick, golden hair coiled loosely about her head.

Before she realised that she was not alone her cousin's wife stood

---

1 Russian sleigh drawn by a team of three horses abreast.

before her, brilliant in colour as an enamel of Petitot, or a Saxe figure of Kaendler;[1] radiant with health, with contentment, with animation, with the satisfaction with all existent things, which is the
most durable, though not the most delicate, form of human happiness. Vere rose to her feet, cold, silent, annoyed, angered; she was in
her own house, at least her own since it was her husband's; she could
say nothing that was discourteous; she would say nothing that was
welcome. She was astonished and stood mute, looking down from
the height of her noble stature on this brilliantly-tinted, porcelain-
like figure. For the only time in all her life she who was Pick-me-up
in the world of fashion was made nervous and held mute.

She was impudent, daring, clever, vain, and always successful; yet,
for the moment, she felt like a frightened child, like a chidden dog,
before the amazed cold rebuke of those grand, grey eyes that she had
once envied to the girl Vere Herbert.

"Well! you don't seem to like the look of me," she said at last, and
there was a nervous quiver in her high, thin voice. "You can't be said
to look pleased no-way, and yet I've come all this way only just to
see you; there aren't many of the others would do as much."

"You have come to triumph over me!" thought her hearer, but,
with the stately old-world courtesy that was habitual to her, she
motioned to her cousin's wife to be seated near her and said, coldly:

"You are very good; I regret that Szarisla can offer you little recompense for so long a journey. My cousin is well?"

"Frank's first rate, and the child too," said Fuschia, Duchess of
Mull, with a severe effort to recover the usual lightheartedness, with
which she faced all things and all subjects, human and divine. "I
called the boy after you, you know, but you never took any notice.
Goodness! if it's not like a convent here; it's a sort of Bastille,[2] isn't
it, and the windows are all barred up, and I thought they'd have never
let me in; if I hadn't had your husband's order they never would have
done till the day of doom; it's very hard on you."

"My husband sent you here?" said Vere, with her teeth closed; she
felt powerless before a studied insult.

"Sent me? My, no! I don't do things for people's sending," said the
young duchess, with some asperity, and her natural courage reviving
in her. "We were bound to come to Berlin, because of Ronald Her-

---

1   Jean Petitot (1607-91) was a French painter of miniature portraits in
    enamel; Johann Joachim Kaendler (1706-75) was a German porcelain
    maker.
2   Fortress in Paris which was used as a prison.

bert's marriage; he is marrying a Prussian princess—didn't you know of that? Doesn't your husband forward you on your letters? And I said to myself when I'm as near as that, I will go on to Poland and see *her*, so I got that order out of your husband; he didn't like it, but he couldn't say no very well anyhow; we saw him as we came through Paris."

"You were very good to take so much trouble," said Vere, but her eyes said otherwise. Her eyes said, "Why do you come to offend me in my solitude and insult me in my captivity?"

But in truth her visitor was innocent of any such thought. Human motives are not unmixed, and in the brilliant young duchess there had been an innocent vanity—a half-conscious conceit—in showing this high-born and high-bred woman, who had always disdained her, that she was above revenge and capable of a noble action. But beyond all vanity and conceit were the wish to make Vere care for her, the indignation at tyranny of a spirited temper, and the loyal impulse to stand by what she knew was stainless and aspersed.

Fuschia Mull, having once recovered her power of speech, was not silenced soon again. She had seated herself opposite the high window, her bright eyes studied the face of Vere with a curiosity tempered by respect and heightened by wonder; she could flirt with princes and jest with sovereigns, and carry her head high in the great world with all the insolence of a born coquette and a born revolutionary, and since the day when she had become a duchess she had never ceased to assert herself in all the prominence and all the audacity that distinguished her; yet before this lonely woman she felt shy and afraid.

"You aren't a bit glad to see me," she said, with a little tremour in her words, that flowed fast from the sheer habit of loquacity. "You never would take to me. No; I know. You've never forgiven me about that coal, nor for my marrying your cousin. Well, that's natural enough; I don't bear malice. There wasn't any cause you should like me, though I think you'd like the baby if you saw him; he's a real true Herbert, but that's neither here nor there. I wanted to see you because you know they say such things in Paris and London, and all the others are such poor dawdles; they'll never do anything. Even Frank himself says I shouldn't interfere between husband and wife; but people always say you shouldn't interfere when they only mean you may do yourself a mischief, and I never was one to be afraid—"

She paused a moment, and her bright eyes roamed over the dark oak panelled monastic chamber, with its carpet of lambs' skins, and beyond its casements the flat and dreary plains and the low woods of endless firs.

"My!" she said, with a little shiver, "if it aren't worse than a clearin' down West! Well, he's a brute, anyhow——"

Vere looked at her with a regard that stopped her.

"It is my own choice," she said, coldly.

"Yes! I know it is your own choice in a way," returned the other with vivacity; "that is what I wanted to say to you. I told Frank the other day in Berlin, 'She never liked me, and there wasn't any particular reason why she should; but I always did like her, and I don't mean to stand still and see her put upon.' You don't mind me speaking so?—you *are* put upon because you are just too good for this world, my dear. Don't look at me so with your terrible eyes; I don't mean any offence. You know they say all sorts of things in society, and some say one thing and some another; but I believe as how the real fact is this, isn't it? Your husband has sent you here because you would not receive Madame de Sonnaz?"

"That is the fact—yes."

'Well, you are quite right. I only know if the duke—but never mind that. You know, or perhaps you don't know, that in the world they say another thing than that; they say Prince Zouroff is jealous of that beautiful creature, Corrèze——"

"I must request that you do not say that to me."

"Well, they say it in your absence, *some*. I thought I'd better tell you. That Sonnaz woman is a bad lot; poisonous as snakes in a swamp *she* is and of course she bruits it abroad. I cannot make out what your husband drives at; 'guess he wants you to divorce him; but it aren't him so much as it's that snake. Men are always what some woman or other makes them. Now you know this is what I came to say. I know you don't like me, but I *am* the wife of the head of your father's house, and nothing can change that now, and in the world I'm some pumpkins—I mean they think a good deal of me. Now what I come to ask you is this, and the duke says it with me with all his heart. We want you to come and live with us at Castle Herbert, or in London, or wherever we are. It will shut people's mouths. It will nonsuit your husband, and you shall never see that hussy of the Faubourg in *my* house, that I promise you. Will you do it? Will you? Folks mind *me*, and when I say to them the Princess Zouroff stays with me because her husband outrages her, the world will know it's a fact. That's so."

She ceased, and awaited the effect of her words anxiously and even nervously; she meant with all sincerity all she said.

Into Vere's colourless face a warmth came; she felt angered, yet she was touched to the quick. She could not endure the pity, the protection; yet the honesty, and the hospitality, and the frank kindness moved her to emotion.

None of her own friends, none of those who had been her debtor for many an act of kindness or hour of pleasure, had ever thought to come to her in her exile; and the journey was one long and tedious, involving discomfort and self-sacrifice, and yet had had no terrors for this woman, whose vulgarities she had always treated with disdain, whose existence she had always ignored, whose rank she had always refused to acknowledge.

"You aren't angry?" said the other humbly.

"Angry? Oh, no; you have been very good."

"Then you will come with us? Say! Your cousin will be as glad as I."

She was silent.

"Do come!" urged the other with wistful eagerness. "We are going straight home. Come with us. Of course your mother ought to be the one, but then she's—; it's no use thinking of her, and, besides, they wouldn't believe her; they'll believe me. I don't lie. And you know I'm an honest woman. I mean to be honest all my days. I flirt, to be sure, but Lord, what's that. I'd never do what my boy would be sorry I had done, when he grows big enough to know. You needn't be afraid of me. I aren't like you. I never shall be. There is something in the old countries,—but I'll be true to you, true as steel. Americans aren't mean!"

She paused once more, half afraid, in all her omnipotent vanity, of the answer she might receive.

Vere was still silent. The great pride natural to her was at war with the justice and generosity that were no less her nature. She was humiliated; yet she was deeply moved. This woman, whom she had always despised, had given her back kindness for unkindness, honour for scorn.

With a frank and gracious gesture she rose and put out her hand to her cousin's wife.

"I thank you. I cannot accept your offer, but I thank you none the less. You revenge yourself very nobly; you rebuke me very generously. I see that in the past I did you wrong. I beg your pardon."

Into the radiant, bold eyes of Fuschia Mull a cloud of sudden tears floated.

She burst out crying.

When she went away from Szarisla in the twilight of the sultry day she had failed to persuade Vere, yet she had had a victory.

"You are a saint!" she said, passionately, as she stood on the threshold of Vere's prison-house. "You are a saint, and I shall tell all the world so. Will you give me some little thing of your own just to take home to my boy from you? I shall have a kind of fancy as it will bring him a blessing. It's nonsense maybe, but still—"

Vere gave her a silver cross.

The long, empty, colourless days went by in that terrible monotony which is a blank in all after remembrance of it. Since the footsteps of Corrèze had passed away over the snow a silence like death seemed to reign round her. She noticed little that was around her; she scarcely kept any count of the flight of time; it seemed to her that she had died when she had sent him from her to the world— the world that she would never revisit. For she knew her husband too well not to know that he would never change in the thing he demanded, and to purchase freedom by the humiliation of public tribunals was impossible to a woman reared, in her childhood, to the austere tenets of an uncompromising honour, an unyielding pride.

"I can live and die here," she mused often. "But I will never meet his mistress as my friend, and I will never sue for a divorce."

When Sergius Zouroff from time to time wrote her brief words bidding her reconsider her choice she did not consider for a moment; she tore up his message.

The worst bitterness of life had passed her when she had bidden Corrèze depart from her. After that, all seemed so easy, so trivial, so slight and poor.

If her husband had sent her into poverty and made her work with her hands for her bread, it would have seemed no matter to her. As the summer came, parching, dusty, unhealthy, after the bitterness of the cold and the dampness of the rainy season, her attendants grew vaguely alarmed, she looked so thin, so tall, so shadowy, her eyes had such heavy darkness under them, and she slept so little. As for the world, it had already almost forgotten her; she was beautiful but strange; she had always been strange, society said, and she chose to live in Poland.

She thought of society now and then, of all that hurry and fever, all that fuss and fume of precedence, all that insatiable appetite for new things, all that frantic and futile effort at distraction, all that stew of calumny and envy and conflict and detraction which together make up the great world; and it all seemed to her as far away as the noise of a village fair in the valley seems to the climber who stands on a mountain height. Was it only one year ago that she had been in it?—it seemed to her as if centuries had passed over her head, since the gates of Szarisla had closed behind her, and its plains and its pinewoods had parted her from the world.

Even still the isolation was precious to her. She accepted it with gratitude and humility.

"If I were seeing him daily in the life of Paris," she thought, "who can tell—I might fall into concealment, deception, falsehood—I might be no stronger than other women, I might learn to despise myself."

And the gloom and the stillness and the lonely unlovely landscapes, and the long empty joyless days were all welcome to her; they saved her from herself. Her loveliness was unseen, her youth was wasting, her portion was solitude, but she did not complain. Since she had accepted this fate she did not murmur at it. Her women wondered at her patience as the exiled court of exiled sovereigns often wonder at their rulers' fortitude.

One day at the close of the month of May, she sat by herself in the long low room, which served her as her chief habitation. She had come in from her ride over the level lands, and was tired; she was very often tired now; a dull slight rain was veiling the horizon always dreary at its best; the sky was grey, the air was heavy with mist.

It was summertime, and all the plains were green with grass and grain, but it was summer without colour and without warmth, dreary and chilly: it was seven o'clock; the sun was setting behind a mass of vapour; she thought of Paris at that hour at that season; with the homeward rolling tide of carriages, with the noise, the laughter, the gaiety; with the light beginning to sparkle everywhere before the daylight had faded, with music on the air, and the scent of the lilacs, and the last glow of the sun shining on the ruined Tuileries.[1] Had she ever been there with the crowd looking after her as her horses went down the Champs Elysées?—it seemed impossible. It seemed so far away.

By the papers that came to her she knew that Corrèze was still there; there in the city that loved him, where his glance was seduction, and his hours were filled with victories; she knew that he was there, she read of the little château at Marly, she comprehended why

---

1   The Tuileries Palace was located on what is now formal gardens. Louis XIV lived there while his palace at Versailles was being built. During the French Revolution, Louis XIV and Marie Antoinette took refuge there. The mob stormed the palace, killed the guards, and looted it. The Palace was restored under Napoleon III, but it was burned down in 1870, during the overthrow of the Paris Commune.

he chose to live so, in the full light of publicity, for her sake. She thought of him this evening, in that dull grey light which spread like a veil over the mournful plains of Poland. Would he not forget as the world forgot her? why not? She had no pride for him.

At that moment as the day declined, a servant brought her letters.

Letters came to Szarisla but twice in the week fetched by a horseman from the little town. The first letter she took out of the leather sack was from her husband. It was very brief. It said merely:

"Paul de Sonnaz died suddenly last week. If you will consent to pay a visit of ceremony and respect to his wife in her retirement at Ruilhières, I shall welcome you to Paris with pleasure. If not, if you still choose to disobey me and insult me, you must remain at Szarisla, which I regret to hear from Ivan does not appear to suit your health."

There was nothing more except his signature.

The letter was the result of the promise he had given to his sister. Vere tore it in two.

The next she opened was a long and tender one from Nadine Nelaguine urging deference to his wishes, and advising concession on this point of a mere visit of condolence to Ruilhières, with all the arguments that tact and affection and unscrupulousness could together supply to the writer.

The next three or four were unimportant, the last was a packet addressed in a hand unknown to her.

She opened it without attention.

Out of the cover fell three letters in her mother's handwriting.

Wondering and aroused, she read them. They were letters ten years old. Letters of her mother to Sergius Zouroff; letters forgotten when others were burned the week before his marriage; forgotten and left in the tortoise-shell casket.

At ten o'clock on the following night as Prince Zouroff sat at dinner in the Grand Circle a telegram was brought to him. It was from his wife.

"Never approach me: let me live and die here."

CHAPTER VIII.

Szarisla had hidden many sad and many tragic lives.

It hid that of Vere.

To her husband she had perished as utterly as though she was dead. From remote districts of the north, news travels slowly; never travels at all, unless it be expressly sent; Vere had so seldom written to anyone that it scarcely seemed strange that she now never wrote at all. The world had almost ceased to inquire for her; it thought she had withdrawn herself into retirement from religious caprice, or from morbid sentiment, or from an unreturned passion, or that she had been sent into that exile for some fault; whenever women spoke of her they preferred to think this, they revived old rumors. For the rest, silence covered her life.

Her sister-in-law wept honest tears, reviled her brother with honest rage, but then played musical intricacies, or gambled at bezique,[1] and tried to forget that the one creature her cynical heart yearned over, and sighed for, was away in that drear captivity in the Polish plains.

"If I went and lived with her," thought Nadine Nelaguine, "I should do her no good, I should not change her: she is *taillée dans le marbre*,[2] I should alter her in nothing, and I should only be miserable myself."

In country houses of England and Scotland her mother went about through summer and autumn unchanged, charming, popular, and said with a little smile and a sigh, "Oh! my dear child—you know she is too good—really too good—wastes all her life in Poland to teach the children and convert the Nihilists; she is happiest so she assures me; you know she was always so terribly serious; it was Bulmer that ruined her!"

And she believed what she said.

Jeanne de Sonnaz mourned at Ruilhières in the austere severity of a great lady's widowhood in France, heard mass every day with her little blonde and brown-headed girls and boys about her in solemn retreat, yet kept her keen glance on the world, which she had quitted perforce for a space, and said to herself, annoyed and baffled, "When will he cease to live at Marly?"

For Corrèze was always there.

Sergius Zouroff had been to Russia. He only went to Livadia, but the world thought he had been to his wife. He returned, and kept open house, at a superb *chasse*[3] he had bought in the Ardennes. When people asked him for his wife, he answered them briefly that she was well; she preferred the north.

Félicité was closed.

---

1 A card game resembling pinochle.
2 Carved in marble.
3 Hunting park.

The old peasant stood by her wall of furze and looked in vain along the field paths under the apple-blossoms.

"Now the lark is dead," she said to her son, "neither of the two comes near."

So the months fled away.

When the autumn was ended, Corrèze, who was always at his little château with other artists about him, said to himself, "Have I not done enough for obedience and honour? I must see her, though she shall never see me."

Corrèze lived his life in the world obedient to her will, but men and women went by him like shadows, and even his art ceased to have power over him.

He was a supreme artist still, since to the genius in him there was added the culture of years, and the facility of long habit. But the joy of the artist was dead in him.

All his heart, all his soul, all his passion, were with that lonely life in the grey plains of Poland, whose youth was passing in solitude, and whose innocence was being slandered by the guilty.

"I obey her;" he thought, "and what is the use? Our lives will go by like a dream, and we shall be divided even in our graves, the world will always think she has some sin—she lives apart from her husband!"

He chafed bitterly at his doom; he grew feverish and nervous; he fancied in every smile there was a mockery of her, in every word a calumny; once he took up a public print which spoke of himself and of his retreat at Marly, and which with a hint and a veiled jest, quoted that line which Jeanne de Sonnaz had by a laugh wafted through Paris after his name.

"Pur amant sur terre égaré!"

Corrèze crushed the paper in his hand, and threw it from him and went out: he longed to do something, to act in some way, all the impetuosity and ardour of his temper were panting to break from this thraldom of silence and inaction.

He would have struck Sergius Zouroff on the cheek in the sight of all Paris, but he had no title to defend her.

He would only harm her more.

She was the wife of Zouroff, and she accepted her exile at her husband's hands; he had no title to resent for her what she would not resent for herself.

"I am not her lover, he thought bitterly; "I am nothing but a man who loves her hopelessly, uselessly, vainly."

It was late in autumn, and ghastly fancies seized him, vague terrors for her, that left him no sleep and no rest, began to visit him. Was she really at Szarisla? Was she indeed living? He could not tell. There were disturbances and bloodshed in the disaffected provinces; winter had begun there in Poland, the long, black silence of winter, which could cover so many nameless graves; he could bear absence, ignorance, apprehension no longer; he went to sing twenty nights in Vienna, and then in Moscow.

"There I shall breathe the same air," he thought.

He went over the Alps, by way of the Jura and Dauphiné; he thought as he passed the peaceful valleys and the snow-covered summits that had been so familiar to him:

"If I could only dwell in the mountains with her, and let the world and fame go by!"

Then he reproached himself for even such dishonour to her as lay in such a thought.

"What am I that she should be mine?" he mused. "I have been the lover of many women, I am not worthy to touch her hand. The world could not harm her—would I?"

In Vienna he had brilliant successes. He thought the people mad. To himself he seemed for ever useless, and powerless for art, his voice sounded in his ears like a bell muffled and out of tune. The cities rejoiced over him and feasted and honoured him; but it seemed to him all like a dream; he seemed only to hear the beating of his own heart that he wished would break and be at peace for ever.

From Moscow he passed away, under public plea that he was bound for Germany, towards those obscure, dull, unvisited plains, that lie towards the borders of East Prussia and the Baltic sea, and have scarce a traveller to notice them, and never a poet or historian to save them from the nations' oblivion, but lie in the teeth of the north wind, vast, ill-populated, melancholy, with the profound unchangeable wretchedness of a captive people.

Once more he saw the wide grey plains that stretched around Szarisla.

For days and weeks he lingered on in the miserable village which alone afforded him a roof and bed; he passed there as a stranger from the south buying furs; he waited and waited in the pinewoods merely to see her face. "If I can see her once drive by me, and she is well, I will go away," he said to himself, and he watched and waited. But she never came.

At length he spoke of her to the archimandrite[1] of the village, as a traveller might of a great princess of whom hearsay had told him. He learned that she was unwell, and rarely left the house.

Corrèze, as he heard, felt his heart numb with fear, as all nature was numbed with frost around him.

He could not bring himself to leave. The village population began to speak with wonder and curiosity of him; he had bought all the fur they had to sell, and sent them through into Silesia; they knew he was no trader, for he never bargained, and poured out his roubles like sand; they began to speak of him, and wonder at him, and he knew that it was needful he should go. But he could not; he lived in wretchedness, with scarcely any of the necessaries, and none of the comforts of life, in the only place that sheltered travellers, but from that cabin, he could see the stone walls of her prison-house across the white sea of the snow-covered plains; it was enough. The spot was dearer to him than the gay, delirious pleasures of his own Paris. In the world wherever he chose to go, he would have luxury, welcome, amusement, the rapture of crowds, the envy of men, the love of women, all the charm that success and art and fame can lend to life at its zenith. But he stayed on at Szarisla for sake of seeing those pale stern walls that rose up from the sea of snow.

Those walls enclosed her life.

The snow had ceased to fall, the frost had set in, in its full intensity; one day the sun poured through the heavy vapours of the cloud-covered sky.

He went nearer the building than he had ever done. He thought it possible the gleam of the sun might tempt her into the open air.

He stood without the gates and looked; the front of the great sombre pile seemed to frown, the casements had iron stanchions; the doors were like the doors of a prison.

"And that brute has shut her here!" he thought, "shut her here while he sups with Casse-une-Croûte!"

Suddenly he seemed to himself to be a coward, because he did not strike Sergius Zouroff, and shame him before the world.

"I have no right," he thought. "But does a man want one when a woman is wronged?"

He stood in the shadow of some great Siberian pines, a century old, and looked "his heart out through his eyes."

As he stood there, one person and then another, and then anoth-

---

1 Abbot (priest).

er, came up and stood there, until they gathered in a little crowd; he asked, in their own tongue, of one of them why they came; they were all poor; the man who was a cripple said to him: "The Princess used to come to us while she could; now she is ill we come to her; she is strong enough sometimes to let us see her face, touch her hand; the sun is out; perhaps she will appear to-day; twice a week the charities are given."

Corrèze cast his furs close about him, so that his face was not seen, and stood in the shadow of the great gateway.

The doors of the building opened; for a moment he could see nothing; his eyes were blind with the intensity of his desire and his fear.

When the mist passed from his sight he saw a tall and slender form, moving with the grace that he knew so well, but very wearily and very slowly, come out from the great doors, and through the gates; the throng of cripples and sufferers and poor of all sorts fell on their knees and blessed her.

He kneeled with them, but he could not move his lips to any blessing; with all the might of his anguish he cursed Sergius Zouroff.

Vere's voice, much weakened, but grave and clear as of old, came to his ear through the rarified air.

"My people, do not kneel to me; you know it pains me. It is long since I saw you; what can I do?"

She spoke feebly; she leaned on a tall cane she bore, and as she moved the thick veil from about her head, the man who would have given his life for hers saw that she was changed and aged as if by the passing of many years. He stifled a cry that rose to his lips, and stood and gazed on her.

The poor had long tales of woe; she listened patiently, and moved from one to another, saying a few words to each; behind her were her women, who gave alms to each as she directed them. She seemed to have little strength; after a time she stood still, leaning on her cane, and the people grouped about her, and kissed the furs she wore.

Corrèze went forward timidly and with hesitation, and kneeled by her, and touched with his lips the hem of the clothes.

"What do you wish?" she said to him, seeing in him only a stranger, for his face was hidden; then as she looked at him a tremor ran through her; she started, and quivered a little.

"Who are you?" she said quickly and faintly; and before he could answer muttered to him, "Is this how you keep your word?—you are cruel!"

"For the love of God let me see you alone, let me speak one

word," he murmured, as he still kneeled on the frozen snow. "You are suffering? you are ill?"

She moved a little away, apart from the people who only saw in him the traveller they knew, and thought he sought some succour from the mistress of Szarisla. He followed her.

"You promised—" she said wearily, and then her voice sank.

"I promised," he murmured, "and I had not strength to keep it; I will go away now that I have seen you. But you are ill, this country kills you, your people say so; it is you who are cruel."

He could scarcely see her in the veils, and the heavy fur-lined robes that screened her from the cold; he could only see the delicate cheeks grown thin and wan, and the lustrous eyes that were so weary and so large.

"I am not ill; I am only weak," she said, while her voice came with effort. "Oh, why did you come? It was cruel!"

She dropped her hood over her face; he heard her weeping—it was the first time he had ever seen her self-control broken.

"Why cruel?" he murmured. "Dear God! how can I bear it? You suffer; you suffer in health as well as in mind. What do you do with your life?—is it to perish here, buried in the snow like a frozen dove's? He is a brute beast; what need to obey him? what need to be faithful—?"

"Hush—hush! there has been sin enough to expiate. Let me live and die here. Go—go—go!"

Corrèze was silent. He gazed at her and loved her as he had never loved her or any other; and yet knew well that she was right. Nay, he thought almost better could he bear the endless night of perpetual separation than be the tempter to lead that fair life down into the devious ways of hidden intrigue, or out into the bald and garish glare of open adultery.

"O my love, my empress, my saint!" he murmured, as all his soul that yearned for her gazed from his aching eyes. "Long ago I said cursed be those who bring you the knowledge of evil. Others have brought it you; I will not bring more. I love you; yes; what of that? I have sung of love all my days, and I have sworn it to many, and I have been its slave often, too often; but my love for you is as unlike those passions as you are unlike the world. Yet you ask me to leave you here in the darkness of these ghastly winters; in the midst of an alien people that curse the name you bear; alone amidst every peril, surrounded by traitors and spies? Ask me any other thing; not that!"

"It must be that," she said; her voice was below her breath, but it was firm.

"No, no—not that, not that!" he cried passionately; "any other thing; not that! Let me stay where I see the roof that shelters you. Let me stay where I breathe the same air as you breathe. Let me stay where, from a distance in the forests, I can watch your horses go by and see the golden gleam of your hair on the mists; I will perish to the world; I will be dead to men; I will come and live here as a hunter or a woodcutter, as a tiller of the fields—what you will; but let me live where I know all that befalls you, where I can be beside you if you need me, where I can kiss the wind as it blows, because in its course it touched your cheek—"

In all the strength of his passion, in all the melody of his voice, the eloquence that was as natural to him as song to a bird poured itself out in that prayer. Only to dwell near her—never to touch her hand, never to meet her eyes, but to be near her where she dwelt, in this land of frost, of silence, of darkness, of danger, of sorrow—that was all he asked. And all the tenderness that was in her, all the youth, all the womanhood, all the need of sympathy and affection that were in her longed to grant his prayer.

To have him remain within call; to feel that in that dark, lone, wintry desert his heart was beating and his courage was watching near her; to think that when the chill stars shone out of the midnight clouds they would shine on some lonely forest cabin where this one creature who loved her would be living in obscurity for her sake;—this was so sweet a thought she dared not look at it, lest her force should fail her. She gathered all her strength. She remembered all that his life was to him—so gay, so great, so full of love, and honour, and triumph,—would she be so weak, so wicked, in her selfishness as to take him from the world for her, to be his living grave, to make him bankrupt in genius, in art, in fame?

She thrust the temptation from her as though it were a coiling snake.

"You mean the thing you say," she murmured faintly. "Yes; and I am grateful; but all that can never be. All you can do for me is—to leave me."

"How can I leave you—leave you to die alone? What need—what use is there in such a waste of life? No! what you bid me do, I do. I will keep the word I gave you; if you tell me to go, I go, but for the pity of heaven, think first what it is you ask; think a little of what I suffer."

"Have I not thought?"

She put her hands out feebly towards him.

"If you love me indeed, leave me; there is sin enough, shame enough, spare me more. If indeed you love me, be my good angel—not my tempter!"

He was pierced to the heart; he, the lover of so many women, knew well that moment in the lives of all women who love, and are loved, when they sink in a trance of ecstasy and pain, and yield without scarce knowing that they yield, and are as easily drawn downward to their doom as a boat into the whirlpool. He saw that this moment had come to her, as it comes to every woman into whose life has entered love. He saw that he might be the master of her fate and her.

For an instant the temptation seized him, like a flame that wrapped him in its fire from head to foot. But the appeal to his strength and to his pity called to him from out that mist and heat of passion and desire. All that was generous, that was chivalrous, that was heroic, in him, answered to the cry. All at once it seemed to him base—base, with the lowest sort of cowardice—to try and drag the pure and lofty spirit to earth, to try and make her one with the women she abhorred. He took her hands, and pressed them close against his aching heart.

"Better angels than I should be with you," he murmured; "but at least I will try and save you from devils. No man's love is fit for you. I will go, and I will never return."

He stooped, and with tremulous lips touched her hands; then once more he left her, and went away over the frozen snow.

CHAPTER IX.

Without pause Corrèze travelled straight to Paris.

He reached there late, and had barely time to dress and pass on to the stage.

It was the opera of "Romeo and Giulietta."

He knew its music as a child knows its cradle-song.

He played, acted, and sang, from one end to the other of the long acts perfectly, but without any consciousness of what he did.

"I am the mechanical nightingale," he thought, bitterly: the crowded opera-house swam before his eyes.

"Are you ill, Corrèze?" murmured the great songstress, who was his Juliet.

"I am cold," he answered her. It seemed to him as if the cold of those bitter plains, which were the prison of Vere, and might be her tomb, had entered his blood and frozen his very heart.

When he went to his carriage the streets were lined with the

throngs of a city that loved him. They pressed to see him, they shouted his name, they flung bouquets of flowers on to him; he was their
Roi Soleil, their prince of song. He wondered was he mad, or were
they? His voice felt strangled in his throat; he saw nothing of the
lighted streets and the joyous multitude, he saw only the piteous eyes
of the woman he loved as she had said to him—

"Be my angel, not my tempter!"

"I cannot be her angel," he said to himself. "But I will try and save
her from devils."

In all his life before he had never been at a loss. He had never
known before what doubt meant, or

What hell it is in waiting to abide.

His victories had all been facile, his love had all been swift and
smooth, his career had been a *via triumphalis*[1] without shadow, he
had been happy always, he had had romance in his life, but no grief,
no loss, no regret; he had been the spoiled child of fate and of the
world.

Now the fatal tenderness, the unavailing regret, which had been
no darker than a summer cloud when he had passed away from the
shores of Calvados, leaving the child, Vere Herbert, in her mother's
hands, had now spread over all his present and hung over all the
horizon of his future in a sunless gloom that nothing would ever
break or lighten.

And he was powerless!

If he could have acted in any way he would have been consoled.
The elasticity and valour of his temperament would have leapt up to
action like a bright sword from the scabbard. But he could do nothing. The woman he adored might perish slowly of those nameless
maladies which kill the body through the mind; and he could do
nothing.

He would not tempt her, and he could not avenge her.

He who knew the world so intimately, who had seen a million
times a laugh, a hint, a word, destroy the honour of a name, knew
well that he would but harm her more by any defence of her innocence, any protest against the tyranny of her husband.

---

1 A triumphant way.

Though he gave his life to defend her fair fame, the world would only laugh.

He drove through the brilliant streets of Paris at midnight, and shut his eyes to the familiar scenes with a heartsick weariness of pain. He loved *cette bonne ville de Paris*,[1] which had smiled on him, played with him, pampered with him, as a mother her favourite child; which always lamented his departure when he left it, which always welcomed him with acclamation when he returned. He loved it with affection, with habit, with the strength of a thousand memories of his glory, of his pleasure, of his youth; yet as he drove through it, almost he cursed it; Paris sheltered the vices of Sergius Zouroff, and worshipped his wealth.

He entered the club of the Grand Circle after the opera. He wished to gather tidings of the husband of Vere and of what the world said of her in her exile.

In one of the rooms Zouroff was seated, his hat was on the table beside him; he was speaking with the Marquis de Merilhac. As Corrèze entered, Zouroff rose and put his hat on his head. "Let us go to a club where there are no comedians," he said in a loud voice to Hervé de Merilhac, and went out. It was an insolence with intention; in the Ganaches men keep their heads uncovered.

All who were present looked at Corrèze. He took no notice. He spoke to his own acquaintances; the insult had no power to move him since he had so long kept his arm motionless, and his lips mute, for her sake.

Some men who knew him well and were curious, made a vague apology for the Russian Prince.

"He is jealous," they added, with a little fatuous laugh. "You come from Poland!"

"I have sung in Moscow and Warsaw," said Corrèze, with an accent that warned them not to pursue the theme. "And it is true," he added, with a grave coldness that had its weight from one so careless, so gay, and so facile of temper as he was. "It is true that in a part of Poland the Princess Vera Zouroff does live on one of her husband's estates, devoting herself to the poor because she prefers solitude and exile to receiving as her friend the widow of Paul de Sonnaz, the sister of Hervé de Merilhac."

For the moment, such is the immediate force of truth, no one laughed. There was the silence of respect.

---

1 This fine city of Paris.

Then they spoke of his return, of the opera that night, of his stay in Vienna, of all the topics of the hour then occupying the scarcely-opened salons of Paris. No man in the Ganaches was bold enough to speak again in his presence of Princess Zouroff.

"Why did you insult Corrèze?" said the Marquis de Merilhac, as Zouroff passed on with him to the Rue Scribe.

"I do not choose to be in the same club with a singer," answered Zouroff, with rough impatience.

"But he belongs to half the great clubs of Europe."

"Then I will insult him in half of them! You may have heart, *il fait la cour à ma femme.*"[1]

"Jeanne told me something at Félicité," said Hervé de Merilhac. "But she said it was only romance."

"Romance! Faust or Edgardo! or, as in a Renaissance dress, he is adored by Leonora![2] *Merci bien!*[3] I am not jealous, I am not unreasonable; I know the destinies of husbands. But I do not accept a rival in the satin and tinsel of the stage! Half a century ago," added Zouroff, as he turned in at the doors of the Jockey Club, "one could have had this man beaten by one's lackeys. Now one is obliged to meet him at one's *cercle* and insult him as though he were a noble."

"He is one," said the Marquis de Merilhac, who was perplexed and dissatisfied.

"Faugh!" said Zouroff, with the scorn of a great prince.

The next morning, as Corrèze passed through the gardens of the Tuileries, he chanced to see the small, spare form of the Princesse Nelaguine; she was seated on a bench in the sunshine of the wintry morning, watching the little children of her eldest son float their boats upon one of the basins. He paused, hesitated, saluted her, and approached. Madame Nelaguine smiled on him.

"Why not?" she thought, "there is nothing true; even were it true she would be justified."

Corrèze spoke to her with the compliment of daily life, which he, better than most men, could divest of the commonplace and invest with grace and dignity. Then abruptly he said to her, "Princesse, I was coming to you this morning; I have been to Szaris-la—"

She started, and looked at him in surprise.

---

1 He is courting my wife.
2 Lover of Don Fernando in Beethoven's *Fidelio*.
3 Thank you very much.

"To Szarisla? You have seen—my brother's wife? It is strange you should tell me."

"I tell you because she is your brother's wife," answered Corrèze; his face was pale and grave, and his tone was sad and cold, with an accent of rebuke, which her quick ear detected. "May I speak to you honestly? I should be your debtor if you would allow me."

She hesitated; then sent the children and their attendants farther away, and motioned to him to sit beside her.

"I suppose you know what they say," she said to him; "my brother would think I did ill to listen to you."

"In what they say, they lie."

"The world always lies, or almost always; I think it lies about you, or I should not speak to you. You have been to Szarisla?"

"I have been there; I have seen her for five minutes, no more, though I lived in the village five weeks. Madame, she had death in her face."

The tears rushed into his hearer's keen, curious eyes, her lips trembled.

"No—no, you exaggerate! Vera dying? You make my heart sick. I have feared for her health always—always—what did you do those five long weeks?"

"I waited to see her face," said Corrèze simply; "Madame, listen to me one moment; I will try not to tire your patience. She is your brother's wife; yes, but she is dealt with as he would never deal with one of his mistresses. Listen; long ago, when she was a child, I met her on a summer morning; I loved her then; call it fancy, caprice, poetry, what you will; her mother gave her, not to me, but to Prince Zouroff. I kept away from her; I would not sing in Russia whilst she was there; I would not approach her in Paris; if I had seen her in peace, seen her even respected, I would have tried to be content, I would for ever have been silent; instead, I have seen her insulted in every way that infidelity can insult a woman—"

"I know! I know! Spare me that; go on—"

"At last I knew that she was sent into exile; and why? because she would no longer receive Jeanne de Sonnaz."

"It was a madness to refuse to receive Jeanne de Sonnaz; after all, what did it matter? women meet their rivals, their foes, every hour, and kiss them. It was madness to refuse!"

"It may have been. It was noble, it was truthful, it was brave, it was befitting the delicacy and the dignity of her nature. For that act, though no one can deny that she is in the right, she is exiled into a land where life is unendurable, even to yourselves, natives of it;

where the year is divided between an endless winter and a short, parching season of heat that it is mockery to call the summer; where the only living creatures that surround her are servants who watch and chronicle her simplest action, and peasants, whose God is a dream, and whose homes are hovels. Did your brother wish for her death, or for her insanity, that he chose Szarisla?"

"My brother wishes that she should meet Jeanne de Sonnaz. I am frank with you; be frank with me. Are you the lover of my brother's wife? Paris says so."

"Madame, that I love her, and shall love no other whilst I live, I do not deny. That I am her lover is a lie, a calumny, a blasphemy, against her."

Madame Nelaguine was silent; she looked at him with searching, piercing eyes.

"What did you do, then, at Szarisla?"

"I went to see her face, to hear her footsteps, to be sure that she lived. I spoke to her; I laid my soul, my honour, all the service of my life, at her feet, and she rejected them. That is all."

"All?"

She was once more silent; she was a suspicious woman and a cynical, and often false herself, and never credulous; yet she believed him.

"You have been unwise, imprudent; you should never have gone there," she said suddenly. "And she is ill you say?"

"The priest said so; she looks so; she is weak; she is all alone. I should never have gone there? I should have been a coward indeed if I had not; if I had known her so deeply wronged, and had not at least offered her vengeance—"

"Her husband is my brother!"

"It is because he is your brother that I asked the grace of your patience to-day. Madame, remember it is very terrible that at twenty years old an innocent creature, lovely as the morning, should be confined in exile till she dies of utter weariness, of utter loneliness, of utter hopelessness! Prince Zouroff is within his rights, but nonetheless is he an assassin. I believe he alleges that she is free to return, but when he couples her return with an unworthy condition that she cannot accept, she is as much his captive as though chains were on her. If she remain there, she will not live, and she will never consent to leave Szarisla, since she can only leave it at the price of affected friendship with the Duchesse de Sonnaz—"

"What would you have me do?" cried his hearer in a sudden agitation very rare with her, in which anger and sorrow strove together; "what is it you ask? what is it you wish? I do not understand—"

"I wish you to speak to Prince Zouroff."

"Speak to Sergius?"

"In my name, yes; he would not hear me or I would speak myself. Madame, your brother knows very well that his wife is as innocent as the angels, but it suits him that all the world should suspect her."

"Then he is a villain!"

"He is under the influence of an unscrupulous woman, that is nearly the same thing. Madame de Sonnaz never forgave his marriage; she now avenges it. Madame, what I wish is that you should speak to your brother as I speak to you. He would not hear me; that is natural. He is her husband, I am nothing; he has the right to refuse to listen to her name from my mouth. But you, he will hear. Tell him what I have told you; tell him that, when the world speaks of me and of her it lies; and tell him—I can think of no better way—that to remove all possibility of suspicion, to put away all semblance of truth from the rumours of society, I myself will die to the world. Why not? I am tired. She will never be mine. Fame is nothing to me. The very music I have adored all my life seems like the mere shaking of dried peas in an empty bladder. I cannot forget one woman's face, a woman who will never be mine. I will leave art and the world of men; I will go back to the mountains where I was born, and live the life my fathers led; in a season Europe will have forgotten that it had ever an idol called Corrèze. Nay, if that fail to content him, if he doubt that I shall keep my word, I will do more; I will enter one of those retreats where men are alone with their memories and with God. There is the Chartreuse[1] that has sheltered greater men than I and nobler lives than mine. It is all alone amidst the hills; I should be in my native air; I could go there. You stare; do you doubt? I give my word that I will die to the world; I can think of no other way to save her name from mine. If that content him I will do it, if he will bring her back into the honour of the world, and never force her to see Jeanne de Sonnaz. Does it seem so much to you to do? it is nothing; I would die in my body for her, or to do her any good. Thus I shall die, only in name."

He ceased to speak, and his hearer was silent. There was no sound but the wind blowing through the scorched ruins of the Tuileries, and scattering on the earth the withered leaves of the trees.

"But what you will do is a martyrdom," she cried abruptly; "it is

---

1 A Carthusian monastery in Grenoble, France.

death ten thousand times over! Retreat from the world? you? the world's idol!"

"I would do more for her if I knew what to do."

She held out her hand to him.

"You are very noble."

"I will do what I say," he answered simply.

She was silent, in the silence of a great amaze; the amazement of a selfish and a corrupt nature at one that is unselfish and uncorrupted.

"You are very noble," she murmured once more, "and she is worthy of your heroism. Alas! it will be of no use; you do not understand my brother's character, nor what is now moving his mind. You do not see that his desire is, not to save his wife from you, but to force her to divorce him."

"If he were not your brother—"

"You would curse him as a scoundrel? He is not that; he is a man, too rich, spoiled by the world, and now dominated by a dangerous woman. I will speak to him; I will tell him what you have said; but I have little hope."

She gave him her hand again, her eyes were wet. He rose, bowed, and left her. He had done what he could.

At that moment Sergius Zouroff, in the smoking-room of the Ganaches, was reading a little letter that had come to him from the château of Ruilhières. It was very short, it said only, "Corrèze has returned to Paris; he has been at Szarisla. Do not let his talent, the trained talent of the stage, deceive you."

Madame Nelaguine an hour later told him of what had been said to her in the gardens of the Tuileries. She spoke with an eloquence she could command at will, with an emotion that was rarely visible in her.

"This man is noble," she said when she had exhausted all argument and all entreaty, and had won no syllable from him in reply. "Have you no nobility to answer his? His sacrifice would be unparalleled, his devotion superb; he will die to the world in the height of his fame, like a king that abdicates in full glory and youth. Can you not rise for once to his height? Will a prince of our blood be surpassed in generosity by an artist?"

He heard his sister speak in unbroken silence. She was afraid with a great fear. His stormy passions usually spent themselves in rage that was too indolent to act, but his silence was always as terrible as the silence of the frost at midnight in his own plains, when men were dying in the snow.

"You may be the dupe of a comedian's *coup de théâtre*," was all that he said when she had ended; "I am not; tell him so."

Sergius Zouroff knew well when he looked into his own heart that he was doing a base thing; he knew well that Vere was as pure of any earthly sin as any earthly creature can be; he did not believe any one of the daughters of men had ever been so innocent as she, or so faithful to the things she deemed her duty. But he stifled his conscience, and let loose only the rage which consumed him; half rage against her because she was for ever lost to him, half rage against himself for this other tyranny, which he had allowed to eat into and absorb his life. He was sullen, angered, dissatisfied, a dull remorse was awake in him, and the savage temper which had been always uncontrolled in him, craved for some victim on which to vent itself. His wife he dared not approach. His fury, though never his suspicions, fell upon Corrèze.

"He is not her lover; she is as pure as the ice," he said impatiently to himself. But she was not there, and Corrèze was before his eyes in Paris. A real and sombre hatred grew up in him; for little, for nothing, he would have killed this man as he killed a bird.

Corrèze sang this night at the Grand Opéra, according to his engagement.

The opera-house was in a tumult of rapture and homage; flowers rained on him; women wept; Paris the cynical, Paris the mocker, Paris the inconstant, was faithful to him, worshipped him, loved him as poets love, and dogs. It was the grandest night that even his triumphal life had ever known. It was the last. When the glittering crowds swam before his eyes, and welcomed his return, in his heart he said to them, "farewell."

As men doomed to death at dawn look at the sunrise of the last day they will ever see, so he looked at the crowds that hung upon his voice. It was for the last time, he said to himself; to-morrow he would keep the word he had given to Sergius Zouroff and would perish to the world. He would sing no more, save in the matin song, in the cold, white dawns, in the monastery of the mountains above Grenoble.

"She said rightly," he thought; "it is so easy to die."

"But to live so would be hard."

He would leave the laugh of the world behind him; a few women would mourn their lost lover, and the nations would mourn their lost music, but the memory of nations is short-lived for the absent, and he knew well that for the most part the world would laugh; laugh at Ruy Blas, who chose to bury his life for a fatal passion in the solitudes of the mountains in days when passion has lost all dignity and solitude all consolation. To the world he would seem but a romantic fool, since in this time there are neither faith nor force, but only a dreary and monotonous triviality that has no fire for hatred and has no soul for sacrifice.

"I can think of nothing else," he said to himself. He could think of no other way by which he could efface himself from the living world without leaving remorse or calumny upon her name. And to him it was not so terrible as it would have been to others. He had had all the uttermost sweetness and perfection of life, he had drunk deeply of all its intoxications, he was now at the zenith of his triumphs. He thought that it would be better to lay aside the cup still full rather than drain it to the lees. He thought that it would not be so very bitter after all to abdicate, not one half so bitter as to await the waning of triumphs, the decay of strength, the gradual change from public idolatry to public apathy, which all genius sees that does not perish in its prime. And he had more of the old faiths in him than most men of his generation. He had something of the enthusiast and of the visionary, of Montalembert and of Pascal.[1] It would not be so hard, he thought, to dwell amidst the silence of the mountains, waiting until the Unknown God should reveal by death the mysteries of life. Beyond all and beneath all, as he had often said, he was a mountaineer; he would be a monk amidst the mountains. Let the world laugh.

As the crowd of the opera house recalled him, and the plaudits that he would never hear again thundered around him, he murmured:

Je briserai sur mon genou
Le sceptre avec le diadème
Comme un enfant casse un joujou,
Moi-même, en plein règne, au grand jour.[2]

And his eyes were wet as he looked for the last time on the people of Paris and said in his heart—farewell.

---

1 Charles Forbes René de Montalembert (1818-70) was a French political leader and writer; Blaise Pascal (1623-62) was a French philosopher and mathematician. He invented the first digital calculator.
2 I will break on my knee / The scepter and the crown / Like a child breaks a toy / Myself, at the height of success, in broad daylight.

As he went away from the theatre, amidst the shouts of the exulting multitude—waiting as when kings pass through cities that hail them as victors—a note was brought to him. It was from Nadine Nelaguine. It said merely: "I have spoken to my brother, but it is of no use. He will hear no reason. Leave Paris."

The face of Corrèze grew dark.

"I will not leave Paris," he said to himself. He saw in the counsel a warning or a threat. "I will not leave Paris until I enter the shroud of the monkish habit."

And he smiled a little wearily, thinking again that when he should have buried himself in the Chartreuse the world would only see in the action a *coup de théâtre*; a fit ending to the histrion who had been so often the Fernando of its lyric triumphs.

He went down the street slowly on foot, the note of Nadine Nelaguine in his hand, his carriage following him filled with the bouquets and wreaths that had covered the stage that night.

He looked up at the stars and thought: "When I am amidst the snows alone in my cell, will these nights seem to me like heaven or like hell?"

An old and intimate friend touched his arm and gave him a journal of the evening.

"Have you read this?" said his friend, and pointed to an article signed, "*Un qui n'y croit pas.*"[1]

It was one of the wittiest papers that was sold upon the Boulevards; there was a brilliant social study; it was called, "*Les anges terrestres.*"[2]

Under thin disguises it made its sport and jest of the Ice-flower away in Poland, and the Romeo of Paris, who was breaking the hearts of women by an anchorite's[3] coldness.

It had been written by a ready writer in the Rue Meyerbeer, but its biting irony, its merciless raillery, its gay incredulity, its sparkling venom, had been inspired from the retreat of Ruilhières.

Corrèze turned into Bignon's, which he was passing, and read it sitting in the light of the great salon.

It would have hurt him less to have had a score of swords buried in his breast.

"If I avenge her I shall but darken her name more!" he thought,

---

1 One who doesn't believe it.
2 The earthly angels.
3 Hermit's.

in that agony of impotence which is the bitterest suffering a bold and fervent temper can ever know.

At that moment Sergius Zouroff entered; he had both men and women with him. Amongst the women were a circus-rider of the Hippodrome, and the quadroon Casse-une-Croûte.

It was midnight.

Corrèze rose to his feet, at a bound, and approached the husband of Vere.

With a movement of his hand he showed him the article he had read.

"Prince Zouroff," he said, between his teeth. "Will you chastise this as it merits, or do you leave it to me?"

Zouroff looked at him with a cold stare. He had already seen the paper. For the moment he was silent.

"I say," repeated Corrèze, still between his teeth. "Do you avenge the honour of the Princess Zouroff? I ask you in public, that your answer may be public."

"The honour of the Princess Zouroff!" echoed her husband, with a loud laugh. "*Mais—c'est à vous, monsieur!*"[1]

Corrèze lifted his hand and struck him on the cheek.

"You are a liar, you are a coward, and you are an adulterer!" he said, in his clear, far-reaching voice, that rang like a bell through the silence of the assembled people; and he struck him three times as he spoke.

CHAPTER X.

To Szarisla, in the intense starlit cold of a winter's night, a horseman, in hot-haste, brought a message that had been borne to the nearest city on the electric wires, and sent on by swift riders over many versts of snow and ice.

It was a message from Sergius Zouroff to his wife, and her women took it to her when she lay asleep; the troubled, weary sleep that comes at morning to those whose eyes have not closed all night.

It was but a few words.

It said only: "I have shot your nightingale in the throat. He will sing no more!"

She read the message.

For a few moments she knew nothing; a great darkness fell upon

---

1 But it is up to you, sir.

her and she saw nothing; it passed away, and the native courage and energy of her character came to life after their long paralysis.

She said no word to any living creature. She lay quite still upon her bed, her hand crushed upon the paper. She bade her women leave her, and they did so, though they were frightened at her look, and reluctant.

It was an hour past midnight.

When all was again still she arose, and clothed herself by the light of the burning lamp. No man can suffer from insult as a woman does who is at once proud and innocent. A man can avenge himself at all times, unless he be a poltroon[1] indeed; but to a woman there is no vengeance possible that will not make her seem guiltier in the eyes of others, and more deeply lowered in her own. As Vere rose and bound her hair closely about her head, and clothed herself in the furs that were to shelter her against the frightful frost, all her veins were on fire with a consuming rage that for the moment almost burnt out the grief that came with it.

She had been made a public sport, a public shame, by her husband, who knew her innocent, and faithful, and in temptation untempted! She had been sacrificed in life, and peace, and name, and fame, to screen the adulterous guilt of another woman! All the courage in her waked up in sudden resurrection; all the haughty strength of her character revived under the unmerited scourge of insult.

They should not dishonour her in her absence. They should not lie without her protest and her presence. He who was also guiltless should not suffer alone. Perhaps already he was dead. She could not tell; she read the message of her husband as meaning death; she said to herself, "Living, I will console him; dead, I will avenge him."

She drew the marriage-ring off her hand, and trampled it under her foot as Sergius Zouroff had trodden the Moth and the Star.

There is a time in all patience when it becomes weakness; a time in all endurance when it becomes cowardice; then with great natures patience breaks and becomes force, endurance rises, and changes into action.

She, proud as great queens are, and blameless as the saints of the ages of faith, had been made the sport of the tongues of the world; and he who had loved her as knights of old loved, in suffering and honour, was dead, or worse than dead.

---

1 Wretched coward.

The fearlessness of her temper leapt to act, as a lightning-flash springs from the storm-cloud to illumine the darkness. "I am not a coward," she said with clenched teeth, while her eyes were dry. She prepared for a long and perilous journey. She put on all her fur-lined garments. She took some rolls of gold, and the papers that proved her identity as the wife of Prince Zouroff, and would enable her to pass the frontier into East Prussia. With these, holding the dog by the collar, she took a lamp in her hand and passed through the vast, dark, silent corridors, that were like the streets of a catacomb. There was no one stirring; the household slept the heavy sleep of brandy-drinkers. No one heard her step down the passages and staircase. She undid noiselessly the bolts and bars of a small side door and went out into the air. It was of a piercing coldness.

It was midwinter and past midnight. The whole landscape was white and frozen. The stars seemed to burn in the steel-hued sky. She went across the stone court to where the stables lay. She would rouse no one, for she knew that they would to a man obey their Prince and refuse to permit her departure without his written order. She went to the stalls of the horses. The grooms were all asleep. She led out the two that she had driven most often since her residence at Szarisla. Her childish training was of use to her now. She harnessed them. They knew her well and were docile to her touch, and she put them into the light, velvet-lined sledge in which she had been used to drive herself through the fir forests and over the plains.

Her feebleness and her feverishness had left her. She felt strong in the intense strength which comes to women in hours of great mental agony. Her slender hands had the force of a Hercules in them. She had driven so often through all the adjacent lands that the plains were as well known to her as the moors of Bulmer had been to her in her childhood. The sledge and the horses' hoofs made no sound on the frozen snow. She entered the sledge, made the dog lie covered at her feet, and, with a world to the swift young horses, she drove them out of the gates and into the woods, between the aisles of birch and pine. The moonlight was strong; the moon was at the full. The blaze of northern lights made the air clear as day. She knew the road and took it unerringly. She drove all night long. No sense of mortal fear reached her. She seemed to herself frozen as the earth was. The howl of wolves came often on her ears in the ghastly solitude of the unending lines of dwarfish and storm-rift trees. At any moment some famished pack might scent her coming on the air and meet her, or pursue her, and then of her life there would be no more trace than some blood upon the snow, that fresher snow would in another hour obliterate. But she never thought of that. All she thought of was of the voice which for her was mute for ever.

When in the faint red of the sullen winter's dawn she arrived at the first posting village with her horses drooping and exhausted, the postmaster was afraid to give her other horses to pass onward. She could show him no order from Prince Zouroff, but she had gold with her, and at length induced him to bring out fresh animals, leaving her own with him to be sent back on the morrow to Szarisla. The postmaster was terrified at what he had done, and shuddered at what might be his chastisement; but the gold had dazzled him. He gazed after her as the sledge flew over the white ground against the crimson glow of the daybreak and prayed for her to St. Nicholas.[1]

Driving on and on, never pausing save to change her horses, never stopping either to eat or rest, taking a draught of tea and an atom of bread here and there at a posthouse, she at length reached the frontiers of East Prussia.

Corrèze lay on his bed in his house at Paris. Crowds, from princes and senators and marshals to workmen and beggars and street-arabs, came and asked for him, and the people stood in the street without, sorrowful and anxious. For the first news they had heard was that he would die; then they were told that the hemorrhage had ceased, that it was possible he might live, but that he would never sing again.

Paris heard, and wept for its darling—wept yet more for its own lost music.

The days and the weeks went on, and the first emotion and excitement waned in time. Then the Crown-Prince of Germany came into the city; there were feasts, reviews, illuminations. Paris, as she forgot her own wrongs, forgot her mute singer, lying in his darkened room; and the bouquets in his hall were faded and dead. No one left fresh ones. Only some score of poor people, amongst them a blind man and a little ugly girl, hung always, trembling and sobbing, about his doors, afraid lest their angel should unfold his wings and leave them for the skies.

Corrèze lay in his darkness, dumb.

He had been shot in the throat; he himself had fired in the air.

When he had fallen, with the blood filling his mouth, he had found voice to say to his adversary: "Your wife is faultless!"

---

1 Nicholas was bishop of the Christian Church in Asia Minor in the fourth century A.D. He is called "wonderworker" or "miracle-worker" for the miracles he performed.

Sergius Zouroff had looked down on him with a cold and fierce contentment.

"I have done you the honour to meet you, but I am not your dupe," he had said, as he turned away: and yet in his soul he knew—knew as well as that the heavens were above him—that this man, whom he believed to be dying, spoke the truth.

They had met in the garden of the house of Corrèze. They had taken only their seconds with them. It had all been arranged and over by sunrise. Sergius Zouroff had hastened out of the city, and over the frontiers, to make his peace with his sovereign in his own country. Corrèze had been carried into his own house and laid in his own bedchamber. Their friends, according to the instructions given them previously, had sent to the newspapers of the hour a story of an accident that had occurred in playing with a pistol; but it had been soon suspected that this was but a cover to a hostile account, and rumours of the truth had soon run through Paris, where the scene at Bignon's had been the sensation of the hour.

He lay now in the gloom and silence of his chamber. Sisters of charity were watching him: it was twilight there, though outside in Paris the sun was shining on multitudes of people and divisions of troops as the city flocked to a review in the Champ de Mars.[1]

He could not speak; they would save his life, perhaps, but he knew that they could never save his voice.

As a singer he was dead.

All the joys of his art and all its powers were perished for evermore, all the triumph and the ecstasy of song were finished as a tale that was told; all the fame of his life and its splendour were snapped asunder in their prime and perfection, as a flower is broken off in full blossom.

"And I did her no good!" he thought; he had lost all and he had done nothing!

He was half delirious; his sight languidly recognised the familiar room about him, and watched the stray lines of sunshine glimmer through the shutters; but his mind was absorbed and full of dull feverish dreams; he thought now of St. Petersburg, with the rain of hothouse flowers on the ice in his nights of triumph, now of the Norman sunshine with the common roses blooming against the fence of furze, now of the bleak snow-plains of Szarisla. All was con-

---

1 Originally a parade ground for young officer cadets, the area was used for mass ceremonies and exhibitions.

fused to him and showed like figures in a mist. Sometimes he thought that he was already dead, already in his tomb, and that about him the crowds of Paris were singing his own Noël. Sometimes he thought that he was in hell walking with Dante and with Virgil,[1] and that devils tried to hold him down as he strove to cry aloud to Christ: "Lord, she is innocent!"

All the while he was mute; he could scarcely breathe, he could not speak.

Unconscious though they thought him, he heard them say around his bed: "he may speak again, perhaps, but he will never be able to sing a note."

They thought him deaf as well as dumb. But he heard and understood.

In his fever and his suffering he said always in his heart: "If only she will think that I did well!"

Then he would grow delirious again and forget, and he fancied that he was called to sing to the people and that his mouth was closed with steel.

The wintry sunshine was brilliant and clear; it was in the afternoon; through the dusk of his room there came the distant sounds of trumpets, and the boom of the cannon of the Invalides. All else was still.

All Paris was interested with the pleasure of a spectacle; the streets were deserted, the houses were emptied, all the city was in the Champ de Mars, and on the cold clear air bursts of distant sounds from clashing cymbals and rolling drums came into the chamber of Corrèze, whom Paris had forgotten.

At the Gare de l'Est[2] with other travellers at that moment, there descended from a sleeping-carriage a woman clothed in furs, and with a dog in a leash beside her.

She walked quickly, and with a haughty movement across the crowded waiting-room; she was alone except for her dog. Her face was very white, her eyes seemed to burn as the stars did in the Polish frost. She was praying with all the might of prayer in her soul.

She might be too late to see him living; too late to tell him that

---

1 Both Eugène Delacroix (1783–1863) and William-Adolphe Bouguereau (1825–1905) have paintings entitled "Dante and Virgil in Hell"; William Blake (1757–1827) has a painting entitled "Dante and Virgil at the Gates of Hell." Ironically, Corrèze, who did not shoot at Zouroff, imagines himself damned in Dante's *Inferno*, still defending Vere's innocence.

2 The eastern Paris train station.

she loved him; she, for whose sake, and in whose defence, he had found death, or worse than death!

All the courage, all the fearlessness, all the generosity, of her soul had leaped up into life and movement; she had ceased to remember herself or the world, she only prayed to heaven, "Grant him his life! his beautiful life, that is like sunlight upon earth!"

She had come across the middle of Europe in the winter weather, over the snow plains and the frozen rivers, unaided, unaccompanied, making no pause, taking no rest either by night or day, as she had come through Poland.

She descended into the noise and dirt of the streets; she who had never been a yard on foot, or unattended, in a city. The movement around her seemed to her ghastly and horrible. Could he lie dying, and the city he loved not be still and stricken a moment?

She mingled with the crowds and was soon lost in them, she who had always gone through Paris with pomp and splendour; she at whose loveliness the mob had always turned to look; she who had been the Princess Zouroff.

The day was drawing to its close; the troops were returning, the multitudes were shouting. In his darkened room Corrèze, disturbed and distressed by the sounds, moved wearily and sighed.

The door of his chamber opened and Vere entered.

She threw her furs and coverings off her as she moved and came to the sisters of charity. The lassitude, the weakness, the sickness which had weighed on her, and suffocated her youth in her, were gone; there was a great anguish in her eyes, but she moved with her old free, proud grace, she bore herself with the courage of one whose resolve is taken and whose peace is made.

"I am the woman for whom he fought," she said to the nuns. "My place is with you."

Then she went to the side of his bed and kneeled there.

"It is I," she said in a low voice.

From the misty darkness of pain and delirium his senses struggled into life; his eyes unclosed and rested on her face, and had such glory in them as shone in the eyes of martyrs who saw the saints descend to them.

He could not speak, he could only gaze at her.

She bent her proud head lower and lower and touched his hand with hers.

"You have lost all for me. If it comfort you—I am here!"

CHAPTER XI.

In the heart of the Alps of the Valais there lies a little lake, nameless to the world but beautiful; green meadows and woods of pine and beech encircle it, and above it rise the snow mountains, the glory nearest heaven that earth knows.

A road winds down between the hills to Sion but it is seldom traversed; the air is pure and clear as crystal, strong as wine; brooks and torrents tumble through a wilderness of ferns, the cattle-maiden sings on the high grass slopes, the fresh-water fisherman answers the song from his boat on the lake, deep down below and darkly green as emeralds are.

The singer, who is mute to the world for ever, listens to the song without pain, for he is happy.

His home is here, above the shadowy water, facing the grand amphitheatre of ice and snow, that at daybreak and at sunset flash like the rose, glow like the fires of a high altar. It is an old house built to resist all storms, yet open for the sun and summer. Simple, yet noble, with treasure of art and graces of colour, and the gifts of kings, and emperors, and cities, given in those years that are gone for ever to Corrèze. The waters wash its walls, the pine-woods shelter it from the winds, its terraces face the Alps.

Here, when the world is remembered, it seems but a confused and foolish dream, a fretting fever, a madness of disordered minds and carking discontent. What is the world beside Nature, and a love that scarcely even fears death since it believes itself to be immortal.

He leans over the stone balustrade of his terrace and watches the rose-leaves, shaken off by the wind, drop down into the green water far below, and float there like pink shells. On a marble table by him there lie some pages of written music, the score of an opera, with which he hopes to achieve a second fame in the kingdom of music which knows him no more. A great genius can never altogether rest without creation, and he is yet young enough to win the ivy-crown twice over in his life.

In the sunset light a woman, with a dog beside her, comes out on to the terrace. She is clothed in white, her face has regained its early loveliness, her eyes have a serious sweet luminance; on her life there will be always the sadness of a noble nature that has borne the burden of others' sins, of a grand temper that has known the bitterness of calumny, and has given back an unjust scorn with a scorn just and severe; those shadows all the tenderness, the reverence, the religious homage of a man's surpassing love can never wholly banish from her.

As with him, amidst his happiness, there will sometimes arise a wistful longing, not for the homage of the world, not for his old hours of triumph, not for the sight of multitudes waiting on the opening of his lips, but for that magical power for ever perished, that empire for ever lost over all the melody of earth, that joy and strength of utterance, which are now for ever as dead in him as the song is dead in the throat of the shot bird, so upon her, for no fault of her own, the weight of a guilt not her own lies heavily, and the ineffaceable past is like a ghost that tracks her steps; from her memory the pollution of her marriage never can pass away, and to her purity her life is for ever defiled by those dead years, which are like mill-stones hung about her neck.

She was innocent always, and yet—. When the moths have gnawed the ermine, no power in heaven or earth can make it ever again altogether what once it was.

"You never regret?" Vere says to him, as they stand together, and see the evening colours of glory shine on the snow summits.

"I? Regret that I lost the gas-glare to live in heaven's light! Can you ask such a thing?"

"Yet you lost so much, and—"

"I have forgotten what I lost. Nay, I lost nothing. I passed away off the world's ear while I was yet great, how well that is—to be spared all the discontent of decadence, all the pain of diminished triumphs, all the restless sting of new rivalries, all the feebleness of a fame that has outlived itself—how well that is!"

She smiles; that grave and tender smile which is rather from the eyes than on the mouth.

"You say that because you are always generous. Yet when I think of all I cost you, I wonder that you love me so well."

"You wonder! That is because you cannot see yourself; humility blinds you, as vanity blinds other women."

"They called me too proud—"

"Because you were not as they were; what could they understand of such a soul as yours?"

"You understand me and God sees me—that is enough."

He takes her hands in his, and his kiss on them has as reverent and knightly a grace as that with which he had bent to her feet in the day of Szarisla.

What is the world to them? what is the bray and the tinsel of a mountebank's show to those who watch the stars and dwell in the gracious silence of the everlasting hills?

★ ★ ★ ★ ★

In the bright evening light of the spring-time at the same hour the crowds go down the Boulevards of Paris. The black horses of Prince Zouroff go with them; he is sitting behind them alone. His face is gloomy, his eyes are sullen. On the morrow he marries his old friend Jeanne, Duchesse de Sonnaz.

Russia, which permits no wife to plead against her husband, set him free and annulled his marriage on the testimony of servants, who, willing to please, and indifferent to a lie the more, or a lie the less, bore the false witness that they thought would be agreeable to their lord.

Too late he repents; too late he regrets; too late, he thinks, as alas! we all think: "Could I have my life back, I would do otherwise!"

In her own carriage, down the Avenue du Bois, drives the Duchesse de Sonnaz, with her children in front of her; her face is sparkling, her eyes are full of malice and entertainment; the Faubourg finds her approaching marriage with her lost Paul's old friend, one natural and fitting. With a satisfied soul she says to herself, as the setting sun gilds Paris:

"Avec un peu d'esprit, on arrive à tout."[1]

For marriage she does not care, but she loves a triumph, she enjoys a vengeance—she has both.

"Je ferai danser mon ours,"[2] she reflects, as the eyes of her mind glance over her future.

The Princess Nelaguine drives also in her turn out of the avenue and down the Champs Elysées; with her is her old comrade, Count Schondorff, who says to her:

"And you alone know your brother's divorced wife! Oh, surely Nadine—"

"I know the wife of Corrèze; I know a very noble woman who was the victim of my own brother and of Jeanne," answers the little Russian lady with asperity and resolve. "My dear Fritz, she had no sin against my brother, no fault in her anywhere, I have told the Emperor the same thing, and I am not a coward, though I shall salute Jeanne on both cheeks to-morrow because life is a long hypocrisy. Yes, I know Vera. I shall always love her; and honour her too. So does the Duchess of Mull. She was the martyr of a false civilisation, of a society as corrupt as that of the Borgias, and far more dishonest. She had chastity, and she had also courage. We, who are all poltroons, and

---

1 With a little intellect (understanding) one gets it all.
2 I will make my bear dance.

most of us adulteresses, when we find a woman like that gibbet her, *pour encourager les autres.*"[1]

At the same hour Lady Dolly, too, rolls home from Hyde Park, and ascends to her little fan-lined boudoir, and cries a little, prettily, with her old friend Adine, because she has just learned that Jura, poor dear Jura, has been killed in the gun-room at Camelot by the explosion of a rifle he had taken down as unloaded.

"Everything is so dreadful," she says with a little sob and shiver. "Only to think that I cannot know my own daughter! And then to have to wear one's hair flat, and the bonnets are not becoming, say what they like, and the season is so stupid; and now poor dear Jack has killed himself, really killed himself, because nobody believes about that rifle being an accident, he has been so morose and so strange for years, and his mother comes and reproaches *me* when it is all centuries ago, centuries! and I am sure I never did him anything but good!"

Other ladies come in, all great ladies, and some men, all young men, and they have tea out of little yellow cups, and sip iced syrups, and sit and talk of the death at Camelot as they chatter between the four walls with the celebrated fans hung all over them, amidst them the fan of Maria Teresa once sent to Félicité.

"She has so much to bear, and she is such a dear little woman!" say all the friends of Lady Dolly. "And it is very dreadful for her not to be able to know her own daughter. She always behaves beautifully about it, she is so kind, so sweet! But how can she know her, you know?—divorced, and living out of the world with Corrèze!"

So the moths eat the ermine; and the world kisses the leper on both cheeks.

THE END.

---

1 In order to encourage the others.

Appendix A: Contemporary Reviews of Moths

1. "Novels of the Week," *The Athenæum* 7 (February 1880): 181–82

The latest inspiration of Ouidà rejoices—if work so earnest as Ouidà's can without flippancy be said to rejoice—in an epigraph from the Book of Psalms.[1] 'Moths' is a solemn and fanciful tale. To read it is to know that no other living writer is capable of such splendid intellectual feats as Ouidà's. In her hands the English language becomes gorgeous, glittering, and highly inexpressive; to satisfy her ardour of expressiveness, her passion for subtlety and exactness, she has invented a French of her own; she is the author of another and a sadder world, where time and space exist not, where men and women are constructed on a new and peculiar pattern, and their only office is to serve as a background for high-souled misfortune and a tomb for love most futile and austere; she is the mistress of an erudition that ranges from all Bohn[2] to the last love song of Sully Prudhomme, and even includes such recondite scraps as the 'Fichtenbaum' of Heine in the original German. In 'Moths' she comes forward once more as the champion of genius against society. Writing under the influence of the romantic Parent-Duchâtelet,[3] she has imagined a world compact of dreadful men ... and ... women.... They dance, they sing, they drink, they gamble, they lie and slander, and smoke cigarettes; they tell each other improper stories, and talk slang, and run into debt; they bet, and paint, and powder, and wear wigs, and bathe in naughty-looking

---

1 "'Like unto moths fretting a garment' (Psalm)." Ouida may have been paraphrasing Job 13:28: "And he, as a rotten thing, consumeth, as a garment that is moth eaten."

2 Henry George Bohn (1796-1884) was a publisher and bookseller, who amassed a valuable collection of rare books. In 1846, he started his popular *Standard Library*, followed by the *Scientific Library*, *Classical Library*, etc. The whole series numbered over 600 volumes.

3 Alexandre-Jean-Baptiste Parent-Duchâtelet (1790-1836) was a French doctor who researched and wrote about prostitutes. In the 1830s, he investigated and interviewed 5,200 street prostitutes.

costumes; there is nothing vicious of which they are not understood to be capable, and they hate all manner of virtue violently; in a word, they are highly objectionable people, and dreadfully given to Sabbath-breaking and the perusal of abominable novels. Pitted against them are the chaste and lovely Vere Herbert—a maid of sixteen summers, devoted to Greek and music and high-toned things in general, and more virginal in thought and utterance than can be expressed in words—and Corrèze, the illustrious tenor, a person of genius, ubiquitous, universal, irresistible, a marquis. How Vere Herbert loves Corrèze and is forced into the arms of Serge Zouroff, the wicked Russian; how she is betrayed for the notorious Casse-une-Croûte and the dreadful Duchesse de Sonnaz; how she revolts in a feeble-minded and August kind of way and is banished to Poland; how she resists the importunities of Corrèze, and with what dignity she refuses, even at the cost of life, to call upon the horrible duchess,—all these things Ouidà's many readers must see for themselves. What is remarkable is that nobody dies, but that matters are somehow righted, Corrèze being let off with the loss of his voice, and allowed to live with Vere (divorced) and compose operas "in the heart of the Alps of the Valais," on the shores of "a little lake, nameless to the world, but beautiful." This fact would seem to indicate that Ouidà is not so stern of mood as she once was. Be this as it may, she is not a whit less amusing; and though at first glance it seems a waste of time to write three volumes of highly cultured eloquence and sadness just to have the pleasure of remarking at the end of them, in a separate paragraph, "So the moths eat the ermine, and the world kisses the leper on both cheeks," yet one has only to stumble across such a delightful Ouidaism as that reference to "the beauty that was Athens' and the glory that was Rome's"—one of many—to recognize that Ouidà does wisely and well, and will, while she lives, so write as to be worth reading.

2. "Moths," *The Saturday Review* 49 (28 February 1880): 287-88 [1]

... By the books that a man reads, almost as much as by his friends, it can be seen what kind of man he is. A woman whose taste was so depraved as to find pleasure in reading some of the stories that women are now writing, would, we should have hoped, at all events

---

1 Ouida attributed this review to Amelia Edwards.

have hidden herself away while she enjoyed her favourite author.... "Does the woman take her readers for a pack of fools," he might very fairly ask, "that she writes for them in a style which a few short years ago would scarcely have been tolerated, even in Bedlam?"[1] Readers, however, seem to be found in greater numbers than ever, and folly that would once have been treated with utter contempt is now highly rewarded.

It is always dangerous to attack a book of this kind. What the author asks for is notoriety, and notoriety is gained whenever a criminal is put in the dock. It is needful, however, now and then fairly to put before the world what kind of literature it is that is being sold on our railway-stalls and sent up and down the country by our circulating libraries. We are not of those who hold that, because the class of rich idlers has lately gained largely in numbers and in shamelessness, English society as a whole is corrupt. Scattered throughout the land in all its length and breadth there is happily still to be found that virtuous home life which has done so much to make our country what it is. It is the honourable duty of the critic to guide those who are living such lives as these in their reading, to introduce them to writers of sense and learning and virtue, and to guard them against both fools and profligates. They might perchance, in their innocence, be misled by the title-page of the novel before us, which they would find adorned with a quotation from the Scriptures. Let them but turn over the leaf, and they will find Scriptures, virtue and common sense left very far behind. They will be at once introduced to Lady Dolly, "who," they will read, "had everything that can constitute the joys of a woman of her epoch." Why *epoch*? may with good reason be asked. The author either means *time of life*, or *age in which this woman was living*. But neither of these meanings belongs to *epoch*. *Epoch* is defined by Johnson as "the time at which a new computation is begun." Perhaps, after all, some excuse might be made for the word as it is here used. Lady Dolly is living at the present time, and from it the computation might well be begun of the age of silly and vicious female writers. However, we have little doubt that the author thought that *epoch* would better round off the first paragraph of her book than either *age* or *time of life*, and that therefore she chose

---

1   Bedlam or Bethlehem is the world's oldest institution caring for people with mental disorders. It was founded in London in 1247. The original name Bethlehem was shortened in popular speech. The confinement of lunatics there led to "Bedlem" also meaning a house of confusion.

it, in full confidence that such readers as she is likely to get would like a word none the less because they only partially understood it. In the second page the dress of this lady of the epoch is described. It was "*baptiste* sublimised and apotheosised by niello buttons, old lace, and genius." A few pages further on we come across brown holland sublimated, canonized, and raised to the empyrean. Outside the author's mongrel English there are, of course, no such words to be found as *sublimised and apotheosised*, whether by buttons or by anything else. But we must not be too hasty. To her may not belong the honour, or the disgrace, of their invention. She is, we little doubt, a diligent student of her sister novelists—for by what other course of study can she have arrived at the very perfection of a foolish style?—and in a rival's book she may first have come across them. They were too good, and too long, and too unmeaning to be let slip....

For the present, however, we shall pass over the author's language, though no doubt we shall have to return to it again. We shall come to her description of society. Society, we assume, she describes as it is known to her. Perhaps this is all that she could do were she to aim at being true to nature. But then we prefer that those who only know a certain kind of society should at all events have the decency to hold their tongues.

The chatter of the world, [she writes] has almost always an element of the amusing in it, because it ruins so many characters, and gossips and chuckles so merrily and so lightly over infamy, incest, or anything else that it thinks only fun, and deal with such impudent personalities. In another passage the author writes:—

> Those who are little children now will have little left to learn when they reach womanhood. The little children that are about us at afternoon tea and at lawn tennis, that are petted by house parties and romped with at pigeon-shooting, will have little left to discover. They are miniature women already; they know the meaning of many a dubious phrase; they know the relative value of social positions; they know much of the science of flirtation which society has substituted for passion; they understand very thoroughly the shades of intimacy, the suggestions of a smile, the degrees of hot and cold, that may be marked by a bow or emphasized with a good-day. All the subtle science of society is learned by them instinctively and unconsciously, as they learn French and German from their maids. When they are women they will at least never have Eve's excuse for sin; they will know everything that any tempter could tell them.

When the author thus utters her shameless slanders against the little children who all around us are growing up to womanhood; when she says that the chatter of the world has in it an element of the amusing because it ruins characters and chuckles merrily over infamy and incest, we turn round upon her and ask her what is the world in which she lives, and to what class of infamy belong the mothers that she knows whose little daughters are being reared in a steady course of vice.... It is indeed astonishing that any women could be found, except the most abandoned, to read this gross libeller of her sex. What indignation ought to be raised in any woman of common decency, or any man who is not ashamed of his own mother, on reading such a passage as the following:—"She had a gown cut *en coeur*, which was as indecent as the heart of woman could desire." Not the heart of some one of the infamous women who crowd these pages, but the heart of woman—woman whom it has been the aim of a long line of writers to surround and defend with thoughts of chivalry and purity, and whom now a base herd of female novelists are trying to drag down to the level of their own coarse imaginations. The whole plot of this story is an abomination in itself. We might indeed despair of society were we to believe that a woman's tale of incest would not be treated with the contempt and disgust that it deserves. It is she, and not the world, who chuckles so merrily and so lightly over this horrible subject. It is she who spreads it out and dwells upon it in three long volumes. It is she who adds to it the utmost aggravation. And then she attacks "the woman of modern society," who is, she says, "too often and once the feeblest and the foulest outcome of a false civilization." She attacks the world, "which always greets with a damnable smile the approach of a foul idea." She is shocked at "the inane cruel chirping laughter of society when it smells a sin." She writes that "society chirped and babbled merrily of all the filth that satirists scarce dare do more than hint at lest they fall under the law." What right has she to take the shameless profligates of one small class and to call them the world and society? There may be a society which babbles merrily of filth, there may be a world which chuckles over infamy and incest. But we will not allow either those who live in this shameless society and form part of this infamous world, or those who pretend to be familiar with it, to put forward the impudent claim that they are society and they are the world. It would indeed have been a great misfortune had the author of this story been really a clever writer. She is very pretentious; but he must be a poor blockhead indeed who cannot discover that she is very silly. She greatly affects knowledge. She has the names of a certain number of classical authors on her tongue. She writes of the vice which "it is the fashion to pretend to believe shut up between the pages of Suetonius and Livy." She can excite the admiration of her readers by speaking familiarly of "the divine caduceus" and "the thronged auditorium." She makes a waiting-maid sit down by the seashore on a nice, smooth stone, which the next moment is called "a madreporic throne." She represents a great duchess when going out shooting as carrying "her own chokebore by Purdy." She calls sea shingles "the disordered detrius of the beach." She says that a great singer was famous "from Neva to Tagus, from Danube to Seine." She makes the hero pick the rare *Wolfinia Carinthiana*. She describes moths as "Burning themselves in feverish frailty." She brings in French with wonderful facility. Perhaps, however, we might object to an excess of accentuation in such a phrase as the following—"qui donc à (*sic*) voulu me mystifier?" Her studies, it will be seen, have been extensive, if not accurate. They have not, however, kept her from writing rant, and from filling her books with folly. Rant, however, might be forgiven, and folly might be laughed at. But there is much in this ignorant, dull, and disgusting story which no person whose mind is not utterly corrupt can either forgive or make a subject of laughter.

3. "Contemporary Literature," *The Westminster Review* 113 (April 1880): 294

Once more we have our old friend "Ouida." She is the same gushing personage as she was when we made her acquaintance some fifteen years ago in "Strathmore." We have the same vast amount of learning, the same bright wit, and the same intimate acquaintance, not merely with the nobility of our own land, but apparently of every country in the world. To be serious, we wish that Ouida could be persuaded to take a leaf out of some quiet, pure tale, like "From Generation to Generation."[1] Such a book does good, "Ouida's" nothing but harm.

4. A.K. Fiske, "Profligacy in Fiction: Zola's 'Nana.' Ouida's 'Moths,'" *The North American Review* 285 (July 1880): 79–88

.... "Zola will want a lower deep before long, I suppose: he will do well to leave his cellars for the drawing-rooms." Thus the profligate

---

1   A novel by Lady Augusta Noel, published in 1880.

Russian prince to the deceitful Englishwoman in Ouida's "Moths," the chief rival on the fashionable book-stalls of Zola's "Nana." But why should "Ouida" think of abdicating in her prime to the upstart Frenchman? Surely there is no profligacy in the drawing-rooms, or in the inmost closets of the houses of fashion, which she can have any delicacy about dealing with. Zola may as well keep to his cellars, while "Ouida," with feminine penetration for the hidden or the merely surmised, makes exploration of the apartments above stairs. Zola professes to describe the vice that dresses in its own garb and passes by its own name.... "Ouida" spies about genteel society in search of vice disguised by rank, by wealth, by culture, or by fashion. It is a task for a woman, but it needs for its performance a woman of great cleverness and no special regard for virtue, real or assumed. "Ouida" is well qualified. She owes society a grudge, possibly because society, whatever secret guiltiness may lurk in its most pretentious walks, is not openly tolerant of a disregard of the canons of morality, whose outer bulwark is conventionality. With the private character or conduct of the woman known as "Ouida" we have nothing to do, but as a writer she shows the result of a peculiar training. It is evident that she has known nothing of home influence, and has no appreciation of the graces of character which it produces. She has no understanding of home relationships or of their value in the conservation of purity and health in human society, and she has no respect for them. A brilliant girl, dependent for her training on a father of irregular habits and no domestic life, brought up at watering-places and in visits to gay capitals, educated among the shows and shams of life, and a stranger to domesticity of any sort, may develop into an entertaining writer, but can have no intimate knowledge of that which is sound and wholesome in the composition of human society. Disregarding the rules and restraints which experience has shown to be necessary for the protection of virtuous character, she is sure to be guilty of offenses whose heinousness she has no appreciation, and the social penalty for which she regards as not only tyranny, but a hypocritical tyranny. She cherishes resentment against society, and is eager to revenge herself upon it. If she wields a keen pen, it is not difficult. What is called society, like the individual man and woman, or the human race as a whole, has its faults and vices. It is only necessary to seize upon these, and, with the coarse satire of caricature, to represent them as the essential elements of its character.

"Ouida" has a very bad opinion of the women of society.... Her opinion of men is no higher, though she is not moved to formulate it in the same ferocious spirit, and her philosophy of marriage is drawn from her opinion of the unfortunate sexes of humanity....

The works of "Ouida" are charged with offending against propriety. She professes to regard them simply as giving truthful pictures of human society as it exists to-day. If this were so, we might as well despair of the human race, and anticipate an impending doomsday which should sweep the corrupt fabric away as the last failure of a disgusted Creator. In her pages, men are swayed by the passions of their lower nature, and women are not merely their weak and willing victims but their artful and ready seducers. A faithful husband is a thing to be laughed at; a faithful wife, a creature who foolishly mopes and suffers when she might gayly avenge. Marriage is a bondage of the law, fatal to love, and hence to fidelity, and the cover of intrigue and inequity. Society is false and corrupt, and knows it, but protects itself from collapse by a common consent to pretend that it is otherwise, until some fool rebels and makes a scandal. Then the fool must be suppressed, the victim of exposure ostracized, and the shallow comedy is resumed. Husbands have mistresses as a matter of course, and wives have their lovers. Why should they not, as love disappears after the honeymoon, and they would otherwise be unendurable to each other? Each knows the other's sins, but pretends to be blind, and so avoids disturbing the serenity of fashionable hypocrisy.

This is human society according to "Ouida"; society itself takes the gross libel without resentment, and "Ouida" is one of the most popular writers of the day. There is no doubt that Zola in his cellars finds a world of reality, full of sinks of pollution and infested with foul vermin.... But the glare which the clever French *feuilletoniste*[1] turns upon the underground world is garish and delusive. In the ranks of respectable society the baser passions of mankind break out in secret or open revolt against the restraints of moral duty or social decency, and "Ouida" has human fact to deal with. But is this the substance of society, even of the showy and frivolous kind over which Fashion reigns? Pampered princes may be monsters of iniquity, and be tolerated because of their rank or wealth. The sins of the rich and powerful may be too easily condoned, and the weaknesses of women of influential families may be covered with a veil that nobody cares to tear away; but is society made up of such, and is this caricature to be taken as a truthful picture, even in the gay capitals

---

1 Serial writer.

of Europe of the resorts of fashionable diversion? A cynical French-man or a much-traveled adventuress of no nationality may gain admission to the ranks of literature with elaborately garnished sto-ries from the slums and bagnios or from the scandals of the divorce courts, but Anglo-Saxon readers at least should shut the vile rubbish from their libraries. Anglo-Saxon ideas of society and of human life are not those of Zola and "Ouida." With that race the sensual was never uppermost even in its rudest days, when brutality of the roughest sort might be laid to its charge. It believes in the purity of woman, the fidelity of man, the sanctity of home and the family, and the possibility of a society in which the passions are controlled by a sense of duty and of right. With them the love of man and woman is not an animal appetite to be sated and then to give place to indif-ference or aversion. It is a holy sentiment on which life-long com-panionship and helpfulness are to be based, and from which spring the sweet influences of domestic life and the graces of personal virtue and integrity. The Anglo-Saxon mind is not tolerant of infi-delity or profligate practices cloaked by social pretensions, nor does it find entertainment in the garbage of the slums and the orts of unseemly households. It regards society as made up of families, in which decency is held in esteem, where the rose remains on the fair forehead of an innocent love and is not displaced by a blister, and where marriage vows are not rated with dicers' oaths. Society has in it healthful currents and the substance of a sound constitution.

English literature from its beginning has truthfully reflected the social life, the character, and the manners of the people whose blood is English, and there is nothing of which we have more right to be proud than the steady purification of the stream. The coarseness of some of the early poets and dramatists may have been "realistic," but it puts their works on neglected shelves in these days of purer man-ners. The first novels were so much given to accounts of disreputable intrigue, and so infected with the baser qualities of human nature, that, for a long time, all novels were under a Puritanic ban not whol-ly without provocation.... Latterly we have had in English novels many inspiring and purifying pictures of home-life and the fairer aspects of society.... English fiction has been a powerful agency of reform and purification.

Upon this fair domain of our literature these foreign purveyors of infection—for "Ouida" has no claim to the title of English-woman—are permitted to intrude. They turn the gutters into our wholesome gardens and cast the uncleanness of the divorce court about our hearthstones. The rubbish which, in flaring pictorial weeklies, is excluded from respectable kitchens, is elaborated and embellished in gilt bindings and admitted to the parlor-table. It is the last tricklings of that ribald literature which has run through history in a happily decreasing current from the old times when human passion was deified and the rule of the senses was hardly resisted.... To the Anglo-Saxon mind and heart it is or ought to be an offense and an insult.

Condemnation is not to be pronounced upon the authors of this sort of fiction more than on its readers. The writers have their gifts, and use them according to their nature. They are the scavengers and scandal-mongers of society, who will exist so long as they are paid and encouraged. They can not be silenced or suppressed; but it is a sorry indication when their books are in demand at the circulating libraries and the fashionable shops for literary pabulum in English and American cities. Their presence in drawing-rooms show that the old infection still asserts itself in the appetite—taste it can not be called—which craves a stimulant for passion, and is tormented with prurient longings. It is the same spirit that leads to the secret traffic in the merely libidinous in literature and art, the same that prompts the collecting of old indecencies at fancy prices under the pretense of "rare and curious," the same that promotes the gross sensuality that Zola pictures, and the yieldings to lust in which "Ouida" revels. The old Adam in the blood of the race, that besets its course with vice and lapses from integrity, is that which finds satisfaction in the perusal of literature wrought from the material of its sin and weakness. Pruriency and that alone is gratified, and at the same time excited and intensified, by this kind of reading. Pure taste and virtuous inclination find nothing congenial in it, and respectable drawing-rooms should as sternly close their doors against it as they would against the characters that pervade it.

Appendix B: The Novels of Society

[Reviewers often ridiculed Ouida for her lavish descriptions of "demoralized sensuality" in the high society world of her fiction. But as Oscar Wilde shrewdly pointed out (below, p. 561), Ouida successfully "caught much of the tone and the temper of the society of our day."]

1. From Vincent E.H. Murray, "Ouida's Novels," *The Contemporary Review* 22 (1878): 921-33

... Ouida's puppets ... are spangled and bedizened;... As to her women: "diamonds of untold price" generally glisten on their "snowy bosoms;" they wear "gem-sewn robes;" their hair is "diamond-studded;" they stretch out their hands to "jewelled letter-baskets," "jewelled fans," jewelled bouquetières;"[1] their letters "smell of gemmed pen-holders, and Buhl writing-cases." ...

The men whom Ouida would have us accept as representatives of the aristocracy of our day wear "dainty dressing-gowns, broidered with gold and seed pearl," with slippers of the same expensive materials; they sleep "under costly canopies of silk and lace and golden broideries;" they enter bets in "dainty jewelled books;... they see the time of day (or rather of night; for nobody in their world seems to go to bed till the every day world is eating its breakfast) on "jewelled watches." ...

Erotic poems ... cannot be enacted without utter destruction to the chance-sown flowers in the path of the poet, who flings them aside to be trodden under foot in the mud of erotic prose. This is of no importance in Ouida's code of morality—which is, in this respect, alas! the world's—so long as the poet abstains from plucking flowers from the garden of men of race. We know that men of race must have ripe scarlet mouths to "kiss in lawless sovereignty, *because they are men;*" but, in the name of all that is moral and proper, Ouida would have them forbear to "poach" in the "preserves" of their fellow-*sovereigns*, or the very foundations of *Society* will be shaken! With this proviso, they are free to "enjoy."

To enjoy.

---

1   Flower vases.

It is because these words—which aptly sum up the aim of Ouida's works—throw an evil light upon the social corruption of which they are an exhalation, that we hold ourselves justified in directing attention to them. Precisely as certain diseased conditions of the body give rise to a craving after unnatural food, so do certain morbid conditions of the mind produce an appetite for literary food which a sound mental organization would reject. Individual instances of such morbid affections are fit subjects of study for the physician only, and the fact that a silly and ignorant woman should write novels which are at once vulgar, nasty, and immoral in tendency, could not, in itself, be matter of interest for readers of the CONTEMPORARY REVIEW. But that such books have a very large and increasing circulation should be matter of painful interest to every decent man and woman in England. The price at which they are published renders them inaccessible to those whom it is customary to call "the people," and it is clear that a writer who tells us that "a gaunt, bull-throated, sanguinary brigand" is "the type of the *popolares*[1] of all time," does not address herself to them. These books are issued by one of the first houses in the trade; they are written for and read by society.

Is not the motto of Ouida's heroes—"to enjoy"—the motto of society, and every day more openly, more shamelessly, avowed? We believe it is, and we believe further that the society which reads and encourages such literature is a "whited sepulchre"[2] which, if it be not speedily cleansed by the joint effort of pure men and women, will breed a pestilence so foul as to poison the very life-blood of our nation.

2. From "Contemporary Literature," *Blackwood's Edinburgh Magazine* 125 (March 1879): 333-35

... [O]ur Englishwomen are at a sad disadvantage, and greatly to be pitied they are. They must deny themselves the unfettered licence of the French romance; and even when they dare to borrow some refinement of depravity, they must tone it down to the English taste. With the most praiseworthy ambition, if they are to sell their books, or obtain admission for their stories into decent magazines, they can

---

1 Popular people.
2 Matthew 23:27: "Whited Sepulchres, which indeed appear beautiful outward, but are within full of dead men's bones."

hardly write up to the disclosures of the divorce trials. The natural alternative is to launch out in the luxurious, to elaborate marvellous types of hopelessly demoralised sensuality, and to shadow out dim possibilities of guilt which may take shape in the fancies of their more imaginative readers. There is nothing the middle and the lower middle classes care for more than to be introduced to those unfamiliar splendours which Providence has placed beyond their reach, and, necessarily, they can never be very critical as to the beings who people these dazzling realms of mystery.... "Ouida," who has a good deal of the French "genius" in her, may be said to have set English-women the example in that respect. She gave us her delicate Life-Guardsmen, who ... could sit up the best part of the night over cigars and Curaçao punch, gambling on credit for fabulous stakes, and rise "fresh as paint" to go on duty in the morning. They walked the streets and went their nightly rounds, as the embodiment of hyper-melodramatic action. For while their aristocratic superciliousness provoked the quarrel which the weakness of their *physique* seemed to make a foregone conclusion, in reality they had muscles of steel, set in motion by the agility of the catamount.[1] ... Brainless sybarites[2] as they might appear to the superficial observer, with soul and body deteriorating apace like those of the confirmed opium-smoker, they could be reckoned upon at a moment's notice for a manly decision in the most momentous question, or for a heroic deed of superb self-sacrifice. For they had a code of honour and virtue of their own, though it was a code that clashed with the old-fashioned decalogue; and if they swindled a friend or seduced his wife, they would always back his bills to any amount, or give him a meeting at the certainty of social extinction with the chances of capital punishment thrown in.

There was a touch of genius in the audacity that first played fast and loose with the confiding innocence and ignorance of the million. Of genius, we say, because these scenes and persons, being as far-fetched as fanciful, must have been invented at no small expenditure of imagination.... And if we have expatiated on them at some length, it is simply because the mischief they must answer for is likely to survive the unnatural excitement and the extreme absurdity which were their redeeming virtues.... But the fact remains, as Thackeray says of one of his own burlesques, that though much of

---

1 Cougar.
2 Hedonists, people addicted to luxury and sensual pleasures.

it all is absolutely unintelligible to us, "yet for the life of us we cannot help thinking that it is mighty pretty writing." The uneducated and thoughtless who have neither knowledge nor discrimination of taste, no doubt feel unmitigated admiration for those eloquent rhapsodies of lurid description. Foolish lads and girls fancy they have a reflection of high society in the most ludicrously distorted pictures and caricatures; virtue and vice are habitually confounded; and notions that might have been borrowed from the melodramas of the transpontine[1] theatres, are developed and even travestied in those sensational novels. Stories written for the gratification of the ordinary subscribers to Mr. Mudie,[2] are passed on in due course to be devoured by the milliners' apprentices and lawyers' clerks. There seems no reason why the young woman who admires her *beauté du diable*[3] daily in the looking-glass, should not make the acquaintance of one of these noblemen or millionaires, who can raise her to the position her charms would adorn.... These stories are circulated or imitated in the columns of the "penny dreadfuls;" and just notions they must give of the rich and the well-born to the intelligent artisan relaxing from his labour.

3. From Harriet Waters Preston,[4] "Ouida," *The Atlantic Monthly* 58 (1886): 47-58

It is no light thing to be a popular writer; and when one has been a popular writer for twenty-five years, more or less, and, under whatever variety and severity of protest, is quite as much read as ever at the end of that time, the phenomenon is undoubtedly worthy of attention. So much I take to be strictly true of the indefatigable novelist who calls herself by the curious name of Ouida. Everybody reads her twenty or thirty books....

I will premise that this inquiry [why Ouida is so popular] is going to be, primarily and chiefly, a search for merits, rather than a citation of defects. There is very much reason to believe that this is in all cases the true method of criticism: to get inside of a subject, and then work outward;...

And first it may be remarked that in the general type of her tales

---

1 The southern side of the Thames in London.
2 Charles Edward Mudie (1818-90) was the proprietor of a "Select Circulating Library." Thousands of families in London subscribed to it.
3 Bloom of youth.
4 Harriet Waters Preston was a distinguished American critic.

she is really the heir, and the legitimate heir, of very high traditions. She is by nature a flagrant romanticist;... They [romance novelists] are all free, and profess to make their readers free, of a world of ardent love and furious war; of vast riches and dazzling pomp; of heroic virtues and brutal crimes; of consummate personal beauty, flower-like, fairy-like, god-like, as the case may be; of tremendous adventures, enormous windfalls, crushing catastrophes, and miraculous escapes.... We smile at the perfumed baths and jeweled hair-brushes of Ouida's young guardsmen; at the cataracts of diamonds which descend from the shoulders of her heroines when they go to the ball, and the curtains of rose-colored Genoa velvet, edged with old Venice point, which the valet or the maid will draw noiselessly aside, in order to let the noontide sun steal in upon her jaded revelers on the morning after a festivity.... [T]he ecstatic sibilation ... with which Ouida dilates on the luxuries which surround her favorites is paralleled, to say the least, by the solemn rapture of the great statesman before the stock-in-trade of a fashionable jeweler. The worship of wealth is vulgar and demoralizing, yet it is not absolutely and entirely vulgar. It is a possible root of all evil, but it is not the one, sole root, and even the apostle[1] never meant to say that it was. It *marches*, as we used to say of the boundaries of a country, with very noble things, the supreme splendors of art, the possibilities of a vast beneficence.... Riches—mere giddy, golden riches, such as Ouida and the romanticists generally so constitutionally dote upon—have always played a great part in the moral development of mankind, and were probably intended, from the beginning, so to do. They are for the possession of the few and the edification of the many; and whoever succeeds ... in reconciling the minds of men to the fact that wealth *must be* where civilization is, but cannot be for all; whoever helps the many, in their need, to acquiesce in the abundance of the few, will have done more for his kind than all the socialists. The conception of Ouida as a moralist of this magnanimous type is doubtless a humorous one, and any good she may do in this direction will probably be indirect and involuntary....

Meanwhile, it may be observed in her favor that ... she does set some limit to the wealth even of her most opulent hero. After having handsomely endowed him with "home estates as noble as any in England, a house in Park Lane, a hotel on the Champs-Élysées, a toy

---

1 Apostle Paul to Timothy: "The love of money is the root of all evil," 1 Timothy 6:10.

villa at Richmond, and a summer palace on the Bosphorus," beside a yacht, "kept always in sailing order, and servants accustomed to travel into Mexico or Asia Minor at a moment's notice," she does, nevertheless, own him subject to the law which entails pecuniary ruin upon the men whose expenditure is exactly four times as great as his income; and he starves, when the time comes, with as much distinction as he had previously squandered....[1]

It is genuine imagination, however, and takes one well away from the "stuffiness" of the mere society column, which is all the small-fry of the later school seem to aspire to....

[I]t must be confessed, by a goodly number of those who claim to constitute "the age," she proceeds to a sort of glorification of sensuality. She has the honor of having, to some extent, anticipated Zola. She is eager to inform us that all her very noblest heroes, even one who ... is made capable of sparing and forgiving a most malignant foe, have been at one time or another "steeped" in degrading indulgence. Nor is ordinary sensuality sufficient for her. Adultery is often too pale, and she must needs hint at something worse....[2]

Taken altogether, these books reveal a truly remarkable wealth of invention and no mean constructive power; an ability, which may well challenge our admiration, to conceive an almost endless variety of striking figures and picturesque situations, combined with an independence of conventionalities, whether moral or literary, which moves one to something like awe. These books have, moreover, beside their intrinsic qualities, a certain interest in the history of fiction, as constituting ... the very last of the strictly romantic novels which can have been written in entire good faith upon the author's part....

The note of sound reality, which Ouida touches almost for the first time in Friendship, continues to vibrate more or less perceptibly though all her subsequent productions; checking their extravagance, reducing their feverish temperature, regulating by the laws, at least, of remote probability their often insane and occasionally indecent action, imparting form and unity to her facile and rapid compositions.... She has by no means ceased to dote upon princes and dukes, but she acknowledges them to be human....

I have, I think, fulfilled my engagement to say all that can fairly

---

1   A reference to Ouida's *Chandos* (1866). The wealthy aristocratic hero is ruined by the machinations of his bastard brother. He lives in poverty and then becomes a successful poet.

2   Incest.

be said in favor of one whose books are in many hands and whose name is on many lips, while it is wholly impossible to dissociate either books or name from a certain persistent odium. Power and variety are two very distinguished qualities in a writer, and these are possessed by Ouida in so large a degree that very few indeed of the female writers now living can rival her....

4. From [Oscar Wilde],[1] "Ouida's New Novel," *The Pall Mall Gazette* (May 1889): 3

Ouida is the last of the romantics. She belongs to the school of Bulwer Lytton and George Sand, though she may lack the learning of the one, and the sincerity of the other. She tries to make passion, imagination, and poetry, part of fiction. She still believes in heroes and in heroines. She is florid, and fervent, and fanciful. Yet even she, the high-priestess of the impossible, is affected by her age. Her last book "Guilderoy" as she calls it, is an elaborate psychological study of modern temperaments. For her, it is realistic, and she has certainly caught much of the tone and temper of the society of our day.... The book may be described as a study of the peerage from a poetical point of view. Those who are tired of mediocre curates who have doubts, of serious young ladies who has [sic] missions, and of the ordinary figureheads of most of the English fiction of our time, might turn with pleasure, if not with profit, to this amazing romance. It is a resplendent picture of our aristocracy. No expense has been spared in gilding.... For the comparatively small sum of £1 11s. 6d. one is introduced to the best society....

5. From Ouida, "The Sins of Society," *Views and Opinions* (London: Methuen, 1895): 1-33

A brilliant and daring thinker lately published some admirable papers called 'Under the Yoke of the Butterflies.' The only thing which I would have changed in those delightful satires would have been the title. There are no butterflies in this fast, furious and fussy age. They all died with the eighteenth century, or if a few still lingered on into this, they perished forever with the dandies. The

---

1 Oscar Wilde (1854-1900) was a British playwright, novelist, and critic. He was a regular guest at Ouida's dinner parties when she held court at the Langham Hotel in 1886. His review is unsigned.

butterfly is a creature of the most perfect taste, arrayed in the most harmonious colours: the butterfly is always graceful, leisurely, aerial, unerring in its selection of fragrance and freshness, lovely as the summer day through which it floats. The dominant classes of the present day have nothing in the least degree akin to the butterflies; would to Heaven that they had! Their pleasures would be more elegant, their example more artistic, their idleness more picturesque than these are now. They would rest peacefully on their roses instead of nailing them to a ballroom wall; they would hover happily above their lilies and carnations without throwing them about in dust and dirt at carnivals.

Butterflies never congregate in swarms; it is only locusts which do that. Butterflies linger with languorous movement, always softly rhythmical and undulating even when most rapid, through the sunny air above the blossoming boughs. The locust is jammed together in a serried host, and tears breathlessly forward without knowing in the least why or where he goes, except that he must move on and must devour. There is considerable analogy between the locust and society; none between society and the butterfly.

Some clever people have of late been writing a great deal about society, taking English society as their especial theme. But there are certain facts and features in all modern society which they do not touch: perhaps they are too polite, or too politic. In the first place they seem to except [sic], even whilst attacking them, smart people as elegant people, and to confuse the two together: the two words are synonymous in their minds, but are far from being so in reality. Many leaders of the smart sets are wholly unrefined in taste, loud in manner, and followed merely because they please certain personages, spend or seem to spend profusely, and are seen at all the conspicuous gatherings of the season in London and wherever else society congregates. This is why the smart sets have so little refining influence on society. They may be common, even vulgar; it is not necessary even for them to speak grammatically; if they give real jewels with their cotillon toys and have a perfect artist at the head of their kitchens, they can become 'smart,' and receive royalty as much and as often as they please. The horrible word smart has been invented on purpose to express this: smartness has been borrowed from the vocabulary of the kitchenmaids to express something which is at the top of the fashion, without being necessarily either well born or well bred. Smart people may be both the latter, but it is not necessary that they should be either....

It is, therefore, impossible for the smart people to have much influence for good on the culture and manners of the society they dominate. A *beau monde*,[1] really exclusive, elegant and of high culture, not to be bought by any amount of mere riches or display, would have a great refining influence on manner and culture, and its morality, or lack of it, would not matter much. Indeed, society cannot be an accurate judge of morality; the naughty clever people know well how to keep their pleasant sins unseen; the candid, warm-hearted people always sin the sole sin which really injures anybody—they get found out....

An incessant and *maladif*[2] restlessness has become the chief characteristic of all cultured society nowadays: it is accounted a calamity beyond human endurance to be six months at a time in one place; to remain a year would be considered cause for suicide. The dissatisfaction and feverishness which are the diseases of the period are attributed to place most wrongly, for change of place does not cure them and only alleviates them temporarily and briefly. Here, again, the royal personages are the first offenders and the worst examples. They are never still. They are never content. They are incessantly discovering pretexts for conveying their royal persons here and there, to and fro, in ceaseless, useless, costly and foolish journeys.

Every event in their lives is a cause or an excuse for their indulgence in the *pérégrinomanie*;[3] if they are well, they want change of scene; if they are ill, they want change of air; if they suffer a bereavement, nothing can console them except some agreeable foreign strand;...

The French expression for being fashionable, *dans le train*, exactly expresses what fashion now is. It is to be remarkable in a crowd indeed, but still always in a crowd, rushing rapidly with that crowd, and no longer attempting to lead, much less to stem it. Life lived at a gallop may be, whilst we are in the first flight, great fun, but it is wholly impossible that it should be very dignified....

There is still time for society, if it care to do so, to justify its own existence ere its despoilers be upon it; and it can only be so justified if it become something which money cannot purchase, and envy, though it may destroy, cannot deride.

---

1 Fashionable world.
2 Unhealthy.
3 Pilgrimania.

Appendix C: Contemporary Responses to Ouida

[The following commentaries span Ouida's career from 1877 to 1908.]

1. From Ella, "Ouidà," *The Victoria Magazine* 28 (March 1877): 369-72

... Rumour credits Ouidà with possessing a great tenderness for the animal creation generally, and for dogs and horses especially. This is easy to imagine, when we bear in mind how prettily and pathetically she can write about beasts and birds. But rumour also credits her with another distinguishing trait less amiable: it says that she is not an enthusiastic admirer of her own sex. This we need find no difficulty in believing either, when we remember that the feminine creations she has given to the world are not all angels....

Ouidà's writings, judged from a literary point of view, abound in extremes, and upon them the shafts of adverse and favourable criticism must necessarily cross. They are marked by beauty and vigour of language, delicacy of thought, and richness of imagination; the descriptions of scenery they contain are often *unique*; and their author strikes off with marvellous felicity, truisms, drawn from the external world around her, and from that internal world, the human heart. But, Ouidà has defects. Like history, she repeats herself; and, like history also, she occasionally contradicts herself. She can fit words to ideas with great terseness, and put forth both clearly cut as crystal; but she does not always do so, and instead sometimes treats her readers to long, overloaded phrases, that need the pruning knife, to a repetition of thought and redundancy of language which become wearisome. Then she ceases to sketch gracefully, but proceeds to over-draw and over-colour. In her books we meet with sentences that might serve as models of English diction, and also with some which, by their construction, might tempt a master of grammar and analysis to draw red ink across them. Her creations of character follow the same rule of extremes. Some are powerfully conceived, powerfully worked out, and true to life; others are vague, uninteresting, and unreal. Ouidà is essentially a careless writer, as her novels prove; but even genius cannot afford to be too careless in its *modus operandi.*[1] If these novels were to be taken collectively, and subjected to a melting process until lessened in quantity and purged of their dross, they might form a stone worthy to be thrown into the Temple of Literature, and remain there.

This is judging the writer from the platform of literary criticism only, but the world has a right to call her to account from another one. Ouidà can describe rural scenery, and rustics, and innocent people, very charmingly, as her readers know; but she does not confine herself to this field of action. On the contrary, she exercises her powers very often in quite an opposite direction, and draws vivid portraits of town life. She knows how to pick out the back scenes of society and bring them to the front, touching them up with gaudy colour; she paints men and manners, not always as they should be, but as they often are; she describes what had better be left undescribed. The result may be instructive, but is not edifying, particularly to those blossoms of the school-room ... who pour and guzzle over these phases of life when they should be puzzling over geography....

Ouidà must be glanced at for a moment from another point of view before this little sketch can be finished. Her works seem covered with a filmy veil of Christianity, but their tendency is anti-Christian. Shafts of doubt shoot forth here and there, which aim at nothing and prove nothing, except that their author is no logician; but they serve to paganize and throw a cold shadow over the beauty of much that she has written....

Ouidà may teach her readers much; she may inspire them with appreciation of the works of nature and of art; but the general influence of her novels is unhealthy. She does not take for her motto, *Excelsior.*[2]

2. From "The 'Whitehall' Portraits. XCVIII.—Ouida," *The Whitehall Review* (5 October 1878): 484

The illustrious prose-poet who elects to veil her identity under the pseudonym Ouida has been throughout her brilliant literary career so resolute in her determination to be to the world nothing if not an author, and individually to seek oblivion among the crowd, that it would be in the worst taste were we to write of her as a member of Society rather than in her own proud *role* as a representative of the

---

1 Manner of working.
2 Ever upward.

republic of letters. Let it suffice, therefore, that she is known to her *intimes*[1] as Ouida, and that her letters are addressed to her simply as Ouida; that in this respect she is the *religieuse*[2] of fiction, who has merged herself in the work of her life. It matters not whether she is English, American, French, Spanish, or Italian. She is Ouida. What more would you, could you, learn concerning her?...

She is, indeed, the Chopin[3] of dramatic narration. Take up a volume ... and you will be thrilled by chords and cadences unlike anything your ear has ever before heard.... With the sad is mingled the ineffably sweet, with the relentless irony of destiny a divine tenderness.... Ouida, in fact, marks just the advance in prose-poetry that Chopin does in tone-poetry. Both create impressions which, but for their gorgeous genius, we should never have known. Both have laid cultured humanity under a debt which cannot sufficiently be acknowledged.

We have avoided mentioning Ouida's merits as a satirist, because her photographs of Society, though quite the best we have had since Thackeray, are not her strongest point. She soars highest when she follows her chiefest luminance, viz., poetic fatalism, when she is dealing seriously with the great growth of love and its fruit so sweet for a moment to the taste, yet soon to cause the death of the soul who grasps it. From every aspect, however, Ouida is both original and superb, a constellation of surpassing brilliance, an author whose light will never be put out.

3. From Marie Corelli,[4] "A Word about 'Ouida,'" *Belgravia* 71 (March 1890): 362–71

There are a large number of self-styled "superior" people in the literary world who make it a sort of rule to treat with vague laughter and somewhat unintelligent contempt the novels of the gifted Mdlle. de la Ramée, known to the reading public as "Ouida." Men, particularly, profess to be vastly amused with the heroes she depicts; the splendid "muscular" types of masculine beauty, the wondrous

---

1 Close friends.

2 Nun.

3 Frédéric François Chopin (1810-49), Polish pianist and composer, has been called the greatest of all piano composers.

4 Marie Corelli (1855-1924) was the pseudonym of Mary Mackay. She studied music, but turned to fiction (romantic melodramas) at the age of 30. She became a popular novelist.

individuals who "drench" their beards and moustaches with perfume, smoke scented cigars and run through millions of money in no time; and it may readily be admitted that numerous excrescences in the shape of over-floridness, unnecessary exaggeration of character and sensuousness of suggestion, do, to a great extent, spoil works that would, but for these defects, take their place in the highest rank of modern literature.

But, when all is said and done, the fact remains, that "Ouida" is a woman of *genius*. Not Talent, merely, but Genius.... And because a few reviewers jest lightly, and more or less sneeringly at the "Ouida" social types, we are apt to pass on the sneer and repeat the jest without giving the author whom we condemn the fair chance of our own unbiassed examination. Yet reviewers, though they pose as Oracles,[1] are, after all, only men; and difficult as it may be to believe a fact so bare of chivalry, it is pretty certain that many a male author is ungallantly jealous of a woman's brain that proves in any respect sharper, quicker, and more subtle than his own....

Now "Ouida" is not a darkly sybilline writer.[2] No one need puzzle over her utterances, for these are in many respects almost *too* plain for the grimly pious satisfaction of good Mother Grundy![3] ... Why, therefore, "Ouida's" characters of good women should, as a rule, be foolish, and come to a miserably undeserved end, while her characters of courtesans and *cocottes*[4] should nearly always be triumphant, is a question that only "Ouida" herself can answer. Recognizing as I do, with respect, the force of her inspiration, it is a matter of both wonder and regret to me that her brilliant pen has so often been used for the depicting of social enormities and moral sores; but while deploring the fact I still assert: Genius, Genius—not mere talent—is in this woman.... I have never met Mdlle. de la Ramée; I have never even corresponded with her. And certain well-intentioned persons have assured me that should I ever venture into her presence, I should probably meet with a rough reception, "as," say the gossips, "she hates her own sex." ... At all events, no *brusquerie*[5] on her part would alter or pervert in the least the current of a certain homage on mine....

---

1   Priest or Priestesses, believed to be infallible, who often make obscure or allegorical prophecies.
2   She is not making obscure, gloomy prophecies.
3   In England, Mrs. Grundy was the symbolic embodiment of rigid conventional propriety.
4   Floozies, prostitutes.
5   Bluntness.

Now, the men-critics, who, as soon as a novel of "Ouida's" comes in for review, murmur, "Ouida! oh, she's always good game!" and scratch off at once a half column of "smart" gibing, would be cleverer than they are ever likely to be, if they could write such a passage of pure, fluent, eloquent English as this; nay, if a man instead of a woman *had* written it, he might (and would!) be proud. Men are far more conceited concerning their literary efforts, than women. And though I do not wish to claim for "Ouida" any position that she is not, in the opinion of more experienced literary judges, entitled to possess, I *do* claim for her simple justice....

Let it not be imagined that I, or any of us, for that matter, seek to defend "Ouida's" system of morals as set forth in her books. Not at all. Bad morals are bad everywhere, whether served up to us at breakfast in our morning-paper accounts of the latest divorce case [or in novels].... "Ouida" has never sinned to a such a nauseous extent of mind-pollution as *that*. Her faults are those of reckless impulse and hurry of writing.... Taking up her descriptive palette, she mixes her brilliant colours too rapidly, and the male beings she draws, beautiful as gods and muscular as Homer's sinewy warriors, become the laughing-stock of men generally; especially of the ugly and wizened ones who compose the majority! Her lovely women are *too* lovely, and invariably start a feeling of discontent in those members of the fair sex who are unable to spend a fortune on gowns. Love is the chief *motif* of all her novels; and love such as she depicts, arising mainly from the attraction of sex to sex is, *of course*, impossible and absurd—and *wicked*! It does not exist, in fact! We love and marry because it is highly respectable so to do, especially where there is plenty of money to live upon....

But though we need not praise the "Ouida" morals, or endorse the "Ouida" exaggerations, we must, if we are not blind, deaf and obstinate, admire the "Ouida" eloquence. There is no living author who has the same rush, fire and beauty of language; we are bound to admit this if we wish to be just. There are plenty of authors, though, who think it no shame to steal whole passages from her books, and transplant them bodily word for word into their own productions, and in the works of one third-rate lady novelist whom I will not name, I have discovered more than twenty prose gems taken sentence for sentence out of "Ouida" without a shadow of difference!... The original conception triumphs in the end; it remains, while its feeble *replicas* perish; and the most painstaking labour can never compass even a paraphrase of one line of sheer *inspiration*.... Her faults, judged by the strictest rules of criticism *may* be manifold, but it should always be remembered that she is a writer of *romance*, and that she deals with the supposed romantic side of life…. Probably the worst that can be said for "Ouida" is that she is a *romancer*, and an answer to that accusation is best given in her own eloquent way:

"When the soldier dies at his post unhonoured, and unpitied, and out of sheer duty, is that *unreal*, because it is noble? When the sister of charity hides her youth under a grey shroud and gives up her whole life to woe and solitude, is that *unreal* because it is wonderful? A man paints a spluttering candle, a greasy cloth, a mouldy cheese, a pewter can, 'how *real!*' the people say. If he paints the spirituality of dawn, the light of the summer sea, the flame of arctic nights, of tropic woods, they are called *unreal*, though they exist no less than the candle and the cloth, the cheese, and the can. All that is heroic, all that is sublime, impersonal or glorious, is now derided as *unreal*. It is a dreary creed; it will make a dreary world. Is not my Venetian glass with its hues of opal as *real* every whit as your pot of pewter? Yet the time is coming when everyone, morally and mentally at least, will be allowed no other than a pewter pot to drink out of under pain of being 'writ down an ass.' It is a dreary prospect!"[1]

True, oh "Ouida!" Pitifully, deplorably true! Our age is one of Prose and Positivism; we take Deity for an ape, and Andrew Lang[2] as its Prophet!

4. From G.S. Street,[3] "An Appreciation of Ouida," *The Yellow Book* 6 (July 1895): 167-76

… In a world of compromises and transitions there is generally much to be said on both sides, and there are few causes or persons for whom a good word, in a fitting place and time, may not be spoken. I acquit myself of impertinence in stating what I find to like and to

---

1   Corelli is quoting *Moths*. This is Corrèze's defense of romance versus realism in Volume III, Chapter III (p. 440-41).

2   Andrew Lang (1844-1912) was a British scholar, man of letters, novelist, and poet. His column in *Longman's Magazine* did much to form literary opinion in the late nineteenth century. Earlier in her essay Corelli wrote: "Talent, like that of Mr. Andrew Lang, who sitting on his little bibliographic dust-heap, discourses pipingly on 'Was Jehova a stone Fetish?' is, we know, at the beck and call of every subject on which it is paid to write; but genius is wilful, often exceedingly irritating in its capricious changes of humour, and never exactly what the world would have it be."

3   G.S. Street (1867-1936) was a British writer of short stories, essays, and reviews.

respect in the novels of Ouida. For many years, with many thousands of readers they have been popular, I know. But ever since I began to read reviews, to learn from the most reputable authorities what I should admire or avoid, I have found them mentioned with simple merriment or a frankly contemptuous patronage. One had, now and then in boyhood, vague ideas of being cultivated, vague aspirations towards superiority: I thought, for my part, that of the many insuperable obstacles in the way of this goal, this contempt of Ouida's novels was one of the most obvious. I enjoyed them as a boy, and I enjoy them now; I place them far above books whose praise is in all critics' mouths, and I think I have reason for the faith that is in me.

One may write directly of "Ouida" as of a familiar institution, without, I hope, an appearance of bad manners, using the pseudonym for the books as a whole. The faults alleged against her are a commonplace of criticism: it is said that her men and her women are absurd, that her style is bad, that her sentiment is crude or mawkish. It is convenient to make those charges points of departure for my championship....

There *is* an air of stupidity about her good and self-sacrificing women, and since there is nobody, not incredibly unfortunate, but has known women good in the most conventional sense, and self-sacrificing, and wise and clever as well, it follows that Ouida has not described the whole of life. But perhaps she has not tried so to do.... Granted, then, that Ouida has not put all the women in the world into her novels: what of those she has?

Certainly her best-drawn women are hateful: are they also absurd? I think they are not. They are over-emphasised beyond doubt, so much so, sometimes, that they come near to being merely an abstract quality—greed, belike, or animal passion—clothed carelessly in flesh. To be that is to be of the lowest class of characters in fiction, but they are never quite that. A side of their nature may be presented alone, but its presentation is not such as to exclude, as in the other case, what of that nature may be left. And, after all, there have been women—or the chroniclers lie sadly—in whom greed and passion seem to have excluded most else. The critics may not have met them, but Messalina and Barbara Villiers,[1] and certain

---

1   Valeria Messalina (c. A.D. 22-48) was the third wife of the Roman emperor Claudius I. In his absence she married Gaius Silius and attempted to place him on the throne. She was killed when the plot failed; Barbara Villiers, Duchess of Cleveland (1641-1709) was the wife of Roger Palmer and the mistress of King Charles II of England.

ladies of the Second Empire, whose histories Ouida seems to have studied, have lived all the same, and it is reasonable to suppose that a few such are living now....

They are not, I think, absurd in Ouida's presentment, but I confess they are not attractive. One's general emotion with regard to them is regret that nobody was able to score off or discomfit them in some way. And that, it seems, was the intention of their creator. She writes with a keenly pronounced bias against them, she seeks to inform you how vile and baneful they are. It is not a large-hearted attitude, and some would say it is not artistic, but it is one we may easily understand and with which in a measure we may sympathise. A novel is not a sermon, but *sæva indignatio*[1] is generally a respectable quality. I am not trying to prove that Ouida's novels are very strict works of art: I am trying to express what from any point of view may be praised in them. In this instance I take Ouida to be an effective preacher. She is enraged with these women because of men, worth better things, who are ruined by them, or because of better women for them discarded. It would have been more philosophical to rail against the folly of the men, and were Ouida a man, the abuse of the women might be contemptible—... but she is a woman, and ... one need not pity for her scourging. It is effective. She is concerned to show you the baseness and meanness possible to a type of woman: at her best she shows you them naturally, analyzing them in action; often her method is, in essentials, simple denunciation, a preacher's rather than a novelist's; but the impression is nearly always distinct....

And if the hateful women are unattractive, is there not in the atmosphere that surrounds their misdeeds something—now and again, just for a minute or two—vastly and vaguely agreeable? I speak of the atmosphere as I suppose it to be, not as idealised in Ouida's fashion. It is not the atmosphere, I should imagine, of what in the dear old snobbish phrase was called "high life"—gay here and there, but mostly ordered and decorous: there is too much ignored. It is the atmosphere, really, of a profuse Bohemianism, of mysterious little houses, of comical lavishness, and unwisdom, and intrigue.... [T]he plodders and timid livers—could not live in it; better ten hours a day in a bank and a dinner of cold mutton; but fancy may wander in it agreeable for a brief time, and I am grateful to Ouida for its suggestion....

The two qualities, I think, which underlie the best of Ouida's work, and which must have always saved it from commonness, are a

---

1 Savage indignation.

genuine and passionate love of beauty, as she conceives it, and a genuine and passionate hatred of injustice and oppression. The former quality is constantly to be found in her, in her descriptions—accurate or not—of the country, in her scorn of elaborate ugliness as contrasted with homely and simple seemliness, in her railings against all the hideous works of man. It is not confined to physical beauty....

In fine, I take the merits in Ouida's books to balance their faults many times over. They are not finished works of art, they do not approach that state so nearly as hundreds of books with a hundred times less talent spent on them. Her faults, which are obvious, have brought it about that she is placed, in the general estimation of critics, below writers without a tenth of her ability. I should be glad if my appreciation may suggest to better critics than myself better arguments than mine for reconsidering their judgment.

5. From Willa Cather,[1] "The Passing Show," *The Courier* [Lincoln, Nebraska] (23 November 1895): 7

The other day I saw an elevator boy intently perusing a work of literature. I glanced at it and saw that it was Ouida's "Under Two Flags." I could remember when I first met that book and read it quite as intently as the elevator boy was doing, and I was inclined to be patient with him when he took me to the wrong floor, for I knew that he was envying Bertie Cecil his beautiful boots or that he was pondering upon the peaches of great price that Bertie used to throw at the swans to please his sweetheart, and it struck me that it is rather tragic that one of the brightest minds of the last generation should descend to become food for elevator boys. Sometimes I wonder why God ever trusts talent in the hands of women, they usually make such an infernal mess of it. I think He must do it as a sort of ghastly joke. Really, it would be hard to find a better plot that is in that same "Under Two Flags," and the book contains the rudiments of a great style, and it also contains some of the most drivelling nonsense and mawkish sentimentality and contemptible feminine weakness to be found anywhere. Preachers have cried out against the immorality of "Ouida," and mammas have forbidden their daughters to read her, and gentlemen of the world have pretended to shudder at her cynicism. Now the truth of the matter is

---

1   Willa Cather (1873-1947) was a distinguished American novelist and literary critic.

that her greatest sins are technical errors, as palpable as bad grammar or bad construction, sins of form and sense. Adjectives and sentimentality ran away with her, as they do with most women's pens. And then she lacked all sense of humor and will never know how magnificently ridiculous her melancholy heroes and suffering women are. Its [sic] a terrible curse to lack a sense of humor, for it reacts on one and makes one gratify the humor of every other living creature. Ouida is Nordau's "degenerate" incarnate.[1]

And the worst of it is that the woman really had a great talent. No less a person than John Ruskin[2] advised all his art students to read "A Village Commune" and said it was the saddest and most perfect picture of peasant life in Modern Italy ever made in English.... There are great passages in "Friendship," but in them there is not one sane, normal, possible man or woman. I hate to read them. I hate to see the pitiable waste and shameful weaknesses in them. They fill me with the same sense of disgust that Oscar Wilde's books do. They are one rank morass of misguided genius and wasted power. They are sinful, not for what they do, but for what they do not do. They are the work of a brilliant mind that never matured, of hectic emotions that never settled into simplicity and naturalness. They are the product of one who was too early old, too long young. Of one who was misled into thinking that words were life, who was tempted by the alluring mazes of melodrama. Of a life that only imagined and strained after effects, that never lived at all; that never laughed with children, toiled with men or wept with women; of a lying, artificial, abnormal existence. Ink and paper are so rigidly exacting. One may lie to one's self, lie to the world, lie to God, even, but to one's pen one cannot lie.... It is a solemn and terrible thing to write a novel. I wish there were a tax levied on every novel published. We would have fewer ones and better.

---

1 Max Nordau (1849-1923) was a philosopher, writer, orator, and physician. He was the co-founder of the World Zionist Organization. His *Degeneration* (1892) was an attack on much of the culture of the late nineteenth century.

2 John Ruskin (1819-1900) was the pre-eminent art critic of his time. He taught style drawing at the Working Man's College in London and was Slade Professor of Art at Oxford. He was also a writer, artist, scientist, poet, environmentalist, and philosopher.

6. From Max Beerbohm, "Ouida," *More* (London and New York: John Lane The Bodley Head, 1899): 101–15[1]

... Simpler, more striking, and more important, as an instance of reviewers' emptiness is the position of Ouida, the latest of whose long novels, *The Massarenes*, had what is technically termed "a cordial reception"—a reception strangely different from that accorded to her novels thitherto. Ouida's novels have always, I believe, sold well. They contain qualities which have gained for them some measure of Corellian success. Probably that is why, for so many years, no good critic took the trouble to praise them. The good critic, with a fastidiousness which is perhaps a fault, often neglects those who can look after themselves; the very fact of popularity—he is not infallible—often repels him; he prefers to champion the deserving weak. And so, for many years, the critics, unreproved were ridiculing a writer who had many qualities obvious to ridicule, many gifts that lifted her beyond their reach. At length it occurred to a critic of distinction, Mr. G.S. Street, to write an "Appreciation of Ouida," which appeared in the *Yellow Book*....

Ouida is not, and never was, an artist. That, strangely enough, is one reason why she had been so little appreciated by the reviewers. The artist presents his ideas in the finest, strictest form, paring, whittling, polishing. In reading his finished work, none but a few persons note his artistic skill, or take pleasure in it for its own sake. Yet it is this very skill of his which enables the reviewers to read his work with pleasure. To a few persons, artistic skill is in itself delightful, insomuch that they tend to overrate its importance, neglecting the matter for the form. Art, in a writer, is not everything. Indeed, it implies a certain limitation. If a list of consciously artistic writers were drawn up, one would find that most of them were lacking in great force of intellect or of emotion; that their intellects were restricted, their emotions not very strong. Writers of enormous vitality never are artistic: they cannot pause, they must always be moving swiftly forward....

I wonder at Ouida's novels, and I wonder still more at Ouida. I am staggered when I think of that lurid sequence of books and short stories and essays which she has poured forth so swiftly, with such irresistible *élan.*[2] What manner of woman can Ouida be? A woman

---

1 Beerbohm dedicated this collection of essays to Ouida with his compliments and his love.
2 Style.

who writes well never writes much.... All her books are amazing in their sustained vitality. Vitality is, indeed, the most patent, potent factor in her work. Her pen is more inexhaustibly prolific than the pen of any other writer; it gathers new strength of its every dip into the ink-pot. Ouida need not, and could not, husband her unique endowments, and a man might as well shake his head over the daily rising of the indefatigable sun, or preach Malthusianism[1] in a rabbit warren, as counsel Ouida to write less. Her every page is a riot of unpolished epigrams and unpolished poetry of vision, with a hundred discursions and redundancies. She cannot say a thing once; she must repeat it again and again, and, with every repetition, so it seems to me, she says it with greater force and charm. Her style is a veritable cascade, in comparison with which the waters come down at Lodore as tamely as they come down at Shanklin.[2] And, all the while, I never lose interest in her story, constructed with that sound professional knowledge, which the romancers of this later generation, with their vague and halting modes, would probably regard as old-fashioned. Ouida grips me with her every plot, and—since she herself so strenuously believes in them—I can believe even in her characters. True, they are not real, when I think of them in cold blood. They are abstractions, like the figures in early Greek tragedies and epics before psychology was thought of—things of black or white, or colourless things to illustrate the working of destiny, elemental puppets for pity or awe. Ouida does not pretend to the finer shades of civilized psychology.... Her books are, in the true sense of the word, romances.... The picturesqueness of modern life, transfigured by imagination, embellished by fancy, that is her *forte*.[3] She involves her stock-figures—the pure girl, the wicked woman, the adorable hero and the rest—in a series of splendid adventures. She makes her protagonist a guardsman that she may describe, as she alone can, steeple-chases and fox-hunts and horses running away with phaetons. Or she makes him a diplomat, like Strathmore, or a great tenor, like Corèze [sic], or ... or something else—anything so that it be lurid and susceptible of romance. She ranges hither and thither over all countries, snatching at all languages, realising all

---

1   Thomas Robert Malthus (1766-1834) was a British economist who wrote that the demand for food inevitably becomes greater then the supply of it. He expected forces like war, famine, and disease to operate as a check on the growing population.
2   Rivers in the Lake District and on the Isle of Wight (England).
3   Strength.

scenes. Her information is as wide as Macaulay's,[1] and her slips in local colour are but the result of a careless omniscience.... But the fact remains that Ouida uses her great information with extraordinary effect. Her delight in beautiful things has been accounted to her for vulgarity by those who think that a writer "should take material luxury for granted." But such people forget, or are unable to appreciate, the difference between the perfunctory faking of description, as practised by the average novelist—as who should say "soft carpets," "choice wines," "priceless Tintorettos"—and description which is the result of true vision. No writer was ever more finely endowed than Ouida with the love and knowledge of all kinds of beauty in art and nature. There is nothing vulgar in having a sense of beauty—so long as you have it. Ouida's descriptions of boudoirs in palaces are no more vulgar nor less beautiful than her descriptions of lakes and mountains....

I am glad that in her later books Ouida has not deserted "the First Life." She is still the same Ouida, has lost none of her romance, none of her wit and poetry, her ebullitions of pity and indignation. The old "naughtiness" and irresponsibility which were so strange a portent in the Medio-Victorian days, and kept her books away from the drawing-room table, seem to have almost disappeared; and, in complement of her love of luxury for its own sake, there is some social philosophy, diatribes against society for its vulgar usage of luxury. But, though she has become a mentor, she is still Ouida, still that unique, flamboyant lady, one of the miracles of modern literature. After all these years, she is still young and swift and strong, towering head and shoulders over all the other women (and all but one or two of the men) who are writing English novels. That the reviewers have tardily trumpeted her is amusing, but no cause for congratulation. I have watched their attitude rather closely. They have the idiot's cunning and seek to explain their behaviour by saying that Ouida has entirely changed. Save in the slight respect I have noted, Ouida has not changed at all. She is still Ouida. That is the high compliment I would pay her.

7. Obituary, *The Times* (27 January 1908): 7

A Reuter telegram from Florence states that Mlle. Louise de la Ramée, the novelist, better known as "Ouida," died on Saturday at Viareggio.

---

1 Thomas Babington Macaulay (1800-59) was a British historian and author of *History of England* (1848-61).

Mlle. Louise de la Ramée, the daughter of a French father and an English mother, was born at Bury St. Edmunds in 1810. She was brought up in England, but spent most of her middle and later life abroad, occasionally paying long visits to the Langham Hotel, in Portland-place, but chiefly residing at Lucca, in Italy, where she had a villa. The name "Ouida" was originally a baby's approximation to "Louisa." It was adopted as a literary pseudonym and achieved a world-wide celebrity. These facts, together with the list of her books, practically constitute the whole of Mlle. de la Ramée's biography. She began to write, as a contributor to *Colburn's Magazine*, at a very early age, and was only 23 when she published her first novel, "Held in Bondage." That was in 1863; and from that year onwards to the early years of the 20th century she continued to write almost without cessation. In 1904 the number of works standing to her credit in the British Museum catalogue was already 41.... There was no period of weary waiting for recognition. The new writer conquered her public with her very first book, and, if she did not retain her vogue until the last, at all events she retained it until the nineties were well advanced. The measure of her success may be partly gauged from the fact that, as long ago as 1865, she received the compliment of parody by Sir Francis Burnand[1] in *Punch*. Ultimately a new public with other tastes grew up, while the quality of her work remained pretty much what it had always been.

The comparative study of her writings, though these cover a period of about 40 years, discloses but little artistic growth. From first to last Ouida, with certain exceptions to be noted, entirely failed to realize the life that was going on around her. Her most famous novels all suggest a schoolgirl's dream of the *grande passion*. She seems to be living and moving in a world, not of men and women, but of demi-gods and demi-reps.[2] She takes her facts from her imagination, and does not check them by inquiry. Almost any one could have told her that it was impossible for a man to sit up all night drinking whisky punch and stroke the Oxford eight to victory in the morning.[3] Almost any one could have corrected most of the other errors which abounded in her novels to the joy of the reviewer. But she refrained from ask-

---

1   Sir Francis Cowley Burnand (1836-1917) was a regular contributor to *Punch*, an illustrated weekly satirical periodical. He was editor from 1880 to 1906.
2   A demi-rep is a courtesan or mistress.
3   The Oxford Eight was a boat race. The racers belonged to the Boat Club of Queen's College, Oxford University.

ing, and perhaps rightly from her own point of view. She wrote as one inspired, and facts might have broken the spell, and checked the flow of eloquence. Her *rôle* was to render not life, but the schoolgirl's dream aforesaid; and the most typical rendering of it is perhaps to be found in "Moths," written when she was 40. No one else could have made quite the book that she made out of the love of a girl for a singer. A man would have known too much about singers and too little about girls. He would have tried to render the singer not only as he appeared to the girl, but also as he appeared to other men, and would have sympathized with the other men's point of view. There would have been an attempt at analysis as well as rhapsody—a suggestion that the girl, however adorable, was silly. But Ouida was able to write from the girl's point of view, seeing nothing more than the girl herself would see. Her story may be taken as the final and perfect expression of the view, natural to a certain sort of romantic girl, that a handsome tenor is the noblest work of God.

In these ways, and to this extent, Ouida was out of touch with life—almost as much out of touch with it at the end of her life as at the beginning. If the function of fiction be the criticism of life, then there is nothing to be said for the greater number of her books. To enjoy her work, it is necessary to forget everything that you know, and resign yourself to hallucinations and deceptions. The young of both sexes are able to do this, having very little to forget; and on them her novels operate like the habit of opium-smoking, conjuring up many beautifully voluptuous visions of scenes with which they can hardly hope ever to have any first-hand acquaintance. That, no doubt, combined with her undeniable gift of story-telling, is the chief secret of a popularity achieved in defiance of critical opinion; and even critical opinion is disarmed when Ouida writes of peasant life in Italy and elsewhere. Her manner in treating of this subject is still that of the rhapsodist; but she is a rhapsodist speaking, not of what she has imagined, but of what she has seen with sympathetic eyes. She has a very true tenderness for those who suffer, and a very true feeling for beauty....

In her later years Ouida appeared in a new character as a contributor to reviews and magazines—chiefly to the *Fortnightly* and *North American Reviews*—and displayed a surprisingly definite attitude towards the burning topics of the day. She denounced Crispi,[1]

---

1   Francesco Crispi (1818-1901) was an Italian statesman. He was among the key figures of Italy's unification in 1860. He went on to become an authoritarian prime minister, an ally and admirer of Bismarck, whose ambitions for Italy brought Europe close to war on several occasions.

who had "dragged his Sovereign into the meshes of the Triple Alliance[1] and the Slough of Despond[2] of a bottomless debt." She entered into controversy with Lord Wolseley[3] on the moral effects of compulsory military service, which she regarded with an aversion based upon personal knowledge of many peasant conscripts. She speculated as to the future of Christianity, holding that "it can become only one of two things—either a nullity, as it is now in all national life, or a dynamic force allied with and ruling power through Socialism, and destroying all civilization as it at present stands." She opposed female suffrage because of "the millions of ordinary women who have as little of the sage in them as of the angel." She attacked the new woman, who "violates in her own person every law alike of common sense and of artistic fitness, and yet comes forward as a fit and proper person to make laws for others." She championed man against Mrs. Sarah Grand's attacks, declaring that, in marriage, "the influence of the woman is constantly injurious and belittling to the intelligence of the man," and that "the idea prevailing among women that they are valuable, admirable, and almost divine, merely because they are women, is one of the most mischievous fallacies born of human vanity and accepted without analysis."[4] Finally, she insisted in several essays that the private lives of literary and other artists are not proper objects of curiosity. "The interviewer," she wrote, "is the vilest spawn of the most ill-bred age that the world has ever seen," and she was consistently faithful to this principle. Not only did she not seek publicity; it was found impossible to thrust publicity upon her. She lived through the golden age of interviewing without ever being interviewed, though her personality was at the time of great interest to a great number of people; and the catalogues of the contents of the periodical publications do not mention a single article of a personal kind concerning her, though Mr. G.S. Street once contributed a critical essay to the *Yellow*

---

1   In 1882, Italy, angry at France, signed a secret treaty, which bound it with Germany and Austria-Hungary and formed the Triple Alliance.
2   In John Bunyan's *Pilgrim's Progress* (1678), Christian has to cross a deep bog (the Slough of Despond) to get to the Wicket Gate on his way to the Celestial City.
3   Field Marshall Garnet Joseph Wolseley, First Viscount (1833–1913), served in battles throughout the world and was instrumental in modernizing the British army.
4   See Appendices E.3 (p. 605) and E.5 (p. 615).

Book, in which, admitting certain faults, he nevertheless insisted that her work had been unjustly depreciated by superior persons.

The last of her life was sad, though the exact truth concerning it cannot easily be ascertained. "Ouida" received a Civil List pension from Sir Henry Campbell-Bannerman[1]—an award that was somewhat criticized at the time. The report was spread that she was in destitute circumstances, and an appeal was made to her admirers to subscribe for her relief. She wrote to the papers, denying that her necessities were pressing and refusing to accept the offered help. We fear that, for all her pride, she needed it; but that is her secret, and it is no part of our task to pry into it....

---

1   Sir Henry Campbell-Bannerman (1836-1908) was a Liberal British politician. He served as Prime Minister from 1906 to 1908.

Appendix D: Marriage and Divorce in the Nineteenth Century

[The "woman question" and marriage and divorce were key issues in the late nineteenth century. This section deals with Ouida's own cynical attitudes towards marriage in her fiction as well as those of some of her feminist contemporaries. It also provides a critique of the divorce laws and reports of actual divorce cases.]

1. Ouida on The Marriage Market and her "Philosophy of Marriage"

a. From *Granville de Vigne (Held in Bondage)* (1863), *Ouida Illustrated* Vol. 2 (New York: Peter Fenelon Collier, 1893): 427

[A young woman is talking to her mother after her mother has told her that a wealthy man asked for her hand in marriage.]

"... You must be mad—absolutely mad!" cried her mother, too horrified for expression. "Don't you know that there is not a girl in the English, or the French, or the Austrian empire who would not take such an offer as his, and accept it with thanksgiving? The Vallenstein diamonds are something magnificent; he is a thorough Parisien in his tastes, most perfect style and—"

"Oh yes! I could not sell myself to better advantage!"

"Sell yourself?" repeated the peeress. Fine ladies are not often fond of hearing things called by their proper names.

"Yes, sell myself," repeated Violet, bitterly, leaning against the mantel-piece with a painful smile upon her lips. "Would you not put me up to auction, knock me down to the highest bidder? Marriage is the mart, mothers the auctioneers, and he who bids the highest wins. Women are like racers, brought up only to run for cups, and win handicaps for their owners."

"Nonsense!" said her mother, impatiently. "You have lost your senses, I think, There is no question of 'selling,' as you term it. Marriage is a social compact, of course, where alliances suitable in position, birth, and wealth, are studied. Why should you pretend to be wiser than all the rest of the world? Most amiable and excellent women have married without thinking love a necessary ingredient. Why should you object to a good alliance if it be a marriage de convenance?"[1]

"Because I consider a marriage de convenance the most gross of all social falsehood. You prostitute the most sacred vows and outrage the closest ties; you carry a lie to your husband's heart and home. You marry him for his money or his rank, and simulate an attachment for him that you knew to be hypocrisy. You stand before God's altar with an untruth upon your life, and either share an unhallowed barter, or deceive and trick an affection that loves and honors you. The Quadroon girl sold in the slave-market is not so utterly polluted as the woman free, educated, and enlightened, who barters herself, for 'a marriage for position.'"

b. From *Princess Napraxine* (1884), *Ouida Illustrated* Vol. 10 (New York: Peter Fenelon Collier, 1893): 469

[Othmar, the hero, responds to his uncle, who is encouraging him to get married to secure an heir.]

"You should marry for the sake of posterity," reiterated Baron Fritz. "You are so happily and exceptionally situated that you can choose wherever you please. No living woman would refuse you. You should seek physical charms for the sake of your offspring, and high lineage also: the rest is a mere matter of taste."

"The rest is only a trifle! Only character, mind, and feeling,—the three things which determine happiness and influence life more than anything else."

Baron Fritz made a little gesture of indifference: "I imagine any one *bien élevée*[2] would not err in any of these points. Happiness one usually finds with the wives of others. Not that I would discourage you if you be inclined—"

"I am not inclined," said Othmar brusquely. "I only say that character is never considered by men and women when they marry; yet it is what makes or mars a life. When a marriage is announced, what is discussed? The respective fortunes of those concerned, then their good looks or their lack of them;... but you never hear a word as to their characters, their sympathies, or their principles. It is why all marriages are at best but a compromise between two ill-assorted dispositions."

---

1 A marriage of convenience or an arranged marriage.
2 Brought up well.

"... Myself, I have always considered that marriage is a means of continuing a race, so that it legally can continue to transmit property: I have never known why people imported fine sentiments into a legal transaction, It is taking a false view of a social duty to look for personal pleasure out of it; indeed, if a man be in love with his wife he will probably communicate his passion to her, which is undesirable, because it awakens her senses, and ultimately leads to her taking a lover, or lovers, which again introduces uncertainty into the legal enjoyment and transmission of property."

c. From *Guilderoy* (1889), *Ouida Illustrated* Vol. XII (New York: Peter Fenelon Collier, 1893): 113

[The heroine's father responds to his son-in-law who now regrets that he is married.]

"What idiocy is marriage!" he thought. "A man sees a woman, a woman a man, with no knowledge, no experience of each other; very often without even any affinity they enter into the closest of all human relations and undertake to pass their lives together. It is the habit of its apologists to say that it works well, idiotic though it looks. It does not work well. It hurries men and women blindly into unions which often become absolutely hateful to them, stifling to their development and intolerably irritating to their inclinations. It flies in the face of all the laws of sex. It is a figment of the social code, irrational, unreal, and setting up a gigantic lie as the scaffolding which supports society. Nominally monogamous, all cultured society is polygamous; sometimes even polyandrous. Why is the fact not recognized and frankly admitted? Why do we adhere to the fiction of a fidelity which is neither in nature nor in feeling possible to man? Because property lays its foundations most easily by means of marriage, therefore the individual is sacrificed to property."

2. From George H. Lewis,[1] "Marriage and Divorce," *The Fortnightly Review* 37 (1885): 640–53

Twenty-seven years have now elapsed since the passing of the Divorce Act by Lord Palmerston's Government.... It may not be amiss if I ... endeavour to show how the hopes and fears which then prevailed have been realised, and to estimate the character of the

---

1 George H. Lewis (1833–1911) was a British lawyer and essayist.

change which the passing of this Act has impressed on our social institutions to-day. Finally, I will attempt to point out the many injustices which have been in operation, notably on women, during the last quarter of a century....

Up to the year 1857 only four divorces had been obtained by women, and these for the most painful causes.... As regards the old jurisdiction it is enough to say that an injured husband who established a case against his wife was entitled to a divorce unless it could be proved that he had been guilty of collusion[1] or connivance,[2] unless he was open to recrimination and had been guilty of acts which would entitle the wife to be separated from him, *a mensa et thoro*,[3] by a decree of the Ecclesiastical Court.[4] It was necessary that a man seeking a divorce should first prove the adultery in the Ecclesiastical Court, and obtain from that tribunal a decree *a mensa et thoro*. He must also bring an action against the adulterer.... In such an action he must again prove the adultery, and having established his case in that proceeding he was entitled to apply to the House of Lords to be again permitted to prove his case before that tribunal. If he was successful in all three cases he was allowed to receive a divorce *a vinculo matrimonii*.[5] It is hardly to be wondered at that under such a procedure the expense alone was sufficient to deter the most aggrieved parties from having a recourse to such an ordeal in litigation....

The object of the ministry in introducing the Divorce Act of 1857 was, according to its promoters, to extend to the people at large the privileges which, owing to expense, were only available to the nobility before that time. One of the chief contentions of the Attorney General was that the Act made no alteration in the existing law, but only simplified the procedure. The one extension which he

---

1 Secret cooperation between the husband and wife by fabricating adultery and deceiving the court into granting them a divorce.
2 A husband or wife sets up a situation to encourage adultery by his/her spouse.
3 Separation from bed and board.
4 Doctor's Commons was the name given to the College of Advocates and Doctors of Law. It consisted of five courts. Between them they dealt with cases on matrimony, divorce, probate of wills, etc. The Court of Arches belonged to the Archbishop of Canterbury and all appeals directed in ecclesiastical (of or associated with a church) matters, such as divorce, were heard there.
5 Divorce from the bond of matrimony.

admitted it gave, was the power it bestowed on women of obtaining a divorce for adultery coupled with cruelty, or desertion for two years, instead of only for adultery coupled with bigamy or incest, as was the old practice. It was largely round this rock that the controversy raged....

Divorce at present is the *perquisite* of the man, on the same principle that the married woman is still in the operation of the law only the man's "chattel," the "femme sole" being the legal expression of the anomaly of the converse condition.[1] The English law empowers a man, however monstrous his conduct may have been, however great his cruelty, desertion, or adultery, to turn his wife out into the street and separate her from every intercourse with her children, and leave her to starve in a workhouse if, in a moment of weakness, she forgets her marriage vow. No act of the husband's entitles the woman to plead in her defence, no number of years of forbearance, or of much trial fidelity gives her protection. She may be turned into the street at an hour's notice, while before the law she has absolutely no remedy.

Such is the Divorce Act of 1857. The old Ecclesiastical Court, which was a Court of Equity as well as of Justice, would not have allowed this. Again, under the present law, a woman who has been cruelly treated or deserted by her husband, or who has been subjected to his open and continual adultery, even under the conjugal roof, is unable to obtain a divorce unless her husband has been guilty of cruelty or desertion as well as the adultery; and if he has been guilty of only one of these offences, however aggravated the form, she can only obtain a judicial separation; while the husband, unless he has committed adultery, can continue to dog the wretched woman's footsteps day by day and year by year, until he can obtain some evidence of adultery against her.... If she ventures to form even a friendship with a man such as would be perfectly allowable so long as she lived in her husband's house, she is liable to be dragged up by this guilty husband in a divorce court on suspicion, and called upon to defend her name against any charge, however unfounded....

[T]he cruelty practised in a house by the husband on his wife might be a more aggravating evil than repeated acts of transient adultery. The act in this respect displays a blind ignorance of domestic tragedies such as any legal practitioner in the Divorce Court is familiarly acquainted with. It is drawn in a spirit of male "grundyism,"

---

1 See Introduction, p. 26.

with the selfish object of ministering to a man's worst "jealousies," without attempting for one moment to give the woman equal claims over the fidelity of her husband. Moreover, its tendency is to create family gulfs, and to expose domestic horrors to the shame of at least two families, without providing any solution of the difficulties. The exposure of the weaknesses and disorders of married lives fill the daily papers, only too often to stamp the wretched couple with the mark of an abortive publication of their family horrors, while it leaves them for life chained to one another, either on the ground that one of the parties has unclean hands, or that the villainy of the husband is not sufficiently extensive. The act assumes that in such cases the law has done its duty when, after raking up every species of horrors, it simply dismisses the petition, or gives to the aggrieved woman the *damnosa hereditas*[1] of a judicial separation. Englishmen are too much prone to turn their heads when a social problem which involves shame on the morals of our civilisation calls for their just and equitable decision. Like many members in these debate [sic], they argue that as these things affect only a small minority of the population, the matter in no way presses on our attention. Yet who of us that has lived in contact with the troubles of the masses does not know the thousands of instances in which the unjust inequality of the sexes before the law in marriage has wrought untold misery on both the women and children of those wretched homes?

It is said that if divorce were accorded to women for the adultery of their husbands, or for cruelty or desertion without adultery, no household would be safe, that children would be left uncared for.... Where there are no children to a marriage, what ground is there for refusing divorce to a woman who has an adulterous or cruel husband? Do our labouring classes never suffer in this respect? It is fortunate for them that the Divorce Court as it is to-day, with its antiquated machinery and costly procedure, is not within their reach....

[I]t is an indisputable fact that the time is not far distant when women will raise an effective outcry against the abuses of the present system.

In addition to their present rights, a woman ought to be entitled to a divorce—

1. For actual cruelty, or cruelty endangering life.
2. For desertion without reasonable excuse for two years and upwards.

---

1 Ruinous inheritance.

3. For adultery committed by her husband in her home, or under disgraceful or aggravating circumstances.

4. For the conviction and sentence of her husband to a term of five years' penal servitude, or upwards, for crime....

3. From Charles Dickens, *Hard Times* (1854) (London: Nelson, 1904): 74-76

[Stephen Blackpool is asking his employer Mr. Bounderby how he can obtain a divorce from his alcoholic wife. The novel is set in the 1850s before the Divorce Act of 1857.]

"I ha' coom to ask yo, Sir, how I am to be ridded o' this woman.... I mun be ridden o' her. I cannot bear 't nommore.... I ha' read i' th' papers that great fok ... are not bonded together for better for worst so fast, but that they can be set free fro' *their* misfortnet marriages, an' marry ower agen. When they dunnot agree, for that their tempers is ill-sorted, they has rooms o' one kind an' another in their houses, above a bit, and they can live asunders. We fok ha' only one room, and we can't. When that won't do, they ha' gowd an' other cash, an' they can say 'This is for yo' an' that for me,' an' they can go their separate ways. We can't. Spite o' all that, they can be set free for smaller wrongs than mine. So, I mun be ridden o' this woman, and I want t' know how?"

"No how," returned Mr. Bounderby.... [I]t's not for you at all. It costs money. It costs a mint of money."

"How much might that be?" Stephen calmly asked.

"Why, you'd have to go to Doctors' Commons with a suit, and you'd have to go to a court of Common Law with a suit, and you'd have to go to the House of Lords with a suit, and you'd have to get an Act of Parliament to enable you to marry again, and it would cost you (if it was a case of very plain sailing), I suppose from a thousand to fifteen hundred pound," said Mr. Bounderby. "Perhaps twice the money."

"There's no other law?"

"Certainly not."

"Well then, Sir," said Stephen, turning white, and motioning with that right hand of his, as if he gave everything to the four winds, "'*tis* a muddle. 'Tis just a muddle a'toogether, an' the sooner I am dead, the better." ...

"[D]on't you call the institutions of your country a muddle, or you'll get yourself into a real muddle one of these fine mornings.

The institutions of your country are not your piece-work, and the only thing you have got to do, is, to mind your piece-work. You didn't take your wife for fast and for loose; but for better for worse. If she has turned out worse—why, all we have got to say is, she might have turned out better."

4. Reports of Divorce Cases, 1884

a. Cranfield v. Cranfield, *The Times*, 4 April 1884

This was a suit of an unusual character. It was one by a husband to obtain a judicial separation from his wife on the ground of her cruelty. The petitioner, John Medhurst Cranfield, married the respondent, Augusta Cranfield, in 1859, and there are seven children of the marriage. He is a clerk in a City house, and he is also the possessor of some house property. In the evidence given by him in support of his petition, he stated that after 1870 the respondent became addicted to habits of intemperance, and that in her drunkenness she was on various occasions guilty of very violent conduct towards him— such as seizing him by the throat, pulling out hairs from his beard, tearing the shirt off his back, and throwing a teapot at him. Mr. Cranfield's evidence was corroborated by two young men, sons of himself and the respondent, by their eldest daughter, and by two domestic servants. Mrs. Cranfield got into the box and swore that she never had been drunk in her life, and that she never had been guilty of violence towards the petitioner, and the landlady of a house, in which the petitioner and the respondent had lived, and a monthly nurse, who had attended Mrs. Cranfield in her confinements, gave evidence to the effect that they never had seen her drunk or violent. A female friend and her daughter were examined to negative the charges that a scene which had occurred in the street between the husband and wife was owing to her.

The PRESIDENT, in summing-up the case, remarked that it was unusual to find a man claiming the protection of that Court against the cruelty of his wife—first, because it rarely happened that a wife was guilty of violence; and next, because, even when there was violence on the part of the wife, it was seldom of such a character as to render the intervention of the Court necessary for the protection of the husband. But the rules of law in respect of cruelty were equally applicable in the case of a woman as they were in that of a man. The question for the jury was whether the party complained of had been guilty of such violence of conduct as, if continued, would be calculated to injure the health of the party against whom it had been exercised. The learned Judge having reviewed the evidence, the jury found that the respondent had been guilty of cruelty.

The PRESIDENT said he would in this instance follow the course he had pursued in similar cases. He would not pronounce a decree of judicial separation until the parties were prepared to submit to him some arrangement to secure a provision for the wife.

Mr. Inderwick, Q.C., and Mr. Searle appeared for the petitioner; Mr. Waddy, Q.C., and Mr. Berkeley Halle for the respondent.

b. Wilson v. Wilson, Grille, and Morley, *The Times*, 10 May 1884

This was a suit by Harry Arthur Wilson for the dissolution of his marriage with Harriet Emma Wilson, whose maiden name was Norman, on the grounds of her adultery with Frederick Grille and James George Morley. The respondent and the co-respondents denied the adultery, and the respondent further pleaded connivance and condonation.[1]

Mr. Searle appeared for the petitioner: Mr. Inderwick, Q.C., and Mr. Lascombe for the respondent: Mr. Bayford for the co-respondent Grille: and Dr. Pritchard for the co-respondent Morley.

The petitioner and the respondent were married in 1876, and there were two children of the marriage. Mr. Wilson keeps a draper's shop in Clare street. For the last four years the petitioner and co-respondent led a very unhappy life, owing, as he swore, to her violent habits and disorderly mode of life. She took a subscriber's ticket for dancing rooms, at which she danced several evenings each week with men who were unknown to her husband. Her subscription ticket was made out in the name of "Kate Norman," and she never was accompanied to the dancing rooms by her husband. With men whom she met there she sometimes supped at a supper house in the neighborhood of the Haymarket, and she visited Grille and Morley at their lodgings. At Ramsgate she frequented dancing rooms as "Kate Norman," and it was there she made the acquaintance of one, if not both of the co-respondents. Letters from Morley to the respondent, in which some of the expressions were indecent, and letters from Grille to her, indicating that there were improper relations between them, formed a portion of the evidence, and two young ladies employed in the petitioner's establishment gave testi-

---

1 Disregarding an offense (i.e., adultery) without protest or censure.

mony in support of the petition. He denied connivance and condonation. To meet the case against her, Mrs. Wilson got into the witness box, and, in reply to Mr. INDERWICK, admitted that she had received the letters from the co-respondent and letters from other gentlemen, all addressed to her in the name of "Kate Norman," and that presents of flowers and gloves had also come to her from her male companions of the dancing rooms; but she positively asserted that all those letters and most of the presents reached her through the hands of her husband, as she was not in the habit of coming down from her bedroom till 11 o'clock in the forenoon. She added that her husband usually read those letters, and frequently laughed at them, and that sometimes she read her answers to them, which assertion by her Wilson indignantly denied in the witness-box. She also said that at Ramsgate, when coming out of the dancing rooms with a man, she met her husband at the door, introduced him as a relative to her companion, and then went off with the latter, leaving the petitioner in the street. She showed that while she was cohabiting with her husband he wrote an introduction for her to a place of business, and in his letter represented that she was his sister. This the petitioner admitted, but he explained that, as his wife would not assist him in his business and was frequently at dancing rooms, he thought it would be better for herself that she should procure a situation in which she would be compelled to employ herself. It was proved that she left her home in July, 1883, and had not lived with the petitioner since that time; but Mr. Inderwick did not ask her whether she had committed adultery with the co-respondents or with any other persons. However, in cross-examination by Mr. SEARLE, she volunteered an emphatic denial of the charge against her, and repeated that denial when the learned counsel directed her attention to the suggestive and indecent passages of letters from Morley and Grille. On this,

THE PRESIDENT asked Mr. Inderwick whether he intended to put any other witness in the box.

MR. INDERWICK replied in the negative.

THE PRESIDENT said that Mr. Searle need not trouble himself further. He did not believe the respondent on her oath. This woman swore that she had not committed adultery. He thought it impossible for anyone to read the letters addressed to her and believe her statement on that point. In his judgement, they showed that she was not the witness of truth, and could not accept any assertion made by her without corroboration. She stated that her husband had wilfully permitted her bad conduct. The facts of the case taken as a whole negatived that charge against the petitioner. No motive had been shown for such conduct on his part. He had not been making money by his wife's prostitution. There were circumstances in the conduct of the petitioner which were not satisfactory. The fact that he gave the respondent an introduction as his sister was not satisfactory; but his object in doing so appeared to have been to find her employment at which she could be earning money, and therefore, though the proceeding was not one which could be approved, it was explained by the desire of the petitioner to find her occupation, as she was leading an irregular life. That she had been leading such a life was proved to his satisfaction, and he held the charge of adultery was proved against the respondent and the co-respondents; but he would not give costs against either of the latter, because they had had every reason to suppose that she was a prostitute, as she was leading the life of one. There would be a decree *nisi*, the petitioner to have the custody of the children of the marriage.

c. Stent v. Stent and Low, *The Times*, 19 June 1884

This was a suit by Mr. Frederick Warburton Stent for the dissolution of his marriage with Mrs. Eliza Stent, whose maiden name was Mannings, on the grounds of her adultery with General Alexander Low.

Mr. Searle appeared for the petitioner; neither the respondent nor the co-respondent defended the suit. Mr. Stent was examined, and stated that he was an architect. He married the respondent in May 1861, and there were two surviving children of the marriage. Up to the 20th of May, 1882, his wife and he had lived most happily. For some time before that date her health had become affected in such a way that Dr. Mathews Duncan was consulted, and he advised that Mrs. Stent should proceed to Kreuznach, in Germany, to take the waters there. As it seemed likely that her sojourn abroad would have to be a long one, it was impossible, owing to his having to attend to his profession, that the witness could go to Kreuznach and there stay with his wife; and General Low being an intimate friend of Mr. and Mrs. Stent's of many years' standing, it was arranged, after a friendly consultation, that the co-respondent should accompany Mrs. Stent and her daughter, who was about 20 years old. "At that time," said the witness, "I had not the slightest suspicion of the co-respondent, who is nearly 70 I should think. I thought I was acting with a gentleman, and not with a scoundrel." From the time of her departure till October, 1883, the witness received about 100 letters from his wife, dated at Kreuznach, Wilabad, and Geneva. All those communications were affectionate, but in them Mrs. Stent did not speak of returning home. Finding that she was about to spend a second winter abroad, he made inquiries, which led to Mr. Hart Smith, his solicitor and friend, proceeding to Geneva. In consequence of what Mr. Smith reported to him the proceedings in this court were initiated.

Mr. Edward Hart Smith was examined, and stated that in October, 1883, he had an interview with Mrs. Stent at Geneva, in the hotel where she, her daughter, and the co-respondent were staying. He asked Mrs. Stent whether she meant to return to her husband and family. She replied that she did not, and that she had thronw [sic] in her lot with the co-respondent. The respondent and the co-respondent made no secret to him of the illicit relations between them, but told him that Miss Stent had no suspicion of them. He subsequently accompanied Miss Stent to Antwerp, where they met the petitioner. In November he again went to Geneva, and served the respondent and the co-respondent with citations.

The evidence of George Muntz, head waiter in a hotel at Bale, Switzerland, was read. It was taken in April, 1884, and Muntz deposed that the respondent and the co-respondent were then living at the hotel as man and wife.

The President pronounced a decree *nisi*, with costs against the co-respondent.

5. From Mona Caird,[1] "Marriage," *The Westminster Review* (August 1888): 186–201

It is not difficult to find people mild and easy-going about religion, and even politics may be regarded with wide-minded tolerance; but broach social subjects, and English men and women at once become alarmed and talk about the foundations of society and the sacredness of the home! Yet the particular form of social life, or of marriage, to which they are so deeply attached, has by no means existed from time immemorial; in fact, modern marriage, with its satellite ideas, only dates as far back as the age of Luther.[2] Of course the institu-

---

1 Mona Caird (1854–1931) was a journalist, prose writer, novelist, and an early radical feminist.
2 Martin Luther (1483–1546) was the leader of the Protestant Revolution and the founder of the Lutheran Church. In "The Estate of Marriage" (1522) he preaches that the major work of woman is motherhood—that she should have many children and regale in her motherly duties.

tion existed long before, but our particular mode of regarding it can be traced to the era of the Reformation, when commerce, competition, the great *bourgeois* class, and that remarkable thing called "Respectability," also began to arise....

In Mongolia there are large cages in the market-place wherein condemned prisoners are kept and starved to death. The people collect in front of these cages to taunt and insult the victims as they die slowly day by day before their eyes. In reading the history of the past, and even the literature of our own day, it is difficult to avoid seeing in that Mongolian market-place a symbol of our own society, with its iron cage, wherein women are held in bondage, suffering moral starvation, while the thoughtless gather round to taunt and to insult their lingering misery. Let any one who thinks this exaggerated and unjust, note the manner in which our own novelists, for instance, past and present, treat all subjects connected with women, marriage, and motherhood, and then ask himself if he does not recognize at once its ludicrous inconsistency and its cruel insults to womanhood, open and implied....

Now we come to the problem of to-day. This is extremely complex. We have a society ruled by Luther's views on marriage; we have girls brought up to regard it as their destiny; and we have, at the same time, such a large majority of women that they cannot all marry, even ... if they had the fascinations of Helen of Troy and Cleopatra rolled into one. We find, therefore, a number of women thrown on the world to earn their own living in the face of every sort of discouragement. Competition runs high for all, and even were there no prejudice to encounter, the struggle would be a hard one; as it is, life for poor and single women becomes a mere treadmill. It is folly to inveigh against mercenary marriages, however degrading they may be, for a glance at the position of affairs shows that there is no reasonable alternative. We cannot ask every woman to be a heroine and choose a hard and thorny path when a comparatively smooth one, (as it seems), offers itself, and when the pressure of public opinion urges strongly in that direction. A few higher natures will resist and swell the crowds of worn-out, underpaid workers, but the majority will take the voice of society for the voice of God, or at any rate of wisdom, and our common respectable marriage—upon which the safety of all social existence is supposed to rest—will remain, as it is now, the worst, because the most hypocritical, form of woman-purchase. Thus we have on the one side a more or less degrading marriage, and on the other side a number of women who cannot command an entry into that profession, but who must give up health and enjoyment of life in a losing battle with the world....

Amongst other absurdities, we have well-meaning husbands and wives harassing one another to death for no reason in the world but the desire of conforming to current notions regarding the proper conduct of married people. These victims are expected to go about perpetually together, as if they were a pair of carriage-horses; to be forever holding claims over one another, exacting or making useless sacrifices, and generally getting in one another's way. The man who marries finds that his liberty has gone, and the woman exchanges one set of restrictions for another. She thinks herself neglected if her husband does not always return to her in the evenings, and the husband and society think her undutiful, frivolous, and so forth if she does not stay at home alone, trying to sigh him back again. The luckless man finds his wife so *very* dutiful and domesticated, and so *very* much confined to her "proper sphere,"[1] that she is, perchance, more exemplary than entertaining. Still, she may look injured and resigned, but she must not seek society and occupation on her own account, adding to the common mental store, bringing new interest and knowledge into the joint existence, and becoming thus a contented, cultivated, and agreeable being. No wonder that while all this is forbidden we have so many unhappy wives and bored husbands. The more admirable the wives the more profoundly bored the husbands!

Of course there are bright exceptions to this picture of married life, but we are not dealing with exceptions. In most cases, the chain of marriage chafes the flesh, if it does not make a serious wound; and where there is happiness the happiness is dearly bought and is not on a very high plane. For husband and wife are then apt to forget everything in the absorbing but narrow interests of their home, to depend entirely upon one another, to steep themselves in the same ideas, till they become mere echoes, half creatures, useless to the world, because they have run into a groove and have let individuality die. There are few things more stolidly irritating than a very "united" couple. The likeness that may often be remarked between married people is a melancholy index of this united degeneration.

We come then to the conclusion that the present form of marriage—exactly in proportion to its conformity with orthodox ideas—is a vexatious failure. If certain people have made it a success

---

1 In *The Enfranchisement of Women* (1851), Harriet Taylor Mill states: "We deny the right of any portion of the species to decide for another portion, or any individual, what is and what is not their 'proper sphere.' The proper sphere for all human beings is the largest and highest which they are able to attain to."

by ignoring those orthodox ideas, such instances afford no argument in favour of the institution as it stands. We are also led to conclude that modern "Respectability" draws its life-blood from the degradation of womanhood in marriage and in prostitution....

6. From Marie Corelli, "The Modern Marriage Market," *The Lady's Realm* (April 1897): 522-27

... It is one of our many hypocrisies to pretend we do not see things that are plainly put before us every day, and also to assume a fastidious disgust and horror when told of certain "barbarisms" still practised in Europe, barbarisms which we consider we have, in our state of ultra civilisation, fortunately escaped. One of these "barbaric" institutions which moves us to shudder gracefully and turn up the whites of our eyes, is slavery. "Britons never, never shall," we say. British women shall never, for example, stand stripped in the market-place to be appraised and labelled at a price, and purchased by a sensualist and ruffian for so much money down. No British man shall ever stand with bound hands and manacled feet, shamed and contemptible in his own eyes, waiting till some luxurious wanton of the world ... buys him with her millions to be her fetch-and-carry slave till death releases him from the unnatural bondage. These things are done in Stamboul.[1] True. Stamboul is barbaric. What of London? What of the "season," when women are as coolly "brought out" to be sold as any unhappy Armenian girl that ever shuddered at the lewd gaze of a Turkish tyrant? What of the mothers and fathers who force their children thus into the open market? Come—face the thing out—don't put it away or behind you as a matter too awkward and difficult of discussion. It is an absolute grim fact that in England, women—those of the upper classes, at any rate—are not to-day married, but bought for a price. The high and noble intention of marriage is entirely lost sight of in the scheming, the bargaining, and the pricing.

What *is* marriage? Many of you have, I think, forgotten. It is not the church, the ritual, the blessing of the clergyman or the ratifying and approving presence of one's friends and relations at the ceremony,—still less is it a matter of "settlements" and expensive millinery. It is the taking of a solemn vow before the Throne of the Eternal,— a vow which declares that the man and woman concerned have discovered in each other his and her true mate....

---

1 Istanbul.

[In] the rush of our time we are trampling sweet emotions and true passions under foot, and marriages are seldom the result of affection nowadays,—they are merely the carrying out of a settled scheme of business. Mothers teach their daughters to marry for a "suitable establishment": fathers, rendered desperate as to what they are to do with their sons in the increasing struggle for life and the incessant demand for luxuries which are not by any means actually necessary to that life, say, "Look out for a woman with money." Heirs to a great name and title sell their birthrights for a mess of American dollar-pottage,—and it is a very common everyday sight to see some Christian virgin sacrificed on the altar of matrimony to a money-lending, money-grubbing son of Israel.

Bargain and sale,—sale and bargain,—it is the whole *raison d'être*[1] of the "season,"—the balls, the dinners, the suppers, the parties to Hurlingham and Ascot....

"A marriage has been arranged" is a common phrase of newspaper parlance,—and it has one advantage over most newspaper forms of speech—namely, that of being strictly and literally true. A marriage is "arranged" as a matter of convenience or social interest; lawyers draft settlements and conclude the sale,—and a priest of the Most High God is called in to bless the bargain. But it is nevertheless a bargain,—a trafficking in human bodies and souls, as open and as shameless as any other similar scene in Stamboul....

The real fact of the matter is that marriage is nothing more nor less than a crime if it is entered upon without that mutual supreme attraction and deep love which makes the union sacred. It is a selling of body into slavery,—it is a dragging down of souls into impurity....

---

1 Purpose.

Appendix E: Ouida and the New Woman Debate

[This appendix provides examples of the important "New Woman" debates and of attempts to define woman's role in the late nineteenth century. It also illustrates Ouida's conservative stance on women—in contrast to the more liberal stance in her fiction.]

1. From Eliza Lynn Lynton,[1] "The Shrieking Sisterhood," *The Saturday Review* (12 March 1870): 341-42

... One of our quarrels with the Advanced Women of our generation is the hysterical parade they make about their wants and their intentions. It never seems to occur to them that the best means of getting what they want is to take it, when not forbidden by the law—to act, not to talk; that all this running hither and thither over the face of the earth, and feverish unrest, and loud acclaim is but the dilution of purpose through much speaking, and not the right way at all; and that to hold their tongues and do would advance them by as many leagues as babble puts them back. A small knot of women, "terribly in earnest," could move multitudes by the silent force of example. One woman alone, quietly taking her life in her own hands, and working out the great problem of self-help and independence practically, not merely stating it theoretically, is worth a score of shrieking sisters frantically calling on men and gods to see them make an effort to stand upright without support, with interludes of reproach to men for the want of help in their attempt. The silent woman who quietly calculates her chances and measures her powers with her difficulties so as to avoid the probability of a *fiasco*, and who therefore achieves a success according to her endeavour, does more for the real emancipation of her sex than any amount of pamphleteering, lecturing, or petitioning by the shrieking sisterhood can do....

And really if we think of it dispassionately, and carefully dissect the great mosaic of hindrances which women say makes up the pavement of their lives, there is very little which they may not do if

---

1 Eliza Lynn Lynton (1822-98) was a novelist, essayist, and an outspoken conservative anti-feminist.

they like—and can.... To be sure, they do not yet sit on the Bench nor plead at the Bar; they are not in Parliament, and they are not even voters; while, as married women with unfriendly husbands and no protection order, they have something to complain of, and wrongs that are in a fair way of being righted if the shrieking sisterhood does not frighten the world prematurely. But, despite these restrictions, they have a very wide circle wherein they can display their power, and witch the world with noble deeds, if they choose—and as some have chosen.

Of the representative "working women" in England, we find none who have shrieked on platforms or made an hysterical parade of their work. Quietly, and with the dignity which comes by self-respect and the consciousness of strength, they have done what it was in their hearts to do, leaving the world to find out the value of their labours, and to applaud or deride their independence.... These are the women to be respected, whether we sympathize with their line of action or not, having shown themselves to be true workers, capable of sustained effort, and therefore worthy of the honour which belongs to strength and endurance.

Of one thing women may be very sure, though they invariably deny it; the world is glad to take good work from whomsoever will supply it. The most certain patent of success is to deserve it; and if women will prove that they can do the world's work as well as men, they will share with them in the labour and the reward, and if they do it better they will distance them.... If they wish to educate public opinion to accept them as equals with men, they can only do so by demonstration, not by shrieks.... While the shrieking sisterhood remain to the front, the world will stop its ears, and for every hysterical advocate "the cause" loses a rational adherent and gains a disgusted opponent. It is our very desire to see women happy, noble, fitly employed, and well remunerated for such work as they can do, which makes us so indignant with the foolish among them who obscure the question they pretend to elucidate, and put back the cause which they say they advance. The earnest and practical workers among women are a very different class from the shriekers; but we wish the world could dissociate them more clearly than it does at present, and discriminate between them, both in its censure and its praise.

2. From Sarah Grand,[1] "The New Aspect of the Woman Question,"[2] *The North American Review* 158 (March 1894): 270–76

It is amusing as well as interesting to note the pause which the new aspect of the woman question has given to the Bawling Brothers who have hitherto tried to howl down every attempt on the part of our sex to make the world a pleasanter place to live in. That woman should ape man and desire to change places with him was conceivable to him as he stood on the hearth-rug in his lord-and-master-monarch-of-all-I-survey attitude, well inflated with his own conceit; but that she should be content to develop the good material which she finds in herself and be only dissatisfied with the poor quality of that which is being offered to her in man, her mate, must appear to him to be a thing as monstrous as it is unaccountable. "If women don't want to be men, what do they want?" asked the Bawling Brotherhood when the first misgiving of the truth flashed upon them; and then, to reassure themselves, they pointed to a certain sort of woman in proof of the contention that we were all unsexing ourselves.

It would be as rational for us now to declare that men generally are Bawling Brothers or to adopt the hasty conclusion which makes all men out to be fiends on the one hand and all women fools on the other. We have our Shrieking Sisterhood,[3] as the counterpart of the Bawling Brotherhood. The latter consists of two sorts of men. First of all is he who is satisfied with the cow-kind of woman as being most convenient; it is the threat of any strike among his domestic cattle for more consideration that irritates him into loud and angry protests. The other sort of Bawling Brother is he who is under the influence of the scum of our sex, who knows nothing better than women of that class in and out of society, preys upon them or ruins himself for them, takes his whole tone from them, and judges us all by them. Both the cow-woman and the scum-woman are well within range of the comprehension of the Bawling Brotherhood, but the new woman is a little above him, and he never even thought of looking up to where she has been sitting apart in silent

---

1 Sarah Grand was the pseudonym of Frances Elizabeth (Clarke) McFall (1854–1943). She was a New Woman novelist and an ardent, vocal feminist.

2 For an excellent analysis of this essay, see Talia Schaffer, "Nothing But Foolscap and Ink" (40–42).

3 See Appendix E.1 (p. 599).

contemplation all these years, thinking and thinking, until at last she solved the problem and proclaimed for herself what was wrong with Home-is-the-Woman's-Sphere, and prescribed the remedy.

What she perceived at the outset was the sudden and violent upheaval of the suffering sex in all parts of the world. Women were awaking from their long apathy, and, as they awoke, like healthy hungry children unable to articulate, they began to whimper for they knew not what. They might have been easily satisfied at that time had not society, like an ill-conditioned and ignorant nurse, instead of finding out what they lacked, shaken them and beaten them and stormed at them until what was once a little wail became convulsive shrieks and roused up the whole human household. Then man, disturbed by the uproar, came upstairs all anger and irritation, and, without waiting to learn what was the matter, added his own old theories to the din, but, finding they did not act rapidly, formed new ones, and made an intolerable nuisance of himself with his opinions and advice. He was in the state of one who cannot comprehend because he has no faculty to perceive the thing in question, and that is why he was so positive. The dimmest perception that you may be mistaken will save you from making an ass of yourself.

We must look upon man's mistakes, however, with some leniency, because we are not blameless in the matter ourselves. We have allowed him to arrange the whole social system and manage or mismanage it all these ages without ever seriously examining his work with a view to considering whether his abilities and his motives were sufficiently good to qualify him for the task. We have listened without a smile to his preachments, about our place in life and all we are good for, on the text that "there is no understanding a woman." We have endured most poignant misery for his sins, and screened him when we should have exposed him and had him punished. We have allowed him to exact all things of us, and have been content to accept the little he grudgingly gave us in return. We have meekly bowed our heads when he called us bad names instead of demanding proofs of the superiority which alone would give him a right to do so. We have listened much edified to man's sermons on the subject of virtue, and have acquiesced uncomplainingly in the convenient arrangement by which this quality has come to be altogether practised for him by us vicariously.... Man deprived us of all proper education, and then jeered at us because we had no knowledge. He narrowed our outlook on life so that our view of it should be all distorted, and then declared that our mistaken impression of it proved us to be senseless creatures. He cramped our minds so that there was no room for reason in them, and then made merry at our want of logic. Our divine intuition was not to be controlled by him, but he did his best to damage it by sneering at it as an inferior feminine method of arriving at conclusions; and finally, after having had his own way until he lost his head completely, he set himself up as a sort of a god and required us to worship him, and, to our eternal shame be it said, we did so. The truth has all along been in us, but we have cared more for man than for truth, and so the whole human race has suffered. We have failed of our effect by neglecting our duty here, and have deserved much of the obloquy that was cast upon us. All that is over now, however, and while on the one hand man has shrunk to his true proportions in our estimation, we, on the other, have been expanding to our own; and now we come confidently forward to maintain, not that this or that was "intended," but that there are in ourselves, in both sexes, possibilities hitherto suppressed or abused, which, when properly developed, will supply to either what is lacking in the other.

The man of the future will be better, while the woman will be stronger and wiser. To bring this about is the whole aim and object of the present struggle, and with the discovery of the means lies the solution of the Woman Question. Man, having no conception of himself as imperfect from the woman's point of view, will find this difficult to understand, but we know his weakness, and will be patient with him, and help him with his lesson. It is the woman's place and pride and pleasure to teach the child, and man morally is in his infancy. There have been times when there was a doubt as to whether he was to be raised or woman was to be lowered, but we have turned that corner at last; and now woman holds out a strong hand to the child-man, and insists, but with infinite tenderness and pity, upon helping him up....

We have been reproached by Ruskin for shutting ourselves up behind park palings and garden walls, regardless of the waste world that moans in misery without, and that has been too much our attitude; but the day of our acquiescence is over.[1] There is that in ourselves which forces us out of our apathy; we have no choice in the

---

1 See John Ruskin's "Of Queen's Gardens" in *Sesame and Lilies* (1865): "Instead of trying to do this [feel the depth of pain] you turn away from it; you shut yourselves within your park walls and garden gates; and you are content to know that there is beyond them a whole world in wilderness—a world of secrets which you dare not penetrate; and of suffering which you dare not conceive."

matter. When we hear the "Help! help! help!" of the desolate and the oppressed, and still more when we see the awful dumb despair of those who have lost even the hope of help, we must respond. This is often inconvenient to man, especially when he has seized upon a defenceless victim whom he would have destroyed had we not come to the rescue; and so, because it is inconvenient to be exposed and thwarted, he snarls about the end of all true womanliness, cants on the subject of the Sphere, and threatens that if we do not sit still at home with cotton-wool in our ears so that we cannot be stirred into having our sympathies aroused by his victims when they shriek, and with shades over our eyes that we may not see him in his degradation, we shall be afflicted with short hair, coarse skins, unsymmetrical figures, loud voices, tastelessness in dress, and an unattractive appearance and character generally, and then he will not love us any more or marry us. And this is one of the most amusing of his threats, because he has said and proved on so many occasions that he cannot live without us whatever we are....

Of course it will be retorted that the past has been improved upon in our day; but that is not a fair comparison. We walk by the electric light: our ancestors had only oil-lamps. We can see what we are doing and where we are going, and should be as much better as we know how to be. But where are our men? Where is the chivalry, the truth, and affection, the earnest purpose, the plain living, high thinking, and noble self-sacrifice that make a man....

There are upwards of a hundred thousand women in London doomed to damnation by the written law of man if they dare to die, and to infamy for a livelihood if they must live; yet the man at the head of affairs wonders what it is that we with the power are protesting against in the name of our sex. But *is* there any wonder we women wail for the dearth of manliness when we find men from end to end of their rotten social system forever doing the most cowardly deed in their own code, striking at the defenceless woman, especially when she is down?

The Bawling Brotherhood have been seeing reflections of themselves lately which did not flatter them, but their conceit survives, and they cling confidently to the delusion that they are truly all that is admirable, and it is the mirror that is in fault. Mirrors may be either a distorting or a flattering medium, but women do not care to see life any longer in a glass darkly.[1] Let there be light. We suffer in the

---

1 See I Corinthians 13:12.

first shock of it. We shriek in horror at what we discover when it is turned on that which was hidden away in dark corners; but the first principle of good housekeeping is to have no dark corners, and as we recover ourselves we go to work with a will to sweep them out. It is for us to set the human household in order, to see to it that all is clean and sweet and comfortable for the men who are fit to help us to make home in it. We are bound to raise the dust while we are at work, but only those who are in it will suffer any inconvenience from it, and the self-sufficing and self-supporting are not afraid. For the rest it will be all benefits. The Woman Question is the Marriage Question, as shall be shown hereafter.

3. From Ouida, "The New Woman,"[1] *The North American Review* 158 (May 1894): 610-19: Rptd. in *Views and Opinions* (London: Methuen, 1895): 205-22

It can scarcely be disputed, I think, that in the English language there are conspicuous at the present moment two words which designate two unmitigated bores: The Workingman and the Woman. The Workingman and the Woman, the New Woman, be it remembered, meet us at every page of literature written in the English tongue; and each is convinced that on its own especial W hangs the future of the world. Both he and she want to have their values artificially raised and rated, and a status given to them by favor in lieu of desert. In an age in which persistent clamor is generally crowned by success they have both obtained considerable attention; is it offensive to say much more of it than either deserves? Your contributor [2] avers that the Cow-Woman and the Scum-Woman, man understands; but that the New Woman is above him. The elegance of these appellatives is not calculated to recommend them to readers of either sex; and as a specimen of style forces one to hint that the New Woman who, we are told, "has been sitting apart in silent contemplation all these years" might in all these years have studied better models of literary composition. We are farther on told "that the dimmest perception that you may be mistaken, will save you from making an ass of yourself." It appears that even this dimmest perception has never dawned upon the New Woman.

---

1 For an excellent analysis of this essay, see Schaffer, "Nothing But Foolscap and Ink" (42-48); See also Gilbert "Ouida and the New Woman" (170-71).
2 Sara Grand. See Appendix E.2 (p. 601).

We are farther told that "thinking and thinking" in her solitary sphynx-like contemplation she solved the problem and prescribed the remedy (the remedy to a problem!); but what this remedy was we are not told, nor did the New Woman apparently disclose it to the rest of womankind, since she still hears them in "sudden and violent upheaval" like "children unable to articulate whimpering for they know not what." It is sad to reflect that they might have been "easily satisfied at that time" (at what time?), "but society stormed at them until what was a little wail became convulsive shrieks"; and we are not told why the New Woman who had "the remedy for the problem," did not immediately produce it. We are not told either in what country or at what epoch this startling upheaval of volcanic womanhood took place in which "man merely made himself a nuisance with his opinions and his advice," but apparently did quell this wailing and gnashing of teeth since it would seem that he has managed still to remain more masterful than he ought to be.

We are further informed that women "have allowed him to arrange the whole social system and manage or mismanage it all these ages without ever seriously examining his work with a view to considering whether his abilities and his methods were sufficiently good to qualify him for the task."

There is something deliciously comical in the idea, thus suggested, that man has only been allowed to "manage or mismanage" the world because woman has graciously refrained from preventing his doing so. But the comic side of this pompous and solemn assertion does not for a moment offer itself to the New Woman sitting aloof and aloft in her solitary meditation on the superiority of her sex. For the New Woman there is no such thing as a joke. She has listened without a smile to her enemy's "preachments"; she has "endured poignant misery for his sins," she has "meekly bowed her head" when he called her bad names; and she has never asked for "any proof of the superiority" which could alone have given him a right to use such naughty expressions. The truth has all along been in the possession of woman; but strange and sad perversity of taste! she has "cared more for man than for truth, and so the whole human race has suffered!"

"All that is over, however," we are told, and "while on the one hand man has shrunk to his true proportions" she has, all the time of this shrinkage, been herself expanding, and has in a word come to "fancy herself" extremely. So that he has no longer the slightest chance of imposing upon her by his game-cock airs.

Man, "having no conception of himself as imperfect," will find this difficult to understand at first; but the New Woman "knows his weakness," and will "help him with his lesson." "*Man morally is in his infancy.*" There have been times when there was a doubt as to whether he was to be raised to her level, or woman to be lowered to his, but we "have turned that corner at last and now woman holds out a strong hand to the child-man and insists upon helping him up." The child-man (Bismarck? Herbert Spencer? Edison? Gladstone? Alexander III.? Lord Dufferin? the Duc d'Aumale?)[1] the child-man must have his tottering baby steps guided by the New Woman, and he must be taught to live up to his ideals. To live up to an ideal, whether our own or somebody else's is a painful process; but man must be made to do it. For, oddly enough, we are assured that despite "all his assumption he does not make the best of himself," which is not wonderful if he be still only in his infancy; and he has the incredible stupidity to be blind to the fact that "woman has self-respect and good sense," and that "she does not in the least intend to sacrifice the privileges she enjoys on the chance of obtaining others."

I have written amongst other *pensées éparses*[2] which will some day see the light, the following reflection:

L'école nouvelle des femmes libres oublée qu'on ne puisse pas à la fois combattre l'homme sur son propre terrain et attendre de lui des politesses, des tendresses et des galanteries. Il ne faut pas aux même moment prendre de l'homme son chaise à l'Université et sa place dans l'omnibus; si on lui arrâche son gagne-pain, on ne peut pas exiger qu'il offre aussi sa parapluie.[3]

---

1   Otto Von Bismark (1815-98) was Chancellor of Germany from 1870 to 1890; Herbert Spencer (1820-1903) was a British philosopher and sociologist; Thomas Edison (1847-1931) was an American scientist and inventor of the light bulb; William Gladstone (1809-98) was a British statesman; Alexander III (1845-94) was Czar of Russia from 1881 to 1894; Frederick Temple Blackwood, Lord Dufferin (1826-1902) was an Irish diplomat and author; Henri Eugène Philippe Louis of Orleans, Duc D'Aumale (1822-97) was a French prince and statesman, son of Louis Philippe.
2   Scattered thoughts (opinions).
3   The new school of liberated women forget that they cannot at the same time fight men on their own terrain and expect politeness, tenderness, or gallantries from them. One (a woman) must not at the same time take a man's position (literally, pulpit, rostrum) in a university and his place in the bus; if we take away his daily bread, we can't demand that he also offer his umbrella. (Ouida's French errors have not been corrected.)

The whole kernel of the question lies in this. Your contributor says that the New Woman will not surrender her present privileges; *i.e.*, she will still expect the man to stand that she may sit; the man to get wet through that she may use his umbrella. But if she retain these privileges she can only do so by an appeal to his chivalry, *i.e.*, by a confession that she is weaker than he. But she does not want to do this: she wants to get the comforts and concessions due to fee-bleness, at the same time as she demands the lion's share of power due to superior force alone. It is this overweening and unreasonable grasping at both positions which will end in making her odious to man and in her being probably kicked back roughly by him into the seclusion of a harem.

Before me lies an engraving in an illustrated journal[1] of a woman's meeting; whereat a woman is demanding in the name of her sovereign sex the right to vote at political elections. The speaker is middle-aged and plain of feature; she wears an inverted plate on her head tied on with strings under her double-chin; she has bal-loon-sleeves, a bodice tight to bursting, a waist of ludicrous dimensions in proportion to her portly person; she is gesticulating with one hand, of which all the fingers are stuck out in ungraceful defi-ance of all artistic laws of gesture. Now, why cannot this orator learn to gesticulate and learn to dress, instead of clamoring for a franchise? She violates in her own person every law, alike of common-sense and artistic fitness, and yet comes forward as a fit and proper person to make laws for others. She is an exact representative of her sex.

Woman, whether new or old, has immense fields of culture untilled, immense areas of influence wholly neglected. She does almost nothing with the resources she possesses, because her whole energy is concentrated on desiring and demanding those she has not. She can write and print anything she chooses; and she scarcely ever takes the pains to acquire correct grammar or elegance of style before wasting ink and paper. She can paint and model any subjects she chooses, but she imprisons herself in men's *ateliers*[2] to endeavor to steal their technique and their methods, and thus loses any originali-ty she might possess.... Her precept and example in the treatment of the animal creation might be of infinite use in mitigating the hideous tyranny of humanity over them, but she does little or nothing to this

---

1   She is probably referring to the 14 June 1884 issue of *Punch* (279); see
    Schaffer, "Nothing But Foolscap and Ink" (43, 51 n. 9, n. 10).
2   Workshops.

effect; she wears dead birds and the skins of dead creatures; she hunts the hare and shoots the pheasant, she drives and rides with more brutal recklessness than men; she watches with delight the struggles of the dying salmon, of the gralloched[1] deer; she keeps her horses standing in snow and fog for hours with the muscles of their heads and necks tied up in the torture of the bearing rein; when asked to do anything for a stray dog, a lame horse, a poor man's donkey, she is very sorry, but she has so many claims on her already; she never attempts by orders to her household, to her *fournisseurs*,[2] to her dependents, to obtain some degree of mercy in the treatment of sentient creatures and in the methods of their slaughter.

The immense area which lies open to her in private life is almost entirely uncultivated, yet she wants to be admitted into public life. Public life is already overcrowded, verbose, incompetent, fussy, and foolish enough without the addition of her in her sealskin coat with the dead humming bird on her hat. Woman in public life would exaggerate the failings of men, and would not have even their few excellencies. Their legislation would be, as that of men is too often, the offspring of panic or prejudice; and she would not put on the drag of common-sense as man frequently does in public assemblies. There would be little to hope from her humanity, nothing from her liberality; for when she is frightened she is more ferocious than he, and when she has power more merciless.

"Men," says your contributor, "deprived us of all proper education and then jeered at us because we had no knowledge." How far is this based on facts? Could not Lady Jane Grey[3] learn Greek and Latin as she chose? Could not Hypatia lecture?[4] ... If the vast majority have not either the mental or physical gifts to become either, that was nature's fault, not man's.... In all eras and all climes a woman of

---

1 Gutted.
2 Tradesmen.
3 As a result of a conspiracy by her father, Lady Jane Grey (1537-54) took the British throne in 1553. She reigned for nine days. After spending a year in prison, she and her husband were beheaded.
4 Hypatia of Alexandria (c. A.D. 370-415) was a mathematician, astronomer, and philosopher. She was a pagan in an increasingly Christian environment. She used to put on her philosopher's cloak, walk through the middle of town, and publicly interpret Plato articulately and eloquently. Hypatia was eventually captured by a band of merciless men who beat her, dragged her body to a church, mutilated her flesh with sharp tiles, and buried her remains.

great genius or of great beauty has done what she chose; and if the majority of women have led obscure lives, so have the majority of men. The chief part of humanity is insignificant, whether it be male or female. In most people there is very little character indeed, and as little mind. Those who have much never fail to make their marks, be they of which sex they may.

The unfortunate idea that there is no good education without a college curriculum is as injurious as it is erroneous. The college education may have excellencies for men in its *frottement*,[1] its preparation for the world, its rough destruction of personal conceit; but for women it can only be hardening and deforming. If study be delightful to a woman, she will find her way to it as the hart to water brooks....

The "Scum-woman" and the "Cow-woman," to quote the elegant phraseology of your contributor, are both of them less of a menace to humankind than the New Woman with her fierce vanity, her undigested knowledge, her over-weening estimate of her own value and her fatal want of all sense of the ridiculous.

When scum comes to the surface it renders a great service to the substance which it leaves behind it; when the cow yields pure nourishment to the young and the suffering, her place is blessed in the realm of nature; but when the New Woman splutters blistering wrath on mankind she is merely odious and baneful.

The error of the New Woman (as of many an old one) lies in speaking of women as the victims of men, and entirely ignoring the frequency with which men are the victims of women. In nine cases out of ten the first to corrupt the youth is the woman. In nine cases out of ten also she becomes corrupt herself because she likes it....

A worse prostitution than that of the streets, *i.e.*, that of loveless marriages of convenience, are brought about by women, not by men. In such unions the man always gives much more than he gains, and the woman in almost every instance is persuaded or driven into it by women—her mother, her sisters, her acquaintances. It is rarely that the father interferes to bring about such a marriage.

In even what is called a well-assorted marriage, the man is frequently sacrificed to the woman. Men of genius are often dragged to earth by their wives.... Woman may help man sometimes, but she certainly more often hinders him. Her self-esteem is immense and her self-knowledge very small. I view with dread for the future of

---

1 Interaction (with other students).

the world the power which modern inventions place in the hands of woman. Hitherto her physical weakness has restrained her in a great measure from violent action; but a woman can make a bomb and throw it, can fling vitriol, and fire a repeating revolver as well as any man can. These are precisely the deadly, secret, easily handled modes of warfare and revenge, which will commend themselves to her ferocious feebleness....

When you have taken [women] into the physiological and chemical laboratories, when you have extinguished pity in her, and given weapons to her dormant cruelty which she can use in secret, you will be hoist with your own petard[1]—your pupil will be your tyrant, and then she will meet with the ultimate fate of all tyrants....

The elegant epithet of Cow-woman implies the contempt with which maternity is viewed by the New Woman who thinks it something fine to vote at vestries, and shout at meetings, and lay bare the spines of living animals, and haul the gasping salmon from the river pool, and hustle male students off the benches of amphitheatres....

Men, moreover, are in all except the very lowest classes more careful of their talk before young girls than women are. It is very rarely that a man does not respect real innocence; but women frequently do not. The jest, the allusion, the story which sullies her mind and awakes her inquisitiveness, will much oftener be spoken by women than men. It is not from her brothers, nor her brother's friends, but from her female companions that she will understand what the grosser laugh of those around her suggests. The biological and pathological curricula complete the loveless disflowering of her maiden soul.

Everything which tends to obliterate the contrast of the sexes, like your mixture of boys and girls in your American common schools, tends to destroy the charm of intercourse, the savor and sweetness of life. Seclusion lends an infinite seduction to the girl, as the rude and bustling publicity of modern life robs woman of her grace....

That mystic charm will long endure despite the efforts to destroy it of orators in tight stays and balloon sleeves, who scream from platforms, and the beings so justly abhorred of Mrs. Lynn Lynton who smoke in public carriages and from the waist upward are indistinguishable from the men they profess to despise.

---

1 From Shakespeare's *Hamlet*, III.iv.210. Rosencrantz and Guildenstern are killed as a result of their own treachery (literally to kill oneself with one's own bomb).

But every word, whether written or spoken, which urges the woman to antagonism against the man, every word which is written or spoken to try and make of her a hybrid, self-contained, opponent of men, makes a rift in the lute to which the world looks for its sweetest music....

4. From Mrs. M. Eastwood, "The New Woman in Fiction and in Fact," *The Humanitarian* 5 (1894): 375-79

As the novel heroine of the New Woman we have already been made extremely familiar with her. She has been flashed upon us in a rapid succession of such startling and vivid pictures as to have thrown the dull, sober-tinted presentations of the old sort entirely into the shade. And to the modern mind, thirsting for whatever is novel and sensational, how sordid, how prosaic that other poor dead-level creature appears when, in the last chapter, she is left clinging fatuously to the male prop she has by dint of many pretty, old-fashioned feminine dodges....

Let us hasten to put the antiquated specimen on the shelf, with her insipid face to the wall, and forget her whilst we lose ourselves in the bewildering contemplation of the weirdly bewitching, the soulful, the mysterious, the tricksy, the tragic, the electrifying, the intensely-intense, and utterly unfathomable new one.

We observe her breathlessly, for she keeps us on the tenter-hooks of delightfully awful expectation. She is kaleidoscopic in the variety of her aspects. Her moods are like sudden gleams of electric fire, alternating with murky darkness, for at last—at last her soul has burst its fetters and is free!

That in the exuberance of a recently acquired freedom, after centuries of suppression by the tyrant man, this soul of hers should run somewhat amuck with her is a perfectly natural consequence.... But mostly does the New Woman of fiction resemble a syren, luring the easy victim to his destruction.[1] She has only to strike a vibrating "key-note"[2] on her seductive lyre, and behold he lies grovelling at

---

1 In classical mythology the sirens are sea nymphs whose songs lure sailors to their doom.

2 This is a reference to New Woman writer George Egerton (Mary Chavelita Dunne Bright, 1859-1945) and her recently published collection of short stories entitled *Keynotes* (1893). The expression was also in the news in a two-part (10 and 17 March) parody entitled "She-Notes" (see Nelson, *A New Woman Reader*).

her feet! And he likes it, for never does she let him feel bored a single minute. Whether in the capacity of lover or husband, she continues to hold him spell-bound. Usually, however, she begins by marrying him; he is easier to manage that way....

What will she do next?

Ah! She is sportively inclined, and falls to nibbling his ear.... Anon she is off into the raging storm to assuage her emotions. What matter about the dainty slippers? *She* never takes a vulgar cold and gets a swollen nose. Romance with her could never die that shuddering death! In her exultant frenzy she loathes the restraint of the conventional hairpin. She plucks it from her head and casts it from her, abandoning the wealth of her glorious tresses to the battling elements....

And all her conversation is delightful.... But mostly she shines as a moral analyst, and the way she keeps on corking herself down with a pin through her middle until she has laid bare every fibre of her being, is truly heroic.

In short, she is "Grand," every "Iota"[1] of her! Quite too much so, however, for the usages of our grossly practical, work-a-day world; therefore, much as she entertains him, it is a relief to the ordinary mortal to discover that she has no existence in it, but is rather a creation of the hyperbolically emancipated woman's riotous imagination.

None the less is the New Woman a positive and tangible fact. Only, she is altogether otherwise. Far from being unfitted for the world in which she lives, she is adapting herself with marvellous rapidity to its altered conditions. And why should she not? Why should the strong current of evolution which bears all else before it, leave woman alone behind?

The average man, being a selfish man, is of a different opinion. "Why," he demands, "should she not continue for ever to be the beautiful exception we made of her? We placed her in peaceful security, out of reach of the tide, high and dry on the shore. We treated her tenderly and nobly, supplying her with whatever we, in our superior judgement, considered it desirable that she should have. It is outrageous that now she should be pushing her way forward into the stream to elbow along with us, and snatch as her right that share in the good things we generously bestowed on her!

---

1   Eastwood has been satirizing the fictional New Women who appear in the novels of Sara Grand and Iota, a pseudonym for Kathleen Caffyn (1855-1926).

"But at least we can make it hot for her, and we will do it! We will deprive her of all chivalrous attentions. We will jostle her; oppose her progress with our more robust persons. We will dig her in the ribs. We will go farther. We will write scathing articles in the papers about her, and put her in *Punch*. Moreover, we will not marry her—unless we cannot help ourselves!"

This is all very dreadful, and how keenly the courageous pioneers of the "New Womanhood" may at first have felt it we do not know, for they have never told us, but this we perceive, that their small and hazardous fleet has swollen to a formidable armament which can well afford to smile at such buffetings, for it is already equipped to venture the treacherous seas alone....

[Men] have awakened in her the instinct of self-preservation, which, to judge from the way she has hitherto permitted you to determine the conditions of her being, must have lain dormant in her. You have compelled her to take the plunge, and *c'est le premier pas qui coute*.[1] Having taken it she has arisen to the emergency. She has reviewed and begun to test her possibilities, which has resulted in some astonishing discoveries, the primal and most important being the discovery of independent staying properties in her back-bone, which enable her to stand upright without male support.

Since then, as was to be expected, her advance has proceeded by leaps and bounds. So rapid has it been that only the most nimble of the hardier species have been able to keep up with her.... Exhilarated with the race, her shining eyes on the goal, she anticipates the crown of her hopes.

And of a surety it will be hers. The New Woman of to day will be the woman of the future. Only more so. At present she is passing through the ugly duckling stage. Like a growing girl, she has too many elbows. Her movements are spasmodic; her manners lack repose, and her voice has not yet acquired that rich and softly modulated cadence which is woman's most irresistible attribute. Her detractors would have us believe that those tender and endearing charms which ought to distinguish her gentler sex will be entirely wanting in her.... Their grimly prejudiced humour sees in her the fast woman who cultivates man's pet vices, drives four-in-hand to the races and snaps her fingers in the face of respectable Mrs. Grundy.

And truly the vagaries of these extraordinary *fin-de-siècle*[2] growths

---

1 It is the first step that is difficult.
2 End of the century.

are calculated to engross the attention of onlookers. Only let not those wild and wayward suckers which have been thrown out from the superabundant vitality of the New Womanhood be mistaken for sound branches of the parent tree. They bear no closer relationship to the actual Evolving She, than the rag-tag and bobtail that careers at the heels of an advancing army bears to the army itself.

The abiding New Woman wears a very different aspect. Her brow is serious, for the brain behind it is crammed as full of high projects as is the satchel she carries of pamphlets on the missions, rights, grievances, and demands of her sex. She has neither the heart nor has she the time for fooling, and if she assumes certain articles of masculine garb on occasion, it is solely on account of their superior utility; if she rides out on a bicycle it is for the purpose of strengthening her muscles and expanding her lungs for the great work she has before her. Young as she is she talks fearlessly and authoritatively on all and every subject of social depravity, for there is nothing which was hitherto hidden from her which she has not revealed. And since she knows the worst her soaring ambition will be content with nothing less than the reformation of the entire male sex....

Here has begun the radical change which is to effect the future generations. She is fortifying its walls against the unworthy invader and has sworn to surrender only at the instance of disinterested love. Upon the strength of her purpose depends the degree of her success.

5. From Ouida, "Female Suffrage," *Views and Opinions* (London: Methuen, 1895): 302-26

It is a singular fact that England, which has been always esteemed the safest and slowest of all factors in European politics, should be now seriously meditating on such a revolutionary course of action as the political emancipation of women. It is a sign, and a very ominous sign, of the restlessness and feverishness which have come upon this century in its last twenty years of life, and from which England is suffering no less than other nations, is perhaps even suffering more than they....

[A]re women prepared to purchase electoral rights by their willingness to fulfil military obligations? If not, how can they expect political privileges unless they are prepared to renounce for them the peculiar privileges which have been awarded to them in view of the physical weakness of their sex?... The much graver and truer objection lies less in the physical than in the mental and moral inferiority of women. I use moral in its broadest sense. Women on an average have little sense of justice, and hardly any sense whatever of awarding to others a freedom for which they do not care themselves.... Women cannot understand that you can make no nation virtuous by act of parliament; they would construct their acts of parliament on purpose to make people virtuous whether they chose or not, and would not see that this would be a form of tyranny as bad as any other. A few years ago a State in America (I think it was Maine or Massachusetts) decreed that because a few Pomeranian dogs were given to biting people, all Pomeranian dogs within the State, ill and well, young and old, should on a certain date be killed; and they were killed, two thousand odd in number. Now, this is precisely the kind of legislation which women would establish in their moments of panic; the disregard of individual rights, the injustice to innocent animals and their owners, the invasion of private property under the doctrinaire's plea of the general good, would all commend themselves to women in their hysterical hours, for women are more tyrannical and more self-absorbed than men....

I do not think the moral and mental qualities of the average woman so inferior to those of the average man as is conventionally supposed. The average man is not an intellectual nor a noble being; neither is the average woman. But there are certain solid qualities in the male creature which are lacking from the female; such qualities as patience and calmness in judgment, which are of infinite value, and in which the female character is almost invariably deficient....

The woman is the enemy of freedom. Give her power and she is at once despotic,... whether she be a beneficent or a malevolent ruler, whether she be a sovereign or a revolutionist. The enormous pretensions to the monopoly of a man's life which women put forward in marriage, are born of the desire to tyrannise. The rage and amazement displayed by the woman when a man, whether her lover or her husband, is inconstant to her, comes from that tenacity over the man as a property which wholly blinds her to her own faults or lack of charm and power to keep him....

It ["the idea prevailing among women that they are valuable, admirable and almost divine, merely because they are women"] has been passed, like many another fallacy, from generation to generation, and the enormous power of evil which lies in the female sex has been underestimated or conventionally disregarded for the sake of a poetic effect. The seducer is continually held up for condemnation, but the temptress is seldom remembered. It is common to write of women as the victims of men, and it is forgotten how many men are the victims in their earliest youth of women. Even in marriage the woman, by her infidelity, can inflict the most poignant, the most torturing dishonour on the man; the man's infidelity does not in the least touch the honour of the woman. She can never be in doubt as to the fact of her children being her own; but he may be perpetually tortured by such a doubt, nay, may be compelled through lack of proof to give his name and shelter to his offspring when he is morally convinced that they are not his. The woman can bring shame into a great race as the man can never do, and ofttimes brings it with impunity. In marriage, moreover, the influence of the woman, whatever popular prejudices plead to the contrary, is constantly belittling and injurious to the intelligence of the man....

If female suffrage become law anywhere, it must be given to all women who have not rendered themselves ineligible for it by criminality. The result will scarcely be other than the emasculation and the confusion of the whole world of politics. The ideal woman is, we know, the type of heroism, fortitude, wisdom, sweetness and light; but even the ideal woman is not always distinguished by breadth of thought, and it is here a question not of the ideal woman at all, but of the millions of ordinary women who have as little of the sage in them as of the angel. Very few women are capable of being the sympathetic mistress of a great man, or the ennobling mother of a child of genius. Most women are the drag on the wheel of the higher aspirations, to the nobler impulses, to the more original and unconventional opinions, of the men whom they influence. The prospect of their increased ascendency over national movements is very ominous. Is the mass of male humanity ready to accept it?...

I have previously used the words 'mental and moral inferiority'; it is perhaps necessary to explain them. By mental inferiority I do not mean that the average women might not, if educated to it, learn as much mathematics or as much metaphysics as the ordinary man. I do not deny that Girton[1] may produce senior wranglers[2] or physiologists in time to come; it may do so. But the female mind has a radical weakness which is often also its peculiar charm; it is intensely subjective, it is only reluctantly forced to be impersonal, and it has

---

1 Girton College was established in 1869 as the first residential college for women in England. It was called the College for Women. In 1872, a site in Cambridge was purchased. The college, renamed Girton College, opened at the new location in 1873.

2 A person placed in the first class in the mathematics tripos at Cambridge.

the strongest possible tendency to tyranny.... In public morality, also, the female mind is unconsciously unscrupulous; it is seldom very frank or honest, and it would burn down a temple to warm its own pannikin.[1] Women of perfect honesty of intentions and antecedents will adopt a dishonest course, if they think it will serve an aim or a person they care for, with a headlong and cynical completeness which leaves men far behind it. In intrigue a man will often have scruples which the woman brushes aside as carelessly as if they were cobwebs, if once her passions or her jealousies are ardently involved. There is not much veracity anywhere in human nature, but it may always be roughly calculated that the man will be more truthful than the woman, in ninety-nine cases out of a hundred; his judgments will be less coloured by personal wishes and emotions, and his instincts towards justice will be straighter and less mobile than hers....

There is in every woman, even in the best woman, a sleeping potentiality for crime, a curious possibility of fiendish evil. Even her maternal love is dangerously near an insane ferocity, which at times breaks out in infanticide or child-murder. Everything which tends to efface in her gentler and softer instincts tends to make of her a worse curse to the world than any man has ever been. If, indeed, in the centuries to come she should develop into the foe of man,... it is by no means improbable that men, in sheer self-defence, will be compelled to turn on her and chain her down into the impotency of servitude once more....

Man has, I repeat, been very fair in his dealings with women, as far as legislation goes; he could easily have kept her from all time to the harem, and it has been a proof of his fairness, if not of his wisdom, that he has not done so. I have but little doubt but that, before long, he will cede to her clamour, and let her seat herself beside him, or opposite to him, on the benches of his representative houses. When he does, he will, I think, regret the loss of the harem....

Women may, will, very possibly, snatch from the nerveless hand of the sick man those legal and legislative rights which she covets. The political movements of modern times have been always in the direction of giving unlimited power to blind and unmeasured masses, whose use of that which is thus rashly given them the boldest prophet dare not predict. Such movement will probably give political power to women.

---

1 A small metal cup.

I confess that I, for one, dread the day which shall see this further development of that crude and restless character of the nineteenth century, which, with sublime self-contentment and self-conceit, it has presumed to call Progress.

6. From Mrs. Morgan-Dockrell, "Is the New Woman a Myth?" *The Humanitarian* 8 (1896): 339-50

The close of the nineteenth century marks an epoch of social revolutions! Humanity is borne more and more rapidly along on the course of the ever-widening, the ever-swifter flowing stream of progress, through scene after scene of novelty, where stupendous events and marvellous discoveries and inventions crowd thickly one upon another....

The remnant of the old order stand aghast, clinging affrightedly to their traditions; meanwhile the new order hastens forth eagerly, heralding and welcoming the fuller entrance of the New Era. That very word "new," strikes as it were the dominant note in the trend of present-day thought; present-day effort and aspiration.

It sounds out from every quarter. The new art, the new literature, the new fiction, the new journalism, the new humour, the new criticism, the new hedonism, the new morality.... Lastly, more discussed, debated, newspaper paragraphed, caricatured, howled down and denied, or acknowledged and approved, as the case may be, than any of them, we have the new woman. The new man has not as yet lifted up announcing voice. But, doubtless, he too is coming; after whom, perhaps, the millennium followed by a new heaven and a new earth.

Of all these new facts and entities, the new woman appears to me to be immeasurably the first in importance.... But before we can arrive at anything at all approximating to a decision on the questions: Is the nineteenth century new woman a myth, as so many people aver—a figment of the journalistic imagination...? Is she, indeed, none other than an intensely aggravated type of the unwomanly, unlovable, unlovely, untidy, undomesticated, revolting, shrieking, man-hating shrew of all the centuries? Or is she on the other hand, verily an altogether new type of woman evolved from out the ages?... [W]ithin recent years we fail to catch but the faintest echo of that note of protest, if you will, of revolt among women, now daily swelling to a louder chorus, that will, that must of necessity, create discord and jar the music of humanity until there is revision and readjustment of all those laws social and political, which put woman at a disadvantage or handicap her in the race of life....

What of those women in all departments of science, in all professions and trades, in art, in literature, who after long striving and always heavily handicapped by convention, and with no hereditary training, have yet won their right and proved their capacity to work successfully side by side with men for honourable livelihood and independence, as well as for the help and benefit of their fellow human beings? Are they of the old order of woman, who must rather fall and perish dumbly by the wayside than take part in the battle of life?...

Some of us have gloomy memories of those lady-like employments and accomplishments. Those nightmare groups of wax flowers and fruits! Those libellous water colours! Those ghastly antimacassars ... save that of goading all mankind when wrestling with them to blaspheme, and those melancholy practisings of little tunes with gigantic variations!

What of those brave pioneers in South Australia, who have beaten us, their English sisters, by a neck, in the race for woman suffrage?[1] Are they, too, of the old order whose politics were for the most part decided by the relative good looks of the parliamentary candidates or their election colours? My space does not admit of anything like a fair review over the whole field of woman's work. But anyone with average intelligence ... must acknowledge ... that for good or evil ... a new distinct order and type of woman is actively among us.

In discussing the new woman it is absolutely necessary to differentiate between the genuine and spurious entities. For there are new women and new women.

The fact is, the cause of emancipation of woman has come to be a sort of Cave of Adullam[2] for a whole host of restless, discontented women, many of whose hearts never quickened for any cause outside the narrowest of mean self interests, whose only aims in life are

---

1   The woman suffrage movement began in Australia in 1890. Women were granted the vote in South Australia in 1894.
2   See 1 Samuel 22:1-2. "David therefore departed thence, and escaped to the cave Adullam: and when his brethren and all his father's house heard it, they went down thither to him. And every one that was in distress, and every one that was in debt, and every one that was discontented, gathered themselves unto him; and he became a captain over them: and there were with him about four hundred men."

excitement, licence, or notoriety. But all of whose idle vapourings, silly exaggerations and absurdities are laid at the door of the new woman.

Thus we have Mrs. Lynn Lynton's bogey new woman, over which we every now and then hear her hysterically shrieking ... but which, like Frankinstein's [sic] monster, seldom afflicts its presence on any one other than its unhappy creator. Quite recently Ouida, too, neglecting for a while her magnificently big and magnificently wicked guardsmen has given to the world her portrayal and ideas of the new woman. Ouida views with dread for the future of the world the power which modern inventions place in the hands of such women. "Hitherto," says this high priestess of the exclusive, "women's physical weakness has restrained her in a great measure from violent action, but a woman can make a bomb and throw it, can fling vitriol, and fire a repeating revolver as well as any man can. These are precisely the deadly, secret, easily-handled modes of warfare and revenge which will commend themselves to her ferocious feebleness."[1] After which it is but playful chiding of everyday little failings to go on to accuse the new woman of immodesty and cruelty, of violating in her own person every law alike of common sense and artistic fitness, of aping all the absurdities and emulating all the cruelties of man.

Mrs. Lynn Lynton's and Ouida's new women are, so far as their appreciable existence, no more types of any order of Englishwoman at least, than, thank heaven, is that fine flower of civilisation, the Masher,[2] ... a fair type of a nineteenth century Englishman. If types they be, all are equally ephemeral, equally despicable and equally unlikely to leave any mark either for good or evil on their generation, which, unhappily, is more than can be said for that foul thing, the so-called new woman of the new fiction.... This loathsome thing ... is a fertile source of contagion, of moral defilement and corruption. Such monstrosities bespeak decadence and moral decomposition, whereas the genuine new woman, her many crudities and errors of immaturity notwithstanding, typifies and makes for ... regeneration and purification....

The genuine new woman is she who, with some of the ablest men of the century, has awakened to the fact that the time has come

---

1 See Appendix E.3 (p. 611).
2 A masher is a man who makes advances to women he does not know with a view to physical intimacy.

when the work of the world in all departments has need of woman...; that in the intellectual sphere as in the physical there cannot be natural and healthy creation without the co-operation and amalgamation of all the mental attributes, male and female. The male superiority in philosophy, science, invention, and conception of abstract justice, blending with the female superiority in intuition, in altruism, and in the fuller and richer flow of the emotional life; the two half and incomplete individualities combining and forming the perfect whole. The new woman maintains that as the needs and desires of the world are not those of men alone, but are those of men, women, and children, so those needs and desires can only be naturally and effectually provided for by man and woman working harmoniously together for those ends.... [B]efore man and woman as peers ... can go forward abreast and hand in hand for the world's regeneration, woman must first of all and of necessity work woman for woman.... The genuine new woman neither asks nor desires sexual superiority or supremacy. Nor is she either ashamed or aweary of her womanhood....

Intellectually she has counted for little in the direction of the world's affairs, unless indeed we take into account that large amount of undignified back stair influence in diplomacy and politics which men have never hesitated to accept from her for their own aims and ends. As a natural consequence her intellectual faculties have to a very large extent become weak or altogether atrophied....

[T]he unpleasant fact remains that technically ... woman's position has socially and legally been that of a slave. Granted that the present state of society, here at least in our own land, has long risen above and outgrown the observance of such conditions. But that in nowise does away with this fundamental fact that by tradition, by convention, by law, and by the churches, woman is to this day branded the inferior, the subjected creature. Her whole training has borne out and emphasised her subjection. From all time a woman has belonged not to herself but to her menkind or guardians, to be by them disposed of in marriage, and married to yield obedience to her lord and master....

The objections taken to woman striving for emancipation are legion! It is urged that the very desire for it divests woman of all those attributes and characteristics which make her womanly and lovable. Well, that of course depends entirely on what those things are that constitute womanliness, and inspire love. If womanliness consists solely of weakness, utter dependence, morally, physically, and intellectually, of total ignorance, miscalled innocence of the realities of life, and in holding the idea that a woman belongs first of all to her father, brother, or guardians, until she becomes her husband's, and so is really never her own at all, and that, failing marriage, woman is more or less a failure, then it must be candidly admitted the new woman is unwomanly and unlovable. For the new woman's faith is that as strength of mind and body, courage and resolution are glorious in man, they are not the less but the more so in woman. She emphatically protests against the idea that her humanity, apart from wife and motherhood, counts for little or nothing. She claims her human right co-equally with her fellow man to full and free development of every power and faculty.... She resents the fact that she is compelled to obey laws, in the making of which she has no voice, share or part, and so is classified with lunatics and criminals. She emphatically denies that there is righteousness, truth, or reason in the morality that demands a higher standard of virtue for woman than for man....

Well, to my mind, if there be one factor more potent than another in such decay it is the traditional unnatural separation between the alleged spheres and interests of the sexes. The theory very generally prevails that man's sphere is the universe. That woman's is the home; that she has few duties outside it, and strangely enough that the man has almost no duties in it.... [Morgan-Dockrell cites other objections voiced against the New Woman: that the majority of women are content with things as they are; that women would soil their white garments if they left the pedestal; that women subjugate themselves by their love for fashion.]

... Look at her, men and women—the woman on the pedestal, decked in furs and feathers, hugging the gilded fetters which so aptly symbolise her degradation—and say which is the likelier to be the nobler human creature, the more useful citizen, the fitter mother of children, the sweeter, the more loyal helpmate for a true man—she or the new woman?

Select Bibliography

Works that Discuss Ouida

Ardis, Ann L. *New Women, New Novels: Feminism and Early Modernism*. New Brunswick: Rutgers UP, 1990.

Bigland, Eileen. *Ouida, The Passionate Victorian*. New York: Duell, Sloan and Pearce, 1951.

Calder, Jenni. *Women and Marriage in Victorian Fiction*. New York: Oxford UP, 1976.

Dictionary of Literary Biography, Vol. 18: Victorian Novelists after 1885. Detroit, MI: Gale, 1983: 239-46. Rptd. in *Contemporary Authors On Line*. Detroit, MI: Gale, 2002.

Dobrée, Bonamy. "Ouida." *Milton to Ouida: A Collection of Essays*. London: Frank Cass, 1970.

Elwin, Malcolm. *Victorian Wallflowers*. London: Jonathan Cape, 1934.

Ffrench, Yvonne. *Ouida, a Study in Ostentation*. New York and London: D. Appleton-Century, 1938.

Gilbert, Pamela K. *Disease, Desire, and the Body in Victorian Women's Popular Novels*. Cambridge, Cambridge UP, 1997.

—. "Ouida and the Other New Woman," *Victorian Women Writers and the Woman Question*. Ed. Nicola Diane Thompson. Cambridge: Cambridge UP, 1999.

Huntington, Henry G. *Memories: Personages, People, Places*. London: Constable, 1911.

Jordan, Ellen. "The Christening of the New Woman: May 1894." *Victorian Newsletter* 63 (Spring 1983): 19-21.

Jordan, Jane. "The Enigma of a Literary Identity. *Princeton Library Chronicle* 57 (Autumn 1995): 75-95.

—. "The Writings of 'Ouida' (Marie Louise de la Ramée 1839-1908)." PhD Thesis. Birkbeck College, University of London, 1995.

Lee, Elizabeth. *Ouida, a Memoir*. London: T. Fisher Unwin, 1914.

Melchiori, Barbara Arnett. *Terrorism in the Late Victorian Novel*. London: Croom Helm, 1985.

Mitchell, Sally. *The Fallen Angel: Chastity, Class and Women's Reading 1835-1880*. Bowling Green, OH: Bowling Green U Popular P, 1982.

Nelson, Carolyn Christensen, ed. *A New Woman Reader: Fiction, Articles, and Drama of the 1890s*. Peterborough, ON: Broadview P, 2001.

Philips, Walter C. *Dickens, Reade, and Collins, Sensation Novelists*. New York: Columbia UP, 1919.

Poster, Carol. "Oxidation is a Feminist Issue: Acidity, Canonicity, and Popular Victorian Female Authors." *College English* 58.3 (March 1996): 287-306.

Powell, Anthony. "Introduction." *Novels of High Society of the Victorian Age*. London: Pilot P, 1947.

Pykett, Lyn. *The 'Improper' Feminine: The Women's Sensation Novel and the New Woman Writing*. London: Routledge, 1992.

Rubinstein, David. *Before the Suffragettes: Women's Emancipation in the 1890s*. New York: St. Martin's P, 1986.

Schaffer, Talia. "'Nothing But Foolscap and Ink': Inventing the New Woman." *The New Woman in Fiction and in Fact: Fin-de-Siècle Feminisms*. Eds. Angelique Richardson and Chris Willis. New York: Palgrave, 2001.

—. *The Forgotten Female Aesthetes: Literary Culture in Late Victorian England*. Charlottesville, VA: UP of Virginia, 2000.

Schaffer, Talia and Kathy Alexis Psomiades, eds. *Women and British Aestheticism*. Charlottesville, VA: UP of Virginia, 1999.

Schroeder, Natalie. "Feminine Sensationalism, Eroticism, and Self Assertion: M.E. Braddon and Ouida." *Tulsa Studies in Women's Literature* 7 (1988): 87–105.

Stirling, Monica. *The Fine and the Wicked: The Life and Times of Ouida*. New York: Coward-McCann, 1958.

Stubbs, Patricia. *Women and Fiction: Feminism and the Novel 1880-1920*. New York: Harper and Row, 1979.

Sutherland, John. "Introduction." *Under Two Flags by Ouida*. Oxford and New York: Oxford UP, 1995.

Terry, R.C. *Victorian Popular Fiction, 1860-80*. Atlantic Highlands, NJ: Humanities P, 1983.

Thompson, Nicola Diane. "Responding to the Woman Questions: Rereading Noncanonical Victorian Women Novelists." *Victorian Women Writers and the Woman Question*. Ed. Nicola Diane Thompson. Cambridge: Cambridge UP, 1999.

General Background

Altick, Richard D. *Victorian People and Ideas*. New York: W. W. Norton, 1973.

Burchell, S.C. *Imperial Masquerade: The Paris of Napoleon III*. New York: Atheneum, 1971.

Cunningham, Gail. *The New Woman and the Victorian Novel*. London and Basingstoke: Macmillan, 1978.

Gilbert, Sandra M. and Susan Gubar. *The Madwoman in the Attic: The Woman Writer and the Nineteenth Century Literary Imagination*. New Haven: Yale UP, 1979.

Gillis, John R. *For Better, For Worse: British Marriages, 1600 to the Present*. New York: Oxford UP, 1985.

Gilmour, Robin. *The Novel in the Victorian Age: A Modern Introduction*. London: Edward Arnold, 1986.

Heilmann, Ann. *New Women Writing: First-Wave Feminism*. New York: St. Martin's P, 2000.

Helsinger, Elizabeth K., Robin Lauterbach Sheets, and William Veeder. *The Woman Question: Society and Literature in Britain and America 1837-1883*. Vol. 3. Chicago: U of Chicago P, 1989.

Hughes, Winifred. *The Maniac in the Cellar: Sensation Novels of the 1860s.* Princeton, NJ: Princeton UP, 1980.

Kern, Stephen. *The Culture of Love: Victorians to Moderns.* Cambridge, MA: Harvard UP, 1992.

Kropotkin, P. *In Russian and French Prisons.* London: Ward and Downey, 1887.

Leckie, Barbara. *Culture and Adultery: The Novel, the Newspaper, and the Law, 1857-1914.* Philadelphia: U of Pennsylvania P, 1999.

Levine, Philippa. *Victorian Feminism: 1850-1900.* Gainesville: UP of Florida, 1994.

Lewis, Jane. *Women in England 1870-1950: Sexual Divisions and Social Change.* Bloomington: Indiana UP, 1984.

MacColl, Gail and Carol McD Wallace. *To Marry an English Lord.* New York: Workman, 1989.

Mintz, Steven. *A Prison of Expectations: The Family in Victorian Culture.* New York: New York UP, 1983.

Peterson, M. Jeanne. *Family, Love, and Work in the Lives of Victorian Gentlewomen.* Bloomington: Indiana UP, 1989.

Reynolds, Kimberly and Nicola Humble. *Victorian Heroines: Representations of Femininity in Nineteenth-Century Literature and Art.* New York: New York UP, 1993.

Shanley, Mary Lyndon. *Feminism, Marriage, and the Law in Victorian England.* Princeton, NJ: Princeton UP, 1989.

Showalter, Elaine. *A Literature of Their Own: British Women Writers from Brontë to Lessing.* Princeton, NJ: Princeton UP, 1977.

Sutherland, John. *The Stanford Companion to Victorian Fiction.* Stanford, CA: Stanford UP, 1989.